PENGUIN ENGLISH LIBRARY

CONINGSBY

BENJAMIN DISRAELI

Thom Braun was born in 1953 and educated at St John's College, Oxford, and University College, London. He is the author of *Disraeli the Novelist* (1981) and has edited *Sybil* for the Penguin English Library.

BENJAMIN DISRAELI

CONINGSBY

OR THE NEW GENERATION

Edited by Thom Braun

PENGUIN BOOKS

Penguin Books Ltd, Harmondsworth, Middlesex, England
Penguin Books, 625 Madison Avenue, New York, New York 10022, U.S.A.
Penguin Books Australia Ltd, Ringwood, Victoria, Australia
Penguin Books Canada Ltd, 2801 John Street, Markham, Ontario, Canada L3R 1B4
Penguin Books (N.Z.) Ltd, 182–190 Wairau Road, Auckland 10, New Zealand

First published 1844
Published in the Penguin English Library 1983

Introduction and Notes copyright © Thom Braun, 1983
All rights reserved

Made and printed in Great Britain by Richard Clay (The Chaucer Press) Ltd,
Bungay, Suffolk
Filmset in Monophoto Photina by Northumberland Press Ltd, Gateshead

Contents

Acknowledgement

I should like to
thank my wife, Jill,
for her great help in
the preparation of
this edition.

T. B.

Introduction

IMAGINATION is not a quality one would normally associate with British politicians. Which is a pity really, because so often it would appear to be a standard requirement for the job, and as important as an appreciation of seriousness, if not more so. History, however, and contemporary thought often judge things differently. Public opinion would nowadays be almost as shocked or surprised if a leading statesman gave way to a flight of fancy, as it was in 1870 when Disraeli published a novel as an ex-Prime-Minister. As the *Saturday Review* of 9 April 1870 said, 'Mr Disraeli has provided a new sensation for a jaded public. The English mind was startled when a retired novelist became Prime Minister. It has been not less surprised at the announcement that a retired Prime Minister is about again to become a novelist.'

Disraeli had indeed been a novelist for forty-four years by the time *Lothair* appeared in 1870. That is to say, his first novel had been published as early as 1826. It had been a literary career of mixed success and one which, from the modern reader's point of view, was highlighted by the publication of his 'political' trilogy between 1844 and 1847: *Coningsby*, *Sybil* and *Tancred*. It was with those three novels that Disraeli apparently eschewed the flippancies of his youthful fictional exploits to create a new literary genre by his virtual invention of the so-called 'political novel'. Such a view, however, misses much of the point. Disraeli has long been forgiven, by his apologists, for the 'seriousness' of his 'political' novels. What those same apologists have always found it harder to forgive in him is his sense of humour, his wit, his lack of reverence (often couched in phrases of assumed appreciation), his individuality and his ability to be always unusual. Of his admirers, some prefer to see his idiosyncrasies as signs of a radical nature. For others they are merely the most tangible indications of a structured egotism. Neither view is wholly right and neither wholly wrong in its attempt to assess an author whose writings sometimes debunked themselves without losing their wit or their seriousness. As one of the characters in *Lothair* says, 'Books are fatal; they are the curse of the human race. Nine-tenths of existing books are nonsense, and the clever books are the refutation of that nonsense.' It does not always matter so much which category Disraeli's novels fall into; more important is the fact that the author was capable of sliding his tongue in and out of his cheek with amazing and sometimes confusing regularity. On the whole, critics still do not understand Disraeli.

His imagination has not, then, been forgiven. Indeed, it has not always even been acknowledged. Robert Blake, in what is now regarded as the standard biography, has said, 'The truth is that Disraeli lacked imagination. This may sound paradoxical. He praises the value of imagination so much that we tend to assume that he had a great deal of it himself. But imagination is not the same as day-dreaming.' There is a good deal of truth in this. Disraeli did not create characters from the inside out, as did the great novelists of the century, for Disraeli was not a great novelist. But he was a good one, and, what is more, he was a politician as well. Beneath the egotistical day-dreaming lurked a sensitive appreciation of his own limitations as an artist. An original and able, and particularly a political, mind, once aware of its own limitations, will often adapt old designs with new methods. It is not enough to suggest that Disraeli was not of the same calibre as Dickens, George Eliot and Mrs Gaskell. The truth is he was not of their ilk. His novels of the 1840s were political, not just in being about politics, but in being themselves manipulative, and in attempting to present disparate, paradoxical and often contradictory views within an artificially created organic whole.

Biographers, reflecting Disraeli's own recollections, often affirm that he was, if not born in a library, then at least raised in one. He was not, however, a bookish man in the same mould as his father. Isaac D'Israeli, a product of the same generation as Wordsworth and Coleridge, was an admirer of Alexander Pope, and, as a youth, had sent one of his early works to Dr Johnson for a critical opinion. By 1791, at the age of twenty-five, Disraeli's father had achieved fame as the author of a collection of literary curiosities. From then on he settled into his life as a man of sedentary habits who, when not ensconced in the library of the British Museum, would be closeted with his own large collection of books. His son, Benjamin Disraeli, was no doubt influenced by such an atmosphere, but the future politician's concept of books was different from his father's. When, in 1849, Disraeli penned a memoir on his father's life and work, he said:

> The traditionary notion that the life of a man of letters is necessarily deficient in incident, appears to have originated in a misconception of the essential nature of human action ... A Book may be as great a thing as a battle, and there are systems of philosophy that have produced as great revolutions as anything that have disturbed even the social and political existence of our centuries.

As with so much of his writing, there exists in this not only an attempt to assert the potency of the writer in general, but also an effort to justify Benjamin Disraeli's own background through his father as part of an heroic process in an historical tradition of philosophical and poetic action. Books, whether nonsense or the refutation of that nonsense, are seen as dynamic and, by their very inventive nature, revolutionary. Through *his* books Disraeli actively contributed to his own dynamic tradition, his own mythological past. As he wrote to his close friend Lady Bradford sometime after the publication of *Lothair*, 'My books are the history of my life. I don't mean a vulgar photograph of incidents, but the psychological development of my character. Self-inspiration may be egotistical, but it is generally true.'

In relation to *Coningsby*, what is important is not so much books in themselves as rather Disraeli's concept of fiction. His first novel, *Vivian Grey*, published in 1826, was written as much for pecuniary gain as for artistic reasons. When the book appeared, Disraeli was still only twenty-one years old. His early life had already shown signs of turbulence and restlessness, and at the end of 1825 he temporarily retired from the hectic world to write what was in many ways a spoof on the 'society' novels which had been popular in fashionable quarters for a number of years. *Vivian Grey* has often been called a 'silver-fork novel', but, even if it is not a fully conscious parody of this genre of fiction, it is too gauche to be considered as much more than a youthful extravagance.

First novels always provide important indications of the turn of mind of a writer, and *Vivian Grey* is no exception. It is full of bravado and slap-dash wit, anecdotes and shameless padding. But above all it is an adventure of ambition and rapid advancement, viewed in such a way that, even though we realize how close this is to the author's own idealized career, we are never prevented from appreciating the great sense of humour which everywhere tinges this story of spectacular radicalism. As in many other cases, it is perhaps Disraeli's lack of restraint which is the paramount feature of the novel, and this in itself is a presentiment of his limitations as a novelist. If this is a failing, however, the enthusiasm behind it is certainly a compelling force in this novel and in his subsequent works. The book is structured, probably unconsciously, to present the kind of grandiose personal mythology which exists in so much of Disraeli's writing. It is through such a presentation that we become aware of how much 'fiction' and 'fictionalizing' meant to him.

In 1830, in an effort to raise some money by a direct appeal to the same audience that had read *Vivian Grey*, Disraeli published *The Young Duke*. Although he was always highly dismissive of the novel, its increased sense of awareness and use of detail showed how much Disraeli had evolved in his presentation of heroic decadence. In an effort to harness his growing self-awareness in fiction to a 'serious' but idealized introspection, hung over from the romantic era, Disraeli produced in 1832 the novel which was always to be among his favourites, even though, in financial terms, it was a disaster. *Contarini Fleming* was subtitled *A Psychological Auto-Biography* (later changed to the less sensitive *Psychological Romance*), and was a flouncy and intriguing examination of the author's poetic character. This time the establishment of a personal myth is conveyed more by earnestness than by inflated wit. As the hero/narrator informs us early in the book:

I am desirous of writing a book which shall be all truth, a work of which the passion, the thought, the action, and even the style, should spring from my own intellect, from my own observation of incident, from my own study of the genius of expression ... I have resolved therefore

to write the history of my own life, because it is the subject of which
I have the truest knowledge.   (II, i)

No one could dispute this; Disraeli was still in his twenties. But
whenever he deals with the subject of himself, or, in later novels,
with national subjects, Disraeli's history is always itself a form of
fiction which dips at one moment into reality, and the next into
imagination. At one point Contarini Fleming can proclaim how
'much more impressive is Reality than Imagination', but he later
bows to the essentially creative nature of imagination and radical
ideas: 'In imagination I shook thrones and founded empires. I felt
myself a being born to breathe in an atmosphere of revolution.'
Behind what may now appear a commonplace Wordsworthian
sentiment lies the key to the often ambivalent nature of the
fictional world Disraeli created around himself.

The same year that *Contarini Fleming* was published Disraeli
fought his first two election campaigns at High Wycombe, both
of which were unsuccessful. Although it would not be true to say,
as his wife was later to claim in 1841, that 'Literature he has
abandoned for politics', the years between 1832 and his election
to Parliament in 1837 provided no example of Disraeli at his best
as a writer of fiction. In 1834 he published a strange and exotic
novel called *The Wondrous Tale of Alroy*, notable mainly for its
stylistic posing, and *A Year at Hartlebury, or The Election*. This
second book, which has only recently been identified as part of
Disraeli's output, was co-written with his sister Sarah under
the pseudonyms 'Cherry' and 'Fair Star', and is a fascinating work
for Disraeli scholars in that the second volume – the account of
the election – draws on the author's experiences in High
Wycombe in 1832.

Certainly, however, by the mid-1830s, Disraeli's energies were
largely being channelled into political activities. Such a change of
direction did not preclude writing, but to some extent the
emphasis had shifted. It was in the form of an open letter to his
friend and confidant, Lord Lyndhurst, that he wrote during 1835
what Robert Blake has described as Disraeli's 'first serious contribution to political literature'. December of that year saw the
appearance of *A Vindication of the English Constitution in a Letter
to a Noble and Learned Lord by Disraeli the Younger*. Despite the

often fanciful and eccentric nature of much of the *Vindication*, it is interesting to compare the text with *Coningsby* and *Sybil*, for it is a mannered exploration of some of the political, constitutional and historical matters which preoccupied Disraeli in his Young England novels. Perhaps the fact that Disraeli never again attempted to produce a serious political treatise of this kind is itself an indication of his dislike of dogma and theory outside the realms of imagination and spectacular personal advancement. When, in the mid-1840s, he decided to resort to the printed word again in order to present another personal and enlarged view of the political and social structure which had evolved in England, his recourse was immediately to the fictional form rather than to any kind of propagandist tract. By then, of course, he had been in Parliament for a number of years, having been finally elected as a member of the House of Commons at his fifth attempt in 1837, the year in which he published two more romantic novels (*Henrietta Temple* and *Venetia*) and the year in which Victoria became Queen.

Disraeli's love of romance, adventure and a rather mythical state of existence was always likely to put him out of step with the qualities which increasingly were becoming associated with the ministrations of the new Queen's governments: centralization, utilitarianism and liberalism. It was as a gesture against such prevailing trends that Young England was conceived in the early 1840s. If Young England was a recognized clique operating within the acceptable limits of parliamentary procedure, it also existed as an imaginative escape, sustained as much by its founders' romantic fancies as it was by practical notions of political and remedial action. In reacting against the rationalism which underpinned the moves towards liberalism, the only real alternative, short of anarchy, appeared to be the sanctification of those qualities which were *irrational*: romance, imagination and emotion. It was through these qualities that Disraeli's radicalism had always shown itself, especially in his fiction.

For Disraeli human progress had always been marked by personal attributes (love, generosity, duty), rather than by what he would have seen as the depersonalized qualities associated with the material development of society. As far as he was concerned, happiness and satisfaction for the greatest number of people would be most likely to be achieved by the actions of a few persons motivated by ideals of individual heroism. This view of life, perhaps in a less than conscious form, had been behind much of his early fiction. It was a view of life which, unable to look forward to the modern values of society, was forced to look back and to erect an altar to tradition. Indeed, there was already established a notable strain of explicit argument which looked back beyond what we now consider the beginnings of modern society, to the medieval age. The fact that such an age depended on feudalism was by no means seen as a failing; the brand of Toryism with which Disraeli was associated in the early 1840s was purposely retrogressive and was not afraid to promulgate eagerly ideas which were, in many cases, notably illiberal. This fact alone does much to account for the mood of Disraeli and his confederates, which, for all its whimsicality, maintained a good deal of revolutionary fervour.

Young England, with the notable exception of Disraeli himself, was a small group of mainly noble young men who sat on the Tory backbenches at the beginning of Sir Robert Peel's premiership in 1841. The main members were George Smythe (later Lord Strangford, and the person on whom Coningsby is said to be modelled), Lord John Manners (later Duke of Rutland, and Lord Henry Sidney in *Coningsby*), Alexander Baillie-Cochrane (later Lord Lamington, and Buckhurst in *Coningsby*) and, of course, Disraeli himself. The aims of this group were broadly to improve the condition of the poor through an increased harmony between the classes and by promoting a respect for the monarchy, the Church and the country's ancient traditions and institutions. It was an atmosphere and a philosophy on which a romantic imagination like Disraeli's could thrive because, for all its shortcomings, it provided a lively, idealistic antidote to the boring seriousness into which Victorian England was always threatening to descend. As such, Young England itself was a 'fiction', and only by viewing it as such could Disraeli have reconciled it to his more practical political designs.

This reconciliation was important, for it meant that Disraeli could give a lively expression to these ideals without them ever becoming the outbursts of fondness. Despite the abstraction inherent in Young England, Disraeli's wit, idiosyncrasies and sense of purpose kept his own 'fiction' anchored firmly to the realities of the 1840s, which is one reason why his Young England novels are no mere escapist adventures. For example, Disraeli and his colleagues were influenced by much of the explicit medieval-ism which, as I have suggested, had been prevalent in one form or another since early in the century. A notable book which they read on the subject was Kenelm Digby's *The Broadstone of Honour, or The True Sense and Practice of Chivalry*, which was first published in 1822 and which gave the following advantages for studies in chivalry:

> In the first place, they serve their country by adorning its peculiar traditions and recollections; preserving alive in the memories of men the magnanimity and greatness of ages that are departed, and cherishing that poetry which lives in every people, until it is stifled by the various and factitious interests of a life devoted to luxury and avarice.

In the desire to preserve the country's 'peculiar traditions' we can see a distinction between what Smythe and particularly Manners sought, and what Disraeli recognized as the limits of such ideals. In 1843 Lord John Manners published *A Plea for National Holy-Days*, which canvassed for, among other things, village maypoles as a traditional form of people's enjoyment which the author felt had been abandoned by modern society. It is a subject to which Disraeli refers in *Coningsby*:

> 'Henry thinks,' said Lord Everingham, 'that the people are to be fed by dancing round a May-pole.'
> 'But will the people be more fed because they do not dance round a May-pole?' urged Lord Henry.
> 'Obsolete customs!' said Lord Everingham.
> 'And why should dancing round a May-pole be more obsolete than holding a Chapter of the Garter?' asked Lord Henry.   (III, iii)

Although Henry Sidney's final riposte is backed by a winning logic, there remains the sense that Disraeli is satirizing the absurd side of his character's ideals. The subject is viewed sympa-thetically, but there is a certain distance between the author and his creation. Lord John Manners had indeed already written of Disraeli in his journal, 'Could I only satisfy myself that D'Israeli believed all that he said, I should be more happy: his historical views are quite mine, but does he believe them?' The answer is probably yes. But then part of Disraeli had also believed in the machinations of Vivian Grey, the dreams of Contarini Fleming and the ambitions of Alroy. Belief or commitment in a fiction need not be harnessed to values which have any immediate or practicable application. Fiction is a playground for fancy and imagination, and we should be aware that *Coningsby* is an expression of Disraeli's fancy and imagination as much as it is a development of his ideas on politics and society.

One of the occasional supporters of Young England was Henry Hope, a millionaire and MP for Gloucester. It was in 1843, while Disraeli and his wife were staying with Hope at his country seat of Deepdene, that much of *Coningsby* was written, and when the novel was published in May 1844 it appeared with a dedication to him. The novel was an immediate success, and the first edition of 1,000 copies was sold within a fortnight. Disraeli was later to claim, in his Preface to the fifth edition, that:

Three considerable editions were sold in this country in three months; it was largely circulated throughout the Continent of Europe, and within a very brief period more than 50,000 copies were required in the United States of America.

That popularity can be explained in a number of ways. Robert Blake, in his biography, examines *Coningsby* together with *Sybil* (1845) and *Tancred* (1847) as the Young England trilogy, and finds them 'quite different from anything [Disraeli] had written before. A wide gulf separates them from his silver fork novels and historical romances of the 'twenties and 'thirties.' To some extent such a view derives from Disraeli's own reflections on the integrated nature of this 'trilogy'. In the General Preface to the collected edition of his novels which appeared in 1870, he considered what his fictional purposes had been in the 1840s:

The derivation and character of political parties; the condition of the people which had been the consequence of them; the duties of the Church as a main remedial agency in our present state; were the principal topics which I intended to treat, but I found they were too vast for the space I had allotted to myself.

They were all launched in 'Coningsby' but the origin and condition of political parties, the first portion of the theme, was the only one completely handled in that work.

Next year (1845), in SYBIL, OR THE TWO NATIONS, I considered the condition of the people, and the whole work, generally speaking, was devoted to that portion of my scheme ...

In recognising the Church as a powerful agent in the previous development of England ... it seemed to me that the time had arrived when it became my duty to ... consider the position of the descendants of that race who had been the founders of Christianity. Familiar as we all are now with such themes, the House of Israel being now freed from the barbarism of mediaeval misconception, and judged like other races by their contributions to the existing sum of human welfare, and the general influence of race on human action being universally recognised as the key of history, the difficulty and hazard of touching for the first time on such topics cannot now be easily appreciated. But public opinion recognised both the truth and sincerity of these views, and, with its sanction, in TANCRED, OR THE NEW CRUSADE, the third portion of the Trilogy, I completed their development.

Such a reflection offers a very schematic view of three novels which were written very quickly at a turbulent time in Disraeli's life. We cannot be certain that Disraeli had such a planned view of his fiction in his mind when, in 1843, he started work on *Coningsby*. It was only in 1849, in the Preface to the fifth edition of the novel, that he began to talk publicly of the 'trilogy' in this context. Such extra-textual comment, however, does not alter the nature of the novels. Indeed, it merely exemplifies the way in which Disraeli was always fascinated by esoteric ideas. All his novels are threaded through with unusual concepts, many of which are presented in a deceptively casual but organized way, and it is sometimes difficult to realize that the notions which rise out of the fiction are not commonplace.

In some ways Disraeli's whole life was a concerted attempt to gain respectability for notions and postures which were instinctively unpalatable to respectable society. That is not to say that he was always a crusader for worthwhile but unpublicized causes. Many of the causes for which he waved the flag were either lost or not worth fighting for, and in a way it was actually Young England's sense of inherent defeat that romanticized it as a movement. Such a cause is perhaps like campaigning for pain in an age of pain-killers. There are arguments to recommend an apparent negation of scientific progress, but they are arguments based largely on a sense of spiritual and moral awareness rather than a desire for that political entity known as 'human happiness'.

An obvious example of the type of esoteric cause which intrigued Disraeli is found in the passage quoted above from the General Preface of 1870, where he claims that 'the general influence of race on human action' is 'universally recognised as the key of history'. Disraeli's seemingly perverse ideas on race (which would not necessarily have been regarded as such at the time), as expressed in *Tancred* and later in his biography of Lord George Bentinck in 1851, are perhaps familiar symptoms of prejudice in that they stem from an insubstantial political theory acting on an individual who feels his own position to be vulnerable. But again the 'cause' is delivered as part of a more complex understanding of society; an understanding based largely on a misrepresentation of history. In *Coningsby*, such a view is set apart through the guise of Sidonia, a character who has been interpreted as a cross between Baron de Rothschild and Disraeli himself.

The most obvious vein of esoteric argument in the novel, however, is, as Disraeli himself pointed out in dealing with his subject matter, 'the origin and condition of political parties'. It is on the basis of this subject that *Coningsby* has been called the first political novel in the language. The fact that such a title has no particular relevance or meaning does not detract from the fact that so much of the novel depends for its motivation on what Disraeli sees as the political malaise which had afflicted the country for more than two centuries.

In *Coningsby*, and then in *Sybil*, Disraeli sought to display personal heroic destinies against a background of political mismanagement. In delineating that background, he fabricated his own alternative to the so-called Whig interpretation of history. The Whigs, we are told by Disraeli, achieved influence and maintained it by excluding from power those ancient institutions which Young England had been so keen to preserve: the Crown, the Church and the 'People'. Charles I was a martyr who died trying to save those institutions. Once the political initiative had been removed from the monarchy, there was only a slight chance of preventing the Whigs from establishing a 'high aristocratic republic on the model of the Venetian'. The remaining Stuart monarchs fought a losing battle. By the time Queen Anne died, the Venetian party (the Whigs) had won, and the subsequent Hanoverian kings were no more than doges.

Such a political take-over was countered only, Disraeli argues, by certain Tory individuals who sought to preserve an English system of government; that is, one which acknowledges the great importance of the monarchy and Church. These individuals included Bolingbroke, Carteret and the younger Pitt. But even Pitt, Disraeli claims, was finally forced to relinquish the 'English' form of government. Nineteenth-century Toryism is therefore seen to be as bad as Whiggism, and it is on the base of Lord Liverpool's mediocrity and the Duke of Wellington's mismanagement that Disraeli regards the Reform Bill as having been built. The Reform Bill itself, the legislation with which the re-emerging Whigs hoped to consolidate their power base, is seen as 'a mean and selfish revolution which emancipated neither the Crown nor the People', and Disraeli spends much of the early part of *Coningsby* discussing the apparently dreaded details of its passing. The political scene resulting from the passing of the Reform Bill is seen to offer only a Whig-Liberal party whose principles Disraeli instinctively loathed, and a Tory-Conservative party which he claimed had bowed to the liberal spirit and therefore had no principles at all.

But what, we might ask, is Disraeli suggesting should counter this state of affairs? *Coningsby* is subtitled *The New Generation*, and on one level the ideas of young men like Smythe and Manners are, as we have seen, to the fore. The perplexity, however, which is shown by some of the novel's minor characters about what exactly the New Generation was seeking to effect will find a response in many modern readers who feel bombarded by the book's historical and political references. One gentleman in *Coningsby* talks of

'a sort of new set; new ideas and all that sort of thing. Beau tells me a good deal about it; and when I was staying with the Everinghams, at Easter, they were full of it. Coningsby had just returned from his travels,

and they were quite on the *qui vive*. Lady Everingham is one of their set.
I don't know what it is exactly; but I think we shall hear more of it.'
  'A sort of animal magnetism, or unknown tongues, I take it from
your description,' said his companion.
  'Well, I don't know what it is,' said Mr Melton; 'but it has got hold
of all the young fellows who have just come out. Beau is a little bit
himself. I had some idea of giving my mind to it, they made such a fuss
about it at Everingham; but it requires a devilish deal of history, I believe,
and all that sort of thing.'   (VIII, i)

In terms of prescription there is not much more perhaps than the
foggy notions which, as we have seen, enlivened the members
of Young England. Certainly several contemporary critics were
scathing of what they considered to be the negative and
retrogressive nature of the novel's 'philosophy', and there is much
of it which cannot be excused its notable illiberality. Yet *Coningsby*
is neither a limited political tract nor a huge practical joke. It is
an extremely articulate and elegantly presented novel, and we
must try to appreciate other facets of its craft which in the past
have often been ignored.

  For example, the novel is perhaps not so completely different
to Disraeli's earlier works as some critics would have us believe.
There are many links with previous fictional worlds and
characters, most notably with *Contarini Fleming*, and once again
we find a hero who seems to have an innate, natural superiority.
Again it seems at first that we have a character who will mature
into another paragon of heroic individualism and a fine example
of the 'influence of individual character' which Sidonia extols.
Yet there *is* a noticeable difference between Contarini Fleming's
situation and that of Coningsby, and it is not just that one is
un-English and that the other is beset by historical theories. As
a character Coningsby has no strong individual characteristics,
especially when compared with Contarini Fleming, and his own
actions play almost no part in his eventual success. But then
what do we mean by 'character'?

  Disraeli's characters were often, if not a projection of the
author's own dreams, then a relatively crude compression of
facets of his imagined society. In *Coningsby*, with the theme
ostensibly being 'The New Generation', character very much
represents the National Character. Coningsby's own apparent

impotence, despite his innate superiority, parallels that of the
nation, and at the end of the novel optimism and faith in
Coningsby as an individual and in the future of the country are
virtually one and the same thing.

Although, in such a fictional setting, it is not always possible to
know for certain whether or not it is Disraeli's *own* view we are
reading, there are obviously certain passages which appear to be
central to this aspect of the novel. For example, there is this
conversation between Coningsby and Sidonia. Coningsby speaks
first:

> 'But tell me, what do you understand by the term national character?'
> 'A character is an assemblage of qualities; the character of England
> should be an assemblage of great qualities.'
> 'But we cannot deny that the English have great virtues.'
> 'The civilisation of a thousand years must produce great virtues; but
> we are speaking of the decline of public virtue, not its existence.'
> 'In what, then, do you trace that decline?'
> 'In the fact that the various classes of this country are arrayed against
> each other.' (IV, xiii)

That the apparent conflict of classes was central to Disraeli's conception of national character is supported by the fact that in *Sybil*
he went on to offer a descriptive interpretation of that particular
problem. It is interesting, however, that, as with most of the
ideas associated with Young England, the problem is not a
narrowly 'political' one, at least not in the way that Disraeli deals
with it. The use of heady, sometimes archaic language, combined
with overtly religious suggestions, contributes to our feeling that
the problem is a lack of faith, spirituality and those unquantifiable
qualities which Young England admired and which seemed to
have been swept away by the progressive liberalism of early
Victorian England.

If the ailment is not political, however, then neither can the cure
be, and from this realization may stem a certain disenchantment
with the term 'political novel'. Politics are obviously to the fore in
Coningsby, but political activity is only one of the legitimate agencies for remedial action. In *Coningsby* Disraeli pushes politics
into the foreground because it was a subject which fascinated him,
and because he saw in politics and political history the most

obvious reflection of the national character. As Coningsby himself says:

'If the nation that elects the Parliament be corrupt, the elected body will resemble it. The nation that is corrupt deserves to fall. But this only shows that there is something to be considered beyond forms of government – national character. And herein mainly should we repose our hopes. If a nation be led to aim at the good and the great, depend upon it, whatever be its form, the government will respond to its convictions and its sentiments.'   (VII, ii)

When, earlier in the novel, the narrator claims 'There is no influence at the same time so powerful and so singular as that of individual character', the statement is made on the understanding that individual character can achieve real success only if it reflects, as well as guides, the aspirations of national character. To a large extent, it seemed, Disraeli had finished with his ideal of the introverted individual like Contarini Fleming, turning away from a wider historical destiny. For all its idiosyncrasies, *Coningsby* is a more impersonal novel than anything Disraeli had written before; and the maturity inherent in that move away from the egocentric was largely due to the author's recognition that the national fate is as compelling a subject as is the fate of an individual.

Suggested Reading

Other Political Novels by Disraeli:

Sybil, or The Two Nations (1845) edited by Thom Braun with an introduction by Lord Butler, (Harmondsworth: Penguin Books, 1980).
Tancred, or The New Crusade (1847).

Biographical Studies:

Robert Blake, *Disraeli* (London: Eyre & Spottiswoode, 1966).
Christopher Hibbert, *Disraeli and his World* (London: Thames & Hudson, 1978).
André Maurois, *Disraeli: A Picture of the Victorian Age*, translated by Hamish Miles (London: Bodley Head, 1927).
W. F. Monypenny and G. E. Buckle, *The Life of Benjamin Disraeli, Earl of Beaconsfield*, 6 vols. (London: John Murray, 1910–20).

Critical Works:

Thom Braun, *Disraeli the Novelist* (London: George Allen & Unwin, 1981).
Michael Foot, 'The Good Tory' in *Debts of Honour* (London: Davis-Poynter, 1980).
Daniel R. Schwarz, *Disraeli's Fiction* (London: Macmillan, 1979).

Historical Background:

Michael Brock, *The Great Reform Act* (London: Hutchinson, 1973).
Norman Gash, *Aristocracy and People* (London: Edward Arnold, 1979).

Note on the Text

CONINGSBY was first published in 1844 in three volumes. The most important collected edition of the novels to be approved by Disraeli was Longmans' revised Collected Edition which appeared in 1870–71. The first volume of this edition was the first one-volume edition of *Lothair*, and the second volume was *Coningsby*. This Penguin edition reproduces the 1870 text, with its sometimes idiosyncratic spelling and punctuation, and any corrections of obvious misprints have been effected silently.

Facsimile of the title page of the 1870 edition of *Coningsby*, by courtesy of the British Library

CONINGSBY

OR

THE NEW GENERATION.

BY THE

RIGHT HONORABLE B. DISRAELI.

NEW EDITION.

LONDON:

LONGMANS, GREEN, AND CO.

1870.

To Henry Hope

IT is not because this work was conceived and partly executed amid the glades and galleries of the DEEPDENE that I have inscribed it with your name. Nor merely because I was desirous to avail myself of the most graceful privilege of an author, and dedicate my work to the friend whose talents I have always appreciated, and whose virtues I have ever admired.

But because in these pages I have endeavoured to picture something of that development of the new and, as I believe, better mind of England, that has often been the subject of our converse and speculation.

In this volume you will find many a thought illustrated and many a principle attempted to be established that we have often together partially discussed and canvassed. Doubtless you may encounter some opinions with which you may not agree, and some conclusions the accuracy of which you may find cause to question. But if I have generally succeeded in my object, to scatter some suggestions that may tend to elevate the tone of public life, ascertain the true character of political parties, and induce us for the future more carefully to distinguish between facts and phrases, realities and phantoms, I believe that I shall gain your sympathy, for I shall find a reflex to their efforts in your own generous spirit and enlightened mind.

Grosvenor Gate: *May Day* 1844

BOOK I

Chapter 1

IT was a bright May morning some twelve years ago, when a youth of still tender age, for he had certainly not entered his teens by more than two years, was ushered into the waiting-room of a house in the vicinity of St James's Square, which, though with the general appearance of a private residence, and that too of no very ambitious character, exhibited at this period symptoms of being occupied for some public purpose.

The house-door was constantly open, and frequent guests even at this early hour crossed the threshold. The hall-table was covered with sealed letters; and the hall-porter inscribed in a book the name of every individual who entered.

The young gentleman we have mentioned found himself in a room which offered few resources for his amusement. A large table amply covered with writing materials, and a few chairs, were its sole furniture, except the grey drugget that covered the floor, and a muddy mezzotinto of the Duke of Wellington that adorned its cold walls. There was not even a newspaper; and the only books were the Court Guide and the London Directory. For some time he remained with patient endurance planted against the wall, with his feet resting on the rail of his chair; but at length in his shifting posture he gave evidence of his restlessness, rose from his seat, looked out of the window into a small side court of the house surrounded with dead walls, paced the room, took up the Court Guide, changed it for the London Directory, then wrote his name over several sheets of foolscap paper, drew various landscapes and faces of his friends; and then, splitting up a pen or two, delivered himself of a yawn which seemed the climax of his weariness.

And yet the youth's appearance did not betoken a character that, if the opportunity had offered, could not have found amusement and even instruction. His countenance, radiant with health and the lustre of innocence, was at the same time thoughtful and resolute. The expression of his deep blue eye was serious. Without extreme regularity of features, the face was one that would never have passed unobserved. His short upper lip indicated a good breed; and his chestnut curls clustered over his open brow, while his shirt-collar thrown over his shoulders was unrestrained by handkerchief or ribbon. Add to this, a limber and graceful figure, which the jacket of his boyish dress exhibited to great advantage.

Just as the youth, mounted on a chair, was adjusting the portrait of the Duke, which he had observed to be awry, the gentleman for whom he had been all this time waiting entered the room.

'Floreat Etona!' hastily exclaimed the gentleman, in a sharp voice; 'you are setting the Duke to rights. I have left you a long time a prisoner; but I found them so busy here, that I made my escape with some difficulty.'

He who uttered these words was a man of middle size and age, originally in all probability of a spare habit, but now a little inclined to corpulency. Baldness, perhaps, contributed to the spiritual expression of a brow, which was, however, essentially intellectual, and gave some character of openness to a countenance which, though not ill-favoured, was unhappily stamped by a sinister cast that was not to be mistaken. His manner was easy, but rather audacious than well-bred. Indeed, while a visage which might otherwise be described as handsome was spoilt by a dishonest glance, so a demeanour that was by no means deficient in self-possession and facility, was tainted by an innate vulgarity, which in the long run, though seldom, yet surely developed itself.

The youth had jumped off his chair on the entrance of the gentleman, and then taking up his hat, said

'Shall we go to grandpapa now, sir?'

'By all means, my dear boy,' said the gentleman, putting his arm within that of the youth; and they were just on the point of leaving the waiting-room, when the door was suddenly thrown open, and two individuals, in a state of great excitement, rushed into the apartment.

'Rigby! Rigby!' they both exclaimed at the same moment. 'By
G— they're out!'[1]

'Who told you?'

'The best authority; one of themselves.'

'Who? who?'

'Paul Evelyn; I met him as I passed Brookes',[2] and he told me
that Lord Grey had resigned, and the King had accepted his
resignation.'

But Mr Rigby, who, though very fond of news, and much
interested in the present, was extremely jealous of any one giving
him information, was sceptical. He declared that Paul Evelyn was
always wrong; that it was morally impossible that Paul Evelyn
ever could be right; that he knew, from the highest authority, that
Lord Grey had been twice yesterday with the King; that on the
last visit nothing was settled; that if he had been at the palace
again to-day, he could not have been there before twelve o'clock;
that it was only now a quarter to one; that Lord Grey would have
called his colleagues together on his return; that at least an hour
must have elapsed before anything could possibly have transpired.
Then he compared and criticised the dates of every rumoured
incident of the last twenty-four hours, and nobody was stronger
in dates than Mr Rigby; counted even the number of stairs which
the minister had to ascend and descend in his visit to the palace,[3]
and the time their mountings and dismountings must have con-
sumed, detail was Mr Rigby's forte; and finally, what with his
dates, his private information, his knowledge of palace localities,
his contempt for Paul Evelyn, and his confidence in himself, he
succeeded in persuading his downcast and disheartened friends
that their comfortable intelligence had not the slightest foundation.

They all left the room together; they were in the hall; the gentlemen who brought the news looked somewhat depressed, but Mr
Rigby gay, even amid the prostration of his party, from the consciousness that he had most critically demolished a piece of
political gossip and conveyed a certain degree of mortification to
a couple of his companions; when a travelling carriage and four
with a ducal coronet drove up to the house. The door was thrown
open, the steps dashed down, and a youthful noble sprang from his
chariot into the hall.

'Good morning, Rigby,' said the Duke.

'I see your Grace well, I am sure,' said Mr Rigby, with a softened manner.

'You have heard the news, gentlemen?' the Duke continued.

'What news? Yes; no; that is to say, Mr Rigby thinks –'

'You know, of course, that Lord Lyndhurst is with the King?'

'It is impossible,' said Mr Rigby.

'I don't think I can be mistaken,' said the Duke, smiling.

'I will show your Grace that it is impossible,' said Mr Rigby. 'Lord Lyndhurst slept at Wimbledon. Lord Grey could not have seen the King until twelve o'clock; it is now five minutes to one. It is impossible, therefore, that any message from the King could have reached Lord Lyndhurst in time for his Lordship to be at the palace at this moment.'

'But my authority is a high one,' said the Duke.

'Authority is a phrase,' said Mr Rigby; 'we must look to time and place, dates and localities, to discover the truth.'

'Your Grace was saying that your authority –' ventured to observe Mr Tadpole, emboldened by the presence of a duke, his patron, to struggle against the despotism of a Rigby, his tyrant.

'Was the highest,' rejoined the Duke, smiling, 'for it was Lord Lyndhurst himself. I came up from Nuneham this morning, passed his Lordship's house in Hyde Park Place as he was getting into his carriage in full dress, stopped my own, and learned in a breath that the Whigs were out, and that the King had sent for the Chief Baron.[4] So I came on here at once.'

'I always thought the country was sound at bottom,' exclaimed Mr Taper, who, under the old system, had sneaked into the Treasury Board.

Tadpole and Taper were great friends. Neither of them ever despaired of the Commonwealth. Even if the Reform Bill were passed, Taper was convinced that the Whigs would never prove men of business; and when his friends confessed among themselves that a Tory Government was for the future impossible, Taper would remark, in a confidential whisper, that for his part he believed before the year was over the Whigs would be turned out by the clerks.[5]

'There is no doubt that there is considerable reaction,' said Mr Tadpole. 'The infamous conduct of the Whigs in the Amersham case has opened the public mind more than anything.'

'Aldborough was worse,' said Mr Taper.

'Terrible,' said Tadpole. 'They said there was no use discussing the Reform Bill in our House. I believe Rigby's great speech on Aldborough has done more towards the reaction than all the violence of the Political Unions put together.'[6]

'Let us hope for the best,' said the Duke, mildly. ' 'Tis a bold step on the part of the Sovereign, and I am free to say I could have wished it postponed; but we must support the King like men. What say you, Rigby? You are silent.'

'I am thinking how very unfortunate it was that I did not break-fast with Lyndhurst this morning, as I was nearly doing, instead of going down to Eton.'

'To Eton! and why to Eton?'

'For the sake of my young friend here, Lord Monmouth's grandson. By the bye, you are kinsmen. Let me present to your Grace, MR CONINGSBY.'

Chapter 2

THE political agitation which for a year and a half had shaken England to its centre, received, if possible, an increase to its intensity and virulence, when it was known, in the early part of the month of May 1832, that the Prime Minister had tendered his resignation to the King, which resignation had been graciously accepted.

The amendment carried by the Opposition in the House of Lords on the evening of the 7th of May, that the enfranchising clauses of the Reform Bill should be considered before entering into the question of disfranchisement, was the immediate cause of this startling event. The Lords had previously consented to the second reading of the Bill with the view of preventing that large increase of their numbers with which they had been long menaced; rather, indeed, by mysterious rumours than by any official declaration; but, nevertheless, in a manner which had carried conviction to no inconsiderable portion of the Opposition that the threat was not without foundation.[1]

During the progress of the Bill through the Lower House, the journals which were looked upon as the organs of the ministry had announced with unhesitating confidence, that Lord Grey was armed with what was then called a 'carte blanche' to create any number of peers necessary to insure its success. But public journalists who were under the control of the ministry, and whose statements were never contradicted, were not the sole authorities for this prevailing belief. Members of the House of Commons, who were strong supporters of the cabinet, though not connected with it by any official tie, had unequivocally stated in their places that the Sovereign had not resisted the advice of his counsellors to create peers, if such creation were required to carry into effect what was then styled 'the great national measure.' In more than one instance, ministers had been warned, that if they did not exercise that power with prompt energy, they might deserve

impeachment. And these intimations and announcements had
been made in the presence of leading members of the Government, and had received from them, at least, the sanction of their
silence.

It did not subsequently appear that the Reform ministers had
been invested with any such power;[2] but a conviction of the
reverse, fostered by these circumstances, had successfully acted
upon the nervous temperament, or the statesman-like prudence,
of a certain section of the peers, who consequently hesitated
in their course; were known as being no longer inclined to pursue
their policy of the preceding session; had thus obtained a title at
that moment in everybody's mouth, the title of 'THE
WAVERERS.'[3]

Notwithstanding, therefore, the opposition of the Duke of
Wellington and of Lord Lyndhurst, the Waverers carried the
second reading of the Reform Bill; and then, scared at the
consequences of their own headstrong timidity, they went in a
fright to the Duke and his able adviser to extricate them from
the inevitable result of their own conduct.[4] The ultimate device
of these distracted counsels, where daring and poltroonery,
principle and expediency, public spirit and private intrigue, each
threw an ingredient into the turbulent spell, was the celebrated
and successful amendment to which we have referred.

But the Whig ministers, who, whatever may have been their
faults, were at least men of intellect and courage, were not to be
beaten by 'the Waverers.' They might have made terms with
an audacious foe; they trampled on a hesitating opponent. Lord
Grey hastened to the palace.

Before the result of this appeal to the Sovereign was known,
for its effects were not immediate, on the second morning
after the vote in the House of Lords, Mr Rigby had made that
visit to Eton which had summoned very unexpectedly the youthful Coningsby to London. He was the orphan child of the youngest
of the two sons of the Marquess of Monmouth. It was a family
famous for its hatreds. The eldest son hated his father; and, it
was said, in spite had married a lady to whom that father was
attached and with whom Lord Monmouth then meditated a
second alliance. This eldest son lived at Naples, and had several

children, but maintained no connection either with his parent or his native country. On the other hand, Lord Monmouth hated his younger son, who had married, against his consent, a woman to whom that son was devoted. A system of domestic persecution, sustained by the hand of a master, had eventually broken up the health of its victim, who died of a fever in a foreign country, where he had sought some refuge from his creditors.

His widow returned to England with her child; and, not having a relation, and scarcely an acquaintance in the world, made an appeal to her husband's father, the wealthiest noble in England, and a man who was often prodigal, and occasionally generous. After some time, and more trouble, after urgent and repeated, and what would have seemed heart-rending, solicitations, the attorney of Lord Monmouth called upon the widow of his client's son, and informed her of his Lordship's decision. Provided she gave up her child, and permanently resided in one of the remotest counties, he was authorised to make her, in four quarterly payments, the yearly allowance of three hundred pounds, that being the income that Lord Monmouth, who was the shrewdest accountant in the country, had calculated a lone woman might very decently exist upon in a small market town in the county of Westmoreland.

Desperate necessity, the sense of her own forlornness, the utter impossibility to struggle with an omnipotent foe, who, her husband had taught her, was above all scruples, prejudices, and fears, and who, though he respected law, despised opinion, made the victim yield. But her sufferings were not long; the separation from her child, the bleak clime, the strange faces around her, sharp memory, and the dull routine of an unimpassioned life, all combined to wear out a constitution originally frail, and since shattered by many sorrows. Mrs Coningsby died the same day that her father-in-law was made a Marquess. He deserved his honours. The four votes he had inherited in the House of Commons[5] had been increased, by his intense volition and unsparing means, to ten; and the very day he was raised to his Marquisate, he commenced sapping fresh corporations, and was working for the strawberry leaf.[6] His honours were proclaimed in the London Gazette, and her decease was not even noticed in the County Chronicle; but the altars of Nemesis are beneath every outraged roof, and the death of this unhappy lady, apparently without an earthly friend or an earthly hope, desolate and deserted, and dying in obscure poverty, was not forgotten.

Coningsby was not more than nine years of age when he lost his last parent; and he had then been separated from her for nearly three years. But he remembered the sweetness of his nursery days. His mother, too, had written to him frequently since he quitted her, and her fond expressions had cherished the tenderness of his heart. He wept bitterly when his schoolmaster broke to him the news of his mother's death. True it was they had been long parted, and their prospect of again meeting was vague and dim; but his mother seemed to him his only link to human society. It was something to have a mother, even if he never saw her. Other boys went to see their mothers! he, at least, could talk of his. Now he was alone. His grandfather was to him only a name. Lord Monmouth resided almost constantly abroad, and during his rare visits to England had found no time or inclination to see the orphan, with whom he felt no sympathy. Even the death of the boy's mother, and the consequent arrangements, were notified to his master by a stranger. The letter which brought the sad intelligence was from Mr Rigby. It was the first time that name had been known to Coningsby.

Mr Rigby was member for one of Lord Monmouth's boroughs. He was the manager of Lord Monmouth's parliamentary influence, and the auditor of his vast estates. He was more; he was Lord Monmouth's companion when in England, his correspondent when abroad; hardly his counsellor, for Lord Monmouth never required advice; but Mr Rigby could instruct him in matters of detail, which Mr Rigby made amusing. Rigby was not a professional man; indeed, his origin, education, early pursuits, and studies, were equally obscure; but he had contrived in good time to squeeze himself into parliament, by means which no one could ever comprehend, and then set up to be a perfect man of business. The world took him at his word, for he was bold, acute, and voluble; with no thought, but a good deal of desultory information; and though destitute of all imagination and noble sentiment, was blessed with a vigorous, mendacious fancy, fruitful in small expedients, and never happier than when devising shifts for great men's scrapes.

They say that all of us have one chance in this life, and so it was with Rigby. After a struggle of many years, after a long series of the usual alternatives of small successes and small failures, after a few cleverish speeches and a good many cleverish pamphlets, with a considerable reputation, indeed, for pasquinades, most of which he never wrote, and articles in reviews to which it was whispered he had contributed, Rigby, who had already intrigued himself into a subordinate office, met with Lord Monmouth.

He was just the animal that Lord Monmouth wanted, for Lord Monmouth always looked upon human nature with the callous eye of a jockey. He surveyed Rigby, and he determined to buy him. He bought him; with his clear head, his indefatigable industry, his audacious tongue, and his ready and unscrupulous pen; with all his dates, all his lampoons; all his private memoirs, and all his political intrigues. It was a good purchase. Rigby became a great personage, and Lord Monmouth's man.

Mr Rigby, who liked to be doing a great many things at the same time, and to astonish the Tadpoles and Tapers with his energetic versatility, determined to superintend the education of Coningsby. It was a relation which identified him with the noble house of his pupil, or, properly speaking, his charge: for Mr Rigby affected rather the graceful dignity of the governor than the duties of a tutor. The boy was recalled from his homely, rural school, where he had been well grounded by a hard-working curate, and affectionately tended by the curate's unsophisticated wife. He was sent to a fashionable school preparatory to Eton, where he found about two hundred youths of noble families and connections, lodged in a magnificent villa, that had once been the retreat of a minister, superintended by a sycophantic Doctor of Divinity, already well beneficed, and not despairing of a bishopric by favouring the children of the great nobles. The doctor's lady, clothed in cashmeres, sometimes inquired after their health, and occasionally received a report as to their linen.

Mr Rigby had a classical retreat, not distant from this establishment, which he esteemed a Tusculum. There, surrounded by his busts and books, he wrote his lampoons and articles; massacred

a she liberal (it was thought that no one could lash a woman like
Rigby), cut up a rising genius whose politics were different from
his own, or scarified some unhappy wretch who had brought his
claims before parliament, proving, by garbled extracts from
official correspondence that no one could refer to, that the mal-
content instead of being a victim, was, on the contrary, a de-
faulter. Tadpole and Taper would back Rigby for a 'slashing reply'
against the field. Here, too, at the end of a busy week, he found
it occasionally convenient to entertain a clever friend or two of
equivocal reputation, with whom he had become acquainted in
former days of equal brotherhood. No one was more faithful to
his early friends than Mr Rigby, particularly if they could write
a squib.

It was in this refined retirement that Mr Rigby found time
enough, snatched from the toils of official life and parliamentary
struggles, to compose a letter on the study of History, addressed
to Coningsby. The style was as much like that of Lord Bolingbroke[7] as if it had been written by the authors of the 'Rejected
Addresses,'[8] and it began, 'My dear young friend.' This polished
composition, so full of good feeling and comprehensive views, and
all in the best taste, was not published. It was only privately
printed, and a few thousand copies were distributed among select
personages as an especial favour and mark of high consideration. Each copy given away seemed to Rigby like a certificate of
character; a property which, like all men of dubious repute, he
thoroughly appreciated. Rigby intrigued very much that the headmaster of Eton should adopt his discourse as a classbook. For this
purpose he dined with the Doctor,[9] told him several anecdotes of
the King, which intimated personal influence at Windsor; but the
headmaster was inflexible, and so Mr Rigby was obliged to be
content with having his Letter on History canonized as a classic
in the Preparatory Seminary, where the individual to whom it was
addressed was a scholar.

This change in the life of Coningsby contributed to his happiness. The various characters which a large school exhibited
interested a young mind whose active energies were beginning to
stir. His previous acquirements made his studies light; and he
was fond of sports, in which he was qualified to excel. He did not

particularly like Mr Rigby. There was something jarring and grating in that gentleman's voice and modes, from which the chords of the young heart shrank. He was not tender, though perhaps he wished to be; scarcely kind: but he was good-natured, at least to children. However, this connection was, on the whole, an agreeable one for Coningsby. He seemed suddenly to have friends; he never passed his holydays again at school. Mr Rigby was so clever that he contrived always to quarter Coningsby on the father of one of his school-fellows, for Mr Rigby knew all his school-fellows and all their fathers. Mr Rigby also called to see him, not unfrequently would give him a dinner at the Star and Garter, or even have him up to town for a week to Whitehall. Compared with his former forlorn existence, these were happy days, when he was placed under the gallery as a member's son, or went to the play with the butler!

When Coningsby had attained his twelfth year, an order was received from Lord Monmouth, who was at Rome, that he should go at once to Eton. This was the first great epoch of his life. There never was a youth who entered into that wonderful little world with more eager zest than Coningsby. Nor was it marvellous.

That delicious plain, studded with every creation of graceful culture; hamlet and hall, and grange; garden and grove, and park; that castle-palace, grey with glorious ages; those antique spires, hoar with faith and wisdom, the chapel and the college; that river winding through the shady meads; the sunny glade and the solemn avenue; the room in the Dame's house where we first order our own breakfast and first feel we are free; the stirring multitude, the energetic groups, the individual mind that leads, conquers, controls; the emulation and the affection; the noble strife and the tender sentiment; the daring exploit and the dashing scrape; the passion that pervades our life, and breathes in everything, from the aspiring study to the inspiring sport: oh! what hereafter can spur the brain and touch the heart like this; can give us a world so deeply and variously interesting; a life so full of quick and bright excitement, passed in a scene so fair?

Chapter 3

LORD MONMOUTH, who detested popular tumults as much as he despised public opinion, had remained during the agitating year of 1831 in his luxurious retirement in Italy, contenting himself with opposing the Reform Bill by proxy. But when his correspondent, Mr Rigby, had informed him, in the early part of the spring of 1832, of the probability of a change in the tactics of the Tory party, and that an opinion was becoming prevalent among their friends, that the great scheme must be defeated in detail rather than again withstood on principle, his Lordship, who was never wanting in energy when his own interests were concerned, immediately crossed the Alps, and travelled rapidly to England. He indulged a hope that the weight of his presence and the influence of his strong character, which was at once shrewd and courageous, might induce his friends to relinquish their half measure, a course to which his nature was repugnant. At all events, if they persisted in their intention, and the Bill went into committee, his presence was indispensable, for in that stage of a parliamentary proceeding proxies become ineffective.

The counsels of Lord Monmouth, though they coincided with those of the Duke of Wellington, did not prevail with the Waverers. Several of these high-minded personages had had their windows broken, and they were of opinion that a man who lived at Naples was not a competent judge of the state of public feeling in England. Besides, the days are gone by for senates to have their beards plucked in the forum. We live in an age of prudence. The leaders of the people, now, generally follow. The truth is, the peers were in a fright. 'Twas a pity; there is scarcely a less dignified entity than a patrician in a panic.

Among the most intimate companions of Coningsby at Eton, was Lord Henry Sydney, his kinsman. Coningsby had frequently passed his holydays of late at Beaumanoir, the seat of the Duke, Lord Henry's father. The Duke sat next to Lord Monmouth during the debate on the enfranchising question, and to while away the time, and from kindness of disposition, spoke, and spoke with warmth and favour, of his grandson. The polished Lord Monmouth bowed as if he were much gratified by this notice of one so dear to him. He had too much tact to admit that he had never yet seen his grandchild; but he asked some questions as to his progress and pursuits, his tastes and habits, which intimated the interest of an affectionate relative.

Nothing, however, was ever lost upon Lord Monmouth. No one had a more retentive memory, or a more observant mind. And the next day, when he received Mr Rigby at his morning levee, Lord Monmouth performed this ceremony in the high style of the old court, and welcomed his visitors in bed, he said with imperturbable calmness, and as if he had been talking of trying a new horse, 'Rigby, I should like to see the boy at Eton.'

There might be some objection to grant leave to Coningsby at this moment; but it was a rule with Mr Rigby never to make difficulties, or at least to persuade his patron that he, and he only, could remove them. He immediately undertook that the boy should be forthcoming, and notwithstanding the excitement of the moment, he went off next morning to fetch him.

They arrived in town rather early; and Rigby, wishing to know how affairs were going on, ordered the servant to drive immediately to the head-quarters of the party;[1] where a permanent committee watched every phasis of the impending revolution; and where every member of the Opposition, of note and trust, was instantly admitted to receive or to impart intelligence.

It was certainly not without emotion that Coningsby contemplated his first interview with his grandfather. All his experience of the ties of relationship, however limited, was full of tenderness and rapture. His memory often dwelt on his mother's sweet embrace; and ever and anon a fitful phantom of some past passage of domestic love haunted his gushing heart. The image of his father was less fresh in his mind; but still it was associated with a vague sentiment of kindness and joy; and the allusions to her husband in his mother's letters had cherished these impressions. To notice lesser sources of influence in his estimate of the domestic tie, he had witnessed under the roof of Beaumanoir the existence of a family bound together by the most beautiful affections. He could not forget how Henry Sydney was embraced by his sisters when he returned home; what frank and fraternal love existed between his kinsman and his elder brother; how affectionately the kind Duke had welcomed his son once more to the house where they had both been born; and the dim eyes, and saddened brows, and tones of tenderness, which rather looked than said farewell, when they went back to Eton.

And these rapturous meetings and these mournful adieus were occasioned only by a separation at the most of a few months, softened by constant correspondence and the communication of mutual sympathy. But Coningsby was to meet a relation, his near, almost his only, relation, for the first time; the relation, too, to whom he owed maintenance, education; it might be said, existence. It was a great incident for a great drama; something tragical in the depth and stir of its emotions. Even the imagination of the boy could not be insensible to its materials; and Coningsby was picturing to himself a beneficent and venerable gentleman pressing to his breast an agitated youth, when his reverie was broken by the carriage stopping before the gates of Monmouth House.

The gates were opened by a gigantic Swiss, and the carriage rolled into a huge court-yard. At its end Coningsby beheld a Palladian palace, with wings and colonnades encircling the court.

A double flight of steps led into a circular and marble hall, adorned with colossal busts of the Cæsars; the staircase in fresco by Sir James Thornhill, breathed with the loves and wars of gods and heroes. It led into a vestibule, painted in arabesque, hung with Venetian girandoles, and looking into gardens. Opening a door in this chamber, and proceeding some little way down a corridor, Mr Rigby and his companion arrived at the base of a private stair-case. Ascending a few steps, they reached a landing-place hung with tapestry. Drawing this aside, Mr Rigby opened a door, and ushered Coningsby through an ante-chamber into a small saloon, of beautiful proportions, and furnished in a brilliant and delicate taste.

'You will find more to amuse you here than where you were

before,' said Mr Rigby, 'and I shall not be nearly so long absent.'
So saying, he entered into an inner apartment.

The walls of the saloon, which were covered with light blue
satin, held, in silver panels, portraits of beautiful women, painted
by Boucher. Couches and easy chairs of every shape invited in
every quarter to luxurious repose; while amusement was afforded
by tables covered with caricatures, French novels, and endless
miniatures of foreign dancers, princesses, and sovereigns.

But Coningsby was so impressed with the impending interview
with his grandfather, that he neither sought nor required diversion. Now that the crisis was at hand, he felt agitated and nervous,
and wished that he was again at Eton. The suspense was sicken-
ing, yet he dreaded still more the summons. He was not long
alone; the door opened; he started, grew pale; he thought it was
his grandfather; it was not even Mr Rigby. It was Lord Monmouth's valet.

'Monsieur Konigby?'

'My name is Coningsby,' said the boy.

'Milor is ready to receive you,' said the valet.

Coningsby sprang forward with that desperation which the
scaffold requires. His face was pale; his hand was moist; his
heart beat with tumult. He had occasionally been summoned by
Dr Keate; that, too, was awful work, but, compared with the
present, a morning visit. Music, artillery, the roar of cannon, and
the blare of trumpets, may urge a man on to a forlorn hope;
ambition, one's constituents, the hell of previous failure, may
prevail on us to do a more desperate thing; speak in the House of
Commons; but there are some situations in life, such, for instance,
as entering the room of a dentist, in which the prostration of the
nervous system is absolute.

The moment had at length arrived when the desolate was to
find a benefactor, the forlorn a friend, the orphan a parent; when
the youth, after a childhood of adversity, was to be formally
received into the bosom of the noble house from which he had
been so long estranged, and at length to assume that social
position to which his lineage entitled him. Manliness might
support, affection might soothe, the happy anguish of such a
meeting; but it was undoubtedly one of those situations which stir

up the deep fountains of our nature, and before which the conventional proprieties of our ordinary manners instantaneously vanish.

Coningsby with an uncertain step followed his guide through a bed-chamber, the sumptuousness of which he could not notice, into the dressing-room of Lord Monmouth. Mr Rigby, facing Coningsby as he entered, was leaning over the back of a large chair, from which as Coningsby was announced by the valet, the Lord of the house slowly rose, for he was suffering slightly from the gout, his left hand resting on an ivory stick. Lord Monmouth was in height above the middle size, but somewhat portly and corpulent. His countenance was strongly marked; sagacity on the brow, sensuality in the mouth and jaw. His head was bald, but there were remains of the rich brown locks on which he once prided himself. His large deep blue eye, madid[2] and yet piercing, showed that the secretions of his brain were apportioned, half to voluptuousness, half to common sense. But his general mien was truly grand; full of a natural nobility, of which no one was more sensible than himself. Lord Monmouth was not in dishabille; on the contrary, his costume was exact, and even careful. Rising as we have mentioned when his grandson entered, and leaning with his left hand on his ivory cane, he made Coningsby such a bow as Louis Quatorze might have bestowed on the ambassador of the United Provinces.[3] Then extending his right hand, which the boy tremblingly touched, Lord Monmouth said:

'How do you like Eton?'

This contrast to the reception which he had imagined, hoped, feared, paralysed the reviving energies of young Coningsby. He felt stupified; he looked almost aghast. In the chaotic tumult of his mind, his memory suddenly seemed to receive some miraculous inspiration. Mysterious phrases heard in his earliest boyhood, unnoticed then, long since forgotten, rose to his ear. Who was this grandfather, seen not before, seen now for the first time? Where was the intervening link of blood between him and this superb and icy being? The boy sank into the chair which had been placed for him, and leaning on the table burst into tears.

Here was a business! If there were one thing which would have made Lord Monmouth travel from London to Naples at four-and-twenty hours' notice, it was to avoid a scene. He hated scenes. He hated feelings. He saw instantly the mistake he had made in sending for his grandchild. He was afraid that Coningsby was tender-hearted like his father. Another tender-hearted Coningsby! Unfortunate family! Degenerate race! He decided in his mind that Coningsby must be provided for in the Church, and looked at Mr Rigby, whose principal business it always was to disembarrass his patron from the disagreeable.

Mr Rigby instantly came forward and adroitly led the boy into the adjoining apartment, Lord Monmouth's bed-chamber, closing the door of the dressing-room behind him.

'My dear young friend,' said Mr Rigby, 'what is all this?'

A sob the only answer.

'What can be the matter?' said Mr Rigby.

'I was thinking,' said Coningsby, 'of poor mamma!'

'Hush!' said Mr Rigby; 'Lord Monmouth never likes to hear of people who are dead; so you must take care never to mention your mother or your father.'

In the meantime Lord Monmouth had decided on the fate of Coningsby. The Marquis thought he could read characters by a glance, and in general he was successful, for his natural sagacity had been nurtured by great experience. His grandson was not to his taste; amiable no doubt, but spooney.

We are too apt to believe that the character of a boy is easily read. 'Tis a mystery the most profound. Mark what blunders parents constantly make as to the nature of their own offspring, bred, too, under their eyes, and displaying every hour their characteristics. How often in the nursery does the genius count as a dunce because he is pensive; while a rattling urchin is invested with almost supernatural qualities because his animal spirits make him impudent and flippant! The school-boy, above all others, is not the simple being the world imagines. In that young bosom are often stirring passions as strong as our own, desires not less violent, a volition not less supreme. In that young bosom what burning love, what intense ambition, what avarice, what lust of power; envy that fiends might emulate, hate that man might fear!

Chapter 4

'Come,' said Mr Rigby, when Coningsby was somewhat composed, 'come with me and we will see the house.'

So they descended once more the private staircase, and again entered the vestibule.

'If you had seen these gardens when they were illuminated for a fête to George IV,' said Rigby, as crossing the chamber he ushered his charge into the state apartments. The splendour and variety of the surrounding objects soon distracted the attention of the boy, for the first time in the palace of his fathers. He traversed saloon after saloon hung with rare tapestry and the gorgeous products of foreign looms; filled with choice pictures and creations of curious art; cabinets that sovereigns might envy, and colossal vases of malachite presented by emperors. Coningsby alternately gazed up to ceilings glowing with colour and with gold, and down upon carpets bright with the fancies and vivid with the tints of Aubusson and of Axminster.

'This grandfather of mine is a great prince,' thought Coningsby, as musing he stood before a portrait in which he recognised the features of the being from whom he had so recently and so strangely parted. There he stood, Philip Augustus, Marquess of Monmouth, in his robes of state, with his new coronet on a table near him, a despatch lying at hand that indicated the special mission of high ceremony of which he had been the illustrious envoy,[1] and the garter beneath his knee.

'You will have plenty of opportunities to look at the pictures,' said Rigby, observing that the boy had now quite recovered himself. 'Some luncheon will do you no harm after our drive;' and he opened the door of another apartment.

It was a pretty room adorned with a fine picture of the chase; at a round table in the centre sat two ladies interested in the meal to which Rigby had alluded.

'Ah, Mr Rigby!' said the eldest, yet young and beautiful, and speaking, though with fluency, in a foreign accent, 'come and tell me some news. Have you seen Milor?' and then she threw a scrutinizing glance from a dark flashing eye at his companion.

'Let me present to your Highness,' said Rigby, with an air of some ceremony, 'Mr Coningsby.'

'My dear young friend,' said the lady, extending her white hand with an air of joyous welcome, 'this is Lucretia, my daughter. We love you already. Lord Monmouth will be so charmed to see you. What beautiful eyes he has, Mr Rigby. Quite like Milor.'

The young lady, who was really more youthful than Coningsby, but of a form and stature so developed that she appeared almost a woman, bowed to the guest with some ceremony, and a faint sullen smile, and then proceeded with her Perigord pie.

'You must be so hungry after your drive,' said the elder lady, placing Coningsby at her side, and herself filling his plate.

This was true enough; and while Mr Rigby and the lady talked an infinite deal about things which he did not understand, and persons of whom he had never heard, our little hero made his first meal in his paternal house with no ordinary zest; and renovated by the pasty and a glass of sherry, felt altogether a different being from what he was, when he had undergone the terrible interview in which he began to reflect he had considerably exposed himself. His courage revived, his senses rallied, he replied to the interrogations of the lady with calmness, but with promptness and propriety. It was evident that he had made a favourable impression on her Highness, for ever and anon she put a truffle or some small delicacy in his plate, and insisted upon his taking some particular confectionary, because it was a favourite of her own. When she rose, she said, –

'In ten minutes the carriage will be at the door; and if you like, my dear young friend, you shall be our beau.'

'There is nothing I should like so much,' said Coningsby.

'Ah!' said the lady, with the sweetest smile, 'he is frank.'

The ladies bowed and retired; Mr Rigby returned to the Marquess, and the groom of the chambers led Coningsby to his room.

This lady, so courteous to Coningsby, was the Princess Colonna, a Roman dame, the second wife of Prince Paul Colonna. The

Prince had first married when a boy, and into a family not inferior to his own. Of this union, in every respect unhappy, the Princess Lucretia was the sole offspring. He was a man dissolute and devoted to play; and cared for nothing much but his pleasures and billiards, in which latter he was esteemed unrivalled. According to some, in a freak of passion, according to others, to cancel a gambling debt, he had united himself to his present wife, whose origin was obscure; but with whom he contrived to live on terms of apparent cordiality, for she was much admired, and made the society of her husband sought by those who contributed to his enjoyment. Among these especially figured the Marquess of Monmouth, between whom and Prince Colonna the world recognised as existing the most intimate and entire friendship, so that his Highness and his family were frequent guests under the roof of the English nobleman, and now accompanied him on a visit to England.

Chapter 5

IN the meantime, while ladies are luncheoning on Perigord pie, or coursing in whirling britskas, performing all the singular ceremonies of a London morning in the heart of the season; making visits where nobody is seen, and making purchases which are not wanted; the world is in agitation and uproar. At present the world and the confusion are limited to St James's Street and Pall Mall; but soon the boundaries and the tumult will be extended to the intended metropolitan boroughs; to-morrow they will spread over the manufacturing districts. It is perfectly evident, that before eight-and-forty hours have passed, the country will be in a state of fearful crisis. And how can it be otherwise? Is it not a truth that the subtle Chief Baron has been closeted one whole hour with the King; that shortly after, with thoughtful brow and compressed lip, he was marked in his daring chariot entering the courtyard of Apsley House?[1] Great was the panic at Brookes', wild the hopes of Carlton Terrace; all the gentlemen who expected to have been made peers perceived that the country was going to be given over to a rapacious oligarchy.

In the meantime Tadpole and Taper, who had never quitted for an instant the mysterious head-quarters of the late Opposition, were full of hopes and fears, and asked many questions, which they chiefly answered themselves.

'I wonder what Lord Lyndhurst will say to the King,' said Taper.

'He has plenty of pluck,' said Tadpole.

'I almost wish now that Rigby had breakfasted with him this morning,' said Taper.

'If the King be firm, and the country sound,' said Tadpole, 'and Lord Monmouth keep his boroughs, I should not wonder to see Rigby made a privy councillor.'

'There is no precedent for an under-secretary being a privy councillor,' said Taper.

'But we live in revolutionary times,' said Tadpole.

'Gentlemen,' said the groom of the chambers, in a loud voice, entering the room, 'I am desired to state that the Duke of Wellington is with the King.'

'There *is* a Providence!' exclaimed an agitated gentleman, the patent of whose intended peerage had not been signed the day that the Duke had quitted office in 1830.

'I always thought the King would be firm,' said Mr Tadpole.

'I wonder who will have the India Board,' said Taper.

At this moment three or four gentlemen entered the room in a state of great bustle and excitement; they were immediately surrounded.

'Is it true?' 'Quite true; not the slightest doubt. Saw him myself. Not at all hissed; certainly not hooted. Perhaps a little hissed. One fellow really cheered him. Saw him myself. Say what they like, there *is* reaction.' 'But Constitution Hill, they say?' 'Well, there was a sort of inclination to a row on Constitution Hill; but the Duke quite firm; pistols, and carriage doors bolted.'

Such may give a faint idea of the anxious inquiries and the satisfactory replies that were occasioned by the entrance of this group.

'Up, guards, and at them!' exclaimed Tadpole, rubbing his hands in a fit of patriotic enthusiasm.

Later in the afternoon, about five o'clock, the high change of political gossip, when the room was crowded, and every one had his rumour, Mr Rigby looked in again to throw his eye over the evening papers, and catch in various chit-chat the tone of public or party feeling on the 'crisis.' Then it was known that the Duke had returned from the King, having accepted the charge of forming an administration. An administration to do what? Portentous question! Were concessions to be made? And if so, what? Was it altogether impossible, and too late, 'stare super vias antiquas?'[2] Questions altogether above your Tadpoles and your Tapers, whose idea of the necessities of the age was that they themselves should be in office.

Lord Eskdale came up to Mr Rigby. This peer was a noble Crœsus,[3] acquainted with all the gradations of life; a voluptuary who could be a Spartan; clear-sighted, unprejudiced, sagacious; the best judge in the world of a horse or a man; he was the universal referee; a quarrel about a bet or a mistress was solved by him in a moment, and in a manner which satisfied both parties. He patronised and appreciated the fine arts, though a jockey; respected literary men, though he only read French novels; and without any affectation of tastes which he did not possess, was looked upon by every singer and dancer in Europe as their natural champion. The secret of his strong character and great influence was his self-composure, which an earthquake or a Reform Bill could not disturb, and which in him was the result of temperament and experience. He was an intimate acquaintance of Lord Monmouth, for they had many tastes in common; were both men of considerable, and in some degree similar, abilities; and were the two greatest proprietors of close boroughs in the country.

'Do you dine at Monmouth House to-day?' inquired Lord Eskdale of Mr Rigby.

'Where I hope to meet your Lordship. The Whig papers are very subdued,' continued Mr Rigby.

'Ah! they have not the cue yet,' said Lord Eskdale.

'And what do you think of affairs?' inquired his companion.

'I think the hounds are too hot to hark off now,' said Lord Eskdale.

'There is one combination,' said Rigby, who seemed meditating an attack on Lord Eskdale's button.

'Give it us at dinner,' said Lord Eskdale, who knew his man, and made an adroit movement forwards, as if he were very anxious to see the *Globe* newspaper.

In the course of two or three hours these gentlemen met again in the green drawing-room of Monmouth House. Mr Rigby was sitting on the sofa by Lord Monmouth, detailing in whispers all his gossip of the morn: Lord Eskdale murmuring quaint inquiries into the ear of the Princess Lucretia. Madame Colonna made remarks alternately to two gentlemen, who paid her assiduous court. One of these was Mr Ormsby; the school, the college, and the club crony of Lord Monmouth, who had been his shadow through life; travelled with him in early days, won money with him at play, had been his colleague in the House of Commons; and was still one of his nominees. Mr Ormsby was a millionaire, which Lord Monmouth liked. He liked his companions to be very rich or very poor; to be his equals, able to play with him at high stakes, or join him in a great speculation; or to be his tools, and to amuse and serve him. There was nothing which he despised and disliked so much as a moderate fortune.

The other gentleman was of a different class and character. Nature had intended Lucian Gay for a scholar and a wit; necessity had made him a scribbler and a buffoon. He had distinguished himself at the University; but he had no patrimony, nor those powers of perseverance which success in any learned profession requires. He was good-looking, had great animal spirits, and a keen sense of enjoyment, and could not drudge. Moreover he had a fine voice, and sang his own songs with considerable taste; accomplishments which made his fortune in society and completed his ruin. In due time he extricated himself from the bench and merged into journalism, by means of which he chanced to become acquainted with Mr Rigby. That worthy individual was not slow in detecting the treasure he had lighted on; a wit, a ready and happy writer, a joyous and tractable being, with the education, and still the feelings and manners, of a gentleman. Frequent were the Sunday dinners which found Gay a guest at Mr Rigby's villa; numerous the airy pasquinades which he left behind, and which made the fortune of his patron. Flattered by the familiar acquaintance of a man of station, and sanguine that he had found the link which would sooner or later restore him to the polished world that he had forfeited, Gay laboured in his vocation with enthusiasm and success. Willingly would Rigby have kept his treasure to himself; and truly he hoarded it for a long time, but it oozed out. Rigby loved the reputation of possessing the complete art of society. His dinners were celebrated at least for their guests. Great intellectual illustrations were found there blended with rank and high station. Rigby loved to patronise; to play the minister unbending and seeking relief from the cares of council in the society of authors, artists, and men of science. He liked dukes to dine with him and hear him scatter his audacious criticisms to Sir Thomas or Sir Humphry. They went away astounded by the powers of their host, who, had he not fortunately devoted those powers to their party, must apparently have rivalled Vandyke, or discovered the safety-lamp.[4]

Now in these dinners, Lucian Gay, who had brilliant conversational powers, and who possessed all the resources of boon companionship, would be an invaluable ally. He was therefore admitted, and inspired both by the present enjoyment, and the future to which it might lead, his exertions were untiring, various, most successful. Rigby's dinners became still more celebrated. It, however, necessarily followed that the guests who were charmed by Gay, wished Gay also to be their guest. Rigby was very jealous of this, but it was inevitable; still by constant manœuvre, by intimations of some exercise, some day or other, of substantial patronage in his behalf, by a thousand little arts by which he carved out work for Gay which often prevented him accepting invitations to great houses in the country, by judicious loans of small sums on Lucian's notes of hand and other analogous devices, Rigby contrived to keep the wit in a fair state of bondage and dependence.

One thing Rigby was resolved on: Gay should never get into Monmouth House. That was an empyrean too high for his wing to soar in. Rigby kept that social monopoly distinctively to mark the relation that subsisted between them as patron and client. It was something to swagger about when they were together after their second bottle of claret. Rigby kept his resolution for some years, which the frequent and prolonged absence of the Marquess rendered not very difficult. But we are the creatures of circumstances; at least the Rigby race particularly. Lord Monmouth returned to England one year, and wanted to be amused. He wanted a jester: a man about him who would make him, not laugh, for that was impossible, but smile more frequently, tell good stories, say good things, and sing now and then, especially French songs. Early in life Rigby would have attempted all this, though he had neither fun, voice, nor ear. But his hold on Lord Monmouth no longer depended on the mere exercise of agreeable qualities, he had become indispensable to his Lordship, by more serious if not higher considerations. And what with auditing his accounts, guarding his boroughs, writing him, when absent, gossip by every post, and when in England deciding on every question and arranging every matter which might otherwise have ruffled the sublime repose of his patron's existence, Rigby might be excused if he shrank a little from the minor part of table wit, particularly when we remember all his subterranean journalism, his acid squibs, and his malicious paragraphs, and, what Tadpole called, his 'slashing articles.'

These 'slashing articles' were, indeed, things which, had they appeared as anonymous pamphlets, would have obtained the contemptuous reception which in an intellectual view no compositions more surely deserved; but whispered as the productions of one behind the scenes, and appearing in the pages of a party review, they were passed off as genuine coin, and took in great numbers of the lieges, especially in the country. They were written in a style apparently modelled on the briefs of those sharp attorneys who weary advocates with their clever commonplace; teasing with obvious comment, and torturing with inevitable inference. The affectation of order in the statement of facts had all the lucid method of an adroit pettifogger. They dealt much in extracts from newspapers, quotations from the *Annual Register*, parallel passages in forgotten speeches, arranged with a formidable array of dates rarely accurate. When the writer was of opinion he had made a point, you may be sure the hit was in italics, that last resource of the Forcible Feebles.[5] He handled a particular in chronology as if he were proving an alibi at the Criminal Court. The censure was coarse without being strong, and vindictive when it would have been sarcastic. Now and then there was a passage which aimed at a higher flight, and nothing can be conceived more unlike genuine feeling, or more offensive to pure taste. And yet, perhaps, the most ludicrous characteristic of these factious gallimaufreys was an occasional assumption of the high moral and admonitory tone, which when we recurred to the general spirit of the discourse, and were apt to recall the character of its writer, irresistibly reminded one of Mrs Cole and her prayer-book.

To return to Lucian Gay. It was a rule with Rigby that no one, if possible, should do anything for Lord Monmouth but himself; and as a jester must be found, he was determined that his Lordship should have the best in the market, and that he should have the credit of furnishing the article. As a reward, therefore, for many past services, and a fresh claim to his future exertions,

Rigby one day broke to Gay that the hour had at length arrived when the highest object of reasonable ambition on his part, and the fulfilment of one of Rigby's long-cherished and dearest hopes, were alike to be realised. Gay was to be presented to Lord Monmouth and dine at Monmouth House.

The acquaintance was a successful one; very agreeable to both parties. Gay became an habitual guest of Lord Monmouth when his patron was in England; and in his absence received frequent and substantial marks of his kind recollection, for Lord Monmouth was generous to those who amused him.

In the meantime the hour of dinner is at hand. Coningsby, who had lost the key of his carpet-bag, which he finally cut open with a penknife that he found on his writing-table, and the blade of which he broke in the operation, only reached the drawing-room as the figure of his grandfather, leaning on his ivory cane, and following his guests, was just visible in the distance. He was soon overtaken. Perceiving Coningsby, Lord Monmouth made him a bow, not so formal a one as in the morning, but still a bow, and said, 'I hope you liked your drive.'

Chapter 6

A LITTLE dinner, not more than the Muses, with all the guests clever, and some pretty, offers human life and human nature under very favourable circumstances. In the present instance, too, every one was anxious to please, for the host was entirely well-bred, never selfish in little things, and always contributed his quota to the general fund of polished sociability.

Although there was really only one thought in every male mind present, still, regard for the ladies, and some little apprehension of the servants, banished politics from discourse during the greater part of the dinner, with the occasional exception of some rapid and flying allusion which the initiated understood, but which remained a mystery to the rest. Nevertheless an old story now and then well told by Mr Ormsby, a new joke now and then well introduced by Mr Gay, some dashing assertion by Mr Rigby, which, though wrong, was startling; this agreeable blending of anecdote, jest, and paradox, kept everything fluent, and produced that degree of mild excitation which is desirable. Lord Monmouth sometimes summed up with an epigrammatic sentence, and turned the conversation by a question, in case it dwelt too much on the same topic. Lord Eskdale addressed himself principally to the ladies; inquired after their morning drive and doings, spoke of new fashions, and quoted a letter from Paris. Madame Colonna was not witty, but she had that sweet Roman frankness which is so charming. The presence of a beautiful woman, natural and good-tempered, even if she be not a L'Espinasse or a De Stael,[1] is animating.

Nevertheless, owing probably to the absorbing powers of the forbidden subject, there were moments when it seemed that a pause was impending, and Mr Ormsby, an old hand, seized one of these critical instants to address a good-natured question to Coningsby, whose acquaintance he had already cultivated by taking wine with him.

'And how do you like Eton?' asked Mr Ormsby.

It was the identical question which had been presented to Coningsby in the memorable interview of the morning, and which had received no reply; or rather had produced on his part a sentimental ebullition that had absolutely destined or doomed him to the Church.

'I should like to see the fellow who did *not* like Eton,' said Coningsby, briskly, determined this time to be very brave.

'Gad I must go down and see the old place,' said Mr Ormsby, touched by a pensive reminiscence. 'One can get a good bed and bottle of port at the Christopher, still?'

'You had better come and try, sir,' said Coningsby. 'If you will come some day and dine with me at the Christopher, I will give you such a bottle of champagne as you never tasted yet.'

The Marquess looked at him, but said nothing.

'Ah! I liked a dinner at the Christopher,' said Mr Ormsby; after mutton, mutton, mutton, every day, it was not a bad thing.'

'We had venison for dinner every week last season,' said Coningsby; 'Buckhurst had it sent up from his park. But I don't care for dinner. Breakfast is my lounge.'

'Ah! those little rolls and pats of butter!' said Mr Ormsby. 'Short commons,[2] though. What do you think we did in my time? We used to send over the way to get a mutton-chop.'

'I wish you could see Buckhurst and me at breakfast,' said Coningsby, 'with a pound of Castle's sausages!'

'What Buckhurst is that, Harry?' inquired Lord Monmouth, in a tone of some interest, and for the first time calling him by his Christian name.

'Sir Charles Buckhurst, sir, a Berkshire man: Shirley Park is his place.'

'Why, that must be Charley's son, Eskdale,' said Lord Monmouth; 'I had no idea he could be so young.'

'He married late, you know, and had nothing but daughters for a long time.'

'Well, I hope there will be no Reform Bill for Eton,' said Lord Monmouth, musingly.

The servants had now retired.

'I think, Lord Monmouth,' said Mr Rigby, 'we must ask permission to drink one toast to-day.'

'Nay, I will myself give it,' he replied. 'Madame Colonna, you
will, I am sure, join us when we drink, THE DUKE!'[3]

'Ah! what a man!' exclaimed the Princess. 'What a pity it is
you have a House of Commons here! England would be the
greatest country in the world if it were not for that House of
Commons. It makes so much confusion!'

'Don't abuse our property,' said Lord Eskdale; 'Lord Monmouth
and I have still twenty votes of that same body between us.'

'And there is a combination,' said Rigby, 'by which you may
still keep them.'

'Ah! now for Rigby's combination,' said Lord Eskdale.

'The only thing that can save this country,' said Rigby, 'is a
coalition on a sliding scale.'[4]

'You had better buy up the Birmingham Union and the other
bodies,'[5] said Lord Monmouth; 'I believe it might all be done for
two or three hundred thousand pounds; and the newspapers too.
Pitt would have settled this business long ago.'

'Well, at any rate, we are in,' said Rigby, 'and we must do
something.'

'I should like to see Grey's list of new peers,'[6] said Lord
Eskdale. 'They say there are several members of our club in it.'

'And the claims to the honour are so opposite,' said Lucian Gay;
'one, on account of his large estate; another, because he has none;
one, because he has a well-grown family to perpetuate the title;
another, because he has no heir, and no power of ever obtaining
one.'

'I wonder how he will form his cabinet,' said Lord Monmouth; 'the old story won't do.'[7]

'I hear that Baring is to be one of the new cards; they say
it will please in the city,' said Lord Eskdale. 'I suppose they
will pick out of hedge and ditch everything that has ever had
the semblance of liberalism.'

'Affairs in my time were never so complicated,' said Mr Ormsby.

'Nay, it appears to me to lie in a nutshell,' said Lucian Gay; 'one
party wishes to keep their old boroughs, and the other to get their
new peers.'

Chapter 7

THE future historian of the country will be perplexed to ascertain what was the distinct object which the Duke of Wellington proposed to himself in the political manœuvres of May 1832.[1] It was known that the passing of the Reform Bill was a condition absolute with the King; it was unquestionable, that the first general election under the new law must ignominiously expel the Anti-Reform Ministry from power; who would then resume their seats on the Opposition benches in both Houses with the loss not only of their boroughs, but of that reputation for political consistency, which might have been some compensation for the parliamentary influence of which they had been deprived. It is difficult to recognise in this premature effort of the Anti-Reform leader to thrust himself again into the conduct of public affairs, any indications of the prescient judgment which might have been expected from such a quarter. It savoured rather of restlessness than of energy; and, while it proved in its progress not only an ignorance on his part of the public mind, but of the feelings of his own party, it terminated under circumstances which were humiliating to the Crown, and painfully significant of the future position of the House of Lords in the new constitutional scheme.

The Duke of Wellington has ever been the votary of circumstances. He cares little for causes. He watches events rather than seeks to produce them. It is a characteristic of the military mind. Rapid combinations, the result of a quick, vigilant, and comprehensive glance, are generally triumphant in the field: but in civil affairs, where results are not immediate; in diplomacy and in the management of deliberative assemblies, where there is much intervening time and many counteracting causes, this velocity of decision, this fitful and precipitate action, are often productive of considerable embarrassment, and sometimes of terrible discomfiture. It is remarkable that men celebrated for military prudence are often found to be headstrong statesmen. In civil life a great general is frequently and strangely the creature of impulse; influenced in his political movements by the last snatch of information; and often the creature of the last aide-de-camp who has his ear.

We shall endeavour to trace in another chapter the reasons which on this, as on previous and subsequent occasions, induced Sir Robert Peel to stand aloof, if possible, from official life, and made him reluctant to re-enter the service of his Sovereign. In the present instance, even temporary success could only have been secured by the utmost decision, promptness, and energy. These were all wanting: some were afraid to follow the bold example of their leader; many were disinclined. In eight-and-forty hours it was known there was a 'hitch.'

The Reform party, who had been rather stupified than appalled by the accepted mission of the Duke of Wellington, collected their scattered senses, and rallied their forces. The agitators harangued, the mobs hooted. The City of London, as if the King had again tried to seize the five members, appointed a permanent committee of the Common Council to watch the fortunes of the 'great national measure,' and to report daily.[2] Brookes', which was the only place that at first was really frightened and talked of compromise, grew valiant again; while young Whig heroes jumped upon club-room tables, and delivered fiery invectives. Emboldened by these demonstrations, the House of Commons met in great force, and passed a vote which struck, without disguise, at all rival powers in the State; virtually announced its supremacy; revealed the forlorn position of the House of Lords under the new arrangement; and seemed to lay for ever the fluttering phantom of regal prerogative.[3]

It was on the 9th of May that Lord Lyndhurst was with the King, and on the 15th all was over. Nothing in parliamentary history so humiliating as the funeral oration delivered that day by the Duke of Wellington over the old constitution, that, modelled on the Venetian,[4] had governed England since the accession of the House of Hanover. He described his Sovereign, when his Grace first repaired to his Majesty, as in a state of the greatest 'difficulty and distress,' appealing to his never-failing loyalty to extricate him from his trouble and vexation. The Duke of Wellington, representing the House of Lords, sympathises with the King, and pledges his utmost efforts for his Majesty's relief. But after five days' exertion, this man of indomitable will and invincible fortunes, resigns the task in discomfiture and despair, and alleges as the only and sufficient reason of his utter and hopeless defeat, that the House of Commons had come to a vote which ran counter to the contemplated exercise of the prerogative.

From that moment power passed from the House of Lords to another assembly. But if the peers have ceased to be magnificoes, may it not also happen that the Sovereign may cease to be a Doge? It is not impossible that the political movements of our time, which seem on the surface to have a tendency to democracy, may have in reality a monarchical bias.

In less than a fortnight's time the House of Lords, like James II,[5] having abdicated their functions by absence, the Reform Bill passed; the ardent monarch, who a few months before had expressed his readiness to go down to Parliament, in a hackney-coach if necessary, to assist its progress, now declining personally to give his assent to its provisions.[6]

In the protracted discussions to which this celebrated measure gave rise, nothing is more remarkable than the perplexities into which the speakers of both sides are thrown, when they touch upon the nature of the representative principle. On one hand it was maintained, that, under the old system, the people were virtually represented; while, on the other, it was triumphantly urged, that if the principle be conceded, the people should not be virtually, but actually, represented. But who are the people? And where are you to draw a line? And why should there be any? It was urged that a contribution to the taxes was the constitutional qualification for the suffrage. But we have established a system of taxation in this country of so remarkable a nature, that the beggar who chews his quid as he sweeps a crossing, is contributing to the imposts! Is he to have a vote? He is one of the people, and he yields his quota to the public burthens.

Amid these conflicting statements, and these confounding conclusions, it is singular that no member of either House should have recurred to the original character of these popular assemblies, which have always prevailed among the northern nations. We still

retain in the antique phraseology of our statutes the term which
might have beneficially guided a modern Reformer in his recon-
structive labours.

When the crowned Northman consulted on the welfare of his
kingdom, he assembled the ESTATES of his realm. Now an estate
is a class of the nation invested with political rights. There
appeared the estate of the clergy, of the barons, of other classes.
In the Scandinavian kingdoms to this day, the estate of the
peasants sends its representatives to the Diet. In England, under
the Normans, the Church and the Baronage were convoked,
together with the estate of the Community, a term which then
probably described the inferior holders of land, whose tenure was
not immediate of the Crown. This Third Estate was so numerous,
that convenience suggested its appearance by representation;
while the others, more limited, appeared, and still appear,
personally. The Third Estate was reconstructed as circumstances
developed themselves. It was a Reform of Parliament when the
towns were summoned.

In treating the House of the Third Estate as the House of the
People, and not as the House of a privileged class, the Ministry
and Parliament of 1831 virtually conceded the principle of
Universal Suffrage. In this point of view the ten-pound franchise[7]
was an arbitrary, irrational, and impolitic qualification. It had,
indeed, the merit of simplicity, and so had the constitutions of
Abbé Siéyès.[8] But its immediate and inevitable result was
Chartism.[9]

But if the Ministry and Parliament of 1831 had announced that
the time had arrived when the Third Estate should be enlarged and
reconstructed, they would have occupied an intelligible position;
and if, instead of simplicity of elements in its reconstruction, they
had sought, on the contrary, various and varying materials which
would have neutralised the painful predominance of any particular interest in the new scheme, and prevented those banded
jealousies which have been its consequences, the nation would
have found itself in a secure condition. Another class not less
numerous than the existing one, and invested with privileges not
less important, would have been added to the public estates of the
realm; and the bewildering phrase 'the People' would have

remained, what it really is, a term of natural philosophy, and not of political science.[10]

During this eventful week of May 1832, when an important revolution was effected in the most considerable of modern kingdoms, in a manner so tranquil, that the victims themselves were scarcely conscious at the time of the catastrophe, Coningsby passed his hours in unaccustomed pleasures, and in novel excitement. Although he heard daily from the lips of Mr Rigby and his friends that England was for ever lost, the assembled guests still contrived to do justice to his grandfather's excellent dinners; nor did the impending ruin that awaited them prevent the Princess Colonna from going to the Opera, whither she very good-naturedly took Coningsby. Madame Colonna, indeed, gave such gratifying accounts of her dear young friend, that Coningsby became daily a greater favourite with Lord Monmouth, who cherished the idea that his grandson had inherited not merely the colour of his eyes, but something of his shrewd and fearless spirit.

With Lucretia, Coningsby did not much advance. She remained silent and sullen. She was not beautiful; pallid, with a lowering brow, and an eye that avoided meeting another's. Madame Colonna, though good-natured, felt for her something of the affection for which step-mothers are celebrated. Lucretia, indeed, did not encourage her kindness, which irritated her step-mother, who seemed seldom to address her but to rate and chide; Lucretia never replied, but looked dogged. Her father, the Prince, did not compensate for this treatment. The memory of her mother, whom he had greatly disliked, did not soften his heart. He was a man still young; slender, not tall; very handsome, but worn; a haggard Antinous;[11] his beautiful hair daily thinning; his dress rich and effeminate; many jewels, much lace. He seldom spoke, but was polished, though moody.

At the end of the week, Coningsby returned to Eton. On the eve of his departure, Lord Monmouth desired his grandson to meet him in his apartments on the morrow, before quitting his roof. This farewell visit was as kind and gracious as the first one had been repulsive. Lord Monmouth gave Coningsby his blessing and ten pounds; desired that he would order a dress, anything he liked, for the approaching Montem,[12] which Lord Monmouth meant to attend; and informed his grandson that he should order that in future a proper supply of game and venison should be forwarded to Eton for the use of himself and his friends.

Chapter 8

AFTER eight o'clock school, the day following the return of Coningsby, according to custom, he repaired to Buckhurst's room, where Henry Sydney, Lord Vere, and our hero held with him their breakfast mess. They were all in the fifth form, and habitual companions, on the river or on the Fives' Wall, at cricket or at foot-ball. The return of Coningsby, their leader alike in sport and study, inspired them to-day with unusual spirits, which, to say the truth, were never particularly depressed. Where he had been, what he had seen, what he had done, what sort of fellow his grandfather was, whether the visit had been a success; here were materials for almost endless inquiry. And indeed, to do them justice, the last question was not the least exciting to them; for the deep and cordial interest which all felt in Coningsby's welfare far outweighed the curiosity which, under ordinary circumstances, they would have experienced on the return of one of their companions from an unusual visit to London. The report of their friend imparted to them unbounded satisfaction, when they learned that his relative was a splendid fellow; that he had been loaded with kindness and favours; that Monmouth House, the wonders of which he rapidly sketched, was hereafter to be his home; that Lord Monmouth was coming down to Montem; that Coningsby was to order any dress he liked, build a new boat if he chose; and, finally, had been pouched in a manner worthy of a Marquess and a grandfather.

'By the bye,' said Buckhurst, when the hubbub had a little subsided, 'I am afraid you will not half like it, Coningsby; but, old fellow, I had no idea you would be back this morning; I have asked Millbank to breakfast here.'

A cloud stole over the clear brow of Coningsby.

'It was my fault,' said the amiable Henry Sydney; 'but I really wanted to be civil to Millbank, and as you were not here, I put Buckhurst up to ask him.'

'Well,' said Coningsby, as if sullenly resigned, 'never mind; but why should you ask an infernal manufacturer?'

'Why the Duke always wished me to pay him some attention,' said Lord Henry, mildly. 'His family were so civil to us when we were at Manchester.'

'Manchester, indeed!' said Coningsby; 'if you knew what I do about Manchester! A pretty state we have been in in London this week past with your Manchesters and Birminghams!'

'Come, come, Coningsby,' said Lord Vere, the son of a Whig minister; 'I am all for Manchester and Birmingham.'

'It is all up with the country I can tell you,' said Coningsby, with the air of one who was in the secret.

'My father says it will all go right now,' rejoined Lord Vere. 'I had a letter from my sister yesterday.'

'They say we shall all lose our estates, though,' said Buckhurst; 'I know I shall not give up mine without a fight. Shirley was besieged, you know, in the civil wars; and the rebels got infernally licked.'

'I think that all the people about Beaumanoir would stand by the Duke,' said Lord Henry, pensively.

'Well, you may depend upon it you will have it very soon,' said Coningsby. 'I know it from the best authority.'

'It depends on whether my father remains in,' said Lord Vere. 'He is the only man who can govern the country now. All say that.'

At this moment Millbank entered. He was a good-looking boy, somewhat shy, and yet with a sincere expression in his countenance. He was evidently not extremely intimate with those who were now his companions. Buckhurst, and Henry Sydney, and Vere, welcomed him cordially. He looked at Coningsby with some constraint, and then said,

'You have been in London, Coningsby?'

'Yes, I have been there during all the row.'

'You must have had a rare lark.'

'Yes, if having your windows broken by a mob be a rare lark. They could not break my grandfather's, though. Monmouth House is in a court-yard. All noblemen's houses should be in court-yards.'

'I was glad to see it all ended very well,' said Millbank.

'It has not begun yet,' said Coningsby.

'What?' said Millbank.

'Why, the revolution.'

'The Reform Bill will prevent a revolution, my father says,' said Millbank.

'By Jove! here's the goose,' said Buckhurst.

At this moment there entered the room a little boy, the scion of a noble house, bearing a roasted goose, which he had carried from the kitchen of the opposite inn, the Christopher. The lower boy or fag, depositing his burthen, asked his master whether he had further need of him; and Buckhurst, after looking round the table, and ascertaining that he had not, gave him permission to retire; but he had scarcely disappeared, when his master singing out, 'Lower boy, St John!' he immediately re-entered, and demanded his master's pleasure, which was, that he should pour some water in the teapot. This being accomplished, St John really made his escape, and retired to a pupil-room, where the bullying of a tutor, because he had no derivations, exceeded in all probability the bullying of his master, had he contrived in his passage from the Christopher to have upset the goose or dropped the sausages.

In their merry meal, the Reform Bill was forgotten. Their thoughts were soon concentred in their little world, though it must be owned that visions of palaces and beautiful ladies did occasionally flit over the brain of one of the company. But for him especially there was much of interest and novelty. So much had happened in his absence! There was a week's arrears for him of Eton annals. They were recounted in so fresh a spirit, and in such vivid colours, that Coningsby lost nothing by his London visit. All the bold feats that had been done, and all the bright things that had been said; all the triumphs, and all the failures, and all the scrapes; how popular one master had made himself, and how ridiculous another; all was detailed with a liveliness, a candour, and a picturesque ingenuousness, which would have made the fortune of a Herodotus or a Froissart.[1]

'I'll tell you what,' said Buckhurst, 'I move that after twelve we five go up to Maidenhead.'

'Agreed; agreed!'

Chapter 9

MILLBANK was the son of one of the wealthiest manufacturers in Lancashire. His father, whose opinions were of a very democratic bent, sent his son to Eton, though he disapproved of the system of education pursued there, to show that he had as much right to do so as any duke in the land. He had, however, brought up his only boy with a due prejudice against every sentiment or institution of an aristocratic character, and had especially impressed upon him in his school career, to avoid the slightest semblance of courting the affections or society of any member of the falsely-held superior class.

The character of the son, as much as the influence of the father, tended to the fulfilment of these injunctions. Oswald Millbank was of a proud and independent nature; reserved, a little stern. The early and constantly-reiterated dogma of his father, that he belonged to a class debarred from its just position in the social system, had aggravated the grave and somewhat discontented humour of his blood. His talents were considerable, though invested with no dazzling quality. He had not that quick and brilliant apprehension, which, combined with a memory of rare retentiveness, had already advanced Coningsby far beyond his age, and made him already looked to as the future hero of the school. But Millbank possessed one of those strong, industrious volitions whose perseverance amounts almost to genius, and nearly attains its results. Though Coningsby was by a year his junior, they were rivals. This circumstance had no tendency to remove the prejudice which Coningsby entertained against him, but its bias on the part of Millbank had a contrary effect.

The influence of the individual is nowhere so sensible as at school. There the personal qualities strike without any intervening and counteracting causes. A gracious presence, noble sentiments, or a happy talent, make their way there at once, without preliminary inquiries as to what set they are in, or what family they are of, how much they have a-year, or where they live. Now, on no spirit had the influence of Coningsby, already the favourite, and soon probably to become the idol, of the school, fallen more effectually than on that of Millbank, though it was an influence that no one could suspect except its votary or its victim.

At school, friendship is a passion. It entrances the being; it tears the soul. All loves of after-life can never bring its rapture, or its wretchedness; no bliss so absorbing, no pangs of jealousy or despair so crushing and so keen! What tenderness and what devotion; what illimitable confidence; infinite revelations of inmost thoughts; what ecstatic present and romantic future; what bitter estrangements and what melting reconciliations; what scenes of wild recrimination, agitating explanations, passionate correspondence; what insane sensitiveness, and what frantic sensibility; what earthquakes of the heart and whirlwinds of the soul are confined in that simple phrase, a schoolboy's friendship! 'Tis some indefinite recollection of these mystic passages of their young emotion that makes grey-haired men mourn over the memory of their schoolboy days. It is a spell that can soften the acerbity of political warfare, and with its witchery can call forth a sigh even amid the callous bustle of fashionable saloons.

The secret of Millbank's life was a passionate admiration and affection for Coningsby. Pride, his natural reserve, and his father's injunctions, had, however, hitherto successfully combined to restrain the slightest demonstration of these sentiments. Indeed, Coningsby and himself were never companions, except in school, or in some public game. The demeanour of Coningsby gave no encouragement to intimacy to one, who, under any circumstances, would have required considerable invitation to open himself. So Millbank fed in silence on a cherished idea. It was his happiness to be in the same form, to join in the same sport, with Coningsby; occasionally to be thrown in unusual contact with him, to exchange slight and not unkind words. In their division they were rivals; Millbank sometimes triumphed, but to be vanquished by Coningsby was for him not without a degree of wild satisfaction. Not a gesture, not a phrase from Coningsby, that he did not watch and ponder over and treasure up. Coningsby was his model, alike in studies, in manners, or in pastimes; the aptest scholar, the gayest wit, the most graceful associate, the most accomplished playmate: his standard of the excellent. Yet Millbank was the very last boy in the school who would have had credit given him by his companions for profound and ardent feeling. He was not indeed unpopular. The favourite of the school like Coningsby, he could, under no circumstances, ever have become; nor was he qualified to obtain that general graciousness among the multitude, which the sweet disposition of Henry Sydney, or the gay profusion of Buckhurst, acquired without an effort. Millbank was not blessed with the charm of manner. He seemed close and cold; but he was courageous, just, and inflexible; never bullied, and to his utmost would prevent tyranny. The little boys looked up to him as a stern protector; and his word, too, throughout the school was a proverb: and truth ranks a great quality among boys. In a word, Millbank was respected by those among whom he lived; and school-boys scan character more nicely than men suppose.

A brother of Henry Sydney, quartered in Lancashire, had been wounded recently in a riot, and had received great kindness from the Millbank family, in whose immediate neighbourhood the disturbance had occurred. The kind Duke had impressed on Henry Sydney to acknowledge with cordiality to the younger Millbank at Eton, the sense which his family entertained of these benefits; but though Henry lost neither time nor opportunity in obeying an injunction, which was grateful to his own heart, he failed in cherishing, or indeed creating, any intimacy with the object of his solicitude. A companionship with one who was Coningsby's relative and most familiar friend, would at the first glance have appeared, independently of all other considerations, a most desirable result for Millbank to accomplish. But, perhaps, this very circumstance afforded additional reasons for the absence of all encouragement with which he received the overtures of Lord Henry. Millbank suspected that Coningsby was not affected in his favour, and his pride recoiled from gaining, by any indirect means, an intimacy which to have obtained in a plain and express manner would have deeply gratified him. However, the urgent invitation of Buckhurst and Henry Sydney, and the fear that a persistence in refusal might be misinterpreted into churlishness, had at length brought Millbank to their breakfast-mess, though, when he accepted their invitation, he did not apprehend that Coningsby would have been present.

It was about an hour before sunset, the day of this very break-fast, and a good number of boys, in lounging groups, were collected in the Long Walk. The sports and matches of the day were over. Criticism had succeeded to action in sculling and in cricket. They talked over the exploits of the morning; canvassed the merits of the competitors, marked the fellow whose play or whose stroke was improving; glanced at another, whose promise had not been fulfilled; discussed the pretensions, and adjudged the palm. Thus public opinion is formed. Some, too, might be seen with their books and exercises, intent on the inevitable and impending tasks. Among these, some unhappy wight in the remove, wandering about with his hat, after parochial fashion, seeking relief in the shape of a verse. A hard lot this, to know that you must be delivered of fourteen verses at least in the twenty-four hours, and to be conscious that you are pregnant of none. The lesser boys, urchins of tender years, clustered like flies round the baskets of certain vendors of sugary delicacies that rested on the Long Walk wall. The pallid countenance, the lack-lustre eye, the hoarse voice clogged with accumulated phlegm, indicated too surely the irreclaimable and hopeless votary of lollypop, the opium-eater of school-boys.

'It is settled, the match to-morrow shall be between Aquatics and Drybobs,'[1] said a senior boy; who was arranging a future match at cricket.

'But what is to be done about Fielding major?' inquired another. 'He has not paid his boating money, and I say he has no right to play among the Aquatics before he has paid his money.'

'Oh! but we must have Fielding major, he is such a devil of a swipe.'

'I declare he shall not play among the Aquatics if he does not pay his boating money. It is an infernal shame.'

'Let us ask Buckhurst. Where is Buckhurst?'

'Have you got any toffy?' inquired a dull-looking little boy, in a hoarse voice, of one of the vendors of scholastic confectionary.

'Tom Trot, sir.'

'No; I want toffy.'

'Very nice Tom Trot, sir.'

'No, I want toffy; I have been eating Tom Trot all day.'

'Where is Buckhurst? We must settle about the Aquatics.'

'Well, I for one will not play if Fielding major plays amongst the Aquatics. That is settled.'

'Oh! nonsense; he will pay his money if you ask him.'

'I shall not ask him again. The captain duns us every day. It is an infernal shame.'

'I say, Burnham, where can one get some toffy? This fellow never has any.'

'I will tell you; at Barnes' on the bridge. The best toffy in the world.'

'I will go at once. I must have some toffy.'

'Just help me with this verse, Collins,' said one boy to another, in an imploring tone, 'that's a good fellow.'

'Well, give it us: first syllable in *fabri* is short; three false quantities in the two first lines! You're a pretty one. There, I have done it for you.'

'That's a good fellow.'

'Any fellow seen Buckhurst?'

'Gone up the river with Coningsby and Henry Sydney.'

'But he must be back by this time. I want him to make the list for the match to-morrow. Where the deuce can Buckhurst be?'

And now, as rumours rise in society we know not how, so there was suddenly a flying report in this multitude the origin of which no one in his alarm stopped to ascertain, that a boy was drowned.

Every heart was agitated.

What boy? When, where, how? Who was absent? Who had been on the river to-day? Buckhurst. The report ran that Buckhurst was drowned. Great were the trouble and consternation. Buckhurst was ever much liked; and now no one remembered anything but his good qualities.

'Who heard it was Buckhurst?' said Sedgwick, captain of the school, coming forward.

'I heard Bradford tell Palmer it was Buckhurst,' said a little boy.

'Where is Bradford?'

'Here.'

'What do you know about Buckhurst?'

'Wentworth told me that he was afraid Buckhurst was drowned. He heard it at the Brocas; a bargeman told him about a quarter of an hour ago.'

'Here is Wentworth! Here is Wentworth!' a hundred voices exclaimed, and they formed a circle round him.

'Well, what did you hear, Wentworth?' asked Sedgwick.

'I was at the Brocas, and a Bargee told me that an Eton fellow had been drowned above Surley, and the only Eton boat above Surley to-day, as I can learn, is Buckhurst's four-oar. That is all.'

There was a murmur of hope.

'Oh! come, come,' said Sedgwick, 'there is some chance. Who is with Buckhurst; who knows?'

'I saw him walk down to the Brocas with Vere,' said a boy.

'I hope it is not Vere,' said a little boy, with a tearful eye; 'he never lets any fellow bully me.'

'Here is Maltravers,' halloed out a boy; 'he knows something.'

'Well, what do you know, Maltravers?'

'I heard Boots at the Christopher say that an Eton fellow was drowned, and that he had seen a person who was there.'

'Bring Boots here,' said Sedgwick.

Instantly a band of boys rushed over the way, and in a moment the witness was produced.

'What have you heard, Sam, about this accident?' said Sedgwick.

'Well, sir, I heard a young gentleman was drowned above Monkey Island,' said Boots.

'And no name mentioned?'

'Well, sir, I believe it was Mr Coningsby.'

A general groan of horror.

'Coningsby, Coningsby! By Heavens I hope not,' said Sedgwick.

'I very much fear so,' said Boots; 'as how the bargeman who told me saw Mr Coningsby in the Lock House laid out in flannels.'

'I had sooner any fellow had been drowned than Coningsby,' whispered one boy to another.

'I liked him, the best fellow at Eton,' responded his companion, in a smothered tone.

'What a clever fellow he was!'

'And so deuced generous!'

'He would have got the medal if he had lived.'

'And how came he to be drowned? for he was such a fine swimmer!'

'I heard Mr Coningsby was saving another's life,' continued Boots in his evidence, 'which makes it in a manner more sorrowful.'

'Poor Coningsby!' exclaimed a boy, bursting into tears: 'I move the whole school goes into mourning.'

'I wish we could get hold of this bargeman,' said Sedgwick. 'Now stop, stop, don't all run away in that mad manner; you frighten the people. Charles Herbert and Palmer, you two go down to the Brocas and inquire.'

But just at this moment, an increased stir and excitement were evident in the Long Walk; the circle round Sedgwick opened, and there appeared Henry Sydney and Buckhurst.

There was a dead silence. It was impossible that suspense could be strained to a higher pitch. The air and countenance of Sydney and Buckhurst were rather excited than mournful or alarmed. They needed no inquiries, for before they had penetrated the circle they had become aware of its cause.

Buckhurst, the most energetic of beings, was of course the first to speak. Henry Sydney indeed looked pale and nervous; but his companion, flushed and resolute, knew exactly how to hit a popular assembly, and at once came to the point.

'It is all a false report, an infernal lie; Coningsby is quite safe, and nobody is drowned.'

There was a cheer that might have been heard at Windsor Castle. Then, turning to Sedgwick, in an under tone Buckhurst added,

'It *is* all right, but, by Jove! we have had a shaver. I will tell you all in a moment, but we want to keep the thing quiet, and so let the fellows disperse, and we will talk afterwards.'

In a few moments the Long Walk had resumed its usual character; but Sedgwick, Herbert, and one or two others turned into the playing fields, where, undisturbed and unnoticed by the multitude, they listened to the promised communication of Buckhurst and Henry Sydney.

'You know we went up the river together,' said Buckhurst. 'Myself, Henry Sydney, Coningsby, Vere, and Millbank. We had breakfasted together, and after twelve agreed to go up to Maidenhead. Well, we went up much higher than we had intended. About a quarter of a mile before we had got to the Lock we pulled up; Coningsby was then steering. Well, we fastened the boat to, and were all of us stretched out on the meadow, when Millbank and Vere said they should go and bathe in the Lock Pool. The rest of us were opposed; but after Millbank and Vere had gone about ten minutes, Coningsby, who was very fresh, said he had changed his mind and should go and bathe too. So he left us. He had scarcely got to the pool when he heard a cry. There was a fellow drowning. He threw off his clothes and was in in a moment. The fact is this, Millbank had plunged in the pool and found himself in some eddies, caused by the meeting of two currents. He called out to Vere not to come, and tried to swim off. But he was beat, and seeing he was in danger, Vere jumped in. But the stream was so strong, from the great fall of water from the lasher[2] above, that Vere was exhausted before he could reach Millbank, and nearly sank himself. Well, he just saved himself; but Millbank sank as Coningsby jumped in. What do you think of that?'

'By Jove!' exclaimed Sedgwick, Herbert, and all. The favourite oath of schoolboys perpetuates the divinity of Olympus.

'And now comes the worst. Coningsby caught Millbank when he rose, but he found himself in the midst of the same strong current that had before nearly swamped Vere. What a lucky thing that he had taken into his head not to pull to-day! Fresher than Vere, he just managed to land Millbank and himself. The shouts of Vere called us, and we arrived to find the bodies of Millbank and Coningsby apparently lifeless, for Millbank was quite gone, and Coningsby had swooned on landing.'

'If Coningsby had been lost,' said Henry Sydney, 'I never would have shown my face at Eton again.'

'Can you conceive a position more terrible?' said Buckhurst. 'I declare I shall never forget it as long as I live. However, there was the Lock House at hand; and we got blankets and brandy. Coningsby was soon all right; but Millbank, I can tell you, gave us some trouble. I thought it was all up. Didn't you, Henry Sydney?'

'The most fishy[3] thing I ever saw,' said Henry Sydney.

'Well, we were fairly frightened here,' said Sedgwick. 'The first report was, that you had gone, but that seemed without foundation; but Coningsby was quite given up. Where are they now?'

'They are both at their tutors'. I thought they had better keep quiet. Vere is with Millbank, and we are going back to Coningsby directly; but we thought it best to show, finding on our arrival that there were all sorts of rumours about. I think it will be best to report at once to my tutor, for he will be sure to hear something.'

'I would if I were you.'

Chapter 10

WHAT wonderful things are events! The least are of greater importance than the most sublime and comprehensive speculations! In what fanciful schemes to obtain the friendship of Coningsby had Millbank in his reveries often indulged! What combinations that were to extend over years and influence their lives! But the moment that he entered the world of action, his pride recoiled from the plans and hopes which his sympathy had inspired. His sensibility and his inordinate self-respect were always at variance. And he seldom exchanged a word with the being whose idea engrossed his affection.

And now, suddenly, an event had occurred, like all events, unforeseen, which in a few, brief, agitating, tumultuous moments had singularly and utterly changed the relations that previously subsisted between him and the former object of his concealed tenderness. Millbank now stood with respect to Coningsby in the position of one who owes to another the greatest conceivable obligation; a favour which time could permit him neither to forget nor to repay. Pride was a sentiment that could no longer subsist before the preserver of his life. Devotion to that being, open, almost ostentatious, was now a duty, a paramount and absorbing tie. The sense of past peril, the rapture of escape, a renewed relish for the life so nearly forfeited, a deep sentiment of devout gratitude to the providence that had guarded over him, for Millbank was an eminently religious boy, a thought of home, and the anguish that might have overwhelmed his hearth; all these were powerful and exciting emotions for a young and fervent mind, in addition to the peculiar source of sensibility on which we have already touched. Lord Vere, who lodged in the same house as Millbank, and was sitting by his bedside, observed, as night fell, that his mind wandered.

The illness of Millbank, the character of which soon transpired, and was soon exaggerated, attracted the public attention with increased interest to the circumstances out of which it had arisen, and from which the parties principally concerned had wished to have diverted notice. The sufferer, indeed, had transgressed the rules of the school by bathing at an unlicensed spot, where there were no expert swimmers in attendance, as is customary, to instruct the practice and to guard over the lives of the young adventurers. But the circumstances with which this violation of rules had been accompanied, and the assurance of several of the party that they had not themselves infringed the regulations, combined with the high character of Millbank, made the authorities not over anxious to visit with penalties a breach of observance which, in the case of the only proved offender, had been attended with such impressive consequences. The feat of Coningsby was extolled by all as an act of high gallantry and skill. It confirmed and increased the great reputation which he already enjoyed.

'Millbank is getting quite well,' said Buckhurst to Coningsby a few days after the accident. 'Henry Sydney and I are going to see him. Will you come?'

'I think we shall be too many. I will go another day,' replied Coningsby.

So they went without him. They found Millbank up and reading.

'Well, old fellow,' said Buckhurst, 'how are you? We should have come up before, but they would not let us. And you are quite right now, eh?'

'Quite. Has there been any row about it?'

'All blown over,' said Henry Sydney; 'C*******y behaved like a trump.'

'I have seen nobody yet,' said Millbank; 'they would not let me till today. Vere looked in this morning and left me this book, but I was asleep. I hope they will let me out in a day or two. I want to thank Coningsby; I never shall rest till I have thanked Coningsby.'

'Oh, he will come to see you,' said Henry Sydney; 'I asked him just now to come with us.'

'Yes!' said Millbank, eagerly; 'and what did he say?'

'He thought we should be too many.'

'I hope I shall see him soon,' said Millbank, 'somehow or other.'

'I will tell him to come,' said Buckhurst.

'Oh! no, no, don't tell him to come,' said Millbank. 'Don't bore him.'

'I know he is going to play a match at fives this afternoon,' said Buckhurst, 'for I am one.'

'And who are the others?' inquired Millbank.

'Herbert and Campbell.'

'Herbert is no match for Coningsby,' said Millbank.

And then they talked over all that had happened since his absence; and Buckhurst gave him a graphic report of the excitement on the afternoon of the accident; at last they were obliged to leave him.

'Well, good-bye, old fellow; we will come and see you every day. What can we do for you? Any books, or anything?'

'If any fellow asks after me,' said Millbank, 'tell him I shall be glad to see him. It is very dull being alone. But do not tell any fellow to come if he does not ask after me.'

Notwithstanding the kind suggestions of Buckhurst and Henry Sydney, Coningsby could not easily bring himself to call on Millbank. He felt a constraint. It seemed as if he went to receive thanks. He would rather have met Millbank again in school, or in the playing fields. Without being able then to analyse his feelings, he shrank unconsciously from that ebullition of sentiment, which in more artificial circles is described as a scene. Not that any dislike of Millbank prompted him to this reserve. On the contrary, since he had conferred a great obligation on Millbank, his prejudice against him had sensibly decreased. How it would have been had Millbank saved Coningsby's life, is quite another affair. Probably, as Coningsby was by nature generous, his sense of justice might have struggled successfully with his painful sense of the overwhelming obligation. But in the present case there was no element to disturb his fair self-satisfaction. He had greatly distinguished himself; he had conferred on his rival an essential service; and the whole world rang with his applause. He began rather to like Millbank; we will not say because Millbank was the unintentional cause of his pleasurable sensations. Really it was that the unusual circumstances had prompted him to a more impartial judgment of his rival's character. In this mood, the day after the visit of Buckhurst and Henry Sydney, Coningsby called on Millbank, but finding his medical attendant with him, Coningsby availed himself of that excuse for going away without seeing him.

The next day he left Millbank a newspaper on his way to school, time not permitting a visit. Two days after, going into his room, he found on his table a letter addressed to 'Harry Coningsby, Esq.'

ETON, *May*—, 1832.

'DEAR CONINGSBY, I very much fear that you must think me a very ungrateful fellow, because you have not heard from me before; but I was in hopes that I might get out and say to you what I feel; but whether I speak or write, it is quite impossible for me to make you understand the feelings of my heart to you. Now, I will say at once, that I have always liked you better than any fellow in the school, and always thought you the cleverest; indeed, I always thought that there was no one like you; but I never would say this or show this, because you never seemed to care for me, and because I was afraid you would think I merely wanted to con with you, as they used to say of some other fellows, whose names I will not mention, because they always tried to do so with Henry Sydney and you. I do not want this at all; but I want, though we may not speak to each other more than before, that we may be friends; and that you will always know that there is nothing I will not do for you, and that I like you better than any fellow at Eton. And I do not mean that this shall be only at Eton, but afterwards, wherever we may be, that you will always remember that there is nothing I will not do for you. Not because you saved my life, though that is a great thing, but because before that I would have done anything for you; only, for the cause above mentioned, I would not show it. I do not expect that we shall be more together than before; nor can I ever suppose that you could like me as you like Henry Sydney and Buckhurst, or even as you like Vere; but still I hope you will always think of me with kindness now, and let me sign myself, if ever I do write to you,

'Your most attached, affectionate, and devoted friend,

'OSWALD MILLBANK'

Chapter 11

ABOUT a fortnight after this nearly fatal adventure on the river, it was Montem. One need hardly remind the reader that this celebrated ceremony, of which the origin is lost in obscurity, and which now occurs triennially, is the tenure by which Eton College holds some of its domains. It consists in the waving of a flag by one of the scholars, on a mount near the village of Salt Hill, which, without doubt, derives its name from the circumstance that on this day every visitor to Eton, and every traveller in its vicinity, from the monarch to the peasant, are stopped on the road by youthful brigands in picturesque costume, and summoned to contribute 'salt,' in the shape of coin of the realm, to the purse collecting for the Captain of Eton, the senior scholar on the Foundation, who is about to repair to King's College, Cambridge.

On this day the Captain of Eton appears in a dress as martial as his title: indeed, each sixth-form boy represents in his uniform, though not perhaps according to the exact rules of the Horse Guards, an officer of the army. One is a marshal, another an ensign. There is a lieutenant, too; and the remainder are sergeants. Each of those who are intrusted with these ephemeral commissions has one or more attendants, the number of these varying according to his rank. These servitors are selected according to the wishes of the several members of the sixth form, out of the ranks of the lower boys, that is, those boys who are below the fifth form; and all these attendants are arrayed in a variety of fancy dresses. The Captain of the Oppidans and the senior Colleger next to the Captain of the school, figure also in fancy costume, and are called 'Saltbearers.' It is their business, together with the twelve senior Collegers of the fifth form, who are called 'Runners,' and whose costume is also determined by the taste of the wearers, to levy the contributions. And all the Oppidans of the fifth form, among whom ranked Coningsby, class as 'Corporals;' and are severally followed by one or more lower boys, who are denominated 'Polemen,' but who appear in their ordinary dress.

It was a fine, bright morning; the bells of Eton and Windsor rang merrily; everybody was astir, and every moment some gay equipage drove into the town. Gaily clustering in the thronged precincts of the College, might be observed many a glistening form: airy Greek or sumptuous Ottoman, heroes of the Holy Sepulchre, Spanish Hidalgos who had fought at Pavia,[1] Highland Chiefs who had charged at Culloden,[2] gay in the tartan of Prince Charlie. The Long Walk was full of busy groups in scarlet coats or fanciful uniforms; some in earnest conversation, some criticising the arriving guests; others encircling some magnificent hero, who astounded them with his slashed doublet or flowing plume.

A knot of boys, sitting on the Long Walk wall, with their feet swinging in the air, watched the arriving guests of the Provost.

'I say, Townshend,' said one, 'there's Grobbleton; he *was* a bully. I wonder if that's his wife? Who's this? The Duke of Agincourt. He wasn't an Eton fellow? Yes, he was. He was called Poictiers then. Oh! ah! his name is in the upper school, very large, under Charles Fox.[3] I say, Townshend, did you see Saville's turban? What was it made of? He says his mother brought it from Grand Cairo. Didn't he just look like the Saracen's Head? Here are some Dons. That's Hallam! We'll give him a cheer. I say, Townshend, look at this fellow. He doesn't think small beer of himself. I wonder who he is? The Duke of Wellington's valet come to say his master is engaged. Oh! by Jove, he heard you! I wonder if the Duke will come? Won't we give him a cheer!'

'By Jove! who is this?' exclaimed Townshend, and he jumped from the wall, and, followed by his companions, rushed towards the road.

Two britskas, each drawn by four grey horses of mettle, and each accompanied by outriders as well mounted, were advancing at a rapid pace along the road that leads from Slough to the College. But they were destined to an irresistible check. About fifty yards before they had reached the gate that leads into

Weston's Yard, a ruthless but splendid Albanian, in crimson and gold embroidered jacket, and snowy camise, started forward, and holding out his silver-sheathed yataghan[4] commanded the postilions to stop. A Peruvian Inca on the other side of the road gave a simultaneous command, and would infallibly have transfixed the outriders with an arrow from his unerring bow, had they for an instant hesitated. The Albanian Chief then advanced to the door of the carriage, which he opened, and in a tone of great courtesy, announced that he was under the necessity of troubling its inmates for 'salt.' There was no delay. The Lord of the equipage, with the amiable condescension of a 'grand monarque,' expressed his hope that the collection would be an ample one, and as an old Etonian, placed in the hands of the Albanian his contribution, a magnificent purse, furnished for the occasion, and heavy with gold.

'Don't be alarmed, ladies,' said a very handsome young officer, laughing, and taking off his cocked hat.

'Ah!' exclaimed one of the ladies, turning at the voice, and starting a little. 'Ah! it is Mr Coningsby.'

Lord Eskdale paid the salt for the next carriage. 'Do they come down pretty stiff?' he inquired, and then, pulling forth a roll of bank-notes from the pocket of his pea-jacket, he wished them good morning.

The courtly Provost, then the benignant Goodall,[5] a man who, though his experience of life was confined to the colleges in which he had passed his days, was naturally gifted with the rarest of all endowments, the talent of reception; and whose happy bearing and gracious manner, a smile ever in his eye and a lively word ever on his lip, must be recalled by all with pleasant recollections, welcomed Lord Monmouth and his friends to an assemblage of the noble, the beautiful, and the celebrated, gathered together in rooms not unworthy of them, as you looked upon their interesting walls, breathing with the portraits of the heroes whom Eton boasts, from Wotton to Wellesley.[6] Music sounded in the quadrangle of the College, in which the boys were already quickly assembling. The Duke of Wellington had arrived, and the boys were cheering a hero, who was also an Eton field-marshal. From an oriel window in one of the Provost's rooms, Lord Monmouth, surrounded by every circumstance that could make life delightful, watched with some intentness the scene in the quadrangle beneath.

'I would give his fame,' said Lord Monmouth, 'if I had it, and my wealth, to be sixteen.'

Five hundred of the youth of England, sparkling with health, high spirits, and fancy dresses, were now assembled in the quadrangle. They formed into rank, and headed by a band of the Guards, thrice they marched round the court. Then quitting the College, they commenced their progress 'ad Montem.' It was a brilliant spectacle to see them defiling through the playing fields, those bowery meads; the river sparkling in the sun, the castled heights of Windsor, their glorious landscape; behind them, the pinnacles of their College.

The road from Eton to Salt Hill was clogged with carriages; the broad fields as far as eye could range were covered with human beings. Amid the burst of martial music and the shouts of the multitude, the band of heroes, as if they were marching from Athens, or Thebes, or Sparta, to some heroic deed, encircled the mount; the ensign reaches its summit, and then, amid a deafening cry of 'Floreat Etona!' he unfurls, and thrice waves the consecrated standard.

'Lord Monmouth,' said Mr Rigby to Coningsby, 'wishes that you should beg your friends to dine with him. Of course you will ask Lord Henry and your friend Sir Charles Buckhurst; and is there any one else that you would like to invite?'

'Why there is Vere,' said Coningsby, hesitating, 'and –'

'Vere! What Lord Vere?' said Mr Rigby. 'Hum! He is one of your friends, is he? His father has done a great deal of mischief, but still he is Lord Vere. Well, of course, you can invite Vere.'

'There is another fellow I should like to ask very much,' said Coningsby, 'if Lord Monmouth would not think I was asking too many.'

'Never fear that; he sent me particularly to tell you to invite as many as you liked.'

'Well, then, I should like to ask Millbank.'

'Millbank!' said Mr Rigby, a little excited, and then he added, 'Is that a son of Lady Albinia Millbank?'

'No; his mother is not a Lady Albinia, but he is a great friend of mine. His father is a Lancashire manufacturer.'

'By no means,' exclaimed Mr Rigby, quite agitated. 'There is nothing in the world that Lord Monmouth dislikes as much as Manchester manufacturers, and particularly if they bear the name of Millbank. It must not be thought of, my dear Harry. I hope you have not spoken to the young man on the subject. I assure you it is quite out of the question. It would make Lord Monmouth quite ill. It would spoil everything, quite upset him.'

It was, of course, impossible for Coningsby to urge his wishes against such representations. He was disappointed, rather amazed; but Madame Colonna having sent for him to introduce her to some of the scenes and details of Eton life, his vexation was soon absorbed in the pride of acting in the face of his companions as the cavalier of a beautiful lady, and becoming the cicerone of the most brilliant party that had attended Montem. He presented his friends, too, to Lord Monmouth, who gave them a cordial invitation to dine with him at his hotel at Windsor, which they warmly accepted. Buckhurst delighted the Marquess by his reckless genius. Even Lucretia deigned to appear amused; especially when, on visiting the upper school, the name of CARDIFF, the title Lord Monmouth bore in his youthful days, was pointed out to her by Coningsby, cut with his grandfather's own knife on the classic panels of that memorable wall in which scarcely a name that has flourished in our history, since the commencement of the eighteenth century, may not be observed with curious admiration.

It was the humour of Lord Monmouth that the boys should be entertained with the most various and delicious banquet that luxury could devise or money could command. For some days beforehand orders had been given for the preparation of this festival. Our friends did full justice to their Lucullus;[7] Buckhurst especially, who gave his opinion on the most refined dishes with all the intrepidity of saucy ignorance, and occasionally shook his head over a glass of Hermitage or Côte Rôtie with a dissatisfaction which a satiated Sybarite could not have exceeded. Considering all things, Coningsby and his friends exhibited a great deal of self-command; but they were gay, even to the verge of

frolic. But then the occasion justified it, as much as their youth.
All were in high spirits. Madame Colonna declared that she had
met nothing in England equal to Montem; that it was a Protestant
Carnival;[8] and that its only fault was that it did not last forty
days. The Prince himself was all animation, and took wine with
every one of the Etonians several times. All went on flowingly
until Mr Rigby contradicted Buckhurst on some point of Eton
discipline, which Buckhurst would not stand. He rallied Mr Rigby
roundly, and Coningsby, full of champagne, and owing Rigby
several years of contradiction, followed up the assault. Lord Monmouth, who liked a butt, and had a weakness for boisterous
gaiety, slyly encouraged the boys, till Rigby began to lose his
temper and get noisy.

The lads had the best of it; they said a great many funny things,
and delivered themselves of several sharp retorts; whereas there
was something ridiculous in Rigby putting forth his 'slashing'
talents against such younkers.[9] However, he brought the inflic-
tion on himself by his strange habit of deciding on subjects of
which he knew nothing, and of always contradicting persons
on the very subjects of which they were necessarily masters.

To see Rigby baited was more amusement to Lord Monmouth
even than Montem. Lucian Gay, however, when the affair was
getting troublesome, came forward as a diversion. He sang an
extemporaneous song on the ceremony of the day, and introduced
the names of all the guests at the dinner, and of a great many
other persons besides. This was capital! The boys were in raptures,
but when the singer threw forth a verse about Dr Keate, the
applause became uproarious.

'Good-bye, my dear Harry,' said Lord Monmouth, when he bade
his grandson farewell. 'I am going abroad again; I cannot remain
in this Radical-ridden country. Remember, though I am away,
Monmouth House is your home, at least so long as it belongs
to me. I understand my tailor has turned Liberal, and is going
to stand for one of the metropolitan districts, a friend of Lord
Durham;[10] perhaps I shall find him in it when I return. I fear
there are evil days for the NEW GENERATION!'

END OF BOOK I

BOOK II

Chapter 1

IT was early in November 1834, and a large shooting party was assembled at Beaumanoir, the seat of that great nobleman, who was the father of Henry Sydney. England is unrivalled for two things, sporting and politics. They were combined at Beaumanoir; for the guests came not merely to slaughter the Duke's pheasants, but to hold council on the prospects of the party, which, it was supposed by the initiated, began at this time to indicate some symptoms of brightening.

The success of the Reform Ministry on their first appeal to the new constituency which they had created, had been fatally complete. But the triumph was as destructive to the victors as to the vanquished.

'We are too strong,' prophetically exclaimed one of the fortunate cabinet, which found itself supported by an inconceivable majority of three hundred. It is to be hoped that some future publisher of private memoirs may have preserved some of the traits of that crude and short-lived parliament, when old Cobbett insolently thrust Sir Robert from the prescriptive seat of the chief of opposition, and treasury understrappers sneered at the 'queer lot' that had arrived from Ireland, little foreseeing what a high bidding that 'queer lot' would eventually command. Gratitude to Lord Grey was the hustings-cry at the end of 1832, the pretext that was to return to the new-modelled House of Commons none but men devoted to the Whig cause. The successful simulation, like everything that is false, carried within it the seeds of its own dissolution. Ingratitude to Lord Grey was more the fashion at the commencement of 1834, and before the close of that eventful year, the once popular Reform Ministry was upset, and the eagerly-sought Reformed Parliament dissolved!

It can scarcely be alleged that the public was altogether unprepared for this catastrophe. Many deemed it inevitable; few thought it imminent. The career of the Ministry, and the existence of the Parliament, had indeed from the first been turbulent and fitful. It was known, from authority, that there were dissensions in the cabinet, while a House of Commons which passed votes on subjects not less important than the repeal of a tax, or the impeachment of a judge, on one night, and rescinded its resolutions on the following, certainly established no increased claims to the confidence of its constituents in its discretion. Nevertheless, there existed at this period a prevalent conviction that the Whig party, by a great stroke of state, similar in magnitude and effect to that which in the preceding century had changed the dynasty, had secured to themselves the government of this country for, at least, the lives of the present generation. And even the well-informed in such matters were inclined to look upon the perplexing circumstances to which we have alluded rather as symptoms of a want of discipline in a new system of tactics, than as evidences of any essential and deeply-rooted disorder.

The startling rapidity, however, of the strange incidents of 1834; the indignant, soon to become vituperative, secession of a considerable section of the cabinet, some of them esteemed too at that time among its most efficient members;[1] the piteous deprecation of 'pressure from without,' from lips hitherto deemed too stately for entreaty, followed by the Trades' Union, thirty thousand strong, parading in procession to Downing-street;[2] the Irish negotiations of Lord Hatherton,[3] strange blending of complex intrigue and almost infantile ingenuousness; the still inexplicable resignation of Lord Althorp,[4] hurriedly followed by his still more mysterious resumption of power, the only result of his precipitate movements being the fall of Lord Grey himself, attended by circumstances which even a friendly historian could scarcely describe as honourable to his party or dignified to himself; latterly, the extemporaneous address of King William to the Bishops;[5] the vagrant and grotesque apocalypse of the Lord Chancellor;[6] and the fierce recrimination and memorable defiance of the Edinburgh banquet,[7] all these impressive instances of public affairs and public conduct had combined to create a predominant opinion that, whatever might be the consequences, the prolonged

continuance of the present party in power was a clear impossibility.

It is evident that the suicidal career of what was then styled
the Liberal party had been occasioned and stimulated by its unnatural excess of strength. The apoplectic plethora of 1834 was
not less fatal than the paralytic tenuity of 1841. It was not
feasible to gratify so many ambitions, or to satisfy so many expectations. Every man had his double; the heels of every placeman[8] were dogged by friendly rivals ready to trip them up. There
were even two cabinets; the one that met in council, and the
one that met in cabal. The consequence of destroying the
legitimate Opposition of the country was, that a moiety of the
supporters of Government had to discharge the duties of
Opposition.

Herein, then, we detect the real cause of all that irregular and
unsettled carriage of public men which so perplexed the nation
after the passing of the Reform Act. No government can be long
secure without a formidable Opposition. It reduces their supporters to that tractable number which can be managed by the
joint influences of fruition and of hope. It offers vengeance to
the discontented, and distinction to the ambitious; and employs
the energies of aspiring spirits, who otherwise may prove traitors
in a division or assassins in a debate.

The general election of 1832 abrogated the Parliamentary
Opposition of England, which had practically existed for more
than a century and a half. And what a series of equivocal transactions and mortifying adventures did the withdrawal of this
salutary restraint entail on the party which then so loudly congratulated themselves and the country that they were at length
relieved from its odious repression! In the hurry of existence one
is apt too generally to pass over the political history of the times
in which we ourselves live. The two years that followed the
Reform of the House of Commons are full of instruction, on
which a young man would do well to ponder. It is hardly possible that he could rise from the study of these annals without
a confirmed disgust for political intrigue; a dazzling practice, apt
at first to fascinate youth, for it appeals at once to our invention
and our courage, but one which really should only be the resource

of the second-rate. Great minds must trust to great truths and great talents for their rise, and nothing else.

While, however, as the autumn of 1834 advanced, the people of this country became gradually sensible of the necessity of some change in the councils of their Sovereign, no man felt capable of predicting by what means it was to be accomplished, or from what quarry the new materials were to be extracted. The Tory party, according to those perverted views of Toryism unhappily too long prevalent in this country, was held to be literarily defunct, except by a few old battered crones of office, crouched round the embers of faction which they were fanning, and muttering 'reaction' in mystic whispers. It cannot be supposed indeed for a moment, that the distinguished personage[9] who had led that party in the House of Commons previously to the passing of the act of 1832, ever despaired in consequence of his own career. His then time of life, the perfection, almost the prime, of manhood; his parliamentary practice, doubly estimable in an inexperienced assembly; his political knowledge; his fair character and reputable position; his talents and tone as a public speaker, which he had always aimed to adapt to the habits and culture of that middle class from which it was concluded the benches of the new Parliament were mainly to be recruited, all these were qualities the possession of which must have assured a mind not apt to be disturbed in its calculations by any intemperate heats, that with time and patience the game was yet for him.

Unquestionably, whatever may have been insinuated, this distinguished person had no inkling that his services in 1834 might be claimed by his Sovereign. At the close of the session of that year he had quitted England with his family, and had arrived at Rome, where it was his intention to pass the winter. The party charges that have imputed to him a previous and sinister knowledge of the intentions of the Court, appear to have been made not only in ignorance of the personal character, but of the real position, of the future minister.

It had been the misfortune of this eminent gentleman when he first entered public life, to become identified with a political connection which, having arrogated to itself the name of an illustrious historical party, pursued a policy which was either founded on no principle whatever, or on principles exactly contrary to those which had always guided the conduct of the great Tory leaders. The chief members of this official confederacy were men distinguished by none of the conspicuous qualities of statesmen. They had none of the divine gifts that govern senates and guide councils. They were not orators; they were not men of deep thought or happy resource, or of penetrative and sagacious minds. Their political ken was essentially dull and contracted. They expended some energy in obtaining a defective, blundering acquaintance with foreign affairs; they knew as little of the real state of their own country as savages of an approaching eclipse. This factious league had shuffled themselves into power by clinging to the skirts of a great minister,[10] the last of Tory statesmen, but who, in the unparalleled and confounding emergencies of his latter years, had been forced, unfortunately for England, to relinquish Toryism. His successors inherited all his errors without the latent genius, which in him might have still rallied and extricated him from the consequences of his disasters. His successors did not merely inherit his errors; they exaggerated, they caricatured them. They rode into power on a spring-tide of all the rampant prejudices and rancorous passions of their time. From the King to the boor their policy was a mere pandering to public ignorance. Impudently usurping the name of that party of which nationality, and therefore universality, is the essence, these pseudo-Tories made Exclusion the principle of their political constitution, and Restriction the genius of the commercial code.

The blind goddess that plays with human fortunes has mixed up the memory of these men with traditions of national glory. They conducted to a prosperous conclusion the most renowned war in which England has ever been engaged. Yet every military conception that emanated from their cabinet was branded by their characteristic want of grandeur. Chance, however, sent them a great military genius,[11] whom they treated for a long time with indifference, and whom they never heartily supported until his career had made him their master. His transcendent exploits, and European events even greater than his achievements, placed in the manikin grasp of the English ministry, the settlement of Europe.

The act of the Congress of Vienna remains the eternal monument of their diplomatic knowledge and political sagacity. Their capital feats were the creation of two kingdoms, both of which are already erased from the map of Europe.[12] They made no single preparation for the inevitable, almost impending, conjunctures of the East.[13] All that remains of the pragmatic arrangements of the mighty Congress of Vienna is the mediatisation of the petty German princes.[14]

But the settlement of Europe by the pseudo-Tories was the dictate of inspiration compared with their settlement of England. The peace of Paris found the government of this country in the hands of a body of men of whom it is no exaggeration to say that they were ignorant of every principle of every branch of political science. So long as our domestic administration was confined merely to the raising of a revenue, they levied taxes with gross facility from the industry of a country too busy to criticise or complain. But when the excitement and distraction of war had ceased, and they were forced to survey the social elements that surrounded them, they seemed, for the first time, to have become conscious of their own incapacity. These men, indeed, were the mere children of routine. They prided themselves on being practical men. In the language of this defunct school of statesmen, a practical man is a man who practises the blunders of his predecessors.

Now commenced that Condition-of-England Question of which our generation hears so much. During five-and-twenty years every influence that can develope the energies and resources of a nation had been acting with concentrated stimulation on the British Isles. National peril and national glory; the perpetual menace of invasion, the continual triumph of conquest; the most extensive foreign commerce that was ever conducted by a single nation; an illimitable currency; an internal trade supported by swarming millions, whom manufactures and inclosure-bills[15] summoned into existence; above all, the supreme control obtained by man over mechanic power, these are some of the causes of that rapid advance of material civilisation in England, to which the annals of the world can afford no parallel. But there was no proportionate advance in our moral civilisation. In the hurry-

skurry of money-making, men-making, and machine-making, we
had altogether outgrown, not the spirit, but the organisation, of
our institutions.

The peace came; the stimulating influences suddenly ceased;
the people, in a novel and painful position, found themselves
without guides. They went to the ministry; they asked to be
guided; they asked to be governed. Commerce requested a code;
trade required a currency; the unfranchised subject solicited his
equal privilege; suffering labour clamoured for its rights; a new
race demanded education. What did the ministry do?

They fell into a panic. Having fulfilled during their lives the
duties of administration, they were frightened because they were
called upon, for the first time, to perform the functions of
government. Like all weak men, they had recourse to what they
called strong measures. They determined to put down the multitude. They thought they were imitating Mr Pitt, because they
mistook disorganisation for sedition.[16]

Their projects of relief were as ridiculous as their system of
coercion was ruthless; both were alike founded in intense
ignorance. When we recall Mr Vansittart with his currency
resolutions; Lord Castlereagh with his plans for the employment
of labour; and Lord Sidmouth with his plots for ensnaring the
laborious; we are tempted to imagine that the present epoch has
been one of peculiar advances in political ability, and marvel how
England could have attained her present pitch under a series of
such governors.[17]

We should, however, be labouring under a very erroneous
impression. Run over the statesmen that have figured in England
since the accession of the present family, and we may doubt
whether there be one, with the exception perhaps of the Duke
of Newcastle,[18] who would have been a worthy colleague of the
council of Mr Perceval,[19] or the early cabinet of Lord Liverpool.[20]
Assuredly the genius of Bolingbroke and the sagacity of Walpole[21]
would have alike recoiled from such men and such measures
And if we take the individuals who were governing England immediately before the French Revolution, one need only refer to
the speeches of Mr Pitt, and especially to those of that profound
statesman and most instructed man, Lord Shelburne,[22] to find

that we can boast no remarkable superiority either in political justice or in political economy. One must attribute this degeneracy, therefore, to the long war and our insular position, acting upon men naturally of inferior abilities, and unfortunately, in addition, of illiterate habits.

In the meantime, notwithstanding all the efforts of the political Panglosses[23] who, in evening Journals and Quarterly Reviews, were continually proving that this was the best of all possible governments, it was evident to the ministry itself that the machine must stop. The class of Rigbys indeed at this period, one eminently favourable to that fungous tribe, greatly distinguished themselves. They demonstrated in a manner absolutely convincing, that it was impossible for any person to possess any ability, knowledge, or virtue, any capacity of reasoning, any ray of fancy or faculty of imagination, who was not a supporter of the existing administration. If any one impeached the management of a department, the public was assured that the accuser had embezzled; if any one complained of the conduct of a colonial governor, the complainant was announced as a returned convict.[24] An amelioration of the criminal code was discountenanced because a search in the parish register of an obscure village proved that the proposer had not been born in wedlock. A relaxation of the commercial system was denounced because one of its principal advocates was a Socinian.[25] The inutility of Parliamentary Reform was ever obvious since Mr Rigby was a member of the House of Commons.

To us, with our *Times* newspaper every morning on our breakfast-table, bringing, on every subject which can interest the public mind, a degree of information and intelligence which must form a security against any prolonged public misconception, it seems incredible that only five-and-twenty years ago the English mind could have been so ridden and hoodwinked, and that, too, by men of mean attainments and moderate abilities. But the war had directed the energies of the English people into channels by no means favourable to political education. Conquerors of the world, with their ports filled with the shipping of every clime, and their manufactories supplying the European continent, in the art of self-government, that art in which their fathers excelled, they had become literally children; and Rigby and his brother hirelings were the nurses that frightened them with hideous fables and ugly words.

Notwithstanding, however, all this successful mystification, the Arch-Mediocrity[26] who presided, rather than ruled, over this Cabinet of Mediocrities, became hourly more conscious that the inevitable transition from fulfilling the duties of an administration to performing the functions of a government could not be conducted without talents and knowledge. The Arch-Mediocrity had himself some glimmering traditions of political science. He was sprung from a laborious stock, had received some training, and though not a statesman, might be classed among those whom the Lord Keeper Williams used to call 'statemongers.'[27] In a subordinate position his meagre diligence and his frigid method might not have been without value; but the qualities that he possessed were misplaced; nor can any character be conceived less invested with the happy properties of a leader. In the conduct of public affairs his disposition was exactly the reverse of that which is the characteristic of great men. He was peremptory in little questions, and great ones he left open.

In the natural course of events, in 1819 there ought to have been a change of government, and another party in the state should have entered into office; but the Whigs, though they counted in their ranks at that period an unusual number of men of great ability, and formed, indeed, a compact and spirited opposition, were unable to contend against the new adjustment of borough influence which had occurred during the war, and under the protracted administration by which that war had been conducted. New families had arisen on the Tory side that almost rivalled old Newcastle himself in their electioneering management; and it was evident that, unless some reconstruction of the House of Commons could be effected, the Whig party could never obtain a permanent hold of official power. Hence, from that period, the Whigs became Parliamentary Reformers.

It was inevitable, therefore, that the country should be governed by the same party; indispensable that the ministry should be renovated by new brains and blood. Accordingly, a Mediocrity,[28] not without repugnance, was induced to withdraw, and the great name of Wellington supplied his place in council. The talents of the Duke, as they were then understood, were not exactly of the kind most required by the cabinet, and his colleagues were careful that he should not occupy too prominent a post; but still it was an impressive acquisition, and imparted to the ministry a semblance of renown.

There was an individual who had not long entered public life, but who had already filled considerable, though still subordinate, offices. Having acquired a certain experience of the duties of administration, and distinction for his mode of fulfilling them, he had withdrawn from his public charge; perhaps because he found it a barrier to the attainment of that parliamentary reputation for which he had already shown both a desire and a capacity; perhaps, because being young and independent, he was not over-anxious irremediably to identify his career with a school of politics of the infallibility of which his experience might have already made him a little sceptical. But he possessed the talents that were absolutely wanted, and the terms were at his own dictation. Another, and a very distinguished Mediocrity, who would not resign, was thrust out, and Mr Peel became Secretary of State.[29]

From this moment dates that intimate connection between the Duke of Wellington and the present First Minister, which has exercised a considerable influence over the career of individuals and the course of affairs. It was the sympathetic result of superior minds placed among inferior intelligences, and was, doubtless, assisted by a then mutual conviction, that the difference of age, the circumstance of sitting in different houses, and the general contrast of their previous pursuits and accomplishments, rendered personal rivalry out of the question. From this moment, too, the domestic government of the country assumed a new character, and one universally admitted to have been distinguished by a spirit of enlightened progress and comprehensive amelioration.

A short time after this, a third and most distinguished Mediocrity died; and Canning, whom they had twice worried out of the cabinet, where they had tolerated him some time in an obscure and ambiguous position, was recalled just in time from his impending banishment, installed in the first place in the Lower

House, and intrusted with the seals of the Foreign Office.[30] The
Duke of Wellington had coveted them, nor could Lord Liverpool
have been insensible to his Grace's peculiar fitness for such
duties; but strength was required in the House of Commons, where
they had only one Secretary of State, a young man already distinguished, yet untried as a leader, and surrounded by colleagues
notoriously incapable to assist him in debate.

The accession of Mr Canning to the cabinet, in a position, too,
of surpassing influence, soon led to a further weeding of the
Mediocrities, and, among other introductions, to the memorable
entrance of Mr Huskisson.[31] In this wise did that cabinet, once
notable only for the absence of all those qualities which
authorise the possession of power, come to be generally esteemed
as a body of men, who, for parliamentary eloquence, official
practice, political information, sagacity in council, and a due
understanding of their epoch, were inferior to none that had
directed the policy of the empire since the Revolution.[32]

If we survey the tenor of the policy of the Liverpool
Cabinet during the latter moiety of its continuance, we shall find
its characteristic to be a partial recurrence to those frank principles of government which Mr Pitt had revived during the latter
part of the last century from precedents that had been set us,
either in practice or in dogma, during its earlier period, by statesmen who then not only bore the title, but professed the opinions,
of Tories. Exclusive principles in the constitution, and restrictive
principles in commerce, have grown up together; and have really
nothing in common with the ancient character of our political
settlement, or the manners and customs of the English people.
Confidence in the loyalty of the nation, testified by munificent
grants of rights and franchises, and favour to an expansive
system of traffic, were distinctive qualities of the English sovereignty, until the House of Commons usurped the better portion
of its prerogatives. A widening of our electoral scheme, great
facilities to commerce, and the rescue of our Roman Catholic
fellow-subjects from the Puritanic yoke,[33] from fetters which have
been fastened on them by English Parliaments in spite of the protests and exertions of English Sovereigns; these were the three
great elements and fundamental truths of the real Pitt system,

a system founded on the traditions of our monarchy, and caught from the writings, the speeches, the councils of those who, for the sake of these and analogous benefits, had ever been anxious that the Sovereign of England should never be degraded into the position of a Venetian Doge.

It is in the plunder of the Church that we must seek for the primary cause of our political exclusion, and our commercial restraint. That unhallowed booty created a factitious aristocracy, ever fearful that they might be called upon to regorge their sacrilegious spoil.[34] To prevent this they took refuge in political religionism, and paltering with the disturbed consciences, or the pious fantasies, of a portion of the people, they organised them into religious sects. These became the unconscious Prætorians[35] of their ill-gotten domains. At the head of these religionists, they have continued ever since to govern, or powerfully to influence, this country. They have in that time pulled down thrones and churches, changed dynasties, abrogated and remodelled parliaments; they have disfranchised Scotland, and confiscated Ireland. One may admire the vigour and consistency of the Whig party, and recognise in their career that unity of purpose that can only spring from a great principle;[36] but the Whigs introduced sectarian religion, sectarian religion led to political exclusion, and political exclusion was soon accompanied by commercial restraint.

It would be fanciful to assume that the Liverpool Cabinet, in their ameliorating career, was directed by any desire to recur to the primordial tenets of the Tory party. That was not an epoch when statesmen cared to prosecute the investigation of principles. It was a period of happy and enlightened practice. A profounder policy is the offspring of a time like the present, when the original postulates of institutions are called in question. The Liverpool Cabinet unconsciously approximated to these opinions, because from careful experiment they were convinced of their beneficial tendency, and they thus bore an unintentional and impartial testimony to their truth. Like many men, who think they are inventors, they were only reproducing ancient wisdom.

But one must ever deplore that this ministry, with all their talents and generous ardour, did not advance to principles. It is always perilous to adopt expediency as a guide; but the choice may be sometimes imperative. These statesmen, however, took expediency for their director, when principle would have given them all that expediency ensured, and much more.

This ministry, strong in the confidence of the sovereign, the parliament, and the people, might, by the courageous promulgation of great historical truths, have gradually formed a public opinion, that would have permitted them to organise the Tory party on a broad, a permanent, and national basis. They might have nobly effected a complete settlement of Ireland, which a shattered section of this very cabinet was forced a few years after to do partially, and in an equivocating and equivocal manner.[37] They might have concluded a satisfactory reconstruction of the third estate, without producing that convulsion[38] with which, from its violent fabrication, our social system still vibrates. Lastly, they might have adjusted the rights and properties of our national industries in a manner which would have prevented that fierce and fatal rivalry that is now disturbing every hearth of the United Kingdom.

We may, therefore, visit on the *laches* of this ministry the introduction of that new principle and power into our constitution which ultimately may absorb all, AGITATION. This cabinet, then, with so much brilliancy on its surface, is the real parent of the Roman Catholic Association, the Political Unions, the Anti-Corn-Law League.[39]

There is no influence at the same time so powerful and so singular as that of individual character. It arises as often from the weakness of the character as from its strength. The dispersion of this clever and showy ministry is a fine illustration of this truth. One morning the Arch-Mediocrity himself died. At the first blush, it would seem that little difficulties could be experienced in finding his substitute. His long occupation of the post proved, at any rate, that the qualification was not excessive. But this cabinet, with its serene and blooming visage, had been all this time charged with fierce and emulous ambitions. They waited the signal, but they waited in grim repose. The death of the nominal leader, whose formal superiority, wounding no vanity, and offending no pride, secured in their councils equality among the able, was the tocsin of their anarchy. There existed in this cabinet two men, who were resolved immediately to be prime ministers; a third who was resolved eventually to be prime minister, but would at any rate occupy no ministerial post without the lead of a House of Parliament; and a fourth,[40] who felt himself capable of being prime minister, but despaired of the revolution which could alone make him one; and who found an untimely end when that revolution had arrived.

Had Mr Secretary Canning remained leader of the House of Commons under the Duke of Wellington, all that he would have gained by the death of Lord Liverpool was a master. Had the Duke of Wellington become Secretary of State under Mr Canning he would have materially advanced his political position, not only by holding the seals of a high department in which he was calculated to excel, but by becoming leader of the House of Lords. But his Grace was induced by certain court intriguers to believe that the King would send for him, and he was also aware that Mr Peel would no longer serve under any minister in the House of Commons. Under any circumstances it would have been impossible to keep the Liverpool Cabinet together. The struggle, therefore, between the Duke of Wellington and 'my dear Mr Canning' was internecine, and ended somewhat unexpectedly.

And here we must stop to do justice to our friend Mr Rigby, whose conduct on this occasion was distinguished by a bustling dexterity which was quite charming. He had, as we have before intimated, on the credit of some clever lampoons written during the Queen's trial,[41] which were, in fact, the effusions of Lucian Gay, wriggled himself into a sort of occasional unworthy favour at the palace, where he was half butt and half buffoon. Here, during the interregnum occasioned by the death, or rather inevitable retirement, of Lord Liverpool, Mr Rigby contrived to scrape up a conviction that the Duke was the winning horse, and in consequence there appeared a series of leading articles in a notorious evening newspaper, in which it was, as Tadpole and Taper declared, most 'slashingly' shown, that the son of an actress[42] could never be tolerated as a Prime Minister of England. Not content with this, and never doubting for a moment the authentic basis of his persuasion, Mr Rigby poured forth his coarse volubility on the subject at several of the new clubs which he was getting up in order to revenge himself for having been black-balled at White's.[43]

What with arrangements about Lord Monmouth's boroughs, and the lucky bottling of some claret which the Duke had imported on Mr Rigby's recommendations, this distinguished gentleman contrived to pay almost hourly visits at Apsley House, and so bullied Tadpole and Taper that they scarcely dared address him. About four-and-twenty hours before the result, and when it was generally supposed that the Duke was in, Mr Rigby, who had gone down to Windsor to ask his Majesty the date of some obscure historical incident, which Rigby, of course, very well knew, found that audiences were impossible, that his Majesty was agitated, and learned, from an humble but secure authority, that in spite of all his slashing articles, and Lucian Gay's parodies of the Irish melodies, Canning was to be Prime Minister.

This would seem something of a predicament! To common minds, there are no such things as scrapes for gentlemen with Mr Rigby's talents for action. He had indeed, in the world, the credit of being an adept in machinations, and was supposed ever to be involved in profound and complicated contrivances. This was quite a mistake. There was nothing profound about Mr Rigby; and his intellect was totally incapable of devising or sustaining an intricate or continuous scheme. He was, in short, a man who neither felt nor thought; but who possessed, in a very remarkable degree, a restless instinct for adroit baseness. On the present occasion he got into his carriage, and drove at the utmost speed from Windsor to the Foreign Office. The Secretary of State was engaged when he arrived; but Mr Rigby would listen to no difficulties. He rushed upstairs, flung open the door, and with agitated countenance, and eyes suffused with tears, threw himself into the arms of the astonished Mr Canning.

'All is right,' exclaimed the devoted Rigby, in broken tones; 'I have convinced the King that the First Minister must be in the House of Commons. No one knows it but myself; but it is certain.'

We have seen that at an early period of his career, Mr Peel withdrew from official life. His course had been one of unbroken prosperity; the hero of the University[44] had become the favourite of the House of Commons. His retreat, therefore, was not prompted by chagrin. Nor need it have been suggested by a calculating ambition, for the ordinary course of events was fast bearing to him all to which man could aspire. One might rather suppose, that he had already gained sufficient experience, perhaps in his Irish Secretaryship,[45] to make him pause in that career of superficial success which education and custom had hitherto chalked out for him, rather than the creative energies of his own mind. A thoughtful intellect may have already detected elements in our social system which required a finer observation, and a more unbroken study, than the gyves and trammels of office would permit. He may have discovered that the representation of the University, looked upon in those days as the blue ribbon of the House of Commons, was a sufficient fetter without unnecessarily adding to its restraint. He may have wished to reserve himself for a happier occasion, and a more progressive period. He may have felt the strong necessity of arresting himself in his rapid career of felicitous routine, to survey his position in calmness, and to comprehend the stirring age that was approaching.

For that, he could not but be conscious that the education which he had consummated, however ornate and refined, was not sufficient. That age of economical statesmanship which Lord Shelburne had predicted in 1787, when he demolished, in the House of Lords, Bishop Watson and the Balance of Trade, which Mr Pitt had comprehended, and for which he was preparing the nation when the French Revolution diverted the public mind into a stronger and more turbulent current, was again impending, while the intervening history of the country had been prolific in events which had aggravated the necessity of investigating the sources of the wealth of nations. The time had arrived when parliamentary pre-eminence could no longer be achieved or maintained by gorgeous abstractions borrowed from Burke,[46] or shallow systems purloined from De Lolme,[47] adorned with Horatian points, or varied with Virgilian passages. It was to be an age of abstruse disquisition, that required a compact and sinewy intellect, nurtured in a class of learning not yet honoured in colleges, and which might arrive at conclusions conflicting with predominant prejudices.

Adopting this view of the position of Mr Peel, strengthened as it is by his early withdrawal for awhile from the direction of public affairs, it may not only be a charitable but a true estimate of the motives which influenced him in his conduct towards Mr Canning, to conclude that he was not guided in that transaction by the disingenuous rivalry usually imputed to him. His statement in Parliament of the determining circumstances of his conduct, coupled with his subsequent and almost immediate policy, may perhaps always leave this a painful and ambiguous passage in his career; but in passing judgment on public men, it behoves us ever to take large and extended views of their conduct; and previous incidents will often satisfactorily explain subsequent events, which, without their illustrating aid, are involved in misapprehension or mystery.

It would seem, therefore, that Sir Robert Peel, from an early period, meditated his emancipation from the political confederacy in which he was implicated, and that he has been continually baffled in this project. He broke loose from Lord Liverpool; he retired from Mr Canning. Forced again into becoming the subordinate leader of the weakest government in parliamentary annals, he believed he had at length achieved his emancipation, when he declared to his late colleagues, after the overthrow of 1830, that he would never again accept a secondary position in office. But the Duke of Wellington was too old a tactician to lose so valuable an ally. So his Grace declared after the Reform Bill was passed, as its inevitable result, that thenceforth the Prime Minister must be a member of the House of Commons; and this aphorism, cited as usual by the Duke's parasites as demonstration of his supreme sagacity, was a graceful mode of resigning the pre-eminence which had been productive of such great party disasters. It is remarkable that the party who devised and passed the Reform Bill, and who, in consequence, governed the nation for ten years, never once had their Prime Minister in the House of Commons: but that does not signify; the Duke's maxim is still quoted as an oracle almost equal in prescience to his famous query, 'How is the King's government to be carried on?' a question to which his Grace by this time has contrived to give a tolerably practical answer.

Sir Robert Peel, who had escaped from Lord Liverpool, escaped from Mr Canning, escaped even from the Duke of Wellington in 1832, was at length caught in 1834; the victim of ceaseless intriguers, who neither comprehended his position, nor that of their country.

Chapter 2

BEAUMANOIR was one of those Palladian palaces, vast and ornate, such as the genius of Kent and Campbell[1] delighted in at the beginning of the eighteenth century. Placed on a noble elevation, yet screened from the northern blast, its sumptuous front, connected with its far-spreading wings by Corinthian colonnades, was the boast and pride of the midland counties. The surrounding gardens, equalling in extent the size of ordinary parks, were crowded with temples dedicated to abstract virtues and to departed friends. Occasionally a triumphal arch celebrated a general whom the family still esteemed a hero; and sometimes a votive column commemorated the great statesman who had advanced the family a step in the peerage. Beyond the limits of this pleasance the hart and hind wandered in a wilderness abounding in ferny coverts and green and stately trees.

The noble proprietor of this demesne had many of the virtues of his class: a few of their failings. He had that public spirit which became his station. He was not one of those who avoided the exertions and the sacrifices which should be inseparable from high position, by the hollow pretext of a taste for privacy, and a devotion to domestic joys. He was munificent, tender, and bounteous to the poor, and loved a flowing hospitality. A keen sportsman, he was not untinctured by letters, and had indeed a cultivated taste for the fine arts. Though an ardent politician, he was tolerant to adverse opinions, and full of amenity to his opponents. A firm supporter of the corn-laws, he never refused a lease. Notwithstanding there ran through his whole demeanour and the habit of his mind, a vein of native simplicity that was full of charm, his manner was finished. He never offended any one's self-love. His good breeding, indeed, sprang from the only sure source of gentle manners, a kind heart. To have pained others would have pained himself. Perhaps, too, this noble sympathy may have been in some degree prompted by the ancient blood in his veins, an accident of lineage rather rare with the English nobility. One could hardly praise him for the strong affections that bound him to his hearth, for fortune had given him the most pleasing family in the world; but, above all, a peerless wife.

The Duchess was one of those women who are the delight of existence. She was sprung from a house not inferior to that with which she had blended, and was gifted with that rare beauty which time ever spares, so that she seemed now only the elder sister of her own beautiful daughters. She, too, was distinguished by that perfect good breeding which is the result of nature and not of education: for it may be found in a cottage, and may be missed in a palace. 'Tis a genial regard for the feelings of others that springs from an absence of selfishness. The Duchess, indeed, was in every sense a fine lady; her manners were refined and full of dignity; but nothing in the world could have induced her to appear bored when another was addressing or attempting to amuse her. She was not one of those vulgar fine ladies who meet you one day with a vacant stare, as if unconscious of your existence, and address you on another in a tone of impertinent familiarity. Her temper, perhaps, was somewhat quick, which made this consideration for the feelings of others still more admirable, for it was the result of a strict moral discipline acting on a good heart. Although the best of wives and mothers, she had some charity for her neighbours. Needing herself no indulgence, she could be indulgent; and would by no means favour that strait-laced morality that would constrain the innocent play of the social body. She was accomplished, well read, and had a lively fancy. Add to this that sunbeam of a happy home, a gay and cheerful spirit in its mistress, and one might form some faint idea of this gracious personage.

The eldest son of this house was now on the Continent; of his two younger brothers, one was with his regiment, and the other was Coningsby's friend at Eton, our Henry Sydney. The two eldest daughters had just married, on the same day, and at the same altar; and the remaining one, Theresa, was still a child.

The Duke had occupied a chief post in the Household under the late administration, and his present guests chiefly consisted of his former colleagues in office. There were several members of the late cabinet, several members for his Grace's late boroughs, looking very much like martyrs, full of suffering and of hope. Mr Tadpole and Mr Taper were also there; they too had lost their seats since 1832; but being men of business, and accustomed from early life to look about them, they had already commenced the combinations which on a future occasion were to bear them back to the assembly where they were so missed.

Taper had his eye on a small constituency which had escaped the fatal schedules, and where he had what they called a 'connection;' that is to say, a section of the suffrages who had a lively remembrance of Treasury favours once bestowed by Mr Taper, and who had not been so liberally dealt with by the existing powers. This connection of Taper was in time to leaven the whole mass of the constituent body, and make it rise in full rebellion against its present liberal representative, who being one of a majority of three hundred, could get nothing when he called at Whitehall or Downing Street.

Tadpole, on the contrary, who was of a larger grasp of mind than Taper, with more of imagination and device but not so safe a man, was coquetting with a manufacturing town and a large constituency, where he was to succeed by the aid of the Wesleyans, of which pious body he had suddenly become a fervent admirer.[2] The great Mr Rigby, too, was a guest out of Parliament, nor caring to be in; but hearing that his friends had some hopes, he thought he would just come down to dash them.

The political grapes were sour for Mr Rigby; a prophet of evil, he preached only mortification and repentance and despair to his late colleagues. It was the only satisfaction left Mr Rigby, except assuring the Duke that the finest pictures in his gallery were copies, and recommending him to pull down Beaumanoir, and rebuild it on a design with which Mr Rigby would furnish him.

The battue and the banquet were over; the ladies had withdrawn; and the butler placed fresh claret on the table.

'And you really think you could give us a majority, Tadpole?' said the Duke.

Mr Tadpole, with some ceremony, took a memorandum-book

out of his pocket, amid the smiles and the faint well-bred merriment of his friends.

'Tadpole is nothing without his book,' whispered Lord Fitz-Booby.

'It is here,' said Mr Tadpole, emphatically patting his volume, 'a clear working majority of twenty-two.'

'Near sailing that!' cried the Duke.

'A far better majority than the present Government have,' said Mr Tadpole.

'There is nothing like a good small majority,' said Mr Taper, 'and a good registration.'[3]

'Ay! register, register, register!' said the Duke. 'Those were immortal words.'

'I can tell your Grace three far better ones,' said Mr Tadpole, with a self-complacent air. 'Object, object, object!'

'You may register, and you may object,' said Mr Rigby, 'but you will never get rid of Schedule A and Schedule B.'[4]

'But who could have supposed two years ago that affairs would be in their present position?' said Mr Taper, deferentially.

'I foretold it,' said Mr Rigby. 'Every one knows that no government now can last twelve months.'

'We may make fresh boroughs,' said Taper. 'We have reduced Shabbyton at the last registration under three hundred.'

'And the Wesleyans!' said Tadpole. 'We never counted on the Wesleyans!'

'I am told these Wesleyans are really a respectable body,' said Lord Fitz-Booby. 'I believe there is no material difference between their tenets and those of the Establishment. I never heard of them much till lately. We have too long confounded them with the mass of Dissenters, but their conduct at several of the later elections prove that they are far from being unreasonable and disloyal individuals. When we come in, something should be done for the Wesleyans, eh, Rigby?'

'All that your Lordship can do for the Wesleyans is what they will very shortly do for themselves, appropriate a portion of the Church Revenues to their own use.'

'Nay, nay,' said Mr Tadpole with a chuckle, 'I don't think we shall find the Church attacked again in a hurry. I only wish they would try! A good Church cry before a registration,' he continued, rubbing his hands; 'eh, my Lord, I think that would do.'

'But how are we to turn them out?' said the Duke.

'Ah!' said Mr Taper, 'that is a great question.'

'What do you think of a repeal of the Malt Tax?' said Lord Fitz-Booby. 'They have been trying it on in —shire, and I am told it goes down very well.'

'No repeal of any tax,' said Taper, sincerely shocked, and shaking his head; 'and the Malt Tax of all others. I am all against that.'

'It is a very good cry though, if there be no other,' said Tadpole.

'I am all for a religious cry,' said Taper. 'It means nothing, and, if successful, does not interfere with business when we are in.'

'You will have religious cries enough in a short time,' said Mr Rigby, rather wearied of any one speaking but himself, and thereat he commenced a discourse, which was, in fact, one of his 'slashing' articles in petto on Church Reform, and which abounded in parallels between the present affairs and those of the reign of Charles I. Tadpole, who did not pretend to know anything but the state of the registration, and Taper, whose political reading was confined to an intimate acquaintance with the Red Book and Beatson's Political Index,[5] which he could repeat backwards, were silenced. The Duke, who was well instructed and liked to be talked to, sipped his claret, and was rather amused by Rigby's lecture, particularly by one or two statements characterised by Rigby's happy audacity, but which the Duke was too indolent to question. Lord Fitz-Booby listened with his mouth open, but rather bored. At length, when there was a momentary pause, he said

'In my time, the regular thing was to move an amendment on the address.'[6]

'Quite out of the question,' exclaimed Tadpole, with a scoff.

'Entirely given up,' said Taper, with a sneer.

'If you will drink no more claret, we will go and hear some music,' said the Duke.

Chapter 3

A BREAKFAST at Beaumanoir was a meal of some ceremony. Every guest was expected to attend, and at a somewhat early hour. Their host and hostess set them the example of punctuality. 'Tis an old form rigidly adhered to in some great houses, but, it must be confessed, does not contrast very agreeably with the easier arrangements of establishments of less pretension and of more modern order.

The morning after the dinner to which we have been recently introduced, there was one individual absent from the breakfast-table whose non-appearance could scarcely be passed over without notice; and several inquired with some anxiety, whether their host were indisposed.

'The Duke has received some letters from London which detain him,' replied the Duchess. 'He will join us.'

'Your Grace will be glad to hear that your son Henry is very well,' said Mr Rigby; 'I heard of him this morning. Harry Coningsby enclosed me a letter for his grandfather, and tells me that he and Henry Sydney had just had a capital run with the King's hounds.'

'It is three years since we have seen Mr Coningsby,' said the Duchess. 'Once he was often here. He was a great favourite of mine. I hardly ever knew a more interesting boy.'

'Yes, I have done a great deal for him,' said Mr Rigby. 'Lord Monmouth is fond of him and wishes that he should make a figure; but how any one is to distinguish himself now, I am really at a loss to comprehend.'

'But are affairs so very bad?' said the Duchess, smiling. 'I thought that we were all regaining our good sense and good temper.'

'I believe all the good sense and all the good temper in England are concentrated in your Grace,' said Mr Rigby, gallantly.

'I should be sorry to be such a monopolist. But Lord Fitz-Booby was giving me last night quite a glowing report of Mr

Tadpole's prospects for the nation. We were all to have our own again; and Percy to carry the county.'

'My dear Madam, before twelve months are past, there will not be a county in England. Why should there be? If boroughs are to be disfranchised, why should not counties be destroyed?'

At this moment the Duke entered, apparently agitated. He bowed to his guests, and apologised for his unusual absence. 'The truth is,' he continued, 'I have just received a very important despatch. An event has occurred which may materially affect affairs. Lord Spencer is dead.'[1]

A thunderbolt in a summer sky, as Sir William Temple says,[2] could not have produced a greater sensation. The business of the repast ceased in a moment. The knives and forks were suddenly silent. All was still.

'It is an immense event,' said Tadpole.

'I don't see my way,' said Taper.

'When did he die?' said Lord Fitz-Booby.

'I don't believe it,' said Mr Rigby.

'They have got their man ready,' said Tadpole.

'It is impossible to say what will happen,' said Taper.

'Now is the time for an amendment on the address,' said Fitz-Booby.

'There are two reasons which convince me that Lord Spencer is not dead,' said Mr Rigby.

'I fear there is no doubt of it,' said the Duke, shaking his head.

'Lord Althorp was the only man who could keep them together,' said Lord Fitz-Booby.

'On the contrary,' said Tadpole 'If I be right in my man, and I have no doubt of it, you will have a radical programme, and they will be stronger than ever.'

'Do you think they can get the steam up again?' said Taper, musingly.

'They will bid high,' replied Tadpole. 'Nothing could be more unfortunate than this death. Things were going on so well and so quietly! The Wesleyans almost with us!'

'And Shabbyton too!' mournfully exclaimed Taper. 'Another registration and quiet times, and I could have reduced the constituency to two hundred and fifty.'

'If Lord Spencer had died on the 10th,' said Rigby, 'it must have been known to Henry Rivers. And I have a letter from Henry Rivers by this post. Now, Althorp is in Northamptonshire, mark that, and Northampton is a county –'

'My dear Rigby,' said the Duke, 'pardon me for interrupting you. Unhappily, there is no doubt Lord Spencer is dead, for I am one of his executors.'

This announcement silenced even Mr Rigby, and the conversation now entirely merged in speculations on what would occur. Numerous were the conjectures hazarded, but the prevailing impression was, that this unforeseen event might embarrass those secret expectations of Court succour in which a certain section of the party had for some time reason to indulge.

From the moment, however, of the announcement of Lord Spencer's death, a change might be visibly observed in the tone of the party at Beaumanoir. They became silent, moody, and restless. There seemed a general, though not avowed, conviction that a crisis of some kind or other was at hand. The post, too, brought letters every day from town teeming with fanciful speculations, and occasionally mysterious hopes.

'I kept this cover for Peel,' said the Duke pensively, as he loaded his gun on the morning of the 14th. 'Do you know, I was always against his going to Rome.'

'It is very odd,' said Tadpole, 'but I was thinking of the very same thing.'

'It will be fifteen years before England will see a Tory Government,' said Mr Rigby, drawing his ramrod, 'and then it will only last five months.'

'Melbourne,[3] Althorp, and Durham, all in the Lords,' said Taper. 'Three leaders! They must quarrel.'

'If Durham come in, mark me, he will dissolve on Household Suffrage and the Ballot,'[4] said Tadpole.

'Not nearly so good a cry as Church,' replied Taper.

'With the Malt Tax,' said Tadpole. 'Church, without the Malt Tax, will not do against Household Suffrage and Ballot.'

'Malt Tax is madness,' said Taper. 'A good farmer's friend cry without Malt Tax would work just as well.'

'They will never dissolve,' said the Duke. 'They are so strong.'

'They cannot go on with three hundred majority,' said Taper. 'Forty is as much as can be managed with open constituencies.'

'If he had only gone to Paris instead of Rome!' said the Duke.

'Yes,' said Mr Rigby, 'I could have written to him then by every post, and undeceived him as to his position.'

'After all he is the only man,' said the Duke; 'and I really believe the country thinks so.'

'Pray, what is the country?' inquired Mr Rigby. 'The country is nothing; it is the constituency you have to deal with.'

'And to manage them you must have a good cry,' said Taper. 'All now depends upon a good cry.'

'So much for the science of politics,' said the Duke, bringing down a pheasant. 'How Peel would have enjoyed this cover!'

'He will have plenty of time for sport during his life,' said Mr Rigby.

On the evening of the 15th of November, a despatch arrived at Beaumanoir, informing his Grace that the King had dismissed the Whig Ministry, and sent for the Duke of Wellington. Thus the first agitating suspense was over; to be succeeded, however, by expectation still more anxious. It was remarkable that every individual suddenly found that he had particular business in London which could not be neglected. The Duke very properly pleaded his executorial duties; but begged his guests on no account to be disturbed by his inevitable absence. Lord Fitz-Booby had just received a letter from his daughter, who was indisposed, at Brighton, and he was most anxious to reach her. Tadpole had to receive deputations from Wesleyans, and well-registered boroughs anxious to receive well-principled candidates. Taper was off to get the first job at the contingent Treasury, in favour of the Borough of Shabbyton. Mr Rigby alone was silent; but he quietly ordered a post-chaise at daybreak, and long before his fellow guests were roused from their slumbers, he was half-way to London, ready to give advice, either at the pavilion⁵ or at Apsley House.

Chapter 4

ALTHOUGH it is far from improbable that, had Sir Robert Peel been in England in the autumn of 1834, the Whig government would not have been dismissed; nevertheless, whatever may now be the opinion of the policy of that measure; whether it be looked on as a premature movement which necessarily led to the compact reorganisation of the Liberal party, or as a great stroke of State, which, by securing at all events a dissolution of the Parliament of 1832, restored the healthy balance of parties in the Legislature, questions into which we do not now wish to enter, it must be generally admitted, that the conduct of every individual eminently concerned in that great historical transaction was characterised by the rarest and most admirable quality of public life, moral courage. The Sovereign who dismissed a Ministry apparently supported by an overwhelming majority in the Parliament and the nation, and called to his councils the absent chief of a parliamentary section, scarcely numbering at that moment one hundred and forty individuals, and of a party in the country supposed to be utterly discomfited by a recent revolution; the two ministers[1] who in this absence provisionally administered the affairs of the kingdom in the teeth of an enraged and unscrupulous Opposition, and perhaps themselves not sustained by a profound conviction, that the arrival of their expected leader would convert their provisional into a permanent position; above all the statesman who accepted the great charge at a time and under circumstances which marred probably the deep projects of his own prescient sagacity and maturing ambition; were all men gifted with a high spirit of enterprise, and animated by that active fortitude which is the soul of free governments.

It was a lively season, that winter of 1834! What hopes, what fears, and what bets! From the day on which Mr Hudson[2] was to arrive at Rome to the election of the Speaker, not a contingency that was not the subject of a wager! People sprang up like mushrooms; town suddenly became full. Everybody who had been in office, and everybody who wished to be in office; everybody who had ever had anything, and everybody who ever expected to have anything, were alike visible. All of course by mere accident; one might meet the same men regularly every day for a month, who were only 'passing through town.'

Now was the time for men to come forward who had never despaired of their country. True they had voted for the Reform Bill, but that was to prevent a revolution. And now they were quite ready to vote against the Reform Bill, but this was to prevent a dissolution. These are the true patriots, whose confidence in the good sense of their countrymen and in their own selfishness is about equal. In the meantime, the hundred and forty threw a grim glance on the numerous waiters on Providence, and amiable trimmers, who affectionately enquired every day when news might be expected of Sir Robert. Though too weak to form a government, and having contributed in no wise by their exertions to the fall of the late, the cohort of Parliamentary Tories felt all the alarm of men who have accidentally stumbled on some treasure-trove, at the suspicious sympathy of new allies. But, after all, who were to form the government, and what was the government to be? Was it to be a Tory government, or an Enlightened-Spirit-of-the-Age Liberal-Moderate-Reform government; was it to be a government of high philosophy or of low practice; of principle or of expediency; of great measures or of little men? A government of statesmen or of clerks? Of Humbug or of Humdrum? Great questions these, but unfortunately there was nobody to answer them. They tried the Duke; but nothing could be pumped out of him. All that he knew, which he told in his curt, husky manner, was, that he had to carry on the King's government. As for his solitary colleague, he listened and smiled, and then in his musical voice asked them questions in return, which is the best possible mode of avoiding awkward inquiries. It was very unfair this; for no one knew what tone to take; whether they should go down to their public dinners and denounce the Reform Act or praise it; whether the Church was to be re-modelled or only admonished; whether Ireland was to be conquered or conciliated.

'This can't go on much longer,' said Taper to Tadpole, as they reviewed together their electioneering correspondence on the 1st of December; 'we have no cry.'

'He is half way by this time,' said Tadpole; 'send an extract from a private letter to the *Standard*, dated Augsburg, and say he will be here in four days.'

At last he came; the great man in a great position, summoned from Rome to govern England. The very day that he arrived he had his audience with the King.

It was two days after this audience; the town, though November, in a state of excitement; clubs crowded, not only morning rooms, but halls and staircases swarming with members eager to give and to receive rumours equally vain; streets lined with cabs and chariots, grooms and horses; it was two days after this audience that Mr Ormsby, celebrated for his political dinners, gave one to a numerous party. Indeed his saloons to-day, during the half-hour of gathering which proceeds dinner, offered in the various groups, the anxious countenances, the inquiring voices, and the mysterious whispers, rather the character of an Exchange or Bourse than the tone of a festive society.

Here might be marked a murmuring knot of greyheaded privy-councillors, who had held fat offices under Perceval and Liverpool, and who looked back to the Reform Act as to a hideous dream; there some middle-aged aspirants might be observed who had lost their seats in the convulsion, but who flattered themselves they had done something for the party in the interval, by spending nothing except their breath in fighting hopeless boroughs, and occasionally publishing a pamphlet, which really produced less effect than chalking the walls. Light as air, and proud as a young peacock, tripped on his toes a young Tory, who had contrived to keep his seat in a Parliament where he had done nothing, but who thought an Under-Secretaryship was now secure, particularly as he was the son of a noble Lord who had also in a public capacity plundered and blundered in the good old time. The true political adventurer, who with dull desperation had stuck at nothing, had never neglected a treasury note, had been present at every division, never spoke when he was asked to be silent, and was always ready on any subject when they wanted him to open his mouth; who had treated his leaders with servility even behind their backs, and was happy for the day if a future Secretary of the Treasury bowed to him; who had not only discountenanced discontent in the party, but had regularly reported in strict confidence every instance of insubordination which came to his knowledge; might there too be detected under all the agonies of the crisis; just beginning to feel the dread misgiving, whether being a slave and a sneak were sufficient qualifications for office, without family or connection. Poor fellow! half the industry he had wasted on his cheerless craft might have made his fortune in some decent trade!

In dazzling contrast with these throes of low ambition, were some brilliant personages who had just scampered up from Melton, thinking it probable that Sir Robert might want some moral lords of the bed-chamber. Whatever may have been their private fears or feelings, all however seemed smiling and significant, as if they knew something if they chose to tell it, and that something very much to their own satisfaction. The only grave countenance that was occasionally ushered into the room belonged to some individual whose destiny was not in doubt, and who was already practising the official air that was in future to repress the familiarity of his former fellow-strugglers.

'Do you hear anything?' said a great noble who wanted something in the general scramble, but what he knew not; only he had a vague feeling he ought to have something, having made such great sacrifices.

'There is a report that Clifford[3] is to be Secretary to the Board of Control,' said Mr Earwig, whose whole soul was in this subaltern arrangement, of which the Minister of course had not even thought; 'but I cannot trace it to any authority.'

'I wonder who will be their Master of the Horse,' said the great noble, loving gossip though he despised the gossiper.

'Clifford has done nothing for the party,' said Mr Earwig.

'I dare say Rambrooke will have the Buckhounds,'[4] said the great noble, musingly.

'Your Lordship has not heard Clifford's name mentioned?' continued Mr Earwig.

'I should think they had not come to that sort of thing,' said the great noble, with ill-disguised contempt. 'The first thing after the Cabinet is formed is the Household: the things you talk of are done last;' and he turned upon his heel, and met the imperturbable countenance and clear sarcastic eye of Lord Eskdale.

'You have not heard anything?' asked the great noble of his brother patrician.

'Yes, a great deal since I have been in this room; but unfortunately it is all untrue.'

'There is a report that Rambrooke is to have the Buckhounds; but I cannot trace it to any authority.'

'Pooh!' said Lord Eskdale.

'I don't see that Rambrooke should have the Buckhounds any more than anybody else. What sacrifices has he made?'

'Past sacrifices are nothing,' said Lord Eskdale. 'Present sacrifices are the thing we want: men who will sacrifice their principles, and join us.'

'You have not heard Rambrooke's name mentioned?'

'When a Minister has no Cabinet, and only one hundred and forty supporters in the House of Commons, he has something else to think of than places at Court,' said Lord Eskdale, as he slowly turned away to ask Lucian Gay whether it were true that Jenny Colon was coming over.

Shortly after this, Henry Sydney's father, who dined with Mr Ormsby, drew Lord Eskdale into a window, and said in an under tone

'So there is to be a kind of programme: something is to be written.'

'Well, we want a cue,' said Lord Eskdale. 'I heard of this last night: Rigby has written something.'

The Duke shook his head.

'No; Peel means to do it himself.'

But at this moment Mr Ormsby begged his Grace to lead them to dinner.

'Something is to be written.' It is curious to recall the vague terms in which the first projection of documents, that are to exercise a vast influence on the course of affairs or the minds of nations, is often mentioned. This 'something to be written' was written; and speedily; and has ever since been talked of.

We believe we may venture to assume that at no period during the movements of 1834–5 did Sir Robert Peel ever believe in the success of his administration. Its mere failure could occasion him little dissatisfaction; he was compensated for it by the noble opportunity afforded to him for the display of those great qualities, both moral and intellectual, which the swaddling-clothes of a routine prosperity had long repressed, but of which his opposition to the Reform Bill had given to the nation a significant intimation. The brief administration elevated him in public opinion, and even in the eye of Europe; and it is probable that a much longer term of power would not have contributed more to his fame.

The probable effect of the premature effort of his party on his future position as a Minister was, however, far from being so satisfactory. At the lowest ebb of his political fortunes, it cannot be doubted that Sir Robert Peel looked forward, perhaps through the vista of many years, to a period when the national mind, arrived by reflection and experience at certain conclusions, would seek in him a powerful expositor of its convictions. His time of life permitted him to be tranquil in adversity, and to profit by its salutary uses. He would then have acceded to power as the representative of a Creed, instead of being the leader of a Confederacy, and he would have been supported by earnest and enduring enthusiasm, instead of by that churlish sufferance which is the result of a supposed balance of advantages in his favour. This is the consequence of the tactics of those short-sighted intriguers, who persisted in looking upon a revolution as a mere party struggle, and would not permit the mind of the nation to work through the inevitable phases that awaited it. In 1834, England, though frightened at the reality of Reform, still adhered to its phrases; it was inclined, as practical England, to maintain existing institutions; but as theoretical England, it was suspicious that they were indefensible.

No one had arisen either in Parliament, the Universities, or the Press, to lead the public mind to the investigation of principles; and not to mistake, in their reformations, the corruption of practice for fundamental ideas. It was this perplexed, ill-informed, jaded, shallow generation, repeating cries which they did not comprehend, and wearied with the endless ebullitions of their own barren conceit, that Sir Robert Peel was summoned to govern. It was from such materials, ample in quantity, but in all spiritual qualities most deficient; with great numbers, largely acred, consoled up to their chins, but without knowledge, genius, thought, truth, or faith, that Sir Robert Peel was to form a 'great Conservative party on a comprehensive basis.' That he did this like a dexterous politician, who can deny? Whether he realised those prescient views of a great statesman in which he had doubtless indulged, and in which, though still clogged by the leadership of 1834, he may yet find fame for himself and salvation for his country, is altogether another question. His difficult attempt was expressed in an address to his constituents, which now ranks among state papers. We shall attempt briefly to consider it with the impartiality of the future.

Chapter 5

THE Tamworth Manifesto[1] of 1834 was an attempt to construct a party without principles; its basis therefore was necessarily Latitudinarianism; and its inevitable consequence has been Political Infidelity.

At an epoch of political perplexity and social alarm, the confederation was convenient, and was calculated by aggregation to encourage the timid and confused. But when the perturbation was a little subsided, and men began to inquire why they were banded together, the difficulty of defining their purpose proved that the league, however respectable, was not a party. The leaders indeed might profit by their eminent position to obtain power for their individual gratification; but it was impossible to secure their followers that which, after all, must be the great recompense of a political party, the putting in practice of their opinions; for they had none.

There was indeed a considerable shouting about what they called Conservative principles; but the awkward question naturally arose, what will you conserve? The prerogatives of the Crown, provided they are not exercised; the independence of the House of Lords, provided it is not asserted; the Ecclesiastical estate, provided it is regulated by a commission of laymen. Everything, in short, that is established, as long as it is a phrase and not a fact.

In the meantime, while forms and phrases are religiously cherished in order to make the semblance of a creed, the rule of practice is to bend to the passion or combination of the hour. Conservatism assumes in theory that everything established should be maintained; but adopts in practice that everything that is established is indefensible. To reconcile this theory and this practice, they produce what they call 'the best bargain;' some arrangement which has no principle and no purpose, except to obtain a temporary lull of agitation, until the mind of the Conservatives, without a guide and without an aim, distracted, tempted, and bewildered, is prepared for another arrangement, equally statesmanlike with the preceding one.

Conservatism was an attempt to carry on affairs by substituting the fulfilment of the duties of office for the performance of the functions of government; and to maintain this negative system by the mere influence of property, reputable private conduct, and what are called good connections. Conservatism discards Prescription, shrinks from Principle, disavows Progress; having rejected all respect for Antiquity, it offers no redress for the Present, and makes no preparation for the Future. It is obvious that for a time, under favourable circumstances, such a confederation might succeed; but it is equally clear, that on the arrival of one of those critical conjunctures that will periodically occur in all states, and which such an unimpassioned system is even calculated ultimately to create, all power of resistance will be wanting: the barren curse of political infidelity will paralyse all action; and the Conservative Constitution will be discovered to be a Caput Mortuum.

Chapter 6

In the meantime, after dinner, Tadpole and Taper, who were among the guests of Mr Ormsby, withdrew to a distant sofa, out of earshot, and indulged in confidential talk.

'Such a strength in debate was never before found on a Treasury bench,' said Mr Tadpole; 'the other side will be dumb-founded.'

'And what do you put our numbers at now?' inquired Mr Taper.

'Would you take fifty-five for our majority?' rejoined Mr Tad-pole.

'It is not so much the tail they have, as the excuse their junction will be for the moderate, sensible men to come over,' said Taper. 'Our friend Sir Everard for example, it would settle him.'

'He is a solemn imposter,' rejoined Mr Tadpole; 'but he is a baronet and a county member, and very much looked up to by the Wesleyans. The other men, I know, have refused him a peerage.'

'And we might hold out judicious hopes,' said Taper.

'No one can do that better than you,' said Tadpole. 'I am apt to say too much about those things.'

'I make it a rule never to open my mouth on such subjects,' said Taper. 'A nod or a wink will speak volumes. An affectionate pressure of the hand will sometimes do a great deal; and I have promised many a peerage without committing myself, by an ingenious habit of deference which cannot be mistaken by the future noble.'

'I wonder what they will do with Rigby,' said Tadpole.

'He wants a good deal,' said Taper.

'I tell you what, Mr Taper, the time is gone by when a Marquess of Monmouth was Letter A, No. 1.'

'Very true, Mr Tadpole. A wise man would do well now to look to the great middle class, as I said the other day to the electors of Shabbyton.'

'I had sooner be supported by the Wesleyans,' said Mr Tadpole, 'than by all the marquesses in the peerage.'

'At the same time,' said Mr Taper, 'Rigby is a considerable man. If we want a slashing article —'

'Pooh!' said Mr Tadpole. 'He is quite gone by. He takes three months for his slashing articles. Give me the man who can write a leader. Rigby can't write a leader.'

'Very few can,' said Mr Taper. 'However, I don't think much of the press. Its power is gone by. They overdid it.'

'There is Tom Chudleigh,' said Tadpole. 'What is he to have?'

'Nothing, I hope,' said Taper. 'I hate him. A coxcomb! Cracking his jokes and laughing at us.'

'He has done a good deal for the party, though,' said Tadpole. 'That, to be sure, is only an additional reason for throwing him over, as he is too far committed to venture to oppose us. But I am afraid from something that dropped to-day, that Sir Robert thinks he has claims.'

'We must stop them,' said Taper, growing pale. 'Fellows like Chudleigh, when they once get in, are always in one's way. I have no objection to young noblemen being put forward, for they are preferred so rapidly, and then their fathers die, that in the long run they do not practically interfere with us.'

'Well, his name was mentioned,' said Tadpole. 'There is no concealing that.'

'I will speak to Earwig,' said Taper. 'He shall just drop into Sir Robert's ear by chance, that Chudleigh used to quiz him in the smoking-room. Those little bits of information do a great deal of good.'

'Well, I leave him to you,' said Tadpole. 'I am heartily with you in keeping out all fellows like Chudleigh. They are very well for opposition; but in office we don't want wits.'

'And when shall we have the answer from Knowsley?' inquired Taper. 'You can anticipate no possible difficulty?'

'I tell you it is "carte blanche," ' replied Tadpole. 'Four places in the cabinet. Two secretaryships at the least. Do you happen to know any gentleman of your acquaintance, Mr Taper, who refuses Secretaryships of State so easily, that you can for an instant doubt of the present arrangement?'

'I know none indeed,' said Mr Taper, with a grim smile.

'The thing is done,' said Mr Tadpole.

'And now for our cry,' said Mr Taper.

'It is not a Cabinet for a good cry,' said Tadpole; 'but then, on the other hand, it is a Cabinet that will sow dissension in the opposite ranks, and prevent them having a good cry.'

'Ancient institutions and modern improvements, I suppose, Mr Tadpole?'

'Ameliorations is the better word; ameliorations. Nobody knows exactly what it means.'

'We go strong on the Church?' said Mr Taper.

'And no repeal of the Malt Tax; you were right, Taper. It can't be listened to for a moment.'

'Something might be done with prerogative,' said Mr Taper; 'the King's constitutional choice.'

'Not too much,' replied Mr Tadpole. 'It is a raw time yet for prerogative.'

'Ah! Tadpole,' said Mr Taper, getting a little maudlin; 'I often think, if the time should ever come, when you and I should be joint Secretaries of the Treasury!'

'We shall see, we shall see. All we have to do is to get into Parliament, work well together, and keep other men down.'

'We will do our best,' said Taper. 'A dissolution you hold inevitable?'

'How are you and I to get into Parliament if there be not one? We must make it inevitable. I tell you what, Taper, the lists must prove a dissolution inevitable. You understand me? If the present Parliament goes on, where shall we be? We shall have new men cropping up every session.'

'True, terribly true,' said Mr Taper. 'That we should ever live to see a Tory government again! We have reason to be very thankful.'

'Hush!' said Mr Tadpole. 'The time has gone by for Tory governments; what the country requires is a sound Conservative government.'

'A sound Conservative government,' said Taper, musingly. 'I understand: Tory men and Whig measures.'

Chapter 7

AMID the contentions of party, the fierce struggles of ambition, and the intricacies of political intrigue, let us not forget our Eton friends. During the period which elapsed from the failure of the Duke of Wellington to form a government in 1832, to the failure of Sir Robert Peel to carry on a government in 1835, the boys had entered, and advanced in youth. The ties of friendship which then united several of them had only been confirmed by continued companionship. Coningsby and Henry Sydney, and Buckhurst and Vere, were still bound together by entire sympathy, and by the affection of which sympathy is the only sure spring. But their intimacies had been increased by another familiar friend. There had risen up between Coningsby and Millbank mutual sentiments of deep, and even ardent, regard. Acquaintance had developed the superior qualities of Millbank. His thoughtful and inquiring mind, his inflexible integrity, his stern independence, and yet the engaging union of extreme tenderness of heart with all this strength of character, had won the goodwill, and often excited the admiration, of Coningsby. Our hero, too, was gratified by the affectionate deference that was often shown to him by one who condescended to no other individual; he was proud of having saved the life of a member of their community whom masters and boys alike considered; and he ended by loving the being on whom he had conferred a great obligation.

The friends of Coningsby, the sweet-tempered and intelligent Henry Sydney, the fiery and generous Buckhurst, and the calm and sagacious Vere, had ever been favourably inclined to Millbank, and had they not been, the example of Coningsby would soon have influenced them. He had obtained over his intimates the ascendant power, which is the destiny of genius. Nor was the submission of such spirits to be held cheap. Although they were willing to take the colour of their minds from him, they were in intellect and attainments, in personal accomplishments and general character, the leaders of the school; an authority not to be won from five hundred high-spirited boys without the possession of great virtues and great talents.

As for the dominion of Coningsby himself, it was not limited to the immediate circle of his friends. He had become the hero of Eton; the being of whose existence everybody was proud, and in whose career every boy took an interest. They talked of him, they quoted him, they imitated him. Fame and power are the objects of all men. Even their partial fruition is gained by very few; and that too at the expense of social pleasure, health, conscience, life. Yet what power of manhood in passionate intenseness, appealing at the same time to the subject and the votary, can rival that which is exercised by the idolised chieftain of a great public school? What fame of after days equals the rapture of celebrity that thrills the youthful poet, as in tones of rare emotion he recites his triumphant verses amid the devoted plaudits of the flower of England? That's fame, that's power; real, unquestioned, undoubted, catholic. Alas! the school-boy, when he becomes a man, finds that power, even fame, like everything else, is an affair of party.

Coningsby liked very much to talk politics with Millbank. He heard things from Millbank which were new to him. Himself, as he supposed, a high Tory, which he was according to the revelation of the Rigbys, he was also sufficiently familiar with the hereditary tenets of his Whig friend, Lord Vere. Politics had as yet appeared to him a struggle whether the country was to be governed by Whig nobles or Tory nobles; and he thought it very unfortunate that he should probably have to enter life with his friends out of power, and his family boroughs destroyed. But in conversing with Millbank, he heard for the first time of influential classes in the country, who were not noble, and were yet determined to acquire power. And although Millbank's views, which were of course merely caught up from his father, without the intervention of his own intelligence, were doubtless crude enough, and were often very acutely canvassed and satisfactorily demolished by the clever prejudices of another school, which Coningsby had at command, still they were, unconsciously to the recipient, materials for thought, and insensibly provoked in his mind a spirit of inquiry into political questions, for which he had a predisposition.

It may be said, indeed, that generally among the upper boys there might be observed at this time, at Eton, a reigning inclination for political discussion. The school truly had at all times been proud of its statesmen and its parliamentary heroes, but this was merely a superficial feeling in comparison with the sentiment which now first became prevalent. The great public questions that were the consequence of the Reform of the House of Commons, had also agitated their young hearts. And especially the controversies that were now rife respecting the nature and character of ecclesiastical establishments, wonderfully addressed themselves to their excited intelligence. They read their newspapers with a keen relish, canvassed debates, and criticised speeches; and although in their debating society, which had been instituted more than a quarter of a century, discussion on topics of the day was prohibited, still by fixing on periods of our history when affairs were analogous to the present, many a youthful orator contrived very effectively to reply to Lord John, or to refute the fallacies of his rival.

As the political opinions predominant in the school were what in ordinary parlance are styled Tory, and indeed were far better entitled to that glorious epithet than the flimsy shifts which their fathers were professing in Parliament and the country; the formation and the fall of Sir Robert Peel's government had been watched by Etonians with great interest, and even excitement. The memorable efforts which the Minister himself made, supported only by the silent votes of his numerous adherents, and contending alone against the multiplied assaults of his able and determined foes, with a spirit equal to the great occasion, and with resources of parliamentary contest which seemed to increase with every exigency; these great and unsupported struggles alone were calculated to gain the sympathy of youthful and generous spirits. The assault on the revenues of the Church[1]; the subsequent crusade against the House of Lords; the display of intellect and courage exhibited by Lord Lyndhurst in that assembly, when all seemed cowed and faint-hearted; all these were incidents or personal traits apt to stir the passions, and create in breasts not yet schooled to repress emotion, a sentiment even of enthusiasm. It is the personal that interests mankind, that fires their imagination, and wins their hearts. A cause is a great abstraction, and fit only for students; embodied in a party, it stirs men to action; but place at the head of that party a leader who can inspire enthusiasm, he commands the world. Divine faculty! Rare and incomparable privilege! A parliamentary leader who possesses it, doubles his majority; and he who has it not, may shroud himself in artificial reserve, and study with undignified arrogance an awkward haughtiness, but he will nevertheless be as far from controlling the spirit as from captivating the hearts of his sullen followers.

However, notwithstanding this general feeling at Eton, in 1835, in favour of 'Conservative principles,' which was, in fact, nothing more than a confused and mingled sympathy with some great political truths, which were at the bottom of every boy's heart, but nowhere else; and with the personal achievements and distinction of the chieftains of the party; when all this hubbub had subsided, and retrospection, in the course of a year, had exercised its moralising influence over the more thoughtful part of the nation, inquiries, at first faint and unpretending, and confined indeed for a long period to limited, though inquisitive, circles, began gently to circulate, what Conservative principles were.

These inquiries, urged indeed with a sort of hesitating scepticism, early reached Eton. They came, no doubt, from the Universities. They were of a character, however, far too subtile and refined to exercise any immediate influence over the minds of youth. To pursue them required previous knowledge and habitual thought. They were not yet publicly prosecuted by any school of politicians, or any section of the public press. They had not a local habitation or a name. They were whispered in conversation by a few. A tutor would speak of them in an esoteric vein to a favourite pupil, in whose abilities he had confidence, and whose future position in life would afford him the opportunity of influencing opinion. Among others, they fell upon the ear of Coningsby. They were addressed to a mind which was prepared for such researches.

There is a Library at Eton formed by the boys and governed by the boys; one of those free institutions which are the just pride of that noble school, which shows the capacity of the boys for self-government, and which has sprung from the large freedom that has been wisely conceded them, the prudence of which confidence has been proved by their rarely abusing it. This Library has been formed by subscriptions of the present and still more by the gifts of old Etonians. Among the honoured names of these donors may be remarked those of the Grenvilles and Lord Wellesley; nor should we forget George IV, who enriched the collection with a magnificent copy of the Delphin Classics.[2] The Institution is governed by six directors, the three first Collegers and the three first Oppidans for the time being; and the subscribers are limited to the one hundred senior members of the school.

It is only to be regretted that the collection is not so extensive as it is interesting and choice. Perhaps its existence is not so generally known as it deserves to be. One would think that every Eton man would be as proud of his name being registered as a donor in the Catalogue of this Library, as a Venetian of his name being inscribed in the Golden Book.[3] Indeed an old Etonian, who still remembers with tenderness the sacred scene of youth, could scarcely do better than build a Gothic apartment for the reception of the collection. It cannot be doubted that the Provost and fellows would be gratified in granting a piece of ground for the purpose.

Great were the obligations of Coningsby to this Eton Library. It introduced him to that historic lore, that accumulation of facts and incidents illustrative of political conduct, for which he had imbibed an early relish. His study was especially directed to the annals of his own country, in which youth, and not youth alone, is frequently so deficient. This collection could afford him Clarendon[4] and Burnet,[5] and the authentic volumes of Coxe;[6] these were rich materials for one anxious to be versed in the great parliamentary story of his country. During the last year of his stay at Eton, when he had completed his eighteenth year, Coningsby led a more retired life than previously; he read much, and pondered with all the pride of acquisition over his increasing knowledge.

And now the hour has come when this youth is to be launched into a new world more vast than that in which he has hitherto sojourned, yet for which this microcosm has been no ill preparation. He will become more wise; will he remain as generous? His ambition may be as great; will it be as noble? What, indeed, is to be the future of this existence that is now to be sent forth into the great aggregate of entities? Is it an ordinary organisation that will jostle among the crowd, and be jostled? Is it a finer temperament, susceptible of receiving the impressions and imbibing the inspirations of superior yet sympathising spirits? Or is it a primordial and creative mind; one that will say to his fellows, 'Behold, God has given me thought; I have discovered truth, and you shall believe?'

The night before Coningsby left Eton, alone in his room, before he retired to rest, he opened the lattice and looked for the last time upon the landscape before him; the stately keep of Windsor, the bowery meads of Eton, soft in the summer moon and still in the summer night. He gazed upon them; his countenance had none of the exultation, that under such circumstances might have distinguished a more careless glance, eager for fancied emancipation and passionate for a novel existence. Its expression was serious, even sad; and he covered his brow with his hand.

END OF BOOK II

BOOK III

Chapter 1

THERE are few things more full of delight and splendour, than to travel during the heat of a refulgent summer in the green district of some ancient forest.

In one of our midland counties there is a region of this character, to which, during a season of peculiar lustre, we would introduce the reader.

It was a fragment of one of those vast sylvan tracts wherein Norman kings once hunted, and Saxon outlaws plundered; and although the plough had for centuries successfully invaded brake and bower, the relics retained all their original character of wildness and seclusion. Sometimes the green earth was thickly studded with groves of huge and vigorous oaks, intersected with those smooth and sunny glades, that seem as if they must be cut for dames and knights to saunter on. Then again the undulating ground spread on all sides, far as the eye could range, covered with copse and fern of immense growth. Anon you found yourself in a turfy wilderness, girt in apparently by dark woods. And when you had wound your way a little through this gloomy belt, the landscape, still strictly sylvan, would beautifully expand with every combination and variety of woodland; while in its centre, the wildfowl covered the waters of a lake, and the deer basked on the knolls that abounded on its banks.

It was in the month of August, some six or seven years ago, that a traveller on foot, touched, as he emerged from the dark wood, by the beauty of this scene, threw himself under the shade of a spreading tree, and stretched his limbs on the turf for enjoyment rather than repose. The sky was deep-coloured and without a cloud, save here and there a minute, sultry, burnished vapour, almost as glossy as the heavens. Everything was still as it was bright; all seemed brooding and basking; the bee upon its wing was the only stirring sight, and its song the only sound.

The traveller fell into a reverie. He was young, and therefore his musings were of the future. He had felt the pride of learning, so ennobling to youth; he was not a stranger to the stirring impulses of a high ambition, though the world to him was as yet only a world of books, and all that he knew of the schemes of statesmen and the passions of the people, were to be found in their annals. Often had his fitful fancy dwelt with fascination on visions of personal distinction, of future celebrity, perhaps even of enduring fame. But his dreams were of another colour now. The surrounding scene, so fair, so still, and sweet; so abstracted from all the tumult of the world, its strife, its passions, and its cares; had fallen on his heart with its soft and subduing spirit; had fallen on a heart still pure and innocent, the heart of one who, notwithstanding all his high resolves and daring thoughts, was blessed with that tenderness of soul which is sometimes linked with an ardent imagination and a strong will. The traveller was an orphan, more than that, a solitary orphan. The sweet sedulousness of a mother's love, a sister's mystical affection, had not cultivated his early susceptibility. No soft pathos of expression had appealed to his childish ear. He was alone, among strangers calmly and coldly kind. It must indeed have been a truly gentle disposition that could have withstood such hard neglect. All that he knew of the power of the softer passions might be found in the fanciful and romantic annals of schoolboy friendship.

And those friends too, so fond, so sympathising, so devoted, where were they now? Already they were dispersed; the first great separation of life had been experienced; the former schoolboy had planted his foot on the threshold of manhood. True, many of them might meet again; many of them the University must again unite, but never with the same feelings. The space of time, passed in the world before they again met, would be an age of sensation, passion, experience to all of them. They would meet again with altered mien, with different manners, different voices. Their eyes would not shine with the same light; they would not speak the same words. The favourite phrases of their intimacy, the mystic sounds that spoke only to their initiated ear, they would be ashamed to use them. Yes, they might meet again, but the gushing and secret tenderness was gone for ever.

Nor could our pensive youth conceal it from himself that it was affection, and mainly affection, that had bound him to these dear companions. They could not be to him what he had been to them. His had been the inspiring mind that had guided their opinions, formed their tastes, directed the bent and tenor of their lives and thoughts. Often, indeed, had he needed, sometimes he had even sighed for, the companionship of an equal or superior mind; one who, by the comprehension of his thought, and the richness of his knowledge, and the advantage of his experience, might strengthen and illuminate and guide his obscure or hesitating or unpractised intelligence. He had scarcely been fortunate in this respect, and he deeply regretted it; for he was one of those who was not content with excelling in his own circle, if he thought there was one superior to it. Absolute, not relative distinction, was his noble aim.

Alone, in a lonely scene, he doubly felt the solitude of his life and mind. His heart and his intellect seemed both to need a companion. Books, and action, and deep thought, might in time supply the want of that intellectual guide; but for the heart, where was he to find solace?

Ah! If she would but come forth from that shining lake like a beautiful Ondine! Ah, if she would but step out from the green shade of that secret grove like a Dryad of sylvan Greece! O mystery of mysteries, when the youth dreams his first dream over some imaginary heroine!

Suddenly the brooding wildfowl rose from the bosom of the lake, soared in the air, and, uttering mournful shrieks, whirled in agitated tumult. The deer started from their knolls, no longer sunny, stared around, and rushed into the woods. Coningsby raised his eyes from the turf on which they had been long fixed in abstraction, and he observed that the azure sky had vanished, a thin white film had suddenly spread itself over the heavens, and the wind moaned with a sad and fitful gust.

He had some reason to believe that on the other side of the opposite wood the forest was intersected by a public road, and that there were some habitations. Immediately rising, he descended at a rapid pace into the valley, passed the lake, and then struck into the ascending wood on the bank opposite to that on which he had mused away some precious time.

The wind howled, the branches of the forest stirred, and sent forth sounds like an incantation. Soon might be distinguished the various voices of the mighty trees, as they expressed their terror or their agony. The oak roared, the beech shrieked, the elm sent forth its deep and long-drawn groan; while ever and anon, amid a momentary pause, the passion of the ash was heard in moans of thrilling anguish.

Coningsby hurried on, the forest became less close. All that he aspired to was to gain more open country. Now he was in a rough flat land, covered only here and there with dwarf underwood; the horizon bounded at no great distance by a barren hill of moderate elevation. He gained its height with ease. He looked over a vast open country like a wild common; in the extreme distance hills covered with woods; the plain intersected by two good roads: the sky entirely clouded, but in the distance black as ebony.

A place of refuge was at hand: screened from his first glance by some elm-trees, the ascending smoke now betrayed a roof, which Coningsby reached before the tempest broke. The forest-inn was also a farmhouse. There was a comfortable-enough looking kitchen; but the ingle[1] nook was full of smokers, and Coningsby was glad to avail himself of the only private room for the simple meal which they offered him, only eggs and bacon; but very welcome to a pedestrian, and a hungry one.

As he stood at the window of his little apartment, watching the large drops that were the heralds of a coming hurricane, and waiting for his repast, a flash of lightning illumined the whole country, and a horseman at full speed, followed by his groom, galloped up to the door.

The remarkable beauty of the animal so attracted Coningsby's attention, that it prevented him catching even a glimpse of the rider, who rapidly dismounted and entered the inn. The host shortly after came in and asked Coningsby whether he had any objection to a gentleman, who was driven there by the storm, sharing his room until it subsided. The consequence of the immediate assent of Coningsby was, that the landlord retired and soon returned, ushering in an individual, who, though perhaps

ten years older than Coningsby, was still, according to Hippo-
crates, in the period of lusty youth. He was above the middle
height, and of a distinguished air and figure; pale, with an impressive brow, and dark eyes of great intelligence.

'I am glad that we have both escaped the storm,' said the
stranger; 'and I am greatly indebted to you for your courtesy.' He
slightly and graciously bowed, as he spoke in a voice of remarkable clearness; and his manner, though easy, was touched with a
degree of dignity that was engaging.

'The inn is a common home,' replied Coningsby, returning his
salute.

'And free from cares,' added the stranger. Then, looking
through the window, he said, 'A strange storm this. I was sauntering in the sunshine, when suddenly I found I had to gallop for
my life. 'Tis more like a white squall in the Mediterranean than
anything else.'

'I never was in the Mediterranean,' said Coningsby. 'There is
nothing I should like so much as to travel.'

'You are travelling,' rejoined his companion. 'Every moment is
travel, if understood.'

'Ah! but the Mediterranean!' exclaimed Coningsby. 'What
would I not give to see Athens!'

'I have seen it,' said the stranger, slightly shrugging his
shoulders; 'and more wonderful things. Phantoms and spectres!
The Age of Ruins is past. Have you seen Manchester?'

'I have seen nothing,' said Coningsby; 'this is my first wandering. I am about to visit a friend who lives in this county, and I
have sent on my baggage as I could. For myself, I determined to
trust to a less common-place conveyance.'

'And seek adventures,' said the stranger, smiling. 'Well, according to Cervantes, they should begin in an inn.'

'I fear that the age of adventures is past, as well as that of ruins,'
replied Coningsby.

'Adventures are to the adventurous,' said the stranger.

At this moment a pretty serving-maid entered the room. She
laid the dapper cloth and arranged the table with a self-possession
quite admirable. She seemed unconscious that any being was in
the chamber except herself, or that there were any other duties

to perform in life beyond filling a salt-cellar or folding a napkin.

'She does not even look at us,' said Coningsby, when she had quitted the room; 'and I dare say is only a prude.'

'She is calm,' said the stranger, 'because she is mistress of her subject; 'tis the secret of self-possession. She is here as a duchess at court.'

They brought in Coningsby's meal, and he invited the stranger to join him. The invitation was accepted with cheerfulness.

' 'Tis but simple fare,' said Coningsby, as the maiden uncovered the still hissing bacon and eggs, that looked like tufts of primroses.

'Nay, a national dish,' said the stranger, glancing quickly at the table, 'whose fame is a proverb. And what more should we expect under a simple roof! How much better than an omelette or a greasy olla,[2] that they would give us in a posada![3] 'Tis a wonderful country this England! What a napkin! How spotless! And so sweet; I declare 'tis a perfume. There is not a princess throughout the South of Europe served with the cleanliness that meets us in this cottage.'

'An inheritance from our Saxon fathers?' said Coningsby. 'I apprehend the northern nations have a greater sense of cleanliness, of propriety, of what we call comfort?'

'By no means,' said the stranger; 'the East is the land of the Bath. Moses and Mahomet made cleanliness religion.'

'You will let me help you?' said Coningsby, offering him a plate which he had filled.

'I thank you,' said the stranger, 'but it is one of my bread days. With your permission this shall be my dish;' and he cut from the large loaf a supply of crusts.

' 'Tis but unsavoury fare after a gallop,' said Coningsby.

'Ah! you are proud of your bacon and your eggs,' said the stranger, smiling, 'but I love corn and wine. They are our chief and our oldest luxuries. Time has brought us substitutes, but how inferior! Man has deified corn and wine! but not even the Chinese or the Irish have raised temples to tea and potatoes.'

'But Ceres without Bacchus,' said Coningsby, 'how does that do? Think you, under this roof, we could invoke the god?'

'Let us swear by his body that we will try,' said the stranger.

Alas! the landlord was not a priest to Bacchus. But then these inquiries led to the finest perry in the world. The young men agreed they had seldom tasted anything more delicious; they sent for another bottle. Coningsby, who was much interested by his new companion, enjoyed himself amazingly.

A cheese, such as Derby alone can produce, could not induce the stranger to be even partially inconstant to his crusts. But his talk was as vivacious as if the talker had been stimulated by the juices of the finest banquet. Coningsby had never met or read of any one like this chance companion. His sentences were so short, his language so racy, his voice rang so clear, his elocution was so complete. On all subjects his mind seemed to be instructed, and his opinions formed. He flung out a result in a few words; he solved with a phrase some deep problem that men muse over for years. He said many things that were strange, yet they immediately appeared to be true. Then, without the slightest air of pretension or parade, he seemed to know everybody as well as everything. Monarchs, statesmen, authors, adventurers, of all descriptions and of all climes, if their names occurred in the conversation, he described them in an epigrammatic sentence, or revealed their precise position, character, calibre, by a curt dramatic trait. All this, too, without any excitement of manner; on the contrary, with repose amounting almost to nonchalance. If his address had any fault in it, it was rather a deficiency of earnestness. A slight spirit of mockery played over his speech even when you deemed him most serious; you were startled by his sudden transitions from profound thought to poignant sarcasm. A very singular freedom from passion and prejudice on every topic on which they treated, might be some compensation for this want of earnestness, perhaps was its consequence. Certainly it was difficult to ascertain his precise opinions on many subjects, though his manner was frank even to abandonment. And yet throughout his whole conversation, not a stroke of egotism, not a word, not a circumstance escaped him, by which you could judge of his position or purposes in life. As little did he seem to care to discover those of his companion. He did not by any means monopolise the conversation. Far from it; he continually asked questions, and while he received answers, or had engaged his fellow-traveller in any exposition of his opinion or feelings, he listened with a serious and fixed attention, looking Coningsby in the face with a steadfast glance.

'I perceive,' said Coningsby, pursuing a strain of thought which the other had indicated, 'that you have great confidence in the influence of individual character. I also have some confused persuasions of that kind. But it is not the Spirit of the Age.'

'The age does not believe in great men, because it does not possess any,' replied the stranger. 'The Spirit of the Age is the very thing that a great man changes.'

'But does he not rather avail himself of it?' inquired Coningsby.

'Parvenus do,' rejoined his companion; 'but not prophets, great legislators, great conquerors. They destroy and they create.'

'But are these times for great legislators and great conquerors?' urged Coningsby.

'When were they wanted more?' asked the stranger. 'From the throne to the hovel all call for a guide. You give monarchs constitutions to teach them sovereignty, and nations Sunday-schools to inspire them with faith.'

'But what is an individual,' exclaimed Coningsby, 'against a vast public opinion?'

'Divine,' said the stranger. 'God made man in His own image; but the Public is made by Newspapers, Members of Parliament, Excise Officers, Poor Law Guardians.[4] Would Philip have succeedded if Epaminondas had not been slain?[5] And if Philip had not succeeded? Would Prussia have existed had Frederick not been born? And if Frederick had not been born? What would have been the fate of the Stuarts if Prince Henry had not died, and Charles I, as was intended, had been Archbishop of Canterbury?'

'But when men are young they want experience,' said Coningsby; 'and when they have gained experience, they want energy.'

'Great men never want experience,' said the stranger.

'But everybody says that experience –'

'Is the best thing in the world, a treasure for you, for me, for millions. But for a creative mind, less than nothing. Almost everything that is great has been done by youth.'

'It is at least a creed flattering to our years,' said Coningsby, with a smile.

'Nay,' said the stranger; 'for life in general there is but one decree. Youth is a blunder; Manhood a struggle; Old Age a regret. Do not suppose,' he added, smiling, 'that I hold that youth is genius; all that I say is, that genius, when young, is divine. Why, the greatest captains of ancient and modern times both conquered Italy at five-and-twenty! Youth, extreme youth, overthrew the Persian Empire. Don John of Austria won Lepanto at twenty-five,[6] the greatest battle of modern time; had it not been for the jealousy of Philip, the next year he would have been Emperor of Mauritania. Gaston de Foix was only twenty-two when he stood a victor on the plain of Ravenna. Every one remembers Condé and Rocroy at the same age. Gustavus Adolphus died at thirty-eight. Look at his captains: that wonderful Duke of Weimar, only thirty-six when he died. Banier himself, after all his miracles, died at forty-five. Cortes was little more than thirty when he gazed upon the golden cupolas of Mexico. When Maurice of Saxony died at thirty-two, all Europe acknowledged the loss of the greatest captain and the profoundest statesman of the age. Then there is Nelson, Clive; but these are warriors, and perhaps you may think there are greater things than war. I do not: I worship the Lord of Hosts. But take the most illustrious achievements of civil prudence. Innocent III, the greatest of the Popes, was the despot of Christendom at thirty-seven. John de Medici was a Cardinal at fifteen, and according to Guicciardini, baffled with his statecraft Ferdinand of Arragon himself.[7] He was Pope as Leo X at thirty-seven. Luther robbed even him of his richest province at thirty-five. Take Ignatius Loyola and John Wesley, they worked with young brains. Ignatius was only thirty when he made his pilgrimage and wrote the "Spiritual Exercises." Pascal wrote a great work at sixteen,[8] and died at thirty-seven, the greatest of Frenchmen.

'Ah! that fatal thirty-seven, which reminds me of Byron, greater even as a man than a writer. Was it experience that guided the pencil of Raphael when he painted the palaces of Rome? He, too, died at thirty-seven. Richelieu was Secretary of State at thirty-one. Well then, there were Bolingbroke and Pitt, both ministers before other men left off cricket. Grotius[9] was in great practice at seventeen, and Attorney-General at twenty-four. And Acquaviva;[10]

Acquaviva was General of the Jesuits, ruled every cabinet in Europe, and colonised America before he was thirty-seven. What a career!' exclaimed the stranger; rising from his chair and walking up and down the room; 'the secret sway of Europe! That was indeed a position! But it is needless to multiply instances! The history of Heroes is the history of Youth.'

'Ah!' said Coningsby, 'I should like to be a great man.'

The stranger threw at him a scrutinising glance. His countenance was serious. He said in a voice of almost solemn melody,

'Nurture your mind with great thoughts. To believe in the heroic makes heroes.'

'You seem to me a hero,' said Coningsby, in a tone of real feeling, which, half ashamed of his emotion, he tried to turn into playfulness.

'I am and must ever be,' said the stranger, 'but a dreamer of dreams.' Then going towards the window, and changing into a familiar tone, as if to divert the conversation, he added, 'What a delicious afternoon! I look forward to my ride with delight. You rest here?'

'No; I go on to Nottingham, where I shall sleep.'

'And I in the opposite direction.' And he rang the bell, and ordered his horses.

'I long to see your mare again,' said Coningsby. 'She seemed to me so beautiful.'

'She is not only of pure race,' said the stranger, 'but of the highest and rarest breed in Arabia. Her name is "the Daughter of the Star." She is a foal of that famous mare, which belonged to the Prince of the Wahabees;[11] and to possess which, I believe, was one of the principal causes of war between that tribe and the Egyptians. The Pacha of Egypt gave her to me, and I would not change her for her statue in pure gold, even carved by Lysippus.[12] Come round to the stable and see her.'

They went out together. It was a soft sunny afternoon; the air fresh from the rain, but mild and exhilarating.

The groom brought forth the mare. 'The Daughter of the Star' stood before Coningsby with her sinewy shape of matchless symmetry; her burnished skin, black mane, legs like those of an antelope, her little ears, dark speaking eye, and tail worthy of a

Pacha. And who was her master, and whither was she about to take him?

Coningsby was so naturally well-bred, that we may be sure it was not curiosity; no, it was a finer feeling that made him hesitate and think a little, and then say

'I am sorry to part.'

'I also,' said the stranger. 'But life is constant separation.'

'I hope we may meet again,' said Coningsby.

'If our acquaintance be worth preserving,' said the stranger, 'you may be sure it will not be lost.'

'But mine is not worth preserving,' said Coningsby, earnestly. 'It is yours that is the treasure. You teach me things of which I have long mused.'

The stranger took the bridle of 'the Daughter of the Star,' and turning round with a faint smile, extended his hand to his companion.

'Your mind at least is nurtured with great thoughts,' said Coningsby; 'your actions should be heroic.'

'Action is not for me,' said the stranger; 'I am of that faith that the Apostles professed before they followed their master.'

He vaulted into his saddle, 'the Daughter of the Star' bounded away as if she scented the air of the Desert from which she and her rider had alike sprung, and Coningsby remained in profound meditation.

Chapter 2

THE day after his adventure at the Forest Inn, Coningsby arrived
at Beaumanoir. It was several years since he had visited the
family of his friend, who were indeed also his kin; and in his
boyish days had often proved that they were not unmindful of the
affinity. This was a visit that had been long counted on, long
promised, and which a variety of circumstances had hitherto prevented. It was to have been made by the schoolboy; it was to be
fulfilled by the man. For no less a character could Coningsby under
any circumstances now consent to claim, since he was closely
verging to the completion of his nineteenth year; and it appeared
manifest that if it were his destiny to do anything great, he had but
few years to wait before the full development of his power. Visions
of Gastons de Foix and Maurices of Saxony, statesmen giving up
cricket to govern nations, beardless Jesuits plunged in profound
abstraction in omnipotent cabinets, haunted his fancy from the
moment he had separated from his mysterious and deeply interesting companion. To nurture his mind with great thoughts had ever
been Coningsby's inspiring habit. Was it also destined that he
should achieve the heroic?

There are some books, when we close them; one or two in the
course of our life, difficult as it may be to analyse or ascertain
the cause; our minds seem to have made a great leap. A thousand
obscure things receive light; a multitude of indefinite feelings are
determined. Our intellect grasps and grapples with all subjects
with a capacity, a flexibility, and a vigour, before unknown to us.
It masters questions hitherto perplexing, which are not even
touched or referred to in the volume just closed. What is this
magic? It is the spirit of the supreme author, by a magnetic
influence blending with our sympathising intelligence, that
directs and inspires it. By that mysterious sensibility we extend to
questions which he has not treated, the same intellectual force
which he has exercised over those which he has expounded. His

genius for a time remains in us. 'Tis the same with human beings as with books. All of us encounter, at least once in our life, some individual who utters words that make us think for ever. There are men whose phrases are oracles; who condense in a sentence the secrets of life; who blurt out an aphorism that forms a character or illustrates an existence. A great thing is a great book; but greater than all is the talk of a great man.

And what is a great man? Is it a Minister of State? Is it a victorious General? A gentleman in the Windsor uniform? A Field Marshal covered with stars? Is it a Prelate, or a Prince? A King, even an Emperor? It may be all these; yet these, as we must all daily feel, are not necessarily great men. A great man is one who affects the mind of his generation: whether he be a monk in his cloister agitating Christendom, or a monarch crossing the Granicus,[1] and giving a new character to the Pagan World.

Our young Coningsby reached Beaumanoir in a state of meditation. He also desired to be great. Not from the restless vanity that sometimes impels youth to momentary exertion, by which they sometimes obtain a distinction as evanescent as their energy. The ambition of our hero was altogether of a different character. It was, indeed, at present not a little vague, indefinite, hesitating, inquiring, sometimes desponding. What were his powers? what should be his aim? were often to him, as to all young aspirants, questions infinitely perplexing and full of pain. But, on the whole, there ran through his character, notwithstanding his many dazzling qualities and accomplishments, and his juvenile celebrity, which has spoiled so much promise, a vein of grave simplicity that was the consequence of an earnest temper, and of an intellect that would be content with nothing short of the profound.

His was a mind that loved to pursue every question to the centre. But it was not a spirit of scepticism that impelled this habit; on the contrary, it was the spirit of faith. Coningsby found that he was born in an age of infidelity in all things, and his heart assured him that a want of faith was a want of nature. But his vigorous intellect could not take refuge in that maudlin substitute for belief which consists in a patronage of fantastic theories. He needed that deep and enduring conviction that the heart and the intellect, feeling and reason united, can alone supply. He asked himself why governments were hated, and religions despised? Why loyalty was dead, and reverence only a galvanised corpse?

These were indeed questions that had as yet presented themselves to his thought in a crude and imperfect form; but their very occurrence showed the strong predisposition of his mind. It was because he had not found guides among his elders, that his thoughts had been turned to the generation that he himself represented. The sentiment of veneration was so developed in his nature, that he was exactly the youth that would have hung with enthusiastic humility on the accents of some sage of old in the groves of Academus, or the porch of Zeno.[2] But as yet he had found age only perplexed and desponding; manhood only callous and desperate. Some thought that systems would last their time; others, that something would turn up. His deep and pious spirit recoiled with disgust and horror from such lax, chance-medley maxims, that would, in their consequences, reduce man to the level of the brutes. Notwithstanding a prejudice which had haunted him from his childhood, he had, when the occasion offered, applied to Mr Rigby for instruction, as one distinguished in the republic of letters, as well as the realm of politics; who assumed the guidance of the public mind, and, as the phrase runs, was looked up to. Mr Rigby listened at first to the inquiries of Coningsby, urged, as they ever were, with a modesty and deference which do not always characterise juvenile investigations, as if Coningsby were speaking to him of the unknown tongues. But Mr Rigby was not a man who ever confessed himself at fault. He caught up something of the subject as our young friend proceeded, and was perfectly prepared, long before he had finished, to take the whole conversation into his own hands.

Mr Rigby began by ascribing everything to the Reform Bill, and then referred to several of his own speeches on Schedule A. Then he told Coningsby that want of religious Faith was solely occasioned by want of churches; and want of Loyalty, by George IV having shut himself up too much at the cottage[3] in Windsor Park, entirely against the advice of Mr Rigby. He assured Coningsby that the Church Commission was operating wonders, and that with private benevolence, he had himself subscribed 1,000*l.*, for Lord Monmouth, we should soon have churches enough. The great question now was their architecture. Had George IV lived all would have been right. They would have been built on the model of the Budhist pagoda. As for Loyalty, if the present King went regularly to Ascot races, he had no doubt all would go right. Finally, Mr Rigby impressed on Coningsby to read the Quarterly Review with great attention; and to make himself master of Mr Wordy's History of the late War, in twenty volumes, a capital work, which proves that Providence was on the side of the Tories.

Coningsby did not apply to Mr Rigby again; but worked on with his own mind, coming often enough to sufficiently crude conclusions, and often much perplexed and harassed. He tried occasionally his inferences on his companions, who were intelligent and full of fervour. Millbank was more than this. He was of a thoughtful mood; had also caught up from a new school some principles, which were materials for discussion. One way or other, however, before he quitted Eton there prevailed among this circle of friends, the initial idea doubtless emanating from Coningsby, an earnest, though a rather vague, conviction that the present state of feeling in matters both civil and religious was not healthy; that there must be substituted for this latitudinarianism something sound and deep, fervent and well defined, and that the priests of this new faith must be found among the New Generation; so that when the bright-minded rider of 'the Daughter of the Star' descanted on the influence of individual character, of great thoughts and heroic actions, and the divine power of youth and genius, he touched a string that was the very heart-chord of his companion, who listened with fascinated enthusiasm as he introduced him to his gallery of inspiring models.

Coningsby arrived at Beaumanoir at a season when men can neither hunt nor shoot. Great internal resources should be found in a country family under such circumstances. The Duke and Duchess had returned from London only a few days with their daughter, who had been presented this year. They were all glad to find themselves again in the country, which they loved and which loved them. One of their sons-in-law and his wife, and Henry Sydney, completed the party.

There are few conjunctures in life of a more startling interest, than to meet the pretty little girl that we have gambolled with in

our boyhood, and to find her changed in the lapse of a very few
years, which in some instances may not have brought a corresponding alteration in our own appearance, into a beautiful
woman. Something of this flitted over Coningsby's mind, as he
bowed, a little agitated from his surprise, to Lady Theresa Sydney.
All that he remembered had prepared him for beauty; but not for
the degree or character of beauty he met. It was a rich, sweet face,
with blue eyes and dark lashes, and a nose that we have no epithet
in English to describe, but which charmed in Roxalana.[4] Her
brown hair fell over her white and well-turned shoulders in long
and luxuriant tresses. One has met something as brilliant and
dainty in a medallion of old Sèvres, or amid the terraces and
gardens of Watteau.[5]

Perhaps Lady Theresa, too, might have welcomed him with
more freedom had his appearance also more accorded with the
image which he had left behind. Coningsby was a boy then, as we
described him in our first chapter. Though only nineteen now, he
had attained his full stature, which was above the middle height,
and time had fulfilled that promise of symmetry in his figure, and
grace in his mien, then so largely intimated. Time, too, which had
not yet robbed his countenance of any of its physical beauty, had
strongly developed the intellectual charm by which it had ever
been distinguished. As he bowed lowly before the Duchess and her
daughter, it would have been difficult to image a youth of a mien
more prepossessing and a manner more finished.

A manner that was spontaneous; nature's pure gift, the reflex
of his feeling. No artifice prompted that profound and polished
homage. Not one of those influences, the aggregate of whose sway
produces, as they tell us, the finished gentleman, had ever exercised its beneficent power on our orphan, and not rarely forlorn,
Coningsby. No clever and refined woman, with her quick perception, and nice criticism that never offends our self-love, had
ever given him that education that is more precious than Universities. The mild suggestions of a sister, the gentle raillery of some
laughing cousin, are also advantages not always appreciated at
the time, but which boys, when they have become men, often
think over with gratitude, and a little remorse at the ungracious
spirit in which they were received. Not even the dancing-master

had afforded his mechanical aid to Coningsby, who, like all Eton boys of this generation, viewed that professor of accomplishments with frank repugnance. But even in the boisterous life of school, Coningsby, though his style was free and flowing, was always well-bred. His spirit recoiled from that gross familiarity that is the characteristic of modern manners, and which would destroy all forms and ceremonies merely because they curb and control their own coarse convenience and ill-disguised selfishness. To women, however, Coningsby instinctively bowed, as to beings set apart for reverence and delicate treatment. Little as his experience was of them, his spirit had been fed with chivalrous fancies, and he entertained for them all the ideal devotion of a Surrey or a Sydney. Instructed, if not learned, as books and thought had already made him in men, he could not conceive that there were any other women in the world than fair Geraldines and Countesses of Pembroke.[6]

There was not a country-house in England that had so completely the air of habitual residence as Beaumanoir. It is a charming trait, and very rare. In many great mansions everything is as stiff, formal, and tedious, as if your host were a Spanish grandee in the days of the Inquisition. No ease, no resources; the passing life seems a solemn spectacle in which you play a part. How delightful was the morning room at Beaumanoir; from which gentlemen were not excluded with that assumed suspicion that they can never enter it but for felonious purposes. Such a profusion of flowers! Such a multitude of books! Such a various prodigality of writing materials! So many easy chairs too, of so many shapes; each in itself a comfortable home; yet nothing crowded. Woman alone can organise a drawing-room; man succeeds sometimes in a library. And the ladies' work! How graceful they look bending over their embroidery frames, consulting over the arrangement of a group, or the colour of a flower. The panniers and fanciful baskets, overflowing with variegated worsted, are gay and full of pleasure to the eye, and give an air of elegant business that is vivifying. Even the sight of employment interests.

Then the morning costume of English women is itself a beautiful work of art. At this period of the day they can find no rivals in other climes. The brilliant complexions of the daughters of the north dazzle in daylight; the illumined saloon levels all distinctions. One should see them in their well-fashioned muslin dresses. What matrons, and what maidens! Full of graceful dignity, fresher than the morn! And the married beauty in her little lace cap. Ah, she is a coquette! A charming character at all times; in a country-house an invaluable one.

A coquette is a being who wishes to please. Amiable being! If you do not like her, you will have no difficulty in finding a female companion of a different mood. Alas! coquettes are but too rare. 'Tis a career that requires great abilities, infinite pains, a gay and airy spirit. 'Tis the coquette that provides all amusement; suggests the riding party, plans the pic-nic, gives and guesses charades, acts them. She is the stirring element amid the heavy congeries of social atoms; the soul of the house, the salt of the banquet. Let any one pass a very agreeable week, or it may be ten days, under any roof, and analyse the cause of his satisfaction, and one might safely make a gentle wager that his solution would present him with the frolic phantom of a coquette.

'It is impossible that Mr Coningsby can remember me!' said a clear voice; and he looked round, and was greeted by a pair of sparkling eyes and the gayest smile in the world.

It was Lady Everingham, the Duke's married daughter.

Chapter 3

'AND you walked here!' said Lady Everingham to Coningsby, when the stir of arranging themselves at dinner had subsided. 'Only think, papa, Mr Coningsby walked here! I also am a great walker.'

'I had heard much of the forest,' said Coningsby.

'Which I am sure did not disappoint you,' said the Duke.

'But forests without adventures!' said Lady Everingham, a little shrugging her pretty shoulders.

'But I had an adventure,' said Coningsby.

'Oh! tell it us by all means!' said the Lady, with great animation. 'Adventures are my weakness. I have had more adventures than any one. Have I not had, Augustus?' she added, addressing her husband.

'But you make everything out to be an adventure, Isabel,' said Lord Everingham. 'I dare say that Mr Coningsby's was more substantial.' And looking at our young friend, he invited him to inform them.

'I met a most extraordinary man,' said Coningsby.

'It should have been a heroine,' exclaimed Lady Everingham.

'Do you know anybody in this neighbourhood who rides the finest Arab in the world?' asked Coningsby. 'She is called "the Daughter of the Star," and was given to her rider by the Pacha of Egypt.'

'This is really an adventure,' said Lady Everingham, interested.

'The Daughter of the Star!' said Lady Theresa. 'What a pretty name! Percy has a horse called "Sunbeam."'

'A fine Arab, the finest in the world!' said the Duke, who was very fond of horses. 'Who can it be?'

'Can you throw any light on this, Mr Lyle?' asked the Duchess of a young man who sat next to her.

He was a neighbour who had joined their dinner-party. Eustace Lyle, a Roman Catholic, and the richest commoner in the county;

for he had succeeded to a great estate early in his minority, which had only this year terminated.

'I certainly do not know the horse,' said Mr Lyle; 'but if Mr Coningsby would describe the rider, perhaps –'

'He is a man something under thirty,' said Coningsby, 'pale, with dark hair. We met in a sort of forest-inn during a storm. A most singular man! Indeed, I never met any one who seemed to me so clever, or to say such remarkable things.'

'He must have been the spirit of the storm,' said Lady Everingham.

'Charles Verney has a great deal of dark hair,' said Lady Theresa. 'But then he is anything but pale, and his eyes are blue.'

'And certainly he keeps his wonderful things for your ear, Theresa,' said her sister.

'I wish that Mr Coningsby would tell us some of the wonderful things he said,' said the Duchess, smiling.

'Take a glass of wine first with my mother, Coningsby,' said Henry Sydney, who had just finished helping them all to fish.

Coningsby had too much tact to be entrapped into a long story. He already regretted that he had been betrayed into any allusion to the stranger. He had a wild, fanciful notion, that their meeting ought to have been preserved as a sacred secret. But he had been impelled to refer to it in the first instance by the chance observation of Lady Everingham; and he had pursued his remark from the hope that the conversation might have led to the discovery of the unknown. When he found that his inquiry in this respect was unsuccessful, he was willing to turn the conversation. In reply to the Duchess, then, he generally described the talk of the stranger as full of lively anecdote and epigrammatic views of life; and gave them, for example, a saying of an illustrious foreign Prince, which was quite new and pointed, and which Coningsby told well. This led to a new train of discourse. The Duke also knew this illustrious foreign Prince, and told another story of him; and Lord Everingham had played whist with this illustrious foreign Prince often at the Travellers',[1] and this led to a third story; none of them too long. Then Lady Everingham came in again, and sparkled agreeably. She, indeed, sustained throughout dinner the principal weight of the conversation; but, as she asked questions of everybody, all seemed to contribute. Even the voice of Mr Lyle, who was rather bashful, was occasionally heard in reply. Coningsby, who had at first unintentionally taken a more leading part than he aspired to, would have retired into the background for the rest of the dinner, but Lady Everingham continually signalled him out for her questions, and as she sat opposite to him, he seemed the person to whom they were principally addressed.

At length the ladies rose to retire. A very great personage in a foreign, but not remote country, once mentioned to the writer of these pages, that he ascribed the superiority of the English in political life, in their conduct of public business and practical views of affairs, in a great measure to 'that little half-hour' that separates, after dinner, the dark from the fair sex. The writer humbly submitted, that if the period of disjunction were strictly limited to a 'little half-hour,' its salutary consequences for both sexes need not be disputed, but that in England the 'little half-hour' was too apt to swell into a term of far more awful character and duration. Lady Everingham was a disciple of the 'very little half-hour' school; for, as she gaily followed her mother, she said to Coningsby, whose gracious lot it was to usher them from the apartment,

'Pray do not be too long at the Board of Guardians to-day.'

These were prophetic words; for no sooner were they all again seated, than the Duke, filling his glass and pushing the claret to Coningsby, observed,

'I suppose Lord Monmouth does not trouble himself much about the New Poor Law?'[2]

'Hardly,' said Coningsby. 'My grandfather's frequent absence from England, which his health, I believe, renders quite necessary, deprives him of the advantage of personal observation on a subject, than which I can myself conceive none more deeply interesting.'

'I am glad to hear you say so,' said the Duke, 'and it does you great credit, and Henry too, whose attention, I observe, is directed very much to these subjects. In my time, the young men did not think so much of such things, and we suffer consequently. By the bye, Everingham, you, who are a Chairman of the Board of

Guardians, can give me some information. Supposing a case of out-door relief –'

'I could not suppose anything so absurd,' said the son-in-law.

'Well,' rejoined the Duke, 'I know your views on that subject, and it certainly is a question on which there is a good deal to be said. But would you under any circumstances give relief out of the Union,[3] even if the parish were to save a considerable sum?'

'I wish I knew the Union where such a system was followed,' said Lord Everingham; and his Grace seemed to tremble under his son-in-law's glance.

The Duke had a good heart, and not a bad head. If he had not made in his youth so many Latin and English verses, he might have acquired considerable information, for he had a natural love of letters, though his pack were the pride of England, his barrel seldom missed, and his fortune on the turf, where he never betted, was a proverb. He was good, and he wished to do good; but his views were confused from want of knowledge, and his conduct often inconsistent because a sense of duty made him immediately active; and he often acquired in the consequent experience a conviction exactly contrary to that which had prompted his activity.

His Grace had been a great patron and a zealous administrator of the New Poor Law. He had been persuaded that it would elevate the condition of the labouring class. His son-in-law, Lord Everingham, who was a Whig, and a clear-headed, cold-blooded man, looked upon the New Poor Law as another Magna Charta. Lord Everingham was completely master of the subject. He was himself the Chairman of one of the most considerable Unions of the kingdom. The Duke, if he ever had a misgiving, had no chance in argument with his son-in-law. Lord Everingham overwhelmed him with quotations from Commissioners' rules and Subcommissioners' reports, statistical tables, and references to dietaries. Sometimes with a strong case, the Duke struggled to make a fight; but Lord Everingham, when he was at fault for a reply, which was very rare, upbraided his father-in-law with the abuses of the old system, and frightened him with visions of rates exceeding rentals.

Of late, however, a considerable change had taken place in the Duke's feelings on this great question. His son Henry entertained strong opinions upon it, and had combated his father with all the fervour of a young votary. A victory over his Grace, indeed, was not very difficult. His natural impulse would have early enlisted him on the side, if not of opposition to the new system, at least of critical suspicion of its spirit and provisions. It was only the statistics and sharp acuteness of his son-in-law that had, indeed, ever kept him to his colours. Lord Henry would not listen to statistics, dietary tables, Commissioners' rules, Sub-commissioners' reports. He went far higher than his father; far deeper than his brother-in-law. He represented to the Duke that the order of the peasantry was as ancient, legal, and recognised an order as the order of the nobility; that it had distinct rights and privileges, though for centuries they had been invaded and violated, and permitted to fall into desuetude. He impressed upon the Duke that the parochial constitution of this country was more important than its political constitution; that it was more ancient, more universal in its influence; and that this parochial constitution had already been shaken to its centre by the New Poor Law. He assured his father that it would never be well for England until this order of the peasantry was restored to its pristine condition; not merely in physical comfort, for that must vary according to the economical circumstances of the time, like that of every class; but to its condition in all those moral attributes which make a recognised rank in a nation; and which, in a great degree, are independent of economics, manners, customs, ceremonies, rights, and privileges.

'Henry thinks,' said Lord Everingham, 'that the people are to be fed by dancing round a May-pole.'

'But will the people be more fed because they do not dance round a May-pole?' urged Lord Henry.

'Obsolete customs!' said Lord Everingham.

'And why should dancing round a May-pole be more obsolete than holding a Chapter of the Garter?' asked Lord Henry.

The Duke, who was a blue ribbon, felt this a home thrust. 'I must say,' said his Grace, 'that I for one deeply regret that our popular customs have been permitted to fall so into desuetude.'

'The Spirit of the Age is against such things,' said Lord Everingham.

'And what is the Spirit of the Age?' asked Coningsby.

'The Spirit of Utility,' said Lord Everingham.

'And you think then that ceremony is not useful?' urged Coningsby, mildly.

'It depends upon circumstances,' said Lord Everingham. 'There are some ceremonies, no doubt, that are very proper, and of course very useful. But the best thing we can do for the labouring classes is to provide them with work.'

'But what do you mean by the labouring classes, Everingham?' asked Lord Henry. 'Lawyers are a labouring class, for instance, and by the bye sufficiently provided with work. But would you approve of Westminster Hall being denuded of all its ceremonies?'

'And the long vacation being abolished?' added Coningsby.

'Theresa brings me terrible accounts of the sufferings of the poor about us,' said the Duke, shaking his head.

'Women think everything to be suffering!' said Lord Everingham.

'How do you find them about you, Mr Lyle?' continued the Duke.

'I have revived the monastic customs at St Geneviève,' said the young man, blushing. 'There is an almsgiving twice a-week.'

'I am sure I wish I could see the labouring classes happy,' said the Duke.

'Oh! pray do not use, my dear father, that phrase, the labouring classes!' said Lord Henry. 'What do you think, Coningsby, the other day we had a meeting in this neighbourhood to vote an agricultural petition that was to comprise all classes. I went with my father, and I was made chairman of the committee to draw up the petition. Of course, I described it as the petition of the nobility, clergy, gentry, yeomanry, and peasantry of the county of —; and, could you believe it, they struck out *peasantry* as a word no longer used, and inserted *labourers*.'

'What can it signify,' said Lord Everingham, 'whether a man be called a labourer or a peasant?'

'And what can it signify,' said his brother-in-law, 'whether a man be called Mr Howard or Lord Everingham?'

They were the most affectionate family under this roof of Beaumanoir, and of all members of it, Lord Henry the sweetest tempered, and yet it was astonishing what sharp skirmishes every day arose between him and his brother-in-law, during that 'little half-hour' that forms so happily the political character of the nation. The Duke, who from experience felt that a guerilla movement was impending, asked his guests whether they would take any more claret; and on their signifying their dissent, moved an adjournment to the ladies.

They joined the ladies in the music-room. Coningsby, not experienced in feminine society, and who found a little difficulty from want of practice in maintaining conversation, though he was desirous of succeeding, was delighted with Lady Everingham, who, instead of requiring to be amused, amused him; and suggested so many subjects, and glanced at so many topics, that there never was that cold, awkward pause, so common with sullen spirits and barren brains. Lady Everingham thoroughly understood the art of conversation, which, indeed, consists of the exercise of two fine qualities. You must originate, and you must sympathise; you must possess at the same time the habit of communicating and the habit of listening. The union is rather rare, but irresistible.

Lady Everingham was not a celebrated beauty, but she was something infinitely more delightful, a captivating woman. There were combined in her, qualities not commonly met together, great vivacity of mind with great grace of manner. Her words sparkled and her movements charmed. There was, indeed, in all she said and did, that congruity that indicates a complete and harmonious organisation. It was the same just proportion which characterised her form: a shape slight and undulating with grace; the most beautifully shaped ear; a small, soft hand; a foot that would have fitted the glass slipper; and which, by the bye, she lost no opportunity of displaying; and she was right, for it was a model.

Then there was music. Lady Theresa sang like a seraph: a rich voice, a grand style. And her sister could support her with grace and sweetness. And they did not sing too much. The Duke took up a review, and looked at Rigby's last slashing article. The country seemed ruined, but it appeared that the Whigs were still worse off than the Tories. The assassins had committed suicide. This poetical justice is pleasing. Lord Everingham, lounging in an easy chair, perused with great satisfaction his *Morning Chronicle*, which contained a cutting reply to Mr Rigby's article, not quite so 'slashing' as the Right Honourable scribe's manifesto, but with some searching mockery, that became the subject and the subject-monger.

Mr Lyle seated himself by the Duchess, and encouraged by her amenity, and speaking in whispers, became animated and agreeable, occasionally patting the lap-dog. Coningsby stood by the singers, or talked with them when the music had ceased: and Henry Sydney looked over a volume of Strutt's *Sports and Pastimes*,[4] occasionally, without taking his eyes off the volume, calling the attention of his friends to his discoveries.

Mr Lyle rose to depart, for he had some miles to return; he came forward with some hesitation, to hope that Coningsby would visit his bloodhounds, which Lord Henry had told him Coningsby had expressed a wish to do. Lady Everingham remarked that she had not been at St Geneviève since she was a girl, and it appeared Lady Theresa had never visited it. Lady Everingham proposed that they should all ride over on the morrow, and she appealed to her husband for his approbation, instantly given, for though she loved admiration, and he apparently was an iceberg, they were really devoted to each other. Then there was a consultation as to their arrangements. The Duchess would drive over in her pony chair with Theresa. The Duke, as usual, had affairs that would occupy him. The rest were to ride. It was a happy suggestion, all anticipated pleasure; and the evening terminated with the prospect of what Lady Everingham called an adventure.

The ladies themselves soon withdrew; the gentlemen lingered for awhile; the Duke took up his candle, and bid his guests good night; Lord Everingham drank a glass of Seltzer water,[5] nodded, and vanished. Lord Henry and his friend sat up talking over the past. They were too young to call them old times; and yet what a life seemed to have elapsed since they had quitted Eton, dear old Eton! Their boyish feelings, and still latent boyish character, developed with their reminiscences.

'Do you remember Bucknall? Which Bucknall? The eldest: I saw him the other day at Nottingham; he is in the Rifles. Do you remember that day at Sirly Hall, that Paulet had that row with Dickinson? Did you like Dickinson? Hum! Paulet was a good fellow. I tell you who was a good fellow, Paulet's little cousin. What! Augustus Le Grange? Oh! I liked Augustus Le Grange. I wonder where Buckhurst is? I had a letter from him the other day. He has gone with his uncle to Paris. We shall find him at Cambridge in October. I suppose you know Millbank has gone to Oriel. Has he, though! I wonder who will have our room at Cookesley's? Cookesley was a good fellow! Oh, capital! How well he behaved when there was that row about our going out with the hounds! Do you remember Vere's face? It makes me laugh now when I think of it. I tell you who was a good fellow, Kangaroo Gray; I liked him. I don't know any fellow who sang a better song!'

'By the bye,' said Coningsby, 'what sort of fellow is Eustace Lyle? I rather liked his look.'

'Oh! I will tell you all about him,' said Lord Henry. 'He is a great ally of mine, and I think you will like him very much. It is a Roman Catholic family, about the oldest we have in the county, and the wealthiest. You see, Lyle's father was the most violent ultra Whig, and so were all Eustace's guardians; but the moment he came of age, he announced that he should not mix himself up with either of the parties in the county, and that his tenantry might act exactly as they thought fit. My father thinks, of course, that Lyle is a Conservative, and that he only waits the occasion to come forward; but he is quite wrong. I know Lyle well, and he speaks to me without disguise. You see 'tis an old Cavalier family, and Lyle has all the opinions and feelings of his race. He will not ally himself with anti-monarchists, and democrats, and infidels, and sectarians; at the same time, why should he support a party who pretend to oppose these, but who never lose an opportunity of insulting his religion, and would deprive him, if possible, of the advantages of the very institutions which his family assisted in establishing?'

'Why, indeed? I am glad to have made his acquaintance,' said Coningsby. 'Is he clever?'

'I think so,' said Lord Henry. 'He is the most shy fellow, especially among women, that I ever knew, but he is very popular in the county. He does an amazing deal of good, and is one of the best riders we have. My father says, the very best; bold, but so very certain.'

'He is older than we are?'

'My senior by a year: he is just of age.'

'Oh, ah! twenty-one. A year younger than Gaston de Foix when he won Ravenna, and four years younger than John of Austria when he won Lepanto,' observed Coningsby, musingly. 'I vote we go to bed, old fellow!'

Chapter 4

IN a valley, not far from the margin of a beautiful river, raised on a lofty and artificial terrace at the base of a range of wooded heights, was a pile of modern building in the finest style of Christian architecture. It was of great extent and richly decorated. Built of a white and glittering stone, it sparkled with its pinnacles in the sunshine as it rose in strong relief against its verdant background. The winding valley, which was studded, but not too closely studded, with clumps of old trees, formed for a great extent on either side of the mansion a grassy demesne, which was called the Lower Park; but it was a region bearing the name of the Upper Park, that was the peculiar and most picturesque feature of this splendid residence. The wooded heights that formed the valley were not, as they appeared, a range of hills. Their crest was only the abrupt termination of a vast and enclosed table-land, abounding in all the qualities of the ancient chase: turf and trees, a wilderness of underwood, and a vast spread of gorse and fern. The deer, that abounded, lived here in a world as savage as themselves: trooping down in the evening to the river. Some of them, indeed, were ever in sight of those who were in the valley, and you might often observe various groups clustered on the green heights above the mansion, the effect of which was most inspiriting and graceful. Sometimes in the twilight, a solitary form, magnified by the illusive hour, might be seen standing on the brink of the steep, large and black against the clear sky.

We have endeavoured slightly to sketch St Geneviève as it appeared to our friends from Beaumanoir, winding into the valley the day after Mr Lyle had dined with them. The valley opened for about half-a-mile opposite the mansion, which gave to the dwellers in it a view over an extensive and richly-cultivated country. It was through this district that the party from Beaumanoir had pursued their way. The first glance at the building, its striking situation, its beautiful form, its brilliant colour, its great extent, a gathering as it seemed of galleries, halls, and chapels, mullioned windows, portals of clustered columns, and groups of airy pinnacles and fretwork spires, called forth a general cry of wonder and of praise.

The ride from Beaumanoir had been delightful; the breath of summer in every breeze, the light of summer on every tree. The gay laugh of Lady Everingham rang frequently in the air; often were her sunny eyes directed to Coningsby, as she called his attention to some fair object or some pretty effect. She played the hostess of Nature, and introduced him to all the beauties.

Mr Lyle had recognised them. He cantered forward with greetings on a fat little fawn-coloured pony, with a long white mane and white flowing tail, and the wickedest eye in the world. He rode by the side of the Duchess, and indicated their gently-descending route.

They arrived, and the peacocks, who were sunning themselves on the turrets, expanded their plumage to welcome them.

'I can remember the old house,' said the Duchess, as she took Mr Lyle's arm; 'and I am happy to see the new one. The Duke had prepared me for much beauty, but the reality exceeds his report.'

They entered by a short corridor into a large hall. They would have stopped to admire its rich roof, its gallery and screen; but their host suggested that they should refresh themselves after their ride, and they followed him through several apartments into a spacious chamber, its oaken panels covered with a series of interesting pictures, representing the siege of St Geneviève by the Parliament forces in 1643: the various assaults and sallies, and the final discomfiture of the rebels. In all these figured a brave and graceful Sir Eustace Lyle, in cuirass and buff jerkin, with gleaming sword and flowing plume. The sight of these pictures was ever a source of great excitement to Henry Sydney, who always lamented his ill-luck in not living in such days; nay, would insist that all others must equally deplore their evil destiny.

'See, Coningsby, this battery on the Upper Park,' said Lord Henry. 'This did the business: how it rakes up the valley; Sir Eustace works it himself. Mother, what a pity Beaumanoir was not besieged!'

'It may be,' said Coningsby.

'I always fancy a siege must be so interesting,' said Lady Everingham. 'It must be so exciting.'

'I hope the next siege may be at Beaumanoir, instead of St Geneviève,' said Lyle, laughing; 'as Henry Sydney has such a military predisposition. Duchess, you said the other day that you liked Malvoisie,[1] and here is some.'

> 'Now broach me a cask of Malvoisie,
> Bring pasty from the doe;'

said the Duchess. 'That has been my luncheon.'

'A poetic repast,' said Lady Theresa.

'Their breeds of sheep must have been very inferior in old days,' said Lord Everingham, 'as they made such a noise about their venison. For my part I consider it a thing as much gone by as tilts and tournaments.'[2]

'I am sorry that they have gone by,' said Lady Theresa.

'Everything has gone by that is beautiful,' said Lord Henry.

'Life is much easier,' said Lord Everingham.

'Life easy!' said Lord Henry. 'Life appears to me to be a fierce struggle.'

'Manners are easy,' said Coningsby, 'and life is hard.'

'And I wish to see things exactly the reverse,' said Lord Henry. 'The means and modes of subsistence less difficult; the conduct of life more ceremonious.'

'Civilisation has no time for ceremony,' said Lord Everingham.

'How very sententious you all are!' said his wife. 'I want to see the hall and many other things.' And they all rose.

There were indeed many other things to see: a long gallery, rich in ancestral portraits, specimens of art and costume from Holbein to Lawrence; courtiers of the Tudors, and cavaliers of the Stuarts, terminating in red-coated squires fresh from the field, and gentlemen buttoned up in black coats, and sitting in library chairs, with their backs to a crimson curtain. Woman, however, is always charming; and the present generation may view their mothers painted by Lawrence, as if they were patronesses of Almacks';[3] or their grandmothers by Reynolds, as Robinettas caressing birds, with as much delight as they gaze on the dewy-eyed matrons of Lely, and the proud bearing of the heroines of Vandyke. But what interested them more than the gallery, or the rich saloons, or even the baronial hall, was the chapel, in which art had exhausted all its invention, and wealth offered all its resources. The walls and vaulted roofs entirely painted in encaustic* by the first artists of Germany, and representing the principal events of the second Testament, the splendour of the mosaic pavement, the richness of the painted windows, the sumptuousness of the altar, crowned by a masterpiece of Carlo Dolce and surrounded by a silver rail, the tone of rich and solemn light that pervaded all, and blended all the various sources of beauty into one absorbing and harmonious whole: all combined to produce an effect which stilled them into a silence that lasted for some minutes, until the ladies breathed their feelings in an almost inarticulate murmur of reverence and admiration; while a tear stole to the eye of the enthusiastic Henry Sydney.

Leaving the chapel, they sauntered through the gardens, until, arriving at their limit, they were met by the prettiest sight in the world; a group of little pony chairs, each drawn by a little fat fawn-coloured pony, like the one that Mr Lyle had been riding. Lord Henry drove his mother; Lord Everingham, Lady Theresa; Lady Everingham was attended by Coningsby. Their host cantered by the Duchess's side, and along winding roads of easy ascent, leading through beautiful woods, and offering charming landscapes, they reached in due time the Upper Park.

'One sees our host to great advantage in his own house,' said Lady Everingham. 'He is scarcely the same person. I have not observed him once blush. He speaks and moves with ease. It is a pity that he is not more graceful. Above all things I like a graceful man.'

'That chapel,' said Coningsby, 'was a fine thing.'

'Very!' said Lady Everingham. 'Did you observe the picture over the altar, the Virgin with blue eyes? I never observed blue eyes before in such a picture. What is your favourite colour for eyes?'

Coningsby felt embarrassed: he said something rather pointless about admiring everything that is beautiful.

'But every one has a favourite style; I want to know yours. Regular features, do you like regular features? Or is it expression that pleases you?'

'Expression; I think I like expression. Expression must be always delightful.'

'Do you dance?'

'No; I am no great dancer. I fear I have few accomplishments. I am fond of fencing.'

'I don't fence,' said Lady Everingham, with a smile. 'But I think you are right not to dance. It is not in your way. You are ambitious, I believe?' she added.

'I was not aware of it; everybody is ambitious.'

'You see I know something of your character. Henry has spoken of you to me a great deal; long before we met, – met again, I should say, for we are old friends, remember. Do you know your career much interests me? I like ambitious men.'

There is something fascinating in the first idea that your career interests a charming woman. Coningsby felt that he was perhaps driving a Madame de Longueville.[5] A woman who likes ambitious men must be no ordinary character; clearly a sort of heroine. At this moment they reached the Upper Park, and the novel landscape changed the current of their remarks.

Far as the eye could reach there spread before them a savage sylvan scene. It wanted, perhaps, undulation of surface, but that deficiency was greatly compensated for by the multitude and prodigious size of the trees; they were the largest, indeed, that could well be met with in England; and there is no part of Europe where the timber is so huge. The broad interminable glades, the vast avenues, the quantity of deer browsing or bounding in all directions, the thickets of yellow gorse and green fern, and the breeze that even in the stillness of summer was ever playing over this table-land, all produced an animated and renovating scene. It was like suddenly visiting another country, living among other manners, and breathing another air. They stopped for a few minutes at a pavilion built for the purposes of the chase, and then returned, all gratified by this visit to what appeared to be the higher regions of the earth.

As they approached the brow of the hill that hung over St Geneviève, they heard the great bell sound.

'What is that?' asked the Duchess.

'It is almsgiving day,' replied Mr Lyle, looking a little embarrassed, and for the first time blushing. 'The people of the parishes with which I am connected come to St Geneviève twice a-week at this hour.'

'And what is your system?' inquired Lord Everingham, who had stopped, interested by the scene. 'What check have you?'

'The rectors of the different parishes grant certificates to those who in their belief merit bounty according to the rules which I have established. These are again visited by my almoner, who countersigns the certificate, and then they present it at the postern-gate. The certificate explains the nature of their necessities, and my steward acts on his discretion.'

'Mamma, I see them!' exclaimed Lady Theresa.

'Perhaps your Grace may think that they might be relieved without all this ceremony,' said Mr Lyle, extremely confused. 'But I agree with Henry and Mr Coningsby, that Ceremony is not, as too commonly supposed, an idle form. I wish the people constantly and visibly to comprehend that Property is their protector and their friend.'

'My reason is with you, Mr Lyle,' said the Duchess, 'as well as my heart.'

They came along the valley, a procession of Nature, whose groups an artist might have studied. The old man, who loved the pilgrimage too much to avail himself of the privilege of a substitute accorded to his grey hairs, came in person with his grandchild and his staff. There also came the widow with her child at the breast, and others clinging to her form; some sorrowful faces, and some pale; many a serious one, and now and then a frolic glance; many a dame in her red cloak, and many a maiden with her light basket; curly-headed urchins with demure looks, and sometimes a stalwart form baffled for a time of the labour which he desired. But not a heart there that did not bless the bell that sounded from the tower of St Geneviève!

Chapter 5

'My fathers perilled their blood and fortunes for the cause of the Sovereignty and Church of England,' said Lyle to Coningsby, as they were lying stretched out on the sunny turf in the park of Beaumanoir, 'and I inherit their passionate convictions. They were Catholics, as their descendant. No doubt they would have been glad to see their ancient faith predominant in their ancient land; but they bowed, as I bow, to an adverse and apparently irrevocable decree. But if we could not have the Church of our fathers, we honoured and respected the Church of their children. It was at least a Church; a "Catholic and Apostolic Church," as it daily declares itself. Besides, it was our friend. When we were persecuted by Puritanic Parliaments, it was the Sovereign and the Church of England that interposed, with the certainty of creating against themselves odium and mistrust, to shield us from the dark and relentless bigotry of Calvinism.'

'I believe,' said Coningsby, 'that if Charles I had hanged all the Catholic priests that Parliament petitioned him to execute, he would never have lost his crown.'

'You were mentioning my father,' continued Lyle. 'He certainly was a Whig. Galled by political exclusion, he connected himself with that party in the State which began to intimate emancipation. After all, they did not emancipate us. It was the fall of the Papacy in England that founded the Whig aristocracy;[1] a fact that must always lie at the bottom of their hearts, as, I assure you, it does of mine.

'I gathered at an early age,' continued Lyle, 'that I was expected to inherit my father's political connections with the family estates. Under ordinary circumstances this would probably have occurred. In times that did not force one to ponder, it is not likely I should have recoiled from uniting myself with a party formed of the best families in England, and ever famous for accomplished men and charming women. But I enter life in the midst of a convulsion in which the very principles of our political and social systems are called in question. I cannot unite myself with the party of destruction. It is an operative cause alien to my being. What, then, offers itself? The Duke talks to me of Conservative principles; but he does not inform me what they are. I observe indeed a party in the State whose rule it is to consent to no change, until it is clamorously called for, and then instantly to yield; but those are Concessionary, not Conservative principles. This party treats institutions as we do our pheasants, they preserve only to destroy them. But is there a statesman among these Conservatives who offers us a dogma for a guide, or defines any great political truth which we should aspire to establish? It seems to me a barren thing, this Conservatism, an unhappy cross-breed; the mule of politics that engenders nothing. What do you think of all this, Coningsby? I assure you I feel confused, perplexed, harassed. I know I have public duties to perform; I am, in fact, every day of my life solicited by all parties to throw the weight of my influence in one scale or another; but I am paralysed. I often wish I had no position in the country. The sense of its responsibility depresses me; makes me miserable. I speak to you without reserve; with a frankness which our short acquaintance scarcely authorises; but Henry Sydney has so often talked to me of you, and I have so long wished to know you, that I open my heart without restraint.'

'My dear fellow,' said Coningsby, 'you have but described my feelings when you depictured your own. My mind on these subjects has long been a chaos. I float in a sea of troubles, and should long ago have been wrecked had I not been sustained by a profound, however vague, conviction, that there are still great truths, if we could but work them out; that Government, for instance, should be loved and not hated, and that Religion should be a faith and not a form.'

The moral influence of residence furnishes some of the most interesting traits of our national manners. The presence of this power was very apparent throughout the district that surrounded Beaumanoir. The ladies of that house were deeply sensible of the responsibility of their position; thoroughly comprehending their duties, they fulfilled them without affectation, with earnestness, and with that effect which springs from a knowledge of the subject. The consequences were visible in the tone of the peasantry being superior to that which we too often witness. The ancient feudal feeling that lingers in these sequestered haunts is an instrument which, when skilfully wielded, may be productive of vast social benefit. The Duke understood this well; and his family had imbibed all his views, and seconded them. Lady Everingham, once more in the scene of her past life, resumed the exercise of gentle offices, as if she had never ceased to be a daughter of the house, and as if another domain had not its claims upon her solicitude. Coningsby was often the companion of herself and her sister in their pilgrimages of charity and kindness. He admired the graceful energy, and thorough acquaintance with details, with which Lady Everingham superintended schools, organised societies of relief, and the discrimination which she brought to bear upon individual cases of suffering or misfortune. He was deeply interested as he watched the magic of her manner, as she melted the obdurate, inspired the slothful, consoled the afflicted, and animated with her smiles and ready phrase the energetic and the dutiful. Nor on these occasions was Lady Theresa seen under less favourable auspices. Without the vivacity of her sister, there was in her demeanour a sweet seriousness of purpose that was most winning; and sometimes a burst of energy, a trait of decision, which strikingly contrasted with the somewhat over-controlled character of her life in drawing-rooms.

In the society of these engaging companions, time for Coningsby glided away in a course which he sometimes wished nothing might disturb. Apart from them, he frequently felt himself pensive and vaguely disquieted. Even the society of Henry Sydney or Eustace Lyle, much as under ordinary circumstances they would have been adapted to his mood, did not compensate for the absence of that indefinite, that novel, that strange, yet sweet excitement, which he felt, he knew not exactly how or why, stealing over his senses. Sometimes the countenance of Theresa Sydney flitted over his musing vision; sometimes the merry voice of Lady Everingham haunted his ear. But to be their companion in ride or ramble; to avoid any arrangement which for many hours should deprive him of their presence; was every day with Coningsby a principal object.

One day he had been out shooting rabbits with Lyle and Henry Sydney, and returned with them late to Beaumanoir to dinner. He had not enjoyed his sport, and he had not shot at all well. He had been dreamy, silent, had deeply felt the want of Lady Everingham's conversation, that was ever so poignant and so interestingly personal to himself; one of the secrets of her sway, though Coningsby was not then quite conscious of it. Talk to a man about himself, and he is generally captivated. That is the real way to win him. The only difference between men and women in this respect is, that most women are vain, and some men are not. There are some men who have no self-love; but if they have, female vanity is but a trifling and airy passion compared with the vast voracity of appetite which in the sterner sex can swallow anything, and always crave for more.

When Coningsby entered the drawing-room, there seemed a somewhat unusual bustle in the room, but as the twilight had descended, it was at first rather difficult to distinguish who was present. He soon perceived that there were strangers. A gentleman of pleasing appearance was near a sofa on which the Duchess and Lady Everingham were seated, and discoursing with some volubility. His phrases seemed to command attention; his audience had an animated glance, eyes sparkling with intelligence and interest; not a word was disregarded. Coningsby did not advance as was his custom; he had a sort of instinct, that the stranger was discoursing of matters of which he knew nothing. He turned to a table, he took up a book, which he began to read upside downwards. A hand was lightly placed on his shoulder. He looked round, it was another stranger; who said, however, in a tone of familiar friendliness,

'How do you do, Coningsby?'

It was a young man about four-and-twenty years of age, tall, good-looking. Old recollections, his intimate greeting, a strong family likeness, helped Coningsby to conjecture correctly who was the person who addressed him. It was, indeed, the eldest son of the Duke, the Marquis of Beaumanoir, who had arrived at his father's unexpectedly with his friend, Mr Melton, on their way to the north.

Mr Melton was a gentleman of the highest fashion, and a great favourite in society. He was about thirty, good-looking, with an air that commanded attention, and manners, though facile, sufficiently finished. He was communicative, though calm, and without being witty, had at his service a turn of phrase, acquired by practice and success, which was, or which always seemed to be, poignant. The ladies seemed especially to be delighted at his arrival. He knew everything of everybody they cared about; and Coningsby listened in silence to names which for the first time reached his ears, but which seemed to excite great interest. Mr Melton frequently addressed his most lively observations and his most sparkling anecdotes to Lady Everingham, who evidently relished all that he said, and returned him in kind.

Throughout the dinner Lady Everingham and Mr Melton maintained what appeared a most entertaining conversation, principally about things and persons which did not in any way interest our hero; who, however, had the satisfaction of hearing Lady Everingham, in the drawing-room, say in a careless tone to the Duchess,

'I am so glad, mamma, that Mr Melton has come; we wanted some amusement.'

What a confession! What a revelation to Coningsby of his infinite insignificance! Coningsby entertained a great aversion for Mr Melton, but felt his spirit unequal to the social contest. The genius of the untutored inexperienced youth quailed before that of the long-practised, skilful man of the world. What was the magic of this man? What was the secret of this ease, that nothing could disturb, and yet was not deficient in deference and good taste? And then his dress, it seemed fashioned by some unearthly artist; yet it was impossible to detect the unobtrusive causes of the general effect that was irresistible. Coningsby's coat was made by Stultz; almost every fellow in the sixth form had his coats made by Stultz; yet Coningsby fancied that his own garment looked as if it had been furnished by some rustic slopseller. He began to wonder where Mr Melton got his boots from, and glanced at his own, which, though made in St James's Street, seemed to him to have a cloddish air.

Lady Everingham was determined that Mr Melton should see

Beaumanoir to the greatest advantage. Mr Melton had never been there before, except at Christmas, with the house full of visitors and factitious gaiety. Now he was to see the country. Accordingly, there were long rides every day, which Lady Everingham called expeditions, and which generally produced some slight incident which she styled an adventure. She was kind to Coningsby, but had no time to indulge in the lengthened conversations which he had previously found so magical. Mr Melton was always on the scene, the monopolising hero, it would seem, of every thought, and phrase, and plan. Coningsby began to think that Beaumanoir was not so delightful a place as he had imagined. He began to think that he had stayed there perhaps too long. He had received a letter from Mr Rigby, to inform him that he was expected at Coningsby Castle at the beginning of September, to meet Lord Monmouth, who had returned to England, and for grave and special reasons was about to reside at his chief seat, which he had not visited for many years. Coningsby had intended to have remained at Beaumanoir until that time; but suddenly it occurred to him, that the Age of Ruins was past, and that he ought to seize the opportunity of visiting Manchester, which was in the same county as the castle of his grandfather. So difficult is it to speculate upon events! Muse as we may, we are the creatures of circumstances; and the unexpected arrival of a London dandy at the country-seat of an English nobleman sent this representative of the New Generation, fresh from Eton, nursed in prejudices, yet with a mind predisposed to inquiry and prone to meditation, to a scene apt to stimulate both intellectual processes; which demanded investigation and induced thought, the great METRO-POLIS of LABOUR.

END OF BOOK III

BOOK IV

Chapter 1

A GREAT city, whose image dwells in the memory of man, is the type of some great idea. Rome represents conquest; Faith hovers over the towers of Jerusalem; and Athens embodies the pre-eminent quality of the antique world, Art.

In modern ages, Commerce has created London; while Manners, in the most comprehensive sense of the word, have long found a supreme capital in the airy and bright-minded city of the Seine.

What Art was to the ancient world, Science is to the modern: the distinctive faculty. In the minds of men the useful has succeeded to the beautiful. Instead of the city of the Violet Crown, a Lancashire village has expanded into a mighty region of factories and warehouses. Yet, rightly understood, Manchester is as great a human exploit as Athens.

The inhabitants, indeed, are not so impressed with their idiosyncrasy as the countrymen of Pericles and Phidias.[1] They do not fully comprehend the position which they occupy. It is the philosopher alone who can conceive the grandeur of Manchester, and the immensity of its future. There are yet great truths to tell, if we had either the courage to announce or the temper to receive them.

Chapter 2

A FEELING of melancholy, even of uneasiness, attends our first entrance into a great town, especially at night. Is it that the sense of all this vast existence with which we have no connection, where we are utterly unknown, oppresses us with our insignificance? Is it that it is terrible to feel friendless where all have friends?

Yet reverse the picture. Behold a community where you are unknown, but where you will be known, perhaps honoured. A place where you have no friends, but where, also, you have no enemies. A spot that has hitherto been a blank in your thoughts, as you have been a cipher in its sensations, and yet a spot, perhaps, pregnant with your destiny!

There is, perhaps, no act of memory so profoundly interesting as to recall the careless mood and moment in which we have entered a town, a house, a chamber, on the eve of an acquaintance or an event, that have given a colour and an impulse to our future life.

What is this Fatality that men worship? Is it a Goddess?

Unquestionably it is a power that acts mainly by female agents. Women are the Priestesses of Predestination.

Man conceives Fortune, but Woman conducts it.

It is the Spirit of Man that says, 'I will be great;' but it is the Sympathy of Woman that usually makes him so.

It was not the comely and courteous hostess of the Adelphi Hotel, Manchester, that gave occasion to these remarks, though she may deserve them, and though she was most kind to our Coningsby as he came in late at night very tired, and not in very good humour.

He had travelled the whole day through the great district of labour, his mind excited by strange sights, and at length wearied by their multiplication. He had passed over the plains where iron and coal supersede turf and corn, dingy as the entrance of Hades, and flaming with furnaces; and now he was among illumined factories, with more windows than Italian palaces, and smoking chimneys taller than Egyptian obelisks. Alone in the great metropolis of machinery itself, sitting down in a solitary coffee-room glaring with gas, with no appetite, a whirling head, and not a plan or purpose for the morrow, why was he there? Because a being, whose name even was unknown to him, had met him in a hedge alehouse during a thunderstorm, and told him that the Age of Ruins was past.

Remarkable instance of the influence of an individual; some evidence of the extreme susceptibility of our hero.

Even his bedroom was lit by gas. Wonderful city! That, however, could be got rid of. He opened the window. The summer air was sweet, even in this land of smoke and toil. He feels a sensation such as in Lisbon or Lima precedes an earthquake. The house appears to quiver. It is a sympathetic affection occasioned by a steam-engine in a neighbouring factory.

Notwithstanding, however, all these novel incidents, Coningsby slept the deep sleep of youth and health, of a brain which, however occasionally perplexed by thought, had never been harassed by anxiety. He rose early, freshened, and in fine spirits. And by the time the devilled chicken and the buttered toast, that mysterious and incomparable luxury, which can only be obtained at an inn, had disappeared, he felt all the delightful excitement of travel.

And now for action! Not a letter had Coningsby; not an individual in that vast city was known to him. He went to consult his kind hostess, who smiled confidence. He was to mention her name at one place, his own at another. All would be right; she seemed to have reliance in the destiny of such a nice young man.

He saw all; they were kind and hospitable to the young stranger, whose thought, and earnestness, and gentle manners attracted them. One recommended him to another; all tried to aid and assist him. He entered chambers vaster than are told of in Arabian fable, and peopled with habitants more wondrous than Afrite or Peri. For there he beheld, in long-continued ranks, those mysterious forms full of existence without life, that perform with facility, and in an instant, what man can fulfil only with difficulty and in days. A machine is a slave that neither brings nor bears degradation; it is a being endowed with the greatest degree of energy, and acting under the greatest degree of excitement, yet free at the same time from all passion and emotion. It is, therefore, not only a slave, but a supernatural slave. And why should one say that the machine does not live? It breathes, for its breath forms the atmosphere of some towns. It moves with more regularity than man. And has it not a voice? Does not the spindle sing like a merry girl at her work, and the steam-engine roar in jolly chorus, like a strong artisan handling his lusty tools, and gaining a fair day's wages for a fair day's toil?

Nor should the weaving-room be forgotten, where a thousand or fifteen hundred girls may be observed in their coral necklaces, working like Penelope in the daytime;[1] some pretty, some pert, some graceful and jocund, some absorbed in their occupation; a little serious some, few sad. And the cotton you have observed in its rude state, that you have seen the silent spinner change into thread, and the bustling weaver convert into cloth, you may now watch as in a moment it is tinted with beautiful colours, or printed with fanciful patterns. And yet the mystery of mysteries is to view machines making machines; a spectacle that fills the mind with curious, and even awful, speculation.

From early morn to the late twilight, our Coningsby for several days devoted himself to the comprehension of Manchester. It was to him a new world, pregnant with new ideas, and suggestive of new trains of thought and feeling. In this unprecedented partnership between capital and science, working on a spot which Nature had indicated as the fitting theatre of their exploits, he beheld a great source of the wealth of nations which had been reserved for these times, and he perceived that this wealth was rapidly developing classes whose power was imperfectly recognised in the constitutional scheme, and whose duties in the social system seemed altogether omitted. Young as he was, the bent of his mind, and the inquisitive spirit of the times, had sufficiently prepared him, not indeed to grapple with these questions, but to be sensible of their existence, and to ponder.

One evening, in the coffee-room of the hotel, having just finished his well-earned dinner, and relaxing his mind for the moment in a fresh research into the Manchester Guide, an individual, who had also been dining in the same apartment, rose from his table, and, after lolling over the empty fireplace, reading the framed announcements, looking at the directions of several letters waiting there for their owners, picking his teeth, turned round to Coningsby, and, with an air of uneasy familiarity, said, —

'First visit to Manchester, sir?'

'My first.'

'Gentleman traveller, I presume?'

'I am a traveller,' said Coningsby.

'Hem! From south?'

'From the south.'

'And pray, sir, how did you find business as you came along? Brisk, I dare say. And yet there is a something, a sort of a something; didn't it strike you, sir, there was a something? A deal of queer paper about, sir!'

'I fear you are speaking on a subject of which I know nothing,' said Coningsby, smiling; 'I do not understand business at all; though I am not surprised that, being at Manchester, you should suppose so.'

'Ah! not in business. Hem! Professional?'

'No,' said Coningsby, 'I am nothing.'

'Ah! an independent gent; hem! and a very pleasant thing, too. Pleased with Manchester, I dare say?' continued the stranger.

'And astonished,' said Coningsby; 'I think, in the whole course of my life, I never saw so much to admire.'

'Seen all the lions, have no doubt?'

'I think I have seen everything,' said Coningsby, rather eager and with some pride.

'Very well, very well,' exclaimed the stranger, in a patronising tone. 'Seen Mr Birley's weaving-room, I dare say?'

'Oh! isn't it wonderful?' said Coningsby.

'A great many people,' said the stranger, with a rather supercilious smile.

'But after all,' said Coningsby, with animation, 'it is the machinery without any interposition of manual power that overwhelms me. It haunts me in my dreams,' continued Coningsby; 'I see cities peopled with machines. Certainly Manchester is the most wonderful city of modern times!'

The stranger stared a little at the enthusiasm of his companion, and then picked his teeth.

'Of all the remarkable things here,' said Coningsby, 'what on the whole, sir, do you look upon as the most so?'

'In the way of machinery?' asked the stranger.

'In the way of machinery.'

'Why, in the way of machinery, you know,' said the stranger, very quietly, 'Manchester is a dead letter.'

'A dead letter!' said Coningsby.

'Dead and buried,' said the stranger, accompanying his words with that peculiar application of his thumb to his nose that signifies so eloquently that all is up.

'You astonish me!' said Coningsby.

'It's a booked place though,' said the stranger, 'and no mistake. We have all of us a very great respect for Manchester, in course; look upon her as a sort of mother, and all that sort of thing. But she is behind the times, sir, and that won't do in this age. The long and short of it is, Manchester is gone by.'

'I thought her only fault might be she was too much in advance of the rest of the country,' said Coningsby, innocently.

'If you want to see life,' said the stranger, 'go to Staley-bridge or Bolton. There's high pressure.'

'But the population of Manchester is increasing,' said Coningsby.

'Why, yes; not a doubt. You see we have all of us a great respect for the town. It is a sort of metropolis of this district, and there is a good deal of capital in the place. And it has some firstrate institutions. There's the Manchester Bank. That's a noble institution, full of commercial enterprise; understands the age, sir; high-pressure to the backbone. I came up to town to see the manager to-day. I am building a new mill now myself at Staley-bridge, and mean to open it by January, and when I do, I'll give you leave to pay another visit to Mr Birley's weaving-room, with my compliments.'

'I am very sorry,' said Coningsby, 'that I have only another day left; but pray tell me, what would you recommend me most to see within a reasonable distance of Manchester?'

'My mill is not finished,' said the stranger musingly, 'and

though there is still a great deal worth seeing at Staley-bridge, still you had better wait to see my new mill. And Bolton, let me see; Bolton, there is nothing at Bolton that can hold up its head for a moment against my new mill; but then it is not finished. Well, well, let us see. What a pity this is not the 1st of January, and then my new mill would be at work! I should like to see Mr Birley's face, or even Mr Ashworth's, that day. And the Oxford Road Works, where they are always making a little change, bit by bit reform, eh! not a very particular fine appetite, I suspect, for dinner, at the Oxford Road Works, the day they hear of my new mill being at work. But you want to see something tip-top. Well, there's Millbank; that's regular slap-up, quite a sight, regular lion; if I were you I would see Millbank.'

'Millbank!' said Coningsby; 'what Millbank?'

'Millbank of Millbank, made the place, made it himself. About three miles from Bolton; train to-morrow morning at 7.25, get a fly at the station, and you will be at Millbank by 8.40.'[2]

'Unfortunately I am engaged to-morrow morning,' said Coningsby, 'and yet I am most anxious, particularly anxious, to see Millbank.'

'Well, there's a late train,' said the stranger, '3.15; you will be there by 4.30.'

'I think I could manage that,' said Coningsby.

'Do,' said the stranger; 'and if you ever find yourself at Staley-bridge, I shall be very happy to be of service. I must be off now. My train goes at 9.15.' And he presented Coningsby with his card as he wished him good night.

> MR G. O. A. HEAD,
> STALEY-BRIDGE

Chapter 3

IN a green valley of Lancaster, contiguous to that district of factories on which we have already touched, a clear and powerful stream flows through a broad meadow land. Upon its margin, adorned, rather than shadowed, by some old elm-trees, for they are too distant to serve except for ornament, rises a vast deep red brick pile, which though formal and monotonous in its general character, is not without a certain beauty of proportion and an artist-like finish in its occasional masonry. The front, which is of great extent, and covered with many tiers of small windows, is flanked by two projecting wings in the same style, which form a large court, completed by a dwarf wall crowned with a light, and rather elegant railing; in the centre, the principal entrance, a lofty portal of bold and beautiful design, surmounted by a statue of Commerce.

This building, not without a degree of dignity, is what is technically, and not very felicitously, called a mill; always translated by the French in their accounts of our manufacturing riots, 'moulin;' and which really was the principal factory of Oswald Millbank, the father of that youth whom, we trust, our readers have not quite forgotten.

At some little distance, and rather withdrawn from the principal stream, were two other smaller structures of the same style. About a quarter of a mile further on, appeared a village of not inconsiderable size, and remarkable from the neatness and even picturesque character of its architecture, and the gay gardens that surrounded it. On a sunny knoll in the background rose a church, in the best style of Christian architecture, and near it was a clerical residence and a school-house of similar design. The village, too, could boast of another public building; an Institute where there were a library and a lecture-room; and a reading-hall, which any one might frequent at certain hours, and under reasonable regulations.

On the other side of the principal factory, but more remote, about half-a-mile up the valley, surrounded by beautiful meadows, and built on an agreeable and well-wooded elevation, was the mansion of the mill-owner; apparently a commodious and not inconsiderable dwelling-house, built in what is called a villa style, with a variety of gardens and conservatories. The atmosphere of this somewhat striking settlement was not disturbed and polluted by the dark vapour, which, to the shame of Manchester, still infests that great town, for Mr Millbank, who liked nothing so much as an invention, unless it were an experiment, took care to consume his own smoke.

The sun was declining when Coningsby arrived at Millbank, and the gratification which he experienced on first beholding it, was not a little diminished, when, on enquiring at the village, he was informed that the hour was past for seeing the works. Determined not to relinquish his purpose without a struggle, he repaired to the principal mill, and entered the counting-house, which was situated in one of the wings of the building.

'Your pleasure, sir?' said one of three individuals sitting on high stools behind a high desk.

'I wish, if possible, to see the works.'

'Quite impossible, sir;' and the clerk, withdrawing his glance, continued his writing. 'No admission without an order, and no admission with an order after two o'clock.'

'I am very unfortunate,' said Coningsby.

'Sorry for it, sir. Give me ledger K. X., will you, Mr Benson?'

'I think, Mr Millbank would grant me permission,' said Coningsby.

'Very likely, sir; to-morrow. Mr Millbank is there, sir, but very much engaged.' He pointed to an inner counting-house, and the glass doors permitted Coningsby to observe several individuals in close converse.

'Perhaps his son, Mr Oswald Millbank, is here?' inquired Coningsby.

'Mr Oswald is in Belgium,' said the clerk.

'Would you give a message to Mr Millbank, and say a friend of his son's at Eton is here, and here only for a day, and wishes very much to see his works?'

'Can't possibly disturb Mr Millbank now, sir; but, if you like to sit down, you can wait and see him yourself.'

Coningsby was content to sit down, though he grew very impatient at the end of a quarter of an hour. The ticking of the clock, the scratching of the pens of the three silent clerks, irritated him. At length, voices were heard, doors opened, and the clerk said, 'Mr Millbank is coming, sir,' but nobody came; voices became hushed, doors were shut; again nothing was heard, save the ticking of the clock and the scratching of the pen.

At length there was a general stir, and they all did come forth, Mr Millbank among them, a well-proportioned, comely man, with a fair face inclining to ruddiness, a quick, glancing, hazel eye, the whitest teeth, and short, curly, chestnut hair, here and there slightly tinged with grey. It was a visage of energy and decision.

He was about to pass through the counting-house with his companions, with whom his affairs were not concluded, when he observed Coningsby, who had risen.

'This gentleman wishes to see me?' he inquired of his clerk, who bowed assent.

'I shall be at your service, sir, the moment I have finished with these gentlemen.'

'The gentleman wishes to see the works, sir,' said the clerk.

'He can see the works at proper times,' said Mr Millbank, somewhat pettishly; 'tell him the regulations;' and he was about to go.

'I beg your pardon, sir,' said Coningsby, coming forward, and with an air of earnestness and grace that arrested the step of the manufacturer. 'I am aware of the regulations, but would beg to be permitted to infringe them.'

'It cannot be, sir,' said Mr Millbank, moving.

'I thought, sir, being here only for a day, and as a friend of your son – '

Mr Millbank stopped and said,

'Oh! a friend of Oswald's, eh? What, at Eton?'

'Yes, sir, at Eton; and I had hoped perhaps to have found him here.'

'I am very much engaged, sir, at this moment,' said Mr Millbank; 'I am sorry I cannot pay you any personal attention, but my clerk will show you everything. Mr Benson, let this gentleman see everything;' and he withdrew.

'Be pleased to write your name here, sir,' said Mr Benson, opening a book, and our friend wrote his name and the date of his visit to Millbank:

'HARRY CONINGSBY, SEPT. 2, 1836.'

Coningsby beheld in this great factory the last and the most refined inventions of mechanical genius. The building had been fitted up by a capitalist as anxious to raise a monument of the skill and power of his order, as to obtain a return for the great investment.

'It is the glory of Lancashire!' exclaimed the enthusiastic Mr Benson.

The clerk spoke freely of his master, whom he evidently idolised, and his great achievements, and Coningsby encouraged him. He detailed to Coningsby the plans which Mr Millbank had pursued, both for the moral and physical well-being of his people; how he had built churches, and schools, and institutes; houses and cottages on a new system of ventilation; how he had allotted gardens; established singing classes.

'Here is Mr Millbank,' continued the clerk, as he and Coningsby, quitting the factory, re-entered the court.

Mr Millbank was approaching the factory, and the moment that he observed them, he quickened his pace.

'Mr Coningsby?' he said, when he reached them. His countenance was rather disturbed, and his voice a little trembled, and he looked on our friend with a glance scrutinising and serious. Coningsby bowed.

'I am sorry that you should have been received at this place with so little ceremony, sir,' said Mr Millbank; 'but had your name been mentioned, you would have found it cherished here.' He nodded to the clerk, who disappeared.

Coningsby began to talk about the wonders of the factory, but Mr Millbank recurred to other thoughts that were passing in his mind. He spoke of his son: he expressed a kind reproach that Coningsby should have thought of visiting this part of the world without giving them some notice of his intention, that he might

have been their guest, that Oswald might have been there to receive him, that they might have made arrangements that he
should see everything, and in the best manner; in short, that they
might all have shown, however slightly, the deep sense of their
obligations to him.

'My visit to Manchester, which led to this, was quite accidental,'
said Coningsby. 'I am bound for the other division of the county,
to pay a visit to my grandfather, Lord Monmouth; but an irresistible desire came over me during my journey to view this
famous district of industry. It is some days since I ought to have
found myself at Coningsby, and this is the reason why I am so
pressed.'

A cloud passed over the countenance of Millbank as the name
of Lord Monmouth was mentioned, but he said nothing. Turning
towards Coningsby, with an air of kindness:

'At least,' said he, 'let not Oswald hear that you did not taste
our salt. Pray dine with me to-day; there is yet an hour to dinner;
and as you have seen the factory, suppose we stroll together
through the village.'

Chapter 4

THE village clock struck five as Mr Millbank and his guest entered the gardens of his mansion. Coningsby lingered a moment to admire the beauty and gay profusion of the flowers.

'Your situation,' said Coningsby, looking up the green and silent valley, 'is absolutely poetic.'

'I try sometimes to fancy,' said Mr Millbank, with a rather fierce smile, 'that I am in the New World.'

They entered the house; a capacious and classic hall, at the end a staircase in the Italian fashion. As they approached it, the sweetest and the clearest voice exclaimed from above, 'Papa! papa!' and instantly a young girl came bounding down the stairs, but suddenly seeing a stranger with her father she stopped upon the landing-place, and was evidently on the point of as rapidly retreating as she had advanced, when Mr Millbank waved his hand to her and begged her to descend. She came down slowly; as she approached them her father said, 'A friend you have often heard of, Edith: this is Mr Coningsby.'

She started; blushed very much; and then, with a trembling and uncertain gait, advanced, put forth her hand with a wild unstudied grace, and said in a tone of sensibility, 'How often have we all wished to see and to thank you!'

This daughter of his host was of tender years; apparently she could scarcely have counted sixteen summers. She was delicate and fragile, but as she raised her still blushing visage to her father's guest, Coningsby felt that he had never beheld a countenance of such striking and such peculiar beauty.

'My only daughter, Mr Coningsby, Edith; a Saxon name, for she is the daughter of a Saxon.'

But the beauty of the countenance was not the beauty of the Saxons. It was a radiant face, one of those that seem to have been touched in their cradle by a sunbeam, and to have retained all their brilliancy and suffused and mantling lustre. One marks sometimes such faces, diaphanous with delicate splendour, in the southern regions of France. Her eye, too, was the rare eye of Aquitaine; soft and long, with lashes drooping over the cheek, dark as her clustering ringlets.

They entered the drawing-room.

'Mr Coningsby,' said Millbank to his daughter, 'is in this part of the world only for a few hours, or I am sure he would become our guest. He has, however, promised to stay with us now and dine.'

'If Miss Millbank will pardon this dress,' said Coningsby, bowing an apology for his inevitable frock and boots; the maiden raised her eyes and bent her head.

The hour of dinner was at hand. Millbank offered to show Coningsby to his dressing-room. He was absent but a few minutes. When he returned he found Miss Millbank alone. He came somewhat suddenly into the room. She was playing with her dog, but ceased the moment she observed Coningsby.

Coningsby, who since his practice with Lady Everingham, flattered himself that he had advanced in small talk, and was not sorry that he had now an opportunity of proving his prowess, made some lively observations about pets and the breeds of lap-dogs, but he was not fortunate in extracting a response or exciting a repartee. He began then on the beauty of Millbank, which he would on no account have avoided seeing, and inquired when she had last heard of her brother. The young lady, apparently much distressed, was murmuring something about Antwerp, when the entrance of her father relieved her from her embarrassment.

Dinner being announced, Coningsby offered his arm to his fair companion, who took it with her eyes fixed on the ground.

'You are very fond, I see, of flowers,' said Coningsby, as they moved along; and the young lady said 'Yes.'

The dinner was plain, but perfect of its kind. The young hostess seemed to perform her office with a certain degree of desperate determination. She looked at a chicken and then at Coningsby, and murmured something which he understood. Sometimes she informed herself of his tastes or necessities in more detail, by the medium of her father, whom she treated as a sort of dragoman;

in this way: 'Would not Mr Coningsby, papa, take this or that, or do so and so?' Coningsby was always careful to reply in a direct manner, without the agency of the interpreter; but he did not advance. Even a petition for the great honour of taking a glass of sherry with her only induced the beautiful face to bow. And yet when she had first seen him, she had addressed him even with emotion. What could it be? He felt less confidence in his increased power of conversation. Why, Theresa Sydney was scarcely a year older than Miss Millbank, and though she did not certainly originate like Lady Everingham, he got on with her perfectly well.

Mr Millbank did not seem to be conscious of his daughter's silence: at any rate, he attempted to compensate for it. He talked fluently and well; on all subjects his opinions seemed to be decided, and his language was precise. He was really interested in what Coningsby had seen, and what he had felt; and his sympathy divested his manner of the disagreeable effect that accompanies a tone inclined to be dictatorial. More than once Coningsby observed the silent daughter listening with extreme attention to the conversation of himself and her father.

The dessert was remarkable. Millbank was proud of his fruit. A bland expression of self-complacency spread over his features as he surveyed his grapes, his peaches, his figs.

'These grapes have gained a medal,' he told Coningsby. 'Those too are prize peaches. I have not yet been so successful with my figs. These however promise, and perhaps this year I may be more fortunate.'

'What would your brother and myself have given for such a dessert at Eton!' said Coningsby to Miss Millbank, wishing to say something, and something too that might interest her.

She seemed infinitely distressed, and yet this time would speak,

'Let me give you some.' He caught by chance her glance immediately withdrawn; yet it was a glance not only of beauty, but of feeling and thought. She added, in a hushed and hurried tone, dividing very nervously some grapes, 'I hardly know whether Oswald will be most pleased or grieved when he hears that you have been here.'

'And why grieved?' said Coningsby.

'That he should not have been here to welcome you, and that your stay is for so brief a time. It seems so strange that after having talked of you for years, we should see you only for hours.'

'I hope I may return,' said Coningsby, 'and that Millbank may be here to welcome me; but I hope I may be permitted to return even if he be not.'

But there was no reply; and soon after, Mr Millbank talking of the American market, and Coningsby helping himself to a glass of claret, the daughter of the Saxon, looking at her father, rose and left the room, so suddenly and so quickly that Coningsby could scarcely gain the door.

'Yes,' said Millbank, filling his glass, and pursuing some previous observations, 'all that we want in this country is to be masters of our own industry; but Saxon industry and Norman manners never will agree; and some day, Mr Coningsby, you will find that out.'

'But what do you mean by Norman manners?' inquired Coningsby.

'Did you ever hear of the Forest of Rossendale?' said Millbank. 'If you were staying here, you should visit the district. It is an area of twenty-four square miles. It was disforested in the early part of the sixteenth century, possessing at that time eighty inhabitants. Its rental in James the First's time was 120*l.* When the woollen manufacture was introduced into the north, the shuttle competed with the plough in Rossendale, and about forty years ago we sent them the Jenny. The eighty souls are now increased to upwards of eighty thousand, and the rental of the forest, by the last county assessment, amounts to more than 50,000*l.*, 41,000 per cent on the value in the reign of James I. Now I call that an instance of Saxon industry competing successfully with Norman manners.'

'Exactly,' said Coningsby, 'but those manners are gone.'

'From Rossendale,' said Millbank, with a grim smile; 'but not from England.'

'Where do you meet them?'

'Meet them! In every place, at every hour; and feel them, too, in every transaction of life.'

'I know, sir, from your son,' said Coningsby, inquiringly, 'that you are opposed to an aristocracy.'

'No, I am not. I am for an aristocracy; but a real one, a natural one.'

'But, sir, is not the aristocracy of England,' said Coningsby, 'a real one? You do not confound our peerage, for example, with the degraded patricians of the Continent.'

'Hum!' said Millbank. 'I do not understand how an aristocracy can exist, unless it be distinguished by some quality which no other class of the community possesses. Distinction is the basis of aristocracy. If you permit only one class of the population, for example, to bear arms, they are an aristocracy; not one much to my taste; but still a great fact. That, however, is not the characteristic of the English peerage. I have yet to learn they are richer than we are, better informed, wiser, or more distinguished for public or private virtue. Is it not monstrous, then, that a small number of men, several of whom take the titles of Duke and Earl from towns in this very neighbourhood, towns which they never saw, which never heard of them, which they did not form, or build, or establish, I say, is it not monstrous, that individuals so circumstanced, should be invested with the highest of conceivable privileges, the privilege of making laws? Dukes and Earls indeed! I say there is nothing in a masquerade more ridiculous.'

'But do you not argue from an exception, sir?' said Coningsby. 'The question is, whether a preponderance of the aristocratic principle in a political constitution be, as I believe, conducive to the stability and permanent power of a State; and whether the peerage, as established in England, generally tends to that end? We must not forget in such an estimate the influence which, in this country, is exercised over opinion by ancient lineage.'

'Ancient lineage!' said Mr Millbank; 'I never heard of a peer with an ancient lineage. The real old families of this country are to be found among the peasantry; the gentry, too, may lay some claim to old blood. I can point you out Saxon families in this county who can trace their pedigrees beyond the Conquest; I know of some Norman gentlemen whose fathers undoubtedly came over with the Conqueror. But a peer with an ancient lineage is to me quite a novelty. No, no; the thirty years of the wars of the Roses freed us from those gentlemen. I take it, after the battle of Tewkesbury,[1] a Norman baron was almost as rare a being in England as a wolf is now.'

'I have always understood,' said Coningsby, 'that our peerage was the finest in Europe.'

'From themselves,' said Millbank, 'and the heralds they pay to paint their carriages. But I go to facts. When Henry VII called his first Parliament, there were only twenty-nine temporal peers to be found, and even some of them took their seats illegally, for they had been attainted.[2] Of those twenty-nine not five remain, and they, as the Howards for instance, are not Norman nobility. We owe the English peerage to three sources: the spoliation of the Church; the open and flagrant sale of its honours by the elder Stuarts; and the boroughmongering of our own times. Those are the three main sources of the existing peerage of England, and in my opinion disgraceful ones. But I must apologise for my frankness in thus speaking to an aristocrat.'

'Oh, by no means, sir, I like discussion. Your son and myself at Eton have had some encounters of this kind before. But if your view of the case be correct,' added Coningsby, smiling, 'you cannot at any rate accuse our present peers of Norman manners.'

'Yes, I do: they adopted Norman manners while they usurped Norman titles. They have neither the right of the Normans, nor do they fulfil the duty of the Normans: they did not conquer the land, and they do not defend it.'

'And where will you find your natural aristocracy?' asked Coningsby.

'Among those men whom a nation recognises as the most eminent for virtue, talents, and property, and, if you please, birth and standing in the land. They guide opinion; and, therefore, they govern. I am no leveller; I look upon an artificial equality as equally pernicious with a factitious aristocracy; both depressing the energies, and checking the enterprise of a nation. I like man to be free, really free: free in his industry as well as his body. What is the use of Habeas Corpus, if a man may not use his hands when he is out of prison?'

'But it appears to me you have, in a great measure, this natural aristocracy in England.'

'Ah, to be sure! If we had not, where should we be? It is the counteracting power that saves us, the disturbing cause in the calculations of short-sighted selfishness. I say it now, and I have said it a hundred times, the House of Commons is a more aristocratic body than the House of Lords. The fact is, a great peer would be a greater man now in the House of Commons than in the House of Lords. Nobody wants a second chamber, except a few disreputable individuals. It is a valuable institution for any member of it who has no distinction, neither character, talents, nor estate. But a peer who possesses all or any of these great qualifications, would find himself an immeasurably more important personage in what, by way of jest, they call the Lower House.'

'Is not the revising wisdom of a senate a salutary check on the precipitation of a popular assembly?'

'Why should a popular assembly, elected by the flower of a nation, be precipitate? If precipitate, what senate could stay an assembly so chosen? No, no, no! the thing has been tried over and over again; the idea of restraining the powerful by the weak is an absurdity; the question is settled. If we wanted a fresh illustration, we need only look to the present state of our own House of Lords. It originates nothing; it has, in fact, announced itself as a mere Court of Registration of the decrees of your House of Commons; and if by any chance it ventures to alter some miserable detail in a clause of a bill that excites public interest, what a clatter through the country, at Conservative banquets got up by the rural attorneys, about the power, authority, and independence of the House of Lords; nine times nine, and one cheer more! No, sir, you may make aristocracies by laws; you can only maintain them by manners. The manners of England preserve it from its laws. And they have substituted for our formal aristocracy an essential aristocracy; the government of those who are distinguished by their fellow-citizens.'

'But then it would appear,' said Coningsby, 'that the remedial action of our manners has removed all the political and social evils of which you complain?'

'They have created a power that may remove them; a power that has the capacity to remove them. But in a great measure they still exist, and must exist yet, I fear, for a long time. The growth of our civilisation has ever been as slow as our oaks; but this tardy development is preferable to the temporary expansion of the gourd.'

'The future seems to me sometimes a dark cloud.'

'Not to me,' said Mr Millbank. 'I am sanguine; I am the Disciple of Progress. But I have cause for my faith. I have witnessed advance. My father has often told me that in his early days the displeasure of a peer of England was like a sentence of death to a man. Why it was esteemed a great concession to public opinion, so late as the reign of George II, that Lord Ferrars should be executed for murder.[3] The king of a new dynasty, who wished to be popular with the people, insisted on it, and even then he was hanged with a silken cord. At any rate we may defend ourselves now,' continued Mr Millbank, 'and, perhaps, do something more. I defy any peer to crush me, though there is one who would be very glad to do it. No more of that; I am very happy to see you at Millbank, very happy to make your acquaintance,' he continued, with some emotion, 'and not merely because you are my son's friend and more than a friend.'

The walls of the dining-room were covered with pictures of great merit, all of the modern English school. Mr Millbank understood no other, he was wont to say! and he found that many of his friends who did, bought a great many pleasing pictures that were copies, and many originals that were very displeasing. He loved a fine free landscape by Lee, that gave him the broad plains, the green lanes, and running streams of his own land; a group of animals by Landseer, as full of speech and sentiment as if they were designed by Æsop; above all, he delighted in the household humour and homely pathos of Wilkie. And if a higher tone of imagination pleased him, he could gratify it without difficulty among his favourite masters. He possessed some specimens of Etty worthy of Venice when it was alive; he could muse amid the twilight ruins of ancient cities raised by the magic pencil of Danby, or accompany a group of fair Neapolitans to a festival by the genial aid of Uwins.

Opposite Coningsby was a portrait, which had greatly attracted his attention during the whole dinner. It represented a woman, young and of a rare beauty. The costume was of that classical character prevalent in this country before the general peace; a blue ribbon bound together as a fillet her clustering chestnut curls. The face was looking out of the canvas, and Coningsby never raised his eyes without catching its glance of blended vivacity and tenderness.

There are moments when our sensibility is affected by circumstances of a trivial character. It seems a fantastic emotion, but the gaze of this picture disturbed the serenity of Coningsby. He endeavoured sometimes to avoid looking at it, but it irresistibly attracted him. More than once during dinner he longed to inquire whom it represented; but it is a delicate subject to ask questions about portraits, and he refrained. Still, when he was rising to leave the room, the impulse was irresistible. He said to Mr Millbank, 'By whom is that portrait, sir?'

The countenance of Millbank became disturbed; it was not an expression of tender reminiscence that fell upon his features. On the contrary, the expression was agitated, almost angry.

'Oh! that is by a country artist,' he said, 'of whom you never heard,' and moved away.

They found Miss Millbank in the drawing-room; she was sitting at a round table covered with working materials, apparently dressing a doll.

'Nay,' thought Coningsby, 'she must be too old for that.'

He addressed her, and seated himself by her side. There were several dolls on the table, but he discovered, on examination, that they were pincushions; and elicited, with some difficulty, that they were making for a fancy fair about to be held in aid of that excellent institution, the Manchester Athenæum. Then the father came up and said,

'My child, let us have some tea;' and she rose and seated herself at the tea-table. Coningsby also quitted his seat, and surveyed the apartment.

There were several musical instruments; among others, he observed a guitar; not such an instrument as one buys in a music shop, but such an one as tinkles at Seville, a genuine Spanish guitar. Coningsby repaired to the tea-table.

'I am glad that you are fond of music, Miss Millbank.'

A blush and a bow.

'I hope after tea you will be so kind as to touch the guitar.'

Signals of great distress.

'Were you ever at Birmingham?'

'Yes:' a sigh.

'What a splendid music-hall! They should build one at Manchester.'

'They ought,' in a whisper.

The tea-tray was removed; Coningsby was conversing with Mr Millbank, who was asking him questions about his son; what he thought of Oxford; what he thought of Oriel; should himself have preferred Cambridge; but had consulted a friend, an Oriel man, who had a great opinion of Oriel; and Oswald's name had been entered some years back. He rather regretted it now; but the thing was done. Coningsby, remembering the promise of the guitar, turned round to claim its fulfilment, but the singer had made her escape. Time elapsed, and no Miss Millbank re-appeared. Coningsby looked at his watch; he had to go three miles to the train, which started, as his friend of the previous night would phrase it, at 9.45.

'I should be happy if you remained with us,' said Mr Millbank; 'but as you say it is out of your power, in this age of punctual travelling a host is bound to speed the parting guest. The carriage is ready for you.'

'Farewell, then, sir. You must make my adieux to Miss Millbank, and accept my thanks for your great kindness.'

'Farewell, Mr Coningsby,' said his host, taking his hand, which he retained for a moment, as if he would say more. Then leaving it, he repeated with a somewhat wandering air, and in a voice of emotion, 'Farewell, farewell, Mr Coningsby.'

Chapter 5

TOWARDS the end of the session of 1836, the hopes of the Conservative party were again in the ascendant. The Tadpoles and the Tapers had infused such enthusiasm into all the country attorneys, who, in their turn, had so bedevilled the registration, that it was whispered in the utmost confidence, but as a flagrant truth, that Reaction was at length 'a great fact.' All that was required was the opportunity; but as the existing parliament was not two years old, and the government had an excellent working majority, it seemed that the occasion could scarcely be furnished. Under these circumstances, the backstairs politicians, not content with having by their premature movements already seriously damaged the career of their leader, to whom in public they pretended to be devoted, began weaving again their old intrigues about the court, and not without effect.

It was said that the royal ear lent itself with no marked repugnance to suggestions which might rid the sovereign of ministers, who, after all, were the ministers not of his choice, but of his necessity. But William IV, after two failures in a similar attempt, after his respective embarrassing interviews with Lord Grey and Lord Melbourne, on their return to office in 1832 and 1835, was resolved never to make another move unless it were a checkmate. The king, therefore, listened and smiled, and loved to talk to his favourites of his private feelings and secret hopes; the first outraged, the second cherished; and a little of these revelations of royalty was distilled to great personages, who in their turn spoke hypothetically to their hangers-on of royal dispositions, and possible contingencies, while the hangers-on and go-betweens, in their turn, looked more than they expressed; took county members by the button into a corner, and advised, as friends, the representatives of boroughs to look sharply after the next registration.

Lord Monmouth, who was never greater than in adversity, and

whose favourite excitement was to aim at the impossible, had never been more resolved on a Dukedom than when the Reform Act deprived him of the twelve votes which he had accumulated to attain that object. While all his companions in discomfiture were bewailing their irretrievable overthrow, Lord Monmouth became almost a convert to the measure, which had furnished his devising and daring mind, palled with prosperity, and satiated with a life of success, with an object, and the stimulating enjoyment of a difficulty.

He had early resolved to appropriate to himself a division of the county in which his chief seat was situate; but what most interested him, because it was most difficult, was the acquisition of one of the new boroughs that was in his vicinity, and in which he possessed considerable property. The borough, however, was a manufacturing town, and returning only one member, it had hitherto sent up to Westminster a radical shopkeeper, one Mr Jawster Sharp, who had taken what is called 'a leading part' in the town on every 'crisis' that occurred since 1830; one of those zealous patriots who had got up penny subscriptions for gold cups to Lord Grey; cries for the bill, the whole bill and nothing but the bill; and public dinners where the victual was devoured before grace was said; a worthy who makes speeches, passes resolutions, votes addresses, goes up with deputations, has at all times the necessary quantity of confidence in the necessary individual; confidence in Lord Grey; confidence in Lord Durham; confidence in Lord Melbourne; and can also, if necessary, give three cheers for the King, or three groans for the Queen.

But the days of the genus Jawster Sharp were over in this borough as well as in many others. He had contrived in his lustre of agitation to feather his nest pretty successfully; by which he had lost public confidence and gained his private end. Three hungry Jawster Sharps, his hopeful sons, had all become commissioners of one thing or another; temporary appointments with interminable duties; a low-church son-in-law found himself comfortably seated in a chancellor's living; and several cousins and nephews were busy in the Excise. But Jawster Sharp himself was as pure as Cato.[1] He had always said he would never touch the public money, and he had kept his word. It was an understood

thing that Jawster Sharp was never to show his face again on
the hustings of Darlford; the Liberal party was determined to be
represented in future by a man of station, substance, character,
a true Reformer, but one who wanted nothing for himself, and
therefore might, if needful, get something for them. They were
looking out for such a man, but were in no hurry. The seat was
looked upon as a good thing; a contest certainly, every place is
contested now, but as certainly a large majority. Notwithstanding all this confidence, however, Reaction or Registration, or some
other mystification, had produced effects even in this creature of
the Reform Bill, the good Borough of Darlford. The borough that
out of gratitude to Lord Grey returned a jobbing shopkeeper twice
to Parliament as its representative without a contest, had now a
Conservative Association, with a banker for its chairman, and a
brewer for its vice-president, and four sharp lawyers nibbing their
pens, noting their memorandum-books, and assuring their neighbours, with a consoling and complacent air, that 'Property must
tell in the long run.' Whispers also were about, that when the
proper time arrived, a Conservative candidate would certainly
have the honour of addressing the electors. No name mentioned,
but it was not concealed that he was to be of no ordinary calibre;
a tried man, a distinguished individual, who had already fought
the battle of the constitution, and served his country in eminent
posts; honoured by the nation, favoured by his sovereign. These
important and encouraging intimations were ably diffused in the
columns of the Conservative journal, and in a style which, from
its high tone, evidently indicated no ordinary source and no
common pen. Indeed, there appeared occasionally in this paper,
articles written with such unusual vigour, that the proprietors of
the Liberal journal almost felt the necessity of getting some eminent hand down from town to compete with them. It was impossible that they could emanate from the rival Editor. They knew
well the length of their brother's tether. Had they been more
versant in the periodical literature of the day, they might in this
'slashing' style have caught perhaps a glimpse of the future candidate for their borough, the Right Honourable Nicholas Rigby.

Lord Monmouth, though he had been absent from England
since 1832, had obtained from his vigilant correspondent a cur-

rent knowledge of all that had occurred in the interval: all the hopes, fears, plans, prospects, manœuvres, and machinations; their rise and fall; how some had bloomed, others were blighted; not a shade of reaction that was not represented to him; not the possibility of an adhesion that was not very duly reported; he could calculate at Naples at any time, within ten, the result of a dissolution. The season of the year had prevented him crossing the Alps in 1834, and after the general election he was too shrewd a practiser in the political world to be deceived as to the ultimate result. Lord Eskdale, in whose judgment he had more confidence than in that of any individual, had told him from the first that the pear was not ripe; Rigby, who always hedged against his interest by the fulfilment of his prophecy of irremediable discomfiture, was never very sanguine. Indeed, the whole affair was always considered premature by the good judges; and a long time elapsed before Tadpole and Taper recovered their secret influence, or resumed their ostentatious loquacity, or their silent insolence.

The pear, however, was now ripe. Even Lord Eskdale wrote that after the forthcoming registration a bet was safe, and Lord Monmouth had the satisfaction of drawing the Whig Minister at Naples into a cool thousand on the event. Soon after this he returned to England, and determined to pay a visit to Coningsby Castle, feast the county, patronise the borough, diffuse that confidence in the party which his presence never failed to do; so great and so just was the reliance in his unerring powers of calculation and his intrepid pluck. Notwithstanding Schedule A, the prestige of his power had not sensibly diminished, for his essential resources were vast, and his intellect always made the most of his influence.

True, however, to his organisation, Lord Monmouth, even to save his party and gain his dukedom, must not be bored. He, therefore, filled his castle with the most agreeable people from London, and even secured for their diversion a little troop of French comedians. Thus supported, he received his neighbours with all the splendour befitting his immense wealth and great position, and with one charm which even immense wealth and great position cannot command, the most perfect manner in the world. Indeed, Lord Monmouth was one of the most finished

gentlemen that ever lived; and as he was good-natured, and for
a selfish man even good-humoured, there was rarely a cloud of
caprice or ill-temper to prevent his fine manners having their fair
play. The country neighbours were all fascinated; they were
received with so much dignity and dismissed with so much grace.
Nobody would believe a word of the stories against him. Had he
lived all his life at Coningsby, fulfilled every duty of a great
English nobleman, benefited the county, loaded the inhabitants
with favours, he would not have been half so popular as he found
himself within a fortnight of his arrival with the worst county
reputation conceivable, and every little squire vowing that he
would not even leave his name at the Castle to show his respect.

Lord Monmouth, whose contempt for mankind was absolute;
not a fluctuating sentiment, not a mournful conviction, ebbing
and flowing with circumstances, but a fixed, profound, unalter-
able instinct; who never loved any one, and never hated any one
except his own children; was diverted by his popularity, but he
was also gratified by it. At this moment it was a great element
of power; he was proud that, with a vicious character, after
having treated these people with unprecedented neglect and con-
tumely, he should have won back their golden opinions in a
moment by the magic of manner and the splendour of wealth.
His experience proved the soundness of his philosophy.

Lord Monmouth worshipped gold, though, if necessary, he
could squander it like a caliph. He had even a respect for very
rich men; it was his only weakness, the only exception to his
general scorn for his species. Wit, power, particular friendships,
general popularity, public opinion, beauty, genius, virtue, all these
are to be purchased; but it does not follow that you can buy a
rich man: you may not be able or willing to spare enough. A
person or a thing that you perhaps could not buy, became invested, in the eyes of Lord Monmouth, with a kind of halo
amounting almost to sanctity.

As the prey rose to the bait, Lord Monmouth resolved they
should be gorged. His banquets were doubled; a ball was announced; a public day fixed; not only the county, but the principal
inhabitants of the neighbouring borough, were encouraged to
attend; Lord Monmouth wished it, if possible, to be without dis-

tinction of party. He had come to reside among his old friends, to live and die where he was born. The Chairman of the Conservative Association and the Vice President exchanged glances, which would have become Tadpole and Taper; the four attorneys nibbed their pens with increased energy, and vowed that nothing could withstand the influence of the aristocracy 'in the long run.' All went and dined at the Castle; all returned home overpowered by the condescension of the host, the beauty of the ladies, several real Princesses, the splendour of his liveries, the variety of his viands, and the flavour of his wines. It was agreed that at future meetings of the Conservative Association, they should always give 'Lord Monmouth and the House of Lords!' superseding the Duke of Wellington, who was to figure in an after-toast with the Battle of Waterloo.

It was not without emotion that Coningsby beheld for the first time the castle that bore his name. It was visible for several miles before he even entered the park, so proud and prominent was its position, on the richly-wooded steep of a considerable eminence. It was a castellated building, immense and magnificent, in a faulty and incongruous style of architecture, indeed, but compensating in some degree for these deficiencies of external taste and beauty by the splendour and accommodation of its interior, and which a Gothic castle, raised according to the strict rules of art, could scarcely have afforded. The declining sun threw over the pile a rich colour as Coningsby approached it, and lit up with fleeting and fanciful tints the delicate foliage of the rare shrubs and tall thin trees that clothed the acclivity on which it stood. Our young friend felt a little embarrassed when, without a servant and in a hack chaise, he drew up to the grand portal, and a crowd of retainers came forth to receive him. A superior servant inquired his name with a stately composure that disdained to be supercilious. It was not without some degree of pride and satisfaction that the guest replied, 'Mr Coningsby.' The instantaneous effect was magical. It seemed to Coningsby that he was borne on the shoulders of the people to his apartment; each tried to carry some part of his luggage; and he only hoped his welcome from their superiors might be as hearty.

Chapter 6

IT appeared to Coningsby in his way to his room, that the Castle was in a state of great excitement; everywhere bustle, preparation, moving to and fro, ascending and descending of stairs, servants in every corner; orders boundlessly given, rapidly obeyed; many desires, equal gratification. All this made him rather nervous. It was quite unlike Beaumanoir. That also was a palace, but it was a home. This, though it should be one to him, seemed to have nothing of that character. Of all the mysteries the social mysteries are the most appalling. Going to an assembly for the first time is more alarming than the first battle. Coningsby had never before been in a great house full of company. It seemed an overwhelming affair. The sight of the servants bewildered him; how then was he to encounter their masters?

That, however, he must do in a moment. A groom of the chambers indicates the way to him, as he proceeds with a hesitating yet hurried step through several ante-chambers and drawing-rooms; then doors are suddenly thrown open, and he is ushered into the largest and most sumptuous saloon that he had ever entered. It was full of ladies and gentlemen. Coningsby for the first time in his life was at a great party. His immediate emotion was to sink into the earth; but perceiving that no one even noticed him, and that not an eye had been attracted to his entrance, he regained his breath and in some degree his composure, and standing aside, endeavoured to make himself, as well as he could, master of the land.

Not a human being that he had ever seen before! The circumstance of not being noticed, which a few minutes since he had felt as a relief, became now a cause of annoyance. It seemed that he was the only person standing alone whom no one was addressing. He felt renewed and aggravated embarrassment, and fancied, perhaps was conscious, that he was blushing. At length his ear caught the voice of Mr Rigby. The speaker was not visible;

he was at a distance surrounded by a wondering group, whom he was severally and collectively contradicting, but Coningsby could not mistake those harsh, arrogant tones. He was not sorry indeed that Mr Rigby did not observe him. Coningsby never loved him particularly, which was rather ungrateful, for he was a person who had been kind, and, on the whole, serviceable to him; but Coningsby writhed, especially as he grew older, under Mr Rigby's patronising air and paternal tone. Even in old days, though attentive, Coningsby had never found him affectionate. Mr Rigby would tell him what to do and see, but never asked him what he wished to do and see. It seemed to Coningsby that it was always contrived that he should appear the *protégé*, or poor relation, of a dependent of his family. These feelings, which the thought of Mr Rigby had revived, caused our young friend, by an inevitable association of ideas, to remember that, unknown and unnoticed as he might be, he was the only Coningsby in that proud Castle, except the Lord of the Castle himself; and he began to be rather ashamed of permitting a sense of his inexperience in the mere forms and fashions of society so to suppress him, and deprive him, as it were, of the spirit and carriage which became alike his character and his position. Emboldened and greatly restored to himself, Coningsby advanced into the body of the saloon.

On his legs, wearing his blue ribbon and bending his head frequently to a lady who was seated on a sofa, and continually addressed him, Coningsby recognised his grandfather. Lord Monmouth was somewhat balder than four years ago, when he had come down to Montem, and a little more portly perhaps; but otherwise unchanged. Lord Monmouth never condescended to the artifices of the toilet, and, indeed, notwithstanding his life of excess, had little need of them. Nature had done much for him, and the slow progress of decay was carried off by his consummate bearing. He looked, indeed, the chieftain of a house of whom a cadet might be proud.

For Coningsby, not only the chief of his house, but his host too. In either capacity he ought to address Lord Monmouth. To sit down to dinner without having previously paid his respects to his grandfather, to whom he was so much indebted, and whom he had not seen for so many years, struck him not only as un-courtly, but as unkind and ungrateful, and, indeed, in the highest degree absurd. But how was he to do it? Lord Monmouth seemed deeply engaged, and apparently with some very great lady. And if Coningsby advanced and bowed, in all probability he would only get a bow in return. He remembered the bow of his first interview. It had made a lasting impression on his mind. For it was more than likely Lord Monmouth would not recognise him. Four years had not sensibly altered Lord Monmouth, but four years had changed Harry Coningsby from a schoolboy into a man. Then how was he to make himself known to his grandfather? To an-nounce himself as Coningsby, as his Lordship's grandson, seemed somewhat ridiculous: to address his grandfather as Lord Mon-mouth would serve no purpose: to style Lord Monmouth 'grand-father' would make every one laugh, and seemed stiff and unnatural. What was he to do? To fall into an attitude and exclaim, 'Behold your grandchild!' or, 'Have you forgotten your Harry?'

Even to catch Lord Monmouth's glance was not an easy affair; he was much occupied on one side by the great lady, on the other were several gentlemen who occasionally joined in the conver-sation. But something must be done.

There ran through Coningsby's character, as we have before mentioned, a vein of simplicity which was not its least charm. It resulted, no doubt, in a great degree from the earnestness of his nature. There never was a boy so totally devoid of affectation, which was remarkable, for he had a brilliant imagination, a quality that, from its fantasies, and the vague and indefinite desires it engenders, generally makes those whose characters are not formed, affected. The Duchess, who was a fine judge of charac-ter, and who greatly regarded Coningsby, often mentioned this trait as one which, combined with his great abilities and acquire-ments so unusual at his age, rendered him very interesting. In the present instance it happened that, while Coningsby was watching his grandfather, he observed a gentleman advance, make his bow, say and receive a few words and retire. This little incident, however, made a momentary diversion in the immediate circle of Lord Monmouth, and before they could all resume their former talk and fall into their previous positions, an impulse sent forth Coningsby, who walked up to Lord Monmouth, and standing before him, said,

'How do you do, grandpapa?'

Lord Monmouth beheld his grandson. His comprehensive and penetrating glance took in every point with a flash. There stood before him one of the handsomest youths he had ever seen, with a mien as graceful as his countenance was captivating; and his whole air breathing that freshness and ingenuousness which none so much appreciates as the used man of the world. And this was his child; the only one of his blood to whom he had been kind. It would be exaggeration to say that Lord Monmouth's heart was touched; but his goodnature effervesced, and his fine taste was deeply gratified. He perceived in an instant such a relation might be a valuable adherent; an irresistible candidate for future elections: a brilliant tool to work out the Dukedom. All these impressions and ideas, and many more, passed through the quick brain of Lord Monmouth ere the sound of Coningsby's words had seemed to cease, and long before the surrounding guests had recovered from the surprise which they had occasioned them, and which did not diminish, when Lord Monmouth, advancing, placed his arms round Coningsby with a dignity of affection that would have become Louis XIV, and then, in the high manner of the old Court, kissed him on each cheek.

'Welcome to your home,' said Lord Monmouth. 'You have grown a great deal.'

Then Lord Monmouth led the agitated Coningsby to the great lady, who was a Princess and an Ambassadress, and then, placing his arm gracefully in that of his grandson, he led him across the room, and presented him in due form to some royal blood that was his guest, in the shape of a Russian Grand-duke. His Imperial Highness received our hero as graciously as the grandson of Lord Monmouth might expect; but no greeting can be imagined warmer than the one he received from the lady with whom the Grand-duke was conversing. She was a dame whose beauty was mature, but still radiant. Her figure was superb; her dark hair crowned with a tiara of curious workmanship. Her rounded arm was covered with costly bracelets, but not a jewel on her finely formed bust, and the least possible rouge on her still oval cheek. Madame Colonna retained her charms.

The party, though so considerable, principally consisted of the guests at the castle. The suite of the Grand-duke included several counts and generals; then there were the Russian Ambassador and his lady; and a Russian Prince and Princess, their relations. The Prince and Princess Colonna and the Princess Lucretia were also paying a visit to the Marquess; and the frequency of these visits made some straight-laced magnificoes mysteriously declare it was impossible to go to Coningsby; but as they were not asked, it did not much signify. The Marquess knew a great many very agreeable people of the highest *ton*, who took a more liberal view of human conduct, and always made it a rule to presume the best motives instead of imputing the worst. There was Lady St Julians, for example, whose position was of the highest; no one more sought; she made it a rule to go everywhere and visit everybody, provided they had power, wealth, and fashion. She knew no crime except a woman not living with her husband; that was past pardon. So long as his presence sanctioned her conduct, however shameless, it did not signify; but if the husband were a brute, neglected his wife first, and then deserted her; then, if a breath but sullies her name she must be crushed; unless, indeed, her own family were very powerful, which makes a difference, and sometimes softens immorality into discretion.

Lord and Lady Gaverstock were also there, who never said an unkind thing of anybody; her ladyship was pure as snow; but her mother having been divorced, she ever fancied she was paying a kind of homage to her parent, by visiting those who might some day be in the same predicament. There were other lords and ladies of high degree; and some who, though neither lords nor ladies, were charming people, which Lord Monmouth chiefly cared about; troops of fine gentlemen who came and went; and some who were neither fine nor gentlemen, but who were very amusing or very obliging, as circumstances required, and made life easy and pleasant to others and themselves.

A new scene this for Coningsby, who watched with interest all that passed before him. The dinner was announced as served; an affectionate arm guides him at a moment of some perplexity.

'When did you arrive, Harry? We shall sit together. How is the Duchess?' inquired Mr Rigby, who spoke as if he had seen Coningsby for the first time; but who indeed had, with that eye which nothing could escape, observed his reception by his grandfather, marked it well, and inwardly digested it.

Chapter 7

THERE was to be a first appearance on the stage of Lord Monmouth's theatre to-night, the expectation of which created considerable interest in the party, and was one of the principal subjects of conversation at dinner. Villebecque, the manager of the troop, had married the actress Stella, once celebrated for her genius and her beauty; a woman who had none of the vices of her craft, for, though she was a fallen angel, there were what her countrymen style extenuating circumstances in her declension. With the whole world at her feet, she had remained unsullied. Wealth and its enjoyments could not tempt her, although she was unable to refuse her heart to one whom she deemed worthy of possessing it. She found her fate in an Englishman, who was the father of her only child, a daughter. She thought she had met in him a hero, a demi-god, a being of deep passion and original and creative mind; but he was only a voluptuary, full of violence instead of feeling, and eccentric, because he had great means with which he could gratify extravagant whims. Stella found she had made the great and irretrievable mistake. She had exchanged devotion for a passionate and evanescent fancy, prompted at first by vanity, and daily dissipating under the influence of custom and new objects. Though not stainless in conduct, Stella was pure in spirit. She required that devotion which she had yielded; and she separated herself from the being to whom she had made the most precious sacrifice. He offered her the consoling compensation of a settlement, which she refused; and she returned with a broken spirit to that profession of which she was still the ornament and the pride.

The animating principle of her career was her daughter, whom she educated with a solicitude which the most virtuous mother could not surpass. To preserve her from the stage, and to secure for her an independence, were the objects of her mother's life; but nature whispered to her, that the days of that life were already numbered. The exertions of her profession had alarmingly developed an inherent tendency to pulmonary disease. Anxious that her child should not be left without some protector, Stella yielded to the repeated solicitations of one who from the first had been her silent admirer, and she married Villebecque, a clever actor, and an enterprising man who meant to be something more. Their union was not of long duration, though it was happy on the side of Villebecque, and serene on that of his wife. Stella was recalled from this world, where she had known much triumph and more suffering; and where she had exercised many virtues, which elsewhere, though not here, may perhaps be accepted as some palliation of one great error.

Villebecque acted becomingly to the young charge which Stella had bequeathed to him. He was himself, as we have intimated, a man of enterprise, a restless spirit, not content to move for ever in the sphere in which he was born. Vicissitudes are the lot of such aspirants. Villebecque became manager of a small theatre, and made money. If Villebecque without a sou had been a schemer, Villebecque with a small capital was the very Chevalier Law[1] of theatrical managers. He took a larger theatre, and even that succeeded. Soon he was recognised as the lessee of more than one, and still he prospered. Villebecque began to dabble in opera-houses. He enthroned himself at Paris; his envoys were heard of at Milan and Naples, at Berlin and St Petersburg. His controversies with the Conservatoire at Paris ranked among state papers. Villebecque rolled in chariots and drove cabriolets; Villebecque gave refined suppers to great nobles, who were honoured by the invitation; Villebecque wore a red ribbon in the button-hole of his frock, and more than one cross in his gala dress.

All this time the daughter of Stella increased in years and stature, and we must add in goodness: a mild, soft-hearted girl, as yet with no decided character, but one who loved calmness and seemed little fitted for the circle in which she found herself. In that circle, however, she ever experienced kindness and consideration. No enterprise however hazardous, no management however complicated, no schemes however vast, ever for a moment induced Villebecque to forget 'La Petite.' If only for one breathless instant, hardly a day elapsed but he saw her; she was his companion in all his rapid movements, and he studied every comfort and convenience that could relieve her delicate frame in some degree from the inconvenience and exhaustion of travel. He was proud to surround her with luxury and refinement; to supply her with the most celebrated masters; to gratify every wish that she could express.

But all this time Villebecque was dancing on a volcano. The catastrophe which inevitably occurs in the career of all great speculators, and especially theatrical ones, arrived to him. Flushed with his prosperity, and confident in his constant success, nothing would satisfy him but universal empire. He had established his despotism at Paris, his dynasties at Naples and at Milan; but the North was not to him, and he was determined to appropriate it. Berlin fell before a successful campaign, though a costly one; but St Petersburg and London still remained. Resolute and reckless, nothing deterred Villebecque. One season all the opera-houses in Europe obeyed his nod, and at the end of it he was ruined. The crash was utter, universal, overwhelming; and under ordinary circumstances a French bed and a brasier of charcoal alone re-mained for Villebecque, who was equal to the occasion. But the thought of La Petite and the remembrance of his promise to Stella deterred him from the deed. He reviewed his position in a spirit becoming a practical philosopher. Was he worse off than before he commenced his career? Yes, because he was older; though to be sure he had his compensating reminiscences. But was he too old to do anything? At forty-five the game was not altogether up; and in a large theatre, not too much lighted, and with the artifices of a dramatic toilet, he might still be able successfully to re-assume those characters of coxcombs and muscadins,[2] in which he was once so celebrated. Luxury had perhaps a little too much enlarged his waist, but diet and rehearsals would set all right.

Villebecque in their adversity broke to La Petite, that the time had unfortunately arrived when it would be wise for her to con-sider the most effectual means for turning her talents and ac-complishments to account. He himself suggested the stage, to which otherwise there were doubtless objections, because her oc-cupation in any other pursuit would necessarily separate them; but he impartially placed before her the relative advantages and disadvantages of every course which seemed to lie open to them, and left the preferable one to her own decision. La Petite, who had wept very much over Villebecque's misfortunes, and often assured him that she cared for them only for his sake, decided for the stage, solely because it would secure their not being parted; and yet, as she often assured him, she feared she had no predisposition for the career.

Villebecque had now not only to fill his own parts at the theatre at which he had obtained an engagement, but he had also to be the instructor of his ward. It was a life of toil; an addition of labour and effort that need scarcely have been made to the exciting exertion of performance, and the dull exercise of rehearsal; but he bore it all without a murmur; with a self-command and a gentle perseverance which the finest temper in the world could hardly account for; certainly not when we remember that its possessor, who had to make all these exertions and endure all this wearisome toil, had just experienced the most shattering vicissitudes of fortune, and been hurled from the possession of absolute power and illimitable self-gratification.

Lord Eskdale, who was always doing kind things to actors and actresses, had a great regard for Villebecque, with whom he had often supped. He had often been kind, too, to La Petite. Lord Eskdale had a plan for putting Villebecque, as he termed it, 'on his legs again.' It was to establish him with a French company in London at some pretty theatre; Lord Eskdale to take a private box and to make all his friends do the same. Villebecque, who was as sanguine as he was good-tempered, was ravished by this friendly scheme. He immediately believed that he should recover his great fortunes as rapidly as he had lost them. He foresaw in La Petite a genius as distinguished as that of her mother, although as yet not developed, and he was boundless in his expressions of gratitude to his patron. And indeed of all friends, a friend in need is the most delightful. Lord Eskdale had the talent of being a friend in need. Perhaps it was because he knew so many worthless persons. But it often happens that worthless persons are merely people who are worth nothing.

Lord Monmouth having written to Mr Rigby of his intention to reside for some months at Coningsby, and having mentioned that he wished a troop of French comedians to be engaged for the summer, Mr Rigby had immediately consulted Lord Eskdale on the subject, as the best current authority. Thinking this a good opportunity of giving a turn to poor Villebecque, and that it might serve as a capital introduction to their scheme of the London company, Lord Eskdale obtained for him the engagement.

Villebecque and his little troop had now been a month at Coningsby, and had hitherto performed three times a-week. Lord Monmouth was content; his guests much gratified; the company, on the whole, much approved of. It was, indeed, considering its limited numbers, a capital company. There was a young lady who played the old woman's parts, nothing could be more garrulous and venerable; and a lady of maturer years who performed the heroines, gay and graceful as May. Villebecque himself was a celebrity in characters of airy insolence and careless frolic. Their old man, indeed, was rather hard, but handy; could take anything either in the high serious, or the low droll. Their sentimental lover was rather too much bewigged, and spoke too much to the audience, a fault rare with the French; but this hero had a vague idea that he was ultimately destined to run off with a princess.

In this wise, affairs had gone on for a month; very well, but not too well. The enterprising genius of Villebecque, once more a manager, prompted him to action. He felt an itching desire to announce a novelty. He fancied Lord Monmouth had yawned once or twice when the heroine came on. Villebecque wanted to make a *coup*. It was clear that La Petite must sooner or later begin. Could she find a more favourable audience, or a more fitting occasion, than were now offered? True it was she had a great repugnance to come out; but it certainly seemed more to her advantage that she should make her first appearance at a private theatre than at a public one; supported by all the encouraging patronage of Coningsby Castle, than subjected to all the cynical criticism of the stalls of St James'.

These views and various considerations were urged and represented by Villebecque to La Petite, with all the practised powers of plausibility of which so much experience as a manager had made him master. La Petite looked infinitely distressed, but yielded, as she ever did. And the night of Coningsby's arrival at the Castle was to witness in its private theatre the first appearance of MADEMOISELLE FLORA.

Chapter 8

THE guests re-assembled in the great saloon before they repaired
to the theatre. A lady on the arm of the Russian Prince bestowed
on Coningsby a haughty, but not ungracious, bow; which he
returned, unconscious of the person to whom he bent. She was,
however, a striking person; not beautiful, her face, indeed, at the
first glance was almost repulsive, yet it ever attracted a second
gaze. A remarkable pallor distinguished her; her features had
neither regularity nor expression; neither were her eyes fine; but
her brow impressed you with an idea of power of no ordinary
character or capacity. Her figure was as fine and commanding
as her face was void of charm. Juno, in the full bloom of her im-
mortality, could have presented nothing more majestic. Coningsby watched her as she swept along like a resistless Fate.

Servants now went round and presented to each of the guests
a billet of the performance. It announced in striking characters
the *début* of Mademoiselle Flora. A principal servant, bearing
branch lights, came forward and bowed to the Marquess. Lord
Monmouth went immediately to the Grand-duke, and notified to
His Imperial Highness that the comedy was ready. The Grand-
duke offered his arm to the Ambassadress; the rest were following;
Coningsby was called; Madame Colonna wished him to be her
beau.

It was a pretty theatre; had been rapidly rubbed up and renovated here and there; the painting just touched; a little gilding
on a cornice. There were no boxes, but the ground-floor, which
gradually ascended, was carpeted and covered with arm-chairs,
and the back of the theatre with a new and rich curtain of green
velvet.

They are all seated; a great artist performs on the violin, accompanied by another great artist on the piano. The lights rise;
somebody evidently crosses the stage behind the curtain. They
are disposing the scene. In a moment the curtain will rise also.

'Have you seen Lucretia?' said the Princess to Coningsby. 'She is so anxious to resume her acquaintance with you.'

But before he could answer the bell rang, and the curtain rose.

The old man, who had a droll part to-night, came forward and maintained a conversation with his housekeeper; not bad. The young woman who played the grave matron performed with great finish. She was a favourite, and was ever applauded. The second scene came; a saloon tastefully furnished; a table with flowers, arranged with grace; birds in cages, a lap-dog on a cushion; some books. The audience were pleased; especially the ladies; they like to recognise signs of *bon ton* in the details of the scene. A rather awful pause, and Mademoiselle Flora enters. She was greeted with even vehement approbation. Her agitation is extreme; she curt-seys and bows her head, as if to hide her face. The face was pleasing, and pretty enough, soft and engaging. Her figure slight and rather graceful. Nothing could be more perfect than her costume; purely white, but the fashion consummate; a single rose her only ornament. All admitted that her hair was arranged to admiration.

At length she spoke; her voice trembled, but she had a good elocution, though her organ wanted force. The gentlemen looked at each other, and nodded approbation. There was something so unobtrusive in her mien, that she instantly became a favourite with the ladies. The scene was not long, but it was successful.

Flora did not appear in the next scene. In the fourth and final one of the act, she had to make a grand display. It was a love-scene, and rather of an impassioned character; Villebecque was her suitor. He entered first on the stage. Never had he looked so well, or performed with more spirit. You would not have given him five-and-twenty years; he seemed redolent of youth. His dress, too, was admirable. He had studied the most distinguished of his audience for the occasion, and had outdone them all. The fact is, he had been assisted a little by a great connoisseur, a celebrated French nobleman, Count D'O—y, who had been one of the guests. The thing was perfect; and Lord Monmouth took a pinch of snuff, and tapped approbation on the top of his box.

Flora now re-appeared, received with renewed approbation. It did not seem, however, that in the interval she had gained courage; she looked agitated. She spoke, she proceeded with her part; it became impassioned. She had to speak of her feelings; to tell the secrets of her heart; to confess that she loved another; her emotion was exquisitely performed, the mournful tenderness of her tones thrilling. There was, throughout the audience, a dead silence; all were absorbed in their admiration of the unrivalled artist; all felt a new genius had visited the stage; but while they were fascinated by the actress, the woman was in torture. The emotion was the disturbance of her own soul; the mournful tenderness of her tones thrilled from the heart: suddenly she clasped her hands with all the exhaustion of woe; an expression of agony flitted over her countenance; and she burst into tears. Villebecque rushed forward, and carried, rather than led, her from the stage; the audience looking at each other, some of them suspecting that this movement was a part of the scene.

'She has talent,' said Lord Monmouth to the Russian Ambassadress, 'but wants practice. Villebecque should send her for a time to the provinces.'

At length M. Villebecque came forward to express his deep regret that the sudden and severe indisposition of Mlle. Flora rendered it impossible for the company to proceed with the piece; but that the curtain would descend to rise again for the second and last piece announced.

All this accordingly took place. The experienced performer who acted the heroines now came forward and disported most jocundly. The failure of Flora had given fresh animation to her perpetual liveliness. She seemed the very soul of elegant frolic. In the last scene she figured in male attire; and in air, fashion, and youth, beat Villebecque out of the field. She looked younger than Coningsby when he went up to his grandpapa.

The comedy was over, the curtain fell; the audience, much amused, chattered brilliant criticism, and quitted the theatre to repair to the saloon, where they were to be diverted to-night with Russian dances. Nobody thought of the unhappy Flora; not a single message to console her in her grief, to compliment her on what she had done, to encourage her future. And yet it was a season for a word of kindness; so, at least, thought one of the audience, as he lingered behind the hurrying crowd, absorbed in their coming amusements.

Coningsby had sat very near the stage; he had observed, with great advantage and attention, the countenance and movements of Flora from the beginning. He was fully persuaded that her woe was genuine and profound. He had felt his eyes moist when she wept. He recoiled from the cruelty and the callousness that, without the slightest symptom of sympathy, could leave a young girl who had been labouring for their amusement, and who was suffering for her trial.

He got on the stage, ran behind the scenes, and asked for Mlle Flora. They pointed to a door; he requested permission to enter. Flora was sitting at a table, with her face resting on her hands. Villebecque was there, resting on the edge of the tall fender, and still in the dress in which he had performed in the last piece.

'I took the liberty,' said Coningsby, 'of inquiring after Mlle Flora;' and then advancing to her, who had raised her head, he added, 'I am sure my grandfather must feel much indebted to you, Mademoiselle, for making such exertions when you were suffering under so much indisposition.'

'This is very amiable of you, sir,' said the young lady, looking at him with earnestness.

'Mademoiselle has too much sensibility,' said Villebecque, making an observation by way of diversion.

'And yet that must be the soul of fine acting,' said Coningsby; 'I look forward, all look forward, with great interest to the next occasion on which you will favour us.'

'Never!' said La Petite, in a plaintive tone; 'oh, I hope, never!'

'Mademoiselle is not aware at this moment,' said Coningsby, 'how much her talent is appreciated. I assure you, sir,' he added, turning to Villebecque, 'I heard but one opinion, but one expression of gratification at her feeling and her fine taste.'

'The talent is hereditary,' said Villebecque.

'Indeed you have reason to say so,' said Coningsby.

'Pardon; I was not thinking of myself. My child reminded me so much of another this evening. But that is nothing. I am glad you are here, sir, to reassure Mademoiselle.'

'I came only to congratulate her, and to lament, for our sakes as well as her own, her indisposition.'

'It is not indisposition,' said La Petite, in a low tone, with her eyes cast down.

'Mademoiselle cannot overcome the nervousness incidental to a first appearance,' said Villebecque.

'A last appearance,' said La Petite; 'yes, it must be the last.' She rose gently, she approached Villebecque, she laid her head on his breast, and placed her arms round his neck, 'My father, my best father, yes, say it is the last.'

'You are the mistress of your lot, Flora,' said Villebecque; 'but with such a distinguished talent –'

'No, no, no; no talent. You are wrong my father. I know myself. I am not of those to whom nature gives talents. I am born only for still life. I have no taste except for privacy. The convent is more suited to me than the stage.'

'But you hear what this gentleman says,' said Villebecque, returning her embrace. 'He tells you that his grandfather, my Lord Marquess, I believe, sir, that every one, that –'

'Oh, no, no, no!' said Flora, shaking her head. 'He comes here because he is generous, because he is a gentleman; and he wished to soothe the soul that he knew was suffering. Thank him, my father, thank him for me and before me, and promise in his presence that the stage and your daughter have parted for ever.'

'Nay, Mademoiselle,' said Coningsby, advancing and venturing to take her hand, a soft hand, 'make no such resolutions to-night. M. Villebecque can have no other thought or object but your happiness; and, believe me, 'tis not I only, but all, who appreciate, and, if they were here, must respect you.'

'I prefer respect to admiration,' said Flora; 'but I fear that respect is not the appanage of such as I am.'

'All must respect those who respect themselves,' said Coningsby. 'Adieu, Mademoiselle; I trust to-morrow to hear that you are yourself.' He bowed to Villebecque and retired.

In the meantime affairs in the drawing-room assumed a very different character from those behind the scenes. Coningsby returned to brilliancy, groups apparently gushing with light-heartedness, universal content, and Russian dances!

'And you too, do you dance the Russian dances, Mr Coningsby?' said Madame Colonna.

'I cannot dance at all,' said Coningsby, beginning a little to lose his pride in the want of an accomplishment which at Eton he had thought it spirited to despise.

'Ah! you cannot dance the Russian dances! Lucretia shall teach you,' said the Princess; 'nothing will please her so much.'

On the present occasion the ladies were not so experienced in the entertainment as the gentlemen; but there was amusement in being instructed. To be disciplined by a Grand-duke or a Russian Princess was all very well; but what even the good-tempered Lady Gaythorpe could not pardon was, that a certain Mrs Guy Flouncey, whom they were all of them trying to put down and to keep down, on this, as almost on every other occasion, proved herself a more finished performer than even the Russians themselves.

Lord Monmouth had picked up the Guy Flounceys during a Roman winter. They were people of some position in society. Mr Guy Flouncey was a man of good estate, a sportsman, proud of his pretty wife. Mrs Guy Flouncey was even very pretty, dressed in a style of ultra fashion. However, she could sing, dance, act, ride, and talk, and all well; and was mistress of the art of flirtation. She had amused the Marquess abroad, and had taken care to call at Monmouth House the instant the *Morning Post* apprised her he had arrived in England; the consequence was an invitation to Coningsby. She came with a wardrobe which, in point of variety, fancy, and fashion, never was surpassed. Morning and evening, every day a new dress equally striking; and a riding habit that was the talk and wonder of the whole neighbourhood. Mrs Guy Flouncey created far more sensation in the borough when she rode down the High Street, than what the good people called the real Princesses.

At first the fine ladies never noticed her, or only stared at her over their shoulders; everywhere sounded, in suppressed whispers, the fatal question, 'Who is she?' After dinner they formed always into polite groups, from which Mrs Guy Flouncey was invariably excluded; and if ever the Princess Colonna, impelled partly by goodnature, and partly from having known her on the Continent, did kindly sit by her, Lady St Julians, or some dame equally benevolent, was sure, by an adroit appeal to Her Highness on some point which could not be decided without moving, to withdraw her from her pretty and persecuted companion.

It was, indeed, rather difficult work the first few days for Mrs Guy Flouncey, especially immediately after dinner. It is not soothing to one's self-love to find oneself sitting alone, pretending to look at prints, in a fine drawing-room, full of fine people who don't speak to you. But Mrs Guy Flouncey, after having taken Coningsby Castle by storm, was not to be driven out of its drawing-room by the tactics even of a Lady St Julians. Experience convinced her that all that was required was a little patience. Mrs Guy had confidence in herself, her quickness, her ever ready accomplishments, and her practised powers of attraction. And she was right. She was always sure of an ally the moment the gentlemen appeared. The cavalier who had sat next to her at dinner was only too happy to meet her again. More than once, too, she had caught her noble host, though a whole garrison was ever on the watch to prevent her, and he was greatly amused, and showed that he was greatly amused by her society. Then she suggested plans to him to divert his guests. In a country-house the suggestive mind is inestimable. Somehow or other, before a week was passed, Mrs Guy Flouncey seemed the soul of everything, was always surrounded by a cluster of admirers, and with what are called 'the best men' ever ready to ride with her, dance with her, act with her, or fall at her feet. The fine ladies found it absolutely necessary to thaw: they began to ask her questions after dinner. Mrs Guy Flouncey only wanted an opening. She was an adroit flatterer, with a temper imperturbable, and gifted with a ceaseless energy of conferring slight obligations. She lent them patterns for new fashions, in all which mysteries she was very versant; and what with some gentle glozing and some gay gossip, sugar for their tongues and salt for their tails, she contrived pretty well to catch them all.

Chapter 9

NOTHING could present a greater contrast than the respective interiors of Coningsby and Beaumanoir. That air of habitual habitation, which so pleasingly distinguished the Duke's family seat, was entirely wanting at Coningsby. Everything, indeed, was vast and splendid; but it seemed rather a gala-house than a dwelling; as if the grand furniture and the grand servants had all come down express from town with the grand company, and were to disappear and to be dispersed at the same time. And truly there were manifold traces of hasty and temporary arrangement; new carpets and old hangings; old paint, new gilding; battalions of odd French chairs, squadrons of queer English tables; and large tasteless lamps and tawdry chandeliers, evidently true cockneys, and only taking the air by way of change. There was, too, throughout the drawing-rooms an absence of all those minor articles of ornamental furniture that are the offering of taste to the home we love. There were no books neither; few flowers; no pet animals; no portfolios of fine drawings by our English artists like the album of the Duchess, full of sketches by Landseer and Stanfield, and their gifted brethren; not a print even, except portfolios of H.B.'s caricatures. The modes and manners of the house were not rural; there was nothing of the sweet order of a country life. Nobody came down to breakfast; the ladies were scarcely seen until dinner-time; they rolled about in carriages together late in the afternoon as if they were in London, or led a sort of factitious boudoir life in their provincial dressing-rooms.

The Marquess sent for Coningsby the morning after his arrival and asked him to breakfast with him in his private rooms. Nothing could be more kind or more agreeable than his grandfather. He appeared to be interested in his grandson's progress, was glad to find Coningsby had distinguished himself at Eton, solemnly adjured him not to neglect his French. A classical education, he said, was a very admirable thing, and one which all gentlemen should

enjoy; but Coningsby would find some day that there were two
educations, one which his position required, and another which
was demanded by the world. 'French, my dear Harry,' he continued, 'is the key to this second education. In a couple of years
or so you will enter the world; it is a different thing to what you
read about. It is a masquerade; a motley, sparkling multitude, in
which you may mark all forms and colours, and listen to all sentiments and opinions; but where all you see and hear has only one
object, plunder. When you get into this crowd you will find that
Greek and Latin are not so much diffused as you imagine. I was
glad to hear you speaking French yesterday. Study your accent.
There are a good many foreigners here with whom you may try
your wing a little; don't talk to any of them too much. Be very
careful of intimacies. All the people here are good acquaintance;
at least pretty well. Now, here,' said the Marquess, taking up a
letter and then throwing it on the table again, 'now here is a man
whom I should like you to know, Sidonia. He will be here in a
few days. Lay yourself out for him if you have the opportunity.
He is a man of rare capacity, and enormously rich. No one knows
the world like Sidonia. I never met his equal; and 'tis so pleasant
to talk with one that can want nothing of you.'

Lord Monmouth had invited Coningsby to take a drive with
him in the afternoon. The Marquess wished to show a part of his
domain to the Ambassadress. Only Lucretia, he said, would be
with them, and there was a place for him. This invitation was
readily accepted by Coningsby, who was not yet sufficiently established in the habits of the house exactly to know how to pass his
morning. His friend and patron, Mr Rigby, was entirely taken up
with the Grand-duke, whom he was accompanying all over the
neighbourhood, in visits to manufactures, many of which Rigby
himself saw for the first time, but all of which he fluently explained to his Imperial Highness. In return for this, he extracted
much information from the Grand-duke on Russian plans and
projects, materials for a 'slashing' article against the Russophobia
that he was preparing, and in which he was to prove that Musco-
vite aggression was an English interest, and entirely to be explained by the want of sea-coast, which drove the Czar, for the
pure purposes of commerce, to the Baltic and the Euxine.

When the hour for the drive arrived, Coningsby found Lucretia, a young girl when he had first seen her only four years back, and still his junior, in that majestic dame who had conceded a superb recognition to him the preceding eve. She really looked older than Madame Colonna; who, very beautiful, very young-looking, and mistress of the real arts of the toilet, those that cannot be detected, was not in the least altered since she first so cordially saluted Coningsby as her dear young friend at Monmouth House.

The day was delightful, the park extensive and picturesque, the Ambassadress sparkling with anecdote, and occasionally, in a low voice, breathing a diplomatic hint to Lord Monmouth, who bowed his graceful consciousness of her distinguished confidence. Coningsby occasionally took advantage of one of those moments, when the conversation ceased to be general, to address Lucretia, who replied in calm, fine smiles, and in affable monosyllables. She indeed generally succeeded in conveying an impression to those she addressed, that she had never seen them before, did not care to see them now, and never wished to see them again. And all this, too, with an air of great courtesy.

They arrived at the brink of a wooded bank; at their feet flowed a fine river, deep and rushing, though not broad; its opposite bank the boundary of a richly-timbered park.

'Ah! this is beautiful!' exclaimed the Ambassadress. 'And is that yours, Lord Monmouth?'

'Not yet,' said the Marquess. 'That is Hellingsley; it is one of the finest places in the county, with a splendid estate; not so considerable as Coningsby, but very great. It belongs to an old, a very old man, without a relative in the world. It is known that the estate will be sold at his death, which may be almost daily expected. Then it is mine. No one can offer for it what I can afford. For it gives me this division of the county, Princess. To possess Hellingsley is one of my objects.' The Marquess spoke with an animation unusual with him, almost with a degree of excitement.

The wind met them as they returned, the breeze blew rather freshly. Lucretia all of a sudden seemed touched with unusual emotion. She was alarmed lest Lord Monmouth should catch cold;

she took a kerchief from her own well-turned throat to tie round his neck. He feebly resisted, evidently much pleased.

The Princess Lucretia was highly accomplished. In the evening, having refused several distinguished guests, but instantly yielding to the request of Lord Monmouth, she sang. It was impossible to conceive a contralto of more thrilling power, or an execution more worthy of the voice. Coningsby, who was not experienced in fine singing, listened as if to a supernatural lay, but all agreed it was of the highest class of nature and of art; and the Grand-duke was in raptures. Lucretia received even his Highness' compliments with a graceful indifference. Indeed, to those who watched her demeanour, it might be remarked that she seemed to yield to none, although all bowed before her.

Madame Colonna, who was always kind to Coningsby, expressed to him her gratification from the party of the morning. It must have been delightful, she assured Coningsby, for Lord Monmouth to have had both Lucretia and his grandson with him; and Lucretia too, she added, must have been so pleased.

Coningsby could not make out why Madame Colonna was always intimating to him that the Princess Lucretia took such great interest in his existence, looked forward with such gratification to his society, remembered with so much pleasure the past, anticipated so much happiness from the future. It appeared to him that he was to Lucretia, if not an object of repugnance, as he sometimes fancied, certainly one only of absolute indifference; but he said nothing. He had already lived long enough to know that it is unwise to wish everything explained.

In the meantime his life was agreeable. Every day, he found, added to his acquaintance. He was never without a companion to ride or shoot with; and of riding Coningsby was very fond. His grandfather, too, was continually giving him goodnatured turns, and making him of consequence in the Castle: so that all the guests were fully impressed with the importance of Lord Monmouth's grandson. Lady St Julians pronounced him distinguished; the Ambassadress thought diplomacy should be his part, as he had a fine person and a clear brain; Madame Colonna spoke of him always as if she took intense interest in his career, and declared that she liked him almost as much as Lucretia did; the

Russians persisted in always styling him 'the young Marquess,' notwithstanding the Ambassador's explanations; Mrs Guy Flouncey made a dashing attack on him; but Coningsby remembered a lesson which Lady Everingham had graciously bestowed on him. He was not to be caught again easily. Besides, Mrs Guy Flouncey laughed a little too much, and talked a little too loud.

As time flew on, there were changes of visitors, chiefly among the single men. At the end of the first week after Coningsby's arrival, Lord Eskdale appeared, bringing with him Lucian Gay; and soon after followed the Marquess of Beaumanoir and Mr Melton. These were all heroes who, in their way, interested the ladies, and whose advent was hailed with general satisfaction. Even Lucretia would relax a little to Lord Eskdale. He was one of her oldest friends, and with a simplicity of manner which amounted almost to plainness, and with rather a cynical nonchalance in his carriage towards men, Lord Eskdale was invariably a favourite with women. To be sure his station was eminent; he was noble, and very rich, and very powerful, and these are qualities which tell as much with the softer as the harsher sex; but there are individuals with all these qualities who are nevertheless unpopular with women. Lord Eskdale was easy, knew the world thoroughly, had no prejudices, and, above all, had a reputation for success. A reputation for success has as much influence with women as a reputation for wealth has with men. Both reputations may be, and often are, unjust; but we see persons daily make good fortunes by them all the same. Lord Eskdale was not an impostor; and though he might not have been so successful a man had he not been Lord Eskdale, still, thrown over by a revolution, he would have lighted on his legs.

The arrival of this nobleman was the occasion of giving a good turn to poor Flora. He went immediately to see his friend Villebecque and his troop. Indeed it was a sort of society which pleased Lord Eskdale more than that which is deemed more refined. He was very sorry about 'La Petite;' but thought that everything would come right in the long run; and told Villebecque that he was glad to hear him well spoken of here, especially by the Marquess, who seemed to take to him. As for Flora, he was entirely against her attempting the stage again, at least for the present, but as she was a good musician, he suggested to the Princess Lucretia one night, that the subordinate aid of Flora might be of service to her, and permit her to favour her friends with some pieces which otherwise she must deny to them. This suggestion was successful; Flora was introduced occasionally, soon often, to their parties in the evening, and her performances were in every respect satisfactory. There was nothing to excite the jealousy of Lucretia either in her style or her person. And yet she sang well enough, and was a quiet, refined, retiring, by no means disagreeable person. She was the companion of Lucretia very often in the morning as well as in the illumined saloon; for the Princess was devoted to the art in which she excelled. This connection on the whole contributed to the happiness of poor Flora. True it was, in the evening she often found herself sitting or standing alone and no one noticing her; she had no dazzling quality to attract men of fashion, who themselves love to worship ever the fashionable. Even their goddesses must be à la mode. But Coningsby never omitted an opportunity to show Flora some kindness under these circumstances. He always came and talked to her, and praised her singing, and would sometimes hand her refreshments and give her his arm if necessary. These slight attentions coming from the grandson of Lord Monmouth were for the world redoubled in their value, though Flora thought only of their essential kindness; all in character with that first visit which dwelt on the poor girl's memory, though it had long ago escaped that of her visitor. For in truth Coningsby had no other impulse for his conduct but kind-heartedness.

Thus we have attempted to give some faint idea how life glided away at the Castle the first fortnight that Coningsby passed there. Perhaps we ought not to omit that Mrs Guy Flouncey, to the infinite disgust of Lady St Julians, who had a daughter with her, successfully entrapped the devoted attentions of the young Marquess of Beaumanoir, who was never very backward if a lady would take trouble enough; while his friend, Mr Melton, whose barren homage Lady St Julians wished her daughter ever particularly to shun, employed all his gaiety, good-humour, frivolity, and fashion in amusing that young lady, and with irresistible effect. For the rest, they continued, though they had only partridges to shoot, to pass the morning without weariness. The weather was fine; the stud numerous; all might be mounted. The Grand-duke and his suite, guided by Mr Rigby, had always some objects to visit, and railroads returned them just in time for the banquet with an appetite which they had earned, and during which Rigby recounted their achievements, and his own opinions.

The dinner was always firstrate; the evening never failed; music, dancing, and the theatre offered great resources independently of the soul-subduing sentiment harshly called flirtation, and which is the spell of a country house. Lord Monmouth was satisfied, for he had scarcely ever felt wearied. All that he required in life was to be amused; perhaps that was not all he required, but it was indispensable. Nor was it wonderful that on the present occasion he obtained his purpose, for there were half a hundred of the brightest eyes and quickest brains ever on the watch or the whirl to secure him distraction. The only circumstance that annoyed him was the non-arrival of Sidonia. Lord Monmouth could not bear to be disappointed. He could not refrain from saying, notwithstanding all the resources and all the exertions of his guests,

'I cannot understand why Sidonia does not come. I wish Sidonia were here.'

'So do I,' said Lord Eskdale; 'Sidonia is the only man who tells one anything new.'

'We saw Sidonia at Lord Studcaster's,' said Lord Beaumanoir. 'He told Melton he was coming here.'

'You know he has bought all Studcaster's horses,' said Mr Melton.

'I wonder he does not buy Studcaster himself,' said Lord Monmouth; 'I would if I were he; Sidonia can buy anything,' he turned to Mrs Guy Flouncey.

'I wonder who Sidonia is,' thought Mrs Guy Flouncey, but she was determined no one should suppose she did not know.

At length one day Coningsby met Madame Colonna in the vestibule before dinner.

'Milor is in such good temper, Mr Coningsby,' she said; 'Monsieur de Sidonia has arrived.'

About ten minutes before dinner there was a stir in the cham-

ber. Coningsby looked round. He saw the Grand-duke advancing,
and holding out his hand in a manner the most gracious. A
gentleman, of distinguished air, but with his back turned to
Coningsby, was bowing as he received his Highness' greeting.
There was a general pause in the room. Several came forward:
even the Marquess seemed a little moved. Coningsby could not
resist the impulse of curiosity to see this individual of whom he
had heard so much. He glided round the room, and caught the
countenance of his companion in the forest inn; he who announced to him, that 'the Age of Ruins was past.'

Chapter 10

SIDONIA was descended from a very ancient and noble family of Arragon, that, in the course of ages, had given to the state many distinguished citizens. In the priesthood its members had been peculiarly eminent. Besides several prelates, they counted among their number an Archbishop of Toledo; and a Sidonia, in a season of great danger and difficulty, had exercised for a series of years the paramount office of Grand Inquisitor.[1]

Yet, strange as it may sound, it is nevertheless a fact, of which there is no lack of evidence, that this illustrious family during all this period, in common with two-thirds of the Arragonese nobility, secretly adhered to the ancient faith and ceremonies of their fathers; a belief in the unity of the God of Sinai, and the rights and observances of the laws of Moses.

Whence came those Mosaic Arabs whose passages across the strait from Africa to Europe long preceded the invasion of the Mohammedan Arabs, it is now impossible to ascertain. Their traditions tell us that from time immemorial they had sojourned in Africa; and it is not improbable that they may have been the descendants of some of the earlier dispersions; like those Hebrew colonies that we find in China, and who probably emigrated from Persia in the days of the great monarchies. Whatever may have been their origin in Africa, their fortunes in Southern Europe are not difficult to trace, though the annals of no race in any age can detail a history of such strange vicissitudes, or one rife with more touching and romantic incident. Their unexampled prosperity in the Spanish Peninsula, and especially in the south, where they had become the principal cultivators of the soil, excited the jealousy of the Goths; and the Councils of Toledo during the sixth and seventh centuries attempted, by a series of decrees worthy of the barbarians who promulgated them, to root the Jewish Arabs out of the land. There is no doubt the Council of Toledo led, as directly as the lust of Roderick, to the invasion of Spain by the

Moslemin Arabs.[2] The Jewish population, suffering under the most sanguinary and atrocious persecution, looked to their sympathising brethren of the Crescent, whose camps already gleamed on the opposite shore. The overthrow of the Gothic kingdoms was as much achieved by the superior information which the Saracens received from their suffering kinsmen, as by the resistless valour of the Desert. The Saracen kingdoms were established. That fair and unrivalled civilisation arose which preserved for Europe arts and letters when Christendom was plunged in darkness. The children of Ishmael rewarded the children of Israel with equal rights and privileges with themselves. During these halcyon centuries, it is difficult to distinguish the follower of Moses from the votary of Mahomet. Both alike built palaces, gardens, and fountains; filled equally the highest offices of the state, competed in an extensive and enlightened commerce, and rivalled each other in renowned universities.

Even after the fall of the principal Moorish kingdoms, the Jews of Spain were still treated by the conquering Goths with tenderness and consideration. Their numbers, their wealth, the fact that, in Arragon especially, they were the proprietors of the soil, and surrounded by warlike and devoted followers, secured for them an usage which, for a considerable period, made them little sensible of the change of dynasties and religions. But the tempest gradually gathered. As the Goths grew stronger, persecution became more bold. Where the Jewish population was scanty they were deprived of their privileges, or obliged to conform under the title of 'Nuevos Christianos.' At length the union of the two crowns under Ferdinand and Isabella, and the fall of the last Moorish kingdom, brought the crisis of their fate both to the New Christian and the nonconforming Hebrew.[3] The Inquisition appeared, the Institution that had exterminated the Albigenses[4] and had desolated Languedoc, and which, it should ever be remembered, was established in the Spanish kingdoms against the protests of the Cortes[5] and amid the terror of the populace. The Dominicans opened their first tribunal at Seville, and it is curious that the first individuals they summoned before them were the Duke of Medina Sidonia, the Marquess of Cadiz, and the Count of Arcos; three of the most considerable personages in Spain. How many were burned alive at Seville during the first year, how many imprisoned for life, what countless thousands were visited with severe though lighter punishments, need not be recorded here. In nothing was the Holy Office more happy than in multiform and subtle means by which they tested the sincerity of the New Christians.

At length the Inquisition was to be extended to Arragon. The high-spirited nobles of that kingdom knew that its institution was for them a matter of life or death. The Cortes of Arragon appealed to the King and to the Pope; they organised an extensive conspiracy; the chief Inquisitor was assassinated in the cathedral of Saragossa. Alas! it was fated that in this, one of the many, and continual, and continuing struggles between the rival organisations of the North and the South, the children of the sun should fall. The fagot and the San Benito[6] were the doom of the nobles of Arragon. Those who were convicted of secret Judaism, and this scarcely three centuries ago, were dragged to the stake; the sons of the noblest houses, in whose veins the Hebrew taint could be traced, had to walk in solemn procession, singing psalms, and confessing their faith in the religion of the fell Torquemada.[7]

This triumph in Arragon, the almost simultaneous fall of the last Moorish kingdom, raised the hopes of the pure Christians to the highest pitch. Having purged the new Christians, they next turned their attention to the old Hebrews. Ferdinand was resolved that the delicious air of Spain should be breathed no longer by any one who did not profess the Catholic faith. Baptism or exile was the alternative. More than six hundred thousand individuals, some authorities greatly increase the amount, the most industrious, the most intelligent, and the most enlightened of Spanish subjects, would not desert the religion of their fathers. For this they gave up the delightful land wherein they had lived for centuries, the beautiful cities they had raised, the universities from which Christendom drew for ages its most precious lore, the tombs of their ancestors, the temples where they had worshipped the God for whom they had made their sacrifice. They had but four months to prepare for eternal exile, after a residence of as many centuries; during which brief period forced sales and glutted markets virtually confiscated their property. It is a calamity that the scattered nation still ranks with the desolations of Nebuchadnezzar and of Titus.[8] Who after this should say the Jews are by nature a sordid people? But the Spanish Goth, then so cruel and so haughty, where is he? A despised suppliant to the very race which he banished, for some miserable portion of the treasure which their habits of industry have again accumulated. Where is that tribunal that summoned Medina Sidonia and Cadiz to its dark inquisition? Where is Spain? Its fall, its unparalleled and its irremediable fall, is mainly to be attributed to the expulsion of the large portion of its subjects, the most industrious and intelligent, who traced their origin to the Mosaic[9] and Mohammedan Arabs.

The Sidonias of Arragon were Nuevos Christianos. Some of them, no doubt, were burned alive at the end of the fifteenth century, under the system of Torquemada; many of them, doubtless, wore the San Benito; but they kept their titles and estates, and in time reached those great offices to which we have referred.

During the long disorders of the Peninsular war, when so many openings were offered to talent, and so many opportunities seized by the adventurous, a cadet of a younger branch of this family made a large fortune by military contracts, and supplying the commissariat of the different armies. At the peace, prescient of the great financial future of Europe, confident in the fertility of his own genius, in his original views of fiscal subjects, and his knowledge of national resources, this Sidonia, feeling that Madrid, or even Cadiz, could never be a base on which the monetary transactions of the world could be regulated, resolved to emigrate to England, with which he had, in the course of years, formed considerable commercial connections. He arrived here after the peace of Paris, with his large capital. He staked all that he was worth on the Waterloo loan;[10] and the event made him one of the greatest capitalists in Europe.

No sooner was Sidonia established in England than he professed Judaism; which Torquemada flattered himself, with the fagot and the San Benito, he had drained out of the veins of his family more than three centuries ago. He sent over, also, for several of his brothers, who were as good Catholics in Spain as Ferdinand and Isabella could have possibly desired, but who made an offering in the synagogue, in gratitude for their safe voyage, on their arrival in England.

Sidonia had foreseen in Spain that, after the exhaustion of a war of twenty-five years, Europe must require capital to carry on peace. He reaped the due reward of his sagacity. Europe did require money, and Sidonia was ready to lend it to Europe. France wanted some; Austria more; Prussia a little; Russia a few millions. Sidonia could furnish them all. The only country which he avoided was Spain; he was too well acquainted with its resources. Nothing, too, would ever tempt him to lend anything to the revolted colonies of Spain.[11] Prudence saved him from being a creditor of the mother-country; his Spanish pride recoiled from the rebellion of her children.

It is not difficult to conceive that, after having pursued the career we have intimated for about ten years, Sidonia had become one of the most considerable personages in Europe. He had established a brother, or a near relative, in whom he could confide, in most of the principal capitals. He was lord and master of the money-market of the world, and of course virtually lord and master of everything else. He literally held the revenues of Southern Italy in pawn; and monarchs and ministers of all countries courted his advice and were guided by his suggestions. He was still in the vigour of life, and was not a mere money-making machine. He had a general intelligence equal to his position, and looked forward to the period when some relaxation from his vast enterprises and exertions might enable him to direct his energies to great objects of public benefit. But in the height of his vast prosperity he suddenly died, leaving only one child, a youth still of tender years, and heir to the greatest fortune in Europe, so great, indeed, that it could only be calculated by millions.

Shut out from universities and schools, those universities and schools which were indebted for their first knowledge of ancient philosophy to the learning and enterprise of his ancestors, the young Sidonia was fortunate in the tutor whom his father had procured for him, and who devoted to his charge all the resources of his trained intellect and vast and various erudition. A Jesuit before the revolution;[12] since then an exiled Liberal leader; now a member of the Spanish Cortes; Rebello was always a Jew. He found in his pupil that precocity of intellectual development which is characteristic of the Arabian organisation. The young Sidonia penetrated the highest mysteries of mathematics with a facility almost instinctive; while a memory, which never had any twilight hours, but always reflected a noontide clearness, seemed to magnify his acquisitions of ancient learning by the promptness with which they could be reproduced and applied.

The circumstances of his position, too, had early contributed to give him an unusual command over the modern languages. An Englishman, and taught from his cradle to be proud of being an Englishman, he first evinced in speaking his native language those remarkable powers of expression, and that clear and happy elocution, which ever afterwards distinguished him. But the son of a Spaniard, the sonorous syllables of that noble tongue constantly resounded in his ear; while the foreign guests who thronged his father's mansion habituated him from an early period of life to the tones of languages that were not long strange to him. When he was nineteen, Sidonia, who had then resided some time with his uncle at Naples, and had made a long visit to another of his father's relatives at Frankfort, possessed a complete mastery over the principal European languages.

At seventeen he had parted with Rebello, who returned to Spain, and Sidonia, under the control of his guardians, commenced his travels. He resided, as we have mentioned, some time in Germany, and then, having visited Italy, settled at Naples, at which city it may be said he made his entrance into life. With an interesting person, and highly accomplished, he availed himself of the gracious attentions of a court of which he was principal creditor; and which, treating him as a distinguished English traveller, were enabled perhaps to show him some favours that the manners of the country might not have permitted them to accord to his Neapolitan relatives. Sidonia thus obtained at an early age that experience of refined and luxurious society, which is a necessary part of a finished education. It gives the last polish to the manners; it teaches us something of the power of the passions, early developed in the hot-bed of self-indulgence; it instils into us that indefinable tact seldom obtained in later life, which prevents us from saying the wrong thing, and often impels us to do the right.

Between Paris and Naples Sidonia passed two years, spent apparently in the dissipation which was perhaps inseparable from his time of life. He was admired by women, to whom he was magnificent, idolised by artists whom he patronised, received in all circles with great distinction, and appreciated for his intellect by the very few to whom he at all opened himself. For, though affable and gracious, it was impossible to penetrate him. Though unreserved in his manner, his frankness was strictly limited to the surface. He observed everything, thought ever, but avoided serious discussion. If you pressed him for an opinion, he took refuge in raillery, or threw out some grave paradox with which it was not easy to cope.

The moment he came of age, Sidonia, having previously, at a great family congress held at Naples, made arrangements with the heads of the houses that bore his name respecting the disposition and management of his vast fortune, quitted Europe.

Sidonia was absent from his connections for five years, during which period he never communicated with them. They were aware of his existence only by the orders which he drew on them for payment, and which arrived from all quarters of the globe. It would appear from these documents that he had dwelt a considerable time in the Mediterranean regions; penetrated Nilotic Africa to Sennaar and Abyssinia; traversed the Asiatic continent to Tartary, whence he had visited Hindostan, and the isles of that Indian Sea which are so little known. Afterwards he was heard of at Valparaiso,[13] the Brazils, and Lima. He evidently remained some time at Mexico, which he quitted for the United States. One morning, without notice, he arrived in London.

Sidonia had exhausted all the sources of human knowledge; he was master of the learning of every nation, of all tongues dead or living, of every literature, Western and Oriental. He had pursued the speculations of science to their last term, and had himself illustrated them by observation and experiment. He had lived in all orders of society, had viewed every combination of Nature and of Art, and had observed man under every phasis of civilisation.

He had even studied him in the wilderness. The influence of creeds and laws, manners, customs, traditions, in all their diversities, had been subjected to his personal scrutiny.

He brought to the study of this vast aggregate of knowledge a penetrative intellect that, matured by long meditation, and assisted by that absolute freedom from prejudice, which was the compensatory possession of a man without a country, permitted Sidonia to fathom, as it were by intuition, the depth of questions apparently the most difficult and profound. He possessed the rare faculty of communicating with precision ideas the most abstruse, and in general a power of expression which arrests and satisfies attention.

With all this knowledge, which no one knew more to prize, with boundless wealth, and with an athletic frame, which sickness had never tried, and which had avoided excess, Sidonia nevertheless looked upon life with a glance rather of curiosity than content. His religion walled him out from the pursuits of a citizen; his riches deprived him of the stimulating anxieties of a man. He perceived himself a lone being, alike without cares and without duties.

To a man in his position there might yet seem one unfailing source of felicity and joy; independent of creed, independent of country, independent even of character. He might have discovered that perpetual spring of happiness in the sensibility of the heart. But this was a sealed fountain to Sidonia. In his organisation there was a peculiarity, perhaps a great deficiency. He was a man without affections. It would be harsh to say he had no heart, for he was susceptible of deep emotions, but not for individuals. He was capable of rebuilding a town that was burned down; of restoring a colony that had been destroyed by some awful visitation of Nature; of redeeming to liberty a horde of captives; and of doing these great acts in secret; for, void of all self-love, public approbation was worthless to him; but the individual never touched him. Woman was to him a toy, man a machine.

The lot the most precious to man, and which a beneficent Providence has made not the least common; to find in another heart a perfect and profound sympathy; to unite his existence with one who could share all his joys, soften all his sorrows, aid him in all his projects, respond to all his fancies, counsel him in his cares, and support him in his perils; make life charming by her charms, interesting by her intelligence, and sweet by the vigilant variety of her tenderness; to find your life blessed by such an influence, and to feel that your influence can bless such a life: this lot, the most divine of divine gifts, that power and even fame can never rival in its delights, all this Nature had denied to Sidonia.

With an imagination as fiery as his native Desert, and an intellect as luminous as his native sky, he wanted, like that land, those softening dews without which the soil is barren, and the sunbeam as often a messenger of pestilence as an angel of regenerative grace.

Such a temperament, though rare, is peculiar to the East. It inspired the founders of the great monarchies of antiquity, the prophets that the Desert had sent forth, the Tartar chiefs who have overrun the world; it might be observed in the great Corsican, who, like most of the inhabitants of the Mediterranean isles, had probably Arab blood in his veins. It is a temperament that befits conquerors and legislators, but, in ordinary times and ordinary situations, entails on its possessor only eccentric aberrations or profound melancholy.

The only human quality that interested Sidonia was Intellect. He cared not whence it came; where it was to be found: creed, country, class, character, in this respect, were alike indifferent to him. The author, the artist, the man of science, never appealed to him in vain. Often he anticipated their wants and wishes. He encouraged their society; was as frank in his conversation as he was generous in his contributions; but the instant they ceased to be authors, artists, or philosophers, and their communications arose from anything but the intellectual quality which had originally interested him, the moment they were rash enough to approach intimacy and appealed to the sympathising man, instead of the congenial intelligence, he saw them no more. It was not however intellect merely in these unquestionable shapes that commanded his notice. There was not an adventurer in Europe with whom he was not familiar. No Minister of State had

such communication with secret agents and political spies as
Sidonia. He held relations with all the clever outcasts of the world.
The catalogue of his acquaintance in the shape of Greeks,
Armenians, Moors, secret Jews, Tartars, Gipsies, wandering Poles
and Carbonari,[14] would throw a curious light on those subterranean agencies of which the world in general knows so little,
but which exercise so great an influence on public events. His
extensive travels, his knowledge of languages, his daring and adventurous disposition, and his unlimited means, had given him
opportunities of becoming acquainted with these characters, in
general so difficult to trace, and of gaining their devotion. To these
sources he owed that knowledge of strange and hidden things
which often startled those who listened to him. Nor was it easy,
scarcely possible, to deceive him. Information reached him from
so many, and such contrary quarters, that with his discrimination
and experience, he could almost instantly distinguish the truth.
The secret history of the world was his pastime. His great pleasure
was to contrast the hidden motive, with the public pretext, of
transactions.

One source of interest Sidonia found in his descent and in the
fortunes of his race. As firm in his adherence to the code of the
great Legislator as if the trumpet still sounded on Sinai, he might
have received in the conviction of divine favour an adequate compensation for human persecution. But there were other and more
terrestrial considerations that made Sidonia proud of his origin,
and confident in the future of his kind. Sidonia was a great
philosopher, who took comprehensive views of human affairs, and
surveyed every fact in its relative position to other facts, the only
mode of obtaining truth.

Sidonia was well aware that in the five great varieties into
which Physiology has divided the human species; to wit, the
Caucasian, the Mongolian, the Malayan, the American, the
Ethiopian; the Arabian tribes rank in the first and superior class,
together, among others, with the Saxon and the Greek. This fact
alone is a source of great pride and satisfaction to the animal
Man. But Sidonia and his brethren could claim a distinction which
the Saxon and the Greek, and the rest of the Caucasian nations,
have forfeited. The Hebrew is an unmixed race. Doubtless, among

the tribes who inhabit the bosom of the Desert, progenitors alike of the Mosaic and the Mohammedan Arabs, blood may be found as pure as that of the descendants of the Scheik Abraham. But the Mosaic Arabs are the most ancient, if not the only, unmixed blood that dwells in cities.

An unmixed race of a firstrate organisation are the aristocracy of Nature. Such excellence is a positive fact; not an imagination, a ceremony, coined by poets, blazoned by cozening heralds, but perceptible in its physical advantages, and in the vigour of its unsullied idiosyncrasy.

In his comprehensive travels, Sidonia had visited and examined the Hebrew communities of the world. He had found, in general, the lower orders debased; the superior immersed in sordid pursuits; but he perceived that the intellectual development was not impaired. This gave him hope. He was persuaded that organisation would outlive persecution. When he reflected on what they had endured, it was only marvellous that the race had not disappeared. They had defied exile, massacre, spoliation, the degrading influence of the constant pursuit of gain; they had defied Time. For nearly three thousand years, according to Archbishop Usher,[15] they have been dispersed over the globe. To the unpolluted current of their Caucasian structure, and to the segregating genius of their great Lawgiver, Sidonia ascribed the fact that they had not been long ago absorbed among those mixed races, who presume to persecute them, but who periodically wear away and disappear, while their victims still flourish in all the primeval vigour of the pure Asian breed.

Shortly after his arrival in England, Sidonia repaired to the principal Courts of Europe, that he might become personally acquainted with the monarchs and ministers of whom he had heard so much. His position insured him a distinguished reception; his personal qualities immediately made him cherished. He could please; he could do more, he could astonish. He could throw out a careless observation which would make the oldest diplomatist start; a winged word that gained him the consideration, sometimes the confidence, of Sovereigns. When he had fathomed the intelligence which governs Europe, and which can only be done by personal acquaintance, he returned to this country.

The somewhat hard and literal character of English life suited one who shrank from sensibility, and often took refuge in sarcasm. Its masculine vigour and active intelligence occupied and interested his mind. Sidonia, indeed, was exactly the character who would be welcomed in our circles. His immense wealth, his unrivalled social knowledge, his clear vigorous intellect, the severe simplicity of his manners, frank, but neither claiming nor brooking familiarity, and his devotion to field-sports, which was the safety-valve of his energy, were all circumstances and qualities which the English appreciate and admire; and it may be fairly said of Sidonia that few men were more popular, and none less understood.

Chapter 11

AT dinner, Coningsby was seated on the same side as Sidonia, and distant from him. There had been, therefore, no mutual recognition. Another guest had also arrived, Mr Ormsby. He came straight from London, full of rumours, had seen Tadpole, who, hearing he was on the wing for Coningsby Castle, had taken him into a dark corner of a club, and shown him his book, a safe piece of confidence, as Mr Ormsby was very near-sighted. It was, however, to be received as an undoubted fact, that all was right, and somehow or other, before very long, there would be national demonstration of the same. This arrival of Mr Ormsby, and the news that he bore, gave a political turn to the conversation after the ladies had left the room.

'Tadpole wants me to stand for Birmingham,' said Mr Ormsby, gravely.

'You!' exclaimed Lord Monmouth, and, throwing himself back in his chair, he broke into a real, hearty laugh.

'Yes; the Conservatives mean to start two candidates; a manufacturer they have got, and they have written up to Tadpole for a "West-end man." '

'A what?'

'A West-end man, who will make the ladies patronise their fancy articles.'

'The result of the Reform Bill, then,' said Lucian Gay, 'will be to give Manchester a bishop, and Birmingham a dandy.'

'I begin to believe the result will be very different from what we expected,' said Lord Monmouth.

Mr Rigby shook his head and was going to prophesy, when Lord Eskdale, who liked talk to be short, and was of opinion that Rigby should keep his amplifications for his slashing articles, put in a brief careless observation, which balked his inspiration.

'Certainly,' said Mr Ormsby, 'when the guns were firing over

Vyvyan's last speech and confession,[1] I never expected to be asked to stand for Birmingham.'

'Perhaps you may be called up to the other house by the title,' said Lucian Gay. 'Who knows?'

'I agree with Tadpole,' said Mr Ormsby, 'that if we only stick to the Registration the country is saved.'

'Fortunate country!' said Sidonia, 'that can be saved by a good registration!'

'I believe, after all, that with property and pluck,' said Lord Monmouth, 'Parliamentary Reform is not such a very bad thing.'

Here several gentlemen began talking at the same time, all agreeing with their host, and proving in their different ways, the irresistible influence of property and pluck; property in Lord Monmouth's mind meaning vassals, and pluck a total disregard for public opinion. Mr Guy Flouncey, who wanted to get into parliament, but why nobody knew, who had neither political abilities nor political opinions, but had some floating idea that it would get himself and his wife to some more balls and dinners, and who was duly ticketed for 'a good thing' in the candidate list of the Tadpoles and the Tapers, was of opinion that an immense deal might be done by properly patronising borough races. That was his specific how to prevent revolution.

Taking advantage of a pause, Lord Monmouth said, 'I should like to know what you think of this question, Sidonia?'

'I am scarcely a competent judge,' he said, as if wishing to disclaim any interference in the conversation, and then added, 'but I have been ever of opinion that revolutions are not to be evaded.'

'Exactly my views,' said Mr Rigby, eagerly; 'I say it now, I have said it a thousand times, you may doctor the registration as you like, but you can never get rid of Schedule A.'

'Is there a person in this room who can now tell us the names of the boroughs in Schedule A?' said Sidonia.

'I am sure I cannot,' said Lord Monmouth, 'though six of them belonged to myself.'

'But the principle,' said Mr Rigby; 'they represented a principle.'

'Nothing else, certainly,' said Lucian Gay.

'And what principle?' inquired Sidonia.

'The principle of nomination.'

'That is a practice, not a principle,' said Sidonia. 'Is it a practice that no longer exists?'

'You think then,' said Lord Eskdale, cutting in before Rigby, 'that the Reform Bill has done us no harm?'

'It is not the Reform Bill that has shaken the aristocracy of this country, but the means by which that Bill was carried,' replied Sidonia.

'Physical force?' said Lord Eskdale.

'Or social power?' said Sidonia.

Upon this, Mr Rigby, impatient at any one giving the tone in a political discussion but himself, and chafing under the vigilance of Lord Eskdale, which to him ever appeared only fortuitous, violently assaulted the argument, and astonished several country gentlemen present by his volubility. They at length listened to real eloquence. At the end of a long appeal to Sidonia, that gentleman only bowed his head and said, 'Perhaps;' and then, turning to his neighbour, inquired whether birds were plentiful in Lancashire this season; so that Mr Rigby was reduced to the necessity of forming the political opinions of Mr Guy Flouncey.

As the gentlemen left the dining-room, Coningsby, though at some distance, was observed by Sidonia, who stopped instantly, then advanced to Coningsby, and extending his hand said, 'I said we should meet again, though I hardly expected so quickly.'

'And I hope we shall not separate so soon,' said Coningsby; 'I was much struck with what you said just now about the Reform Bill. Do you know that the more I think the more I am perplexed by what is meant by Representation?'

'It is a principle of which a limited definition is only current in this country,' said Sidonia, quitting the room with him. 'People may be represented without periodical elections of neighbours who are incapable to maintain their interests, and strangers who are unwilling.'

The entrance of the gentlemen produced the same effect on the saloon as sunrise on the world; universal animation, a general though gentle stir. The Grand-duke, bowing to every one, devoted himself to the daughter of Lady St Julians, who herself pinned Lord Beaumanoir before he could reach Mrs Guy Flouncey. Con-

ingsby instead talked nonsense to that lady. Brilliant cavaliers,
including Mr Melton, addressed a band of beautiful damsels
grouped on a large ottoman. Everywhere sounded a delicious
murmur, broken occasionally by a silver-sounding laugh not too
loud. Sidonia and Lord Eskdale did not join the ladies. They stood
for a few moments in conversation, and then threw themselves
on a sofa.

'Who is that?' asked Sidonia of his companion rather earnestly,
as Coningsby quitted them.

' 'Tis the grandson of Monmouth; young Coningsby.'

'Ah! The new generation then promises. I met him once before,
by chance; he interests me.'

'They tell me he is a lively lad. He is a prodigious favourite here,
and I should not be surprised if Monmouth made him his heir.'

'I hope he does not dream of inheritance,' said Sidonia. ' 'Tis
the most enervating of visions.'

'Do you admire Lady Augustina St Julians?' said Mrs Guy
Flouncey to Coningsby.

'I admire no one except yourself.'

'Oh! how very gallant, Mr Coningsby!'

'When should men be gallant, if not to the brilliant and the
beautiful!' said Coningsby.

'Ah! you are laughing at me.'

'No, I am not. I am quite grave.'

'Your eyes laugh. Now tell me, Mr Coningsby, Lord Henry
Sydney is a very great friend of yours?'

'Very.'

'He is very amiable.'

'Very.'

'He does a great deal for the poor at Beaumanoir. A very fine
place, is it not?'

'Very.'

'As fine as Coningsby?'

'At present, with Mrs Guy Flouncey at Coningsby, Beaumanoir
would have no chance.'

'Ah! you laugh at me again! Now tell me, Mr Coningsby, what
do you think we shall do to-night? I look upon you, you know,
as the real arbiter of our destinies.'

'You shall decide,' said Coningsby.

'Mon cher Harry,' said Madame Colonna, coming up, 'they wish Lucretia to sing and she will not. You must ask her, she cannot refuse you.'

'I assure you she can,' said Coningsby.

'Mon cher Harry, your grandpapa did desire me to beg you to ask her to sing.'

So Coningsby unwillingly approached Lucretia, who was talking with the Russian Ambassador.

'I am sent upon a fruitless mission,' said Coningsby, looking at her, and catching her glance.

'What, and why?' she replied.

'The mission is to entreat you to do us all a great favour; and the cause of its failure will be that I am the envoy.'

'If the favour be one to yourself, it is granted; and if you be the envoy, you need never fear failure with me.'

'I must presume then to lead you away,' said Coningsby, bending to the Ambassador.

'Remember,' said Lucretia, as they approached the instrument, 'that I am singing to you.'

'It is impossible ever to forget it,' said Coningsby, leading her to the piano with great politeness, but only with great politeness.

'Where is Mademoiselle Flora?' she inquired.

Coningsby found La Petite crouching as it were behind some furniture, and apparently looking over some music. She looked up as he approached, and a smile stole over her countenance. 'I am come to ask a favour,' he said, and he named his request.

'I will sing,' she replied; 'but only tell me what you like.'

Coningsby felt the difference between the courtesy of the head and of the heart, as he contrasted the manner of Lucretia and Flora. Nothing could be more exquisitely gracious than the daughter of Colonna was to-night; Flora, on the contrary, was rather agitated and embarrassed; and did not express her readiness with half the facility and the grace of Lucretia; but Flora's arm trembled as Coningsby led her to the piano.

Meantime Lord Eskdale and Sidonia are in deep converse.

'Hah! that is a fine note!' said Sidonia, and he looked round. 'Who is that singing? Some new *protégée* of Lord Monmouth?'

' 'Tis the daughter of the Colonnas,' said Lord Eskdale, 'the Princess Lucretia.'

'Why, she was not at dinner to-day.'

'No, she was not there.'

'My favourite voice; and of all, the rarest to be found. When I was a boy, it made me almost in love even with Pisaroni.'

'Well, the Princess is scarcely more lovely. 'Tis a pity the plumage is not as beautiful as the note. She is plain.'

'No; not plain with that brow.'

'Well, I rather admire her myself,' said Lord Eskdale. 'She has fine points.'

'Let us approach,' said Sidonia.

The song ceased, Lord Eskdale advanced, made his compliments, and then said, 'You were not at dinner to-day.'

'Why should I be?' said the Princess.

'For our sakes, for mine, if not for your own,' said Lord Eskdale, smiling. 'Your absence has been remarked, and felt, I assure you, by others as well as myself. There is my friend Sidonia so enraptured with your thrilling tones, that he has abruptly closed a conversation which I have been long counting on. Do you know him? May I present him to you?'

And having obtained a consent, not often conceded, Lord Eskdale looked round, and calling Sidonia, he presented his friend to the Princess.

'You are fond of music, Lord Eskdale tells me?' said Lucretia.

'When it is excellent,' said Sidonia.

'But that is so rare,' said the Princess.

'And precious as Paradise,' said Sidonia. 'As for indifferent music, 'tis Purgatory; but when it is bad, for my part I feel myself –'

'Where?' said Lord Eskdale.

'In the last circle of the Inferno,' said Sidonia.

Lord Eskdale turned to Flora.

'And in what circle do you place us who are here?' the Princess inquired of Sidonia.

'One too polished for his verse,' replied her companion.

'You mean too insipid,' said the Princess. 'I wish that life were a little more Dantesque.'

'There is not less treasure in the world,' said Sidonia, 'because we use paper currency; and there is not less passion than of old, though it is *bon ton* to be tranquil.'

'Do you think so?' said the Princess, inquiringly, and then looking round the apartment, 'Have these automata, indeed, souls?'

'Some of them,' said Sidonia. 'As many as would have had souls in the fourteenth century.'

'I thought they were wound up every day,' said the Princess.

'Some are self-impelling,' said Sidonia.

'And you can tell at a glance?' inquired the Princess. 'You are one of those who can read human nature?'

' 'Tis a book open to all.'

'But if they cannot read?'

'Those must be your automata.'

'Lord Monmouth tells me you are a great traveller?'

'I have not discovered a new world.'

'But you have visited it?'

'It is getting old.'

'I would sooner recall the old than discover the new,' said the Princess.

'We have both of us cause,' said Sidonia. 'Our names are the names of the Past.'

'I do not love a world of Utility,' said the Princess.

'You prefer to be celebrated to being comfortable,' said Sidonia.

'It seems to me that the world is withering under routine.'

' 'Tis the inevitable lot of humanity,' said Sidonia. 'Man must ever be the slave of routine: but in old days it was a routine of great thoughts, and now it is a routine of little ones.'

The evening glided on; the dance succeeded the song; the ladies were fast vanishing; Coningsby himself was meditating a move-ment, when Lord Beaumanoir, as he passed him, said, 'Come to Lucian Gay's room; we are going to smoke a cigar.'

This was a favourite haunt, towards midnight, of several of the younger members of the party at the Castle, who loved to find relaxation from the decorous gravities of polished life in the fumes of tobacco, the inspiration of whiskey toddy, and the infinite amusement of Lucian Gay's conversation and company. This was the genial hour when the good story gladdened, the pun flashed, and the song sparkled with jolly mirth or saucy mimicry. To-night, being Coningsby's initiation, there was a special general meeting of the Grumpy Club, in which everybody was to say the gayest things with the gravest face, and every laugh carried a forfeit. Lucian was the inimitable president. He told a tale for which he was famous, of 'the very respectable county family who had been established in the shire for several generations, but who, it was a fact, had been ever distinguished by the strange and humiliating peculiarity of being born with sheep's tails.' The remarkable circumstances under which Lucian Gay had become acquainted with this fact; the traditionary mysteries by which the family in question had succeeded for generations in keeping it secret; the decided measures to which the chief of the family had recourse to stop for ever the rumour when it first became preva-lent; and finally the origin and result of the legend; were details which Lucian Gay, with the most rueful countenance, loved to expend upon the attentive and expanding intelligence of a new member of the Grumpy Club. Familiar as all present were with the story whose stimulus of agonising risibility they had all in turn experienced, it was with extreme difficulty that any of them could resist the fatal explosion which was to be attended with the dreaded penalty. Lord Beaumanoir looked on the table with desperate seriousness, an ominous pucker quivering round his lip; Mr Melton crammed his handkerchief into his mouth with one hand, while he lighted the wrong end of a cigar with the other; one youth hung over the back of his chair pinching himself like a faquir, while another hid his countenance on the table.

'It was at the Hunt dinner,' continued Lucian Gay, in an almost solemn tone, 'that an idea for a moment was prevalent, that Sir Mowbray Cholmondeley Fetherstonehaugh, as the head of the family, had resolved to terminate for ever these mysterious asper-sions on his race, that had circulated in the county for more than two centuries; I mean that the highly respectable family of the Cholmondeley Fetherstonehaughs had the misfortune to be graced with that appendage to which I have referred. His health being drunk, Sir Mowbray Cholmondeley Fetherstonehaugh rose. He was a little unpopular at the moment, from an ugly story about killing foxes, and the guests were not as quiet as orators generally desire, so the Honourable Baronet prayed particular attention to a matter personal to himself. Instantly there was a dead silence –' but here Coningsby, who had moved for some time very restlessly on his chair, suddenly started up, and struggling for a moment against the inward convulsion, but in vain, stamped against the floor, and gave a shout.

'A song from Mr Coningsby,' said the president of the Grumpy Club, amid an universal, and now permissible roar of laughter.

Coningsby could not sing; so he was to favour them as a substitute with a speech or a sentiment. But Lucian Gay always let one off these penalties easily, and, indeed, was ever ready to fulfil them for all. Song, speech, or sentiment, he poured them all forth; nor were pastimes more active wanting. He could dance a Tarantalla like a Lazzarone, and execute a Cracovienne[2] with all the mincing graces of a ballet heroine.

His powers of mimicry, indeed, were great and versatile. But in nothing was he so happy as in a Parliamentary debate. And it was remarkable that, though himself a man who on ordinary occasions was quite incapable without infinite perplexity of publicly expressing his sense of the merest courtesy of society, he was not only a master of the style of every speaker of distinction in either house, but he seemed in his imitative play to appropriate their intellectual as well as their physical peculiarities, and presented you with their mind as well as their manner. There were several attempts to-night to induce Lucian to indulge his guests with a debate, but he seemed to avoid the exertion, which was great. As the night grew old, however, and every hour he grew more lively, he suddenly broke without further pressure into the promised diversion; and Coningsby listened really with admiration to a discussion, of which the only fault was that it was more parliamentary than the original, 'plus Arabe que l'Arabie.'

The Duke was never more curt, nor Sir Robert more specious; he was as fiery as Stanley,[3] and as bitter as Graham.[4] Nor did he do their opponents less justice. Lord Palmerston[5] himself never treated a profound subject with a more pleasant volatility; and when Lucian rose at an early hour of morn, in a full house alike exhausted and excited, and after having endured for hours, in sarcastic silence, the menacing finger of Sir Robert, shaking over the green table and appealing to his misdeeds in the irrevocable records of Hansard, Lord John[6] himself could not have afforded a more perfect representative of pluck.

But loud as was the laughter, and vehement the cheering, with which Lucian's performances were received, all these ebullitions sank into insignificance compared with the reception which greeted what he himself announced was to be the speech of the night. Having quaffed full many a quaigh of toddy, he insisted on delivering it on the table, a proposition with which his auditors immediately closed.

The orator appeared, the great man of the night, who was to answer everybody on both sides. Ah! that harsh voice, that arrogant style, that saucy superficiality which decided on everything, that insolent ignorance that contradicted everybody; it was impossible to mistake them! And Coningsby had the pleasure of seeing reproduced before him the guardian of his youth and the patron of the mimic, the Right Honourable Nicholas Rigby!

Chapter 12

MADAME Colonna, with that vivacious energy which charac-
terises the south, had no sooner seen Coningsby, and heard his
praises celebrated by his grandfather, than she resolved that an
alliance should sooner or later take place between him and her
step-daughter. She imparted her projects without delay to
Lucretia, who received them in a different spirit from that in which
they were communicated. Lucretia bore as little resemblance to
her step-mother in character, as in person. If she did not possess
her beauty, she was born with an intellect of far greater capacity
and reach. She had a deep judgment. A hasty alliance with a
youth, arranged by their mutual relatives, might suit very well
the clime and manners of Italy, but Lucretia was well aware that
it was altogether opposed to the habits and feelings of this country.
She had no conviction that either Coningsby would wish to marry
her, or, if willing, that his grandfather would sanction such a step
in one as yet only on the threshold of the world. Lucretia therefore received the suggestions and proposals of Madame Colonna
with coldness and indifference; one might even say contempt, for
she neither felt respect for this lady, nor was she sedulous to evince
it. Although really younger than Coningsby, Lucretia felt that a
woman of eighteen is, in all worldly considerations, ten years older
than a youth of the same age. She anticipated that a considerable
time might elapse before Coningsby would feel it necessary to seal
his destiny by marriage, while, on the other hand, she was not
only anxious, but resolved, not to delay on her part her emancipation from the galling position in which she very frequently
found herself.

Lucretia felt rather than expressed these ideas and impressions.
She was not naturally communicative, and conversed with no
one with less frankness and facility than with her step-mother.
Madame Colonna therefore found no reasons in her conversation
with Lucretia to change her determination. As her mind was not

ingenious she did not see questions in those various lights which make us at the same time infirm of purpose and tolerant. What she fancied ought to be done, she fancied must be done; for she perceived no middle course or alternative. For the rest, Lucretia's carriage towards her gave her little discomfort. Besides, she herself, though good-natured, was obstinate. Her feelings were not very acute; nothing much vexed her. As long as she had fine dresses, good dinners, and opera-boxes, she could bear her plans to be crossed like a philosopher; and her consolation under her unaccomplished devices was her admirable consistency, which always assured her that her projects were wise, though unfulfilled.

She broke her purpose to Mr Rigby, that she might gain not only his adhesion to her views, but his assistance in achieving them. As Madame Colonna, in Mr Rigby's estimation, exercised more influence over Lord Monmouth than any other individual, faithful to his policy or practice, he agreed with all Madame Colonna's plans and wishes, and volunteered instantly to further them. As for the Prince, his wife never consulted him on any subject, nor did he wish to be consulted. On the contrary, he had no opinion about anything. All that he required was that he should be surrounded by what contributed to his personal enjoyment, that he should never be troubled, and that he should have billiards. He was not inexpert in field-sports, rode indeed very well for an Italian, but he never cared to be out-of-doors; and there was only one room in the interior which passionately interested him. It was where the echoing balls denoted the sweeping hazard or the effective cannonade. That was the chamber where the Prince Colonna literally existed. Half-an-hour after breakfast he was in the billiard-room; he never quitted it until he dressed for dinner; and he generally contrived, while the world were amused or amusing themselves at the comedy or in the dance, to steal down with some congenial sprites to the magical and illumined chamber, and use his cue until bedtime.

Faithful to her first impressions, Lucretia had made no difference in her demeanour to Coningsby to that which she offered to the other guests. Polite, but uncommunicative; ready to answer, but never originating conversation; she charmed him as little by her manner as by her person; and after some attempts, not very painstaking, to interest her, Coningsby had ceased to address her. The day passed by with only a faint recognition between them; even that sometimes omitted.

When, however, Lucretia observed that Coningsby had become one of the most notable persons in the Castle; when she heard everywhere of his talents and accomplishments, his beauty and grace and great acquirements, and perceived that he was courted by all; that Lord Monmouth omitted no occasion publicly to evince towards him his regard and consideration; that he seemed generally looked upon in the light of his grandfather's heir; and that Lady St Julians, more learned in that respect than any lady in the kingdom, was heard more than once to regret that she had not brought another daughter with her, Clara Isabella, as well as Augustina; the Princess Lucretia began to imagine that Madame Colonna, after all, might not be so extravagant in her purpose as she had first supposed. She, therefore, surprised Coningsby with the almost affectionate moroseness with which, while she hated to sing, she yet found pleasure in singing for him alone. And it is impossible to say what might not have been the next move in her tactics in this respect, had not the very night on which she had resolved to commence the enchantment of Coningsby introduced to her Sidonia.

The Princess Lucretia encountered the dark still glance of the friend of Lord Eskdale. He, too, beheld a woman unlike other women, and with his fine experience, both as a man and as a physiologist, felt that he was in the presence of no ordinary organisation. From the evening of his introduction Sidonia sought the society of the Princess Lucretia. He could not complain of her reserve. She threw out her mind in various and highly-cultivated intelligence. He recognised in her a deep and subtile spirit, considerable reading for a woman, habits of thought, and a soul passionate and daring. She resolved to subdue one whose appreciation she had gained, and who had subdued her. The profound meaning and the calm manner of Sidonia combined to quell her spirit. She struggled against the spell. She tried to rival his power; to cope with him, and with the same weapons. But prompt as was her thought and bright as was its expression, her heart beat in tumult; and, with all her apparent serenity, her agitated soul was a prey of absorbing passion. She could not contend with that intelligent, yet inscrutable, eye; with that manner so full of interest and respect, and yet so tranquil. Besides, they were not on equal terms. Here was a girl contending with a man learned in the world's way.

Between Sidonia and Coningsby there at once occurred companionship. The morning after his arrival they went out shooting together. After a long ramble they would stretch themselves on the turf under a shady tree, often by the side of some brook where the cresses grow, that added a luxury to their sporting meal; and then Coningsby would lead their conversation to some subject on which Sidonia would pour out his mind with all that depth of reflection, variety of knowledge, and richness of illustrative memory, which distinguished him; and which offered so striking a contrast to the sharp talent, the shallow information, and the worldly cunning, that make a Rigby.

This fellowship between Sidonia and Coningsby elevated the latter still more in the estimation of Lucretia, and rendered her still more desirous of gaining his good will and opinion. A great friendship seemed to have arisen between them, and the world began to believe that there must be some foundation for Madame Colonna's innuendos. That lady herself was not in the least alarmed by the attention which Sidonia paid her step-daughter. It was, of course, well known that Sidonia was not a marrying man. He was, however, a great friend of Mr Coningsby, his presence and society brought Coningsby and Lucretia more together; and however flattered her daughter might be for the moment by Sidonia's homage, still, as she would ultimately find out, if indeed she ever cared so to do, that Sidonia could only be her admirer, Madame Colonna had no kind of doubt that ultimately Coningsby would be Lucretia's husband, as she had arranged from the first.

The Princess Lucretia was a fine horse-woman, though she rarely joined the various riding-parties that were daily formed at the Castle. Often, indeed, attended only by her groom, she met the equestrians. Now she would ride with Sidonia and Coningsby, and as a female companion was indispensable, she insisted upon La Petite accompanying her. This was a fearful trial for Flora, but she encountered it, encouraged by the kind solicitude of Coningsby, who always seemed her friend.

Very shortly after the arrival of Sidonia, the Grand-duke and his suite quitted the Castle, which had been his Highness' head-quarters during his visit to the manufacturing districts; but no other great change in the assembled company occurred for some little time.

Chapter 13

'You will observe one curious trait,' said Sidonia to Coningsby, 'in the history of this country: the depository of power is always unpopular; all combine against it; it always falls. Power was deposited in the great Barons; the Church, using the King for its instrument, crushed the great Barons. Power was deposited in the Church; the King, bribing the Parliament, plundered the Church. Power was deposited in the King; the Parliament, using the People, beheaded the King, expelled the King, changed the King, and, finally, for a King substituted an administrative officer. For one hundred and fifty years Power has been deposited in the Parliament, and for the last sixty or seventy years it has been becoming more and more unpopular. In 1830 it was endeavoured by a reconstruction to regain the popular affection; but, in truth, as the Parliament then only made itself more powerful, it has only become more odious. As we see that the Barons, the Church, the King, have in turn devoured each other, and that the Parliament, the last devourer, remains, it is impossible to resist the impression that this body also is doomed to be destroyed; and he is a sagacious statesman who may detect in what form and in what quarter the great consumer will arise.'

'You take, then, a dark view of our position?'

'Troubled, not dark. I do not ascribe to political institutions that paramount influence which it is the feeling of this age to attribute to them. The Senate that confronted Brennus[1] in the Forum was the same body that registered in an after-age the ribald decrees of a Nero. Trial by jury, for example, is looked upon by all as the Palladium of our liberties; yet a jury, at a very recent period of our own history, the reign of Charles II, was a tribunal as iniquitous as the Inquisition.'[2] And a graver expression stole over the countenance of Sidonia as he remembered what that Inquisition had operated on his own race and his own destiny. 'There are families in this country,' he continued, 'of both the great historical parties, that in the persecution of their houses, the murder and proscription of some of their most illustrious members, found judges as unjust and relentless in an open jury of their countrymen as we did in the conclaves of Madrid and Seville.'

'Where, then, would you look for hope?'

'In what is more powerful than laws and institutions, and without which the best laws and the most skilful institutions may be a dead letter, or the very means of tyranny in the national character. It is not in the increased feebleness of its institutions that I see the peril of England; it is in the decline of its character as a community.'

'And yet you could scarcely describe this as an age of corruption?'

'Not of political corruption. But it is an age of social disorganisation, far more dangerous in its consequences, because far more extensive. You may have a corrupt government and a pure community; you may have a corrupt community and a pure administration. Which would you elect?'

'Neither,' said Coningsby; 'I wish to see a people full of faith, and a government full of duty.'

'Rely upon it,' said Sidonia, 'that England should think more of the community and less of the government.'

'But tell me, what do you understand by the term national character?'

'A character is an assemblage of qualities; the character of England should be an assemblage of great qualities.'

'But we cannot deny that the English have great virtues.'

'The civilisation of a thousand years must produce great virtues; but we are speaking of the decline of public virtue, not its existence.'

'In what, then, do you trace that decline?'

'In the fact that the various classes of this country are arrayed against each other.'

'But to what do you attribute those reciprocal hostilities?'

'Not entirely, not even principally, to those economical causes of which we hear so much. I look upon all such as secondary causes, which, in a certain degree, must always exist, which obtrude themselves in troubled times, and which at all times it is the business of wise statesmen to watch, to regulate, to ameliorate, to modify.'

'I am speaking to elicit truth, not to maintain opinions,' said Coningsby; 'for I have none,' he added, mournfully.

'I think,' said Sidonia, 'that there is no error so vulgar as to believe that revolutions are occasioned by economical causes. They come in, doubtless, very often to precipitate a catastrophe; very rarely do they occasion one. I know no period, for example, when physical comfort was more diffused in England than in 1640. England had a moderate population, a very improved agriculture, a rich commerce; yet she was on the eve of the greatest and most violent changes that she has yet experienced.'

'That was a religious movement.'

'Admit it; the cause, then, was not physical. The imagination of England rose against the government. It proves, then, that when the faculty is astir in a nation, it will sacrifice even physical comfort to follow its impulses.'

'Do you think, then, there is a wild desire for extensive political change in the country?'

'Hardly that: England is perplexed at the present moment, not inventive. That will be the next phasis in her moral state, and to that I wish to draw your thoughts. For myself, while I ascribe little influence to physical causes for the production of this perplexity, I am still less of opinion that it can be removed by any new disposition of political power. It would only aggravate the evil. That would be recurring to the old error of supposing you can necessarily find national content in political institutions. A political institution is a machine; the motive power is the national character. With that it rests whether the machine will benefit society, or destroy it. Society in this country is perplexed, almost paralysed; in time it will move, and it will devise. How are the elements of the nation to be again blended together? In what spirit is that reorganisation to take place?'

'To know that would be to know everything.'

'At least let us free ourselves from the double ignorance of the Platonists. Let us not be ignorant that we are ignorant.'

'I have emancipated myself from that darkness for a long time,' said Coningsby. 'Long has my mind been musing over these thoughts, but to me all is still obscurity.'

'In this country,' said Sidonia, 'since the peace, there has been an attempt to advocate a reconstruction of society on a purely rational basis. The principle of Utility has been powerfully developed. I speak not with lightness of the labours of the disciples of that school. I bow to intellect in every form: and we should be grateful to any school of philosophers, even if we disagree with them; doubly grateful in this country, where for so long a period our statesmen were in so pitiable an arrear of public intelligence. There has been an attempt to reconstruct society on a basis of material motives and calculations. It has failed. It must ultimately have failed under any circumstances; its failure in an ancient and densely-peopled kingdom was inevitable. How limited is human reason, the profoundest inquirers are most conscious. We are not indebted to the Reason of man for any of the great achievements which are the landmarks of human action and human progress. It was not Reason that besieged Troy; it was not Reason that sent forth the Saracen from the Desert to conquer the world; that inspired the Crusades; that instituted the Monastic orders; it was not Reason that produced the Jesuits; above all, it was not Reason that created the French Revolution. Man is only truly great when he acts from the passions; never irresistible but when he appeals to the imagination. Even Mormon[3] counts more votaries than Bentham.'[4]

'And you think, then, that as Imagination once subdued the State, Imagination may now save it?'

'Man is made to adore and to obey: but if you will not command him, if you give him nothing to worship, he will fashion his own divinities, and find a chieftain in his own passions.'

'But where can we find faith in a nation of sectaries? Who can feel loyalty to a sovereign of Downing Street?'

'I speak of the eternal principles of human nature, you answer me with the passing accidents of the hour. Sects rise and sects disappear. Where are the Fifth-Monarchy men?[5] England is governed by Downing Street; once it was governed by Alfred and Elizabeth.'

Chapter 14

About this time a steeple-chase in the West of England had attracted considerable attention. This sport was then of recent introduction in England, and is, in fact, an importation of Irish growth, although it has flourished in our soil. A young guardsman, who was then a guest at the Castle, and who had been in garrison in Ireland, had some experience of this pastime in the Kildare country, and he proposed that they should have a steeple-chase at Coningsby. This was a suggestion very agreeable to the Marquess of Beaumanoir, celebrated for his feats of horsemanship, and, indeed, to most of the guests. It was agreed that the race should come off at once, before any of the present company, many of whom gave symptoms of being on the wing, had quitted the Castle. The young guardsman and Mr Guy Flouncey had surveyed the country, and had selected a line which they esteemed very appropriate for the scene of action. From a hill of common land you looked down upon the valley of Coningsby, richly cultivated, deeply ditched, and stiffly fenced; the valley was bounded by another rising ground, and the scene was admirably calculated to give an extensive view to a multitude.

The distance along the valley was to be two miles out, and home again; the starting-post being also the winning-post, and the flags, which were placed on every fence which the horses were to pass, were to be passed on the left hand of the rider both going and coming; so that although the horses had to leap the same fences forward and backward, they could not come over the same place twice. In the last field before they turned, was a brook seventeen feet clear from side to side, with good taking off on both banks. Here real business commenced.

Lord Monmouth highly approved the scheme, but mentioned that the stakes must be moderate, and open to the whole county. The neighbourhood had a week of preparation, and the entries for the Coningsby steeple-chase were numerous. Lord Monmouth, after a reserve for his own account, placed his stable at the service of his guests. For himself, he offered to back his horse, Sir Robert, which was to be ridden by his grandson.

Now, nothing was spoken or thought of at Coningsby Castle except the coming sport. The ladies shared the general excitement. They embroidered handkerchiefs, and scarfs, and gloves, with the respective colours of the rivals, and tried to make jockey-caps. Lady St Julians postponed her intended departure in consequence. Madame Colonna wished that some means could be contrived by which they might all win.

Sidonia, with the other competitors, had ridden over the ground and glanced at the brook with the eye of a workman. On his return to the Castle he sent a despatch for some of his stud.

Coningsby was all anxiety to win. He was proud of the confidence of his grandfather in backing him. He had a powerful horse and a first-rate fencer, and he was resolved himself not to flinch. On the night before the race, retiring somewhat earlier than usual to his chamber, he observed on his dressing-table a small packet addressed to his name, and in an unknown handwriting. Opening it, he found a pretty racing-jacket embroidered with his colours of pink and white. This was a perplexing circumstance, but he fancied it on the whole a happy omen. And who was the donor? Certainly not the Princess Lucretia, for he had observed her fashioning some maroon ribbons, which were the colours of Sidonia. It could scarcely be from Mrs Guy Flouncey. Perhaps Madame Colonna to please the Marquess? Thinking over this incident he fell asleep.

The morning before the race Sidonia's horses arrived. All went to examine them at the stables. Among them was an Arab mare. Coningsby recognised the Daughter of the Star. She was greatly admired for her points; but Guy Flouncey whispered to Mr Melton that she never could do the work.

'But Lord Beaumanoir says he is all for speed against strength in these affairs,' said Mr Melton.

Guy Flouncey smiled incredulously.

The night before the race it rained rather heavily.

'I take it the country will not be very like the Deserts of Arabia,' said Mr Guy Flouncey, with a knowing look to Mr Melton, who was noting a bet in his memorandum-book.

The morning was fine, clear, and sunny, with a soft western breeze. The starting-post was about three miles from the Castle; but, long before the hour, the surrounding hills were covered with people; squire and farmer; with no lack of their wives and daughters; many a hind in his smock-frock, and many an 'operative' from the neighbouring factories. The 'gentlemen riders' gradually arrived. The entries were very numerous, though it was understood that not more than a dozen would come to the post, and half of these were the guests of Lord Monmouth. At half-past one the *cortège* from the Castle arrived, and took up the post which had been prepared for them on the summit of the hill. Lord Monmouth was much cheered on his arrival. In the carriage with him were Madame Colonna and Lady St Julians. The Princess Lucretia, Lady Gaythorpe, Mrs Guy Flouncey, accompanied by Lord Eskdale and other cavaliers, formed a brilliant company. There was scarcely a domestic in the Castle who was not there. The comedians, indeed, did not care to come, but Villebecque prevailed upon Flora to drive with him to the race in a buggy he borrowed of the steward.

The start was to be at two o'clock. The 'gentlemen jockeys' are mustered. Never were riders mounted and appointed in better style. The stewards and the clerk of the course attend them to the starting-post. There they are now assembled. Guy Flouncey takes up his stirrup-leathers a hole; Mr Melton looks at his girths. In a few moments, the irrevocable monosyllable will be uttered.

The bugle sounds for them to face about; the clerk of the course sings out, 'Gentlemen, are you all ready?' No objection made, the word given to go, and fifteen riders start in excellent style.

Prince Colonna, who rode like Prince Rupert, took the lead, followed close by a stout yeoman on an old white horse of great provincial celebrity, who made steady running, and, from his appearance and action, an awkward customer. The rest, with two exceptions, followed in a cluster at no great distance, and in this order they continued, with very slight variation, for the first two miles, though there were several ox-fences, and one or two of them remarkably stiff. Indeed, they appeared more like horses running over a course than over a country. The two exceptions were Lord

Beaumanoir on his horse Sunbeam, and Sidonia on the Arab. These kept somewhat slightly in the rear.

Almost in this wise they approached the dreaded brook. Indeed, with the exception of the last two riders, who were about thirty yards behind, it seemed that you might have covered the rest of the field with a sheet. They arrived at the brook at the same moment: seventeen feet of water between strong sound banks is no holiday work; but they charged with unfaltering intrepidity. But what a revolution in their spirited order did that instant produce! A masked battery of canister and grape could not have achieved more terrible execution. Coningsby alone clearly lighted on the opposing bank; but, for the rest of them, it seemed for a moment that they were all in the middle of the brook, one over another, splashing, kicking, swearing; every one trying to get out and keep others in. Mr Melton and the stout yeoman regained their saddles and were soon again in the chase. The Prince lost his horse, and was not alone in his misfortune. Mr Guy Flouncey lay on his back with a horse across his diaphragm; only his head above the water, and his mouth full of chickweed and dockleaves. And if help had not been at hand, he and several others might have remained struggling in their watery bed for a considerable period. In the midst of this turmoil, the Marquess and Sidonia at the same moment cleared the brook.

Affairs now became interesting. Here Coningsby took up the running, Sidonia and the Marquess lying close at his quarters. Mr Melton had gone the wrong side of a flag, and the stout yeoman, though close at hand, was already trusting much to his spurs. In the extreme distance might be detected three or four stragglers. Thus they continued until within three fields of home. A ploughed field finished the old white horse; the yeoman struck his spurs to the rowels, but the only effect of the experiment was, that the horse stood stock-still. Coningsby, Sidonia, and the Marquess were now altogether. The winning-post is in sight, and a high and strong gate leads to the last field. Coningsby, looking like a winner, gallantly dashed forward and sent Sir Robert at the gate, but he had over-estimated his horse's powers at this point of the game, and a rattling fall was the consequence: however, horse and rider were both on the right side, and Coningsby was in his saddle and at work again in a moment. It seemed that the Marquess was winning. There was only one more fence; and that the foot people had made a breach in by the side of a gate-post, and wide enough, as was said, for a broad-wheel waggon to travel by. Instead of passing straight over this gap, Sunbeam swerved against the gate and threw his rider. This was decisive. The Daughter of the Star, who was still going beautifully, pulling double, and her jockey sitting still, sprang over the gap and went in first; Coningsby, on Sir Robert, being placed second. The distance measured was about four miles; there were thirty-nine leaps; and it was done under fifteen minutes.

Lord Monmouth was well content with the prowess of his grandson, and his extreme cordiality consoled Coningsby under a defeat which was very vexatious. It was some alleviation that he was beaten by Sidonia. Madame Colonna even shed tears at her young friend's disappointment, and mourned it especially for Lucretia, who had said nothing, though a flush might be observed on her usually pale countenance. Villebecque, who had betted, was so extremely excited by the whole affair, especially during the last three minutes, that he quite forgot his quiet companion, and when he looked round he found Flora fainting.

'You rode well,' said Sidonia to Coningsby; 'but your horse was more strong than swift. After all, this thing is a race; and, notwithstanding Solomon,[1] in a race speed must win.'

Chapter 15

NOTWITHSTANDING the fatigues of the morning, the evening was passed with great gaiety at the Castle. The gentlemen all vowed that, far from being inconvenienced by their mishaps, they felt, on the whole, rather better for them. Mr Guy Flouncey, indeed, did not seem quite so limber and flexible as usual; and the young guardsman, who had previously discoursed in an almost alarming style of the perils and feats of the Kildare country, had subsided into a remarkable reserve. The Provincials were delighted with Sidonia's riding, and even the Leicestershire gentlemen admitted that he was a 'customer.'

Lord Monmouth beckoned to Coningsby to sit by him on the sofa, and spoke of his approaching University life. He gave his grandson a great deal of good advice: told him to avoid drinking, especially if he ever chanced to play cards, which he hoped he never would; urged the expediency of never borrowing money, and of confining his loans to small sums, and then only to friends of whom he wished to get rid; most particularly impressed on him never to permit his feelings to be engaged by any woman; nobody, he assured Coningsby, despised that weakness more than women themselves. Indeed, feeling of any kind did not suit the present age: it was not *bon ton*; and in some degree always made a man ridiculous. Coningsby was always to have before him the possible catastrophe of becoming ridiculous. It was the test of conduct, Lord Monmouth said; a fear of becoming ridiculous is the best guide in life, and will save a man from all sorts of scrapes. For the rest, Coningsby was to appear at Cambridge as became Lord Monmouth's favourite grandson. His grandfather had opened an account for him with Drummonds', on whom he was to draw for his considerable allowance; and if by any chance he found himself in a scrape, no matter of what kind, he was to be sure to write to his grandfather, who would certainly get him out of it.

'Your departure is sudden,' said the Princess Lucretia, in a low deep tone to Sidonia, who was sitting by her side and screened from general observation by the waltzers who whirled by.

'Departures should be sudden.'

'I do not like departures,' said the Princess.

'Nor did the Queen of Sheba when she quitted Solomon. You know what she did?'

'Tell me.'

'She wept very much, and let one of the King's birds fly into the garden. "You are freed from your cage," she said; "but I am going back to mine." '

'But you never weep?' said the Princess.

'Never.'

'And are always free?'

'So are men in the Desert.'

'But your life is not a Desert?'

'It at least resembles the Desert in one respect: it is useless.'

'The only useless life is woman's.'

'Yet there have been heroines,' said Sidonia.

'The Queen of Sheba,' said the Princess, smiling.

'A favourite of mine,' said Sidonia.

'And why was she a favourite of yours?' rather eagerly inquired Lucretia.

'Because she thought deeply, talked finely, and moved gracefully.'

'And yet might be a very unfeeling dame at the same time,' said the Princess.

'I never thought of that,' said Sidonia.

'The heart, apparently, does not reckon in your philosophy.'

'What we call the heart,' said Sidonia, 'is a nervous sensation, like shyness, which gradually disappears in society. It is fervent in the nursery, strong in the domestic circle, tumultuous at school. The affections are the children of ignorance; when the horizon of our experience expands, and models multiply, love and admiration imperceptibly vanish.'

'I fear the horizon of your experience has very greatly expanded. With your opinions, what charm can there be in life?'

'The sense of existence.'

'So Sidonia is off to-morrow, Monmouth,' said Lord Eskdale.

'Hah!' said the Marquess. 'I must get him to breakfast with me before he goes.'

The party broke up. Coningsby, who had heard Lord Eskdale announce Sidonia's departure, lingered to express his regret, and say farewell.

'I cannot sleep,' said Sidonia, 'and I never smoke in Europe. If you are not stiff with your wounds, come to my rooms.'

This invitation was willingly accepted.

'I am going to Cambridge in a week,' said Coningsby. 'I was almost in hopes you might have remained as long.'

'I, also; but my letters of this morning demand me. If it had not been for our chase, I should have quitted immediately. The minister cannot pay the interest on the national debt; not an unprecedented circumstance, and has applied to us. I never permit any business of State to be transacted without my personal interposition; and so I must go up to town immediately.'

'Suppose you don't pay it,' said Coningsby, smiling.

'If I followed my own impulse, I would remain here,' said Sidonia. 'Can anything be more absurd than that a nation should apply to an individual to maintain its credit, and, with its credit, its existence as an empire, and its comfort as a people; and that individual one to whom its laws deny the proudest rights of citizenship, the privilege of sitting in its senate and of holding land? for though I have been rash enough to buy several estates, my own opinion is, that, by the existing law of England, an Englishman of Hebrew faith cannot possess the soil.'

'But surely it would be easy to repeal a law so illiberal –'

'Oh! as for illiberality, I have no objection to it if it be an element of power. Eschew political sentimentalism. What I contend is, that if you permit men to accumulate property, and they use that permission to a great extent, power is inseparable from that property, and it is in the last degree impolitic to make it the interest of any powerful class to oppose the institutions under which they live. The Jews, for example, independently of the capital qualities for citizenship which they possess in their industry, temperance, and energy and vivacity of mind, are a race essentially monarchical, deeply religious, and shrinking themselves from converts as from a calamity, are ever anxious to see the religious systems of the countries in which they live flourish; yet, since your society has become agitated in England, and powerful combinations menace your institutions, you find the once loyal Hebrew invariably arrayed in the same ranks as the leveller and the latitudinarian, and prepared to support the policy which may even endanger his life and property, rather than tamely continue under a system which seeks to degrade him. The Tories lose an important election at a critical moment; 'tis the Jews come forward to vote against them. The Church is alarmed at the scheme of a latitudinarian university, and learns with relief that funds are not forthcoming for its establishment; a Jew immediately advances and endows it. Yet the Jews, Coningsby, are essentially Tories. Toryism, indeed, is but copied from the mighty prototype which has fashioned Europe. And every generation they must become more powerful and more dangerous to the society which is hostile to them. Do you think that the quiet humdrum persecution of a decorous representative of an English university can crush those who have successfully baffled the Pharaohs, Nebuchadnezzar, Rome, and the Feudal ages? The fact is, you cannot destroy a pure race of the Caucasian organisation. It is a physiological fact; a simple law of nature, which has baffled Egyptian and Assyrian Kings, Roman Emperors, and Christian Inquisitors. No penal laws, no physical tortures, can effect that a superior race should be absorbed in an inferior, or be destroyed by it. The mixed persecuting races disappear; the pure persecuted race remains. And at this moment, in spite of centuries, of tens of centuries, of degradation, the Jewish mind exercises a vast influence on the affairs of Europe. I speak not of their laws, which you still obey; of their literature, with which your minds are saturated; but of the living Hebrew intellect.

'You never observe a great intellectual movement in Europe in which the Jews do not greatly participate. The first Jesuits were Jews; that mysterious Russian Diplomacy which so alarms Western Europe is organised and principally carried on by Jews; that mighty revolution which is at this moment preparing in Germany, and which will be, in fact, a second and greater Reformation, and of which so little is as yet known in England, is entirely developing under the auspices of Jews, who almost monopolise

the professorial chairs of Germany. Neander, the founder of Spiritual Christianity, and who is Regius Professor of Divinity in the
University of Berlin, is a Jew. Benary, equally famous, and in the
same University, is a Jew. Wehl, the Arabic Professor of Heidel-
berg, is a Jew. Years ago, when I was in Palestine, I met a German student who was accumulating materials for the History of
Christianity, and studying the genius of the place; a modest and
learned man. It was Wehl; then unknown, since become the first
Arabic scholar of the day, and the author of the life of Mahomet.
But for the German professors of this race, their name is Legion.
I think there are more than ten at Berlin alone.

'I told you just now that I was going up to town to-morrow,
because I always made it a rule to interpose when affairs of State
were on the carpet. Otherwise, I never interfere. I hear of peace
and war in newspapers, but I am never alarmed, except when
I am informed that the Sovereigns want treasure; then I know
that monarchs are serious.

'A few years back we were applied to by Russia. Now, there
has been no friendship between the Court of St Petersburgh and
my family. It has Dutch connections, which have generally supplied it; and our representations in favour of the Polish Hebrews,
a numerous race, but the most suffering and degraded of all the
tribes, have not been very agreeable to the Czar. However, circumstances drew to an approximation between the Romanoffs and
the Sidonias. I resolved to go myself to St Petersburgh. I had, on
my arrival, an interview with the Russian Minister of Finance,
Count Cancrin; I beheld the son of a Lithuanian Jew. The loan
was connected with the affairs of Spain; I resolved on repairing
to Spain from Russia. I travelled without intermission. I had an
audience immediately on my arrival with the Spanish Minister,
Senor Mendizabel; I beheld one like myself, the son of a Nuevo
Christiano, a Jew of Arragon. In consequence of what transpired
at Madrid, I went straight to Paris to consult the President of the
French Council; I beheld the son of a French Jew, a hero, an imperial marshal, and very properly so, for who should be military
heroes if not those who worship the Lord of Hosts?'

'And is Soult a Hebrew?'

'Yes, and others of the French marshals, and the most famous;

Massena, for example; his real name was Manasseh: but to my anecdote. The consequence of our consultations was, that some Northern power should be applied to in a friendly and mediative capacity. We fixed on Prussia; and the President of the Council made an application to the Prussian Minister, who attended a few days after our conference. Count Arnim entered the cabinet, and I beheld a Prussian Jew. So you see, my dear Coningsby, that the world is governed by very different personages from what is imagined by those who are not behind the scenes.'

'You startle, and deeply interest me.'

'You must study physiology, my dear child. Pure races of Caucasus may be persecuted, but they cannot be despised, except by the brutal ignorance of some mongrel breed, that brandishes fagots and howls extermination, but is itself exterminated without persecution, by that irresistible law of Nature which is fatal to curs.'

'But I come also from Caucasus,' said Coningsby.

'Verily; and thank your Creator for such a destiny: and your race is sufficiently pure. You come from the shores of the Northern Sea, land of the blue eye, and the golden hair, and the frank brow: 'tis a famous breed, with whom we Arabs have contended long; from whom we have suffered much: but these Goths, and Saxons, and Normans were doubtless great men.'

'But so favoured by Nature, why has not your race produced great poets, great orators, great writers?'

'Favoured by Nature and by Nature's God, we produced the lyre of David; we gave you Isaiah and Ezekiel; they are our Olynthians, our Philippics. Favoured by Nature we still remain: but in exact proportion as we have been favoured by Nature we have been persecuted by Man. After a thousand struggles; after acts of heroic courage that Rome has never equalled; deeds of divine patriotism that Athens, and Sparta, and Carthage have never excelled; we have endured fifteen hundred years of supernatural slavery, during which, every device that can degrade or destroy man has been the destiny that we have sustained and baffled. The Hebrew child has entered adolescence only to learn that he was the Pariah of that ungrateful Europe that owes to him the best part of its laws, a fine portion of its literature, all its religion. Great poets require a public; we have been content with the immortal melodies that we sung more than two thousand years ago by the waters of Babylon and wept. They record our triumphs; they solace our affliction. Great orators are the creatures of popular assemblies; we were permitted only by stealth to meet even in our temples. And as for great writers, the catalogue is not blank. What are all the schoolmen, Aquinas himself, to Maimonides?[1] And as for modern philosophy, all springs from Spinoza.[2]

'But the passionate and creative genius, that is the nearest link to Divinity, and which no human tyranny can destroy, though it can divert it; that should have stirred the hearts of nations by its inspired sympathy, or governed senates by its burning eloquence; has found a medium for its expression, to which, in spite of your prejudices and your evil passions, you have been obliged to bow. The ear, the voice, the fancy teeming with combinations, the imagination fervent with picture and emotion, that came from Caucasus, and which we have preserved unpolluted, have endowed us with almost the exclusive privilege of Music; that science of harmonious sounds, which the ancients recognised as most divine, and deified in the person of their most beautiful creation. I speak not of the past; though, were I to enter into the history of the lords of melody, you would find it the annals of Hebrew genius. But at this moment even, musical Europe is ours. There is not a company of singers, not an orchestra in a single capital, that is not crowded with our children under the feigned names which they adopt to conciliate the dark aversion which your posterity will some day disclaim with shame and disgust. Almost every great composer, skilled musician, almost every voice that ravishes you with its transporting strains, springs from our tribes. The catalogue is too vast to enumerate; too illustrious to dwell for a moment on secondary names, however eminent. Enough for us that the three great creative minds to whose exquisite inventions all nations at this moment yield, Rossini, Meyerbeer, Mendelssohn, are of Hebrew race; and little do your men of fashion, your muscadins of Paris, and your dandies of London, as they thrill into raptures at the notes of a Pasta or a Grisi,[3] little do they suspect that they are offering their homage to "the sweet singers of Israel!"'

Chapter 16

IT was the noon of the day on which Sidonia was to leave the Castle. The wind was high; the vast white clouds scudded over the blue heaven; the leaves yet green, and tender branches snapped like glass, were whirled in eddies from the trees; the grassy sward undulated like the ocean with a thousand tints and shadows. From the window of the music-room Lucretia Colonna gazed on the turbulent sky.

The heaven of her heart, too, was disturbed.

She turned from the agitated external world to ponder over her inward emotion. She uttered a deep sigh.

Slowly she moved towards her harp; wildly, almost unconsciously, she touched with one hand its strings, while her eyes were fixed on the ground. An imperfect melody resounded; yet plaintive and passionate. It seemed to attract her soul. She raised her head, and then, touching the strings with both her hands, she poured forth tones of deep, yet thrilling power.

'I am a stranger in the halls of a stranger! Ah! whither shall I flee?
To the castle of my fathers in the green mountains; to the palace of my
    fathers in the ancient city?
There is no flag on the castle of my fathers in the green mountains: silent
    is the palace of my fathers in the ancient city.
Is there no home for the homeless? Can the unloved never find love?
Ah! thou fliest away fleet cloud: he will leave us swifter than thee! Alas!
    cutting wind, thy breath is not so cold as his heart!
I am a stranger in the halls of a stranger! Ah! whither shall I flee?'

The door of the music-room slowly opened. It was Sidonia. His hat was in his hand; he was evidently on the point of departure.

'Those sounds assured me,' he said calmly, but kindly, as he advanced, 'that I might find you here, on which I scarcely counted at so early an hour.'

'You are going then?' said the Princess.

'My carriage is at the door; the Marquess has delayed me; I

must be in London to-night. I conclude more abruptly than I could have wished one of the most agreeable visits I ever made; and I hope you will permit me to express to you how much I am indebted to you for a society which those should deem themselves fortunate who can more frequently enjoy.'

He held forth his hand; she extended hers, cold as marble, which he bent over, but did not press to his lips.

'Lord Monmouth talks of remaining here some time,' he observed; 'but I suppose next year, if not this, we shall all meet in some city of the earth?'

Lucretia bowed; and Sidonia, with a graceful reverence, withdrew.

The Princess Lucretia stood for some moments motionless; a sound attracted her to the window; she perceived the equipage of Sidonia whirling along the winding roads of the park. She watched it till it disappeared; then quitting the window, she threw herself into a chair, and buried her face in her shawl.

END OF BOOK IV

BOOK V

Chapter 1

AN University life did not bring to Coningsby that feeling of emancipation usually experienced by freshmen. The contrast between school and college life is perhaps, under any circumstances, less striking to the Etonian than to others: he has been prepared for becoming his own master by the liberty wisely entrusted to him in his boyhood, and which is, in general, discreetly exercised. But there were also other reasons why Coningsby should have been less impressed with the novelty of his life, and have encountered less temptations than commonly are met with in the new existence which an University opens to youth. In the interval which had elapsed between quitting Eton and going to Cambridge, brief as the period may comparatively appear, Coningsby had seen much of the world. Three or four months, indeed, may not seem, at the first blush, a course of time which can very materially influence the formation of character; but time must not be counted by calendars, but by sensations, by thought. Coningsby had felt a good deal, reflected more. He had encountered a great number of human beings, offering a vast variety of character for his observation. It was not merely manners, but even the intellectual and moral development of the human mind, which in a great degree, unconsciously to himself, had been submitted to his study and his scrutiny. New trains of ideas had been opened to him; his mind was teeming with suggestions. The horizon of his intelligence had insensibly expanded. He perceived that there were other opinions in the world, besides those to which he had been habituated. The depths of his intellect had been stirred. He was a wiser man.

He distinguished three individuals whose acquaintance had greatly influenced his mind; Eustace Lyle, the elder Millbank, above all, Sidonia. He curiously meditated over the fact, that three English subjects, one of them a principal landed proprietor, another one of the most eminent manufacturers, and the third the greatest capitalist in the kingdom, all of them men of great intelligence, and doubtless of a high probity and conscience, were in their hearts disaffected with the political constitution of the country. Yet, unquestionably, these were the men among whom we ought to seek for some of our first citizens. What, then, was this repulsive quality in those institutions which we persisted in calling national, and which once were so? Here was a great question.

There was another reason, also, why Coningsby should feel a little fastidious among his new habits, and, without being aware of it, a little depressed. For three or four months, and for the first time in his life, he had passed his time in the continual society of refined and charming women. It is an acquaintance which, when habitual, exercises a great influence over the tone of the mind, even if it does not produce any more violent effects. It refines the taste, quickens the perception, and gives, as it were, a grace and flexibility to the intellect. Coningsby in his solitary rooms arranging his books, sighed when he recalled the Lady Everinghams and the Lady Theresas; the gracious Duchess; the frank, good-natured Madame Colonna; that deeply interesting enigma the Princess Lucretia; and the gentle Flora. He thought with disgust of the impending dissipation of an University, which could only be an exaggeration of their coarse frolics at school. It seemed rather vapid this mighty Cambridge, over which they had so often talked in the playing fields of Eton, with such anticipations of its vast and absorbing interest. And those University honours that once were the great object of his aspirations, they did not figure in that grandeur with which they once haunted his imagination.

What Coningsby determined to conquer was knowledge. He had watched the influence of Sidonia in society with an eye of unceasing vigilance. Coningsby perceived that all yielded to him; that Lord Monmouth even, who seemed to respect none, gave place to his intelligence; appealed to him, listened to him, was guided by him. What was the secret of this influence? Knowledge. On all subjects, his views were prompt and clear, and this not more from his native sagacity and reach of view, than from the aggregate of facts which rose to guide his judgment and illustrate his

meaning, from all countries and all ages, instantly at his command.

The friends of Coningsby were now hourly arriving. It seemed
when he met them again, that they had all suddenly become men
since they had separated; Buckhurst especially. He had been at
Paris, and returned with his mind very much opened, and trousers
made quite in a new style. All his thoughts were, how soon he
could contrive to get back again; and he told them endless stories
of actresses, and dinners at fashionable *cafés*. Vere enjoyed Cambridge most, because he had been staying with his family since
he quitted Eton. Henry Sydney was full of church architecture,
national sports, restoration of the order of the Peasantry, and
was to maintain a constant correspondence on these and similar
subjects with Eustace Lyle. Finally, however, they all fell into a
very fair, regular, routine life. They all read a little, but not with
the enthusiasm which they had once projected. Buckhurst drove
four-in-hand, and they all of them sometimes assisted him; but
not immoderately. Their suppers were sometimes gay, but never
outrageous; and, among all of them, the school friendship was
maintained unbroken, and even undisturbed.

The fame of Coningsby preceded him at Cambridge. No man
ever went up from whom more was expected in every way. The
dons awaited a sucking member for the University, the under-
graduates were prepared to welcome a new Alcibiades.[1] He was
neither: neither a prig nor a profligate; but a quiet, gentlemanlike,
yet spirited young man, gracious to all, but intimate only with his
old friends, and giving always an impression in his general tone
that his soul was not absorbed in his University.

And yet, perhaps, he might have been coddled into a prig, or
flattered into a profligate, had it not been for the intervening experience which he gained between his school and college life. That
had visibly impressed upon him, what before he had only faintly
acquired from books, that there was a greater and more real world
awaiting him, than to be found in those bowers of Academus to
which youth is apt at first to attribute an exaggerated importance.
A world of action and passion, of power and peril; a world for
which a great preparation was indeed necessary, severe and profound, but not altogether such an one as was now offered to him.

Yet this want must be supplied, and by himself. Coningsby had already acquirements sufficiently considerable, with some formal application, to ensure him at all times his degree. He was no longer engrossed by the intention he once proudly entertained of trying for honours, and he chalked out for himself that range of reading, which, digested by his thought, should furnish him in some degree with that various knowledge of the history of man to which he aspired. No, we must not for a moment believe that accident could have long diverted the course of a character so strong. The same desire that prevented the Castle of his grandfather from proving a Castle of Indolence[2] to him, that saved him from a too early initiation into the seductive distractions of a refined and luxurious society, would have preserved Coningsby from the puerile profligacy of a college life, or from being that idol of private tutors, a young pedant. It was that noble ambition, the highest and the best, that must be born in the heart and organised in the brain, which will not let a man be content, unless his intellectual power is recognised by his race, and desires that it should contribute to their welfare. It is the heroic feeling; the feeling that in old days produced demi-gods; without which no State is safe; without which political institutions are meat without salt; the Crown a bauble, the Church an establishment, Parliaments debating-clubs, and Civilisation itself but a fitful and transient dream.

Chapter 2

LESS than a year after the arrival of Coningsby at Cambridge, and which he had only once quitted in the interval, and that to pass a short time in Berkshire with his friend Buckhurst, occurred the death of King William IV. This event necessarily[1] induced a dissolution of the Parliament, elected under the auspices of Sir Robert Peel in 1834, and after the publication of the Tamworth Manifesto.

The death of the King was a great blow to what had now come to be generally styled the 'Conservative Cause.' It was quite unexpected; within a fortnight of his death, eminent persons still believed that 'it was only the hay-fever.' Had his Majesty lived until after the then impending registration, the Whigs would have been again dismissed. Nor is there any doubt that, under these circumstances, the Conservative Cause would have secured for the new ministers a parliamentary majority. What would have been the consequences to the country, if the four years of Whig rule, from 1837 to 1841, had not occurred? It is easier to decide what would have been the consequences to the Whigs. Some of their great friends might have lacked blue ribbons and lord-lieutenancies, and some of their little friends comfortable places in the Customs and Excise. They would have lost, undoubtedly, the distribution of four years' patronage; we can hardly say the exercise of four years' power; but they would have existed at this moment as the most powerful and popular Opposition that ever flourished in this country, if, indeed, the course of events had not long ere this carried them back to their old posts in a proud and intelligible position. The Reform Bill did not do more injury to the Tories, than the attempt to govern this country without a decided Parliamentary majority did the Whigs. The greatest of all evils is a weak government. They cannot carry good measures, they are forced to carry bad ones.

The death of the King was a great blow to the Conservative

Cause; that is to say, it darkened the brow of Tadpole, quailed the heart of Taper, crushed all the rising hopes of those numerous statesmen who believe the country must be saved if they receive twelve hundred a-year. It is a peculiar class, that; 1,200*l.* per annum, paid quarterly, is their idea of political science and human nature. To receive 1,200*l.* per annum is government; to try to receive 1,200*l.* per annum is opposition; to wish to receive 1,200*l.* per annum is ambition. If a man wants to get into Parliament, and does not want to get 1,200*l.* per annum, they look upon him as daft; as a benighted being. They stare in each other's face, and ask, 'What can * * * * * want to get into Parliament for?' They have no conception that public reputation is a motive power, and with many men the greatest. They have as much idea of fame or celebrity, even of the masculine impulse of an honourable pride, as eunuchs of manly joys.

The twelve-hundred-a-yearers were in despair about the King's death. Their loyal souls were sorely grieved that his gracious Majesty had not outlived the Registration. All their happy inventions about 'hay-fever,' circulated in confidence, and sent by post to chairmen of Conservative Associations, followed by a royal funeral! General election about to take place with the old registration; government boroughs against them, and the young Queen for a cry. What a cry! Youth, beauty, and a Queen! Taper grew pale at the thought. What could they possibly get up to countervail it? Even Church and Corn-laws together would not do; and then Church was sulky, for the Conservative Cause had just made it a present of a commission,[2] and all that the country gentlemen knew of Conservatism was, that it would not repeal the Malt Tax, and had made them repeal their pledges. Yet a cry must be found. A dissolution without a cry, in the Taper philosophy, would be a world without a sun. A rise might be got by 'Independence of the House of Lords;' and Lord Lyndhurst's summaries might be well circulated at one penny per hundred, large discount allowed to Conservative Associations, and endless credit. Tadpole, however, was never very fond of the House of Lords; besides, it was too limited. Tadpole wanted the young Queen brought in; the rogue! At length, one morning, Taper came up to him with a slip of paper, and a smile of complacent austerity on his dull visage. 'I think, Mr Tadpole, that will do!'

Tadpole took the paper and read, 'Our Young Queen, and our Old Institutions.'

The eyes of Tadpole sparkled as if they had met a gnomic sentence of Periander or Thales;[3] then turning to Taper, he said,

'What do you think of "ancient," instead of "old"?'

'You cannot have "Our modern Queen and our ancient Institutions,"' said Mr Taper.

The dissolution was soon followed by an election for the borough of Cambridge. The Conservative Cause candidate was an old Etonian. That was a bond of sympathy which imparted zeal even to those who were a little sceptical of the essential virtues of Conservatism. Every undergraduate especially who remembered 'the distant spires,' became enthusiastic. Buckhurst took a very decided part. He cheered, he canvassed, he brought men to the poll whom none could move; he influenced his friends and his companions. Even Coningsby caught the contagion, and Vere, who had imbibed much of Coningsby's political sentiment, prevailed on himself to be neutral. The Conservative Cause triumphed in the person of its Eton champion. The day the member was chaired,[4] several men in Coningsby's rooms were talking over their triumph.

'By Jove!' said the panting Buckhurst, throwing himself on the sofa, 'it was well done; never was any thing better done. An immense triumph! The greatest triumph the Conservative Cause has had. And yet,' he added, laughing, 'if any fellow were to ask me what the Conservative Cause is, I am sure I should not know what to say.'

'Why, it is the cause of our glorious institutions,' said Coningsby. 'A Crown robbed of its prerogatives; a Church controlled by a commission; and an Aristocracy that does not lead.'

'Under whose genial influence the order of the Peasantry, "a country's pride," has vanished from the face of the land,' said Henry Sydney, 'and is succeeded by a race of serfs, who are called labourers, and who burn ricks.'

'Under which,' continued Coningsby, 'the Crown has become a cipher; the Church a sect; the Nobility drones; and the People drudges.'

'It is the great constitutional cause,' said Lord Vere, 'that refuses everything to opposition; yields everything to agitation; conservative in Parliament, destructive out-of-doors; that has no objection to any change provided only it be effected by un-authorised means.'

'The first public association of men,' said Coningsby, 'who have worked for an avowed end without enunciating a single principle.'

'And who have established political infidelity throughout the land,' said Lord Henry.

'By Jove!' said Buckhurst, 'what infernal fools we have made ourselves this last week!'

'Nay,' said Coningsby, smiling, 'it was our last school-boy weakness. Floreat Etona, under all circumstances.'

'I certainly, Coningsby,' said Lord Vere, 'shall not assume the Conservative Cause, instead of the cause for which Hampden died in the field, and Sydney on the scaffold.'[5]

'The cause for which Hampden died in the field and Sydney on the scaffold,' said Coningsby, 'was the cause of the Venetian Republic.'

'How, how?' said Buckhurst.

'I repeat it,' said Coningsby. 'The great object of the Whig leaders in England from the first movement under Hampden to the last most successful one in 1688, was to establish in England a high aristocratic republic on the model of the Venetian, then the study and admiration of all speculative politicians. Read Harrington;[6] turn over Algernon Sydney;[7] and you will see how the minds of the English leaders in the seventeenth century were saturated with the Venetian type. And they at length succeeded. William III found them out. He told the Whig leaders, "I will not be a Doge." He balanced parties; he baffled them as the Puritans baffled them fifty years before. The reign of Anne was a struggle between the Venetian and the English systems. Two great Whig nobles, Argyle and Somerset, worthy of seats in the Council of Ten, forced their Sovereign on her deathbed to change the ministry.[8] They accomplished their object. They brought in a new family on their own terms. George I was a Doge; George II was a Doge; they were what William III, a great man, would not be. George III tried not to be a Doge, but it was impossible materially to resist the deeply-laid combination. He might get rid of the Whig magnificoes, but he could not rid himself of the Venetian constitution. And a Venetian constitution did govern England from the accession of the House of Hanover until 1832. Now I do not ask you, Vere, to relinquish the political tenets which in ordinary times would have been your inheritance. All I say is, the constitution introduced by your ancestors having been subverted by their descendants your contemporaries, beware of still holding Venetian principles of government when you have not a Venetian constitution to govern with. Do what I am doing, what Henry Sydney and Buckhurst are doing, what other men that I could mention are doing, hold yourself aloof from political parties which, from the necessity of things, have ceased to have distinctive principles, and are therefore practically only factions; and wait and see, whether with patience, energy, honour, and Christian faith, and a desire to look to the national welfare and not to sectional and limited interests; whether, I say, we may not discover some great principles to guide us, to which we may adhere, and which then, if true, will ultimately guide and control others.'

'The Whigs are worn out,' said Vere, 'Conservatism is a sham, and Radicalism is pollution.'

'I certainly,' said Buckhurst, 'when I get into the House of Commons, shall speak my mind without reference to any party whatever; and all I hope is, we may all come in at the same time, and then we may make a party of our own.'

'I have always heard my father say,' said Vere, 'that there was nothing so difficult as to organise an independent party in the House of Commons.'

'Ay! but that was in the Venetian period, Vere,' said Henry Sydney, smiling.

'I dare say,' said Buckhurst, 'the only way to make a party in the House of Commons is just the one that succeeds anywhere else. Men must associate together. When you are living in the same set, dining together every day, and quizzing the Dons, it is astonishing how well men agree. As for me, I never would enter into a conspiracy, unless the conspirators were fellows who had been at Eton with me; and then there would be no treachery.'

'Let us think of principles, and not of parties,' said Coningsby.

'For my part,' said Buckhurst, 'whenever a political system is breaking up, as in this country at present, I think the very best thing is to brush all the old Dons off the stage. They never take to the new road kindly. They are always hampered by their exploded prejudices and obsolete traditions. I don't think a single man, Vere, that sat in the Venetian Senate ought to be allowed to sit in the present English House of Commons.'

'Well, no one does in our family except my uncle Philip,' said Lord Henry; 'and the moment I want it, he will resign; for he detests Parliament. It interferes so with his hunting.'

'Well, we all have fair parliamentary prospects,' said Buckhurst. 'That is something. I wish we were in now.'

'Heaven forbid!' said Coningsby. 'I tremble at the responsibility of a seat at any time. With my present unsettled and perplexed views, there is nothing from which I should recoil so much as the House of Commons.'

'I quite agree with you,' said Henry Sydney. 'The best thing we can do is to keep as clear of political party as we possibly can. How many men waste the best part of their lives in painfully apologising for conscientious deviation from a parliamentary course which they adopted when they were boys, without thought, or prompted by some local connection, or interest, to secure a seat.'

It was the midnight following the morning when this conversation took place, that Coningsby, alone, and having just quitted a rather boisterous party of wassailers who had been celebrating at Buckhurst's rooms the triumph of 'Eton Statesmen,' if not of Conservative principles, stopped in the precincts of that Royal College that reminded him of his school-days, to cool his brow in the summer air, that even at that hour was soft, and to calm his mind in the contemplation of the still, the sacred, and the beauteous scene that surrounded him.

There rose that fane, the pride and boast of Cambridge, not unworthy to rank among the chief temples of Christendom. Its vast form was exaggerated in the uncertain hour; part shrouded in the deepest darkness, while a flood of silver light suffused its southern side, distinguished with revealing beam the huge ribs of its buttresses, and bathed with mild lustre its airy pinnacles.

'Where is the spirit that raised these walls?' thought Coningsby. 'Is it indeed extinct? Is then this civilisation, so much vaunted, inseparable from moderate feelings and little thoughts? If so, give me back barbarism! But I cannot believe it. Man that is made in the image of the Creator, is made for God-like deeds. Come what come may, I will cling to the heroic principle. It can alone satisfy my soul.'

Chapter 3

WE must now revert to the family, or rather the household, of Lord Monmouth, in which considerable changes and events had occurred since the visit of Coningsby to the Castle in the preceding autumn.

In the first place, the earliest frost of the winter had carried off the aged proprietor of Hellingsley, that contiguous estate which Lord Monmouth so much coveted, the possession of which was indeed one of the few objects of his life, and to secure which he was prepared to pay far beyond its intrinsic value, great as that undoubtedly was. Yet Lord Monmouth did not become its possessor. Long as his mind had been intent upon the subject, skilful as had been his combinations to secure his prey, and unlimited the means which were to achieve his purpose, another stepped in, and without his privity, without even the consolation of a struggle, stole away the prize; and this too a man whom he hated, almost the only individual out of his own family that he did hate; a man who had crossed him before in similar enterprises; who was his avowed foe; had lavished treasure to oppose him in elections; raised associations against his interest; established journals to assail him; denounced him in public; agitated against him in private; had declared more than once that he would make 'the county too hot for him;' his personal, inveterate, indomitable foe, Mr Millbank of Millbank.

The loss of Hellingsley was a bitter disappointment to Lord Monmouth; but the loss of it to such an adversary touched him to the quick. He did not seek to control his anger; he could not succeed even in concealing his agitation. He threw upon Rigby that glance so rare with him, but under which men always quailed; that play of the eye which Lord Monmouth shared in common with Henry VIII, that struck awe into the trembling Commons when they had given an obnoxious vote, as the King entered the gallery of his palace, and looked around him.

It was a look which implied that dreadful question, 'Why have I bought you that such things should happen? Why have I unlimited means and unscrupulous agents?' It made even Rigby feel; even his brazen tones were hushed.

To fly from everything disagreeable was the practical philosophy of Lord Monmouth; but he was as brave as he was sensual. He would not shrink before the new proprietor of Hellingsley. He therefore remained at the Castle with an aching heart, and redoubled his hospitalities. An ordinary mind might have been soothed by the unceasing consideration and the skilful and delicate flattery that ever surrounded Lord Monmouth; but his sagacious intelligence was never for a moment the dupe of his vanity. He had no self-love, and as he valued no one, there were really no feelings to play upon. He saw through everybody and everything; and when he had detected their purpose, discovered their weakness or their vileness, he calculated whether they could contribute to his pleasure or his convenience in a degree that counterbalanced the objections which might be urged against their intentions, or their less pleasing and profitable qualities. To be pleased was always a principal object with Lord Monmouth; but when a man wants vengeance, gay amusement is not exactly a satisfactory substitute.

A month elapsed. Lord Monmouth with a serene or smiling visage to his guests, but in private taciturn and morose, scarcely ever gave a word to Mr Rigby, but continually bestowed on him glances which painfully affected the appetite of that gentleman. In a hundred ways it was intimated to Mr Rigby that he was not a welcome guest, and yet something was continually given him to do which rendered it impossible for him to take his departure. In this state of affairs, another event occurred which changed the current of feeling, and by its possible consequences distracted the Marquess from his brooding meditations over his discomfiture in the matter of Hellingsley. The Prince Colonna, who, since the steeple-chase, had imbibed a morbid predilection for such amusements, and indeed for every species of rough-riding, was thrown from his horse and killed on the spot.

This calamity broke up the party at Coningsby, which was not at the moment very numerous. Mr Rigby, by command, instantly seized the opportunity of preventing the arrival of other guests who were expected. This catastrophe was the cause of Mr Rigby resuming in a great measure his old position in the Castle. There were a great many things to be done, and all disagreeable; he achieved them all, and studied everybody's convenience. Coroners' inquests, funerals especially, weeping women, these were all spectacles which Lord Monmouth could not endure, but he was so high-bred, that he would not for the world that there should be in manner or degree the slightest deficiency in propriety or even sympathy. But he wanted somebody to do everything that was proper; to be considerate and consoling and sympathetic. Mr Rigby did it all; gave evidence at the inquest, was chief mourner at the funeral, and arranged everything so well that not a single emblem of death crossed the sight of Lord Monmouth; while Madame Colonna found submission in his exhortations, and the Princess Lucretia, a little more pale and pensive than usual, listened with tranquillity to his discourse on the vanity of all sublunary things.

When the tumult had subsided, and habits and feelings had fallen into their old routine and relapsed into their ancient channels, the Marquess proposed that they should all return to London, and with great formality, though with warmth, begged that Madame Colonna would ever consider his roof as her own. All were glad to quit the Castle, which now presented a scene so different from its former animation, and Madame Colonna, weeping, accepted the hospitality of her friend, until the impending expansion of the spring would permit her to return to Italy. This notice of her return to her own country seemed to occasion the Marquess great disquietude.

After they had remained about a month in London, Madame Colonna sent for Mr Rigby one morning to tell him how very painful it was to her feelings to remain under the roof of Monmouth House without the sanction of a husband; that the circumstances of being a foreigner, under such unusual affliction, might have excused, though not authorised, the step at first, and for a moment; but that the continuance of such a course was quite out of the question; that she owed it to herself, to her stepchild, no longer to trespass on this friendly hospitality, which, if persisted in, might be liable to misconstruction. Mr Rigby listened with great attention to this statement, and never in the least interrupted Madame Colonna; and then offered to do that which he was convinced the lady desired, namely, to make the Marquess acquainted with the painful state of her feelings. This he did according to his fashion, and with sufficient dexterity. Mr Rigby himself was anxious to know which way the wind blew, and the mission with which he had been entrusted, fell in precisely with his inclinations and necessities. The Marquess listened to the communication and sighed, then turned gently round and surveyed himself in the mirror and sighed again, then said to Rigby

'You understand exactly what I mean, Rigby. It is quite ridiculous their going, and infinitely distressing to me. They must stay.'

Rigby repaired to the Princess full of mysterious bustle, and with a face beaming with importance and satisfaction. He made much of the two sighs; fully justified the confidence of the Marquess in his comprehension of unexplained intentions; prevailed on Madame Colonna to have some regard for the feelings of one so devoted; expatiated on the insignificance of worldly misconstructions, when replied to by such honourable intentions; and fully succeeded in his mission. They did stay. Month after month rolled on, and still they stayed; every month all the family becoming more resigned or more content, and more cheerful. As for the Marquess himself, Mr Rigby never remembered him more serene and even joyous. His Lordship scarcely ever entered general society. The Colonna family remained in strict seclusion; and he preferred the company of these accomplished and congenial friends to the mob of the great world.

Between Madame Colonna and Mr Rigby there had always subsisted considerable confidence. Now, that gentleman seemed to have achieved fresh and greater claims to her regard. In the pleasure with which he looked forward to her approaching alliance with his patron, he reminded her of the readiness with which he had embraced her suggestions for the marriage of her daughter with Coningsby. Always obliging, she was never wearied of chanting his praises to her noble admirer, who was apparently much gratified she should have bestowed her esteem on one of whom she would necessarily in after-life see so much. It is seldom the lot of husbands that their confidential friends gain the regards of their brides.

'I am glad you all like Rigby,' said Lord Monmouth, 'as you will see so much of him.'

The remembrance of the Hellingsley failure seemed to be erased from the memory of the Marquess. Rigby never recollected him more cordial and confidential, and more equable in his manner. He told Rigby one day, that he wished that Monmouth House should possess the most sumptuous and the most fanciful boudoir in London or Paris. What a hint for Rigby! That gentleman consulted the first artists, and gave them some hints in return; his researches on domestic decoration ranged through all ages; he even meditated a rapid tour to mature his inventions; but his confidence in his native taste and genius ultimately convinced him that this movement was unnecessary.

The summer advanced; the death of the King occurred; the dissolution summoned Rigby to Coningsby and the borough of Darlford. His success was marked certain in the secret books of Tadpole and Taper. A manufacturing town, enfranchised under the Reform Act, already gained by the Conservative cause! Here was reaction; here influence of property! Influence of character, too; for no one was so popular as Lord Monmouth; a most distinguished nobleman of strict Conservative principles, who, if he carried the county and the manufacturing borough also, merited the strawberry-leaf.

'There will be no holding Rigby,' said Taper; 'I'm afraid he will be looking for something very high.'

'The higher the better,' rejoined Tadpole, 'and then he will not interfere with us. I like your high-flyers; it is your plodders I detest, wearing old hats and high-lows,[1] speaking in committee, and thinking they are men of business: d—n them!'

Rigby went down, and made some impressive speeches; at least they read very well in some of his second-rate journals, where all the uproar figured as loud cheering, and the interruption of a cabbage-stalk was represented as a question from some intelligent individual in the crowd. The fact is, Rigby bored his audience too much with history, especially with the French

Revolution, which he fancied was his 'forte,' so that the people at last, whenever he made any allusion to the subject, were almost as much terrified as if they had seen the guillotine.

Rigby had as yet one great advantage; he had no opponent; and without personal opposition, no contest can be very bitter. It was for some days Rigby *versus* Liberal principles; and Rigby had much the best of it; for he abused Liberal principles roundly in his harangues, who, not being represented on the occasion, made no reply; while plenty of ale, and some capital songs by Lucian Gay, who went down express, gave the right cue to the mob, who declared in chorus, beneath the windows of Rigby's hotel, that he was 'a fine old English gentleman!'

But there was to be a contest; no question about that, and a sharp one, although Rigby was to win, and well. The Liberal party had been so fastidious about their new candidate, that they had none ready though several biting. Jawster Sharp thought at one time that sheer necessity would give him another chance still; but even Rigby was preferable to Jawster Sharp, who, finding it would not do, published his long-prepared valedictory address, in which he told his constituents, that having long sacrificed his health to their interests, he was now obliged to retire into the bosom of his family. And a very well-provided-for family, too.

All this time the Liberal deputation from Darlford, two aldermen, three town-councillors, and the Secretary of the Reform Association, were walking about London like mad things, eating luncheons and looking for a candidate. They called at the Reform Club twenty times in the morning, badgered whips and red-tapers; were introduced to candidates, badgered candidates; examined would-be members as if they were at a cattle-show, listened to political pedigrees, dictated political pledges, referred to Hansard to see how men had voted, inquired whether men had spoken, finally discussed terms. But they never could hit the right man. If the principles were right, there was no money; and if money were ready, money would not take pledges. In fact, they wanted a Phœnix: a very rich man, who would do exactly as they liked, with extremely low opinions and with very high connections.

'If he would go for the ballot and had a handle to his name, it would have the best effect,' said the secretary of the Reform

Association, 'because you see we are fighting against a Right Honourable, and you have no idea how that takes with the mob.'

The deputation had been three days in town, and urged by despatches by every train to bring affairs to a conclusion; jaded, perplexed, confused, they were ready to fall into the hands of the first jobber or bold adventurer. They discussed over their dinner at a Strand coffee-house the claims of the various candidates who had presented themselves. Mr Donald Macpherson Macfarlane, who would only pay the legal expenses; he was soon despatched. Mr Gingerly Browne, of Jermyn Street, the younger son of a baronet, who would go as far as 1,000*l.* provided the seat was secured. Mr Juggins, a distiller, 2,000*l.* man; but would not agree to any annual subscriptions. Sir Baptist Placid, vague about expenditure, but repeatedly declaring that 'there could be no difficulty on that head.' He however had a moral objection to subscribing to the races, and that was a great point at Darlford. Sir Baptist would subscribe a guinea per annum to the Infirmary, and the same to all religious societies without any distinction of sects; but races, it was not the sum, 100*l.* per annum, but the principle. He had a moral objection.

In short, the deputation began to suspect, what was the truth, that they were a day after the fair, and that all the electioneering rips that swarm in the purlieus of political clubs during an impending dissolution of Parliament, men who become political characters in their small circle because they have been talked of as once having an intention to stand for places for which they never offered themselves, or for having stood for places where they never could by any circumstance have succeeded, were in fact nibbling at their dainty morsel.

At this moment of despair, a ray of hope was imparted to them by a confidential note from a secretary of the Treasury, who wished to see them at the Reform Club on the morrow. You may be sure they were punctual to their appointment. The secretary received them with great consideration. He had got them a candidate, and one of high mark, the son of a Peer, and connected with the highest Whig houses. Their eyes sparkled. A real honourable. If they liked he would introduce them immediately to the Honourable Alberic de Crecy. He had only to introduce them, as there was no difficulty either as to means or opinions, expenses or pledges.

The secretary returned with a young gentleman, whose diminutive stature would seem, from his smooth and singularly puerile countenance, to be merely the consequence of his very tender years; but Mr de Crecy was really of age, or at least would be by nomination-day. He did not say a word, but looked like the rosebud which dangled in the button-hole of his frock-coat. The aldermen and town-councillors were what is sometimes emphatically styled flabbergasted: they were speechless from bewilderment. 'Mr de Crecy will go for the ballot,' said the secretary of the Treasury, with an audacious eye and a demure look, 'and for Total and Immediate, if you press him hard; but don't, if you can help it, because he has an uncle, an old county member, who has prejudices, and might disinherit him. However, we answer for him. And I am very happy that I have been the means of bringing about an arrangement which, I feel, will be mutually advantageous.' And so saying, the secretary effected his escape.

Circumstances, however, retarded for a season the political career of the Honourable Alberic de Crecy. While the Liberal party at Darlford were suffering under the daily inflictions of Mr Rigby's slashing style, and the post brought them very unsatisfactory prospects of a champion, one offered himself, and in an address which intimated that he was no man of straw, likely to recede from any contest in which he chose to embark. The town was suddenly placarded with a letter to the Independent Electors from Mr Millbank, the new proprietor of Hellingsley.

He expressed himself as one not anxious to obtrude himself on their attention, and founding no claim to their confidence on his recent acquisition; but at the same time as one resolved that the free and enlightened community, with which he must necessarily hereafter be much connected, should not become the nomination borough of any Peer of the realm without a struggle, if they chose to make one. And so he offered himself if they could not find a better candidate, without waiting for the ceremony of a requisition. He was exactly the man they wanted; and though he had 'no handle to his name,' and was somewhat impracticable about pledges, his fortune was so great, and his character so high, that it might be hoped that the people would be almost as content as if they were appealed to by some obscure scion of factitious nobility, subscribing to political engagements which he could not comprehend, and which, in general, are vomited with as much facility as they are swallowed.

Chapter 4

THE people of Darlford, who, as long as the contest for their representation remained between Mr Rigby and the abstraction called Liberal Principles, appeared to be very indifferent about the result, the moment they learned that for the phrase had been substituted a substance, and that, too, in the form of a gentleman who was soon to figure as their resident neighbour, became excited, speedily enthusiastic. All the bells of all the churches rang when Mr Millbank commenced his canvass; the Conservatives, on the alert, if not alarmed, insisted on their champion also showing himself in all directions; and in the course of four-and-twenty hours, such is the contagion of popular feeling, the town was divided into two parties, the vast majority of which were firmly convinced that the country could only be saved by the return of Mr Rigby, or preserved from inevitable destruction by the election of Mr Millbank.

The results of the two canvasses were such as had been anticipated from the previous reports of the respective agents and supporters. In these days the personal canvass of a candidate is a mere form. The whole country that is to be invaded has been surveyed and mapped out before entry; every position reconnoitred; the chain of communications complete. In the present case, as was not unusual, both candidates were really supported by numerous and reputable adherents; and both had good grounds for believing that they would be ultimately successful. But there was a body of the electors sufficiently numerous to turn the election, who would not promise their votes: conscientious men who felt the responsibility of the duty that the constitution had entrusted to their discharge, and who would not make up their minds without duly weighing the respective merits of the two rivals. This class of deeply meditative individuals are distinguished not only by their pensive turn of mind, but by a charitable vein that seems to pervade their being. Not only will they think of your request, but for their parts they wish both sides equally well. Decision, indeed, as it must dash the hopes of one of their solicitors, seems infinitely painful to them; they have always a good reason for postponing it. If you seek their suffrage during the canvass, they reply, that the writ not having come down, the day of election is not yet fixed. If you call again to inform them that the writ has arrived, they rejoin, that perhaps after all there may not be a contest. If you call a third time, half dead with fatigue, to give them friendly notice that both you and your rival have pledged yourselves to go to the poll, they twitch their trousers, rub their hands, and with a dull grin observe,

'Well, sir, we shall see.'

'Come, Mr Jobson,' says one of the committee, with an insinuating smile, 'give Mr Millbank one.'

'Jobson, I think you and I know each other,' says a most influential supporter, with a knowing nod.

'Yes, Mr Smith, I should think we did.'

'Come, come, give us one.'

'Well, I have not made up my mind yet, gentlemen.'

'Jobson!' says a solemn voice, 'didn't you tell me the other night you wished well to this gentleman?'

'So I do; I wish well to everybody,' replies the imperturbable Jobson.

'Well, Jobson,' exclaims another member of the committee, with a sigh, 'who could have supposed that you would have been an enemy?'

'I don't wish to be no enemy to no man, Mr Trip.'

'Come, Jobson,' says a jolly tanner, 'if I wanted to be a Parliament man, I don't think you could refuse me one!'

'I don't think I could, Mr Oakfield.'

'Well, then, give it to my friend.'

'Well, sir, I'll think about it.'

'Leave him to me,' says another member of the committee, with a significant look. 'I know how to get round him. It's all right.'

'Yes, leave him to Hayfield, Mr Millbank; he knows how to manage him.'

But all the same, Jobson continues to look as little tractable and lamb-like as can be well fancied.

And here, in a work which, in an unpretending shape, aspires to take neither an uninformed nor a partial view of the political history of the ten eventful years of the Reform struggle, we should pause for a moment to observe the strangeness, that only five years after the reconstruction of the electoral body by the Whig party, in a borough called into political existence by their policy, a manufacturing town, too, the candidate comprising in his person every quality and circumstance which could recommend him to the constituency, and his opponent the worst specimen of the Old Generation, a political adventurer, who owed the least disreputable part of his notoriety to his opposition to the Reform Bill; that in such a borough, under such circumstances, there should be a contest, and that, too, one of a very doubtful issue.

What was the cause of this? Are we to seek it in the 'Reaction' of the Tadpoles and the Tapers? That would not be a satisfactory solution. Reaction, to a certain extent, is the law of human existence. In the particular state of affairs before us, England after the Reform Act, it never could be doubtful that Time would gradually, and in some instances rapidly, counteract the national impulse of 1832. There never could have been a question, for example, that the English counties would have reverted to their natural allegiance to their proprietors; but the results of the appeals to the third Estate in 1835 and 1837 are not to be accounted for by a mere readjustment of legitimate influences.

The truth is, that, considerable as are the abilities of the Whig leaders, highly accomplished as many of them un-questionably must be acknowledged in parliamentary debate, experienced in council, sedulous in office, eminent as scholars, powerful from their position, the absence of individual influence, and of the pervading authority of a commanding mind, have been the cause of the fall of the Whig party.

Such a supremacy was generally acknowledged in Lord Grey on the accession of this party to power: but it was the supremacy of a tradition rather than of a fact. Almost at the outset of his authority his successor[1] was indicated. When the crisis arrived, the intended successor was not in the Whig ranks. It is in this virtual absence of a real and recognised leader, almost from the moment that they passed their great measure, that we must seek a chief cause of all that insubordination, all those distempered ambitions, and all those dark intrigues, that finally broke up, not only the Whig government, but the Whig party; demoralised their ranks, and sent them to the country, both in 1835 and 1837, with every illusion, which had operated so happily in their favour in 1832, scattered to the winds. In all things we trace the irresistible influence of the individual.

And yet the interval that elapsed between 1835 and 1837 proved, that there was all this time in the Whig array one entirely competent to the office of leading a great party, though his capacity for that fulfilment was too tardily recognised.

LORD JOHN RUSSELL has that degree of imagination, which, though evinced rather in sentiment than expression, still enables him to generalise from the details of his reading and experience; and to take those comprehensive views, which, however easily depreciated by ordinary men in an age of routine, are indispensable to a statesman in the conjunctures in which we live. He understands, therefore, his position; and he has the moral intrepidity which prompts him ever to dare that which his intellect assures him is politic. He is consequently, at the same time, sagacious and bold in council. As an administrator he is prompt and indefatigable. He is not a natural orator, and labours under physical deficiencies which even a Demosthenic impulse[2] could scarcely overcome. But he is experienced in debate, quick in reply, fertile in resource, takes large views, and frequently compensates for a dry and hesitating manner by the expression of those noble truths that flash across the fancy, and rise spontaneously to the lip, of men of poetic temperament when addressing popular assemblies. If we add to this, a private life of dignified repute, the accidents of his birth and rank, which never can be severed from the man, the scion of a great historic family, and born, as it were, to the hereditary service of the State, it is difficult to ascertain at what period, or under what circumstances, the Whig party have ever possessed, or could obtain, a more efficient leader.

But we must return to the Darlford election. The class of thoughtful voters was sufficiently numerous in that borough to render the result of the contest doubtful to the last; and on the eve of the day of nomination both parties were equally sanguine.

Nomination-day altogether is an unsatisfactory affair. There is little to be done, and that little mere form. The tedious hours remain, and no one can settle his mind to anything. It is not a holiday, for every one is serious; it is not business, for no one can attend to it; it is not a contest, for there is no canvassing; nor an election, for there is no poll. It is a day of lounging without an object, and luncheons without an appetite; of hopes and fears; confidence and dejection; bravado bets and secret hedging; and, about midnight, of furious suppers of grilled bones, brandy-and-water, and recklessness.

The president and vice-president of the Conservative Association, the secretary and the four solicitors who were agents, had impressed upon Mr Rigby that it was of the utmost importance, and must produce a great moral effect, if he obtained the show of hands. With his powers of eloquence and their secret organisation, they flattered themselves it might be done. With this view, Rigby inflicted a speech of more than two hours' duration on the electors, who bore it very kindly, as the mob likes, above all things, that the ceremonies of nomination-day should not be cut short: moreover, there is nothing that the mob likes so much as a speech. Rigby therefore had, on the whole, a far from unfavourable audience, and he availed himself of their forbearance. He brought in his crack theme, the guillotine, and dilated so elaborately upon its qualities, that one of the gentlemen below could not refrain from exclaiming, 'I wish you may get it.' This exclamation gave Mr Rigby what is called a great opening, which, like a practised speaker, he immediately seized. He denounced the sentiment as 'un-English,' and got much cheered. Excited by this success, Rigby began to call everything else 'un-English' with which he did not agree, until menacing murmurs began to rise, when he shifted the subject, and rose into a grand peroration, in which he assured them that the eyes of the whole empire were on this particular election; cries of 'That's true,' from all sides; and that England expected every man to do his duty.

'And who do you expect to do yours?' inquired a gentleman below, 'about that ere pension?'

'Rigby,' screeched a hoarse voice, 'don't you mind; you guv it them well.'

'Rigby, keep up your spirits, old chap: we will have you.'

'Now!' said a stentorian voice; and a man as tall as Saul looked round him. This was the engaged leader of the Conservative mob; the eye of every one of his minions was instantly on him. 'Now! Our young Queen and our Old Institutions! Rigby for ever!'

This was a signal for the instant appearance of the leader of the Liberal mob. Magog Wrath, not so tall as Bully Bluck, his rival, had a voice almost as powerful, a back much broader, and a countenance far more forbidding. 'Now, my boys, the Queen and Millbank for ever!'

These rival cries were the signals for a fight between the two bands of gladiators in the face of the hustings, the body of the people little interfering. Bully Bluck seized Magog Wrath's colours; they wrestled, they seized each other; their supporters were engaged in mutual contest; it appeared to be a most alarming and perilous fray; several ladies from the windows screamed, one fainted; a band of special constables pushed their way through the mob; you heard their staves resounding on the skulls of all who opposed them, especially the little boys: order was at length restored; and, to tell the truth, the only hurts inflicted were those which came from the special constables. Bully Bluck and Magog Wrath, with all their fierce looks, flaunting colours, loud cheers, and desperate assaults, were, after all, only a couple of Condottieri, who were cautious never to wound each other. They were, in fact, a peaceful police, who kept the town in awe, and prevented others from being mischievous who were more inclined to do harm. Their hired gangs were the safety-valves for all the scamps of the borough, who, receiving a few shillings per head for their nominal service, and as much drink as they liked after the contest, were bribed and organised into peace and sobriety on the days in which their excesses were most to be apprehended.

Now Mr Millbank came forward: he was brief compared with Mr Rigby; but clear and terse. No one could misunderstand him.

He did not favour his hearers with any history, but gave them his views about taxes, free trade, placemen, and pensioners, whoever and whatever they might be.

'Hilloa, Rigby, about that ere pension?'

'Millbank for ever! We will have him.'

'Never mind, Rigby, you'll come in next time.'

Mr Millbank was energetic about resident representatives, but did not understand that a resident representative meant the nominee of a great Lord, who lived in a great castle; great cheering. There was a Lord once who declared that, if he liked, he would return his negro valet to Parliament; but Mr Millbank thought those days were over. It remained for the people of Darlford to determine whether he was mistaken.

'Never!' exclaimed the mob. 'Millbank for ever! Rigby in the river! No niggers, no walets!'

'Three groans for Rigby.'

'His language ain't as purty as the Lunnun chap's,' said a critic below; 'but he speaks from his 'art: and give me the man who 'as got a 'art.'

'That's your time of day, Mr Robinson.'

'Now!' said Magog Wrath, looking around. 'Now, the Queen and Millbank for ever! Hurrah!'

The show of hands was entirely in favour of Mr Millbank. Scarcely a hand was held up for Mr Rigby below, except by Bully Bluck and his prætorians. The Chairman and the Deputy Chairman of the Conservative Association, the Secretary, and the four agents, severally and respectively went up to Mr Rigby and congratulated him on the result, as it was a known fact, 'that the show of hands never won.'

The eve of polling-day was now at hand. This is the most critical period of an election. All night parties in disguise were perambulating the different wards, watching each other's tactics; masks, wigs, false noses, gentles in livery coats, men in female attire, a silent carnival of manœuvre, vigilance, anxiety, and trepidation. The thoughtful voters about this time make up their minds; the enthusiasts who have told you twenty times a-day for the last fortnight, that they would get up in the middle of the night to serve you, require the most watchful cooping; all the individuals who have assured you that 'their word is their bond,' change sides.

Two of the Rigbyites met in the market-place about an hour after midnight.

'Well, how goes it?' said one.

'I have been the rounds. The blunt's going like the ward-pump.[3] I saw a man come out of Moffatt's house, muffled up with a mask on. I dodged him. It was Biggs.'

'You don't mean that, do you? D—e, I'll answer for Moffatt.'

'I never thought he was a true man.'

'Told Robins?'

'I could not see him; but I met young Gunning and told him.'

'Young Gunning! That won't do.'

'I thought he was as right as the town clock.'

'So did I, once. Hush! who comes here? The enemy, Franklin and Sampson Potts. Keep close.'

'I'll speak to them. Good night, Potts. Up rather late to-night?'

'All fair election time. You ain't snoring, are you?'

'Well, I hope the best man will win.'

'I am sure he will.'

'You must go for Moffatt early, to breakfast at the White Lion; that's your sort. Don't leave him, and poll him yourself. I am going off to Solomon Lacey's. He has got four Millbankites cooped up very drunk, and I want to get them quietly into the country before daybreak.'

'Tis polling day! The candidates are roused from their slumbers at an early hour by the music of their own bands perambulating the town, and each playing the 'conquering hero' to sustain the courage of their jaded employers, by depriving them of that rest which can alone tranquillise the nervous system. There is something in that matin burst of music, followed by a shrill cheer from the boys of the borough, the only inhabitants yet up, that is very depressing.

The committee-rooms of each candidate are soon rife with black reports; each side has received fearful bulletins of the preceding night campaign; and its consequences as exemplified in the morning, unprecedented tergiversations, mysterious absences; men who breakfast with one side and vote with the other;

men who won't come to breakfast; men who won't leave breakfast.

At ten o'clock Mr Rigby was in a majority of twenty-eight.

The polling was brisk and equal until the middle of the day,
when it became slack. Mr Rigby kept a majority, but an
inconsiderable one. Mr Millbank's friends were not disheartened,
as it was known that the leading members of Mr Rigby's
committee had polled; whereas his opponent's were principally
reserved. At a quarter-past two there was great cheering and
uproar. The four voters in favour of Millbank, whom Solomon
Lacey had cooped up, made drunk, and carried into the country,
had recovered their senses, made their escape, and voted as they
originally intended. Soon after this, Mr Millbank was declared
by his committee to be in a majority of one, but the committee
of Mr Rigby instantly posted a placard, in large letters, to
announce that, on the contrary, their man was in a majority
of nine.

'If we could only have got another registration,' whispered the
principal agent to Mr Rigby, at a quarter-past four.

'You think it's all over then?'

'Why, I do not see now how we can win. We have polled all
our dead men, and Millbank is seven a-head.'

'I have no doubt we shall be able to have a good petition,'
said the consoling chairman of the Conservative Association.

Chapter 5

IT was not with feelings of extreme satisfaction that Mr Rigby returned to London. The loss of Hellingsley, followed by the loss of the borough to Hellingsley's successful master, were not precisely the incidents which would be adduced as evidence of Mr Rigby's good management or good fortune. Hitherto that gentleman had persuaded the world that he was not only very clever, but that he was also always in luck; a quality which many appreciate more even than capacity. His reputation was unquestionably damaged, both with his patron and his party. But what the Tapers and the Tadpoles thought or said, what even might be the injurious effect on his own career of the loss of this election, assumed an insignificant character when compared with its influence on the temper and disposition of the Marquess of Monmouth.

And yet his carriage is now entering the courtyard of Monmouth House, and, in all probability, a few minutes would introduce him to that presence before which he had, ere this, trembled. The Marquess was at home, and anxious to see Mr Rigby. In a few minutes that gentleman was ascending the private staircase, entering the antechamber, and waiting to be received in the little saloon, exactly as our Coningsby did more than five years ago, scarcely less agitated, but by feelings of a very different character.

'Well, you made a good fight of it,' exclaimed the Marquess, in a cheerful and cordial tone, as Mr Rigby entered his dressing-room. 'Patience! We shall win the next time.'

This reception instantly reassured the defeated candidate, though its contrast to that which he expected rather perplexed him. He entered into the details of the election, talked rapidly of the next registration, the propriety of petitioning; accustomed himself to hearing his voice with its habitual volubility in a chamber where he had feared it might not sound for some time.

'D—n politics!' said the Marquess. 'These fellows are in for this Parliament, and I am really weary of the whole affair. I begin to think the Duke was right, and it would have been best to have left them to themselves. I am glad you have come up at once, for I want you. The fact is, I am going to be married.'

This was not a startling announcement to Mr Rigby; he was prepared for it, though scarcely could have hoped that he would have been favoured with it on the present occasion, instead of a morose comment on his misfortunes. Marriage, then, was the predominant idea of Lord Monmouth at the present moment, in whose absorbing interest all vexations were forgotten. Fortunate Rigby! Disgusted by the failure of his political combinations, his disappointments in not dictating to the county and not carrying the borough, and the slight prospect at present of obtaining the great object of his ambition, Lord Monmouth had resolved to precipitate his fate, was about to marry immediately, and quit England.

'You will be wanted, Rigby,' continued the Marquess. 'We must have a couple of trustees, and I have thought of you as one. You know you are my executor; and it is better not to bring in unnecessarily new names into the management of my affairs. Lord Eskdale will act with you.'

Rigby then, after all, was a lucky man. After such a succession of failures, he had returned only to receive fresh and the most delicate marks of his patron's good feeling and consideration. Lord Monmouth's trustee and executor! 'You know you are my executor.' Sublime truth! It ought to be blazoned in letters of gold in the most conspicuous part of Rigby's library, to remind him perpetually of his great and impending destiny. Lord Monmouth's executor, and very probably one of his residuary legatees! A legatee of some sort he knew he was. What a splendid *memento mori*! What cared Rigby for the borough of Darlford? And as for his political friends, he wished them joy of their barren benches. Nothing was lost by not being in this Parliament.

It was then with sincerity that Rigby offered his congratulations to his patron. He praised the judicious alliance, accompanied by every circumstance conducive to worldly happiness; distinguished beauty, perfect temper, princely rank. Rigby, who had hardly got out of his hustings' vein, was most eloquent in his praises of Madame Colonna.

'An amiable woman,' said Lord Monmouth, 'and very handsome. I always admired her; and an agreeable person too; I dare say a very good temper, but I am not going to marry her.'

'Might I then ask who is –'

'Her step-daughter, the Princess Lucretia,' replied the Marquess, quietly, and looking at his ring.

Here was a thunderbolt! Rigby had made another mistake. He had been working all this time for the wrong woman! The consciousness of being a trustee alone sustained him. There was an inevitable pause. The Marquess would not speak however, and Rigby must. He babbled rather incoherently about the Princess Lucretia being admired by everybody; also that she was the most fortunate of women, as well as the most accomplished; he was just beginning to say he had known her from a child, when discretion stopped his tongue, which had a habit of running on somewhat rashly; but Rigby, though he often blundered in his talk, had the talent of extricating himself from the consequence of his mistakes.

'And Madame must be highly gratified by all this?' observed Mr Rigby, with an inquiring accent. He was dying to learn how she had first received the intelligence, and congratulated himself that his absence at his contest had preserved him from the storm.

'Madame Colonna knows nothing of our intentions,' said Lord Monmouth. 'And by the bye, that is the very business on which I wish to see you, Rigby. I wish you to communicate them to her. We are to be married, and immediately. It would gratify me that the wife of Lucretia's father should attend our wedding. You understand exactly what I mean, Rigby; I must have no scenes. Always happy to see the Princess Colonna under my roof: but then I like to live quietly, particularly at present; harassed as I have been by the loss of these elections, by all this bad management, and by all these disappointments on subjects in which I was led to believe success was certain. Madame Colonna is at home;' and the Marquess bowed Mr Rigby out of the room.

Chapter 6

THE departure of Sidonia from Coningsby Castle, in the autumn, determined the Princess Lucretia on a step which had for some time before his arrival occupied her brooding imagination. Nature had bestowed on this lady an ambitious soul and a subtle spirit; she could dare much and could execute finely. Above all things she coveted power; and though not free from the characteristic susceptibility of her sex, the qualities that could engage her passions or fascinate her fancy must partake of that intellectual eminence which distinguished her. Though the Princess Lucretia in a short space of time had seen much of the world, she had as yet encountered no hero. In the admirers whom her rank, and sometimes her intelligence, assembled around her, her master had not yet appeared. Her heart had not trembled before any of those brilliant forms whom she was told her sex admired; nor did she envy any one the homage which she did not appreciate. There was, therefore, no disturbing element in the worldly calculations which she applied to that question which is, to woman, what a career is to man, the question of marriage. She would marry to gain power, and therefore she wished to marry the powerful. Lord Eskdale hovered around her, and she liked him. She admired his incomparable shrewdness; his freedom from ordinary prejudices; his selfishness which was always good-natured, and the imperturbability that was not callous. But Lord Eskdale had hovered round many; it was his easy habit. He liked clever women, young, but who had seen something of the world. The Princess Lucretia pleased him much; with the form and mind of a woman even in the nursery. He had watched her development with interest; and had witnessed her launched in that world where she floated at once with as much dignity and consciousness of superior power, as if she had braved for seasons its waves and its tempests.

Musing over Lord Eskdale, the mind of Lucretia was drawn to

the image of his friend; her friend; the friend of her parents. And why not marry Lord Monmouth? The idea pleased her. There was something great in the conception; difficult and strange. The result, if achieved, would give her all that she desired. She devoted her mind to this secret thought. She had no confidants. She concentrated her intellect on one point, and that was to fascinate the grandfather of Coningsby, while her step-mother was plotting that she should marry his grandson. The volition of Lucretia Colonna was, if not supreme, of a power most difficult to resist. There was something charming and alluring in the conversation of one who was silent to all others; something in the tones of her low rich voice which acted singularly on the nervous system. It was the voice of the serpent; indeed, there was an undulating movement in Lucretia, when she approached you, which irresistibly reminded you of that mysterious animal.

Lord Monmouth was not insensible to the spell, though totally unconscious of its purpose. He found the society of Lucretia very agreeable to him; she was animated, intelligent, original; her inquiries were stimulating; her comments on what she saw, and heard, and read, racy and often indicating a fine humour. But all this was reserved for his ear. Before her parents, as before all others, Lucretia was silent, a little scornful, never communicating, neither giving nor seeking amusement, shut up in herself.

Lord Monmouth fell therefore into the habit of riding and driving with Lucretia alone. It was an arrangement which he found made his life more pleasant. Nor was it displeasing to Madame Colonna. She looked upon Lord Monmouth's fancy for Lucretia as a fresh tie for them all. Even the Prince, when his wife called his attention to the circumstance, observed it with satisfaction. It was a circumstance which represented in his mind a continuance of good eating and good drinking, fine horses, luxurious baths, unceasing billiards.

In this state of affairs appeared Sidonia, known before to her step-mother, but seen by Lucretia for the first time. Truly, he came, saw, and conquered. Those eyes that rarely met another's were fixed upon his searching yet unimpassioned glance. She listened to that voice, full of music yet void of tenderness; and the spirit of Lucretia Colonna bowed before an intelligence that commanded sympathy, yet offered none.

Lucretia naturally possessed great qualities as well as great talents. Under a genial influence, her education might have formed a being capable of imparting and receiving happiness. But she found herself without a guide. Her father offered her no love; her step-mother gained from her no respect. Her literary education was the result of her own strong mind and inquisitive spirit. She valued knowledge, and she therefore acquired it. But not a single moral principle or a single religious truth had ever been instilled into her being. Frequent absence from her own country had by degrees broken off even an habitual observance of the forms of her creed; while a life of undisturbed indulgence, void of all anxiety and care, while it preserved her from many of the temptations to vice, deprived her of that wisdom 'more precious than rubies,' which adversity and affliction, the struggles and the sorrows of existence, can alone impart.

Lucretia had passed her life in a refined, but rather dissolute, society. Not indeed that a word that could call forth a maiden blush, conduct that could pain the purest feelings, could be heard or witnessed in those polished and luxurious circles. The most exquisite taste pervaded their atmosphere; and the uninitiated who found themselves in those perfumed chambers and those golden saloons, might believe, from all that passed before them, that their inhabitants were as pure, as orderly, and as irreproachable as their furniture. But among the habitual dwellers in these delicate halls there was a tacit understanding, a prevalent doctrine that required no formal exposition, no proofs and illustrations, no comment and no gloss; which was indeed rather a traditional conviction than an imparted dogma; that the exoteric public were, on many subjects, the victims of very vulgar prejudices, which these enlightened personages wished neither to disturb nor to adopt.

A being of such a temper, bred in such a manner; a woman full of intellect and ambition, daring and lawless, and satiated with prosperity, is not made for equable fortunes and an uniform existence. She would have sacrificed the world for Sidonia, for he had touched the fervent imagination that none before could approach; but that inscrutable man would not read the secret of her heart; and prompted alike by pique, the love of power, and a weariness of her present life, Lucretia resolved on that great result which Mr Rigby is now about to communicate to the Princess Colonna.

About half-an-hour after Mr Rigby had entered that lady's apartments it seemed that all the bells of Monmouth House were ringing at the same time. The sound even reached the Marquess in his luxurious recess; who immediately took a pinch of snuff, and ordered his valet to lock the door of the ante-chamber. The Princess Lucretia, too, heard the sounds; she was lying on a sofa, in her boudoir, reading the *Inferno*, and immediately mustered her garrison in the form of a French maid, and gave directions that no one should be admitted. Both the Marquess and his intended bride felt that a crisis was at hand, and resolved to participate in no scenes.

The ringing ceased; there was again silence. Then there was another ring; a short, hasty, and violent pull; followed by some slamming of doors. The servants, who were all on the alert, and had advantages of hearing and observation denied to their secluded master, caught a glimpse of Mr Rigby endeavouring gently to draw back into her apartments Madame Colonna, furious amid his deprecatory exclamations.

'For heaven's sake, my dear Madame; for your own sake; now really; now I assure you; you are quite wrong; you are indeed; it is a complete misapprehension; I will explain everything. I entreat, I implore, whatever you like, just what you please; only listen.'

Then the lady, with a mantling visage and flashing eye, violently closing the door, was again lost to their sight. A few minutes after there was a moderate ring, and Mr Rigby, coming out of the apartments, with his cravat a little out of order, as if he had had a violent shaking, met the servant who would have entered.

'Order Madame Colonna's travelling carriage,' he exclaimed in a loud voice, 'and send Mademoiselle Conrad here directly. I don't think the fellow hears me,' added Mr Rigby, and following the servant, he added in a low tone and with a significant glance, 'No travelling carriage; no Mademoiselle Conrad; order the britska round as usual.'

Nearly another hour passed; there was another ring; very moderate indeed. The servant was informed that Madame Colonna was coming down, and she appeared as usual. In a beautiful morning dress, and leaning on the arm of Mr Rigby, she descended the stairs, and was handed into her carriage by that gentleman, who, seating himself by her side, ordered them to drive to Richmond.

Lord Monmouth having been informed that all was calm, and that Madame Colonna, attended by Mr Rigby, had gone to Richmond, ordered his carriage, and accompanied by Lucretia and Lucian Gay, departed immediately for Blackwall, where, in whitebait, a quiet bottle of claret, the society of his agreeable friends, and the contemplation of the passing steamers, he found a mild distraction and an amusing repose.

Mr Rigby reported that evening to the Marquess on his return, that all was arranged and tranquil. Perhaps he exaggerated the difficulties, to increase the service; but according to his account they were considerable. It required some time to make Madame Colonna comprehend the nature of his communication. All Rigby's diplomatic skill was expended in the gradual development. When it was once fairly put before her, the effect was appalling. That was the first great ringing of bells. Rigby softened a little what he had personally endured; but he confessed she sprang at him like a tigress balked of her prey, and poured forth on him a volume of epithets, many of which Rigby really deserved. But after all, in the present instance, he was not treacherous, only base, which he always was. Then she fell into a passion of tears, and vowed frequently that she was not weeping for herself, but only for that dear Mr Coningsby, who had been treated so infamously and robbed of Lucretia, and whose heart she knew must break. It seemed that Rigby stemmed the first violence of her emotion by mysterious intimations of an important communication that he had to make; and piquing her curiosity, he calmed her passion. But really having nothing to say, he was nearly involved in fresh dangers. He took refuge in the affectation of great agitation which prevented exposition. The lady then insisted on her travelling carriage being ordered and packed, as she was determined to set out for Rome that afternoon. This little occurrence gave Rigby some few minutes to collect himself, at the end of which he made the Princess several announcements of intended arrangements, all of which pleased her mightily, though they were so inconsistent with each other, that if she had not been a woman in a passion, she must have detected that Rigby was lying. He assured her almost in the same breath, that she was never to be separated from them, and that she was to have any establishment in any country she liked. He talked wildly of equipages, diamonds, shawls, opera-boxes; and while her mind was bewildered with these dazzling objects, he, with intrepid gravity, consulted her as to the exact amount she would like to have apportioned, independent of her general revenue, for the purposes of charity.

At the end of two hours, exhausted by her rage and soothed by these visions, Madame Colonna having grown calm and reasonable, sighed and murmured a complaint, that Lord Monmouth ought to have communicated this important intelligence in person. Upon this Rigby instantly assured her, that Lord Monmouth had been for some time waiting to do so, but in consequence of her lengthened interview with Rigby, his Lordship had departed for Richmond with Lucretia, where he hoped that Madame Colonna and Mr Rigby would join him. So it ended, with a morning drive and suburban dinner; Rigby, after what he had gone through, finding no difficulty in accounting for the other guests not being present, and bringing home Madame Colonna in the evening, at times almost as gay and good-tempered as usual, and almost oblivious of her disappointment.

When the Marquess met Madame Colonna he embraced her with great courtliness, and from that time consulted her on every arrangement. He took a very early occasion of presenting her with a diamond necklace of great value. The Marquess was fond of making presents to persons to whom he thought he had not behaved very well, and who yet spared him scenes.

The marriage speedily followed by special license,[1] at the villa of the Right Hon. Nicholas Rigby, who gave away the bride.

The wedding was very select, but brilliant as the diamond necklace: a royal Duke and Duchess, Lady St Julians, and a few others. Mr Ormsby presented the bride with a bouquet of precious stones, and Lord Eskdale with a French fan in a diamond frame. It was a fine day; Lord Monmouth, calm as if he were winning the St Leger; Lucretia, universally recognised as a beauty; all the guests gay, the Princess Colonna especially.

The travelling carriage is at the door which is to bear away the happy pair. Madame Colonna embraces Lucretia; the Marquess gives a grand bow: they are gone. The guests remain awhile. A Prince of the blood will propose a toast; there is another glass of champagne quaffed, another ortolan devoured: and then they rise and disperse. Madame Colonna leaves with Lady St Julians, whose guest for a while she is to become. And in a few minutes their host is alone.

Mr Rigby retired into his library: the repose of the chamber must have been grateful to his feelings after all this distraction. It was spacious, well-stored, classically adorned, and opened on a beautiful lawn. Rigby threw himself into an ample chair, crossed his legs, and resting his head on his arm, apparently fell into deep contemplation.

He had some cause for reflection, and though we did once venture to affirm that Rigby never either thought or felt, this perhaps may be the exception that proves the rule.

He could scarcely refrain from pondering over the strange event which he had witnessed, and at which he had assisted.

It was an incident that might exercise considerable influence over his fortunes. His patron married, and married to one who certainly did not offer to Mr Rigby such a prospect of easy management as her step-mother! Here were new influences arising; new characters, new situations, new contingencies. Was he thinking of all this? He suddenly jumps up, hurries to a shelf and takes down a volume. It is his interleaved peerage, of which for twenty years he had been threatening an edition. Turning to the Marquisate of Monmouth, he took up his pen and thus made the necessary entry:

'*Married, second time, August 3rd, 1837, The Princess Lucretia Colonna, daughter of Prince Paul Colonna, born at Rome, February 16th, 1819.*'

That was what Mr Rigby called 'a great fact.' There was not a peerage-compiler in England who had that date save himself.

Before we close this slight narrative of the domestic incidents that occurred in the family of his grandfather since Coningsby quitted the Castle, we must not forget to mention what happened to Villebecque and Flora. Lord Monmouth took a great liking to the manager. He found him very clever in many things independently of his profession; he was useful to Lord Monmouth, and did his work in an agreeable manner. And the future Lady Monmouth was accustomed to Flora, and found her useful too, and did not like to lose her. And so the Marquess, turning all the circumstances in his mind, and being convinced that Villebecque could never succeed to any extent in England in his profession, and probably nowhere else, appointed him, to Villebecque's infinite satisfaction, intendant of his household, with a considerable salary, while Flora still lived with her kind stepfather.

Chapter 7

ANOTHER year elapsed; not so fruitful in incidents to Coningsby as the preceding ones, and yet not unprofitably passed. It had been spent in the almost unremitting cultivation of his intelligence. He had read deeply and extensively, digested his acquisitions, and had practised himself in surveying them, free from those conventional conclusions and those traditionary inferences that surrounded him. Although he had renounced his once cherished purpose of trying for University honours, an aim which he found discordant with the investigations on which his mind was bent, he had rarely quitted Cambridge. The society of his friends, the great convenience of public libraries, and the general tone of studious life around, rendered an University for him a genial residence. There is a moment in life, when the pride and thirst of knowledge seem to absorb our being, and so it happened now to Coningsby, who felt each day stronger in his intellectual resources, and each day more anxious and avid to increase them. The habits of public discussion fostered by the Debating Society were also for Coningsby no inconsiderable tie to the University. This was the arena in which he felt himself at home. The promise of his Eton days was here fulfilled. And while his friends listened to his sustained argument or his impassioned declamation, the prompt reply or the apt retort, they looked forward with pride through the vista of years to the time when the hero of the youthful Club should convince or dazzle in the senate. It is probable then that he would have remained at Cambridge with slight intervals until he had taken his degree, had not circumstances occurred which gave altogether a new turn to his thoughts.

When Lord Monmouth had fixed his wedding-day he had written himself to Coningsby to announce his intended marriage, and to request his grandson's presence at the ceremony. The letter was more than kind; it was warm and generous. He assured his grandson that his alliance should make no difference in the very ample provision which he had long intended for him; that he should ever esteem Coningsby his nearest relative; and that, while his death would bring to Coningsby as considerable an independence as an English gentleman need desire, so in his life-time Coningsby should ever be supported as became his birth, breeding, and future prospects. Lord Monmouth had mentioned to Lucretia, that he was about to invite his grandson to their wedding, and the lady had received the intimation with satis-faction. It so happened that a few hours after, Lucretia, who now entered the private rooms of Lord Monmouth without previously announcing her arrival, met Villebecque with the letter to Coningsby in his hand. Lucretia took it away from him, and said it should be posted with her own letters. It never reached its destination. Our friend learnt the marriage from the news-papers, which somewhat astounded him; but Coningsby was fond of his grandfather, and he wrote Lord Monmouth a letter of congratulation, full of feeling and ingenuousness, and which, while it much pleased the person to whom it was addressed, unintentionally convinced him that Coningsby had never received his original communication. Lord Monmouth spoke to Villebecque, who could throw sufficient light upon the subject, but it was never mentioned to Lady Monmouth. The Marquess was a man who always found out everything, and enjoyed the secret.

Rather more than a year after the marriage, when Coningsby had completed his twenty-first year, the year which he had passed so quietly at Cambridge, he received a letter from his grandfather, informing him that after a variety of movements Lady Monmouth and himself were established in Paris for the season, and desiring that he would not fail to come over as soon as practicable, and pay them as long a visit as the regulations of the University would permit. So, at the close of the December term, Coningsby quitted Cambridge for Paris.

Passing through London, he made his first visit to his banker at Charing Cross, on whom he had periodically drawn since he commenced his college life. He was in the outer counting-house, making some inquiries about a letter of credit, when one of the partners came out from an inner room, and invited him to enter.

This firm had been for generations the bankers of the Coningsby family; and it appeared that there was a sealed box in their possession, which had belonged to the father of Coningsby, and they wished to take this opportunity of delivering it to his son. This communication deeply interested him; and as he was alone in London, at an hotel, and on the wing for a foreign country, he requested permission, at once to examine it, in order that he might again deposit it with them: so he was shown into a private room for that purpose. The seal was broken; the box was full of papers, chiefly correspondence: among them was a packet described as letters from 'my dear Helen,' the mother of Coningsby. In the interior of this packet there was a miniature of that mother. He looked at it; put it down; looked at it again and again. He could not be mistaken. There was the same blue fillet in the bright hair. It was an exact copy of that portrait which had so greatly excited his attention when at Millbank! This was a mysterious and singularly perplexing incident. It greatly agitated him. He was alone in the room when he made the discovery. When he had recovered himself, he sealed up the contents of the box, with the exception of his mother's letters and the miniature, which he took away with him, and then re-delivered it to his banker for custody until his return.

Coningsby found Lord and Lady Monmouth in a splendid hotel in the Faubourg St Honoré, near the English Embassy. His grand-father looked at him with marked attention, and received him with evident satisfaction. Indeed, Lord Monmouth was greatly pleased that Harry had come to Paris; it was the University of the World, where everybody should graduate. Paris and London ought to be the great objects of all travellers; the rest was mere landscape.

It cannot be denied that between Lucretia and Coningsby there existed from the first a certain antipathy; and though circum-stances for a short time had apparently removed or modified the aversion, the manner of the lady when Coningsby was ushered into her boudoir, resplendent with all that Parisian taste and luxury could devise, was characterised by that frigid polite-ness which had preceded the days of their more genial acquain-tance. If the manner of Lucretia were the same as before her marriage, a considerable change might however be observed in her appearance. Her fine form had become more developed; while her dress, that she once neglected, was elaborate and gorgeous, and of the last mode. Lucretia was the fashion at Paris; a great lady, greatly admired. A guest under such a roof, however, Coningsby was at once launched into the most brilliant circles of Parisian society, which he found fascinating.

The art of society is, without doubt, perfectly comprehended and completely practised in the bright metropolis of France. An Englishman cannot enter a saloon without instantly feeling he is among a race more social than his compatriots. What, for example, is more consummate than the manner in which a French lady receives her guests! She unites graceful repose and unaffected dignity, with the most amiable regard for others. She sees every one; she speaks to every one; she sees them at the right moment; she says the right thing; it is utterly impossible to detect any difference in the position of her guests by the spirit in which she welcomes them. There is, indeed, throughout every circle of Parisian society, from the *château* to the *cabaret*, a sincere homage to intellect; and this without any maudlin sentiment. None sooner than the Parisians can draw the line between factitious notoriety and honest fame; or sooner distinguish between the counterfeit celebrity and the standard reputation. In England, we too often alternate between a supercilious neglect of genius and a rhapsodical pursuit of quacks. In England when a new character appears in our circles, the first question always is, 'Who is he?' In France it is, 'What is he?' In England, 'How much a-year?' In France, 'What has he done?'

Chapter 8

ABOUT a week after Coningsby's arrival in Paris, as he was sauntering on the soft and sunny Boulevards, soft and sunny though
Christmas, he met Sidonia.

'So you are here?' said Sidonia. 'Turn now with me, for I
see you are only lounging, and tell me when you came, where you
are, and what you have done since we parted. I have been here
myself but a few days.'

There was much to tell. And when Coningsby had rapidly
related all that had passed, they talked of Paris. Sidonia had offered
him hospitality, until he learned that Lord Monmouth was in
Paris, and that Coningsby was his guest.

'I am sorry you cannot come to me,' he remarked; 'I would have
shown you everybody and everything. But we shall meet often.'

'I have already seen many remarkable things,' said Coningsby;
'and met many celebrated persons. Nothing strikes me more in
this brilliant city than the tone of its society, so much higher than
our own. What an absence of petty personalities! How much
conversation, and how little gossip! Yet nowhere is there less
pedantry. Here all women are as agreeable as is the remarkable
privilege in London of some half-dozen. Men too, and great men,
develope their minds. A great man in England, on the contrary,
is generally the dullest dog in company. And yet, how piteous
to think that so fair a civilisation should be in such imminent
peril!'

'Yes! that is a common opinion; and yet I am somewhat
sceptical of its truth,' replied Sidonia. 'I am inclined to believe
that the social system of England is in infinitely greater danger
than that of France. We must not be misled by the agitated surface
of this country. The foundations of its order are deep and
sure. Learn to understand France. France is a Kingdom with a
Republic for its capital. It has been always so, for centuries. From
the days of the League to the days of the Sections, to the days

of 1830. It is still France, little changed; and only more national, for it is less Frank and more Gallic; as England has become less Norman and more Saxon.'

'And it is your opinion, then, that the present King[1] may maintain himself?'

'Every movement in this country, however apparently discordant, seems to tend to that inevitable end. He would not be on the throne if the nature of things had not demanded his presence. The Kingdom of France required a Monarch; the Republic of Paris required a Dictator. He comprised in his person both qualifications; lineage and intellect; blood for the provinces, brains for the city.'

'What a position! what an individual!' exclaimed Coningsby. 'Tell me,' he added, eagerly, 'what is he? This Prince of whom one hears in all countries at all hours; on whose existence we are told the tranquillity, almost the civilisation, of Europe depends, yet of whom we receive accounts so conflicting, so contradictory; tell me, you who can tell me, tell me what he is.'

Sidonia smiled at his earnestness. 'I have a creed of mine own,' he remarked, 'that the great characters of antiquity are at rare epochs reproduced for our wonder, or our guidance. Nature, wearied with mediocrity, pours the warm metal into an heroic mould. When circumstances at length placed me in the presence of the King of France, I recognised, ULYSSES!'

'But is there no danger,' resumed Coningsby, after the pause of a few moments, 'that the Republic of Paris may absorb the Kingdom of France?'

'I suspect the reverse,' replied Sidonia. 'The tendency of advanced civilisation is in truth to pure Monarchy. Monarchy is indeed a government which requires a high degree of civilisation for its full development. It needs the support of free laws and manners, and of a widely-diffused intelligence. Political compromises are not to be tolerated except at periods of rude transition. An educated nation recoils from the imperfect vicariate of what is called a representative government. Your House of Commons, that has absorbed all other powers in the State, will in all probability fall more rapidly than it rose. Public opinion has a more direct, a more comprehensive, a more efficient organ for its utterance, than a body of men sectionally chosen. The Printing-press is a political element unknown to classic or feudal times. It absorbs in a great degree the duties of the Sovereign, the Priest, the Parliament; it controls, it educates, it discusses. That public opinion, when it acts, would appear in the form of one who has no class interests. In an enlightened age the Monarch on the throne, free from the vulgar prejudices and the corrupt interests of the subject, becomes again divine!'

At this moment they reached that part of the Boulevards which leads into the Place of the Madeleine, whither Sidonia was bound; and Coningsby was about to quit his companion, when Sidonia said:

'I am only going a step over to the Rue Tronchet to say a few words to a friend of mine, M. P——s. I shall not detain you five minutes; and you should know him, for he has some capital pictures, and a collection of Limoges ware that is the despair of the dilettanti.'

So saying they turned down by the Place of the Madeleine, and soon entered the court of the hotel of M. P——s. That gentleman received them in his gallery. After some general conversation, Coningsby turned towards the pictures, and left Sidonia with their host. The collection was rare, and interested Coningsby, though unacquainted with art. He sauntered on from picture to picture until he reached the end of the gallery, where an open door invited him into a suite of rooms also full of pictures and objects of curiosity and art. As he was entering a second chamber, he observed a lady leaning back in a cushioned chair, and looking earnestly on a picture. His entrance was unheard and unnoticed, for the lady's back was to the door; yet Coningsby, advancing in an angular direction, obtained nearly a complete view of her countenance. It was upraised, gazing on the picture with an expression of delight; the bonnet thrown back, while the large sable cloak of the gazer had fallen partly off. The countenance was more beautiful than the beautiful picture. Those glowing shades of the gallery to which love, and genius, and devotion had lent their inspiration, seemed without life and lustre by the radiant and expressive presence which Coningsby now beheld.

The finely-arched brow was a little elevated, the soft dark eyes were fully opened, the nostril of the delicate nose slightly dilated, the small, yet rich, full lips just parted; and over the clear, transparent visage, there played a vivid glance of gratified intelligence.

The lady rose, advanced towards the picture, looked at it earnestly for a few moments, and then, turning in a direction opposite to Coningsby, walked away. She was somewhat above the middle stature, and yet could scarcely be called tall; a quality so rare, that even skilful dancers do not often possess it, was hers; that elastic gait that is so winning, and so often denotes the gaiety and quickness of the spirit.

The fair object of his observation had advanced into other chambers, and as soon as it was becoming, Coningsby followed her. She had joined a lady and gentleman, who were examining an ancient carving in ivory. The gentleman was middle-aged and portly; the elder lady tall and elegant, and with traces of interesting beauty. Coningsby heard her speak; the words were English, but the accent not of a native.

In the remotest part of the room, Coningsby, apparently engaged in examining some of that famous Limoges ware of which Sidonia had spoken, watched with interest and intentness the beautiful being whom he had followed, and whom he concluded to be the child of her companions. After some little time, they quitted the apartment on their return to the gallery; Coningsby remained behind, caring for none of the rare and fanciful objects that surrounded him, yet compelled, from the fear of seeming obtrusive, for some minutes to remain. Then he too returned to the gallery, and just as he had gained its end, he saw the portly gentleman in the distance shaking hands with Sidonia, the ladies apparently expressing their thanks and gratification to M. P—s, and then all vanishing by the door through which Coningsby had originally entered.

'What a beautiful countrywoman of yours!' said M. P—s, as Coningsby approached him.

'Is she my countrywoman? I am glad to hear it; I have been admiring her,' he replied.

'Yes,' said M. P—s, 'it is Sir Wallinger: one of your deputies; don't you know him?'

'Sir Wallinger!' said Coningsby, 'no, I have not that honour.'
He looked at Sidonia.

'Sir Joseph Wallinger,' said Sidonia, 'one of the new Whig
baronets, and member for —. I know him. He married a Spaniard.
That is not his daughter, but his niece; the child of his wife's
sister. It is not easy to find any one more beautiful.'

END OF BOOK V

BOOK VI

Chapter 1

THE knowledge that Sidonia was in Paris greatly agitated Lady Monmouth. She received the intimation indeed from Coningsby at dinner with sufficient art to conceal her emotion. Lord Monmouth himself was quite pleased at the announcement. Sidonia was his especial favourite; he knew so much, had such an excellent judgment, and was rich. He had always something to tell you, was the best man in the world to bet on, and never wanted anything. A perfect character according to the Monmouth ethics.

In the evening of the day that Coningsby met Sidonia, Lady Monmouth made a little visit to the charming Duchess de G—t who was 'at home' every other night in her pretty hotel, with its embroidered white satin draperies, its fine old cabinets, and ancestral portraits of famous name, brave marshals and bright princesses of the olden time, on its walls. These receptions without form, yet full of elegance, are what English 'at homes' were before the Continental war, though now, by a curious perversion of terms, the easy domestic title distinguishes in England a formally-prepared and elaborately-collected assembly, in which everything and every person are careful to be as little 'homely' as possible. In France, on the contrary, 'tis on these occasions, and in this manner, that society carries on that degree and kind of intercourse which in England we attempt awkwardly to maintain by the medium of that unpopular species of visitation styled a morning call; which all complain that they have either to make or to endure.

Nowhere was this species of reception more happily conducted than at the Duchess de G—t's. The rooms, though small, decorated with taste, brightly illumined; a handsome and gracious hostess, the Duke the very pearl of gentlemen, and sons and daughters worthy of such parents. Every moment some one came in, and some one went away. In your way from a dinner to a ball, you stopped to exchange agreeable *on dits*. It seemed that every woman was pretty, every man a wit. Sure you were to find yourself surrounded by celebrities, and men were welcomed there, if they were clever, before they were famous, which showed it was a house that regarded intellect, and did not seek merely to gratify its vanity by being surrounded by the distinguished.

Enveloped in a rich Indian shawl, and leaning back on a sofa, Lady Monmouth was engaged in conversation with the courtly and classic Count M—é, when, on casually turning her head, she observed entering the saloon, Sidonia. She just caught his form bowing to the Duchess, and instantly turned her head and replunged into her conversation with increased interest. Lady Monmouth was a person who had the power of seeing all about her, everything and everybody, without appearing to look. She was conscious that Sidonia was approaching her neighbourhood. Her heart beat in tumult; she dreaded to catch the eye of that very individual whom she was so anxious to meet. He was advancing towards the sofa. Instinctively, Lady Monmouth turned from the Count, and began speaking earnestly to her other neighbour, a young daughter of the house, innocent and beautiful, not yet quite fledged, trying her wings in society under the maternal eye. She was surprised by the extreme interest which her grand neighbour suddenly took in all her pursuits, her studies, her daily walks in the Bois de Boulogne. Sidonia, as the Marchioness had anticipated, had now reached the sofa. But no, it was to the Count, and not to Lady Monmouth that he was advancing; and they were immediately engaged in conversation. After some little time, when she had become accustomed to his voice, and found her own heart throbbing with less violence, Lucretia turned again, as if by accident, to the Count, and met the glance of Sidonia. She meant to have received him with haughtiness, but her self-command deserted her; and slightly rising from the sofa, she welcomed him with a countenance of extreme pallor and with some awkwardness.

His manner was such as might have assisted her, even had she been more troubled. It was marked by a degree of respectful friendliness. He expressed without reserve his pleasure at meeting her again; inquired much how she had passed her time since they last parted; asked more than once after the Marquess. The Count moved away; Sidonia took his seat. His ease and homage combined greatly relieved her. She expressed to him how kind her Lord would consider his society, for the Marquess had suffered in health since Sidonia last saw him. His periodical gout had left him, which made him ill and nervous. The Marquess received his friends at dinner every day. Sidonia, particularly amiable, offered himself as a guest for the following one.

'And do you go to the great ball to-morrow?' inquired Lucretia, delighted with all that had occurred.

'I always go to their balls,' said Sidonia, 'I have promised.'

There was a momentary pause; Lucretia happier than she had been for a long time, her face a little flushed, and truly in a secret tumult of sweet thoughts, remembered she had been long there, and offering her hand to Sidonia, bade him adieu until to-morrow, while he, as was his custom, soon repaired to the refined circle of the Countess de C—s—l—ne, a lady whose manners he always mentioned as his fair ideal, and whose house was his favourite haunt.

Before to-morrow comes, a word or two respecting two other characters of this history connected with the family of Lord Monmouth. And first of Flora. La Petite was neither very well nor very happy. Her hereditary disease developed itself; gradually, but in a manner alarming to those who loved her. She was very delicate, and suffered so much from the weakness of her chest, that she was obliged to relinquish singing. This was really the only tie between her and the Marchioness, who, without being a petty tyrant, treated her often with unfeeling haughtiness. She was, therefore, now rarely seen in the chambers of the great. In her own apartments she found, indeed, some distraction in music, for which she had a natural predisposition, but this was a pursuit that only fed the morbid passion of her tender soul. Alone, listening only to sweet sounds, or indulging in soft dreams that never could be realised, her existence glided away like a vision, and she seemed to become every day more fair and fragile. Alas! hers was the sad and mystic destiny to love one whom she never met, and by whom, if she met him, she would scarcely, perhaps, be recognised. Yet in that passion, fanciful, almost ideal, her life was absorbed; nor for her did the world contain an existence, a thought, a sensation, beyond those that sprang from the image of the noble youth who had sympathised with her in her sorrows, and had softened the hard fortunes of dependence by his generous sensibility. Happy that, with many mortifications, it was still her lot to live under the roof of one who bore his name, and in whose veins flowed the same blood! She felt indeed for the Marquess, whom she so rarely saw, and from whom she had never received much notice, prompted, it would seem, by her fantastic passion, a degree of reverence, almost of affection, which seemed occasionally, even to herself, as something inexplicable and without reason.

As for her fond step-father, M. Villebecque, the world fared very differently with him. His lively and enterprising genius, his ready and multiform talents, and his temper which defied disturbance, had made their way. He had become the very right hand of Lord Monmouth; his only counsellor, his only confidant; his secret agent; the minister of his will. And well did Villebecque deserve this trust, and ably did he maintain himself in the difficult position which he achieved. There was nothing which Villebecque did not know, nothing which he could not do, especially at Paris. He was master of his subject; in all things the secret of success, and without which, however they may from accident dazzle the world, the statesman, the orator, the author, all alike feel the damning consciousness of being charlatans.

Coningsby had made a visit to M. Villebecque and Flora the day after his arrival. It was a recollection and a courtesy that evidently greatly gratified them. Villebecque talked very much and amusingly; and Flora, whom Coningsby frequently addressed, very little, though she listened with great earnestness. Coningsby told her that he thought, from all he heard, she was too much alone, and counselled her to gaiety. But nature, that had made her mild, had denied her that constitutional liveliness of being which is the graceful property of French women. She was a lily of the valley, that loved seclusion and the tranquillity of virgin glades. Almost every day, as he passed their *entresol*, Coningsby would look into Villebecque's apartments for a moment, to ask after Flora.

Chapter 2

SIDONIA was to dine at Lord Monmouth's the day after he met Lucretia, and afterwards they were all to meet at a ball much talked of, and to which invitations were much sought; and which was to be given that evening by the Baroness S. de R——d.

Lord Monmouth's dinners at Paris were celebrated. It was generally agreed that they had no rivals; yet there were others who had as skilful cooks, others who, for such a purpose, were equally profuse in their expenditure. What, then, was the secret spell of his success? The simplest in the world, though no one seemed aware of it. His Lordship's plates were always hot: whereas at Paris, in the best appointed houses, and at dinners which, for costly materials and admirable art in their preparation, cannot be surpassed, the effect is always considerably lessened, and by a mode the most mortifying: by the mere circumstance that every one at a French dinner is served on a cold plate. The reason of a custom, or rather a necessity, which one would think a nation so celebrated for their gastronomical taste would recoil from, is really, it is believed, that the ordinary French porcelain is so very inferior that it cannot endure the preparatory heat for dinner. The common white pottery, for example, which is in general use, and always found at the cafés, will not bear vicinage to a brisk kitchen fire for half-an-hour. Now, if we only had that treaty of commerce with France which has been so often on the point of completion, the fabrics of our unrivalled potteries, in exchange for their capital wines, would be found throughout France. The dinners of both nations would be improved: the English would gain a delightful beverage, and the French, for the first time in their lives, would dine off hot plates. An unanswerable instance of the advantages of commercial reciprocity!

The guests at Lord Monmouth's to-day were chiefly Carlists,[1] individuals bearing illustrious names, that animate the page of history, and are indissolubly bound up with the glorious annals of their great country. They are the phantoms of a past, but real Aristocracy; an Aristocracy that was founded on an intelligible principle; which claimed great privileges for great purposes; whose hereditary duties were such, that their possessors were perpetually in the eye of the nation, and who maintained, and, in a certain point of view justified, their pre-eminence by constant illustration.

It pleased Lord Monmouth to show great courtesies to a fallen race with whom he sympathised; whose fathers had been his friends in the days of his hot youth; whose mothers he had made love to; whose palaces had been his home; whose brilliant fêtes he remembered; whose fanciful splendour excited his early imagination; and whose magnificent and wanton luxury had developed his own predisposition for boundless enjoyment. Soubise[2] and his suppers; his cutlets and his mistresses; the profuse and embarrassed De Lauragais,[3] who sighed for 'entire ruin,' as for a strange luxury, which perpetually eluded his grasp; these were the heroes of the olden time that Lord Monmouth worshipped; the wisdom of our ancestors which he appreciated; and he turned to their recollection for relief from the vulgar prudence of the degenerate days on which he had fallen: days when nobles must be richer than other men, or they cease to have any distinction.

It was impossible not to be struck by the effective appearance of Lady Monmouth as she received her guests in grand toilet preparatory to the ball; white satin and minever, a brilliant tiara. Her fine form, her costume of a fashion as perfect as its materials were sumptuous, and her presence always commanding and distinguished, produced a general effect to which few could be insensible. It was the triumph of mien over mere beauty of countenance.

The hotel of Madame S. de R—d is not more distinguished by its profuse decoration, than by the fine taste which has guided the vast expenditure. Its halls of arabesque are almost without a rival; there is not the slightest embellishment in which the hand and feeling of art are not recognised. The rooms were very crowded; everybody distinguished in Paris was there: the lady of the Court, the duchess of the Faubourg, the wife of the rich financier, the constitutional Throne, the old Monarchy, the modern Bourse, were alike represented. Marshals of the Empire, Ministers of the Crown, Dukes and Marquesses, whose ancestors lounged in the Œil de Bœuf;[4] diplomatists of all countries, eminent foreigners of all nations, deputies who led sections, members of learned and scientific academies, occasionally a stray poet; a sea of sparkling tiaras, brilliant bouquets, glittering stars, and glowing ribbons, many beautiful faces, many famous ones: unquestionably the general air of a firstrate Parisian saloon, on a great occasion, is not easily equalled. In London there is not the variety of guests; nor the same size and splendour of saloons. Our houses are too small for reception.

Coningsby, who had stolen away from his grandfather's before the rest of the guests, was delighted with the novelty of the splendid scene. He had been in Paris long enough to make some acquaintances, and mostly with celebrated personages. In his long fruitless endeavour to enter the saloon in which they danced, he found himself hustled against the illustrious Baron von H—t, whom he had sat next to at dinner a few days before at Count M—é's.

'It is more difficult than cutting through the Isthmus of Panama,[5] Baron,' said Coningsby, alluding to a past conversation.

'Infinitely,' replied M. de H., smiling; 'for I would undertake to cut through the Isthmus, and I cannot engage that I shall enter this ball-room.'

Time, however, brought Coningsby into that brilliant chamber. What a blaze of light and loveliness! How coquettish are the costumes! How vivid the flowers! To sounds of stirring melody, beautiful beings move with grace. Grace, indeed, is beauty in action.

Here, where all are fair and everything is attractive, his eye is suddenly arrested by one object, a form of surpassing grace among the graceful, among the beauteous a countenance of unrivalled beauty.

She was young among the youthful; a face of sunshine amid all that artificial light; her head placed upon her finely-moulded shoulders with a queen-like grace; a coronet of white roses on her dark brown hair; her only ornament. It was the beauty of the picture-gallery.

The eye of Coningsby never quitted her. When the dance ceased, he had an opportunity of seeing her nearer. He met her walking with her cavalier, and he was conscious that she observed him. Finally he remarked that she resumed a seat next to the lady whom he had mistaken for her mother, but had afterwards understood to be Lady Wallinger.

Coningsby returned to the other saloons: he witnessed the entrance and reception of Lady Monmouth, who moved on towards the ball-room. Soon after this, Sidonia arrived; he came in with the still handsome and ever courteous Duke D——s. Observing Coningsby, he stopped to present him to the Duke. While thus conversing, the Duke, who is fond of the English, observed, 'See, here is your beautiful countrywoman that all the world are talking of. That is her uncle. He brings to me letters from one of your lords, whose name I cannot recollect.'

And Sir Joseph and his lovely niece veritably approached. The Duke addressed them: asked them in the name of his Duchess to a concert on the next Thursday; and, after a thousand compliments, moved on. Sidonia stopped; Coningsby could not refrain from lingering, but stood a little apart, and was about to move away, when there was a whisper, of which, without hearing a word, he could not resist the impression that he was the subject. He felt a little embarrassed, and was retiring, when he heard Sidonia reply to an inquiry of the lady, 'The same,' and then, turning to Coningsby, said aloud, 'Coningsby, Miss Millbank says that you have forgotten her.'

Coningsby started, advanced, coloured a little, could not conceal his surprise. The lady, too, though more prepared, was not without confusion, and for an instant looked down. Coningsby recalled at that moment the long dark eyelashes, and the beautiful, bashful countenance that had so charmed him at Millbank; but two years had otherwise effected a wonderful change in the sister of his school-day friend, and transformed the silent, embarrassed girl into a woman of surpassing beauty and of the most graceful and impressive mien.

'It is not surprising that Mr Coningsby should not recollect my niece,' said Sir Joseph, addressing Sidonia, and wishing to cover their mutual embarrassment: 'but it is impossible for her, or for anyone connected with her, not to be anxious at all times to express to him our sense of what we all owe him.'

Coningsby and Miss Millbank were now in full routine conversation, consisting of questions; how long she had been at Paris; when she had heard last from Millbank; how her father was; also, how was her brother. Sidonia made an observation to Sir Joseph on a passer-by, and then himself moved on; Coningsby accompanying his new friends, in a contrary direction, to the refreshment-room, to which they were proceeding.

'And you have passed a winter at Rome,' said Coningsby. 'How I envy you! I feel that I shall never be able to travel?'

'And why not?'

'Life has become so stirring, that there is ever some great cause that keeps one at home.'

'Life, on the contrary, so swift, that all may see now that of which they once could only read.'

'The golden and silver sides of the shield,' said Coningsby, with a smile.

'And you, like a good knight, will maintain your own.'

'No, I would follow yours.'

'You have not heard lately from Oswald?'

'Oh, yes; I think there are no such faithful correspondents as we are; I only wish we could meet.'

'You will soon; but he is such a devotee of Oxford; quite a monk; and you, too, Mr Coningsby, are much occupied.'

'Yes, and at the same time as Millbank. I was in hopes, when I once paid you a visit, I might have found your brother.'

'But that was such a rapid visit,' said Miss Millbank.

'I always remember it with delight,' said Coningsby.

'You were willing to be pleased; but Millbank, notwithstanding Rome, commands my affections, and in spite of this surrounding splendour, I could have wished to have passed my Christmas in Lancashire.'

'Mr Millbank has lately purchased a very beautiful place in the county. I became acquainted with Hellingsley when staying at my grandfather's.'

'Ah! I have never seen it; indeed, I was much surprised that papa became its purchaser, because he never will live there; and

Oswald, I am sure, could never be tempted to quit Millbank. You know what enthusiastic ideas he has of his order?'

'Like all his ideas, sound, and high, and pure. I always duly appreciated your brother's great abilities, and, what is far more important, his lofty mind. When I recollect our Eton days, I cannot understand how more than two years have passed away without our being together. I am sure the fault is mine. I might now have been at Oxford instead of Paris. And yet,' added Coningsby, 'that would have been a sad mistake, since I should not have had the happiness of being here.'

'Oh, yes, that would have been a sad mistake,' said Miss Millbank.

'Edith,' said Sir Joseph, rejoining his niece, from whom he had been momentarily separated, 'Edith, that is Monsieur Thiers.'[6]

In the meantime, Sidonia reached the ball-room, and sitting near the entrance was Lady Monmouth, who immediately addressed him. He was, as usual, intelligent and unimpassioned, and yet not without a delicate deference which is flattering to women, especially if not altogether unworthy of it. Sidonia always admired Lucretia, and preferred her society to that of most persons. But the Lady was in error in supposing that she had conquered or could vanquish his heart. Sidonia was one of those men, not so rare as may be supposed, who shrink, above all things, from an adventure of gallantry with a woman in a position. He had neither time nor temper for sentimental circumvolutions. He detested the diplomacy of passion: protocols, protracted negotiations, conferences, correspondence, treaties projected, ratified, violated. He had no genius for the tactics of intrigue; your reconnoiterings, and marchings, and counter-marchings, sappings and minings, assaults, sometimes surrenders, and sometimes repulses. All the solemn and studied hypocrisies were to him infinitely wearisome; and if the movements were not merely formal, they irritated him, distracted his feelings, disturbed the tenor of his mind, deranged his nervous system. Something of the old Oriental vein influenced him in his carriage towards women. He was oftener behind the scenes of the Opera House than in his box; he delighted, too, in the society of ἑταῖραι;[7] Aspasia[8] was his heroine. Obliged to appear much in what is esteemed pure society, he cultivated the acquaintance of clever women, because they interested him; but in such saloons his feminine acquaintances were merely psychological. No lady could accuse him of trifling with her feelings, however decided might be his predilection for her conversation. He yielded at once to an admirer; never trespassed by any chance into the domain of sentiment; never broke, by any accident or blunder, into the irregular paces of flirtation; was a man who notoriously would never diminish by marriage the purity of his race; and one who always maintained that passion and polished life were quite incompatible. He liked the drawing-room, and he liked the Desert, but he would not consent that either should trench on their mutual privileges.

The Princess Lucretia had yielded herself to the spell of Sidonia's society at Coningsby Castle, when she knew that marriage was impossible. But she loved him; and with an Italian spirit. Now they met again, and she was the Marchioness of Monmouth, a very great lady, very much admired, and followed, and courted, and very powerful. It is our great moralist who tells us, in the immortal page, that an affair of gallantry with a great lady is more delightful than with ladies of a lower degree. In this he contradicts the good old ballad; but certain it is that Dr Johnson announced to Boswell, 'Sir, in the case of a Countess the imagination is more excited.'

But Sidonia was a man on whom the conventional superiorities of life produced as little effect as a flake falling on the glaciers of the high Alps. His comprehension of the world and human nature was too vast and complete; he understood too well the relative value of things to appreciate anything but essential excellence; and that not too much. A charming woman was not more charming to him because she chanced to be an empress in a particular district of one of the smallest planets; a charming woman under any circumstances was not an unique animal. When Sidonia felt a disposition to be spell-bound, he used to review in his memory all the charming women of whom he had read in the books of all literatures, and whom he had known himself in every court and clime, and the result of his reflections ever was, that the charming woman in question was by no means the paragon, which some who had read, seen, and thought less, might be inclined to esteem her. There was, indeed, no subject on which Sidonia discoursed so felicitously as on woman, and none on which Lord Eskdale more frequently endeavoured to attract him. He would tell you Talmudical[9] stories about our mother Eve and the Queen of Sheba, which would have astonished you. There was not a free lady of Greece, Leontium and Phryne, Lais, Danae, and Lamia, the Egyptian girl Thonis, respecting whom he could not tell you as many diverting tales as if they were ladies of Loretto; not a nook of Athenæus,[10] not an obscure scholiast, not a passage in a Greek orator, that could throw light on these personages, which was not at his command. What stories he would tell you about Marc Antony and the actress Cytheris in their chariot drawn by tigers! What a character would he paint of that Flora who gave her gardens to the Roman people! It would draw tears to your eyes. No man was ever so learned in the female manners of the last centuries of polytheism as Sidonia. You would have supposed that he had devoted his studies peculiarly to that period if you had not chanced to draw him to the Italian middle ages. And even these startling revelations were almost eclipsed by his anecdotes of the Court of Henry III of France, with every character of which he was as familiar as with the brilliant groups that at this moment filled the saloons of Madame de R—d.

Chapter 3

THE image of Edith Millbank was the last thought of Coningsby, as he sank into an agitated slumber. To him had hitherto in general been accorded the precious boon of dreamless sleep. Homer tells us these phantasmas come from Jove; they are rather the children of a distracted soul. Coningsby this night lived much in past years, varied by painful perplexities of the present, which he could neither subdue nor comprehend. The scene flitted from Eton to the castle of his grandfather; and then he found himself among the pictures of the Rue de Tronchet, but their owner bore the features of the senior Millbank. A beautiful countenance that was alternately the face in the mysterious picture, and then that of Edith, haunted him under all circumstances. He woke little refreshed; restless, and yet sensible of some secret joy.

He woke to think of her of whom he had dreamed. The light had dawned on his soul. Coningsby loved.

Ah! what is that ambition that haunts our youth, that thirst for power or that lust of fame that forces us from obscurity into the sunblaze of the world, what are these sentiments so high, so vehement, so ennobling? They vanish, and in an instant, before the glance of a woman!

Coningsby had scarcely quitted her side the preceding eve. He hung upon the accents of that clear sweet voice, and sought, with tremulous fascination, the gleaming splendour of those soft dark eyes. And now he sat in his chamber, with his eyes fixed upon vacancy. All thoughts and feelings, pursuits, desires, life, merge in one absorbing sentiment.

It is impossible to exist without seeing her again, and instantly. He had requested and gained permission to call on Lady Wallinger; he would not lose a moment in availing himself of it. As early as was tolerably decorous, and before, in all probability, they could quit their hotel, Coningsby repaired to the Rue de Rivoli to pay his respects to his new friends.

As he walked along, he indulged in fanciful speculations which connected Edith and the mysterious portrait of his mother. He felt himself, as it were, near the fulfilment of some fate, and on the threshold of some critical discovery. He recalled the impatient, even alarmed, expressions of Rigby at Montem six years ago, when he proposed to invite young Millbank to his grandfather's dinner; the vindictive feud that existed between the two families, and for which political opinion, or even party passion, could not satisfactorily account; and he reasoned himself into a conviction, that the solution of many perplexities was at hand, and that all would be consummated to the satisfaction of every one, by his unexpected but inevitable agency.

Coningsby found Sir Joseph alone. The worthy Baronet was at any rate no participator in Mr Millbank's vindictive feelings against Lord Monmouth. On the contrary, he had a very high respect for a Marquess, whatever might be his opinions, and no mean consideration for a Marquess' grandson. Sir Joseph had inherited a large fortune made by commerce, and had increased it by the same means. He was a middle-class Whig, had faithfully supported that party in his native town during the days they wandered in the wilderness, and had well earned his share of the milk and honey when they vanquished the promised land. In the spring-tide of Liberalism, when the world was not analytical of free opinions, and odious distinctions were not drawn between Finality men and progressive Reformers,[1] Mr Wallinger had been the popular leader of a powerful body of his fellow-citizens, who had returned him to the first Reformed Parliament, and where, in spite of many a menacing registration, he had contrived to remain. He had never given a Radical vote without the permission of the Secretary of the Treasury, and was not afraid of giving an unpopular one to serve his friends. He was not like that distinguished Liberal, who, after dining with the late Whig Premier, expressed his gratification and his gratitude, by assuring his Lordship that he might count on his support on all popular questions.

'I want men who will support the government on all unpopular questions,' replied the witty statesman.

Mr Wallinger was one of these men. His high character and

strong purse were always in the front rank in the hour of danger. His support in the House was limited to his votes; but in other places equally important, at a meeting at a political club, or in Downing Street, he could find his tongue, take what is called a 'practical' view of a question, adopt what is called an 'independent tone,' reanimate confidence in ministers, check mutiny, and set a bright and bold example to the wavering. A man of his property, and high character, and sound views, so practical and so independent, this was evidently the block from which a Baronet should be cut, and in due time he figured Sir Joseph.

A Spanish gentleman of ample means, and of a good Catalan family, flying during a political convulsion to England, arrived with his two daughters at Liverpool, and bore letters of introduction to the house of Wallinger. Some little time after this, by one of those stormy vicissitudes of political fortune, of late years not unusual in the Peninsula, he returned to his native country, and left his children, and the management of that portion of his fortune that he had succeeded in bringing with him, under the guardianship of the father of the present Sir Joseph. This gentleman was about again to become an exile, when he met with an untimely end in one of those terrible tumults of which Barcelona is the frequent scene.

The younger Wallinger was touched by the charms of one of his father's wards. Her beauty of a character to which he was unaccustomed, her accomplishments of society, and the refinement of her manners, conspicuous in the circle in which he lived, captivated him; and though they had no heir, the union had been one of great felicity. Sir Joseph was proud of his wife; he secretly considered himself, though his 'tone' was as liberal and independent as in old days, to be on the threshold of aristocracy, and was conscious that Lady Wallinger played her part not unworthily in the elevated circles in which they now frequently found themselves. Sir Joseph was fond of great people, and not averse to travel; because, bearing a title, and being a member of the British Parliament, and always moving with the appendages of wealth, servants, carriages, and couriers, and fortified with no lack of letters from the Foreign Office, he was everywhere acknowledged, and received, and treated as a personage; was invited to court-balls, dined with ambassadors, and found himself and his lady at every festival of distinction.

The elder Millbank had been Joseph Wallinger's youthful friend. Different as were their dispositions and the rate of their abilities, their political opinions were the same; and commerce habitually connected their interests. During a visit to Liverpool, Millbank had made the acquaintance of the sister of Lady Wallinger, and had been a successful suitor for her hand. This lady was the mother of Edith and of the schoolfellow of Coningsby. It was only within a very few years that she had died; she had scarcely lived long enough to complete the education of her daughter, to whom she was devoted, and on whom she lavished the many accomplishments that she possessed. Lady Wallinger having no children, and being very fond of her niece, had watched over Edith with infinite solicitude, and finally had persuaded Mr Millbank, that it would be well that his daughter should accompany them in their somewhat extensive travels. It was not, therefore, only that nature had developed a beautiful woman out of a bashful girl since Coningsby's visit to Millbank; but really, every means and every opportunity that could contribute to render an individual capable of adorning the most accomplished circles of life, had naturally, and without effort, fallen to the fortunate lot of the manufacturer's daughter. Edith possessed an intelligence equal to those occasions. Without losing the native simplicity of her character, which sprang from the heart, and which the strong and original bent of her father's mind had fostered, she had imbibed all the refinement and facility of the polished circles in which she moved. She had a clear head, a fine taste, and a generous spirit; had received so much admiration, that, though by no means insensible to homage, her heart was free; was strongly attached to her family; and, notwithstanding all the splendour of Rome, and the brilliancy of Paris, her thoughts were often in her Saxon valley, amid the green hills and busy factories of Millbank.

Sir Joseph, finding himself alone with the grandson of Lord Monmouth, was not very anxious that the ladies should immediately appear. He thought this a good opportunity of getting at what are called 'the real feelings of the Tory party:' and he began to pump with a seductive semblance of frankness.

For his part, he had never doubted that a Conservative government was ultimately inevitable; had told Lord John so two years ago, and, between themselves, Lord John was of the same opinion. The present position of the Whigs was the necessary fate of all progressive parties; could not see exactly how it would end; thought sometimes it must end in a fusion of parties; but could not well see how that could be brought about, at least at present. For his part, should be happy to witness an union of the best men of all parties, for the preservation of peace and order, without any reference to any particular opinions. And, in that sense of the word, it was not at all impossible he might find it his duty some day to support a Conservative government.

Sir Joseph was much astonished when Coningsby, who being somewhat impatient for the entrance of the ladies was rather more abrupt than his wont, told the worthy Baronet that he looked upon a government without distinct principles of policy as only a stop-gap to a widespread and demoralising anarchy; that he for one could not comprehend how a free government could endure without national opinions to uphold it; and that governments for the preservation of peace and order, and nothing else, had better be sought in China, or among the Austrians, the Chinese of Europe. As for Conservative government, the natural question was, What do you mean to conserve? Do you mean to conserve things or only names, realities or merely appearances? Or, do you mean to continue the system commenced in 1834, and, with a hypocritical reverence for the principles, and a superstitious adhesion to the forms, of the old exclusive constitution, carry on your policy by latitudinarian practice?

Sir Joseph stared; it was the first time that any inkling of the views of the New Generation had caught his ear. They were strange and unaccustomed accents. He was extremely perplexed; could by no means make out what his companion was driving at; at length, with a rather knowing smile, expressive as much of compassion as comprehension, he remarked,

'Ah! I see; you are a regular Orangeman.'[2]

'I look upon an Orangeman,' said Coningsby, 'as a pure Whig; the only professor and practiser of unadulterated Whiggism.'

This was too much for Sir Joseph, whose political knowledge

did not reach much further back than the ministry of the Mediocrities; hardly touched the times of the Corresponding Society.[3] But he was a cautious man, and never replied in haste. He was about feeling his way, when he experienced the golden advantage of gaining time, for the ladies entered.

The heart of Coningsby throbbed as Edith appeared. She extended to him her hand; her face radiant with kind expression. Lady Wallinger seemed gratified also by his visit. She had much elegance in her manner; a calm, soft address; and she spoke English with a sweet Doric irregularity. They all sat down, talked of the last night's ball, of a thousand things. There was something animating in the frank, cheerful spirit of Edith. She had a quick eye both for the beautiful and the ridiculous, and threw out her observations in terse and vivid phrases. An hour, and more than an hour, passed away, and Coningsby still found some excuse not to depart. It seemed that on this morning they were about to make an expedition into the antique city of Paris, to visit some old hotels which retained their character; especially they had heard much of the hotel of the Archbishop of Sens, with its fortified courtyard. Coningsby expressed great interest in the subject, and showed some knowledge. Sir Joseph invited him to join the party, which of all things in the world was what he most desired.

Chapter 4

NOT a day elapsed without Coningsby being in the company of Edith. Time was precious for him, for the spires and pinnacles of Cambridge already began to loom in the distance, and he resolved to make the most determined efforts not to lose a day of his liberty. And yet to call every morning in the Rue de Rivoli was an exploit which surpassed even· the audacity of love! More than once, making the attempt, his courage failed him, and he turned into the gardens of the Tuileries, and only watched the windows of the house. Circumstances, however, favoured him: he received a letter from Oswald Millbank; he was bound to communicate in person this evidence of his friend's existence; and when he had to reply to the letter, he must necessarily inquire whether his friend's relatives had any message to transmit to him. These, however, were only slight advantages. What assisted Coningsby in his plans and wishes was the great pleasure which Sidonia, with whom he passed a great deal of his time, took in the society of the Wallingers and their niece. Sidonia presented Lady Wallinger with his opera-box during her stay at Paris; invited them frequently to his agreeable dinner-parties; and announced his determination to give a ball, which Lady Wallinger esteemed a delicate attention to Edith; while Lady Monmouth flattered herself that the festival sprang from the desire she had expressed of seeing the celebrated hotel of Sidonia to advantage.

Coningsby was very happy. His morning visits to the Rue de Rivoli seemed always welcome, and seldom an evening elapsed in which he did not find himself in the society of Edith. She seemed not to wish to conceal that his presence gave her pleasure, and though she had many admirers, and had an airy graciousness for all of them, Coningsby sometimes indulged the exquisite suspicion that there was a flattering distinction in her carriage to himself. Under the influence of these feelings, he began daily to be more conscious that separation would be an intolerable calamity; he began to meditate upon the feasibility of keeping a half term, and of postponing his departure to Cambridge to a period nearer the time when Edith would probably return to England.

In the meanwhile, the Parisian world talked much of the grand fête which was about to be given by Sidonia. Coningsby heard much of it one day when dining at his grandfather's. Lady Monmouth seemed very intent on the occasion. Even Lord Monmouth half talked of going, though, for his part, he wished people would come to him, and never ask him to their houses. That was his idea of society. He liked the world, but he liked to find it under his own roof. He grudged them nothing, so that they would not insist upon the reciprocity of cold-catching, and would eat his good dinners instead of insisting on his eating their bad ones.

'But Monsieur Sidonia's cook is a gem, they say,' observed an Attaché of an embassy.

'I have no doubt of it; Sidonia is a man of sense, almost the only man of sense I know. I never caught him tripping. He never makes a false move. Sidonia is exactly the sort of man I like; you know you cannot deceive him, and that he does not want to deceive you. I wish he liked a rubber more. Then he would be perfect.'

'They say he is going to be married,' said the Attaché.

'Poh!' said Lord Monmouth.

'Married!' exclaimed Lady Monmouth. 'To whom?'

'To your beautiful countrywoman, "la belle Anglaise," that all the world talks of,' said the Attaché.

'And who may she be, pray?' said the Marquess. 'I have so many beautiful countrywomen.'

'Mademoiselle Millbank,' said the Attaché.

'Millbank!' said the Marquess, with a lowering brow. 'There are so many Millbanks. Do you know what Millbank this is, Harry?' he inquired of his grandson, who had listened to the conversation with a rather embarrassed and even agitated spirit.

'What, sir; yes, Millbank?' said Coningsby.

'I say, do you know who this Millbank is?'

'Oh! Miss Millbank: yes, I believe, that is, I know a daughter of the gentleman who purchased some property near you.'

'Oh! that fellow! Has he got a daughter here?'

'The most beautiful girl in Paris,' said the Attaché.

'Lady Monmouth, have you seen this beauty, that Sidonia is going to marry?' he added, with a fiendish laugh.

'I have seen the young lady,' said Lady Monmouth; 'but I had not heard that Monsieur Sidonia was about to marry her.'

'Is she so very beautiful?' inquired another gentleman.

'Yes,' said Lady Monmouth, calm, but pale.

'Poh!' said the Marquess again.

'I assure you that it is a fact,' said the Attaché, 'not at least an *on-dit*. I have it from a quarter that could not well be mistaken.'

Behold a little snatch of ordinary dinner gossip that left a very painful impression on the minds of three individuals who were present.

The name of Millbank revived in Lord Monmouth's mind a sense of defeat, discomfiture, and disgust; Hellingsley, lost elections, and Mr Rigby; three subjects which Lord Monmouth had succeeded for a time in expelling from his sensations. His Lordship thought that, in all probability, this beauty of whom they spoke so highly was not really the daughter of his foe; that it was some confusion which had arisen from the similarity of names: nor did he believe that Sidonia was going to marry her, whoever she might be; but a variety of things had been said at dinner, and a number of images had been raised in his mind that touched his spleen. He took his wine freely, and, the usual consequence of that proceeding with Lord Monmouth, became silent and sullen. As for Lady Monmouth, she had learnt that Sidonia, whatever might be the result, was paying very marked attention to another woman, for whom undoubtedly he was giving that very ball which she had flattered herself was a homage to her wishes, and for which she had projected a new dress of eclipsing splendour.

Coningsby felt quite sure that the story of Sidonia's marriage with Edith was the most ridiculous idea that ever entered into the imagination of man; at least he thought he felt quite sure. But the idlest and wildest report that the woman you love is about to marry another is not comfortable. Besides, he could not conceal from himself that, between the Wallingers and Sidonia there existed a remarkable intimacy, fully extended to their niece. He had seen her certainly on more than one occasion in lengthened and apparently earnest conversation with Sidonia, who, by the bye, spoke with her often in Spanish, and never concealed his admiration of her charms or the interest he found in her society. And Edith; what, after all, had passed between Edith and himself which should at all gainsay this report, which he had been particularly assured was not a mere report, but came from a quarter that could not well be mistaken? She had received him with kindness. And how should she receive one who was the friend and preserver of her only brother, and apparently the intimate and cherished acquaintance of her future husband? Coningsby felt that sickness of the heart that accompanies one's first misfortune. The illusions of life seemed to dissipate and disappear. He was miserable; he had no confidence in himself, in his future. After all, what was he? A dependent on a man of very absolute will and passions. Could he forget the glance with which Lord Monmouth caught the name of Millbank, and received the intimation of Hellingsley? It was a glance for a Spagnoletto or a Caravaggio to catch and immortalise. Why, if Edith were not going to marry Sidonia, how was he ever to marry her, even if she cared for him? Oh! what a future of unbroken, continuous, interminable misery awaited him! Was there ever yet born a being with a destiny so dark and dismal? He was the most forlorn of men, utterly wretched! He had entirely mistaken his own character. He had no energy, no abilities, not a single eminent quality. All was over!

Chapter 5

IT was fated that Lady Monmouth should not be present at that ball, the anticipation of which had occasioned her so much pleasure and some pangs.

On the morning after that slight conversation, which had so disturbed the souls, though unconsciously to each other, of herself and Coningsby, the Marquess was driving Lucretia up the avenue Marigny in his phaeton. About the centre of the avenue the horses took fright, and started off at a wild pace. The Marquess was an experienced whip, calm, and with exertion still very powerful. He would have soon mastered the horses, had not one of the reins unhappily broken. The horses swerved; the Marquess kept his seat; Lucretia, alarmed, sprang up, the carriage was dashed against the trunk of a tree, and she was thrown out of it, at the very instant that one of the outriders had succeeded in heading the equipage and checking the horses.

The Marchioness was senseless. Lord Monmouth had descended from the phaeton; several passengers had assembled; the door of a contiguous house was opened; there were offers of service, sympathy, inquiries, a babble of tongues, great confusion.

'Get surgeons and send for her maid,' said Lord Monmouth to one of his servants.

In the midst of this distressing tumult, Sidonia, on horseback, followed by a groom, came up the avenue from the Champs Elysées. The empty phaeton, reins broken, horses held by strangers, all the appearances of a misadventure, attracted him. He recognised the livery. He instantly dismounted. Moving aside the crowd, he perceived Lady Monmouth senseless and prostrate, and her husband, without assistance, restraining the injudicious efforts of the bystanders.

'Let us carry her in, Lord Monmouth,' said Sidonia, exchanging a recognition as he took Lucretia in his arms, and bore her into the dwelling that was at hand. Those who were standing at the door assisted him. The woman of the house and Lord Monmouth only were present.

'I would hope there is no fracture,' said Sidonia, placing her on a sofa, 'nor does it appear to me that the percussion of the head, though considerable, could have been fatally violent. I have caught her pulse. Keep her in a horizontal position, and she will soon come to herself.'

The Marquess seated himself in a chair by the side of the sofa, which Sidonia had advanced to the middle of the room. Lord Monmouth was silent and very serious. Sidonia opened the window, and touched the brow of Lucretia with water. At this moment M. Villebecque and a surgeon entered the chamber.

'The brain cannot be affected, with that pulse,' said the surgeon; 'there is no fracture.'

'How pale she is!' said Lord Monmouth, as if he were examining a picture.

'The colour seems to me to return,' said Sidonia.

The surgeon applied some restoratives which he had brought with him. The face of the Marchioness showed signs of life; she stirred.

'She revives,' said the surgeon.

The Marchioness breathed with some force; again; then half-opened her eyes, and then instantly closed them.

'If I could but get her to take this draught,' said the surgeon.

'Stop! moisten her lips first,' said Sidonia.

They placed the draught to her mouth; in a moment she put forth her hand as if to repress them, then opened her eyes again, and sighed.

'She is herself,' said the surgeon.

'Lucretia!' said the Marquess.

'Sidonia!' said the Marchioness.

Lord Monmouth looked round to invite his friend to come forward.

'Lady Monmouth!' said Sidonia, in a gentle voice.

She started, rose a little on the sofa, stared around her. 'Where am I?' she exclaimed.

'With me,' said the Marquess; and he bent forward to her, and took her hand.

'Sidonia!' she again exclaimed, in a voice of inquiry.

'Is here,' said Lord Monmouth. 'He carried you in after our accident.'

'Accident! Why is he going to marry?'

The Marquess took a pinch of snuff.

There was an awkward pause in the chamber.

'I think now,' said Sidonia to the surgeon, 'that Lady Monmouth would take the draught.'

She refused it.

'Try you, Sidonia,' said the Marquess, rather drily.

'You feel yourself again?' said Sidonia, advancing.

'Would I did not!' said the Marchioness, with an air of stupor. 'What has happened? Why am I here? Are you married?'

'She wanders a little,' said Sidonia.

The Marquess took another pinch of snuff.

'I could have borne even repulsion,' said Lady Monmouth, in a voice of desolation, 'but not for another!'

'M. Villebecque!' said the Marquess.

'My Lord?'

Lord Monmouth looked at him with that irresistible scrutiny which would daunt a galley-slave; and then, after a short pause, said, 'The carriage should have arrived by this time. Let us get home.'

Chapter 6

AFTER the conversation at dinner which we have noticed, the restless and disquieted Coningsby wandered about Paris, vainly seeking in the distraction of a great city some relief from the excitement of his mind. His first resolution was immediately to depart for England; but when, on reflection, he was mindful that, after all, the assertion which had so agitated him might really be without foundation, in spite of many circumstances that to his regardful fancy seemed to accredit it, his firm resolution began to waver.

These were the first pangs of jealousy that Coningsby had ever experienced, and they revealed to him the immensity of the stake which he was hazarding on a most uncertain die.

The next morning he called in the Rue Rivoli, and was informed that the family were not at home. He was returning under the arcades, towards the Rue St Florentin, when Sidonia passed him in an opposite direction, on horseback, and at a rapid rate. Coningsby, who was not observed by him, could not resist a strange temptation to watch for a moment his progress. He saw him enter the court of the hotel where the Wallinger family were staying. Would he come forth immediately? No. Coningsby stood still and pale. Minute followed minute. Coningsby flattered himself that Sidonia was only speaking to the porter. Then he would fain believe Sidonia was writing a note. Then, crossing the street, he mounted by some steps the terrace of the Tuileries, nearly opposite the Hotel of the Minister of Finance, and watched the house. A quarter of an hour elapsed; Sidonia did not come forth. They were at home to him; only to him. Sick at heart, infinitely wretched, scarcely able to guide his steps, dreading even to meet an acquaintance, and almost feeling that his tongue would refuse the office of conversation, he contrived to reach his grandfather's hotel, and was about to bury himself in his chamber, when on the staircase he met Flora.

Coningsby had not seen her for the last fortnight. Seeing her now, his heart smote him for his neglect, excusable as it really was. Any one else at this time he would have hurried by without recognition, but the gentle and suffering Flora was too meek to be rudely treated by so kind a heart as Coningsby's.

He looked at her; she was pale and agitated. Her step trembled, while she still hastened on.

'What is the matter?' inquired Coningsby.

'My Lord, the Marchioness, are in danger, thrown from their carriage.' Briefly she detailed to Coningsby all that had occurred; that M. Villebecque had already repaired to them; that she herself only this moment had learned the intelligence that seemed to agitate her to the centre. Coningsby instantly turned with her; but they had scarcely emerged from the courtyard when the carriage approached that brought Lord and Lady Monmouth home. They followed it into the court. They were immediately at its door.

'All is right, Harry,' said the Marquess, calm and grave.

Coningsby pressed his grandfather's hand. Then he assisted Lucretia to alight.

'I am quite well,' she said, 'now.'

'But you must lean on me, dearest Lady Monmouth,' Coningsby said in a tone of tenderness, as he felt Lucretia almost sinking from him. And he supported her into the hall of the hotel.

Lord Monmouth had lingered behind. Flora crept up to him, and with unwonted boldness offered her arm to the Marquess. He looked at her with a glance of surprise, and then a softer expression, one indeed of an almost winning sweetness, which, though rare, was not a stranger to his countenance, melted his features, and taking the arm so humbly presented, he said,

'Ma Petite, you look more frightened than any of us. Poor child!'

He had reached the top of the flight of steps; he withdrew his arm from Flora, and thanked her with all his courtesy.

'You are not hurt, then, sir?' she ventured to ask with a look that expressed the infinite solicitude which her tongue did not venture to convey.

'By no means, my good little girl;' and he extended his hand to her, which she reverently bent over and embraced.

Chapter 7

WHEN Coningsby had returned to his grandfather's hotel that morning, it was with a determination to leave Paris the next day for England; but the accident to Lady Monmouth, though, as it ultimately appeared, accompanied by no very serious consequences, quite dissipated this intention. It was impossible to quit them so crudely at such a moment. So he remained another day, and that was the day preceding Sidonia's fête, which he particularly resolved not to attend. He felt it quite impossible that he could again endure the sight of either Sidonia or Edith. He looked upon them as persons who had deeply injured him; though they really were individuals who had treated him with invariable kindness. But he felt their existence was a source of mortification and misery to him. With these feelings, sauntering away the last hours at Paris, disquieted, uneasy; no present, no future; no enjoyment, no hope; really, positively, undeniably unhappy; unhappy too for the first time in his life; the first unhappiness; what a companion piece for the first love! Coningsby, of all places in the world, in the gardens of the Luxembourg, encountered Sir Joseph Wallinger and Edith.

To avoid them was impossible; they met face to face; and Sir Joseph stopped, and immediately reminded him that it was three days since they had seen him, as if to reproach him for so unprecedented a neglect. And it seemed that Edith, though she said not as much, felt the same. And Coningsby turned round and walked with them. He told them he was going to leave Paris on the morrow.

'And miss Monsieur de Sidonia's fête, of which we have all talked so much!' said Edith, with unaffected surprise, and an expression of disappointment which she in vain attempted to conceal.

'The festival will not be less gay for my absence,' said Coningsby, with that plaintive moroseness not unusual to despairing lovers.

'If we were all to argue from the same premises, and act accordingly,' said Edith, 'the saloons would be empty. But if any person's absence would be remarked, I should really have thought it would be yours. I thought you were one of Monsieur de Sidonia's great friends?'

'He has no friends,' said Coningsby. 'No wise man has. What are friends? Traitors.'

Edith looked much astonished. And then she said,

'I am sure you have not quarrelled with Monsieur de Sidonia, for we have just parted with him.'

'I have no doubt you have,' thought Coningsby.

'And it is impossible to speak of another in higher terms than he spoke of you.' Sir Joseph observed how unusual it was for Monsieur de Sidonia to express himself so warmly.

'Sidonia is a great man, and carries everything before him,' said Coningsby. 'I am nothing; I cannot cope with him; I retire from the field.'

'What field?' inquired Sir Joseph, who did not clearly catch the drift of these observations. 'It appears to me that a field for action is exactly what Sidonia wants. There is no vent for his abilities and intelligence. He wastes his energy in travelling from capital to capital like a King's messenger. The morning after his fête he is going to Madrid.'

This brought some reference to their mutual movements. Edith spoke of her return to Lancashire, of her hope that Mr Coningsby would soon see Oswald; but Mr Coningsby informed her that though he was going to leave Paris, he had no intention of returning to England; that he had not yet quite made up his mind whither he should go; but thought that he should travel direct to St Petersburgh. He wished to travel overland to Astrachan. That was the place he was particularly anxious to visit.

After this incomprehensible announcement, they walked on for some minutes in silence, broken only by occasional monosyllables, with which Coningsby responded at hazard to the sound remarks of Sir Joseph. As they approached the Palace a party of English who were visiting the Chamber of Peers, and who were acquainted with the companions of Coningsby, encountered them. Amid the mutual recognitions, Coningsby was about to take his leave somewhat ceremoniously, but Edith held forth her hand, and said,

'Is this indeed farewell?'

His heart was agitated, his countenance changed; he retained her hand amid the chattering tourists, too full of their criticisms and their egotistical commonplaces to notice what was passing. A sentimental ebullition seemed to be on the point of taking place. Their eyes met. The look of Edith was mournful and inquiring.

'We will say farewell at the ball,' said Coningsby, and she rewarded him with a radiant smile.

Chapter 8

SIDONIA lived in the Faubourg St Germain, in a large hotel that, in old days, had belonged to the Crillons; but it had received at his hands such extensive alterations, that nothing of the original decoration, and little of its arrangement, remained.

A flight of marble steps, ascending from a vast court, led into a hall of great dimensions, which was at the same time an orangery and a gallery of sculpture. It was illumined by a distinct, yet soft and subdued light, which harmonised with the beautiful repose of the surrounding forms, and with the exotic perfume that was wafted about. A gallery led from this hall to an inner hall of quite a different character; fantastic, glittering, variegated; full of strange shapes and dazzling objects.

The roof was carved and gilt in that honeycomb style prevalent in the Saracenic buildings; the walls were hung with leather stamped in rich and vivid patterns; the floor was a flood of mosaic; about were statues of negroes of human size with faces of wild expression, and holding in their outstretched hands silver torches that blazed with an almost painful brilliancy.

From this inner hall a double staircase of white marble led to the grand suite of apartments.

These saloons, lofty, spacious, and numerous, had been decorated principally in encaustic by the most celebrated artists of Munich. The three principal rooms were only separated from each other by columns, covered with rich hangings, on this night drawn aside. The decoration of each chamber was appropriate to its purpose. On the walls of the ball-room nymphs and heroes moved in measure in Sicilian landscapes, or on the azure shores of Ægean waters. From the ceiling beautiful divinities threw garlands on the guests, who seemed surprised that the roses, unwilling to quit Olympus, would not descend on earth. The general effect of this fair chamber was heightened, too, by that regulation of the house which did not permit any benches in the ball-room. That dignified assemblage who are always found ranged in precise discipline against the wall, did not here mar the flowing grace of the festivity. The chaperons had no cause to complain. A large saloon abounded in ottomans and easy chairs at their service, where their delicate charges might rest when weary, or find distraction when not engaged.

All the world were at this fête of Sidonia. It exceeded in splendour and luxury every entertainment that had yet been given. The highest rank, even Princes of the blood, beauty, fashion, fame, all assembled in a magnificent and illuminated palace, resounding with exquisite melody.

Coningsby, though somewhat depressed, was not insensible to the magic of the scene. Since the passage in the gardens of the Luxembourg, that tone, that glance, he had certainly felt much relieved, happier. And yet if all were, with regard to Sidonia, as unfounded as he could possibly desire, where was he then? Had he forgotten his grandfather, that fell look, that voice of intense detestation? What was Millbank to him? Where, what was the mystery? for of some he could not doubt. The Spanish parentage of Edith had only more perplexed Coningsby. It offered no solution. There could be no connection between a Catalan family and his mother, the daughter of a clergyman in a midland county. That there was any relationship between the Millbank family and his mother was contradicted by the conviction in which he had been brought up, that his mother had no relations; that she returned to England utterly friendless; without a relative, a connection, an acquaintance to whom she could appeal. Her complete forlornness was stamped upon his brain. Tender as were his years when he was separated from her, he could yet recall the very phrases in which she deplored her isolation; and there were numerous passages in her letters which alluded to it. Coningsby had taken occasion to sound the Wallingers on this subject; but he felt assured, from the manner in which his advances were met, that they knew nothing of his mother, and attributed the hostility of Mr Millbank to his grandfather, solely to political emulation and local rivalries. Still there were the portrait and the miniature. That was a fact; a clue which ultimately, he was persuaded, must lead to some solution.

Coningsby had met with great social success at Paris. He was at once a favourite. The Parisian dames decided in his favour. He was a specimen of the highest style of English beauty, which is popular in France. His air was acknowledged as distinguished. The men also liked him; he had not quite arrived at that age when you make enemies. The moment, therefore, that he found himself in the saloons of Sidonia, he was accosted by many whose notice was flattering; but his eye wandered, while he tried to be courteous and attempted to be sprightly. Where was she? He had nearly reached the ball-room when he met her. She was on the arm of Lord Beaumanoir, who had made her acquaintance at Rome, and originally claimed it as the member of a family who, as the reader may perhaps not forget, had experienced some kindnesses from the Millbanks.

There were mutual and hearty recognitions between the young men; great explanations where they had been, what they were doing, where they were going. Lord Beaumanoir told Coningsby he had introduced steeple-chases at Rome, and had parted with Sunbeam to the nephew of a Cardinal. Coningsby securing Edith's hand for the next dance, they all moved on together to her aunt.

Lady Wallinger was indulging in some Roman reminiscences with the Marquess.

'And you are not going to Astrachan to-morrow?' said Edith.

'Not to-morrow,' said Coningsby.

'You know that you said once that life was too stirring in these days to permit travel to a man?'

'I wish nothing was stirring,' said Coningsby. 'I wish nothing to change. All that I wish is, that this fête should never end.'

'Is it possible that you can be capricious? You perplex me very much.'

'Am I capricious because I dislike change?'

'But Astrachan?'

'It was the air of the Luxembourg that reminded me of the Desert,' said Coningsby.

Soon after this Coningsby led Edith to the dance. It was at a ball that he had first met her at Paris, and this led to other reminiscences; all most interesting. Coningsby was perfectly happy. All mysteries, all difficulties, were driven from his recollection; he lived only in the exciting and enjoyable present. Twenty-one and in love!

Some time after this, Coningsby, who was inevitably separated from Edith, met his host.

'Where have you been, child,' said Sidonia, 'that I have not seen you for some days? I am going to Madrid to-morrow.'

'And I must think, I suppose, of Cambridge.'

'Well, you have seen something; you will find it more profitable when you have digested it; and you will have opportunity. That's the true spring of wisdom: meditate over the past. Adventure and Contemplation share our being like day and night.'

The resolute departure for England on the morrow had already changed into a supposed necessity of thinking of returning to Cambridge. In fact, Coningsby felt that to quit Paris and Edith was an impossibility. He silenced the remonstrance of his conscience by the expedient of keeping a half-term, and had no difficulty in persuading himself that a short delay in taking his degree could not really be of the slightest consequence.

It was the hour for supper. The guests at a French ball are not seen to advantage at this period. The custom of separating the sexes for this refreshment, and arranging that the ladies should partake of it by themselves, though originally founded in a feeling of consideration and gallantry, and with the determination to secure, under all circumstances, the convenience and comfort of the fair sex, is really, in its appearance and its consequences, anything but European, and produces a scene which rather reminds one of the harem of a sultan than a hall of chivalry. To judge from the countenances of the favoured fair, they are not themselves particularly pleased; and when their repast is over they necessarily return to empty halls, and are deprived of the dance at the very moment when they may feel most inclined to participate in its graceful excitement.

These somewhat ungracious circumstances, however, were not attendant on the festival of this night. There was opened in the Hotel of Sidonia for the first time a banqueting-room which could contain with convenience all the guests. It was a vast chamber of white marble, the golden panels of the walls containing festive sculptures by Schwanthaler, relieved by encaustic tinting. In its centre was a fountain, a group of Bacchantes encircling Dionysos; and from this fountain, as from a star, diverged the various tables from which sprang orange-trees in fruit and flower.

The banquet had but one fault; Coningsby was separated from Edith. The Duchess of Grand Cairo, the beautiful wife of the heir of one of the Imperial illustrations, had determined to appropriate Coningsby as her cavalier for the moment. Distracted, he made his escape; but his wandering eye could not find the object of its search; and he fell prisoner to the charming Princess de Petitpoix, a Carlist chieftain, whose witty words avenged the cause of fallen dynasties and a cashiered nobility.

Behold a scene brilliant in fancy, magnificent in splendour! All the circumstances of his life at this moment were such as acted forcibly on the imagination of Coningsby. Separated from Edith, he had still the delight of seeing her, the paragon of that bright company, the consummate being whom he adored! and who had spoken to him in a voice sweeter than a serenade, and had bestowed on him a glance softer than moonlight! The lord of the palace, more distinguished even for his capacity than his boundless treasure, was his chosen friend; gained under circumstances of romantic interest, when the reciprocal influence of their personal qualities was affected by no accessory knowledge of their worldly positions. He himself was in the very bloom of youth and health; the child of a noble house, rich for his present wants, and with a future of considerable fortunes. Entrancing love and dazzling friendship, a high ambition and the pride of knowledge, the consciousness of a great prosperity, the vague, daring energies of the high pulse of twenty-one, all combined to stimulate his sense of existence, which, as he looked around him at the beautiful objects and listened to the delicious sounds, seemed to him a dispensation of almost supernatural ecstasy.

About an hour after this, the ball-room still full, but the other saloons gradually emptying, Coningsby entered a chamber which seemed deserted. Yet he heard sounds, as it were, of earnest conversation. It was a voice that invited his progress; he advanced another step, then suddenly stopped. There were two individuals in the room, by whom he was unnoticed. They were Sidonia and Miss Millbank. They were sitting on a sofa, Sidonia holding her hand and endeavouring, as it seemed, to soothe her. Her tones were tremulous; but the expression of her face was fond and confiding. It was all the work of a moment. Coningsby instantly withdrew, yet could not escape hearing an earnest request from Edith to her companion that he would write to her.

In a few seconds Coningsby had quitted the hotel of Sidonia, and the next day found him on his road to England.

END OF BOOK VI

BOOK VII

Chapter 1

IT was one of those gorgeous and enduring sunsets that seemed to linger as if they wished to celebrate the mid-period of the year. Perhaps the beautiful hour of impending twilight never exercises a more effective influence on the soul than when it descends on the aspect of some distant and splendid city. What a contrast between the serenity and repose of our own bosoms and the fierce passions and destructive cares girt in the walls of that multitude whose domes and towers rise in purple lustre against the resplendent horizon!

And yet the disturbing emotions of existence and the bitter inheritance of humanity should exercise but a modified sway, and entail but a light burden, within the circle of the city into which the next scene of our history leads us. For it is the sacred city of study, of learning, and of faith; and the declining beam is resting on the dome of the Radcliffe, lingering on the towers of Christchurch and Magdalen, sanctifying the spires and pinnacles of holy St Mary's.

A young Oxonian, who had for some time been watching the city in the sunset, from a rising ground in its vicinity, lost, as it would seem, in meditation, suddenly rose, and looking at his watch, as if remindful of some engagement, hastened his return at a rapid pace. He reached the High Street as the Blenheim light post coach dashed up to the Star Hotel, with that brilliant precision which even the New Generation can remember, and yet which already ranks among the traditions of English manners. A peculiar and most animating spectacle used to be the arrival of a first-rate light coach in a country town! The small machine, crowded with so many passengers, the foaming and curvetting leaders, the wheelers more steady and glossy, as if they had not done their ten miles in the hour, the triumphant bugle of the guard, and the haughty routine with which the driver, as he reached his goal, threw his whip to the obedient ostlers in attendance; and, not least, the staring crowd, a little awestruck, and looking for the moment at the lowest official of the stable with considerable respect, altogether made a picture which one recollects with cheerfulness, and misses now in many a dreary market-town.

Our Oxonian was a young man about the middle height, and naturally of a thoughtful expression and rather reserved mien. The general character of his countenance was, indeed, a little stern, but it broke into an almost bewitching smile, and a blush suffused his face, as he sprang forward and welcomed an individual about the same age, who had jumped off the Blenheim.

'Well, Coningsby!' he exclaimed, extending both his hands.

'By Jove! my dear Millbank, we have met at last,' said his friend.

And here we must for a moment revert to what had occurred to Coningsby since he so suddenly quitted Paris at the beginning of the year. The wound he had received was deep to one unused to wounds. Yet, after all, none had outraged his feelings, no one had betrayed his hopes. He had loved one who had loved another. Misery, but scarcely humiliation. And yet 'tis a bitter pang under any circumstances to find another preferred to yourself. It is about the same blow as one would probably feel if falling from a balloon. Your Icarian flight[1] melts into a grovelling existence, scarcely superior to that of a sponge or a coral, or redeemed only from utter insensibility by your frank detestation of your rival. It is quite impossible to conceal that Coningsby had imbibed for Sidonia a certain degree of aversion, which, in these days of exaggerated phrase, might even be described as hatred. And Edith was so beautiful! And there had seemed between them a sympathy so native and spontaneous, creating at once the charm of intimacy without any of the disenchanting attributes that are occasionally its consequence. He would recall the tones of her voice, the expression of her soft dark eye, the airy spirit and frank graciousness, sometimes even the flattering blush, with which she had ever welcomed one of whom she had heard so long and so kindly. It seemed, to use a sweet and homely phrase, that they were made for each other; the circumstances of their mutual destinies might have combined into one enchanting fate.

And yet, had she accorded him that peerless boon, her heart, with what aspect was he to communicate this consummation of all his hopes to his grandfather, ask Lord Monmouth for his blessing, and the gracious favour of an establishment for the daughter of his foe, of a man whose name was never mentioned except to cloud his visage? Ah! what was that mystery that connected the haughty house of Coningsby with the humble blood of the Lancashire manufacturer? Why was the portrait of his mother beneath the roof of Millbank? Coningsby had delicately touched upon the subject both with Edith and the Wallingers, but the result of his inquiries only involved the question in deeper gloom. Edith had none but maternal relatives: more than once she had mentioned this, and the Wallingers, on other occasions, had confirmed the remark. Coningsby had sometimes drawn the conversation to pictures, and he would remind her with playfulness of their first unconscious meeting in the gallery of the Rue Tronchet; then he remembered that Mr Millbank was fond of pictures; then he recollected some specimens of Mr Millbank's collection, and after touching on several which could not excite suspicion, he came to 'a portrait, a portrait of a lady; was it a portrait or an ideal countenance?'

Edith thought she had heard it was a portrait, but she was by no means certain, and most assuredly was quite unacquainted with the name of the original, if there were an original.

Coningsby addressed himself to the point with Sir Joseph. He inquired of the uncle explicitly whether he knew anything on the subject. Sir Joseph was of opinion that it was something that Millbank had somewhere 'picked up.' Millbank used often to 'pick up' pictures.

Disappointed in his love, Coningsby sought refuge in the excitement of study, and in the brooding imagination of an aspiring spirit. The softness of his heart seemed to have quitted him for ever. He recurred to his habitual reveries of political greatness and public distinction. And as it ever seemed to him that no preparation could be complete for the career which he planned for himself, he devoted himself with increased ardour to that digestion of knowledge which converts it into wisdom. His life at Cambridge was now a life of seclusion. With the exception of a few Eton friends, he avoided all society. And, indeed, his acquisitions during this term were such as few have equalled, and could only have been mastered by a mental discipline of a severe and exalted character. At the end of the term Coningsby took his degree, and in a few days was about to quit that university where, on the whole, he had passed three serene and happy years in the society of fond and faithful friends, and in ennobling pursuits. He had many plans for his impending movements, yet none of them very mature ones. Lord Vere wished Coningsby to visit his family in the north, and afterwards to go to Scotland together: Coningsby was more inclined to travel for a year. Amid this hesitation a circumstance occurred which decided him to adopt neither of these courses.

It was Commencement, and coming out of the quadrangle of St John's, Coningsby came suddenly upon Sir Joseph and Lady Wallinger, who were visiting the marvels and rarities of the university. They were alone. Coningsby was a little embarrassed, for he could not forget the abrupt manner in which he had parted from them; but they greeted him with so much cordiality that he instantly recovered himself, and, turning, became their companion. He hardly ventured to ask after Edith: at length, in a depressed tone and a hesitating manner, he inquired whether they had lately seen Miss Millbank. He was himself surprised at the extreme light-heartedness which came over him the moment he heard she was in England, at Millbank, with her family. He always very much liked Lady Wallinger, but this morning he hung over her like a lover, lavished on her unceasing and the most delicate attentions, seemed to exist only in the idea of making the Wallingers enjoy and understand Cambridge; no one else was to be their guide at any place or under any circumstances. He told them exactly what they were to see; how they were to see it; when they were to see it. He told them of things which nobody did see, but which they should. He insisted that Sir Joseph should dine with him in hall; Sir Joseph could not think of leaving Lady Wallinger; Lady Wallinger could not think of Sir Joseph missing an opportunity that might never offer again. Besides, they might both join her after dinner. Except to give her husband a dinner, Coningsby evidently intended never to leave her side.

And the next morning, the occasion favourable, being alone with the lady, Sir Joseph bustling about a carriage, Coningsby said suddenly, with a countenance a little disturbed, and in a low voice, 'I was pleased, I mean surprised, to hear that there was still a Miss Millbank; I thought by this time she might have borne another name?'

Lady Wallinger looked at him with an expression of some perplexity, and then said, 'Yes, Edith was much admired; but she need not be precipitate in marrying. Marriage is for a woman *the* event. Edith is too precious to be carelessly bestowed.'

'But I understood,' said Coningsby, 'when I left Paris,' and here he became very confused, 'that Miss Millbank was engaged, on the point of marriage.'

'With whom?'

'Our friend Sidonia.'

'I am sure that Edith would never marry Monsieur de Sidonia, nor Monsieur de Sidonia, Edith. 'Tis a preposterous idea!' said Lady Wallinger.

'But he very much admired her?' said Coningsby with a searching eye.

'Possibly,' said Lady Wallinger; 'but he never even intimated his admiration.'

'But he was very attentive to Miss Millbank?'

'Not more than our intimate friendship authorized, and might expect.'

'You have known Sidonia a long time?'

'It was Monsieur de Sidonia's father who introduced us to the care of Mr Wallinger,' said Lady Wallinger, 'and therefore I have ever entertained for his son a sincere regard. Besides, I look upon him as a compatriot. Recently he has been even more than usually kind to us, especially to Edith. While we were at Paris he recovered for her a great number of jewels which had been left to her by her uncle in Spain; and, what she prized infinitely more, the whole of her mother's correspondence which she maintained with this relative since her marriage. Nothing but the influence of Sidonia could have effected this. Therefore, of course, Edith is attached to him almost as much as I am. In short, he is our dearest friend; our counsellor in all our cares. But as for marrying him, the idea is ridiculous to those who know Monsieur Sidonia. No earthly consideration would ever induce him to impair that purity of race on which he prides himself. Besides, there are other obvious objections which would render an alliance between him and my niece utterly impossible: Edith is quite as devoted to her religion as Monsieur Sidonia can be to his race.'

A ray of light flashed on the brain of Coningsby as Lady Wallinger said these words. The agitated interview, which never could be explained away, already appeared in quite a different point of view. He became pensive, remained silent, was relieved when Sir Joseph, whose return he had hitherto deprecated, re-appeared. Coningsby learnt in the course of the day that the Wallingers were about to make, and immediately, a visit to Hellingsley; their first visit; indeed, this was the first year that Mr Millbank had taken up his abode there. He did not much like the change of life, Sir Joseph told Coningsby, but Edith was delighted with Hellingsley, which Sir Joseph understood was a very distinguished place, with fine gardens, of which his niece was particularly fond.

When Coningsby returned to his rooms, those rooms which he was soon about to quit for ever, in arranging some papers preparatory to his removal, his eye lighted on a too-long unanswered letter of Oswald Millbank. Coningsby had often projected a visit to Oxford, which he much desired to make, but hitherto it had been impossible for him to effect it, except in the absence of Millbank; and he had frequently postponed it that he might combine his first visit to that famous seat of learning with one to his old schoolfellow and friend. Now that was practicable. And immediately Coningsby wrote to apprise Millbank that he had taken his degree, was free, and prepared to pay to him immediately the long-projected visit. Three years and more had elapsed since they had quitted Eton. How much had happened in the interval! What new ideas, new feelings, vast and novel knowledge! Though they had not met, they were nevertheless familiar with the progress and improvement of each other's minds. Their suggestive correspondence was too valuable to both of them to have been otherwise than cherished. And now they were to meet on the eve of entering that world for which they had made so sedulous a preparation.

Chapter 2

THERE are few things in life more interesting than an unrestrained interchange of ideas with a congenial spirit, and there are few things more rare. How very seldom do you encounter in the world a man of great abilities, acquirements, experience, who will unmask his mind, unbutton his brains, and pour forth in careless and picturesque phrase all the results of his studies and observation; his knowledge of men, books, and nature. On the contrary, if a man has by any chance what he conceives an original idea, he hoards it as if it were old gold; and rather avoids the subject with which he is most conversant, from fear that you may appropriate his best thoughts. One of the principal causes of our renowned dulness in conversation is our extreme intellectual jealousy. It must be admitted that in this respect authors, but especially poets, bear the palm. They never think they are sufficiently appreciated, and live in tremor lest a brother should distinguish himself. Artists have the repute of being nearly as bad. And as for a small rising politician, a clever speech by a supposed rival or suspected candidate for office destroys his appetite and disturbs his slumbers.

One of the chief delights and benefits of travel is, that one is perpetually meeting men of great abilities, of original mind, and rare acquirements, who will converse without reserve. In these discourses the intellect makes daring leaps and marvellous advances. The tone that colours our after-life is often caught in these chance colloquies, and the bent given that shapes a career.

And yet perhaps there is no occasion when the heart is more open, the brain more quick, the memory more rich and happy, or the tongue more prompt and eloquent, than when two school-day friends, knit by every sympathy of intelligence and affection, meet at the close of their college careers, after a long separation, hesitating, as it were, on the verge of active life, and compare together their conclusions of the interval; impart to each other all their thoughts and secret plans and projects; high fancies and noble aspirations; glorious visions of personal fame and national regeneration.

Ah! why should such enthusiasm ever die! Life is too short to be little. Man is never so manly as when he feels deeply, acts boldly, and expresses himself with frankness and with fervour.

Most assuredly there never was a congress of friendship wherein more was said and felt than in this meeting, so long projected, and yet perhaps on the whole so happily procrastinated, between Coningsby and Millbank. In a moment they seemed as if they had never parted. Their faithful correspondence indeed had maintained the chain of sentiment unbroken. But details are only for conversation. Each poured forth his mind without stint. Not an author that had influenced their taste or judgment but was canvassed and criticised; not a theory they had framed or a principle they had adopted that was not confessed. Often, with boyish glee still lingering with their earnest purpose, they shouted as they discovered that they had formed the same opinion or adopted the same conclusion. They talked all day and late into the night. They condensed into a week the poignant conclusions of three years of almost unbroken study. And one night, as they sat together in Millbank's rooms at Oriel, their conversation having for some time taken a political colour, Millbank said,

'Now tell me, Coningsby, exactly what you conceive to be the state of parties in this country; for it seems to me that if we penetrate the surface, the classification must be more simple than their many names would intimate.'

'The principle of the exclusive constitution of England having been conceded by the Acts of 1827–8–32,'[1] said Coningsby, 'a party has arisen in the State who demand that the principle of political liberalism shall consequently be carried to its extent; which it appears to them is impossible without getting rid of the fragments of the old constitution that remain. This is the destructive party; a party with distinct and intelligible principles. They seek a specific for the evils of our social system in the general suffrage of the population.

'They are resisted by another party, who, having given up

exclusion, would only embrace as much liberalism as is necessary for the moment; who, without any embarrassing promulgation of principles, wish to keep things as they find them as long as they can, and then will manage them as they find them as well as they can; but as a party must have the semblance of principles, they take the names of the things that they have destroyed. Thus they are devoted to the prerogatives of the Crown, although in truth the Crown has been stripped of every one of its prerogatives; they affect a great veneration for the constitution in Church and State, though every one knows that the constitution in Church and State no longer exists; they are ready to stand or fall with the "independence of the Upper House of Parliament," though, in practice, they are perfectly aware that, with their sanction, "the Upper House" has abdicated its initiatory functions, and now serves only as a court of review of the legislation of the House of Commons. Whenever public opinion, which this party never attempts to form, to educate, or to lead, falls into some violent perplexity, passion, or caprice, this party yields without struggle to the impulse, and, when the storm has passed, attempts to obstruct and obviate the logical and, ultimately, the inevitable results of the very measures they have themselves originated, or to which they have consented. This is the Conservative party.

'I care not whether men are called Whigs or Tories, Radicals or Chartists, or by what nickname a bustling and thoughtless race may designate themselves; but these two divisions comprehend at present the English nation.

'With regard to the first school, I for one have no faith in the remedial qualities of a government carried on by a neglected democracy, who, for three centuries, have received no education. What prospect does it offer us of those high principles of conduct with which we have fed our imaginations and strengthened our will? I perceive none of the elements of government that should secure the happiness of a people and the greatness of a realm.

'But in my opinion, if Democracy be combated only by Conservatism, Democracy must triumph, and at no distant date. This, then, is our position. The man who enters public life at this epoch has to choose between Political Infidelity and a Destructive Creed.'

'This, then,' said Millbank, 'is the dilemma to which we are brought by nearly two centuries of Parliamentary Monarchy and Parliamentary Church.'

' 'Tis true,' said Coningsby. 'We cannot conceal it from ourselves, that the first has made Government detested, and the second Religion disbelieved.'

'Many men in this country,' said Millbank, 'and especially in the class to which I belong, are reconciled to the contemplation of democracy; because they have accustomed themselves to believe, that it is the only power by which we can sweep away those sectional privileges and interests that impede the intelligence and industry of the community.'

'And yet,' said Coningsby, 'the only way to terminate what, in the language of the present day, is called Class Legislation, is not to entrust power to classes. You would find a locofoco[2] majority as much addicted to Class Legislation as a factitious aristocracy. The only power that has no class sympathy is the Sovereign.'

'But suppose the case of an arbitrary Sovereign, what would be your check against him?'

'The same as against an arbitrary Parliament.'

'But a Parliament is responsible.'

'To whom?'

'To their constituent body.'

'Suppose it was to vote itself perpetual?'

'But public opinion would prevent that.'

'And is public opinon of less influence on an individual than on a body?'

'But public opinon may be indifferent. A nation may be misled, may be corrupt.'

'If the nation that elects the Parliament be corrupt, the elected body will resemble it. The nation that is corrupt deserves to fall. But this only shows that there is something to be considered beyond forms of government, national character. And herein mainly should we repose our hopes. If a nation be led to aim at the good and the great, depend upon it, whatever be its form, the government will respond to its convictions and its sentiments.'

'Do you then declare against Parliamentary government?'

'Far from it: I look upon political change as the greatest of evils, for it comprehends all. But if we have no faith in the permanence of the existing settlement; if the very individuals who established it are, year after year, proposing their modifications or their reconstructions; so also, while we uphold what exists, ought we to prepare ourselves for the change we deem impending?

'Now I would not that either ourselves, or our fellow-citizens, should be taken unawares as in 1832, when the very men who opposed the Reform Bill offered contrary objections to it which destroyed each other, so ignorant were they of its real character, its historical causes, its political consequences. We should now so act that, when the occasion arrives, we should clearly comprehend what we want, and have formed an opinion as to the best means by which that want can be supplied.

'For this purpose I would accustom the public mind to the contemplation of an existing though torpid power in the constitution, capable of removing our social grievances, were we to transfer to it those prerogatives which the Parliament has gradually usurped, and used in a manner which has produced the present material and moral disorganisation. The House of Commons is the house of a few; the Sovereign is the sovereign of all. The proper leader of the people is the individual who sits upon the throne.'

'Then you abjure the Representative principle?'

'Why so? Representation is not necessarily, or even in a principal sense, Parliamentary. Parliament is not sitting at this moment, and yet the nation is represented in its highest as well as in its most minute interests. Not a grievance escapes notice and redress. I see in the newspaper this morning that a pedagogue has brutally chastised his pupil. It is a fact known over all England. We must not forget that a principle of government is reserved for our days that we shall not find in our Aristotles, or even in the forests of Tacitus, nor in our Saxon Wittenagemotes, nor in our Plantagenet parliaments. Opinion is now supreme, and Opinion speaks in print. The representation of the Press is far more complete than the representation of Parliament. Parliamentary representation was the happy device of a ruder age, to which it was admirably adapted: an age of semi-civilisation, when there was a leading class in the community; but it exhibits many symptoms of desuetude. It is controlled by a system of representation more vigorous and comprehensive; which absorbs its duties and fulfils them more efficiently, and in which discussion is pursued on fairer terms, and often with more depth and information.'

'And to what power would you entrust the function of Taxation?'

'To some power that would employ it more discreetly than in creating our present amount of debt, and in establishing our present system of imposts.

'In a word, true wisdom lies in the policy that would effect its ends by the influence of opinion, and yet by the means of existing forms. Nevertheless, if we are forced to revolutions, let us propose to our consideration the idea of a free monarchy, established on fundamental laws, itself the apex of a vast pile of municipal and local government, ruling an educated people, represented by a free and intellectual press. Before such a royal authority, supported by such a national opinion, the sectional anomalies of our country would disappear. Under such a system, where qualification would not be parliamentary, but personal, even statesmen would be educated; we should have no more diplomatists who could not speak French, no more bishops ignorant of theology, no more generals-in-chief who never saw a field.

'Now there is a polity adapted to our laws, our institutions, our feelings, our manners, our traditions; a polity capable of great ends and appealing to high sentiments; a polity which, in my opinion, would render government an object of national affection, which would terminate sectional anomalies, assuage religious heats, and extinguish Chartism.'

'You said to me yesterday,' said Millbank after a pause, 'quoting the words of another, which you adopted, that Man was made to adore and to obey. Now you have shown to me the means by which you deem it possible that government might become no longer odious to the subject; you have shown how man may be induced to obey. But there are duties and interests for man beyond political obedience, and social comfort, and national greatness, higher interests and greater duties. How would you deal with their spiritual necessities? You think you can combat political infidelity in a nation by the principle of enlightened loyalty; how would you encounter religious infidelity in a state? By what means is the principle of profound reverence to be revived? How, in short, is man to be led to adore?'

'Ah! that is a subject which I have not forgotten,' replied Coningsby. 'I know from your letters how deeply it has engaged your thoughts. I confess to you that it has often filled mine with perplexity and depression. When we were at Eton, and both of us impregnated with the contrary prejudices in which we had been brought up, there was still between us one common ground of sympathy and trust; we reposed with confidence and affection in the bosom of our Church. Time and thought, with both of us, have only matured the spontaneous veneration of our boyhood. But time and thought have also shown me that the Church of our heart is not in a position, as regards the community, consonant with its original and essential character, or with the welfare of the nation.'

'The character of a Church is universality,' replied Millbank. 'Once the Church in this country was universal in principle and practice; when wedded to the State, it continued at least universal in principle, if not in practice. What is it now? All ties between the State and the Church are abolished, except those which tend to its danger and degradation.

'What can be more anomalous than the present connection between State and Church? Every condition on which it was originally consented to has been cancelled. That original alliance was, in my view, an equal calamity for the nation and the Church; but, at least, it was an intelligible compact. Parliament, then consisting only of members of the Established Church, was, on ecclesiastical matters, a lay synod, and might, in some points of view, be esteemed a necessary portion of Church government. But you have effaced this exclusive character of Parliament; you have determined that a communion with the Established Church shall no longer be part of the qualification for sitting in the House of Commons. There is no reason, so far as the constitution avails, why every member of the House of Commons should not be a dissenter. But the whole power of the country is concentrated in the House of Commons. The House of Lords, even the Monarch himself, has openly announced and confessed, within these ten years, that the will of the House of Commons is supreme. A single vote of the House of Commons, in 1832, made the Duke of Wellington declare, in the House of Lords, that he was obliged to abandon his sovereign in "the most difficult and distressing circumstances." The House of Commons is absolute. It is the State. "L'État c'est moi."[3] The House of Commons virtually appoints the bishops. A sectarian assembly appoints the bishops of the Established Church. They may appoint twenty Hoadleys.[4] James II was expelled the throne because he appointed a Roman Catholic to an Anglican see.[5] A Parliament might do this to-morrow with impunity. And this is the constitution in Church and State which Conservative dinners toast! The only consequences of the present union of Church and State are, that, on the side of the State, there is perpetual interference in ecclesiastical government, and on the side of the Church a sedulous avoidance of all those principles on which alone Church government can be established, and by the influence of which alone can the Church of England again become universal.'

'But it is urged that the State protects its revenues?'

'No ecclesiastical revenues should be safe that require protection. Modern history is a history of Church spoliation. And by whom? Not by the people; not by the democracy. No; it is the emperor, the king, the feudal baron, the court minion. The estate of the Church is the estate of the people, so long as the Church is governed on its real principles. The Church is the medium by which the despised and degraded classes assert the native equality of man, and vindicate the rights and power of intellect. It made, in the darkest hour of Norman rule, the son of a Saxon pedlar Primate of England, and placed Nicholas Breakspear,[6] a Hertfordshire peasant, on the throne of the Cæsars. It would do as great things now, if it were divorced from the degrading and tyrannical connection that enchains it. You would have other sons of peasants Bishops of England, instead of men appointed to that sacred office solely because they were the needy scions of a factitious aristocracy; men of gross ignorance, profligate habits, and grinding extortion, who have disgraced the episcopal throne, and profaned the altar.'

'But surely you cannot justly extend such a description to the present bench?'

'Surely not: I speak of the past, of the past that has produced so much present evil. We live in decent times; frigid, latitudinarian, alarmed, decorous. A priest is scarcely deemed in our days a fit successor to the authors of the gospels, if he be not the editor of a Greek play; and he who follows St Paul must now at least have been private tutor of some young nobleman who has taken a good degree! And then you are all astonished that the Church is not universal! Why! nothing but the indestructibleness of its principles, however feebly pursued, could have maintained even the disorganised body that still survives.

'And yet, my dear Coningsby, with all its past errors and all its present deficiencies, it is by the Church; I would have said until I listened to you to-night; by the Church alone that I see any chance of regenerating the national character. The parochial system, though shaken by the fatal poor-law, is still the most ancient, the most comprehensive, and the most popular institution of the country; the younger priests are, in general, men whose souls are awake to the high mission which they have to fulfil, and which their predecessors so neglected; there is, I think, a rising feeling in the community, that parliamentary intercourse in matters ecclesiastical has not tended either to the spiritual or the material elevation of the humbler orders. Divorce the Church from the State, and the spiritual power that struggled against the brute force of the dark ages, against tyrannical monarchs and barbarous barons, will struggle again in opposition to influences of a different form, but of a similar tendency; equally selfish, equally insensible, equally barbarising. The priests of God are the tribunes of the people. O, ignorant! that with such a mission they should ever have cringed in the antechambers of ministers, or bowed before parliamentary committees!'

'The Utilitarian system is dead,' said Coningsby. 'It has passed through the heaven of philosophy like a hailstorm, cold, noisy, sharp, and peppering, and it has melted away. And yet can we wonder that it found some success, when we consider the political ignorance and social torpor which it assailed? Anointed kings turned into chief magistrates, and therefore much overpaid; estates of the realm changed into parliaments of virtual representation, and therefore requiring real reform; holy Church transformed into national establishment, and therefore grumbled at by all the nation for whom it was not supported. What an inevitable harvest of sedition, radicalism, infidelity! I really think there is no society, however great its resources, that could long resist the united influences of chief magistrate, virtual representation, and Church establishment!'

'I have immense faith in the new generation,' said Millbank, eagerly.

'It is a holy thing to see a state saved by its youth,' said Coningsby; and then he added, in a tone of humility, if not of depression, 'But what a task! What a variety of qualities, what a combination of circumstances is requisite! What bright abilities and what noble patience! What confidence from the people, what favour from the Most High!'

'But He will favour us,' said Millbank. 'And I say to you as Nathan said unto David, "Thou art the man!"[7] You were our leader at Eton; the friends of your heart and boyhood still cling and cluster round you! they are all men whose position forces them into public life. It is a nucleus of honour, faith, and power. You have only to dare. And will you not dare? It is our privilege to live in an age when the career of the highest ambition is identified with the performance of the greatest good. Of the present epoch it may be truly said, "Who dares to be good, dares to be great."'

'Heaven is above all,' said Coningsby. 'The curtain of our fate is still undrawn. We are happy in our friends, dear Millbank, and whatever lights, we will stand together. For myself, I prefer fame to life; and yet, the consciousness of heroic deeds to the most wide-spread celebrity.'

Chapter 3

THE beautiful light of summer had never shone on a scene and surrounding landscape which recalled happier images of English nature, and better recollections of English manners, than that to which we would now introduce our readers. One of those true old English Halls, now unhappily so rare, built in the time of the Tudors, and in its elaborate timber-framing and decorative woodwork indicating, perhaps, the scarcity of brick and stone at the period of its structure, as much as the grotesque genius of its fabricator, rose on a terrace surrounded by ancient and very formal gardens. The hall itself, during many generations, had been vigilantly and tastefully preserved by its proprietors. There was not a point which was not as fresh as if it had been renovated but yesterday. It stood a huge and strange blending of Grecian, Gothic, and Italian architecture, with a wild dash of the fantastic in addition. The lantern watch-towers of a baronial castle were placed in juxtaposition with Doric columns employed for chimneys, while under oriel windows might be observed Italian doorways with Grecian pediments. Beyond the extensive gardens an avenue of Spanish chestnuts at each point of the compass approached the mansion, or led into a small park which was table-land, its limits opening on all sides to beautiful and extensive valleys, sparkling with cultivation, except at one point, where the river Darl formed the boundary of the domain, and then spread in many a winding through the rich country beyond.

Such was Hellingsley, the new home that Oswald Millbank was about to visit for the first time. Coningsby and himself had travelled together as far as Darlford, where their roads diverged, and they had separated with an engagement on the part of Coningsby to visit Hellingsley on the morrow. As they had travelled along, Coningsby had frequently led the conversation to domestic topics; gradually he had talked and talked much, of

Edith. Without an obtrusive curiosity, he extracted, unconsciously to his companion, traits of her character and early days, which filled him with a wild and secret interest. The thought that in a few hours he was to meet her again, infused into his being a degree of transport, which the very necessity of repressing before his companion rendered more magical and thrilling. How often it happens in life that we have with a grave face to discourse of ordinary topics, while all the time our heart and memory are engrossed with some enchanting secret!

The castle of his grandfather presented a far different scene on the arrival of Coningsby from that which it had offered on his first visit. The Marquess had given him a formal permission to repair to it at his pleasure, and had instructed the steward accordingly. But he came without notice, at a season of the year when the absence of all sports made his arrival unexpected. The scattered and sauntering household roused themselves into action, and contemplated the conviction that it might be necessary to do some service for their wages. There was a stir in that vast, sleepy castle. At last the steward was found, and came forward to welcome their young master, whose simple wants were limited to the rooms he had formerly occupied.

Coningsby reached the castle a little before sunset, almost the same hour that he had arrived there more than three years ago. How much had happened in the interval! Coningsby had already lived long enough to find interest in pondering over the past. That past too must inevitably exercise a great influence over his present. He recalled his morning drive with his grandfather, to the brink of that river which was the boundary between his own domain and Hellingsley. Who dwelt at Hellingsley now?

Restless, excited, not insensible to the difficulties, perhaps the dangers, of his position, yet full of an entrancing emotion in which all thoughts and feelings seemed to merge, Coningsby went forth into the fair gardens to muse over his love amid objects as beautiful. A rosy light hung over the rare shrubs and tall fantastic trees; while a rich yet darker tint suffused the distant woods. This euthanasia of the day exercises a strange influence on the hearts of those who love. Who has not felt it? Magical emotions that touch the immortal part!

But as for Coningsby, the mitigating hour that softens the heart made his spirit brave. Amid the ennobling sympathies of nature, the pursuits and purposes of worldly prudence and conventional advantage subsided into their essential nothingness. He willed to blend his life and fate with a being beautiful as that nature that subdued him, and he felt in his own breast the intrinsic energies that in spite of all obstacles should mould such an imagination into reality.

He descended the slopes, now growing dimmer in the fleeting light, into the park. The stillness was almost supernatural; the jocund sounds of day had died, and the voices of the night had not commenced. His heart too was still. A sacred calm had succeeded to that distraction of emotion which had agitated him the whole day, while he had mused over his love and the infinite and insurmountable barriers that seemed to oppose his will. Now he felt one of those strong groundless convictions that are the inspirations of passion, that all would yield to him as to one holding an enchanted wand.

Onward he strolled; it seemed without purpose, yet always proceeding. A pale and then gleaming tint stole over the masses of mighty timber; and soon a glittering light flooded the lawns and glades. The moon was high in her summer heaven, and still Coningsby strolled on. He crossed the broad lawns, he traversed the bright glades: amid the gleaming and shadowy woods, he traced his prescient way.

He came to the bank of a rushing river, foaming in the moonlight, and wafting on its blue breast the shadow of a thousand stars.

'O river!' he said, 'that rollest to my mistress, bear her, bear her my heart!'

Chapter 4

LADY WALLINGER and Edith were together in the morning room of Hellingsley, the morrow after the arrival of Oswald. Edith was arranging flowers in a vase, while her aunt was embroidering a Spanish peasant in correct costume. The daughter of Millbank looked as bright and fragrant as the fair creations that surrounded her. Beautiful to watch her as she arranged their forms and composed their groups; to mark her eye glance with gratification at some happy combination of colour, or to listen to her delight as they wafted to her in gratitude their perfume. Oswald and Sir Joseph were surveying the stables; Mr Millbank, who had been daily expected for the last week from the factories, had not yet arrived.

'I must say he gained my heart from the first,' said Lady Wallinger.

'I wish the gardener would send us more roses,' said Edith.

'He is so very superior to any young man I ever met,' continued Lady Wallinger.

'I think we must have this vase entirely of roses; don't you think so, aunt?' inquired her niece.

'I am fond of roses,' said Lady Wallinger. 'What beautiful bouquets Mr Coningsby gave us at Paris, Edith!'

'Beautiful!'

'I must say, I was very happy when I met Mr Coningsby again at Cambridge,' said Lady Wallinger. 'It gave me much greater pleasure than seeing any of the colleges.'

'How delighted Oswald seems at having Mr Coningsby for a companion again!' said Edith.

'And very naturally,' said Lady Wallinger. 'Oswald ought to deem himself fortunate in having such a friend. I am sure the kindness of Mr Coningsby when we met him at Cambridge is what I never shall forget. But he always was my favourite from the first time I saw him at Paris. Do you know, Edith, I liked him best of all your admirers.'

'Oh! no, aunt,' said Edith, smiling, 'not more than Lord Beaumanoir; you forget your great favourite, Lord Beaumanoir.'

'But I did not know Mr Coningsby at Rome,' said Lady Wallinger; 'I cannot agree that anybody is equal to Mr Coningsby. I cannot tell you how pleased I am that he is our neighbour!'

As Lady Wallinger gave a finishing stroke to the jacket of her Andalusian, Edith, vividly blushing, yet speaking in a voice of affected calmness, said,

'Here is Mr Coningsby, aunt.'

And, truly, at this moment our hero might be discerned, approaching the hall by one of the avenues; and in a few minutes there was a ringing at the hall bell, and then, after a short pause, the servants announced Mr Coningsby, and ushered him into the morning room.

Edith was embarrassed; the frankness and the gaiety of her manner had deserted her; Coningsby was rather earnest than self-possessed. Each felt at first that the presence of Lady Wallinger was a relief. The ordinary topics of conversation were in sufficient plenty; reminiscences of Paris, impressions of Hellingsley, his visit to Oxford, Lady Wallinger's visit to Cambridge. In ten minutes their voices seemed to sound to each other as they did in the Rue de Rivoli, and their mutual perplexity had in a great degree subsided.

Oswald and Sir Joseph now entered the room, and the conversation became general. Hellingsley was the subject on which Coningsby dwelt; he was charmed with all that he had seen! wished to see more. Sir Joseph was quite prepared to accompany him; but Lady Wallinger, who seemed to read Coningsby's wishes in his eyes, proposed that the inspection should be general; and in the course of half an hour Coningsby was walking by the side of Edith, and sympathising with all the natural charms to which her quick taste and lively expression called his notice and appreciation. Few things more delightful than a country ramble with a sweet companion! Exploring woods, wandering over green commons, loitering in shady lanes, resting on rural stiles; the air full of perfume, the heart full of bliss!

It seemed to Coningsby that he had never been happy before.

A thrilling joy pervaded his being. He could have sung like a bird. His heart was as sunny as the summer scene. Past and Future were absorbed in the flowing hour; not an allusion to Paris, not a speculation on what might arrive; but infinite expressions of agreement, sympathy; a multitude of slight phrases, that, however couched, had but one meaning, congeniality. He felt each moment his voice becoming more tender; his heart gushing in soft expressions; each moment he was more fascinated; her step was grace, her glance was beauty. Now she touched him by some phrase of sweet simplicity; or carried him spell-bound by her airy merriment.

Oswald assumed that Coningsby remained to dine with them. There was not even the ceremony of invitation. Coningsby could not but remember his dinner at Millbank, and the timid hostess whom he then addressed so often in vain, as he gazed upon the bewitching and accomplished woman whom he now passionately loved. It was a most agreeable dinner. Oswald, happy in his friend being his guest, under his own roof, indulged in unwonted gaiety.

The ladies withdrew; Sir Joseph began to talk politics, although the young men had threatened their fair companions immediately to follow them. This was the period of the Bed-Chamber Plot, when Sir Robert Peel accepted and resigned power in the course of three days.[1] Sir Joseph, who had originally made up his mind to support a Conservative government when he deemed it inevitable, had for the last month endeavoured to compensate for this trifling error by vindicating the conduct of his friends, and reprobating the behaviour of those who would deprive her Majesty of the 'friends-of-her-youth.' Sir Joseph was a most chivalrous champion of the 'friends-of-her-youth' principle. Sir Joseph, who was always moderate and conciliatory in his talk, though he would go, at any time, any lengths for his party, expressed himself to-day with extreme sobriety, as he was determined not to hurt the feelings of Mr Coningsby, and he principally confined himself to urging temperate questions, somewhat in the following fashion:–

'I admit that, on the whole, under ordinary circumstances, it would perhaps have been more convenient that these appointments should have remained with Sir Robert; but don't you think that, under the peculiar circumstances, being friends of her Majesty's youth?' &c. &c.

Sir Joseph was extremely astonished when Coningsby replied that he thought, under no circumstances, should any appointment in the Royal Household be dependent on the voice of the House of Commons, though he was far from admiring the 'friends-of-her-youth' principle, which he looked upon as impertinent.

'But surely,' said Sir Joseph, 'the Minister being responsible to Parliament, it must follow that all great offices of State should be filled at his discretion.'

'But where do you find this principle of Ministerial responsibility?' inquired Coningsby.

'And is not a Minister responsible to his Sovereign?' inquired Millbank.

Sir Joseph seemed a little confused. He had always heard that Ministers were responsible to Parliament; and he had a vague conviction, notwithstanding the reanimating loyalty of the Bed-Chamber Plot, that the Sovereign of England was a nonentity. He took refuge in indefinite expressions, and observed, 'The Responsibility of Ministers is surely a constitutional doctrine.'

'The Ministers of the Crown are responsible to their master; they are not the Ministers of Parliament.'

'But then you know virtually,' said Sir Joseph, 'the Parliament, that is, the House of Commons, governs the country.'

'It did before 1832,' said Coningsby; 'but that is all past now. We got rid of that with the Venetian Constitution.'

'The Venetian Constitution!' said Sir Joseph.

'To be sure,' said Millbank. 'We were governed in this country by the Venetian Constitution from the accession of the House of Hanover. But that yoke is past. And now I hope we are in a state of transition from the Italian Dogeship to the English Monarchy.'

'Kings, Lords, and Commons, the Venetian Constitution!' exclaimed Sir Joseph.

'But they were phrases,' said Coningsby, 'not facts. The King was a Doge; the Cabinet the Council of Ten. Your Parliament, that you call Lords and Commons, was nothing more than the Great Council of Nobles.'

'The resemblance was complete,' said Millbank, 'and no wonder, for it was not accidental; the Venetian Constitution was intentionally copied.'

'We should have had the Venetian Republic in 1640,' said Coningsby, 'had it not been for the Puritans. Geneva beat Venice.'[2]

'I am sure these ideas are not very generally known,' said Sir Joseph, bewildered.

'Because you have had your history written by the Venetian party,' said Coningsby, 'and it has been their interest to conceal them.'

'I will venture to say that there are very few men on our side in the House of Commons,' said Sir Joseph, 'who are aware that they were born under a Venetian Constitution.'

'Let us go to the ladies,' said Millbank, smiling.

Edith was reading a letter as they entered.

'A letter from papa,' she exclaimed, looking up at her brother with great animation. 'We may expect him every day; and yet, alas! he cannot fix one.'

They now all spoke of Millbank, and Coningsby was happy that he was familiar with the scene. At length he ventured to say to Edith, 'You once made me a promise which you never fulfilled. I shall claim it to-night.'

'And what can that be?'

'The song that you promised me at Millbank more than three years ago.'

'Your memory is good.'

'It has dwelt upon the subject.'

Then they spoke for awhile of other recollections, and then Coningsby appealing to Lady Wallinger for her influence, Edith rose and took up her guitar. Her voice was rich and sweet; the air she sang gay, even fantastically frolic, such as the girls of Granada chaunt trooping home from some country festival; her soft, dark eye brightened with joyous sympathy; and ever and anon, with an arch grace, she beat the guitar, in chorus, with her pretty hand.

The moon wanes; and Coningsby must leave these enchanted

halls. Oswald walked homeward with him until he reached the domain of his grandfather. Then mounting his horse, Coningsby bade his friend farewell till the morrow, and made his best way to the Castle.

Chapter 5

THERE is a romance in every life. The emblazoned page of Coningsby's existence was now open. It had been prosperous before, with some moments of excitement, some of delight; but they had all found, as it were, their origin in worldly considerations, or been inevitably mixed up with them. At Paris, for example, he loved, or thought he loved. But there not an hour could elapse without his meeting some person, or hearing something, which disturbed the beauty of his emotions, or broke his spell-bound thoughts. There was his grandfather hating the Millbanks, or Sidonia loving them; and common people, in the common world, making common observations on them; asking who they were, or telling who they were; and brushing the bloom off all life's fresh delicious fancies with their coarse handling.

But now his feelings were ethereal. He loved passionately, and he loved in a scene and in a society as sweet, as pure, and as refined as his imagination and his heart. There was no malicious gossip, no callous chatter to profane his ear and desecrate his sentiment. All that he heard or saw was worthy of the summer sky, the still green woods, the gushing river, the gardens and terraces, the stately and fantastic dwellings, among which his life now glided as in some dainty and gorgeous masque.

All the soft, social, domestic sympathies of his nature, which, however abundant, had never been cultivated, were developed by the life he was now leading. It was not merely that he lived in the constant presence, and under the constant influence of one whom he adored, that made him so happy. He was surrounded by beings who found felicity in the interchange of kind feelings and kind words, in the cultivation of happy talents and refined tastes, and the enjoyment of a life which their own good sense and their own good hearts made them both comprehend and appreciate. Ambition lost much of its splendour, even his lofty aspirations something of their hallowing impulse of paramount duty, when Coningsby felt how much ennobling delight was consistent with the seclusion of a private station; and mused over an existence to be passed amid woods and waterfalls with a fair hand locked in his, or surrounded by his friends in some ancestral hall.

The morning after his first visit to Hellingsley Coningsby rejoined his friends, as he had promised Oswald, at their breakfast-table; and day after day he came with the early sun, and left them only when the late moon silvered the keep of Coningsby Castle. Mr Millbank, who wrote daily, and was daily expected, did not arrive. A week, a week of unbroken bliss, had vanished away, passed in long rides and longer walks, sunset saunter-ings, and sometimes moonlit strolls; talking of flowers, and think-ing of things even sweeter; listening to delicious songs, and sometimes reading aloud some bright romance or some inspiring lay.

One day Coningsby, who arrived at the hall unexpectedly late; indeed it was some hours past noon, for he had been detained by despatches which arrived at the Castle from Mr Rigby, and which required his interposition; found the ladies alone, and was told that Sir Joseph and Oswald were at the fishing-cottage where they wished him to join them. He was in no haste to do this; and Lady Wallinger proposed that when they felt inclined to ramble they should all walk down to the fishing-cottage together. So, seating himself by the side of Edith, who was tinting a sketch which she had made of a rich oriel of Hellingsley, the morning passed away in that slight and yet subtle talk in which a lover delights, and in which, while asking a thousand questions, that seem at the first glance sufficiently trifling, he is indeed often conveying a meaning that is not expressed, or attempting to discover a feeling that is hidden. And these are occasions when glances meet and glances are withdrawn: the tongue may speak idly, the eye is more eloquent, and often more true.

Coningsby looked up; Lady Wallinger, who had more than once announced that she was going to put on her bonnet, was gone. Yet still he continued to talk trifles; and still Edith listened.

'Of all that you have told me,' said Edith, 'nothing pleases me so much as your description of St Geneviève. How much I should

like to catch the deer at sunset on the heights! What a pretty
drawing it would make!'

'You would like Eustace Lyle,' said Coningsby. 'He is so shy and
yet so ardent.'

'You have such a band of friends! Oswald was saying this
morning there was no one who had so many devoted friends.'

'We are all united by sympathy. It is the only bond of friendship; and yet friendship –'

'Edith,' said Lady Wallinger, looking into the room from the
garden, with her bonnet on, 'you will find me roaming on the
terrace.'

'We come, dear aunt.'

And yet they did not move. There were yet a few pencil touches
to be given to the tinted sketch; Coningsby would cut the pencils.

'Would you give me,' he said, 'some slight memorial of
Hellingsley and your art? I would not venture to hope for anything
half so beautiful as this; but the slightest sketch. It would
make me so happy when away to have it hanging in my room.'

A blush suffused the cheek of Edith; she turned her head a little
aside, as if she were arranging some drawings. And then she said,
in a somewhat hushed and hesitating voice,

'I am sure I will do so; and with pleasure. A view of the
hall itself; I think that would be the best memorial. Where shall
we take it from? We will decide on our walk?' and she rose,
and promising immediately to return, left the room.

Coningsby leant over the mantel-piece in deep abstraction,
gazing vacantly on a miniature of the father of Edith. A light step
roused him; she had returned. Unconsciously he greeted her with
a glance of ineffable tenderness.

They went forth; it was a grey, sultry day. Indeed it was the
covered sky which had led to the fishing scheme of the morning.
Sir Joseph was an expert and accomplished angler, and the
Darl was renowned for its sport. They lingered before they
reached the terrace where they were to find Lady Wallinger,
observing the different points of view which the Hall presented,
and debating which was to form the subject of Coningsby's
drawing; for already it was to be not merely a sketch, but a
drawing, the most finished that the bright and effective pencil of

Edith could achieve. If it really were to be placed in his room, and were to be a memorial of Hellingsley, her artistic reputation demanded a masterpiece.

They reached the terrace: Lady Wallinger was not there, nor could they observe her in the vicinity. Coningsby was quite certain that she had gone onward to the fishing-cottage, and expected them to follow her; and he convinced Edith of the justness of his opinion. To the fishing-cottage, therefore, they bent their steps. They emerged from the gardens into the park, sauntering over the table land, and seeking as much as possible the shade, in the soft but oppressive atmosphere. At the limit of the table land their course lay by a wild but winding path through a gradual and wooded declivity. While they were yet in this craggy and romantic woodland, the big fervent drops began to fall. Coningsby urged Edith to seek at once a natural shelter; but she, who knew the country, assured him that the fishing-cottage was close by, and that they might reach it before the rain could do them any harm.

And truly, at this moment emerging from the wood, they found themselves in the valley of the Darl. The river here was narrow and winding, but full of life; rushing, and clear but for the dark sky it reflected; with high banks of turf and tall trees; the silver birch, above all others, in clustering groups; infinitely picturesque. At the turn of the river, about two hundred yards distant, Coningsby observed the low, dark roof of the fishing-cottage on its banks. They descended from the woods to the margin of the stream by a flight of turfen steps, Coningsby holding Edith's hand as he guided her progress.

The drops became thicker. They reached, at a rapid pace, the cottage. The absent boat indicated that Sir Joseph and Oswald were on the river. The cottage was an old building of rustic logs, with a shelving roof, so that you might obtain sufficient shelter without entering its walls. Coningsby found a rough garden seat for Edith. The shower was now violent.

Nature, like man, sometimes weeps from gladness. It is the joy and tenderness of her heart that seek relief; and these are summer showers. In this instance the vehemence of her emotion was transient, though the tears kept stealing down her cheek for a long time, and gentle sighs and sobs might for some period be distinguished. The oppressive atmosphere had evaporated; the grey, sullen tint had disappeared; a soft breeze came dancing up the stream; a glowing light fell upon the woods and waters; the perfume of trees and flowers and herbs floated around. There was a carolling of birds; a hum of happy insects in the air; freshness and stir, and a sense of joyous life, pervaded all things; it seemed that the heart of all creation opened.

Coningsby, after repeatedly watching the shower with Edith, and speculating on its progress, which did not much annoy them, had seated himself on a log almost at her feet. And assuredly a maiden and a youth more beautiful and engaging had seldom met before in a scene more fresh and fair. Edith on her rustic seat watched the now blue and foaming river, and the birch-trees with a livelier tint, and quivering in the sunset air; an expression of tranquil bliss suffused her beautiful brow, and spoke from the thrilling tenderness of her soft dark eye. Coningsby gazed on that countenance with a glance of entranced rapture. His cheek was flushed, his eye gleamed with dazzling lustre. She turned her head; she met that glance, and, troubled, she withdrew her own.

'Edith!' he said in a tone of tremulous passion, 'Let me call you Edith! Yes,' he continued, gently taking her hand, 'let me call you my Edith! I love you!'

She did not withdraw her hand; but turned away a face flushed as the impending twilight.

Chapter 6

IT was past the dinner hour when Edith and Coningsby reached the Hall; an embarrassing circumstance, but mitigated by the conviction that they had not to encounter a very critical inspection. What, then, were their feelings when the first servant that they met informed them that Mr Millbank had arrived! Edith never could have believed that the return of her beloved father to his home could ever have been to her other than a cause of delight. And yet now she trembled when she heard the announcement. The mysteries of love were fast involving her existence. But this was not the season of meditation. Her heart was still agitated by the tremulous admission that she responded to that fervent and adoring love whose eloquent music still sounded in her ear, and the pictures of whose fanciful devotion flitted over her agitated vision. Unconsciously she pressed the arm of Coningsby as the servant spoke, and then, without looking into his face, whispering him to be quick, she sprang away.

As for Coningsby, notwithstanding the elation of his heart, and the ethereal joy which flowed in all his veins, the name of Mr Millbank sounded something like a knell. However, this was not the time to reflect. He obeyed the hint of Edith; made the most rapid toilet that ever was consummated by a happy lover, and in a few minutes entered the drawing-room of Hellingsley, to encounter the gentleman whom he hoped by some means or other, quite inconceivable, might some day be transformed into his father-in-law, and the fulfilment of his consequent duties towards whom he had commenced by keeping him waiting for dinner.

'How do you do, sir,' said Mr Millbank, extending his hand to Coningsby. 'You seem to have taken a long walk.'

Coningsby looked round to the kind Lady Wallinger, and half addressed his murmured answer to her, explaining how they had lost her, and their way, and were caught in a storm or a shower, which, as it terminated about three hours back, and the fishing cottage was little more than a mile from the Hall, very satisfactorily accounted for their not being in time for dinner.

Lady Wallinger then said something about the lowering clouds having frightened her from the terrace, and Sir Joseph and Oswald talked a little of their sport, and of their having seen an otter; but there was, or at least there seemed to Coningsby, a tone of general embarrassment which distressed him. The fact is, keeping people from dinner under any circumstances is distressing. They are obliged to talk at the very moment when they wish to use their powers of expression for a very different purpose. They are faint, and conversation makes them more exhausted. A gentleman, too, fond of his family, who in turn are devoted to him, making a great and inconvenient effort to reach them by dinner time, to please and surprise them; and finding them all dispersed, dinner so late that he might have reached home in good time without any great inconvenient effort; his daughter, whom he has wished a thousand times to embrace, taking a singularly long ramble with no other companion than a young gentleman, whom he did not exactly expect to see; all these circumstances, individually perhaps slight, and yet, encountered collectively, it may be doubted whether they would not a little ruffle even the sweetest temper.

Mr Millbank, too, had not the sweetest temper, though not a bad one; a little quick and fiery. But then he had a kind heart. And when Edith, who had providentially sent down a message to order dinner, entered and embraced him at the very moment that dinner was announced, her father forgot everything in his joy in seeing her, and his pleasure in being surrounded by his friends. He gave his hand to Lady Wallinger, and Sir Joseph led away his niece. Coningsby put his arm around the astonished neck of Oswald, as if they were once more in the playing fields of Eton.

'By Jove! my dear fellow,' he exclaimed, 'I am so sorry we kept your father from dinner.'

As Edith headed her father's table, according to his rigid rule, Coningsby was on one side of her. They never spoke so little; Coningsby would have never unclosed his lips, had he followed his humour. He was in a stupor of happiness; the dining room took the appearance of the fishing-cottage; and he saw nothing but the flowing river. Lady Wallinger was however next to him, and that was a relief; for he felt always she was his friend. Sir Joseph, a good-hearted man, and on subjects with which he was acquainted full of sound sense, was invaluable to-day, for he entirely kept up the conversation, speaking of things which greatly interested Mr Millbank. And so their host soon recovered his good temper; he addressed several times his observations to Coningsby, and was careful to take wine with him. On the whole, affairs went on flowingly enough. The gentlemen, indeed, stayed much longer over their wine than on the preceding days, and Coningsby did not venture on the liberty of quitting the room before his host. It was as well. Edith required repose. She tried to seek it on the bosom of her aunt, as she breathed to her the delicious secret of her life. When the gentlemen returned to the drawing-room the ladies were not there.

This rather disturbed Mr Millbank again; he had not seen enough of his daughter; he wished to hear her sing. But Edith managed to reappear; and even to sing. Then Coningsby went up to her and asked her to sing the song of the Girls of Granada. She said in a low voice, and with a fond yet serious look

'I am not in the mood for such a song, but if you wish me –'

She sang it, and with inexpressible grace, and with an arch vivacity, that to a fine observer would have singularly contrasted with the almost solemn and even troubled expression of her countenance a moment afterwards.

The day was about to die; the day the most important, the most precious in the lives of Harry Coningsby and Edith Millbank. Words had been spoken, vows breathed, which were to influence their careers for ever. For them hereafter there was to be but one life, one destiny, one world. Each of them was still in such a state of tremulous excitement, that neither had found time or occasion to ponder over the mighty result. They both required solitude; they both longed to be alone. Coningsby rose to depart. He pressed the soft hand of Edith, and his glance spoke his soul.

'We shall see you at breakfast to-morrow, Coningsby!' said

Oswald, very loud, knowing that the presence of his father would make Coningsby hesitate about coming. Edith's heart fluttered; but she said nothing. It was with delight she heard her father, after a moment's pause, say

'Oh! I beg we may have that pleasure.'

'Not quite at so early an hour,' said Coningsby; 'but if you will permit me, I hope to have the pleasure of hearing from you to-morrow, sir, that your journey has not fatigued you.'

Chapter 7

To be alone; to have no need of feigning a tranquillity he could not feel; of coining common-place courtesy when his heart was gushing with rapture; this was a great relief to Coningsby, though gained by a separation from Edith.

The deed was done; he had breathed his long-brooding passion, he had received the sweet expression of her sympathy, he had gained the long-coveted heart. Youth, beauty, love, the innocence of unsophisticated breasts, and the inspiration of an exquisite nature, combined to fashion the spell that now entranced his life. He turned to gaze upon the moonlit towers and peaked roofs of Hellingsley. Silent and dreamlike, the picturesque pile rested on its broad terrace flooded with the silver light and surrounded by the quaint bowers of its fantastic gardens tipped with the glittering beam. Half hid in deep shadow, half sparkling in the midnight blaze, he recognised the oriel window that had been the subject of the morning's sketch. Almost he wished there should be some sound to assure him of his reality. But nothing broke the all-pervading stillness. Was his life to be as bright and as tranquil? And what was to be his life?

Whither was he to bear the beautiful bride he had gained? Were the portals of Coningsby the proud and hospitable gates that were to greet her? How long would they greet him after the achievement of the last four-and-twenty hours was known to their lord? Was this the return for the confiding kindness of his grandsire? That he should pledge his troth to the daughter of that grandsire's foe?

Away with such dark and scaring visions! Is it not the noon of a summer night fragrant with the breath of gardens, bright with the beam that lovers love, and soft with the breath of Ausonian breezes?[1] Within that sweet and stately residence, dwells there not a maiden fair enough to revive chivalry; who is even now thinking of him as she leans on her pensive hand, or, if perchance she dream, recals him in her visions? And himself, is he one who would cry craven with such a lot? What avail his golden youth, his high blood, his daring and devising spirit, and all his stores of wisdom, if they help not now? Does not he feel the energy divine that can confront Fate and carve out fortunes? Besides it is nigh Midsummer Eve, and what should fairies reign for but to aid such a bright pair as this?

He recals a thousand times the scene, the moment, in which but a few hours past he dared to tell her that he loved; he recals a thousand times the still, small voice, that murmured her agitated felicity: more than a thousand times, for his heart clenched the idea as a diver grasps a gem, he recals the enraptured yet gentle embrace, that had sealed upon her blushing cheek his mystical and delicious sovereignty.

Chapter 8

THE morning broke lowering and thunderous; small white clouds,
dull and immovable, studded the leaden sky; the waters of the
rushing Darl seemed to have become black and almost stagnant;
the terraces of Hellingsley looked like the hard lines of a model;
and the mansion itself had a harsh and metallic character. Before
the chief portal of his Hall, the elder Millbank, with an air of some
anxiety, surveyed the landscape and the heavens, as if he were
speculating on the destiny of the day.

Often his eye wandered over the park; often with an uneasy
and restless step he paced the raised walk before him. The clock
of Hellingsley church had given the chimes of noon. His son and
Coningsby appeared at the end of one of the avenues. His eye
lightened; his lip became compressed; he advanced to meet them.

'Are you going to fish to-day, Oswald?' he inquired of his son.

'We had some thoughts of it, sir.'

'A fine day for sport, I should think,' he observed, as he turned
towards the Hall with them.

Coningsby remarked the fanciful beauty of the portal; its twisted
columns, and Caryatides[1] carved in dark oak.

'Yes, it's very well,' said Millbank; 'but I really do not know
why I came here; my presence is an effort. Oswald does not
care for the place; none of us do, I believe.'

'Oh! I like it now, father; and Edith doats on it.'

'She was very happy at Millbank,' saith the father, rather
sharply.

'We are all of us happy at Millbank,' said Oswald.

'I was much struck with the valley and the whole settlement
when I first saw it,' said Coningsby.

'Suppose you go and see about the tackle, Oswald,' said
Mr Millbank, 'and Mr Coningsby and I will take a stroll on the
terrace in the meantime.'

The habit of obedience, which was supreme in his family,

instantly carried Oswald away, though he was rather puzzled why his father should be so anxious about the preparation of the fishing-tackle, as he rarely used it. His son had no sooner departed than Mr Millbank turned to Coningsby, and said very abruptly,

'You have never seen my own room here, Mr Coningsby; step in, for I wish to say a word to you.' And thus speaking, he advanced before the astonished, and rather agitated Coningsby, and led the way through a door and long passage to a room of moderate dimensions, partly furnished as a library, and full of parliamentary papers and blue-books.[2] Shutting the door with some earnestness and pointing to a chair, he begged his guest to be seated. Both in their chairs, Mr Millbank, clearing his throat, said without preface, 'I have reason to believe, Mr Coningsby, that you are attached to my daughter?'

'I have been attached to her for a long time most ardently,' replied Coningsby, in a calm and rather measured tone, but looking very pale.

'And I have reason to believe that she returns your attachment?' said Mr Millbank.

'I believe she deigns not to disregard it,' said Coningsby, his white cheek becoming scarlet.

'It is then a mutual attachment, which, if cherished, must produce mutual unhappiness,' said Mr Millbank.

'I would fain believe the reverse,' said Coningsby.

'Why?' inquired Mr Millbank.

'Because I believe she possesses every charm, quality, and virtue, that can bless man; and because, though I can make her no equivalent return, I have a heart, if I know myself, that would struggle to deserve her.'

'I know you to be a man of sense; I believe you to be a man of honour,' replied Mr Millbank. 'As the first, you must feel that an union between you and my daughter is impossible; what then should be your duty as a man of correct principle is obvious.'

'I could conceive that our union might be attended with difficulties,' said Coningsby, in a somewhat deprecating tone.

'Sir, it is impossible,' repeated Mr Millbank, interrupting him, though not with harshness; 'that is to say, there is no conceivable marriage which could be effected at greater sacrifices, and which would occasion greater misery.'

'The sacrifices are more apparent to me than the misery,' said Coningsby, 'and even they may be imaginary.'

'The sacrifices and the misery are certain and inseparable,' said Mr Millbank. 'Come now, see how we stand! I speak without reserve, for this is a subject which cannot permit misconception, but with no feelings towards you, sir, but fair and friendly ones. You are the grandson of my Lord Monmouth; at present enjoying his favour, but dependent on his bounty. You may be the heir of his wealth to-morrow, and to-morrow you may be the object of his hatred and persecution. Your grandfather and myself are foes; bitter, irreclaimable, to the death. It is idle to mince phrases; I do not vindicate our mutual feelings, I may regret that they have ever arisen; I may regret it especially at this exigency. They are not the feelings of good Christians; they may be altogether to be deplored and unjustifiable; but they exist, mutually exist; and have not been confined to words. Lord Monmouth would crush me, had he the power, like a worm; and I have curbed his proud fortunes often. Were it not for this feeling I should not be here; I purchased this estate merely to annoy him, as I have done a thousand other acts merely for his discomfiture and mortification. In our long encounter I have done him infinitely more injury than he could do me; I have been on the spot, I am active, vigilant, the maker of my fortunes. He is an epicurean, continually in foreign parts, obliged to leave the fulfilment of his will to others. But, for these very reasons, his hate is more intense. I can afford to hate him less than he hates me; I have injured him more. Here are feelings to exist between human beings! But they do exist; and now you are to go to this man, and ask his sanction to marry my daughter!'

'But I would appease these hatreds; I would allay these dark passions, the origin of which I know not, but which never could justify the end, and which lead to so much misery. I would appeal to my grandfather; I would show him Edith.'

'He has looked upon as fair even as Edith,' said Mr Millbank, rising suddenly from his seat, and pacing the room, 'and did that melt his heart? The experience of your own lot should have guarded you from the perils that you have so rashly meditated encountering, and the misery which you have been preparing for others besides yourself. Is my daughter to be treated like your mother? And by the same hand? Your mother's family were not Lord Monmouth's foes. They were simple and innocent people, free from all the bad passions of our nature, and ignorant of the world's ways. But because they were not noble, because they could trace no mystified descent from a foreign invader, or the sacrilegious minion of some spoliating despot, their daughter was hunted from the family which should have exulted to receive her, and the land of which she was the native ornament. Why should a happier lot await you than fell to your parents? You are in the same position as your father; you meditate the same act. The only difference being aggravating circumstances in your case, which, even if I were a member of the same order as my Lord Monmouth, would prevent the possibility of a prosperous union. Marry Edith, and you blast all the prospects of your life, and entail on her a sense of unceasing humiliation. Would you do this? Should I permit you to do this?'

Coningsby, with his head resting on his arm, his face a little shaded, his eyes fixed on the ground, listened in silence. There was a pause; broken by Coningsby, as in a low voice, without changing his posture or raising his glance, he said, 'It seems, sir, that you were acquainted with my mother!'

'I knew sufficient of her,' replied Mr Millbank, with a kindling cheek, 'to learn the misery that a woman may entail on herself by marrying out of her condition. I have bred my children in a respect for their class. I believe they have imbibed my feeling; though it is strange how in the commerce of the world, chance, in their friendships, has apparently baffled my designs:'

'Oh! do not say it is chance, sir,' said Coningsby, looking up, and speaking with much fervour. 'The feelings that animate me towards your family are not the feelings of chance: they are the creation of sympathy; tried by time, tested by thought. And must they perish? Can they perish? They were inevitable; they are indestructible. Yes, sir, it is in vain to speak of the enmities that are fostered between you and my grandfather; the love that exists between your daughter and myself is stronger than all your hatreds.'

'You speak like a young man, and a young man that is in love,' said Mr Millbank. 'This is mere rhapsody; it will vanish in an instant before the reality of life. And you have arrived at that reality,' he continued, speaking with emphasis, leaning over the back of his chair, and looking steadily at Coningsby with his grey, sagacious eye; 'my daughter and yourself can meet no more.'

'It is impossible you can be so cruel!' exclaimed Coningsby.

'So kind; kind to you both; for I wish to be kind to you as well as to her. You are entitled to kindness from us all; though I will tell you now, that, years ago, when the news arrived that my son's life had been saved, and had been saved by one who bore the name of Coningsby, I had a presentiment, great as was the blessing, that it might lead to unhappiness.'

'I can answer for the misery of one,' said Coningsby, in a tone of great despondency. 'I feel as if my sun were set. Oh! why should there be such wretchedness? Why are there family hatreds and party feuds? Why am I the most wretched of men?'

'My good young friend, you will live, I doubt not, to be a happy one. Happiness is not, as we are apt to fancy, entirely dependent on these contingencies. It is the lot of most men to endure what you are now suffering, and they can look back to such conjunctures through the vista of years with calmness.'

'I may see Edith now?'

'Frankly, I should say, no. My daughter is in her room; I have had some conversation with her. Of course she suffers not less than yourself. To see her again will only aggravate woe. You leave under this roof, sir, some sad memories, but no unkind ones. It is not likely that I can serve you, or that you may want my aid; but whatever may be in my power, remember you may command it; without reserve and without restraint. If I control myself now, it is not because I do not respect your affliction, but because, in the course of my life, I have felt too much not to be able to command my feelings.'

'You never could have felt what I feel now,' said Coningsby, in a tone of anguish.

'You touch on delicate ground,' said Millbank; 'yet from me you may learn to suffer. There was a being once, not less fair than the peerless girl that you would fain call your own, and her heart was my proud possession. There were no family feuds to baffle our union, nor was I dependent on anything, but the energies which had already made me flourishing. What happiness was mine! It was the first dream of my life, and it was the last; my solitary passion, the memory of which softens my heart. Ah! you dreaming scholars, and fine gentlemen who saunter through life, you think there is no romance in the loves of a man who lives in the toil and turmoil of business. You are in deep error. Amid my career of travail, there was ever a bright form which animated exertion, inspired my invention, nerved my energy, and to gain whose heart and life I first made many of those discoveries, and entered into many of those speculations, that have since been the foundation of my wide prosperity.

'Her faith was pledged to me; I lived upon her image; the day was even talked of when I should bear her to the home that I had proudly prepared for her.

'There came a young noble, a warrior who had never seen war, glittering with gewgaws. He was quartered in the town where the mistress of my heart, and who was soon to share my life and my fortunes, resided. The tale is too bitter not to be brief. He saw her, he sighed; I will hope that he loved her; she gave him with rapture the heart which perhaps she found she had never given to me; and instead of bearing the name I had once hoped to have called her by, she pledged her faith at the altar to one who, like you, was called, CONINGSBY.'

'My mother!'

'You see, I too have had my griefs.'

'Dear sir,' said Coningsby, rising and taking Mr Millbank's hand, 'I am most wretched; and yet I wish to part from you even with affection. You have explained circumstances that have long perplexed me. A curse, I fear, is on our families. I have not mind enough at this moment even to ponder on my situation. My head is a chaos. I go; yes, I quit this Hellingsley, where I came to be so happy, where I have been so happy. Nay, let me go, dear sir! I must be alone, I must try to think. And tell her, no, tell her nothing. God will guard over us!'

Proceeding down the avenue with a rapid and distempered

step, his countenance lost, as it were, in a wild abstraction,
Coningsby encountered Oswald Millbank. He stopped, collected
his turbulent thoughts, and throwing on Oswald one look that
seemed at the same time to communicate woe and to demand
sympathy, flung himself into his arms.

'My friend!' he exclaimed, and then added, in a broken voice,
'I need a friend.'

Then in a hurried, impassioned, and somewhat incoherent
strain, leaning on Oswald's arm, as they walked on together,
he poured forth all that had occurred, all of which he had
dreamed; his baffled bliss, his actual despair. Alas! there was
little room for solace, and yet all that earnest affection could
inspire, and a sagacious brain and a brave spirit, were offered
for his support, if not his consolation, by the friend who was
devoted to him.

In the midst of this deep communion, teeming with every
thought and sentiment that could enchain and absorb the
spirit of man, they came to one of the park-gates of Coningsby.
Millbank stopped. The command of his father was peremptory,
that no member of his family, under any circumstances, or for
any consideration, should set his foot on that domain. Lady
Wallinger had once wished to have seen the Castle, and
Coningsby was only too happy in the prospect of escorting her
and Edith over the place; but Oswald had then at once put his
veto on the project, as a thing forbidden; and which, if put in
practice, his father would never pardon. So it passed off, and
now Oswald himself was at the gates of that very domain with
his friend who was about to enter them, his friend whom he might
never see again; that Coningsby who, from their boyish days,
had been the idol of his life; whom he had lived to see appeal
to his affections and his sympathy, and whom Oswald was
now going to desert in the midst of his lonely and unsolaced
woe.

'I ought not to enter here,' said Oswald, holding the hand of
Coningsby as he hesitated to advance; 'and yet there are duties
more sacred even than obedience to a father. I cannot leave you
thus, friend of my best heart!'

The morning passed away in unceasing yet fruitless speculation on the future. One moment something was to happen, the next nothing could occur. Sometimes a beam of hope flashed over the fancy of Coningsby, and jumping up from the turf, on which they were reclining, he seemed to exult in his renovated energies; and then this sanguine paroxysm was succeeded by a fit of depression so dark and dejected that nothing but the presence of Oswald seemed to prevent Coningsby from flinging himself into the waters of the Darl.

The day was fast declining, and the inevitable moment of separation was at hand. Oswald wished to appear at the dinner-table of Hellingsley, that no suspicion might arise in the mind of his father of his having accompanied Coningsby home. But just as he was beginning to mention the necessity of his departure, a flash of lightning seemed to transfix the heavens. The sky was very dark; though studded here and there with dingy spots. The young men sprang up at the same time.

'We had better get out of these trees,' said Oswald.

'We had better get to the Castle,' said Coningsby.

A clap of thunder that seemed to make the park quake broke over their heads, followed by some thick drops. The Castle was close at hand; Oswald had avoided entering it; but the impending storm was so menacing that, hurried on by Coningsby, he could make no resistance; and, in a few minutes, the companions were watching the tempest from the windows of a room in Coningsby Castle.

The fork-lightning flashed and scintillated from every quarter of the horizon: the thunder broke over the Castle, as if the keep were rocking with artillery: amid the momentary pauses of the explosion, the rain was heard descending like dissolving water-spouts.

Nor was this one of those transient tempests that often agitate the summer. Time advanced, and its fierceness was little mitigated. Sometimes there was a lull, though the violence of the rain never appeared to diminish; but then, as in some pitched fight between contending hosts, when the fervour of the field seems for a moment to allay, fresh squadrons arrive and renew the hottest strife, so a low moaning wind that was now at intervals faintly heard bore up a great reserve of electric vapour, that formed, as it were, into field in the space between the Castle and Hellingsley, and then discharged its violence on that fated district.

Coningsby and Oswald exchanged looks. 'You must not think of going home at present, my dear fellow,' said the first. 'I am sure your father would not be displeased. There is not a being here who even knows you, and if they did, what then?'

The servant entered the room, and inquired whether the gentlemen were ready for dinner.

'By all means; come, my dear Millbank, I feel reckless as the tempest; let us drown our cares in wine!'

Coningsby, in fact, was exhausted by all the agitation of the day, and all the harassing spectres of the future. He found wine a momentary solace. He ordered the servants away, and for a moment felt a degree of wild satisfaction in the company of the brother of Edith.

Thus they sat for a long time, talking only of one subject, and repeating almost the same things, yet both felt happier in being together. Oswald had risen, and opening the window, examined the approaching night. The storm had lulled, though the rain still fell; in the west was a streak of light. In a quarter of an hour, he calculated on departing. As he was watching the wind he thought he heard the sound of wheels, which reminded him of Coningsby's promise to lend him a light carriage for his return.

They sat down once more; they had filled their glasses for the last time; to pledge to their faithful friendship, and the happiness of Coningsby and Edith; when the door of the room opened, and there appeared, Mr R IGBY.

END OF BOOK VII

BOOK VIII

Chapter 1

IT was the heart of the London season, nearly four years ago, twelve months having almost elapsed since the occurrence of those painful passages at Hellingsley which closed the last book of this history, and long lines of carriages an hour before midnight, up the classic mount of St James and along Piccadilly, intimated that the world were received at some grand entertainment in Arlington Street.

It was the town mansion of the noble family beneath whose roof at Beaumanoir we have more than once introduced the reader, to gain whose courtyard was at this moment the object of emulous coachmen, and to enter whose saloons was to reward the martyr-like patience of their lords and ladies.

Among the fortunate who had already succeeded in bowing to their hostess were two gentlemen, who, ensconced in a good position, surveyed the scene, and made their observations on the passing guests. They were gentlemen who, to judge from their general air and the great consideration with which they were treated by those who were occasionally in their vicinity, were personages whose criticism bore authority.

'I say, Jemmy,' said the eldest, a dandy who had dined with the Regent, but who was still a dandy, and who enjoyed life almost as much as in the days when Carlton House[1] occupied the terrace which still bears its name, 'I say, Jemmy, what a load of young fellows there are! Don't know their names at all. Begin to think fellows are younger than they used to be. Amazing load of young fellows, indeed!'

At this moment an individual who came under the fortunate designation of a young fellow, but whose assured carriage hardly intimated that this was his first season in London, came up to the junior of the two critics, and said, 'A pretty turn you played us yesterday at White's, Melton. We waited dinner nearly an hour.'

'My dear fellow, I am infinitely sorry; but I was obliged to go down to Windsor, and I missed the return train. A good dinner? Who had you?'

'A capital party, only you were wanted. We had Béaumanoir and Vere, and Jack Tufton and Spraggs.'

'Was Spraggs rich?'

'Wasn't he! I have not done laughing yet. He told us a story about the little Biron who was over here last year; I knew her at Paris; and an Indian screen. Killing! Get him to tell it you. The richest thing you ever heard!'

'Who's your friend?' inquired Mr Melton's companion, as the young man moved away.

'Sir Charles Buckhurst.'

'A–h! That is Sir Charles Buckhurst. Glad to have seen him. They say he is going it.'

'He knows what he is about.'

'Egad! so they all do. A young fellow now of two or three and twenty knows the world as men used to do after as many years of scrapes. I wonder where there is such a thing as a greenhorn. Effie Crabbs says the reason he gives up his house is, that he has cleaned out the old generation, and that the new generation would clean him.'

'Buckhurst is not in that sort of way: he swears by Henry Sydney, a younger son of the Duke, whom you don't know; and young Coningsby; a sort of new set; new ideas and all that sort of thing. Beau tells me a good deal about it; and when I was staying with the Everinghams, at Easter, they were full of it. Coningsby had just returned from his travels, and they were quite on the *qui vive*.[2] Lady Everingham is one of their set. I don't know what it is exactly; but I think we shall hear more of it.'

'A sort of animal magnetism, or unknown tongues, I take it from your description,' said his companion.

'Well, I don't know what it is,' said Mr Melton; 'but it has got hold of all the young fellows who have just come out. Beau is a little bit himself. I had some idea of giving my mind to it, they made such a fuss about it at Everingham; but it requires a devilish deal of history, I believe, and all that sort of thing.'

'Ah! that's a bore,' said his companion. 'It is difficult to turn to with a new thing when you are not in the habit of it. I never could manage charades.'

Mr Ormsby, passing by, stopped. 'They told me you had the gout, Cassilis?' he said to Mr Melton's companion.

'So I had; but I have found out a fellow who cures the gout instanter. Tom Needham sent him to me. A German fellow. Pumicestone pills; sort of a charm, I believe, and all that kind of thing: they say it rubs the gout out of you. I sent him to Luxborough, who was very bad; cured him directly. Luxborough swears by him.'

'Luxborough believes in the Millennium,' said Mr Ormsby.

'But here's a new thing that Melton has been telling me of, that all the world is going to believe in,' said Mr Cassilis, 'something patronised by Lady Everingham.'

'A very good patroness,' said Mr Ormsby.

'Have you heard anything about it?' continued Mr Cassilis. 'Young Coningsby brought it from abroad; didn't you say so, Jemmy?'

'No, no, my dear fellow; it is not at all that sort of thing.'

'But they say it requires a deuced deal of history,' continued Mr Cassilis. 'One must brush up one's Goldsmith.[3] Canterton used to be the fellow for history at White's. He was always boring one with William the Conqueror, Julius Cæsar, and all that sort of thing.'

'I tell you what,' said Mr Ormsby, looking both sly and solemn, 'I should not be surprised if, some day or another, we have a history about Lady Everingham and young Coningsby.'

'Poh!' said Mr Melton; 'he is engaged to be married to her sister, Lady Theresa.'

'The deuce!' said Mr Ormsby; 'well, you are a friend of the family, and I suppose you know.'

'He is a devilish good-looking fellow, that young Coningsby,' said Mr Cassilis. 'All the women are in love with him, they say. Lady Eleanor Ducie quite raves about him.'

'By the bye, his grandfather has been very unwell,' said Mr Ormsby, looking mysteriously.

'I saw Lady Monmouth here just now,' said Mr Melton.

'Oh! he is quite well again,' said Mr Ormsby.

'Got an odd story at White's that Lord Monmouth was going to separate from her,' said Mr Cassilis.

'No foundation,' said Mr Ormsby, shaking his head.

'They are not going to separate, I believe,' said Mr Melton; 'but I rather think there was a foundation for the rumour.'

Mr Ormsby still shook his head.

'Well,' continued Mr Melton, 'all I know is, that it was looked upon last winter at Paris as a settled thing.'

'There was some story about some Hungarian,' said Mr Cassilis.

'No, that blew over,' said Mr Melton; 'it was Trautsmansdorff the row was about.'

All this time Mr Ormsby, as the friend of Lord and Lady Monmouth, remained shaking his head; but as a member of society, and therefore delighting in small scandal, appropriating the gossip with the greatest avidity.

'I should think old Monmouth was not the sort of fellow to blow up a woman,' said Mr Cassilis.

'Provided she would leave him quietly,' said Mr Melton.

'Yes, Lord Monmouth never could live with a woman more than two years,' said Mr Ormsby, pensively. 'And that I thought at the same time rather an objection to his marriage.'

We must now briefly revert to what befell our hero after those unhappy occurrences in the midst of whose first woe we left him.

The day after the arrival of Mr Rigby at the Castle, Coningsby quitted it for London, and before a week had elapsed had embarked for Cadiz. He felt a romantic interest in visiting the land to which Edith owed some blood, and in acquiring the language which he had often admired as she spoke it. A favourable opportunity permitted him in the autumn to visit Athens and the Ægean, which he much desired. In the pensive beauties of that delicate land, where perpetual autumn seems to reign, Coningsby found solace. There is something in the character of Grecian scenery which blends with the humour of the melancholy and the feelings of the sorrowful. Coningsby passed his winter at Rome. The wish of his grandfather had rendered it necessary for him to return to England somewhat abruptly. Lord Monmouth had not visited his native country since his marriage; but the period that had elapsed since that event had considerably improved the prospects of his party. The majority of the Whig Cabinet in the House of Commons by 1840 had become little more than nominal; and though it was circulated among their friends, as if from the highest authority, that 'one was enough,' there seemed daily a better chance of their being deprived even of that magical unit. For the first time in the history of this country since the introduction of the system of parliamentary sovereignty, the Government of England depended on the fate of single elections; and indeed, by a single vote, it is remarkable to observe, the fate of the Whig Government was ultimately decided.

This critical state of affairs, duly reported to Lord Monmouth, revived his political passions, and offered him that excitement which he was ever seeking, and yet for which he had often sighed. The Marquess, too, was weary of Paris. Every day he found it more difficult to be amused. Lucretia had lost her charm. He, from whom nothing could be concealed, perceived that often, while she elaborately attempted to divert him, her mind was wandering elsewhere. Lord Monmouth was quite superior to all petty jealousy and the vulgar feelings of inferior mortals, but his sublime selfishness required devotion. He had calculated that a wife or a mistress who might be in love with another man, however powerfully their interests might prompt them, could not be so agreeable or amusing to their friends and husbands as if they had no such distracting hold upon their hearts or their fancy. Latterly at Paris, while Lucretia became each day more involved in the vortex of society, where all admired and some adored her, Lord Monmouth fell into the easy habit of dining in his private rooms, sometimes tête-à-tête with Villebecque, whose inexhaustible tales and adventures about a kind of society which Lord Monmouth had always preferred infinitely to the polished and somewhat insipid circles in which he was born, had rendered him the prime favourite of his great patron. Sometimes Villebecque, too, brought a friend, male or otherwise, whom he thought invested with the rare faculty of distraction: Lord Monmouth cared not who or what they were, provided they were diverting.

Villebecque had written to Coningsby at Rome, by his grandfather's desire, to beg him to return to England and meet Lord Monmouth there. The letter was couched with all the respect and good feeling which Villebecque really entertained for him whom he addressed; still a letter on such a subject from such a person was not agreeable to Coningsby, and his reply to it was direct to his grandfather; Lord Monmouth, however, had entirely given over writing letters.

Coningsby had met at Paris, on his way to England, Lord and Lady Everingham, and he had returned with them. This revival of an old acquaintance was both agreeable and fortunate for our hero. The vivacity of a clever and charming woman pleasantly disturbed the brooding memory of Coningsby. There is no mortification however keen, no misery however desperate, which the spirit of woman cannot in some degree lighten or alleviate. About, too, to make his formal entrance into the great world, he could not have secured a more valuable and accomplished female friend. She gave him every instruction, ever intimation that was necessary; cleared the social difficulties which in some degree are experienced on their entrance into the world even by the most highly connected, unless they have this benign assistance; planted him immediately in the position which was expedient; took care that he was invited at once to the right houses; and, with the aid of her husband, that he should become a member of the right clubs.

'And who is to have the blue ribbon, Lord Eskdale?' said the Duchess to that nobleman, as he entered and approached to pay his respects.

'If I were Melbourne, I would keep it open,' replied his Lordship. 'It is a mistake to give away too quickly.'

'But suppose they go out,' said her Grace.

'Oh! there is always a last day to clear the House. But they will be in another year. The cliff will not be sapped before then. We made a mistake last year about the ladies.'⁴

'I know you always thought so.'

'Quarrels about women are always a mistake. One should make it a rule to give up to them, and then they are sure to give up to us.'

'You have no great faith in our firmness?'

'Male firmness is very often obstinacy: women have always something better, worth all qualities; they have tact.'

'A compliment to the sex from so finished a critic as Lord Eskdale is appreciated.'

But at this moment the arrival of some guests terminated the conversation, and Lord Eskdale moved away, and approached a group which Lady Everingham was enlightening.

'My dear Lord Fitz-Booby,' her Ladyship observed, 'in politics we require faith as well as in all other things.'

Lord Fitz-Booby looked rather perplexed; but, possessed of considerable official experience, having held high posts, some in the cabinet, for nearly a quarter of a century, he was too versed to acknowledge that he had not understood a single word that had been addressed to him for the last ten minutes. He looked on with the same grave, attentive stolidity, occasionally nodding his head, as he was wont of yore when he received a deputation on sugar duties or joint-stock banks, and when he made, as was his custom when particularly perplexed, an occasional note on a sheet of foolscap paper.

'An Opposition in an age of revolution;' continued Lady Everingham, 'must be founded on principles. It cannot depend on mere personal ability and party address taking advantage of circumstances. You have not enunciated a principle for the last ten years; and when you seemed on the point of acceding to power, it was not on a great question of national interest, but a technical dispute respecting the constitution of an exhausted sugar colony.'

'If you are a Conservative party, we wish to know what you want to conserve,' said Lord Vere.

'If it had not been for the Whig abolition of slavery,' said Lord Fitz-Booby, goaded into repartee, 'Jamaica would not have been an exhausted sugar colony.'

'Then what you do want to conserve is slavery?' said Lord Vere.

'No,' said Lord Fitz-Booby, 'I am never for retracing our steps.'

'But will you advance, will you move? And where will you advance, and how will you move?' said Lady Everingham.

'I think we have had quite enough of advancing,' said his Lordship. 'I had no idea your Ladyship was a member of the Movement party,' he added, with a sarcastic grin.

'But if it were bad, Lord Fitz-Booby, to move where we are, as you and your friends have always maintained, how can you reconcile it to principle to remain there?' said Lord Vere.

'I would make the best of a bad bargain,' said Lord Fitz-Booby. 'With a Conservative government, a reformed Constitution would be less dangerous.'

'Why?' said Lady Everingham. 'What are your distinctive principles that render the peril less?'

'I appeal to Lord Eskdale,' said Lord Fitz-Booby; 'there is Lady Everingham turned quite a Radical, I declare. Is not your Lordship of opinion that the country must be safer with a Conservative government than with a Liberal?'

'I think the country is always tolerably secure,' said Lord Eskdale.

Lady Theresa, leaning on the arm of Mr Lyle, came up at this moment, and unconsciously made a diversion in favour of Lord Fitz-Booby.

'Pray, Theresa,' said Lady Everingham, 'where is Mr Coningsby?'

Let us endeavour to ascertain. It so happened that on this day Coningsby and Henry Sydney dined at Grillion's, at an university club, where, among many friends whom Coningsby had not met for a long time, and among delightful reminiscences, the unconscious hours stole on. It was late when they quitted Grillion's, and Coningsby's brougham was detained for a considerable time before its driver could insinuate himself into the line, which indeed he would never have succeeded in doing had not he fortunately come across the coachman of the Duke of Agincourt, who being of the same politics as himself, belonging to the same club, and always black-balling the same men, let him in from a legitimate party feeling; so they arrived in Arlington Street at a very late hour.

Coningsby was springing up the staircase, now not so crowded as it had been, and met a retiring party; he was about to say a passing word to a gentleman as he went by, when, suddenly, Coningsby turned deadly pale. The gentleman could hardly be the cause, for it was the gracious and handsome presence of Lord Beaumanoir: the lady resting on his arm was Edith. They moved on while he was motionless; yet Edith and himself exchanged glances. His was one of astonishment; but what was the expression of hers? She must have recognised him before he had observed her. She was collected, and she expressed the purpose of her mind in a distant and haughty recognition. Coningsby remained for a moment stupified; then suddenly turning back, he bounded downstairs and hurried into the cloak-room. He met Lady Wallinger; he spoke rapidly, he held her hand, did not listen to her answers, his eyes wandered about. There were many persons present; at length he recognised Edith enveloped in her mantle. He went forward, he looked at her, as if he would have read her soul; he said something. She changed colour as he addressed her, but seemed instantly by an effort to rally and regain her equanimity; replied to his inquiries with extreme brevity, and Lady Wallinger's carriage being announced, moved away with the same slight haughty salute as before, on the arm of Beaumanoir.

Chapter 2

SADNESS fell over the once happy family of Millbank after the departure of Coningsby from Hellingsley. When the first pang was over, Edith had found some solace in the sympathy of her aunt, who had always appreciated and admired Coningsby; but it was a sympathy which aspired only to soften sorrow, and not to create hope. But Lady Wallinger, though she lengthened her visit for the sake of her niece, in time quitted them; and then the name of Coningsby was never heard by Edith. Her brother, shortly after the sorrowful and abrupt departure of his friend, had gone to the factories, where he remained, and of which, in future, it was intended that he should assume the principal direction. Mr Millbank himself, sustained at first by the society of his friend Sir Joseph, to whom he was attached, and occupied with daily reports from his establishments and the transaction of the affairs of his numerous and busy constituents, was for a while scarcely conscious of the alteration which had taken place in the demeanour of his daughter. But when they were once more alone together, it was impossible any longer to be blind to the great change. That happy and equable gaiety of spirit, which seemed to spring from an innocent enjoyment of existence, and which had ever distinguished Edith, was wanting. Her sunny glance was gone. She was not indeed always moody and dispirited, but she was fitful, unequal in her tone. That temper whose sweetness had been a domestic proverb had become a little uncertain. Not that her affection for her father was diminished, but there were snatches of unusual irritability which momentarily escaped her, followed by bursts of tenderness that were the creatures of compunction. And often, after some hasty word, she would throw her arms round her father's neck with the fondness of remorse. She pursued her usual avocations, for she had really too well-regulated a mind, she was in truth a person of too strong an intellect, to neglect any source of occupation and distraction. Her flowers, her pencil, and her books supplied her with these; and music soothed, and at times beguiled, her agitated thoughts. But there was no joy in the house, and in time Mr Millbank felt it.

Mr Millbank was vexed, irritated, grieved. Edith, his Edith, the pride and delight of his existence, who had been to him only a source of exultation and felicity, was no longer happy, was perhaps pining away; and there was the appearance, the unjust appearance that he, her fond father, was the cause and occasion of all this wretchedness. It would appear that the name of Coningsby, to which he now owed a great debt of gratitude, was still doomed to bear him mortification and misery. Truly had the young man said that there was a curse upon their two families. And yet, on reflection, it still seemed to Mr Millbank that he had acted with as much wisdom and real kindness as decision. How otherwise was he to have acted? The union was impossible; the speedier their separation, therefore, clearly the better. Unfortunate, indeed, had been his absence from Hellingsley; unquestionably his presence might have prevented the catastrophe. Oswald should have hindered all this. And yet Mr Millbank could not shut his eyes to the devotion of his son to Coningsby. He felt he could count on no assistance in this respect from that quarter. Yet how hard upon him that he should seem to figure as a despot or a tyrant to his own children, whom he loved, when he had absolutely acted in an inevitable manner! Edith seemed sad, Oswald sullen; all was changed. All the objects for which this clear-headed, strong-minded, kind-hearted man had been working all his life, seemed to be frustrated. And why? Because a young man had made love to his daughter, who was really in no manner entitled to do so.

As the autumn drew on, Mr Millbank found Hellingsley, under existing circumstances, extremely wearisome; and he proposed to his daughter that they should pay a visit to their earlier home. Edith assented without difficulty, but without interest. And yet, as Mr Millbank immediately perceived, the change was a judicious one; for certainly the spirits of Edith seemed to improve after her return to their valley. There were more objects of interest: change, too, is always beneficial. If Mr Millbank had been aware that

Oswald had received a letter from Coningsby, written before he quitted Spain, perhaps he might have recognised a more satisfactory reason for the transient liveliness of his daughter which had so greatly gratified him.

About a month after Christmas, the meeting of Parliament summoned Mr Millbank up to London; and he had wished Edith to accompany him. But London in February to Edith, without friends or connections, her father always occupied and absent from her day and night, seemed to them all, on reflection, to be a life not very conducive to health or cheerfulness, and therefore she remained with her brother. Oswald had heard from Coningsby again from Rome; but at the period he wrote he did not anticipate his return to England. His tone was affectionate, but dispirited.

Lady Wallinger went up to London after Easter for the season, and Mr Millbank, now that there was a constant companion for his daughter, took a house and carried Edith back with him to London. Lady Wallinger, who had great wealth and great tact, had obtained by degrees a not inconsiderable position in society. She had a fine house in a fashionable situation, and gave profuse entertainments. The Whigs were under obligations to her husband, and the great Whig ladies were gratified to find in his wife a polished and pleasing person, to whom they could be courteous without any annoyance. So that Edith, under the auspices of her aunt, found herself at once in circles which otherwise she might not easily have entered, but which her beauty, grace, and experience of the most refined society of the Continent, qualified her to shine in. One evening they met the Marquis of Beaumanoir, their friend of Rome and Paris, and admirer of Edith, who from that time was seldom from their side. His mother, the Duchess, immediately called both on the Millbanks and the Wallingers; glad, not only to please her son, but to express that consideration for Mr Millbank which the Duke always wished to show. It was, however, of no use; nothing would induce Mr Millbank ever to enter what he called aristocratic society. He liked the House of Commons; never paired off;[1] never missed a moment of it; worked at committees all the morning, listened attentively to debates all the night; always dined at

Bellamy's when there was a house; and when there was not, liked dining at the Fishmongers' Company, the Russia Company, great Emigration banquets, and other joint-stock festivities. That was his idea of rational society; business and pleasure combined; a good dinner, and good speeches afterwards.

Edith was aware that Coningsby had returned to England, for her brother had heard from him on his arrival; but Oswald had not heard since. A season in London only represented in the mind of Edith the chance, perhaps the certainty, of meeting Coningsby again; of communing together over the catastrophe of last summer; of soothing and solacing each other's unhappiness, and perhaps, with the sanguine imagination of youth, foreseeing a more felicitous future. She had been nearly a fortnight in town, and though moving frequently in the same circles as Coningsby, they had not yet met. It was one of those results which could rarely occur; but even chance enters too frequently in the league against lovers. The invitation to the assembly at — House was therefore peculiarly gratifying to Edith, since she could scarcely doubt that if Coningsby were in town, which her casual inquiries of Lord Beaumanoir induced her to believe was the case, he would be present. Never, therefore, had she repaired to an assembly with such a fluttering spirit; and yet there was a fascinating anxiety about it that bewilders the young heart.

In vain Edith surveyed the rooms to catch the form of that being, whom for a moment she had never ceased to cherish and muse over. He was not there; and at the very moment when, disappointed and mortified, she most required solace, she learned from Mr Melton that Lady Theresa Sydney, whom she chanced to admire, was going to be married, and to Mr Coningsby!

What a revelation! His silence, perhaps his shunning of her were no longer inexplicable. What a return for all her romantic devotion in her sad solitude at Hellingsley. Was this the end of their twilight rambles, and the sweet pathos of their mutual loves? There seemed to be no truth in man, no joy in life! All the feelings that she had so generously lavished, all returned upon herself. She could have burst into a passion of tears and buried herself in a cloister.

Instead of that, civilisation made her listen with a serene though tortured countenance; but as soon as it was in her power, pleading a headache to Lady Wallinger, she effected, or thought she had effected, her escape from a scene which harrowed her heart.

As for Coningsby, he passed a sleepless night, agitated by the unexpected presence of Edith and distracted by the manner in which she had received him. To say that her appearance had revived all his passionate affection for her would convey an unjust impression of the nature of his feelings. His affection had never for a moment swerved; it was profound and firm. But unquestionably this sudden vision had brought before him, in startling and more vivid colours, the relations that subsisted between them. There was the being whom he loved and who loved him; and whatever were the barriers which the circumstances of life placed against their union, they were partakers of the solemn sacrament of an unpolluted heart.

Coningsby, as we have mentioned, had signified to Oswald his return to England: he had hitherto omitted to write again; not because his spirit faltered, but he was wearied of whispering hope without foundation, and mourning over his chagrined fortunes. Once more in England, once more placed in communication with his grandfather, he felt with increased conviction the difficulties which surrounded him. The society of Lady Everingham and her sister, who had been at the same time her visitor, had been a relaxation, and a beneficial one, to a mind suffering too much from the tension of one idea. But Coningsby had treated the matrimonial project of his gay-minded hostess with the courteous levity in which he believed it had at first half originated. He admired and liked Lady Theresa; but there was a reason why he could not marry her, even had his own heart not been absorbed by one of those passions from which men of deep and earnest character never emancipate themselves.

After musing and meditating again and again over everything that had occurred, Coningsby fell asleep when the morning had far advanced, resolved to rise when a little refreshed and find out Lady Wallinger, who, he felt sure, would receive him with kindness.

Yet it was fated that this step should not be taken, for while he was at breakfast, his servant brought him a letter from Monmouth House, apprising him that his grandfather wished to see him as soon as possible on urgent business.

Chapter 3

LORD MONMOUTH was sitting in the same dressing-room in which he was first introduced to the reader; on the table were several packets of papers that were open and in course of reference; and he dictated his observations to Monsieur Villebecque, who was writing at his left hand.

Thus were they occupied when Coningsby was ushered into the room.

'You see, Harry,' said Lord Monmouth, 'that I am much occupied to-day, yet the business on which I wish to communicate with you is so pressing that it could not be postponed.' He made a sign to Villebecque, and his secretary instantly retired.

'I was right in pressing your return to England,' continued Lord Monmouth to his grandson, who was a little anxious as to the impending communication, which he could not in any way anticipate. 'These are not times when young men should be out of sight. Your public career will commence immediately. The Government have resolved on a dissolution. My information is from the highest quarter. You may be astonished, but it is a fact. They are going to dissolve their own House of Commons. Notwithstanding this and the Queen's name, we can beat them; but the race requires the finest jockeying. We can't give a point. Tadpole has been here to me about Darlford; he came specially with a message, I may say an appeal, from one to whom I can refuse nothing; the Government count on the seat, though with the new Registration 'tis nearly a tie. If we had a good candidate we could win. But Rigby won't do. He is too much of the old clique; used up; a hack; besides, a beaten horse. We are assured the name of Coningsby would be a host; there is a considerable section who support the present fellow who will not vote against a Coningsby. They have thought of you as a fit person, and I have approved of the suggestion. You will, therefore, be the candidate for Darlford with my entire sanction and support, and I have no doubt you will be successful. You may be sure I shall spare nothing: and it will be very gratifying to me, after being robbed of all our boroughs, that the only Coningsby who cares to enter Parliament, should nevertheless be able to do so as early as I could fairly desire.'

Coningsby the rival of Mr Millbank on the hustings of Darlford! Vanquished or victorious, equally a catastrophe! The fierce passions, the gross insults, the hot blood and the cool lies, the ruffianism and the ribaldry, perhaps the domestic discomforture and mortification, which he was about to be the means of bringing on the roof he loved best in the world, occurred to him with anguish. The countenance of Edith, haughty and mournful as last night, rose to him again. He saw her canvassing for her father, and against him. Madness! And for what was he to make this terrible and costly sacrifice? For his ambition? Not even for that Divinity or Dæmon for which we all immolate so much! Mighty ambition, forsooth, to succeed to the Rigbys! To enter the House of Commons a slave and a tool; to move according to instructions, and to labour for the low designs of petty spirits, without even the consolation of being a dupe. What sympathy could there exist between Coningsby and the 'great Conservative party,' that for ten years in an age of revolution had never promulgated a principle; whose only intelligible and consistent policy seemed to be an attempt, very grateful of course to the feelings of an English Royalist, to revive Irish Puritanism; who when in power in 1835 had used that power only to evince their utter ignorance of Church principles; and who were at this moment, when Coningsby was formally solicited to join their ranks, in open insurrection against the prerogatives of the English Monarchy?

'Do you anticipate then an immediate dissolution, sir?' inquired Coningsby after a moment's pause.

'We must anticipate it; though I think it doubtful. It may be next month; it may be in the autumn; they may tide over another year, as Lord Eskdale thinks, and his opinion always weighs with me. He is very safe. Tadpole believes they will dissolve at once. But whether they dissolve now, or in a month's time, or in the autumn, or next year, our course is clear. We must declare our intentions immediately. We must hoist our flag. Monday next, there is a great Conservative dinner at Darlford. You must attend it; that will be the finest opportunity in the world for you to announce yourself.'

'Don't you think, sir,' said Coningsby, 'that such an announcement would be rather premature? It is, in fact, embarking in a contest which may last a year; perhaps more.'

'What you say is very true,' said Lord Monmouth; 'no doubt it is very troublesome; very disgusting; any canvassing is. But we must take things as we find them. You cannot get into Parliament now in the good old gentlemanlike way; and we ought to be thankful that this interest has been fostered for our purpose.'

Coningsby looked on the carpet, cleared his throat as if about to speak, and then gave something like a sigh.

'I think you had better be off the day after to-morrow,' said Lord Monmouth. 'I have sent instructions to the steward to do all he can in so short a time, for I wish you to entertain the principal people.'

'You are most kind, you are always most kind to me, dear sir,' said Coningsby, in a hesitating tone, and with an air of great embarrassment, 'but, in truth, I have no wish to enter Parliament.'

'What?' said Lord Monmouth.

'I feel that I am not yet sufficiently prepared for so great a responsibility as a seat in the House of Commons,' said Coningsby.

'Responsibility!' said Lord Monmouth, smiling. 'What responsibility is there? How can any one have a more agreeable seat? The only person to whom you are responsible is your own relation, who brings you in. And I don't suppose there can be any difference on any point between us. You are certainly still young; but I was younger by nearly two years when I first went in; and I found no difficulty. There can be no difficulty. All you have got to do is to vote with your party. As for speaking, if you have a talent that way, take my advice; don't be in a hurry. Learn to know the House; learn the House to know you. If a man be discreet, he cannot enter Parliament too soon.'

'It is not exactly that, sir,' said Coningsby.

'Then what is it, my dear Harry? You see to-day I have much to do; yet as your business is pressing, I would not postpone seeing you an hour. I thought you would have been very much gratified.'

'You mentioned that I had nothing to do but to vote with my party, sir,' replied Coningsby. 'You mean, of course, by that term what is understood by the Conservative party.'

'Of course; our friends.'

'I am sorry,' said Coningsby, rather pale, but speaking with firmness, 'I am sorry that I could not support the Conservative party.'

'By — !' exclaimed Lord Monmouth, starting in his seat, 'some woman has got hold of him, and made him a Whig!'

'No, my dear grandfather,' said Coningsby, scarcely able to repress a smile, serious as the interview was becoming, 'nothing of the kind, I assure you. No person can be more anti-Whig.'

'I don't know what you are driving at, sir,' said Lord Monmouth, in a hard, dry tone.

'I wish to be frank, sir,' said Coningsby, 'and am very sensible of your goodness in permitting me to speak to you on the subject. What I mean to say is, that I have for a long time looked upon the Conservative party as a body who have betrayed their trust; more from ignorance, I admit, than from design; yet clearly a body of individuals totally unequal to the exigencies of the epoch, and indeed unconscious of its real character.'

'You mean giving up those Irish corporations?'[1] said Lord Monmouth. 'Well, between ourselves, I am quite of the same opinion. But we must mount higher; we must go to '28 for the real mischief.[2] But what is the use of lamenting the past? Peel is the only man; suited to the times and all that; at least we must say so, and try to believe so; we can't go back. And it is our own fault that we have let the chief power out of the hands of our own order. It was never thought of in the time of your great-grandfather, sir. And if a commoner were for a season permitted to be the nominal Premier to do the detail, there was always a secret committee of great 1688 nobles to give him his instructions.'

'I should be very sorry to see secret committees of great 1688 nobles again,' said Coningsby.

'Then what the devil do you want to see?' said Lord Monmouth.

'Political faith,' said Coningsby, 'instead of political infidelity.'

'Hem!' said Lord Monmouth.

'Before I support Conservative principles,' continued Coningsby, 'I merely wish to be informed what those principles aim to conserve. It would not appear to be the prerogative of the Crown, since the principal portion of a Conservative oration now is an invective against a late royal act which they describe as a Bed-chamber plot. Is it the Church which they wish to conserve? What is a threatened Appropriation Clause against an actual Church Commission in the hands of Parliamentary Laymen? Could the Long Parliament have done worse? Well, then, if it is neither the Crown nor the Church, whose rights and privileges this Conservative party propose to vindicate, is it your House, the House of Lords, whose powers they are prepared to uphold? Is it not notorious that the very man whom you have elected as your leader in that House, declares among his Conservative adherents, that henceforth the assembly that used to furnish those very Committees of great revolution nobles that you mention, is to initiate nothing; and, without a struggle, is to subside into that undisturbed repose which resembles the Imperial tranquillity that secured the frontiers by paying tribute?'

'All this is vastly fine,' said Lord Monmouth; 'but I see no means by which I can attain my object but by supporting Peel. After all, what is the end of all parties and all politics? To gain your object. I want to turn our coronet into a ducal one, and to get your grandmother's barony called out of abeyance in your favour. It is impossible that Peel can refuse me. I have already purchased an ample estate with the view of entailing it on you and your issue. You will make a considerable alliance; you may marry, if you please, Lady Theresa Sydney. I hear the report with pleasure. Count on my at once entering into any arrangement conducive to your happiness.'

'My dear grandfather, you have ever been to me only too kind and generous.'

'To whom should I be kind but to you, my own blood, that has never crossed me, and of whom I have reason to be proud? Yes, Harry, it gratifies me to hear you admired and to learn your success. All I want now is to see you in Parliament. A man should be in Parliament early. There is a sort of stiffness about every man, no matter what may be his talents, who enters Parliament late in life; and now, fortunately, the occasion offers. You will go down on Friday; feed the notabilities well; speak out; praise Peel; abuse O'Connell[3] and the ladies of the Bed-chamber; anathematise all waverers; say a good deal about Ireland; stick to the Irish Registration Bill,[4] that's a good card; and, above all, my dear Harry, don't spare that fellow Millbank. Remember, in turning him out you not only gain a vote for the Conservative cause and our coronet, but you crush my foe. Spare nothing for that object; I count on you, boy.'

'I should grieve to be backward in anything that concerned your interest or your honour, sir,' said Coningsby, with an air of great embarrassment.

'I am sure you would, I am sure you would,' said Lord Monmouth, in a tone of some kindness.

'And I feel at this moment,' continued Coningsby, 'that there is no personal sacrifice which I am not prepared to make for them, except one. My interests, my affections, they should not be placed in the balance, if yours, sir, were at stake, though there are circumstances which might involve me in a position of as much mental distress as a man could well endure; but I claim for my convictions, my dear grandfather, a generous tolerance.'

'I can't follow you, sir,' said Lord Monmouth, again in his hard tone. 'Our interests are inseparable, and therefore there can never be any sacrifice of conduct on your part. What you mean by sacrifice of affections, I don't comprehend; but as for your opinions, you have no business to have any other than those I uphold. You are too young to form opinions.'

'I am sure I wish to express them with no unbecoming confidence,' replied Coningsby; 'I have never intruded them on your ear before; but this being an occasion when you yourself said, sir, I was about to commence my public career, I confess I thought it was my duty to be frank; I would not entail on myself long years of mortification by one of those ill-considered entrances into political life which so many public men have cause to deplore.'

'You go with your family, sir, like a gentleman; you are not to consider your opinions, like a philosopher or a political adventurer.'

'Yes, sir,' said Coningsby, with animation, 'but men going with their families like gentlemen, and losing sight of every principle on which the society of this country ought to be established produced the Reform Bill.'

'D— the Reform Bill!' said Lord Monmouth; 'if the Duke had not quarrelled with Lord Grey on a Coal Committee, we should never have had the Reform Bill. And Grey would have gone to Ireland.'[5]

'You are in as great peril now as you were in 1830,' said Coningsby.

'No, no, no,' said Lord Monmouth; 'the Tory party is organised now; they will not catch us napping again: these Conservative Associations[6] have done the business.'

'But what are they organised for?' said Coningsby. 'At the best to turn out the Whigs. And when you have turned out the Whigs, what then? You may get your ducal coronet, sir. But a duke now is not so great a man as a baron was but a century back. We cannot struggle against the irresistible stream of circumstances. Power has left our order; this is not an age for factitious aristocracy. As for my grandmother's barony, I should look upon the termination of its abeyance in my favour as the act of my political extinction. What we want, sir, is not to fashion new dukes and furbish up old baronies, but to establish great principles which may maintain the realm and secure the happiness of the people. Let me see authority once more honoured; a solemn reverence again the habit of our lives; let me see property acknowledging, as in the old days of faith, that labour is his twin brother, and that the essence of all tenure is the performance of duty; let results such as these be brought about, and let me participate, however feebly, in the great fulfilment, and public life then indeed becomes a noble career, and a seat in Parliament an enviable distinction.'

'I tell you what it is, Harry,' said Lord Monmouth, very drily, 'members of this family may think as they like, but they must act as I please. You must go down on Friday to Darlford and declare yourself a candidate for the town, or I shall reconsider our mutual positions. I would say, you must go to-morrow; but it is only courteous to Rigby to give him a previous intimation of your movement. And that cannot be done to-day. I sent for Rigby this morning on other business which now occupies me, and find he is out of town. He will return to-morrow; and will be here at three o'clock, when you can meet him. You will meet him, I doubt not, like a man of sense,' added Lord Monmouth, looking at Coningsby with a glance such as he had never before encountered, 'who is not prepared to sacrifice all the objects of life for the pursuit of some fantastical puerilities.'

His Lordship rang a bell on his table for Villebecque; and to prevent any further conversation, resumed his papers.

Chapter 4

IT would have been difficult for any person, unconscious of crime, to have felt more dejected than Coningsby when he rode out of the court-yard of Monmouth House. The love of Edith would have consoled him for the destruction of his prosperity; the proud fulfilment of his ambition might in time have proved some compensation for his crushed affections; but his present position seemed to offer no single source of solace. There came over him that irresistible conviction that is at times the dark doom of all of us, that the bright period of our life is past; that a future awaits us only of anxiety, failure, mortification, despair; that none of our resplendent visions can ever be realised; and that we add but one more victim to the long and dreary catalogue of baffled aspirations.

Nor could he indeed by any combination see the means to extricate himself from the perils that were encompassing him. There was something about his grandfather that defied persuasion. Prone as eloquent youth generally is to believe in the resistless power of its appeals, Coningsby despaired at once of ever moving Lord Monmouth. There had been a callous dryness in his manner, an unswerving purpose in his spirit, that at once baffled all attempts at influence. Nor could Coningsby forget the look he received when he quitted the room. There was no possibility of mistaking it; it said at once, without periphrasis, 'Cross my purpose, and I will crush you!'

This was the moment when the sympathy, if not the counsels, of friendship might have been grateful. A clever woman might have afforded even more than sympathy; some happy device that might have even released him from the mesh in which he was involved. And once Coningsby had turned his horse's head to Park Lane to call on Lady Everingham. But surely if there were a sacred secret in the world, it was the one which subsisted between himself and Edith. No, that must never be violated. Then there was Lady Wallinger; he could at least speak with freedom to her. He resolved to tell her all. He looked in for a moment at a club to take up the 'Court Guide' and find her direction. A few men were standing in a bow window. He heard Mr Cassilis say,

'So Beau, they say, is booked at last; the new beauty, have you heard?'

'I saw him very sweet on her last night,' rejoined his companion. 'Has she any tin?'

'Deuced deal, they say,' replied Mr Cassilis. 'The father is a cotton lord, and they all have loads of tin, you know. Nothing like them now.'

'He is in Parliament, is not he?'

''Gad, I believe he is,' said Mr Cassilis; 'I never know who is in Parliament in these days. I remember when there were only ten men in the House of Commons who were not either members of Brookes' or this place. Everything is so deuced changed.'

'I hear 'tis an old affair of Beau,' said another gentleman. 'It was all done a year ago at Rome or Paris.'

'They say she refused him then,' said Mr Cassilis.

'Well, that is tolerably cool for a manufacturer's daughter,' said his friend. 'What next?'

'I wonder how the Duke likes it?' said Mr Cassilis.

'Or the Duchess?' added one of his friends.

'Or the Everinghams?' added the other.

'The Duke will be deuced glad to see Beau settled, I take it,' said Mr Cassilis.

'A good deal depends on the tin,' said his friend.

Coningsby threw down the 'Court Guide' with a sinking heart. In spite of every insuperable difficulty, hitherto the end and object of all his aspirations and all his exploits, sometimes even almost unconsciously to himself, was Edith. It was over. The strange manner of last night was fatally explained. The heart that once had been his was now another's. To the man who still loves there is in that conviction the most profound and desolate sorrow of which our nature is capable. All the recollection of the past, all the once-cherished prospects of the future, blend into one bewildering anguish. Coningsby quitted the club, and mounting his horse, rode rapidly out of town, almost unconscious of his direction. He found himself at length in a green lane near Willesden, silent and undisturbed; he pulled up his horse, and summoned all his mind to the contemplation of his prospects.

Edith was lost. Now, should he return to his grandfather, accept his mission, and go down to Darlford on Friday? Favour and fortune, power, prosperity, rank, distinction would be the consequence of this step; might not he add even vengeance? Was there to be no term to his endurance? Might not he teach this proud, prejudiced manufacturer, with all his virulence and despotic caprices, a memorable lesson? And his daughter, too, this betrothed, after all, of a young noble, with her flush futurity of splendour and enjoyment, was she to hear of him only, if indeed she heard of him at all, as of one toiling or trifling in the humbler positions of existence; and wonder, with a blush, that he ever could have been the hero of her romantic girlhood? What degradation in the idea? His cheek burnt at the possibility of such ignominy!

It was a conjuncture in his life that required decision. He thought of his companions who looked up to him with such ardent anticipations of his fame, of delight in his career, and confidence in his leading; were all these high and fond fancies to be baulked? On the very threshold of life was he to blunder? 'Tis the first step that leads to all, and his was to be a wilful error. He remembered his first visit to his grandfather, and the delight of his friends at Eton at his report on his return. After eight years of initiation was he to lose that favour then so highly prized, when the results which they had so long counted on were on the very eve of accomplishment? Parliament and riches, and rank and power; these were facts, realities, substances, that none could mistake. Was he to sacrifice them for speculations, theories, shadows, perhaps the vapours of a green and conceited brain? No, by heaven, no! He was like Cæsar by the starry river's side, watching the image of the planets on its fatal waters. The die was cast.[1]

The sun set; the twilight spell fell upon his soul; the exaltation of his spirit died away. Beautiful thoughts, full of sweetness and tranquillity and consolation, came clustering round his heart like seraphs. He thought of Edith in her hours of fondness; he thought of the pure and solemn moments when to mingle his name with the heroes of humanity was his aspiration, and to achieve immortal fame the inspiring purpose of his life. What were the tawdry accidents of vulgar ambition to him? No domestic despot could deprive him of his intellect, his knowledge, the sustaining power of an unpolluted conscience. If he possessed the intelligence in which he had confidence, the world would recognise his voice even if not placed upon a pedestal. If the principles of his philosophy were true, the great heart of the nation would respond to their expression. Coningsby felt at this moment a profound conviction which never again deserted him, that the conduct which would violate the affections of the heart, or the dictates of the conscience, however it may lead to immediate success, is a fatal error. Conscious that he was perhaps verging on some painful vicissitude of his life, he devoted himself to a love that seemed hopeless, and to a fame that was perhaps a dream.

It was under the influence of these solemn resolutions that he wrote, on his return home, a letter to Lord Monmouth, in which he expressed all that affection which he really felt for his grandfather, and all the pangs which it cost him to adhere to the conclusions he had already announced. In terms of tenderness, and even humility, he declined to become a candidate for Darlford, or even to enter Parliament, except as the master of his own conduct.

Chapter 5

LADY Monmouth was reclining on a sofa in that beautiful boudoir which had been fitted up under the superintendence of Mr Rigby, but as he then believed for the Princess Colonna. The walls were hung with amber satin, painted by Delaroche with such subjects as might be expected from his brilliant and picturesque pencil. Fair forms, heroes and heroines in dazzling costume, the offspring of chivalry merging into what is commonly styled civilisation, moved in graceful or fantastic groups amid palaces and gardens. The ceiling, carved in the deep honeycomb fashion of the Saracens, was richly gilt and picked out in violet. Upon a violet carpet of velvet was represented the marriage of Cupid and Psyche.

It was about two hours after Coningsby had quitted Monmouth House, and Flora came in, sent for by Lady Monmouth as was her custom, to read to her as she was employed with some light work.

"Tis a new book of Sue,'¹ said Lucretia. 'They say it is good.'

Flora, seated by her side, began to read. Reading was an accomplishment which distinguished Flora; but to-day her voice faltered, her expression was uncertain; she seemed but imperfectly to comprehend her page. More than once Lady Monmouth looked round at her with an inquisitive glance. Suddenly Flora stopped and burst into tears.

'O! madam,' she at last exclaimed, 'if you would but speak to Mr Coningsby, all might be right!'

'What is this?' said Lady Monmouth, turning quickly on the sofa; then, collecting herself in an instant, she continued with less abruptness, and more suavity than usual, 'Tell me, Flora, what is it; what is the matter?'

'My Lord,' sobbed Flora, 'has quarrelled with Mr Coningsby.'

An expression of eager interest came over the countenance of Lucretia.

'Why have they quarrelled?'

'I do not know they have quarrelled; it is not, perhaps, a right term; but my Lord is very angry with Mr Coningsby.'

'Not very angry, I should think, Flora; and about what?'

'Oh! very angry, madam,' said Flora, shaking her head mournfully. 'My Lord told M. Villebecque that perhaps Mr Coningsby would never enter the house again.'

'Was it to-day?' asked Lucretia.

'This morning. Mr Coningsby has only left this hour or two. He will not do what my Lord wishes, about some seat in the Chamber. I do not know exactly what it is; but my Lord is in one of his moods of terror: my father is frightened even to go into his room when he is so.'

'Has Mr Rigby been here to-day?' asked Lucretia.

'Mr Rigby is not in town. My father went for Mr Rigby this morning before Mr Coningsby came, and he found that Mr Rigby was not in town. That is why I know it.'

Lady Monmouth rose from her sofa, and walked once or twice up and down the room. Then turning to Flora, she said, 'Go away now: the book is stupid; it does not amuse me. Stop: find out all you can for me about the quarrel before I speak to Mr Coningsby.'

Flora quitted the room. Lucretia remained for some time in meditation; then she wrote a few lines, which she despatched at once to Mr Rigby.

Chapter 6

WHAT a great man was the Right Honourable Nicholas Rigby! Here was one of the first peers of England, and one of the finest ladies in London, both waiting with equal anxiety his return to town; and unable to transact two affairs of vast importance, yet wholly unconnected, without his interposition! What was the secret of the influence of this man, confided in by everybody, trusted by none? His counsels were not deep, his expedients were not felicitous; he had no feeling, and he could create no sympathy. It is that, in most of the transactions of life, there is some portion which no one cares to accomplish, and which everybody wishes to be achieved. This was always the portion of Mr Rigby. In the eye of the world he had constantly the appearance of being mixed up with high dealings, and negotiations and arrangements of fine management, whereas in truth, notwithstanding his splendid livery and the airs he gave himself in the servants' hall, his real business in life had ever been, to do the dirty work.

Mr Rigby had been shut up much at his villa of late. He was concocting, you could not term it composing, an article, a 'very slashing article,' which was to prove that the penny postage must be the destruction of the aristocracy. It was a grand subject, treated in his highest style. His parallel portraits of Rowland Hill the conqueror of Almarez and Rowland Hill the deviser of the cheap postage[1] were enormously fine. It was full of passages in italics, little words in great capitals, and almost drew tears. The statistical details also were highly interesting and novel. Several of the old postmen, both twopenny and general, who had been in office with himself, and who were inspired with an equal zeal against that spirit of reform of which they had alike been victims, supplied him with information which nothing but a breach of ministerial duty could have furnished. The prophetic peroration as to the irresistible progress of democracy was almost as powerful as one of Rigby's speeches on Aldborough or Amersham. There never was a fellow for giving a good hearty kick to the people like Rigby. Himself sprung from the dregs of the populace, this was disinterested. What could be more patriotic and magnanimous than his Jeremiads over the fall of the Montmorencis and the Crillons, or the possible catastrophe of the Percys and the Manners! The truth of all this hullaballoo was that Rigby had a sly pension which, by an inevitable association of ideas, he always connected with the maintenance of an aristocracy. All his rigmarole dissertations on the French revolution were impelled by this secret influence; and when he wailed over 'la guerre aux châteaux,' and moaned like a mandrake over Nottingham Castle in flames,[2] the rogue had an eye all the while to quarter-day!

Arriving in town the day after Coningsby's interview with his grandfather, Mr Rigby found a summons to Monmouth House waiting him, and an urgent note from Lucretia begging that he would permit nothing to prevent him seeing her for a few minutes before he called on the Marquess.

Lucretia, acting on the unconscious intimation of Flora, had in the course of four-and-twenty hours obtained pretty ample and accurate details of the cause of contention between Coningsby and her husband. She could inform Mr Rigby not only that Lord Monmouth was highly incensed against his grandson, but that the cause of their misunderstanding arose about a seat in the House of Commons, and that seat too the one which Mr Rigby had long appropriated to himself, and over whose registration he had watched with such affectionate solicitude.

Lady Monmouth arranged this information like a first-rate artist, and gave it a grouping and a colour which produced the liveliest effect upon her confederate. The countenance of Rigby was almost ghastly as he received the intelligence: a grin, half of malice, half of terror, played over his features.

'I told you to beware of him long ago,' said Lady Monmouth. 'He is, he has ever been, in the way of both of us.'

'He is in my power,' said Rigby. 'We can crush him!'

'How?'

'He is in love with the daughter of Millbank, the man who bought Hellingsley.'

'Hah!' exclaimed Lady Monmouth, in a prolonged tone.

'He was at Coningsby all last summer, hanging about her. I found the younger Millbank quite domiciliated at the Castle; a fact which, of itself, if known to Lord Monmouth, would ensure the lad's annihilation.'

'And you kept this fine news for a winter campaign, my good Mr Rigby,' said Lady Monmouth, with a subtle smile. 'It was a weapon of service. I give you my compliments.'

'The time is not always ripe,' said Mr Rigby.

'But it is now most mature. Let us not conceal it from ourselves that, since his first visit to Coningsby, we have neither of us really been in the same position which we then occupied, or believed we should occupy. My Lord, though you would scarcely believe it, has a weakness for this boy; and though I by my marriage, and you by your zealous ability, have apparently secured a permanent hold upon his habits, I have never doubted that when the crisis comes we shall find that the golden fruit is plucked by one who has not watched the garden. You take me? There is no reason why we two should clash together: we can both of us find what we want, and more securely if we work in company.'

'I trust my devotion to you has never been doubted, dear madam.'

'Nor to yourself, dear Mr Rigby. Go now: the game is before you. Rid me of this Coningsby, and I will secure you all that you want. Doubt not me. There is no reason. I want a firm ally. There must be two.'

'It shall be done,' said Rigby; 'it must be done. If once the notion gets wind that one of the Castle family may perchance stand for Darlford, all the present combinations will be disorganised. It must be done at once. I know that the Government will dissolve.'

'So I hear for certain,' said Lucretia. 'Be sure there is no time to lose. What does he want with you to-day?'

'I know not: there are so many things.'

'To be sure; and yet I cannot doubt he will speak of this quarrel. Let not the occasion be lost. Whatever his mood, the subject may be introduced. If good, you will guide him more easily; if dark, the love for the Hellingsley girl, the fact of the brother being in his castle, drinking his wine, riding his horses, ordering about

his servants; you will omit no details: a Millbank quite at home at
Coningsby will lash him to madness! 'Tis quite ripe. Not a word
that you have seen me. Go, go, or he may hear that you have
arrived. I shall be at home all the morning. It will be but gallant
that you should pay me a little visit when you have transacted
your business. You understand. *Au revoir!*'

Lady Monmouth took up again her French novel; but her eyes
soon glanced over the page, unattached by its contents. Her
own existence was too interesting to find any excitement in fiction.
It was nearly three years since her marriage; that great step which
she ever had a conviction was to lead to results still greater. Of
late she had often been filled with a presentiment that they were
near at hand; never more so than on this day. Irresistible was the
current of associations that led her to meditate on freedom,
wealth, power; on a career which should at the same time dazzle
the imagination and gratify her heart. Notwithstanding the gossip
of Paris, founded on no authentic knowledge of her husband's
character or information, based on the haphazard observations
of the floating multitude, Lucretia herself had no reason to fear
that her influence over Lord Monmouth, if exerted, was materially
diminished. But satisfied that he had formed no other tie, with her
ever the test of her position, she had not thought it expedient, and
certainly would have found it irksome, to maintain that influence
by any ostentatious means. She knew that Lord Monmouth was
capricious, easily wearied, soon palled; and that on men who have
no affections, affection has no hold. Their passions or their
fancies, on the contrary, as it seemed to her, are rather
stimulated by neglect or indifference, provided that they are not
systematic; and the circumstance of a wife being admired by one
who is not her husband sometimes wonderfully revives the
passion or renovates the respect of him who should be devoted to
her.

The health of Lord Monmouth was the subject which never was
long absent from the vigilance or meditation of Lucretia. She
was well assured that his life was no longer secure. She knew that
after their marriage he had made a will, which secured to her a
large portion of his great wealth in case of their having no issue,
and after the accident at Paris all hope in that respect was

over. Recently the extreme anxiety which Lord Monmouth had evinced about terminating the abeyance of the barony to which his first wife was a co-heiress in favour of his grandson, had alarmed Lucretia. To establish in the land another branch of the house of Coningsby was evidently the last excitement of Lord Monmouth, and perhaps a permanent one. If the idea were once accepted, notwithstanding the limit to its endowment which Lord Monmouth might at the first start contemplate, Lucretia had sufficiently studied his temperament to be convinced that all his energies and all his resources would ultimately be devoted to its practical fulfilment. Her original prejudice against Coningsby and jealousy of his influence had therefore of late been considerably aggravated; and the intelligence that for the first time there was a misunderstanding between Coningsby and her husband filled her with excitement and hope. She knew her Lord well enough to feel assured that the cause for the displeasure in the present instance could not be a light one; she resolved instantly to labour that it should not be transient; and it so happened that she had applied for aid in this endeavour to the very individual in whose power it rested to accomplish all her desire, while in doing so he felt at the same time he was defending his own position and advancing his own interests.

Lady Monmouth was now awaiting with some excitement the return of Mr Rigby. His interview with his patron was of unusual length. An hour, and more than an hour, had elapsed. Lady Monmouth again threw aside the book which more than once she had discarded. She paced the room, restless rather than disquieted. She had complete confidence in Rigby's ability for the occasion; and with her knowledge of Lord Monmouth's character, she could not contemplate the possibility of failure, if the circumstances were adroitly introduced to his consideration. Still time stole on: the harassing and exhausting process of suspense was acting on her nervous system. She began to think that Rigby had not found the occasion favourable for the catastrophe; that Monmouth, from apprehension of disturbing Rigby and entailing explanations on himself, had avoided the necessary communication; that her skilful combination for the moment had missed. Two hours had now elapsed, and Lucretia, in a state of considerable irritation, was about to inquire whether Mr Rigby were with his Lordship, when the door of her boudoir opened, and that gentleman appeared.

'How long you have been!' exclaimed Lady Monmouth. 'Now sit down and tell me what has passed.'

Lady Monmouth pointed to the seat which Flora had occupied.

'I thank your Ladyship,' said Mr Rigby, with a somewhat grave and yet perplexed expression of countenance, and seating himself at some little distance from his companion, 'but I am very well here.'

There was a pause. Instead of responding to the invitation of Lady Monmouth to communicate with his usual readiness and volubility, Mr Rigby was silent, and, if it were possible to use such an expression with regard to such a gentleman, apparently embarrassed.

'Well,' said Lady Monmouth, 'does he know about the Millbanks?'

'Everything,' said Mr Rigby.

'And what did he say?'

'His Lordship was greatly shocked,' replied Mr Rigby, with a pious expression of features. 'Such monstrous ingratitude! As his Lordship very justly observed, "It is impossible to say what is going on under my own roof, or to what I can trust."'

'But he made an exception in your favour, I dare say, my dear Mr Rigby,' said Lady Monmouth.

'Lord Monmouth was pleased to say that I possessed his entire confidence,' said Mr Rigby, 'and that he looked to me in his difficulties.'

'Very sensible of him. And what is to become of Mr Coningsby?'

'The steps which his Lordship is about to take with reference to the establishment generally,' said Mr Rigby, 'will allow the connection that at present subsists between that gentleman and his noble relative, now that Lord Monmouth's eyes are open to his real character, to terminate naturally, without the necessity of any formal explanation.'

'But what do you mean by the steps he is going to take in his establishment generally?'

'Lord Monmouth thinks he requires change of scene.'

'Oh! is he going to drag me abroad again?' exclaimed Lady Monmouth, with great impatience.

'Why, not exactly,' said Mr Rigby, rather demurely.

'I hope he is not going again to that dreadful castle in Lancashire.'

'Lord Monmouth was thinking that, as you were tired of Paris, you might find some of the German Baths agreeable.'

'Why, there is nothing that Lord Monmouth dislikes so much as a German bathing-place!'

'Exactly,' said Mr Rigby.

'Then how capricious in him wanting to go to them!'

'He does not want to go to them!'

'What do you mean, Mr Rigby?' said Lady Monmouth, in a lower voice, and looking him full in the face with a glance seldom bestowed.

There was a churlish and unusual look about Rigby. It was as if malignant, and yet at the same time a little frightened, he had screwed himself into doggedness.

'I mean what Lord Monmouth means. He suggests that if your Ladyship were to pass the summer at Kissengen, for example, and a paragraph in the *Morning Post* were to announce that his Lordship was about to join you there, all awkwardness would be removed; and no one could for a moment take the liberty of supposing, even if his Lordship did not ultimately reach you, that anything like a separation had occurred.'

'A separation!' said Lady Monmouth.

'Quite amicable,' said Mr Rigby. 'I would never have consented to interfere in the affair, but to secure that most desirable point.'

'I will see Lord Monmouth at once,' said Lucretia, rising, her natural pallor aggravated into a ghoul-like tint.

'His Lordship has gone out,' said Mr Rigby, rather stubbornly.

'Our conversation, sir, then finishes: I wait his return.' She bowed haughtily.

'His Lordship will never return to Monmouth House again.'

Lucretia sprang from the sofa.

'Miserable craven!' she exclaimed. 'Has the cowardly tyrant fled? And he really thinks that I am to be crushed by such an instrument as this! Pah! He may leave Monmouth House, but I shall not. Begone, sir!'

'Still anxious to secure an amicable separation,' said Mr Rigby, 'your Ladyship must allow me to place the circumstances of the case fairly before your excellent judgment. Lord Monmouth has decided upon a course: you know as well as I that he never swerves from his resolutions. He has left peremptory instructions, and he will listen to no appeal. He has empowered me to represent to your Ladyship that he wishes in every way to consider your convenience. He suggests that everything, in short, should be arranged as if his Lordship were himself unhappily no more; that your Ladyship should at once enter into your jointure, which shall be made payable quarterly to your order, provided you can find it convenient to live upon the Continent,' added Mr Rigby, with some hesitation.

'And suppose I cannot?'

'Why, then, we will leave your Ladyship to the assertion of your rights.'

'We!'

'I beg your Ladyship's pardon. I speak as the friend of the family, the trustee of your marriage settlement, well known also as Lord Monmouth's executor,' said Mr Rigby, his countenance gradually regaining its usual callous confidence, and some degree of self-complacency, as he remembered the good things which he enumerated.

'I have decided,' said Lady Monmouth. 'I will assert my rights. Your master has mistaken my character and his own position. He shall rue the day that he assailed me.'

'I should be sorry if there were any violence,' said Mr Rigby, 'especially as everything is left to my management and control. An office, indeed, which I only accepted for your mutual advantage. I think, upon reflection, I might put before your Ladyship some considerations which might induce you, on the whole, to be of opinion that it will be better for us to draw together in this business, as we have hitherto, indeed, throughout an acquaintance now of some years.' Rigby was resuming all his usual tone of brazen familiarity.

'Your self-confidence exceeds even Lord Monmouth's estimate of it,' said Lucretia.

'Now, now, you are unkind. Your Ladyship mistakes my position. I am interfering in this business for your sake. I might have refused the office. It would have fallen to another, who would have fulfilled it without any delicacy and consideration for your feelings. View my interposition in that light, my dear Lady Monmouth, and circumstances will assume altogether a new colour.'

'I beg that you will quit the house, sir.'

Mr Rigby shook his head. 'I would with pleasure, to oblige you, were it in my power; but Lord Monmouth has particularly desired that I should take up my residence here permanently. The servants are now my servants. It is useless to ring the bell. For your Ladyship's sake, I wish everything to be accomplished with tranquillity, and, if possible, friendliness and good feeling. You can have even a week for the preparations for your departure, if necessary. I will take that upon myself. Any carriages, too, that you desire; your jewels, at least all those that are not at the bankers'. The arrangement about your jointure, your letters of credit, even your passport, I will attend to myself; only too happy if, by this painful interference, I have in any way contributed to soften the annoyance which, at the first blush, you may naturally experience, but which, like everything else, take my word, will wear off.'

'I shall send for Lord Eskdale,' said Lady Monmouth. 'He is a gentleman.'

'I am quite sure,' said Mr Rigby, 'that Lord Eskdale will give you the same advice as myself, if he only reads your Ladyship's letters,' he added slowly, 'to Prince Trautsmandorff.'

'My letters?' said Lady Monmouth.

'Pardon me,' said Rigby, putting his hand in his pocket, as if to guard some treasure, 'I have no wish to revive painful associations; but I have them, and I must act upon them, if you persist in treating me as a foe, who am in reality your best friend; which indeed I ought to be, having the honour of acting as trustee under your marriage settlement, and having known you so many years.'

'Leave me for the present alone,' said Lady Monmouth. 'Send me my servant, if I have one. I shall not remain here the week which you mention, but quit at once this house, which I wish I had never entered. Adieu! Mr Rigby, you are now lord of Monmouth House, and yet I cannot help feeling you too will be discharged before he dies.'

Mr Rigby made Lady Monmouth a bow such as became the master of the house, and then withdrew.

Chapter 7

A PARAGRAPH in the *Morning Post*, a few days after his interview with his grandfather, announcing that Lord and Lady Monmouth had quitted town for the baths of Kissengen, startled Coningsby, who called the same day at Monmouth House in consequence. There he learnt more authentic details of their unexpected movements. It appeared that Lady Monmouth had certainly departed; and the porter, with a rather sceptical visage, informed Coningsby that Lord Monmouth was to follow; but when, he could not tell. At present his Lordship was at Brighton, and in a few days was about to take possession of a villa at Richmond, which had for some time been fitting up for him under the superintendence of Mr Rigby, who, as Coningsby also learnt, now permanently resided at Monmouth House. All this intelligence made Coningsby ponder. He was sufficiently acquainted with the parties concerned to feel assured that he had not learnt the whole truth. What had really taken place, and what was the real cause of the occurrences, were equally mystical to him: all he was convinced of was, that some great domestic revolution had been suddenly effected.

Coningsby entertained for his grandfather a sincere affection. With the exception of their last unfortunate interview, he had experienced from Lord Monmouth nothing but kindness both in phrase and deed. There was also something in Lord Monmouth, when he pleased it, rather fascinating to young men; and as Coningsby had never occasioned him any feelings but pleasurable ones, he was always disposed to make himself delightful to his grandson. The experience of a consummate man of the world, advanced in life, detailed without rigidity to youth, with frankness and facility, is bewitching. Lord Monmouth was never garrulous: he was always pithy, and could be picturesque. He revealed a character in a sentence, and detected the ruling passion with the hand of a master. Besides, he had seen everybody and had done everything; and though, on the whole, too indolent for conversation, and loving to be talked to, these were circumstances which made his too rare communications the more precious.

With these feelings, Coningsby resolved, the moment that he learned that his grandfather was established at Richmond, to pay him a visit. He was informed that Lord Monmouth was at home, and he was shown into a drawing-room, where he found two French ladies in their bonnets, whom he soon discovered to be actresses. They also had come down to pay a visit to his grandfather, and were by no means displeased to pass the interval that must elapse before they had that pleasure in chatting with his grandson. Coningsby found them extremely amusing; with the finest spirits in the world, imperturbable good temper, and an unconscious practical philosophy that defied the devil Care and all his works. And well it was that he found such agreeable companions, for time flowed on, and no summons arrived to call him to his grandfather's presence, and no herald to announce his grandfather's advent. The ladies and Coningsby had exhausted badinage; they had examined and criticised all the furniture, had rifled the vases of their prettiest flowers; and Clotilde, who had already sung several times, was proposing a duet to Ermengarde, when a servant entered, and told the ladies that a carriage was in attendance to give them an airing, and after that Lord Monmouth hoped they would return and dine with him; then turning to Coningsby, he informed him, with his Lord's compliments, that Lord Monmouth was sorry he was too much engaged to see him.

Nothing was to be done but to put a tolerably good face upon it. 'Embrace Lord Monmouth for me,' said Coningsby to his fair friends, 'and tell him I think it very unkind that he did not ask me to dinner with you.'

Coningsby said this with a gay air, but really with a depressed spirit. He felt convinced that his grandfather was deeply displeased with him; and as he rode away from the villa, he could not resist the strong impression that he was destined never to re-enter it. Yet it was decreed otherwise. It so happened that the idle message which Coningsby had left for his grandfather, and which he never seriously supposed for a moment that his late companions would have given their host, operated entirely in his favour. Whatever were the feelings with respect to Coningsby at the bottom of Lord Monmouth's heart, he was actuated in his refusal to see him not more from displeasure than from an anticipatory horror of something like a scene. Even a surrender from Coningsby without terms, and an offer to declare himself a candidate for Darlford, or to do anything else that his grandfather wished, would have been disagreeable to Lord Monmouth in his present mood. As in politics a revolution is often followed by a season of torpor, so in the case of Lord Monmouth the separation from his wife, which had for a long period occupied his meditation, was succeeded by a vein of mental dissipation. He did not wish to be reminded by anything or any person that he had still in some degree the misfortune of being a responsible member of society. He wanted to be surrounded by individuals who were above or below the conventional interests of what is called 'the World.' He wanted to hear nothing of those painful and embarrassing influences which from our contracted experience and want of enlightenment we magnify into such undue importance. For this purpose he wished to have about him persons whose knowledge of the cares of life concerned only the means of existence, and whose sense of its objects referred only to the sources of enjoyment; persons who had not been educated in the idolatry of Respectability; that is to say, of realising such an amount of what is termed Character by a hypocritical deference to the prejudices of the community as may enable them, at suitable times, and under convenient circumstances and disguises, to plunder the public. This was the Monmouth Philosophy.

With these feelings, Lord Monmouth recoiled at this moment from grandsons and relations and ties of all kinds. He did not wish to be reminded of his identity, but to swim unmolested and undisturbed in his Epicurean dream. When, therefore, his fair visitors; Clotilde, who opened her mouth only to breathe roses and diamonds, and Ermengarde, who was so good-natured that she sacrificed even her lovers to her friends; saw him merely to exclaim at the same moment, and with the same voices of thrilling joyousness, –

'Why did not you ask him to dinner?'

And then, without waiting for his reply, entered with that rapidity of elocution which Frenchwomen can alone command into the catalogue of his charms and accomplishments, Lord Monmouth began to regret that he really had not seen Coningsby, who, it appeared, might have greatly contributed to the pleasure of the day. The message, which was duly given, however, settled the business. Lord Monmouth felt that any chance of explanations, or even allusions to the past, was out of the question; and to defend himself from the accusations of his animated guests, he said,

'Well, he shall come to dine with you next time.'

There is no end to the influence of woman on our life. It is at the bottom of everything that happens to us. And so it was, that, in spite of all the combinations of Lucretia and Mr Rigby, and the mortification and resentment of Lord Monmouth, the favourable impression he casually made on a couple of French actresses occasioned Coningsby, before a month had elapsed since his memorable interview at Monmouth House, to receive an invitation again to dine with his grandfather.

The party was agreeable. Clotilde and Ermengarde had wits as sparkling as their eyes. There was the manager of the Opera, a great friend of Villebecque, and his wife, a splendid lady, who had been a prima donna of celebrity, and still had a commanding voice for a chamber; a Carlist nobleman who lived upon his traditions, and who, though without a sou, could tell of a festival given by his family, before the revolution, which had cost a million of francs; and a Neapolitan physician, in whom Lord Monmouth had great confidence, and who himself believed in the elixir vitæ, made up the party, with Lucian Gay, Coningsby, and Mr Rigby. Our hero remarked that Villebecque on this occasion sat at the bottom of the table, but Flora did not appear.

In the meantime, the month which brought about this satisfactory and at one time unexpected result was fruitful also in other circumstances still more interesting. Coningsby and Edith met frequently, if to breathe the same atmosphere in the same crowded saloons can be described as meeting; ever watching each other's movements, and yet studious never to encounter each other's glance. The charms of Miss Millbank had become an universal topic, they were celebrated in ball-rooms, they were discussed at clubs: Edith was the beauty of the season. All admired her, many sighed even to express their admiration; but the devotion of Lord Beaumanoir, who always hovered about her, deterred them from a rivalry which might have made the boldest despair. As for Coningsby, he passed his life principally with the various members of the Sydney family, and was almost daily riding with Lady Everingham and her sister, generally accompanied by Lord Henry and his friend Eustace Lyle, between whom, indeed, and Coningsby there were relations of intimacy scarcely less inseparable. Coningsby had spoken to Lady Everingham of the rumoured marriage of her elder brother, and found, although the family had not yet been formally apprised of it, she entertained little doubt of its ultimate occurrence. She admired Miss Millbank, with whom her acquaintance continued slight; and she wished, of course, that her brother should marry and be happy. 'But Percy is often in love,' she would add, 'and never likes us to be very intimate with his inamoratas. He thinks it destroys the romance; and that domestic familiarity may compromise his heroic character. However,' she added, 'I really believe that will be a match.'

On the whole, though he bore a serene aspect to the world, Coningsby passed this month in a state of restless misery. His soul was brooding on one subject, and he had no confidant: he could not resist the spell that impelled him to the society where Edith might at least be seen, and the circle in which he lived was one in which her name was frequently mentioned. Alone, in his solitary rooms in the Albany,[1] he felt all his desolation; and often a few minutes before he figured in the world, apparently followed and courted by all, he had been plunged in the darkest fits of irremediable wretchedness.

He had, of course, frequently met Lady Wallinger, but their salutations, though never omitted, and on each side cordial, were brief. There seemed to be a tacit understanding between them not to refer to a subject fruitful in painful reminiscences.

The season waned. In the fulfilment of a project originally formed in the playing-fields of Eton, often recurred to at Cambridge, and cherished with the fondness with which men cling to a scheme of early youth, Coningsby, Henry Sydney, Vere, and Buckhurst had engaged some moors together this year; and in a few days they were about to quit town for Scotland. They had pressed Eustace Lyle to accompany them, but he, who in general seemed to have no pleasure greater than their society, had surprised them by declining their invitation, with some vague mention that he rather thought he should go abroad.

It was the last day of July, and all the world were at a breakfast given, at a fanciful cottage situate in beautiful gardens on the banks of the Thames, by Lady Everingham. The weather was as bright as the romances of Boccaccio;[2] there were pyramids of strawberries, in bowls colossal enough to hold orange-trees; and the choicest band filled the air with enchanting strains, while a brilliant multitude sauntered on turf like velvet, or roamed in desultory existence amid the quivering shades of winding walks.

'My fête was prophetic,' said Lady Everingham, when she saw Coningsby. 'I am glad it is connected with an incident. It gives it a point.'

'You are mystical as well as prophetic. Tell me what we are to celebrate.'

'Theresa is going to be married.'

'Then I, too, will prophesy, and name the hero of the romance, Eustace Lyle.'

'You have been more prescient than I,' said Lady Everingham, 'perhaps because I was thinking too much of some one else.'

'It seems to me an union which all must acknowledge perfect. I hardly know which I love best. I have had my suspicions a long time; and when Eustace refused to go to the moors with us, though I said nothing, I was convinced.'

'At any rate,' said Lady Everingham, sighing, with a rather smiling face, 'we are kinsfolk, Mr Coningsby; though I would gladly have wished to have been more.'

'Were those your thoughts, dear lady? Ever kind to me! Happiness,' he added, in a mournful tone, 'I fear can never be mine.'

'And why?'

'Ah! 'tis a tale too strange and sorrowful for a day when, like Seged, we must all determine to be happy.'

'You have already made me miserable.'

'Here comes a group that will make you gay,' said Coningsby as he moved on. Edith and the Wallingers, accompanied by Lord Beaumanoir, Mr Melton, and Sir Charles Buckhurst, formed the party. They seemed profuse in their congratulations to Lady Everingham, having already learnt the intelligence from her brother.

Coningsby stopped to speak to Lady St Julians, who had still a daughter to marry. Both Augustina, who was at Coningsby Castle, and Clara Isabella, who ought to have been there, had each secured the right man. But Adelaide Victoria had now appeared, and Lady St Julians had a great regard for the favourite grandson of Lord Monmouth, and also for the influential friend of Lord Vere and Sir Charles Buckhurst. In case Coningsby did not determine to become her son-in-law himself, he might counsel either of his friends to a judicious decision on an inevitable act.

'Strawberries and cream?' said Lord Eskdale to Mr Ormsby, who seemed occupied with some delicacies.

'Egad! no, no, no; those days are passed. I think there is a little easterly wind with all this fine appearance.'

'I am for in-door nature myself,' said Lord Eskdale. 'Do you know, I do not half like the way Monmouth is going on? He never gets out of that villa of his. He should change his air more. Tell him.'

'It is no use telling him anything. Have you heard anything of Miladi?'

'I had a letter from her to-day: she writes in good spirits. I am sorry it broke up, and yet I never thought it would last so long.'

'I gave them two years,' said Mr Ormsby. 'Lord Monmouth lived with his first wife two years. And afterwards with the Mirandola at Milan, at least nearly two years; it was a year and ten months. I must know, for he called me in to settle affairs. I took the lady to the baths at Lucca, on the pretence that Monmouth would meet us there. He went to Paris. All his great affairs have been two years. I remember I wanted to bet Cassilis, at White's, on it when he married; but I thought, being his intimate friend; the oldest friend he has, indeed, and one of his trustees; it was perhaps as well not to do it.'

'You should have made the bet with himself,' said Lord Eskdale, 'and then there never would have been a separation.'

'Hah, hah, hah! Do you know, I feel the wind?'

About an hour after this, Coningsby, who had just quitted the Duchess, met, on a terrace by the river, Lady Wallinger, walking with Mrs Guy Flouncey and a Russian Prince, whom that lady was enchanting. Coningsby was about to pass with some slight courtesy, but Lady Wallinger stopped and would speak to him, on slight subjects, the weather and the fête, but yet adroitly enough managed to make him turn and join her. Mrs Guy Flouncey walked on a little before with her Russian admirer. Lady Wallinger followed with Coningsby.

'The match that has been proclaimed to-day has greatly surprised me,' said Lady Wallinger.

'Indeed!' said Coningsby: 'I confess I was long prepared for it. And it seems to me the most natural alliance conceivable, and one that every one must approve.'

'Lady Everingham seems much surprised at it.'

'Ah! Lady Everingham is a brilliant personage, and cannot deign to observe obvious circumstances.'

'Do you know, Mr Coningsby, that I always thought you were engaged to Lady Theresa?'

'I!'

'Indeed, we were informed more than a month ago that you were positively going to be married to her.'

'I am not one of those who can shift their affections with such rapidity, Lady Wallinger.'

Lady Wallinger looked distressed. 'You remember our meeting you on the stairs at — House, Mr Coningsby?'

'Painfully. It is deeply graven on my brain.'

'Edith had just been informed that you were going to be married to Lady Theresa.'

'Not surely by him to whom she is herself going to be married?' said Coningsby, reddening.

'I am not aware that she is going to be married to any one. Lord Beaumanoir admires her, has always admired her. But Edith has given him no encouragement, at least gave him no encouragement as long as she believed; but why dwell on such an unhappy subject, Mr Coningsby? I am to blame; I have been to blame perhaps before, but indeed I think it cruel, very cruel, that Edith and you are kept asunder.'

'You have always been my best, my dearest friend, and are the most amiable and admirable of women. But tell me, is it indeed true that Edith is not going to be married?'

At this moment Mrs Guy Flouncey turned round, and assuring Lady Wallinger that the Prince and herself had agreed to refer some point to her about the most transcendental ethics of flirtation, this deeply interesting conversation was arrested, and Lady Wallinger, with becoming suavity, was obliged to listen to the lady's lively appeal of exaggerated nonsense and the Prince's affected protests, while Coningsby walked by her side, pale and agitated, and then offered his arm to Lady Wallinger, which she accepted with an affectionate pressure. At the end of the terrace they met some other guests, and soon were immersed in the multitude that thronged the lawn.

'There is Sir Joseph,' said Lady Wallinger, and Coningsby looked up, and saw Edith on his arm. They were unconsciously approaching them. Lord Beaumanoir was there, but he seemed to shrink into nothing to-day before Buckhurst, who was captivated for the moment by Edith, and hearing that no knight was resolute enough to try a fall with the Marquess, was impelled by his talent for action to enter the lists. He had talked down everybody, unhorsed every cavalier. Nobody had a chance against him: he answered all your questions before you asked them; contradicted everybody with the intrepidity of a Rigby; annihilated your anecdotes by historiettes infinitely more piquant; and if anybody chanced to make a joke which he could not excel, declared immediately that it was a Joe Miller.[3] He was absurd, extravagant, grotesque, noisy; but he was young, rattling, and interesting, from his health and spirits. Edith was extremely amused by him, and was encouraging by her smile his spiritual excesses, when they all suddenly met Lady Wallinger and Coningsby.

The eyes of Edith and Coningsby met for the first time since they so cruelly encountered on the staircase of — House. A deep, quick blush suffused her face, her eyes gleamed with a sudden coruscation; suddenly and quickly she put forth her hand.

Yes! he presses once more that hand which permanently to retain is the passion of his life, yet which may never be his! It seemed that for the ravishing delight of that moment he could have borne with cheerfulness all the dark and harrowing misery of the year that had passed away since he embraced her in the woods of Hellingsley, and pledged his faith by the waters of the rushing Darl.

He seized the occasion which offered itself, a moment to walk by her side, and to snatch some brief instants of unreserved communion.

'Forgive me!' she said.

'Ah! how could you ever doubt me?' said Coningsby.

'I was unhappy.'

'And now we are to each other as before?'

'And will be, come what come may.'

END OF BOOK VIII

BOOK IX

Chapter 1

It was merry Christmas at St Geneviève. There was a yule log blazing on every hearth in that wide domain, from the hall of the squire to the peasant's roof. The Buttery Hatch was open for the whole week from noon to sunset; all comers might take their fill, and each carry away as much bold beef, white bread, and jolly ale as a strong man could bear in a basket with one hand. For every woman a red cloak, and a coat of broadcloth for every man. All day long, carts laden with fuel and warm raiment were traversing the various districts, distributing comfort and dispensing cheer. For a Christian gentleman of high degree was Eustace Lyle.

Within his hall, too, he holds his revel, and his beauteous bride welcomes their guests, from her noble parents to the faithful tenants of the house. All classes are mingled in the joyous equality that becomes the season, at once sacred and merry. There are carols for the eventful eve, and Mummers for the festive day.

The Duke and Duchess, and every member of the family, had consented this year to keep their Christmas with the newly-married couple. Coningsby, too, was there, and all his friends. The party was numerous, gay, hearty, and happy; for they were all united by sympathy.

They were planning that Henry Sydney should be appointed Lord of Misrule, or ordained Abbot of Unreason[1] at the least, so successful had been his revival of the Mummers, the Hobby-horse not forgotten.[2] Their host had entrusted to Lord Henry the restoration of many old observances; and the joyous feeling which this celebration of Christmas had diffused throughout an extensive district was a fresh argument in favour of Lord Henry's principle, that a mere mechanical mitigation of the material necessities of the humbler classes, a mitigation which must inevitably be

limited, can never alone avail sufficiently to ameliorate their condition; that their condition is not merely 'a knife and fork
question,'³ to use the coarse and shallow phrase of the Utilitarian
school; that a simple satisfaction of the grosser necessities of our
nature will not make a happy people; that you must cultivate the
heart as well as seek to content the belly; and that the surest
means to elevate the character of the people is to appeal to their
affections.

There is nothing more interesting than to trace predisposition.
An indefinite, yet strong sympathy with the peasantry of the realm
had been one of the characteristic sensibilities of Lord Henry at
Eton. Yet a schoolboy, he had busied himself with their pastimes
and the details of their cottage economy. As he advanced in life
the horizon of his views expanded with his intelligence and his
experience; and the son of one of the noblest of our houses, to
whom the delights of life are offered with fatal facility, on the
very threshold of his career he devoted his time and thought,
labour and life, to one vast and noble purpose, the elevation of
the condition of the great body of the people.

'I vote for Buckhurst being Lord of Misrule,' said Lord Henry:
'I will be content with being his gentleman usher.'

'It shall be put to the vote,' said Lord Vere.

'No one has a chance against Buckhurst,' said Coningsby.

'Now, Sir Charles,' said Lady Everingham, 'your absolute sway
is about to commence. And what is your will?'

'The first thing must be my formal installation,' said Buckhurst.
'I vote the Boar's head be carried in procession thrice round the
hall, and Beau shall be the champion to challenge all who
question my right. Duke, you shall be my chief butler, the Duchess
my herb-woman. She is to walk before me, and scatter rosemary.
Coningsby shall carry the Boar's head; Lady Theresa and Lady
Everingham shall sing the canticle; Lord Everingham shall be
marshal of the lists, and put all in the stocks who are found sober
and decorous; Lyle shall be the palmer from the Holy Land, and
Vere shall ride the Hobby-horse. Some must carry cups of Hippocras,⁴ some lighted tapers; all must join in chorus.'

He ceased his instructions, and all hurried away to carry them
into effect. Some hastily arrayed themselves in fanciful dresses,

the ladies in robes of white, with garlands of flowers; some drew
pieces of armour from the wall, and decked themselves with helm
and hauberk; others waved ancient banners. They brought in the
Boar's head on a large silver dish, and Coningsby raised it aloft.
They formed into procession, the Duchess distributing rosemary;
Buckhurst swaggering with all the majesty of Tamerlane, his
mock court irresistibly humorous with their servility; and the
sweet voice of Lady Everingham chanting the first verse of the
canticle, followed in the second by the rich tones of Lady Theresa:

I.

Caput Apri defero
Reddens laudes Domino.
The Boar's heade in hande bring I,
With garlandes gay and rosemary:
I pray you all singe merrily,
Qui estis in conbibio.

II.

Caput Apri defero
Reddens laudes Domino.
The Boar's heade I understande
Is the chief serbyce in this lande
Loke whereeber it be fande,
Serbite cum cantico.

The procession thrice paraded the hall. Then they stopped; and
the Lord of Misrule ascended his throne, and his courtiers formed
round him in circle. Behind him they held the ancient banners
and waved their glittering arms, and placed on a lofty and
illuminated pedestal the Boar's head covered with garlands. It was
a good picture, and the Lord of Misrule sustained his part with
untiring energy. He was addressing his court in a pompous
rhapsody of merry nonsense, when a servant approached
Coningsby, and told him that he was wanted without.

Our hero retired unperceived. A despatch had arrived for him
from London. Without any prescience of its purpose, he nevertheless broke the seal with a trembling hand. His presence was
immediately desired in town: Lord Monmouth was dead.

Chapter 2

THIS was a crisis in the life of Coningsby; yet, like many critical epochs, the person most interested in it was not sufficiently aware of its character. The first feeling which he experienced at the intelligence was sincere affliction. He was fond of his grandfather; had received great kindness from him, and at a period of life when it was most welcome. The neglect and hardships of his early years, instead of leaving a prejudice against one who, by some, might be esteemed their author, had by their contrast only rendered Coningsby more keenly sensible of the solicitude and enjoyment which had been lavished on his happy youth.

The next impression on his mind was undoubtedly a natural and reasonable speculation on the effect of this bereavement on his fortunes. Lord Monmouth had more than once assured Coningsby that he had provided for him as became a near relative to whom he was attached, and in a manner which ought to satisfy the wants and wishes of an English gentleman. The allowance which Lord Monmouth had made him, as considerable as usually accorded to the eldest sons of wealthy peers, might justify him in estimating his future patrimony as extremely ample. He was aware, indeed, that at a subsequent period his grandfather had projected for him fortunes of a still more elevated character. He looked to Coningsby as the future representative of an ancient barony, and had been purchasing territory with the view of supporting the title. But Coningsby did not by any means firmly reckon on these views being realised. He had a suspicion that in thwarting the wishes of his grandfather in not becoming a candidate for Darlford, he had at the moment arrested arrangements which, from the tone of Lord Monmouth's communication, he believed were then in progress for that purpose; and he thought it improbable, with his knowledge of his grandfather's habits, that Lord Monmouth had found either time or inclination to resume before his decease the completion of these

plans. Indeed there was a period when, in adopting the course
which he pursued with respect to Darlford, Coningsby was well
aware that he perilled more than the large fortune which was to
accompany the barony. Had not a separation between Lord Monmouth and his wife taken place simultaneously with Coningsby's
difference with his grandfather, he was conscious that the consequences might have been even altogether fatal to his prospects;
but the absence of her evil influence at such a conjuncture, its
permanent removal, indeed, from the scene, coupled with his
fortunate though not formal reconciliation with Lord Monmouth,
had long ago banished from his memory all those apprehensions
to which he had felt it impossible at the time to shut his eyes.
Before he left town for Scotland he had made a farewell visit to his
grandfather, who, though not as cordial as in old days, had been
gracious; and Coningsby, during his excursion to the moors, and
his various visits to the country, had continued at intervals to
write to his grandfather, as had been for some years his custom.
On the whole, with an indefinite feeling which, in spite of many
a rational effort, did nevertheless haunt his mind, that this great
and sudden event might exercise a vast and beneficial influence
on his worldly position, Coningsby could not but feel some consolation in the affliction which he sincerely experienced, in the
hope that he might at all events now offer to Edith a home worthy
of her charms, her virtues, and her love.

Although he had not seen her since their hurried yet sweet
reconciliation in the gardens of Lady Everingham, Coningsby was
never long without indirect intelligence of the incidents of her
life; and the correspondence between Lady Everingham and Henry
Sydney, while they were at the moors, had apprised him that Lord
Beaumanoir's suit had terminated unsuccessfully almost immediately after his brother had quitted London.

It was late in the evening when Coningsby arrived in town:
he called at once on Lord Eskdale, who was one of Lord
Monmouth's executors; and he persuaded Coningsby, whom he
saw depressed, to dine with him alone.

'You should not be seen at a club,' said the good-natured
peer; 'and I remember myself in old days what was the wealth
of an Albanian larder.'

Lord Eskdale, at dinner, talked frankly of the disposition of Lord Monmouth's property. He spoke as a matter of course that Coningsby was his grandfather's principal heir.

'I don't know whether you will be happier with a large fortune?' said Lord Eskdale. 'It is a troublesome thing: nobody is satisfied with what you do with it; very often not yourself. To maintain an equable expenditure; not to spend too much on one thing, too little on another, is an art. There must be a harmony, a keeping, in disbursement, which very few men have. Great wealth wearies. The thing to have is about ten thousand a year, and the world to think you have only five. There is some enjoyment then; one is let alone. But the instant you have a large fortune, duties commence. And then impudent fellows borrow your money; and if you ask them for it again, they go about town saying you are a screw.'

Lord Monmouth had died suddenly at his Richmond villa, which latterly he never quitted, at a little supper, with no persons near him but those who were amusing. He suddenly found he could not lift his glass to his lips, and being extremely polite, waited a few minutes before he asked Clotilde, who was singing a sparkling drinking-song, to do him that service. When, in accordance with his request, she reached him, it was too late. The ladies shrieked, being frightened: at first they were in despair, but, after reflection, they evinced some intention of plundering the house. Villebecque, who was absent at the moment, arrived in time; and everybody became orderly and broken-hearted.

The body had been removed to Monmouth House, where it had been embalmed and laid in state. The funeral was not numerously attended. There was nobody in town; some distinguished connections, however, came up from the country, though it was a period inconvenient for such movements. After the funeral, the will was to be read in the principal saloon of Monmouth House, one of those gorgeous apartments that had excited the boyish wonder of Coningsby on his first visit to that paternal roof, and now hung in black, adorned with the escutcheon of the deceased peer.

The testamentary dispositions of the late lord were still unknown, though the names of his executors had been announced by his family solicitor, in whose custody the will and codicils had always remained. The executors under the will were Lord Eskdale, Mr Ormsby, and Mr Rigby. By a subsequent appointment Sidonia had been added. All these individuals were now present. Coningsby, who had been chief mourner, stood on the right hand of the solicitor, who sat at the end of a long table, round which, in groups, were ranged all who had attended the funeral, including several of the superior members of the household, among them M. Villebecque.

The solicitor rose and explained that though Lord Monmouth had been in the habit of very frequently adding codicils to his will, the original will, however changed or modified, had never been revoked; it was therefore necessary to commence by reading that instrument. So saying, he sat down, and breaking the seals of a large packet, he produced the will of Philip Augustus, Marquess of Monmouth, which had been retained in his custody since its execution.

By this will, of the date of 1829, the sum of 10,000*l*. was left to Coningsby, then unknown to his grandfather; the same sum to Mr Rigby. There was a great number of legacies, none of superior amount, most of them of less: these were chiefly left to old male companions, and women in various countries. There was an almost inconceivable number of small annuities to faithful servants, decayed actors, and obscure foreigners. The residue of his personal estate was left to four gentlemen, three of whom had quitted this world before the legator; the bequests, therefore, had lapsed. The fourth residuary legatee, in whom, according to the terms of the will, all would have consequently centred, was Mr Rigby.

There followed several codicils which did not materially affect the previous disposition; one of them leaving a legacy of 20,000*l*. to the Princess Colonna; until they arrived at the latter part of the year 1832, when a codicil increased the 10,000*l*. left under the will to Coningsby to 50,000*l*.

After Coningsby's visit to the Castle in 1836 a very important change occurred in the disposition of Lord Monmouth's estate. The legacy of 50,000*l*. in his favour was revoked, and the same sum left to the Princess Lucretia. A similar amount was bequeathed to Mr Rigby; and Coningsby was left sole residuary legatee.

The marriage led to a considerable modification. An estate of about nine thousand a year, which Lord Monmouth had himself purchased, and was therefore in his own disposition, was left to Coningsby. The legacy to Mr Rigby was reduced to 20,000*l.*, and the whole of his residue left to his issue by Lady Monmouth. In case he died without issue, the estate bequeathed to Coningsby to be taken into account, and the residue then to be divided equally between Lady Monmouth and his grandson. It was under this instrument that Sidonia had been appointed an executor, and to whom Lord Monmouth left, among others, the celebrated picture of the Holy Family by Murillo, as his friend had often admired it. To Lord Eskdale he left all his female miniatures, and to Mr Ormsby his rare and splendid collection of French novels, and all his wines, except his Tokay, which he left, with his library, to Sir Robert Peel; though this legacy was afterwards revoked, in consequence of Sir Robert's conduct about the Irish corporations.

The solicitor paused and begged permission to send for a glass of water. While this was arranging there was a murmur at the lower part of the room, but little disposition to conversation among those in the vicinity of the lawyer. Coningsby was silent, his brow a little knit. Mr Rigby was pale and restless, but said nothing. Mr Ormsby took a pinch of snuff, and offered his box to Lord Eskdale, who was next to him. They exchanged glances, and made some observation about the weather. Sidonia stood apart, with his arms folded. He had not, of course, attended the funeral, nor had he as yet exchanged any recognition with Coningsby.

'Now, gentlemen,' said the solicitor, 'if you please, I will proceed.'

They came to the year 1839, the year Coningsby was at Hellingsley. This appeared to be a critical period in the fortunes of Lady Monmouth; while Coningsby's reached to the culminating point. Mr Rigby was reduced to his original legacy under the will of 10,000*l.*; a sum of equal amount was bequeathed to Armand Villebecque, in acknowledgment of faithful services; all the dispositions in favour of Lady Monmouth were revoked, and she was limited to her moderate jointure of 3,000*l.* per annum, under the marriage settlement; while everything, without reserve, was left absolutely to Coningsby.

A subsequent codicil determined that the 10,000*l.* left to Mr Rigby should be equally divided between him and Lucian Gay; but as some compensation Lord Monmouth left to the Right Honourable Nicholas Rigby the bust of that gentleman, which he had himself presented to his Lordship, and which, at his desire, had been placed in the vestibule at Coningsby Castle, from the amiable motive that after Lord Monmouth's decease Mr Rigby might wish, perhaps, to present it to some other friend.

Lord Eskdale and Mr Ormsby took care not to catch the eye of Mr Rigby. As for Coningsby, he saw nobody. He maintained, during the extraordinary situation in which he was placed, a firm demeanour; but serene and regulated as he appeared to the spectators, his nerves were really strung to a high pitch.

There was yet another codicil. It bore the date of June 1840, and was made at Brighton, immediately after the separation with Lady Monmouth. It was the sight of this instrument that sustained Rigby at this great emergency. He had a wild conviction that, after all, it must set all right. He felt assured that, as Lady Monmouth had already been disposed of, it must principally refer to the disinheritance of Coningsby, secured by Rigby's well-timed and malignant misrepresentations of what had occurred in Lancashire during the preceding summer. And then to whom could Lord Monmouth leave his money? However he might cut and carve up his fortunes, Rigby, and especially at a moment when he had so served him, must come in for a considerable slice.

His prescient mind was right. All the dispositions in favour of 'my grandson Harry Coningsby' were revoked; and he inherited from his grandfather only the interest of the sum of 10,000*l.* which had been originally bequeathed to him in his orphan boyhood. The executors had the power of investing the principal in any way they thought proper for his advancement in life, provided always it was not placed in 'the capital stock of any manufactory.'

Coningsby turned pale; he lost his abstracted look; he caught the eye of Rigby; he read the latent malice of that nevertheless

anxious countenance. What passed through the mind and being
of Coningsby was thought and sensation enough for a year; but
it was as the flash that reveals a whole country, yet ceases to
be ere one can say it lightens. There was a revelation to him
of an inward power that should baffle these conventional calamities, a natural and sacred confidence in his youth and health,
and knowledge and convictions. Even the recollection of Edith was
not unaccompanied with some sustaining associations. At least
the mightiest foe to their union was departed.

All this was the impression of an instant, simultaneous with
the reading of the words of form with which the last testamentary disposition of the Marquess of Monmouth left the sum
of 30,000*l.* to Armand Villebecque; and all the rest, residue, and
remainder of his unentailed property, wheresoever, and whatso-
ever it might be, amounting in value to nearly a million sterling,
was given, devised, and bequeathed to Flora, commonly called
Flora Villebecque, the step-child of the said Armand Villebecque,
'but who is my natural daughter by Marie Estelle Matteau, an
actress at the Théâtre Français in the years 1811–15, by the
name of Stella.'

Chapter 3

'THÍS is a crash!' said Coningsby, with a grave rather than agitated countenance, to Sidonia, as his friend came up to greet him, without, however, any expression of condolence.

'This time next year you will not think so,' said Sidonia.

Coningsby shrugged his shoulders.

'The principal annoyance of this sort of miscarriage,' said Sidonia, 'is the condolence of the gentle world. I think we may now depart. I am going home to dine. Come, and discuss your position. For the present we will not speak of it.' So saying, Sidonia good-naturedly got Coningsby out of the room.

They walked together to Sidonia's house in Carlton Gardens, neither of them making the slightest allusion to the catastrophe; Sidonia inquiring where he had been, what he had been doing, since they last met, and himself conversing in his usual vein, though with a little more feeling in his manner than was his custom. When they had arrived there, Sidonia ordered their dinner instantly, and during the interval between the command and its appearance, he called Coningsby's attention to an old German painting he had just received, its brilliant colouring and quaint costumes.

'Eat, and an appetite will come,' said Sidonia, when he observed Coningsby somewhat reluctant. 'Take some of that Chablis: it will put you right; you will find it delicious.'

In this way some twenty minutes passed; their meal was over, and they were alone together.

'I have been thinking all this time of your position,' said Sidonia.

'A sorry one I fear,' said Coningsby.

'I really cannot see that,' said his friend. 'You have experienced this morning a disappointment, but not a calamity. If you had lost your eye it would have been a calamity: no combination of circumstances could have given you another. There are really no miseries except natural miseries; conventional misfortunes are mere illusions. What seems conventionally, in a limited view, a great misfortune, if subsequently viewed in its results, is often the happiest incident in one's life.'

'I hope the day may come when I may feel this.'

'Now is the moment when philosophy is of use; that is to say, now is the moment when you should clearly comprehend the circumstances which surround you. Holiday philosophy is mere idleness. You think, for example, that you have just experienced a great calamity, because you have lost the fortune on which you counted?'

'I must say I do.'

'I ask you again, which would you have rather lost, your grandfather's inheritance or your right leg?'

'Most certainly my inheritance.'

'Or your left arm?'

'Still the inheritance.'

'Would you have received the inheritance on condition that your front teeth should be knocked out?'

'No.'

'Would you have given up a year of your life for that fortune trebled?'

'Even at twenty-three I would have refused the terms.'

'Come, come, Coningsby, the calamity cannot be very great.'

'Why, you have put it in an ingenious point of view; and yet it is not so easy to convince a man, that he should be content who has lost everything.'

'You have a great many things at this moment that you separately prefer to the fortune that you have forfeited. How then can you be said to have lost everything?'

'What have I?' said Coningsby, despondingly.

'You have health, youth, good looks, great abilities, considerable knowledge, a fine courage, a lofty spirit, and no contemptible experience. With each of these qualities one might make a fortune; the combination ought to command the highest.'

'You console me,' said Coningsby, with a faint blush and a fainter smile.

'I teach you the truth. That is always solacing. I think you are a most fortunate young man; I should not have thought you more fortunate if you had been your grandfather's heir; perhaps less so. But I wish you to comprehend your position: if you understand it you will cease to lament.'

'But what should I do?'

'Bring your intelligence to bear on the right object. I make you no offers of fortune, because I know you would not accept them, and indeed I have no wish to see you a lounger in life. If you had inherited a great patrimony, it is possible your natural character and previous culture might have saved you from its paralysing influence; but it is a question, even with you. Now you are free; that is to say, you are free, if you are not in debt. A man who has not seen the world, whose fancy is harassed with glittering images of pleasures he has never experienced, cannot live on 300*l.* per annum; but you can. You have nothing to haunt your thoughts, or disturb the abstraction of your studies. You have seen the most beautiful women; you have banqueted in palaces; you know what heroes, and wits, and statesmen are made of: and you can draw on your memory instead of your imagination for all those dazzling and interesting objects that make the inexperienced restless, and are the cause of what are called scrapes. But you can do nothing if you be in debt. You must be free. Before, therefore, we proceed, I must beg you to be frank on this head. If you have any absolute or contingent incumbrances, tell me of them without reserve, and permit me to clear them at once to any amount. You will sensibly oblige me in so doing: because I am interested in watching your career, and if the racer start with a clog my psychological observations will be imperfect.'

'You are, indeed, a friend; and had I debts I would ask you to pay them. I have nothing of the kind. My grandfather was so lavish in his allowance to me that I never got into difficulties. Besides, there are horses and things without end which I must sell, and money at Drummonds'.'

'That will produce your outfit, whatever the course you adopt. I conceive there are two careers which deserve your consideration. In the first place there is Diplomacy. If you decide upon that, I can assist you. There exist between me and the Minister such relations that I can at once secure you that first step which is so difficult to obtain. After that, much, if not all, depends on your-self. But I could advance you, provided you were capable. You should, at least, not languish for want of preferment. In an important post, I could throw in your way advantages which would soon permit you to control cabinets. Information com-mands the world. I doubt not your success, and for such a career, speedy. Let us assume it as a fact. Is it a result satisfactory? Suppose yourself in a dozen years a Plenipotentiary at a chief court, or at a critical post, with a red ribbon[1] and the Privy Council in immediate perspective; and, after a lengthened career, a pension and a peerage. Would that satisfy you? You don't look excited. I am hardly surprised. In your position it would not satisfy me. A Diplomatist is, after all, a phantom. There is a want of nationality about his being. I always look upon Diplomatists as the Hebrews of politics; without country, political creeds, popular convictions, that strong reality of existence which pervades the career of an eminent citizen in a free and great country.'

'You read my thoughts,' said Coningsby. 'I should be sorry to sever myself from England.'

'There remains then the other, the greater, the nobler career,' said Sidonia, 'which in England may give you all, the Bar. I am absolutely persuaded that with the requisite qualifications, and with perseverance, success at the Bar is certain. It may be retarded or precipitated by circumstances, but cannot be ulti-mately affected. You have a right to count with your friends on no lack of opportunities when you are ripe for them. You appear to me to have all the qualities necessary for the Bar; and you may count on that perseverance which is indispensable, for the reason I have before mentioned, because it will be sustained by your experience.'

'I have resolved,' said Coningsby; 'I will try for the Great Seal.'[2]

Chapter 4

ALONE in his chambers, no longer under the sustaining influence of Sidonia's converse and counsel, the shades of night descending and bearing gloom to the gloomy, all the excitement of his spirit evaporated, the heart of Coningsby sank. All now depended on himself, and in that self he had no trust. Why should he succeed? Success was the most rare of results. Thousands fail; units triumph. And even success could only be conducted to him by the course of many years. His career, even if prosperous, was now to commence by the greatest sacrifice which the heart of man could be called upon to sustain. Upon the stern altar of his fortunes he must immolate his first and enduring love. Before, he had a perilous position to offer Edith; now he had none. The future might then have aided them; there was no combination which could improve his present. Under any circumstances he must, after all his thoughts and studies, commence a new novitiate, and before he could enter the arena must pass years of silent and obscure preparation. 'Twas very bitter. He looked up, his eye caught that drawing of the towers of Hellingsley which she had given him in the days of their happy hearts. That was all that was to remain of their loves. He was to bear it to the future scene of his labours, to remind him through revolving years of toil and routine, that he too had had his romance, had roamed in fair gardens, and whispered in willing ears the secrets of his passion. That drawing was to become the altar-piece of his life.

Coningsby passed an agitated night of broken sleep, waking often with a consciousness of having experienced some great misfortune, yet with an indefinite conception of its nature. He woke exhausted and dispirited. It was a gloomy day, a raw north-easter blowing up the cloisters of the Albany, in which the fog was lingering, the newspaper on his breakfast-table, full of rumoured particulars of his grandfather's will, which had of course been duly digested by all who knew him. What a contrast to St Geneviève! To the bright, bracing morn of that merry Christmas! That radiant and cheerful scene, and those gracious and beaming personages, seemed another world and order of beings to the one he now inhabited, and the people with whom he must now commune. The Great Seal indeed! It was the wild excitement of despair, the frenzied hope that blends inevitably with absolute ruin, that could alone have inspired such a hallucination! His unstrung heart deserted him. His energies could rally no more. He gave orders that he was at home to no one; and in his morning gown and slippers, with his feet resting on the fireplace, the once high-souled and noble-hearted Coningsby delivered himself up to despair.

The day passed in a dark trance rather than a reverie. Nothing rose to his consciousness. He was like a particle of chaos; at the best, a glimmering entity of some shadowy Hades. Towards evening the wind changed, the fog dispersed, there came a clear starry night, brisk and bright. Coningsby roused himself, dressed, and wrapping his cloak around him, sallied forth. Once more in the mighty streets, surrounded by millions, his petty griefs and personal fortunes assumed their proper position. Well had Sidonia taught him, view everything in its relation to the rest. 'Tis the secret of all wisdom. Here was the mightiest of modern cities; the rival even of the most celebrated of the ancient. Whether he inherited or forfeited fortunes, what was it to the passing throng? They would not share his splendour, or his luxury, or his comfort. But a word from his lip, a thought from his brain, expressed at the right time, at the right place, might turn their hearts, might influence their passions, might change their opinions, might affect their destiny. Nothing is great but the personal. As civilisation advances, the accidents of life become each day less important. The power of man, his greatness and his glory, depend on essential qualities. Brains every day become more precious than blood. You must give men new ideas, you must teach them new words, you must modify their manners, you must change their laws, you must root out prejudices, subvert convictions, if you wish to be great. Greatness no longer depends on rentals, the world is too rich; nor on pedigrees, the world is too knowing.

'The greatness of this city destroys my misery,' said Coningsby, 'and my genius shall conquer its greatness!'

This conviction of power in the midst of despair was a revelation of intrinsic strength. It is indeed the test of a creative spirit. From that moment all petty fears for an ordinary future quitted him. He felt that he must be prepared for great sacrifices, for infinite suffering; that there must devolve on him a bitter inheritance of obscurity, struggle, envy, and hatred, vulgar prejudice, base criticism, petty hostilities, but the dawn would break, and the hour arrive, when the welcome morning hymn of his success and his fame would sound and be re-echoed.

He returned to his rooms; calm, resolute. He slept the deep sleep of a man void of anxiety, that has neither hope nor fear to haunt his visions, but is prepared to rise on the morrow collected for the great human struggle.

And the morning came. Fresh, vigorous, not rash or precipitate, yet determined to lose no time in idle meditation, Coningsby already resolved at once to quit his present residence, was projecting a visit to some legal quarter, where he intended in future to reside, when his servant brought him a note. The handwriting was feminine. The note was from Flora. The contents were brief. She begged Mr Coningsby, with great earnestness, to do her the honour and the kindness of calling on her at his earliest convenience, at the hotel in Brook Street where she now resided.

It was an interview which Coningsby would rather have avoided; yet it seemed to him, after a moment's reflection, neither just, nor kind, nor manly, to refuse her request. Flora had not injured him. She was, after all, his kin. Was it for a moment to be supposed that he was envious of her lot? He replied, therefore, that in an hour he would wait upon her.

In an hour, then, two individuals are to be brought together whose first meeting was held under circumstances most strangely different. Then Coningsby was the patron, a generous and spontaneous one, of a being obscure, almost friendless, and sinking under bitter mortification. His favour could not be the less appreciated because he was the chosen relative of a powerful noble. That noble was no more; his vast inheritance had devolved on the disregarded, even despised actress, whose suffering emotions Coningsby had then soothed, and whose fortune had risen on the destruction of all his prospects, and the balk of all his aspirations.

Flora was alone when Coningsby was ushered into the room. The extreme delicacy of her appearance was increased by her deep mourning; and seated in a cushioned chair, from which she seemed to rise with an effort, she certainly presented little of the character of a fortunate and prosperous heiress.

'You are very good to come to me,' she said, faintly smiling.

Coningsby extended his hand to her affectionately, in which she placed her own, looking down much embarrassed.

'You have an agreeable situation here,' said Coningsby, trying to break the first awkwardness of their meeting.

'Yes; but I hope not to stop here long.'

'You are going abroad?'

'No; I hope never to leave England!'

There was a slight pause; and then Flora sighed and said, 'I wish to speak to you on a subject that gives me pain; yet of which I must speak. You think I have injured you?'

'I am sure,' said Coningsby, in a tone of great kindness, 'that you could injure no one.'

'I have robbed you of your inheritance.'

'It was not mine by any right, legal or moral. There were others who might have urged an equal claim to it; and there are many who will now think that you might have preferred a superior one.'

'You had enemies; I was not one. They sought to benefit themselves by injuring you. They have not benefited themselves; let them not say that they have at least injured you.'

'We will care not what they say,' said Coningsby; 'I can sustain my lot.'

'Would that I could mine!' said Flora. She sighed again with a downcast glance. Then looking up embarrassed and blushing deeply, she added, 'I wish to restore to you that fortune of which I have unconsciously and unwillingly deprived you.'

'The fortune is yours, dear Flora, by every right,' said Coningsby, much moved; 'and there is no one who wishes more fervently that it may contribute to your happiness than I do.'

'It is killing me,' said Flora, mournfully; then speaking with unusual animation, with a degree of excitement, she continued, 'I must tell what I feel. This fortune is yours. I am happy in the inheritance, if you generously receive it from me, because Providence has made me the means of baffling your enemies. I never thought to be so happy as I shall be if you will generously accept this fortune, always intended for you. I have lived then for a purpose; I have not lived in vain; I have returned to you some service, however humble, for all your goodness to me in my unhappiness.'

'You are, as I have ever thought you, the kindest and most tender-hearted of beings. But you misconceive our mutual positions, my gentle Flora. The custom of the world does not permit such acts to either of us as you contemplate. The fortune is yours. It is left you by one on whose affections you had the highest claim. I will not say that so large an inheritance does not bring with it an alarming responsibility; but you are not unequal to it. Have confidence in yourself. You have a good heart; you have good sense; you have a well-principled being. Your spirit will mount with your fortunes, and blend with them. You will be happy.'

'And you?'

'I shall soon learn to find content, if not happiness, from other sources,' said Coningsby; 'and mere riches, however vast, could at no time have secured my felicity.'

'But they may secure that which brings felicity,' said Flora, speaking in a choking voice, and not meeting the glance of Coningsby. 'You had some views in life which displeased him who has done all this; they may be, they must be, affected by this fatal caprice. Speak to me, for I cannot speak, dear Mr Coningsby; do not let me believe that I, who would sacrifice my life for your happiness, am the cause of such calamities!'

'Whatever be my lot, I repeat I can sustain it,' said Coningsby, with a cheek of scarlet.

'Ah! he is angry with me,' exclaimed Flora; 'he is angry with me!' and the tears stole down her pale cheek.

'No, no, no! dear Flora; I have no other feelings to you than those of affection and respect,' and Coningsby, much agitated, drew his chair nearer to her, and took her hand. 'I am gratified by these kind wishes, though they are utterly impracticable; but they are the witnesses of your sweet disposition and your noble spirit. There never shall exist between us, under any circumstances, other feelings than those of kin and kindness.'

He rose as if to depart. When she saw that, she started, and seemed to summon all her energies.

'You are going,' she exclaimed, 'and I have said nothing, I have said nothing; and I shall never see you again. Let me tell you what I mean. This fortune is yours; it must be yours. It is an arrow in my heart. Do not think I am speaking from a momentary impulse. I know myself. I have lived so much alone, I have had so little to deceive or to delude me, that I know myself. If you will not let me do justice you declare my doom. I cannot live if my existence is the cause of all your prospects being blasted, and the sweetest dreams of your life being defeated. When I die, these riches will be yours; that you cannot prevent. Refuse my present offer, and you seal the fate of that unhappy Flora whose fragile life has hung for years on the memory of your kindness.'

'You must not say these words, dear Flora; you must not indulge in these gloomy feelings. You must live, and you must live happily. You have every charm and virtue which should secure happiness. The duties and the affections of existence will fall to your lot. It is one that will always interest me, for I shall ever be your friend. You have conferred on me one of the most delightful of feelings, gratitude, and for that I bless you. I will soon see you again.' Mournfully he bade her farewell.

Chapter 5

ABOUT a week after this interview with Flora, as Coningsby one morning was about to sally forth from the Albany to visit some chambers in the Temple, to which his notice had been attracted, there was a loud ring, a bustle in the hall, and Henry Sydney and Buckhurst were ushered in.

There never was such a cordial meeting; and yet the faces of his friends were serious. The truth is, the paragraphs in the newspapers had circulated in the country, they had written to Coningsby, and after a brief delay he had confirmed their worst apprehensions. Immediately they came up to town. Henry Sydney, a younger son, could offer little but sympathy, but he declared it was his intention also to study for the bar, so that they should not be divided. Buckhurst, after many embraces and some ordinary talk, took Coningsby aside, and said, 'My dear fellow, I have no objection to Henry Sydney hearing everything I say, but still these are subjects which men like to be discussed in private. Of course I expect you to share my fortune. There is enough for both. We will have an exact division.'

There was something in Buckhurst's fervent resolution very lovable and a little humorous, just enough to put one in good temper with human nature and life. If there were any fellow's fortune in the world that Coningsby would share, Buckhurst's would have had the preference; but while he pressed his hand, and with a glance in which a tear and a smile seemed to contend for mastery, he gently indicated why such arrangements were, with our present manners, impossible.

'I see,' said Buckhurst, after a moment's thought, 'I quite agree with you. The thing cannot be done; and, to tell you the truth, a fortune is a bore. What I vote that we three do at once is, to take plenty of ready-money, and enter the Austrian service. By Jove! it is the only thing to do.'

'There is something in that,' said Coningsby. 'In the meantime, suppose you two fellows walk with me to the Temple, for I have an appointment to look at some chambers.'

It was a fine day, and it was by no means a gloomy walk. Though the two friends had arrived full of indignation against Lord Monmouth, and miserable about their companion, once more in his society, and finding little difference in his carriage, they assumed unconsciously their habitual tone. As for Buckhurst, he was delighted with the Temple, which he visited for the first time. The name enchanted him. The tombs in the church convinced him that the Crusades were the only career. He would have himself become a law student if he might have prosecuted his studies in chain armour. The calmer Henry Sydney was consoled for the misfortunes of Coningsby by a fanciful project himself to pass a portion of his life amid these halls and courts, gardens and terraces, that maintain in the heart of a great city in the nineteenth century, so much of the grave romance and picturesque decorum of our past manners. Henry Sydney was sanguine; he was reconciled to the disinheritance of Coningsby by the conviction that it was a providential dispensation to make him a Lord Chancellor.

These faithful friends remained in town with Coningsby until he was established in Paper Buildings, and had become a pupil of a celebrated special pleader. They would have remained longer had not he himself suggested that it was better that they should part. It seemed a terrible catastrophe after all the visions of their boyish days, their college dreams, and their dazzling adventures in the world.

'And this is the end of Coningsby, the brilliant Coningsby, that we all loved, that was to be our leader!' said Buckhurst to Lord Henry as they quitted him. 'Well, come what may, life has lost something of its bloom.'

'The great thing now,' said Lord Henry, 'is to keep up the chain of our friendship. We must write to him very often, and contrive to be frequently together. It is dreadful to think that in the ways of life our hearts may become estranged. I never felt more wretched than I do at this moment, and yet I have faith that we shall not lose him.'

'Amen!' said Buckhurst; 'but I feel my plan about the Austrian

service was, after all, the only thing. The Continent offers a career.
He might have been prime minister; several strangers have been;
and as for war, look at Brown and Laudohn,[1] and half a hundred
others. I had a much better chance of being a field-marshal than
he has of being a Lord Chancellor.'

'I feel quite convinced that Coningsby will be Lord Chancellor,'
said Henry Sydney, gravely.

This change of life for Coningsby was a great social revolution.
It was sudden and complete. Within a month after the death of
his grandfather his name had been erased from all his fashionable
clubs, his horses and carriages sold, and he had become a student
of the Temple. He entirely devoted himself to his new pursuit. His
being was completely absorbed in it. There was nothing to haunt
his mind; no unexperienced scene or sensation of life to distract
his intelligence. One sacred thought alone indeed there remained,
shrined in the innermost sanctuary of his heart and consciousness. But it was a tradition, no longer a hope. The moment that
he had fairly recovered from the first shock of his grandfather's
will; had clearly ascertained the consequences to himself, and had
resolved on the course to pursue; he had communicated un-
reservedly with Oswald Millbank, and had renounced those pretensions to the hand of his sister which it ill became the destitute
to prefer.

His letter was answered in person. Millbank met Henry Sydney
and Buckhurst at the chambers of Coningsby. Once more they
were all four together; but under what different circumstances,
and with what different prospects from those which attended
their separation at Eton! Alone with Coningsby, Millbank spoke to
him things which letters could not convey. He bore to him all
the sympathy and devotion of Edith; but they would not conceal
from themselves that, at this moment, and in the present state of
affairs, all was hopeless. In no way did Coningsby ever permit
himself to intimate to Oswald the cause of his disinheritance. He
was, of course, silent on it to his other friends; as any communication of the kind must have touched on a subject that was
consecrated in his inmost soul.

Chapter 6

THE state of political parties in England in the spring of 1841 offered a most remarkable contrast to their condition at the period commemorated in the first chapter of this work. The banners of the Conservative camp at this moment lowered on the Whig forces, as the gathering host of the Norman invader frowned on the coast of Sussex. The Whigs were not yet conquered, but they were doomed; and they themselves knew it. The mistake which was made by the Conservative leaders in not retaining office in 1839; and, whether we consider their conduct in a national and constitutional light, or as a mere question of political tactics and party prudence, it was unquestionably a great mistake; had infused into the corps of Whig authority a kind of galvanic action, which only the superficial could mistake for vitality. Even to form a basis for their future operations, after the conjecture of '39, the Whigs were obliged to make a fresh inroad on the revenue, the daily increasing debility of which was now arresting attention and exciting public alarm. It was clear that the catastrophe of the government would be financial.

Under all the circumstances of the case, the conduct of the Whig Cabinet, in their final propositions, cannot be described as deficient either in boldness or prudence. The policy which they recommended was in itself a sagacious and spirited policy; but they erred in supposing that, at the period it was brought forward, any measure promoted by the Whigs could have obtained general favour in the country. The Whigs were known to be feeble; they were looked upon as tricksters. The country knew they were opposed by a powerful party; and though there certainly never was any authority for the belief, the country did believe that that powerful party were influenced by great principles; had in their view a definite and national policy; and would secure to England, instead of a feeble administration and fluctuating opinions, energy and a creed.

The future effect of the Whig propositions of '41 will not be detrimental to that party, even if in the interval they be appropriated piecemeal, as will probably be the case, by their Conservative successors. But for the moment, and in the plight in which the Whig party found themselves, it was impossible to have devised measures more conducive to their precipitate fall. Great interests were menaced by a weak government. The consequence was inevitable. Tadpole and Taper saw it in a moment. They snuffed the factious air, and felt the coming storm. Notwithstanding the extreme congeniality of these worthies, there was a little latent jealousy between them. Tadpole worshipped Registration: Taper adored a Cry. Tadpole always maintained that it was the winnowing of the electoral lists that could alone gain the day; Taper, on the contrary, faithful to ancient traditions, was ever of opinion that the game must ultimately be won by popular clamour. It always seemed so impossible that the Conservative party could ever be popular; the extreme graciousness and personal popularity of the leaders not being sufficiently apparent to be esteemed an adequate set-off against the inveterate odium that attached to their opinions; that the Tadpole philosophy was the favoured tenet in high places; and Taper had had his knuckles well rapped more than once for manœuvring too actively against the New Poor-law, and for hiring several link-boys[1] to bawl a much-wronged lady's name[2] in the Park when the Court prorogued Parliament.

And now, after all, in 1841, it seemed that Taper was right. There was a great clamour in every quarter, and the clamour was against the Whigs and in favour of Conservative principles. What Canadian timber-merchants meant by Conservative principles, it is not difficult to conjecture; or West Indian planters. It was tolerably clear on the hustings what squires and farmers, and their followers, meant by Conservative principles. What they mean by Conservative principles now is another question: and whether Conservative principles mean something higher than a perpetuation of fiscal arrangements, some of them impolitic, none of them important. But no matter what different bodies of men understood by the cry in which they all joined, the Cry existed. Taper beat Tadpole; and the great Conservative party beat the shattered and exhausted Whigs.

Notwithstanding the abstraction of his legal studies, Coningsby could not be altogether insensible to the political crisis. In the political world of course he never mixed, but the friends of his boyhood were deeply interested in affairs, and they lost no opportunity which he would permit them, of cultivating his society. Their occasional fellowship, a visit now and then to Sidonia, and a call sometimes on Flora, who lived at Richmond, comprised his social relations. His general acquaintance did not desert him, but he was out of sight, and did not wish to be remembered. Mr Ormsby asked him to dinner, and occasionally mourned over his fate in the bow window of White's; while Lord Eskdale even went to see him in the Temple, was interested in his progress, and said, with an encouraging look, that, when he was called to the bar, all his friends must join and get up the steam. Coningsby had once met Mr Rigby, who was walking with the Duke of Agincourt, which was probably the reason he could not notice a lawyer. Mr Rigby cut Coningsby.

Lord Eskdale had obtained from Villebecque accurate details as to the cause of Coningsby being disinherited. Our hero, if one in such fallen fortunes may still be described as a hero, had mentioned to Lord Eskdale his sorrow that his grandfather had died in anger with him; but Lord Eskdale, without dwelling on the subject, had assured him that he had reason to believe that if Lord Monmouth had lived, affairs would have been different. He had altered the disposition of his property at a moment of great and general irritation and excitement; and had been too indolent, perhaps really too indisposed, which he was unwilling ever to acknowledge, to recur to a calmer and more equitable settlement. Lord Eskdale had been more frank with Sidonia, and had told him all about the refusal to become a candidate for Darlford against Mr Millbank; the communication of Rigby to Lord Monmouth, as to the presence of Oswald Millbank at the castle, and the love of Coningsby for his sister; all these details, furnished by Villebecque to Lord Eskdale, had been truly transferred by that nobleman to his co-executor; and Sidonia, when he had sufficiently digested them, had made Lady Wallinger acquainted with the whole history.

The dissolution of the Whig Parliament by the Whigs, the project of which had reached Lord Monmouth a year before, and yet in which nobody believed to the last moment, at length took place. All the world was dispersed in the heart of the season, and our solitary student of the Temple, in his lonely chambers, notwithstanding all his efforts, found his eye rather wander over the pages of Tidd and Chitty[3] as he remembered that the great event to which he had so looked forward was now occurring, and he, after all, was no actor in the mighty drama. It was to have been the epoch of his life; when he was to have found himself in that proud position for which all the studies, and meditations, and higher impulses of his nature had been preparing him. It was a keen trial of a man. Every one of his friends and old companions were candidates, and with sanguine prospects. Lord Henry was certain for a division of his county; Buckhurst harangued a large agricultural borough in his vicinity; Eustace Lyle and Vere stood in coalition for a Yorkshire town; and Oswald Millbank solicited the suffrages of an important manufacturing constituency. They sent their addresses to Coningsby. He was deeply interested as he traced in them the influence of his own mind; often recognised the very expressions to which he had habituated them. Amid the confusion of a general election, no unimpassioned critic had time to canvass the language of an address to an isolated constituency; yet an intelligent speculator on the movements of political parties might have detected in these public declarations some intimation of new views, and of a tone of political feeling that has unfortunately been too long absent from the public life of this country.

It was the end of a sultry July day, the last ray of the sun shooting down Pall Mall sweltering with dust; there was a crowd round the doors of the Carlton and the Reform Clubs, and every now and then an express arrived with the agitating bulletin of a fresh defeat or a new triumph. Coningsby was walking up Pall Mall. He was going to dine at the Oxford and Cambridge Club, the only club on whose list he had retained his name, that he might occasionally have the pleasure of meeting an Eton or Cambridge friend without the annoyance of encountering any of his former fashionable acquaintances. He lighted in his walk on Mr Tadpole and Mr Taper, both of whom he knew. The latter did not notice him, but Mr Tadpole, more good-natured, bestowed on him a rough nod, not unmarked by a slight expression of coarse pity.

Coningsby ordered his dinner, and then took up the evening papers, where he learnt the return of Vere and Lyle; and read a speech of Buckhurst denouncing the Venetian Constitution, to the amazement of several thousand persons, apparently not a little terrified by this unknown danger, now first introduced to their notice. Being true Englishmen, they were all against Buckhurst's opponent, who was of the Venetian party, and who ended by calling out Buckhurst for his personalities.

Coningsby had dined, and was reading in the library, when a waiter brought up a third edition of the *Sun*, with electioneering bulletins from the manufacturing districts to the very latest hour. Some large letters which expressed the name of Darlford caught his eye. There seemed great excitement in that borough; strange proceedings had happened. The column was headed, 'Extraordinary Affair! Withdrawal of the Liberal Candidate! Two Tory Candidates in the field!!!'

His eye glanced over an animated speech of Mr Millbank, his countenance changed, his heart palpitated. Mr Millbank had resigned the representation of the town, but not from weakness; his avocations demanded his presence; he had been requested to let his son supply his place, but his son was otherwise provided for; he should always take a deep interest in the town and trade of Darlford; he hoped the link between the borough and Hellingsley would be ever cherished; loud cheering; he wished in parting from them to take a step which should conciliate all parties, put an end to local heats and factious contentions, and secure the town an able and worthy representative. For these reasons he begged to propose to them a gentleman who bore a name which many of them greatly honoured; for himself, he knew the individual, and it was his firm opinion that whether they considered his talents, his character, or the ancient connection of his family with the district, he could not propose a candidate more worthy of their confidence than HARRY CONINGSBY, ESQ.

This proposition was received with that wild enthusiasm which occasionally bursts out in the most civilised communities. The contest between Millbank and Rigby was equally balanced, neither party was over-confident. The Conservatives were not particularly zealous in behalf of their champion; there was no Marquess of Monmouth and no Coningsby Castle now to back him; he was fighting on his own resources, and he was a beaten horse. The Liberals did not like the prospect of a defeat, and dreaded the mortification of Rigby's triumph. The Moderate men, who thought more of local than political circumstances, liked the name of Coningsby. Mr Millbank had dexterously prepared his leading supporters for the substitution. Some traits of the character and conduct of Coningsby had been cleverly circulated. Thus there was a combination of many favourable causes in his favour. In half an hour's time his image was stamped on the brain of every inhabitant of the borough as an interesting and accomplished youth, who had been wronged, and who deserved to be rewarded. It was whispered that Rigby was his enemy. Magog Wrath and his mob offered Mr Millbank's committee to throw Mr Rigby into the river, or to burn down his hotel, in case he was prudent enough not to show. Mr Rigby determined to fight to the last. All his hopes were now staked on the successful result of this contest. It were impossible if he were returned that his friends could refuse him high office. The whole of Lord Monmouth's reduced legacy was devoted to this end. The third edition of the *Sun* left Mr Rigby in vain attempting to address an infuriated populace.

Here was a revolution in the fortunes of our forlorn Coningsby! When his grandfather first sent for him to Monmouth House, his destiny was not verging on greater vicissitudes. He rose from his seat, and was surprised that all the silent gentlemen who were about him did not mark his agitation. Not an individual there that he knew. It was now an hour to midnight, and to-morrow the almost unconscious candidate was to go to the poll. In a tumult of suppressed emotion, Coningsby returned to his chambers. He found a letter in his box from Oswald Millbank, who had been twice at the Temple. Oswald had been returned without a contest, and had reached Darlford in time to hear Coningsby nominated. He set off instantly to London, and left at his friend's chambers a rapid narrative of what had happened, with information that he should call on him again on the morrow at nine o'clock, when they were to repair together immediately to Darlford in time for Coningsby to be chaired, for no one entertained a doubt of his triumph.

Coningsby did not sleep a wink that night, and yet when he rose early felt fresh enough for any exploit, however difficult or hazardous. He felt as an Egyptian does when the Nile rises after its elevation had been despaired of. At the very lowest ebb of his fortunes, an event had occurred which seemed to restore all. He dared not contemplate the ultimate result of all these wonderful changes. Enough for him, that when all seemed dark, he was about to be returned to Parliament by the father of Edith, and his vanquished rival who was to bite the dust before him was the author of all his misfortunes. Love, Vengeance, Justice, the glorious pride of having acted rightly, the triumphant sense of complete and absolute success, here were chaotic materials from which order was at length evolved; and all subsided in an overwhelming feeling of gratitude to that Providence that had so signally protected him.

There was a knock at the door. It was Oswald. They embraced. It seemed that Oswald was as excited as Coningsby. His eye sparkled, his manner was energetic.

'We must talk it all over during our journey. We have not a minute to spare.'

During that journey Coningsby learned something of the course of affairs which gradually had brought about so singular a revolution in his favour. We mentioned that Sidonia had acquired a thorough knowledge of the circumstances which had occasioned and attended the disinheritance of Coningsby. These he had told to Lady Wallinger, first by letter, afterwards in more detail on her arrival in London. Lady Wallinger had conferred with her husband. She was not surprised at the goodness of Coningsby, and she sympathised with all his calamities. He had ever been the favourite of her judgment, and her romance had always consisted in blending his destinies with those of her beloved Edith. Sir Joseph was a judicious man, who never cared to commit himself; a little selfish, but good, just, and honourable, with some impulses, only a little afraid of them; but then his wife stepped in like an angel, and gave them the right direction. They were both absolutely impressed with Coningsby's admirable conduct, and Lady Wallinger was determined that her husband should express to others the convictions which he acknowledged in unison with herself. Sir Joseph spoke to Mr Millbank, who stared; but Sir Joseph spoke feebly. Lady Wallinger conveyed all this intelligence, and all her impressions, to Oswald and Edith. The younger Millbank talked with interest, inveighed against Lord Monmouth, and condemned his will.

After some time, Mr Millbank made inquiries about Coningsby, took an interest in his career, and, like Lord Eskdale, declared that when he was called to the bar, his friends would have an opportunity to evince their sincerity. Affairs remained in this state, until Oswald thought that circumstances were sufficiently ripe to urge his father on the subject. The position which Oswald had assumed at Millbank had necessarily made him acquainted with the affairs and fortune of his father. When he computed the vast wealth which he knew was at his parent's command, and recalled Coningsby in his humble chambers, toiling after all his noble efforts without any results, and his sister pining in a provincial solitude, Oswald began to curse wealth, and to ask himself what was the use of all their marvellous industry and supernatural skill? He addressed his father with that irresistible frankness which a strong faith can alone inspire. What are the objects of wealth, if not to bless those who possess our hearts? The only daughter, the friend to whom the only son was indebted for his life, here are two beings surely whom one would care to bless, and both are unhappy. Mr Millbank listened without prejudice, for he was already convinced. But he felt some interest in the present conduct of Coningsby. A Coningsby working for his bread was a novel incident for him. He wished to be assured of its authenticity. He was resolved to convince himself of the fact. And perhaps he would have gone on yet for a little time, and watched the progress of the experiment, already interested and delighted by what had reached him, had not the dissolution brought affairs to a crisis. The misery of Oswald at the position of Coningsby, the silent sadness of Edith, his own conviction, which assured him that he could do nothing wiser or better than take this young man to his heart, so

ordained it that Mr Millbank, who was after all the creature of
impulse, decided suddenly, and decided rightly. Never making a
single admission to all the representations of his son, Mr Millbank
in a moment did all that his son could have dared to desire.

This is a very imperfect and crude intimation of what had
occurred at Millbank and Hellingsley; yet it conveys a faint sketch
of the enchanting intelligence that Oswald conveyed to Coningsby
during their rapid travel. When they arrived at Birmingham,
they found a messenger and a despatch, informing Coningsby,
that at mid-day, at Darlford, he was at the head of the poll by an
overwhelming majority, and that Mr Rigby had resigned. He was,
however, requested to remain at Birmingham, as they did not
wish him to enter Darlford, except to be chaired, so he was to
arrive there in the morning. At Birmingham, therefore, they
remained.

There was Oswald's election to talk of as well as Coningsby's.
They had hardly had time for this. Now they were both Members
of Parliament. Men must have been at school together, to enjoy
the real fun of meeting thus, and realising boyish dreams. Often,
years ago, they had talked of these things, and assumed these
results; but those were words and dreams, these were positive
facts; after some doubts and struggles, in the freshness of their
youth, Oswald Millbank and Harry Coningsby were members of
the British Parliament; public characters, responsible agents, with
a career.

This afternoon, at Birmingham, was as happy an afternoon as
usually falls to the lot of man. Both of these companions were
labouring under that degree of excitement which is necessary to
felicity. They had enough to talk about. Edith was no longer a
forbidden or a sorrowful subject. There was rapture in their again
meeting under such circumstances. Then there were their friends;
that dear Buckhurst, who had just been called out for styling his
opponent a Venetian, and all their companions of early days.
What a sudden and marvellous change in all their destinies!
Life was a pantomime; the wand was waved, and it seemed that
the schoolfellows had of a sudden become elements of power,
springs of the great machine.

A train arrived; restless they sallied forth, to seek diversion in the dispersion of the passengers. Coningsby and Millbank, with that glance, a little inquisitive, even impertinent, if we must confess it, with which one greets a stranger when he emerges from a public conveyance, were lounging on the platform. The train arrived; stopped; the doors were thrown open, and from one of them emerged Mr Rigby! Coningsby, who had dined, was greatly tempted to take off his hat and make him a bow, but he refrained. Their eyes met. Rigby was dead beat. He was evidently used up; a man without a resource; the sight of Coningsby his last blow; he had met his fate.

'My dear fellow,' said Coningsby, 'I remember I wanted you to dine with my grandfather at Montem, and that fellow would not ask you. Such is life!'

About eleven o'clock the next morning they arrived at the Darlford station. Here they were met by an anxious deputation, who received Coningsby as if he were a prophet, and ushered him into a car covered with satin and blue ribbons, and drawn by six beautiful grey horses, caparisoned in his colours, and ridden by postilions, whose very whips were blue and white. Triumphant music sounded; banners waved; the multitude were marshalled; the Freemasons, at the first opportunity, fell into the procession; the Odd Fellows[4] joined it at the nearest corner. Preceded and followed by thousands, with colours flying, trumpets sounding, and endless huzzas, flags and handkerchiefs waving from every window, and every balcony filled with dames and maidens bedecked with his colours, Coningsby was borne through enthusiastic Darlford like Paulus Emilius returning from Macedon.[5] Uncovered, still in deep mourning, his fine figure, and graceful bearing, and his intelligent brow, at once won every female heart.

The singularity was, that all were of the same opinion: everybody cheered him, every house was adorned with his colours. His triumphal return was no party question. Magog Wrath and Bully Bluck walked together like lambs at the head of his procession.

The car stopped before the principal hotel in the High Street. It was Mr Millbank's committee. The broad street was so crowded, that, as every one declared, you might have walked on the heads of the people. Every window was full; the very roofs were peopled. The car stopped, and the populace gave three cheers for Mr Millbank. Their late member, surrounded by his friends, stood in the balcony, which was fitted up with Coningsby's colours, and bore his name on the hangings in gigantic letters formed of dahlias. The flashing and inquiring eye of Coningsby caught the form of Edith, who was leaning on her father's arm.

The hustings were opposite the hotel, and here, after a while, Coningsby was carried, and, stepping from his car, took up his post to address, for the first time, a public assembly. Anxious as the people were to hear him, it was long before their enthusiasm could subside into silence. At length that silence was deep and absolute. He spoke; his powerful and rich tones reached every ear. In five minutes' time every one looked at his neighbour, and without speaking they agreed that there never was anything like this heard in Darlford before.

He addressed them for a considerable time, for he had a great deal to say; not only to express his gratitude for the unprecedented manner in which he had become their representative, and for the spirit in which they had greeted him, but he had to offer them no niggard exposition of the views and opinions of the member whom they had so confidingly chosen, without even a formal declaration of his sentiments.

He did this with so much clearness, and in a manner so pointed and popular, that the deep attention of the multitude never wavered. His lively illustrations kept them often in continued merriment. But when, towards his close, he drew some picture of what he hoped might be the character of his future and lasting connection with the town, the vast throng was singularly affected. There were a great many present at that moment who, though they had never seen Coningsby before, would willingly have then died for him. Coningsby had touched their hearts, for he had spoken from his own. His spirit had entirely magnetised them. Darlford believed in Coningsby: and a very good creed.

And now Coningsby was conducted to the opposite hotel. He walked through the crowd. The progress was slow, as every one wished to shake hands with him. His friends, however, at last safely landed him. He sprang up the stairs; he was met by Mr

Millbank, who welcomed him with the greatest warmth, and offered his hearty congratulations.

'It is to you, dear sir, that I am indebted for all this,' said Coningsby.

'No,' said Mr Millbank, 'it is to your own high principles, great talents, and good heart.'

After he had been presented by the late member to the principal personages in the borough, Mr Millbank said,

'I think we must now give Mr Coningsby a little rest. Come with me,' he added, 'here is some one who will be very glad to see you.'

Speaking thus, he led our hero a little away, and placing his arm in Coningsby's with great affection opened the door of an apartment. There was Edith, radiant with loveliness and beaming with love. Their agitated hearts told at a glance the tumult of their joy. The father joined their hands, and blessed them with words of tenderness.

Chapter 7

THE marriage of Coningsby and Edith took place early in the autumn. It was solemnised at Millbank, and they passed their first moon at Hellingsley, which place was in future to be the residence of the member for Darlford. The estate was to devolve to Coningsby after the death of Mr Millbank, who in the meantime made arrangements which permitted the newly-married couple to reside at the Hall in a manner becoming its occupants. All these settlements, as Mr Millbank assured Coningsby, were effected not only with the sanction, but at the express instance, of his son.

An event, however, occurred not very long after the marriage of Coningsby, which rendered this generous conduct of his father-in-law no longer necessary to his fortunes, though he never forgot its exercise. The gentle and unhappy daughter of Lord Monmouth quitted a scene with which her spirit had never greatly sympathised. Perhaps she might have lingered in life for yet a little while, had it not been for that fatal inheritance which disturbed her peace and embittered her days, haunting her heart with the recollection that she had been the unconscious instrument of injuring the only being whom she loved, and embarrassing and encumbering her with duties foreign to her experience and her nature. The marriage of Coningsby had greatly affected her, and from that day she seemed gradually to decline. She died towards the end of the autumn, and, subject to an ample annuity to Villebecque, she bequeathed the whole of her fortune to the husband of Edith. Gratifying as it was to him to present such an inheritance to his wife, it was not without a pang that he received the intelligence of the death of Flora. Edith sympathised in his affectionate feelings, and they raised a monument to her memory in the gardens of Hellingsley.

Coningsby passed his next Christmas in his own hall, with his beautiful and gifted wife by his side, and surrounded by the friends of his heart and his youth.

They stand now on the threshold of public life. They are in the leash, but in a moment they will be slipped. What will be their fate? Will they maintain in august assemblies and high places the great truths which, in study and in solitude, they have embraced? Or will their courage exhaust itself in the struggle, their enthusiasm evaporate before hollow-hearted ridicule, their generous impulses yield with a vulgar catastrophe to the tawdry temptations of a low ambition? Will their skilled intelligence subside into being the adroit tool of a corrupt party? Will Vanity confound their fortunes, or Jealousy wither their sympathies? Or will they remain brave, single, and true; refuse to bow before shadows and worship phrases; sensible of the greatness of their position, recognise the greatness of their duties; denounce to a perplexed and disheartened world the frigid theories of a generalising age that have destroyed the individuality of man, and restore the happiness of their country by believing in their own energies, and daring to be great?

Notes

Coningsby is an extremely allusive novel, and a 'complete' annotation would be cumbersome, as well as a possible distraction to the reader. I have therefore tried to discriminate in my annotation, and have not attempted to label every reference. I have not usually provided notes for words which might be traced with the help of a dictionary, and I have not sought to amplify allusions which in themselves do not blur the sense of the text. For example, I have not thought it necessary to annotate *Aubusson* in the context of its carpets which are mentioned in passing and I have not provided notes on personages like Sir Thomas Lawrence and Sir David Wilkie where the text provides a sufficient indication of background or profession for an understanding of the passage concerned.

BOOK I

Chapter 1

1. (p. 33) *By G— they're out!* On the morning of 9 May 1832 it was learned that King William IV had accepted the resignation of Lord Grey and the Whig cabinet. The King had refused the alternative – the creation of fifty or sixty new peers – after the government had lost by 151 to 116 a division in the House of Lords on Lord Lyndhurst's motion to postpone the disfranchising clauses of the Reform Bill. This is explicitly referred to at the beginning of Chapter 2.

2. (p. 33) *Brookes'*. Originally founded in 1764, this was the major Whig club.

3. (p. 33) *the palace.* The King had received Grey's resignation at Windsor. He only travelled to London on the morning of 9 May.

4. (p. 34) *the Chief Baron.* Although a Tory, Lyndhurst had accepted the Chief Barony of the Exchequer (a judgeship) from Grey, having failed to keep his Lord Chancellorship in 1830.

5. (p. 34) *the clerks.* The Tories exaggerated the amount of influence that would pass to the urban middle classes upon the passing of the Reform Act.

6. (p. 35) *the Political Unions put together.* These localized associations of working-class and middle-class radicals were behind such organized militancy as existed during the passage through Parliament of the Reform Bill, and through 'the days of May', as the period following Grey's resignation soon became known, they were a major source of agitation in favour of the return to office of the Whigs.

Chapter 2

1. (p. 36) *not without foundation*. The rumour related to the creation of a further fifty or sixty peers with a view to securing a Whig majority for the Reform Bill in the House of Lords.

2. (p. 37) *with any such power*. The Times of 9 January 1832 had been mainly responsible for spreading the news that the King would not object to a large creation of peers, but, during the crisis of the following May, Grey and Lord Brougham agreed that he 'had never encouraged them to expect that he could consent' to fifty or sixty.

3. (p. 37) 'THE WAVERERS'. Led by Lord Wharncliffe, the 'waverers' had come together counting on some reaction to the Bill which would effect a compromise, guaranteeing a measure of reform without the creation of any more peers.

4. (p. 37) *their own conduct*. By the time the second-reading debate began in the House of Lords on 9 April 1832, the waverers felt that the resignation of the government would have been as bad as the creation of new peers, and at the division the Bill was given a second reading by 184 votes to 175. Soon after, however, Wharncliffe was looking for the cooperation of Wellington to carry amendments to the Bill.

5. (p. 38) *votes he had inherited in the House of Commons*. Large amounts of money could be spent in attempts to gain and retain the control of constituencies, and several rich aristocrats would have been in the same situation as Monmouth in having a clientele of MPs. Prior to the passing of the Reform Act, the naming of MPs could be bought or inherited in those boroughs with small electorates, and borough-mongering was a common feature of political life. Although such boroughs were poor investments in themselves, the power they conferred on their 'owners' could be used to obtain places and promotions.

6. (p. 38) *the strawberry leaf*. i.e. a dukedom. A row of figures of the strawberry leaf appears on the coronet of a duke.

7. (p. 41) *Lord Bolingbroke*. Henry St John, 1st Viscount Bolingbroke (1678–1751), was a prominent politician during the reign of Queen Anne, and a political writer admired by Disraeli.

8. (p. 41) *authors of the 'Rejected Addresses'*. A collection of parodies of contemporary writers by James (1775–1839) and Horace Smith (1779–1849), published in 1812.

9. (p. 41) *the Doctor*. John Keate (1773–1852).

Chapter 3

1. (p. 44) *the head-quarters of the party*. The Carlton Club, which had recently been founded by the Duke of Wellington.

2. (p. 47) *madid*. Rare word for wet or moist.

3. (p. 47) *such a bow as ... ambassador of the United Provinces*. i.e. it showed no more warmth than ceremony demanded. The United Provinces (the Dutch) had been to the fore in imposing arbitration on Louis XIV after

his invasion of the Spanish Netherlands in 1667. Louis invaded the
Provinces five years later.

Chapter 4

1. (p. 49) *the illustrious envoy.* As the British envoy at the second Treaty
of Paris in November 1815 after the Battle of Waterloo. In Book IV Chapter
11 of *Sybil* Lord Deloraine talks of when he was in Paris 'with Monmouth
at the peace'.

Chapter 5

1. (p. 52) *Apsley House.* Wellington's residence.
2. (p. 53) *stare super vias antiquas.* To stay in old ways.
3. (p. 53) *Crœsus.* The extremely rich king of Lydia (in Asia Minor)
from 561 to 546 BC.
4. (p. 55) *the safety-lamp.* The safety-lamp for miners was invented by
Sir Humphry Davy (1778–1829).
5. (p. 57) *the Forcible Feebles.* Falstaff applies the word 'forcible' to
Feeble in *Henry IV, Part 2*, III, ii.

Chapter 6

1. (p. 59) *a l'Espinasse or a De Stael.* Julie de Lespinasse (1732–76) was
hostess of one of the most emancipated Parisian salons and authoress of
several volumes of passionate letters. Madame de Staël (1766–1817),
hostess of a salon for leading intellectuals, was a most accomplished
conversationalist and woman of letters.
2. (p. 60) *Short commons.* Short rations.
3. (p. 61) THE DUKE. Wellington.
4. (p. 61) *a coalition on a sliding scale.* A reference to the form of a
sliding scale of duties on corn, first drawn up by Lord Liverpool before the
collapse of his ministry, and then introduced by Canning in a Bill in
March 1827.
5. (p. 61) *Birmingham Union and the other bodies.* The Birmingham
'Political Union for the Protection of Public Rights', founded by Thomas
Attwóod (1783–1856) and fifteen others on 14 December 1829, was the
most influential of the unions and provided a model for several others in
the years of the Reform crisis.
6. (p. 61) *list of new peers.* i.e. resignation honours.
7. (p. 61) *the old story won't do.* Wellington's formation of a ministry in
1828 had been designed to be something of a reunification of Lord
Liverpool's administration, which Wellington saw as having been disrupted by the premierships of Canning and Goderich. Canningites like
Huskisson, Palmerston, Grant, Dudley and Lamb were retained while men
like Eldon, Westmorland and Vansittart were omitted, and the ultra-
Tories who sought reaction found themselves disappointed. Monmouth is

hopeful that Wellington will now form a cabinet along more reactionary lines.

Chapter 7

1. (p. 62) *May 1832*. Following the resignation of Grey, Wellington's loyalty to the King prompted him to accept a commission to form a government, even though by so doing he would be sacrificing his adherence to the principle of no reform. Public opinion was strongly against accepting any measure of reform from an administration other than Grey's, and the delay in forming a new government under Wellington allowed that opinion to demonstrate itself forcefully. Wellington was also seriously handicapped by the refusal of Peel to join a new administration, and on the morning of 15 May he bowed to the inevitable and resigned his commission, advising the King to recall Grey. The period of time spanning the crisis between the acceptance of Grey's resignation on 9 May and Wellington's withdrawal is known as 'the days of May'.

2. (p. 63) *The City of London ... to report daily*. The Common Council of the City of London petitioned the House of Commons on 10 May for the reinstatement of the reformers and appointed a standing committee to watch events. The City's pro-Reform stance during the days of May was a major factor in convincing the anti-reformers of the futility of their mission. (Charles I attempted to seize the five members of the House of Commons on 4 January 1642. The Common Council of London first formed itself into a joint Committee for Public Safety with Parliament on Saturday 8 January.)

3. (p. 63) *the House of Commons met ... regal prerogative*. On the evening of 9 May Viscount Ebrington, in the House of Commons, gave notice of a motion for the next day in support of the outgoing ministers. Despite pleas that this might embarrass the new government, 180 reforming MPs met at Brooks's to decide on the terms of the motion. On the following day Ebrington's motion was passed by 288 to 208. Disraeli regarded this as a clear flouting of the authority of the role of the House of Lords (in that the passing of Lyndhurst's motion of postponement in that chamber had effectively forced Grey to resign) and of the authority of the King (in that William IV had accepted Grey's resignation and sought a new government).

4. (p. 64) *modelled on the Venetian*. Disraeli used the term 'Venetian constitution' to describe what he saw as the oligarchy of power in England at the end of the eighteenth century; that is, the king reduced to the status of a doge, subject to the will of the great Whig families, whom he compared with the Council of Ten that governed Venice in the fourteenth century.

5. (p. 64) *like James II*. William of Orange entered London and James II fled the country in the week before Christmas 1688. A Convention Parliament met on 22 January 1689, and the Commons voted that

James II had 'endeavoured to subvert the constitution by breaking the original contract between king and people' and had therefore 'abdicated' the throne. The Lords also assented to the theory that the King had 'abdicated' and that the throne was vacant, although in fact James never did abdicate other than by his absence.

6. (p. 64) *assent to its provisions*. The third reading of the Reform Bill was carried in the House of Lords by 106 to 22 on 4 June 1832. The King refused to give the royal consent in person, and it was given by commission on 7 June. When William IV had been waiting to go to Westminster to dissolve Parliament on 23 April the previous year, following the government's defeat on Isaac Gascoyne's motion forbidding any reduction in the number of MPs for England and Wales, he is supposed to have said that if the state coach were not ready in time he would go in a hackney coach.

7. (p. 65) *the ten-pound franchise*. The Reform Act enfranchised the occupiers of houses worth £10 a year.

8. (p. 65) *Abbé Siéyès*. Emmanuel-Joseph Sieyès (1748–1836), church-man and constitutional theorist, whose concept of popular sovereignty was to the fore at the beginning of the French Revolution. Disraeli is thinking in particular of Sieyès's distinction between 'active' (those eligible to vote) and 'passive' citizens, which was adopted in the National Assembly's decrees establishing qualifications for voting – thereby guaranteeing that the bourgeoisie would retain political power.

9. (p. 65) *Chartism*. Taking its name from the People's Charter, which was drafted in 1838 by William Lovett, Chartism was a working-class movement which arose as a response to the economic climate of severe depression and high unemployment in the late 1830s. The Charter made six political demands: universal male suffrage, equal electoral districts, ballot voting, annually elected Parliaments, the payment of Members of Parliament and the abolition of the property qualification for membership.

10. (p. 66) *'the People' ... not of political science*. Disraeli uses 'the people' to include the working classes, but the phraseology of the time of the Reform Act tended to ascribe the term to the middle classes, whilst using the word 'populace' of the workers.

11. (p. 66) *Antinous*. Antinous (AD 110–30), favourite of the Roman emperor Hadrian, and deified by him after his death, was regarded as a model of youthful beauty.

12. (p. 67) *Montem*. 'The earliest account of Montem, in [William] Malim's *Consuetudinarium*, 1560, describes it as an initiation of new boys at Salt Hill by sprinkling them with *salt* in its double meaning of "salt" and "wit". Later it became a festival for the purpose of collecting "salt", i.e. money contributions towards the University expenses of the Senior Colleger ... The senior boys were dressed as officers in the army of different ranks [which explains some of the latter references] ... The increased publicity caused by the introduction of railways made its

continuance undesirable, and it was abolished in 1847 ...' (from the catalogue of the *Loan Collection ... connected with the History of Eton*, 1891).

Chapter 8

1. (p. 70) *a Herodotus or a Froissart.* Herodotus (*c.*484–*c.*420 BC), great historian of Halicarnassus in Asia Minor, known as 'the father of history'. Jean Froissart (1333?–1400/01), poet and court historian. His *Chronicles* of the fourteenth century remain the most important and detailed documents of feudal times.

Chapter 9

1. (p. 74) *Aquatics and Drybobs.* Drybobs were boys who preferred cricket to boating (as opposed to Wetbobs or Aquatics).

2. (p. 78) *the lasher.* A body of water that lashes or rushes over an opening in a barrier or weir.

3. (p. 79) *fishy.* i.e. dull and lifeless.

Chapter 11

1. (p. 85) *Hidalgos ... at Pavia.* The hidalgos were hereditary nobles. Disraeli uses the term to denote the military commanders of the Spanish forces who, as part of the Habsburg army, virtually wiped out the French army under Francis I on 24 February 1525 at Pavia in Northern Italy.

2. (p. 85) *Culloden.* The last battle of the Jacobite rebellion of 1745 on 16 April 1746, when the Scots forces of Prince Charles Edward Stuart were defeated by the British under the Duke of Cumberland.

3. (p. 85) *Charles Fox.* (1749–1806), leading Whig politician who long stood in opposition to the policies of George III.

4. (p. 86) *yataghan.* A Turkish sword with a curved single-edged blade.

5. (p. 86) *Goodall.* Joseph Goodall (1760–1840).

6. (p. 86) *Wotton to Wellesley.* Sir Henry Wotton (1568–1639), poet, diplomat and art connoisseur, became provost of Eton in 1624. Arthur Wellesley became the Duke of Wellington.

7. (p. 88) *Lucullus.* (*c.*117–55 BC), Roman senator and general who served under the dictator Sulla. He later devoted himself to gracious living and his name became synonymous with sybaritic luxury.

8. (p. 89) *a Protestant Carnival.* The word carnival was originally and most commonly used of the Catholic festivities in the week preceding Lent, which may explain Disraeli's reference to forty days. (The old Italian word *carnelevare* meant the removing of meat.)

9. (p. 89) *younkers.* Originally meaning 'young gentlemen', by the middle of the nineteenth century this word was used commonly of all boys.

10. (p. 89) *Lord Durham.* John George Lambton, 1st Earl of Durham (1792–1840), reformist Whig, sometimes known as 'Radical Jack', who was prominent in formulating the early drafts of the Reform Bill.

BOOK II
Chapter 1

1. (p. 92) *its most efficient members.* The resignation of Stanley, Graham, Lord Ripon and the Duke of Richmond, precipitated by the Appropriation Clause of the Irish Church Act of 1833.

2. (p. 92) *in procession to Downing-street.* On 21 April 1834 a large number of trade-unionists marched from Copenhagen Fields to Whitehall to present a petition to the Home Secretary, Lord Melbourne, in support of the Dorchester labourers sentenced to seven years transportation for attempting to form a union using secret oaths.

3. (p. 92) *Irish negotiations of Lord Hatherton.* Edward John Littleton (1791–1863) was only created Lord Hatherton in 1835.

4. (p. 92) *Lord Althorp.* Viscount Althorp (1782–1845), feeling his position over Irish Coercion to be intolerable, resigned in July as Leader of the House of Commons. Grey decided to use the opportunity to tender his own resignation with that of Althorp, and he recommended that Melbourne should follow him as Prime Minister. Relieved of his obligation to Irish Coercion, Althorp consented to resume his post.

5. (p. 92) *King William to the Bishops.* i.e. the Irish prelates, headed by the Archbishop of Armagh, who presented an address to the King complaining of the attacks on the Irish Church and imploring his protection. The King's emotional reply was calculated to embarrass the government.

6. (p. 92) *apocalypse of the Lord Chancellor.* An impolitic attack on Daniel O'Connell made by Lord Brougham during an oratorical tour of Scotland in August 1834.

7. (p. 92) *the Edinburgh banquet.* At this banquet on 15 September in honour of Grey, the ex-Prime-Minister, Brougham and Durham all reiterated their belief in amelioration and reform and derided the idea of a reaction in favour of Tory principles of government.

8. (p. 93) *placeman.* A person holding a public office, probably gaining from it some personal profit for political support rendered.

9. (p. 94) *distinguished personage.* Peel.

10. (p. 95) *a great minister.* William Pitt the younger (1759–1806), Prime Minister from 1783 to 1801 and from 1804 to 1806.

11. (p. 95) *a great military genius.* Wellington.

12. (p. 96) *two kingdoms ... erased from the map of Europe.* The joint kingdom of Norway and Sweden, which was never more than nominal, and the merging of the United Provinces and the old Austrian Netherlands into the kingdom of the Netherlands under the House of Orange. The allotting of Norway to Sweden in 1814 was a major factor

in the increase in Norwegian nationalism, and by 1830 Norway was practically an independent state. That same year saw the confirmation of Belgian independence after several years of Catholic, French and Flemish resentment against the Dutch dominance of the joint kingdom of the Netherlands.

13. (p. 96) *conjunctures of the East.* i.e. the expansion of Russia.

14. (p. 96) *mediatisation of the petty German princes.* The annexing of principalities to another state, leaving the former princes their titles and some restricted rights.

15. (p. 96) *inclosure-bills.* As large-scale farming was seen to be more profitable than the traditional system where each labourer had his strip of land, so the landowners bought out or evicted their tenants and created enclosed fields. Between 1750 and 1810 there were 2,921 Enclosure Acts passed in Parliament, all of which were in favour of the great landowners. The yeoman, who had had a tiny stake in the agricultural community, disappeared, and, without land, was forced into the growing towns to find work in the new factories.

16. (p. 97) *disorganisation for sedition.* Disorders in 1816, including political reform meetings and the Spa Fields riot in December, decided the government to act against further 'sedition'. By the end of March 1817 there was legislation for the compulsory licensing of rooms used for political meetings, a prohibition on federations of societies and meetings of more than fifty people that did not have magistrates' permission, the dissolution of the Spencean societies, the suspension of habeas corpus for people charged with treason, and the death penalty for inciting members of the armed forces to mutiny.

17. (p. 97) *a series of such governors.* Disraeli's view of the endeavours of Lord Liverpool's government in its early years is typically unsympathetic, but reflects the feelings of much of the population in the wake of the war against Napoleon. Nicholas Vansittart was the Chancellor of the Exchequer faced with extreme financial straits after the war. By the beginning of 1819 the government had set up two select committees, one on currency and one on public finance, and Vansittart's budget of that year incorporated the overall principles of the recommendations of these committees. The economic situation provoked much social unrest during the first years of Liverpool's premiership, and 1812 saw the first of several coercion bills introduced by Castlereagh in an attempt to stem the movement towards what was seen by some as revolution. In the event, such measures served only to provoke the working classes even more, and the unrest grew until it reached a kind of climax at the Peterloo 'massacre' on 16 August 1819. Lord Sidmouth, as Home Secretary, was responsible for the series of Acts which, although regarded at the time as repressive, contributed to the restoration of order as economic conditions gradually improved.

18. (p. 97) *the Duke of Newcastle.* (1693–1768), Prime Minister from 1754 to 1756 and from 1757 to 1762.

19. (p. 97) *Mr Perceval*. Spencer Perceval (1762–1812), Prime Minister from 1809 until his assassination in the House of Commons on 11 May 1832.

20. (p. 97) *Lord Liverpool*. Robert Banks Jenkinson, 2nd Earl of Liverpool (1770–1828), Prime Minister from June 1812 until February 1827.

21. (p. 97) *Walpole*. Robert Walpole (1676–1745), generally regarded as the first British Prime Minister, was in power between 1721 and 1742.

22. (p. 97) *Lord Shelburne*. William Petty Fitzmaurice, 1st Marquess of Lansdowne and 2nd Earl of Shelburne (1737–1805), was Prime Minister from July 1782 to February 1783.

23. (p. 98) *Panglosses*. Optimistic philosophers. Pangloss, in Voltaire's *Candide*, holds that all is for the best in the best of all possible worlds, in spite of a series of distressing adventures.

24. (p. 98) *returned convict*. i.e. from transportation, as Magwitch in Dickens's *Great Expectations*.

25. (p. 98) *Socinian*. A member of a religious group that arose in the sixteenth century. Socinians rejected the doctrine of the Trinity and considered Jesus divine by office rather than by nature.

26. (p. 99) *Arch-Mediocrity*. Lord Liverpool

27. (p. 99) *used to call 'statemongers'*. John Williams (1582–1650) succeeded Francis Bacon to the lord-keepership, or chancellorship, after Bacon's fall from power over allegations of bribery in 1621. Although he did not coin the word 'statemonger' (it was first used in 1616), it was still new when he used it in a letter written on 17 September 1622: 'I would therefore see the most subtile State-monger in the world chalk out a way for his Majestie to mediate for Grace, and favour for the Protestants.'

28. (p. 99) *a Mediocrity*. Henry Phipps, 1st Earl of Mulgrave, retired from his post as Master of the Ordnance in 1818 to make way for Wellington.

29. (p. 100) *became Secretary of State*. Peel replaced Sidmouth at the Home Office.

30. (p. 101) *the seals of the Foreign Office*. Canning's reliance on his own ability, rather than on any 'connections', was largely responsible for the antagonism felt towards him by many of his fellow politicians. His ambition for high office at home was seen with distrust, and it seemed that a compromise had been reached when it was agreed that he would go to India as Governor-General – a post which Canning himself had always regarded as an alternative ambition to a high ministerial position at home. However, Castlereagh's suicide, in August 1822, changed the situation and Canning was 'recalled from his impending banishment' and made Foreign Secretary and Leader of the House of Commons.

31. (p. 101) *Mr Huskisson*. William Huskisson (1770–1830) became President of the Board of Trade.

32. (p. 101) *the Revolution*. i.e. of 1688.

33. (p. 101) *Catholic fellow-subjects from the Puritanic yoke*. The Catholic Emancipation Act of 1829.

34. (p. 102) *their sacrilegious spoil*. The lands accruing from the

Dissolution of the Monasteries, which Disraeli sees as forming the basis of the Whig aristocracy.

35. (p. 102) *Prætorians*. Originally the guards or select troops who attended the general of the Roman army, and subsequently instituted by Augustus for the protection of Italy.

36. (p. 102) *a great principle*. 'Civil and religious liberty', the toast of the Whig families who were behind the Revolution of 1688.

37. (p. 103) *complete settlement of Ireland ... equivocal manner*. i.e. Catholic emancipation.

38. (p. 103) *that convulsion*. i.e. the Reform Act.

39. (p. 103) *the Anti-Corn-Law League*. An association formed in London in 1836 and in Manchester in 1838 to organize agitation for the repeal of the Corn Laws.

40. (p. 104) *a fourth*. The four men are respectively Canning, Wellington, Peel and Huskisson, who was knocked down and fatally injured by a locomotive at the opening of the Liverpool—Manchester railway in September 1830.

41. (p. 104) *the Queen's trial*. George IV married, in 1795 (while he was still Prince of Wales), Caroline of Brunswick, but they soon separated. Caroline lived chiefly in Italy, where she was believed to have had an adulterous affair with her courier. When George acceded to the throne on 29 January 1820, she returned to England, whereupon the government introduced a Bill to dissolve the marriage and deprive her of the title of Queen. A lengthy hearing ended with the abandonment of the Bill by the House of Lords, but Caroline was, nevertheless, prevented from attending George's coronation. The problem was solved when she became ill and died nineteen days later.

42. (p. 105) *the son of an actress*. Canning's mother, Mary Anne Costello, went on the stage after her husband's death in 1771. She married twice more and achieved no great success on the stage, quitting it in 1801 when her son, who had by then been Under Secretary of State for five years, arranged to have his pension of £500 a year settled on his mother and sisters.

43. (p. 105) *White's*. John Timbs in *Club Life of London* (1866) says that White's Club was formerly composed of members of the high Tory party.

44. (p. 106) *the hero of the University*. Peel gained a double first in classics and mathematics from Oxford in 1808. He was the Member of Parliament for Oxford from 1817 to 1829.

45. (p. 106) *his Irish Secretaryship*. Peel became Chief Secretary for Ireland in July 1812, a post he held until 1818.

46. (p. 106) *Burke*. Edmund Burke (1729–97), statesman and political thinker, entered the top rank of public life by being elected to Parliament in 1766, where he remained until 1794.

47. (p. 106) *De Lolme*. John Louis De Lolme (1740?–1807), writer on the English constitution. He was born in Geneva but came to England in about 1769.

Chapter 2

1. (p. 109) *Kent and Campbell.* William Kent (1685–1748), architect, landscape gardener, interior decorator and furniture designer, and Colen Campbell (1676?–1729), the first great architect of British eighteenth-century Palladianism.

2. (p. 111) *a fervent admirer.* The spread of Methodism in industrial districts in the fifty years preceding Waterloo was considerable, as was the work of the Methodist Sunday schools in spreading literacy among the industrial poor. Many of the radicals and Chartists prominent in the years Disraeli is writing about came from Methodist families, and several of the reform movements of the time in their moral fervour resembled a secular religion.

3. (p. 112) *a good registration.* There had been no system of registering voters before 1832, and the slow process of voting involved firstly the proving of an entitlement to vote. The Reform Act introduced registration.

4. (p. 112) *Schedule A and Schedule B.* The disfranchising schedules of the Reform Bill. Fifty-six Schedule A boroughs lost a total of 111 Members of Parliament, and thirty Schedule B boroughs lost a total of thirty Members. These schedules were composed according to the number of houses in each borough and the amount of tax paid there. (There were also enfranchising schedules whereby twenty-two unrepresented boroughs gained two Members each, and twenty-one unrepresented boroughs gained one Member each.)

5. (p. 113) *the Red Book and Beatson's Political Index.* The Red Book was a popular name for the 'Royal Kalendar, or Complete ... Annual Register' (published from 1767 to 1893). Beatson's Political Register, compiled by Robert Beatson (1742–1818) was 'A Chronological Register of both Houses of the British Parliament from the Union in 1708, to the third parliament of the United Kingdom of Great Britain and Ireland, in 1807'.

6. (p. 113) *the address.* The formal speech on the government's programme outlined in the Royal Speech at the opening of Parliament.

Chapter 3

1. (p. 115) *Lord Spencer is dead.* Althorp's father, the 2nd Earl Spencer, died on 10 November 1834, and Althorp succeeded him as the 3rd Earl. When Althorp, who had been the key unifying person for the Whigs in the House of Commons, left to take up his seat in the House of Lords, William IV took the opportunity to dismiss the government of Grey's successor, Lord Melbourne.

2. (p. 115) *Sir William Temple says.* Sir William Temple (1628–1699) used the word 'thunderclap' in his *Memoirs* to describe the unexpected attack by France on Holland in 1672.

3. (p. 116) *Melbourne.* William Lamb, 2nd Viscount Melbourne (1799–

1848), was Prime Minister from July to November 1834, and from April 1835 to August 1841.

4. (p. 116) *If Durham ... the Ballot.* Durham, one of the four members of the committee which formulated the first Reform Bill, was a convinced radical, and the highly contentious proposal for a ballot (i.e. voting by secret ballot) which emerged in the committee's report was the result of his insistence. The proposal was not accepted and open voting was retained.

5. (p. 117) *the pavilion.* The Royal Pavilion at Brighton. Rigby would have to travel from Beaumanoir to London en route for Brighton.

Chapter 4

1. (p. 118) *the two ministers.* Wellington and Lyndhurst.

2. (p. 118) *Mr Hudson.* Sir James Hudson (1810–85), as he became, the diplomatist who was the messenger sent to summon Peel home on the dismissal of Melbourne in 1834.

3. (p. 121) *Clifford.* Hugh Charles Clifford, 7th Lord Clifford of Chudleigh (1790–1858), gave his general support to the ministries of Grey and Melbourne, but seldom took part in debates.

4. (p. 121) *Buckhounds.* The Master of the Buckhounds was an officer of the Royal Household. The pack of staghounds existed until 1897.

Chapter 5

1. (p. 125) THE TAMWORTH MANIFESTO. This 'manifesto', which took the form of an election address to his constituents, outlined Peel's plea in December 1834 'to that great and intelligent class of society ... which is far less interested in the contentions of party, than in the maintenance of order and the course of good government'. Although much of what Peel said has been accepted as standard policy by his political descendants, the manifesto was important not so much as a statement of 'new' Conservative ideals, but rather as a demonstration of how such a document could be seen as the official pronouncement of the party which gathered around him.

Chapter 7

1. (p. 132) *revenues of the Church.* The only real achievement of Peel's abortive ministry was the establishment of the ecclesiastical commission, and the English Tithe Bill and Irish Tithe Bill which he tried to put through were eventually carried, with additions, in 1836 and 1838 by the Whigs.

2. (p. 134) *the Delphin Classics.* The edition of the Latin classics *ad usum Delphini* (1674) was prepared for the son of Louis XIV.

3. (p. 134) *the Golden Book.* A registry of the nobility of the state of Venice.

4. (p. 134) *Clarendon.* Edward Hyde, Earl of Clarendon (1609–74). His 'History' – *The True Historical Narrative of the Rebellion and Civil Wars in England* – was first printed in 1702–4.

5. (p. 134) *Burnet.* Gilbert Burnet (1643–1715), Scottish-born bishop of Salisbury and historian who wrote a *History of His Own Time* (1724–34).

6. (p. 134) *Coxe.* The historian William Coxe (1747–1828).

BOOK III

Chapter 1

1. (p. 140) *ingle.* Fireplace.

2. (p. 142) *olla.* Spanish cooking-pot.

3. (p. 142) *posada.* An inn.

4. (p. 144) *Poor Law Guardians.* The Poor Law Amendment Act of 1834 shifted the responsibility for the relief of the poor from the parish vestries to new elected boards of Guardians, who were to work under the general direction and instruction of a new central authority, the Poor Law Commissioners.

5. (p. 144) *Would Philip ... not been slain.* Epaminondas of Thebes (c.410–362 BC) had been the most inventive tactician of all Greek generals. Philip II (382–336 BC) succeeded to the throne of Macedonia three years before Epaminondas's death and made his country the new ruling power in Greece, laying the foundations for Macedonia's expansion under his son Alexander the Great.

6. (p. 145) *Don John ... Lepanto at twenty-five.* In this naval engagement on 7 October 1571, Don John of Austria (then aged twenty-four), the half-brother of Philip II of Spain, led the allied Christian forces against those of the Ottoman Turks during an Ottoman campaign to acquire the Venetian island of Cyprus. The victory fired Don John's personal ambitions, which Philip tried to restrain over a number of years. John's early death at the age of thirty-one released him from an increasingly unrealistic position.

7. (p. 145) *John de Medici ... of Arragon himself.* Giovanni de Medici (1475–1521) became, as Leo X, one of the most extravagant of the Renaissance popes. He was made a cardinal in 1492. Francesco Guicciardini (1483–1540) was the author of the most important contemporary history of Italy.

8. (p. 145) *at sixteen.* An essay on mathematics which was highly regarded by the academic community and praised by Descartes.

9. (p. 145) *Grotius.* Hugo Grotius (1583–1645), scholar and jurist, whose works are of fundamental importance to international law.

10. (p. 145) *Acquaviva.* Claudio Acquaviva (1543–1615) was the fifth and youngest general of the Society of Jesus.

11. (p. 146) *the Wahabees.* The Wahhabis were members of a Muslim puritan movement founded by Muhammad ibn 'Abd al-Wahhab in the

eighteenth century, and adopted in 1744 by the Sa'udi family, with
whose fortunes they became closely allied.

12. (p. 146) *Lysippus*. Fourth-century BC Greek sculptor, particularly
active during the reign of Alexander the Great.

Chapter 2

1. (p. 149) *crossing the Granicus*. The Battle of the Granicus (the
modern River Kocabas) in the early summer of 334 BC was Alexander
the Great's first victory in his invasion of the Persian Empire.

2. (p. 150) *Zeno*. (335–263 BC) Founder of the Stoic school.

3. (p. 150) *the cottage*. Afterwards known as the Royal Lodge, the
cottage was built by George IV. It was designed by Nash and built between
1812 and 1814.

4. (p. 152) *Roxalana*. A reference to Alexander the Great's first wife,
Roxana, the daughter of a Persian satrap.

5. (p. 152) *Watteau*. (Jean-)Antoine Watteau (1648–1721), French
painter known mainly for his *fêtes galantes*.

6. (p. 153) *fair Geraldines and Countesses of Pembroke*. 'The fair Geraldine',
Elizabeth, daughter of the 9th Earl of Kildare, was the subject of many of
the love poems of Henry Howard, Earl of Surrey (1517–47). Mary Herbert,
Countess of Pembroke, was the sister of Sir Philip Sidney (1544–86), who
dedicated *Arcadia* to her.

Chapter 3

1. (p. 156) *Travellers'*. Club in Pall Mall, founded in 1819 by Lord
Castlereagh.

2. (p. 157) *New Poor Law*. i.e. the Poor Law Amendment Act of 1834.

3. (p. 158) *the Union*. Unions of parishes were instituted by the Poor Law
Amendment Act.

4. (p. 162) *Strutt's Sports and Pastimes*. Joseph Strutt, *The Sports and
Pastimes of the People of England*, first published in 1801.

5. (p. 162) *Seltzer water*. The medicinal mineral water from Selters in
Germany, or a substitute, like soda-water.

Chapter 4

1. (p. 167) *Malvoisie*. An amber dessert wine made in France, similar to
malmsey.

2. (p. 167) *tilts and tournaments*. The medieval spirit associated with
Young England reached its apogee in the mock tournament organized by
Lord Eglinton in 1839. Disraeli was on his honeymoon at the time and did
not attend, and his description of it in chapters 59 and 60 of *Endymion*
is inaccurate.

3. (p. 167) *Almacks'*. The temple of fashion at the beginning of the
reign of George IV. It was presided over by the so-called lady patronesses

who included the Ladies Castlereagh, Jersey, Cowper and Sefton, and Princess Esterhazy. They gave the tone to the *beau monde* and it was considered a great privilege to gain admittance to Almacks'.

4. (p. 168) *encaustic.* Decorated by any process involving burning in colours, especially by inlaying coloured clays and baking, or by fusing wax colours to the surface.

5. (p. 169) *Madame de Longueville.* French princess (1619–79) famous for her beauty and intrigues, she was the sister of Condé.

Chapter 5

1. (p. 171) *the Whig aristocracy.* Disraeli traces the 'Whig aristocracy' back to the first secular landlords of the Church lands which changed hands after the Dissolution of the Monasteries.

BOOK IV
Chapter 1

1. (p. 177) *Pericles and Phidias.* Pericles (c.495–429 BC), statesman who brought ancient Athenian democracy to its height. Phidias (c.490–430 BC), Athenian sculptor who directed the construction of the marble statues of the Parthenon.

Chapter 2

1. (p. 180) *Penelope in the daytime.* The wife of Odysseus who, when her husband did not return to Ithaca after the Trojan War, worked at a tapestry in the daytime, telling her many suitors that she would choose one of them when the tapestry was finished. To prolong the period she undid during the night the work that she had done during the day, until the return of Odysseus after twenty years delivered her from her suitors.

2. (p. 183) *by 8.40.* This way of expressing the time was popularized by the railway timetables.

Chapter 4

1. (p. 194) *the battle of Tewkesbury.* 4 May 1471, when the Yorkist King Edward IV gained his final victory over his Lancastrian opponents.

2. (p. 194) *attainted.* i.e. deprived of their estates and forced to forfeit their right of descent.

3. (p. 196) *be executed for murder.* Laurence Shirley, 4th Earl Ferrers (1720–60), was the last nobleman in England to suffer a felon's death. He was tried by his peers and allegedly hanged with a rope of silk in deference to his rank.

Chapter 5

1. (p. 200) *as pure as Cato.* The name of Marcus Porcius Cato (234–

149 BC), known as 'the Censor', became a byword for austerity and puritanism. His great-grandson of the same name (95–46 BC), who maintained the family name for obstinacy and rectitude, inspired Addison's tragedy *Cato*.

Chapter 7

1. (p. 212) *Chevalier Law*. John Law (1671–1729), the Scot who became controller-general of French finance.

2. (p. 213) *muscadins*. Parisian term for dandies. Between the years 1794 and 1796 of the French Revolution it was applied to the members of the moderate party, which was composed chiefly of young men of the upper-middle classes.

Chapter 10

1. (p. 232) *Grand Inquisitor*. The Spanish Inquisition was established by the pope in the latter half of the fifteenth century at the request of the Catholic kings to combat apostate former Jews and Muslims as well as those accused of witchcraft.

2. (p. 233) *Council of Toledo ... by the Moslemin Arabs*. There were eighteen councils of the Catholic Church in Spain, held in Toledo, from c.400 to 702, and they laid the foundation for the establishment of Catholicism as the state religion. Roderick, otherwise known as Don Rodrigo (d.711), was the last Visigothic king of Spain. Following the desertion of much of his army, he was defeated near the Rio Barbate on 19 July 711 by the Islamic invaders from North Africa.

3. (p. 233) *the union of the two crowns ... and the nonconforming Hebrew*. The marriage of Ferdinand II of Aragon to Princess Isabella of Castile in October 1469 initiated the process of Spanish unification. For centuries the Jewish community in Spain had flourished, though anti-Semitism had sometimes made itself felt and pressure to convert was brought to bear on the Jews. Nominal converts from Judaism were called Marranos. After Aragon and Castile were united, the Marranos were denounced as a danger to the existence of Christian Spain, and a bill of Sixtus IV in 1478 authorized the Catholic kings to name inquisitors. Ferdinand supported the Spanish Inquisition and conquered the Kingdom of Granada, the final seat of the Moors in Spain, in 1492. The same year the Spanish Jews were given the choice of exile or baptism.

4. (p. 233) *the Albigenses*. A heretical Christian sect in southern France in the twelfth and thirteenth centuries.

5. (p. 233) *the Cortes*. The Spanish Parliament.

6. (p. 234) *the San Benito.* A penitential garment of yellow cloth, resembling a scapular in shape, ornamented with a red St Andrew's cross before and behind, worn by a confessed and penitent heretic.

7. (p. 234) *Torquemada.* The Dominican Tomás de Torquemada was the first Grand Inquisitor. Although he became the symbol of the inquisitor who uses torture and terror, his methods were those of a time in which judicial procedure itself was cruel. The number of burnings at the stake during his tenure has been exaggerated, although it was probably about 2,000.

8. (p. 235) *of Nebuchadnezzar and of Titus.* Nebuchadnezzar II (*c.*630–562 BC), king of the Chaldean Empire, captured Jerusalem in August 586 BC and deported its prominent citizens. The Roman Emperor Titus (AD 39–81) led a campaign in which a million Jews reputedly died and which culminated in the capture and destruction of Jerusalem in AD 70.

9. (p. 235) *Mosaic.* i.e. the Jews.

10. (p. 235) *the Waterloo loan.* A loan of £36 million raised from private sources by the Exchequer to help finance the coalition against Napoleon in 1815.

11. (p. 236) *revolted colonies of Spain.* Spain's South American colonies revolted during the early 1820s.

12. (p. 236) *the revolution.* The revolution of 1820 brought power to the liberals, but the new system collapsed in the face of conservative reaction and the liberals were forced into exile. The resulting Carlist Wars, which polarized the forces of urban liberalism and rural traditionalism, disrupted Spain for more than fifty years.

13. (p. 238) *Valparaiso.* A port in central Chile.

14. (p. 241) *Carbonari.* Members of a secret political society with liberal republican aims, originating in southern Italy about 1811.

15. (p. 242) *Archbishop Usher.* James Ussher (1581–1656), Archbishop of Armagh.

Chapter 11

1. (p. 245) *Vyvyan's last speech and confession.* Sir Richard Rawlinson Vyvyan was the leader of the ultra-Tories. The reference is to the fact that while the King was on his way to dissolve Parliament on 23 April 1831, Vyvyan was in the middle of a speech passionately attacking the Reform Bill. The approach of the monarch for the purpose of a dissolution was marked by the firing of guns, and these shots could be heard interspersing Vyvyan's harangue.

2. (p. 252) *Cracovienne. Cracovians and the Highlanders*, a Polish opera, written by Jan Stefani (1746–1829).

3. (p. 252) *Stanley.* Edward George Geoffrey Smith Stanley, later 14th Earl of Derby (1799–1869). Although a member of Lord Grey's Reform government, he resigned over the Irish Church question in 1834 and joined the Tories. He was Prime Minister in 1852, 1858 and 1866, during

which ministries Disraeli was Chancellor of the Exchequer and leader of the Conservatives in the House of Commons.

4. (p. 252) *Graham*. Sir James Robert George, 2nd Baronet Graham (1792–1861). At first an advanced liberal member of the Whig party, Graham was, by the time *Coningsby* was written, a confidant and adviser of Peel and was a leading Peelite in the House of Commons after Peel's death in 1850.

5. (p. 252) *Lord Palmerston*. (1784–1865), Whig-Liberal statesman whose long and eminent career included more than thirty years as Foreign Secretary or Prime Minister.

6. (p. 253) *Lord John*. John Russell, 1st Earl Russell (1792–1878), an aristocratic Liberal prominent in the fight for the Reform Bill, was Prime Minister from 1846 to 1852 and from 1865 to 1866.

Chapter 13

1. (p. 259) *Brennus*. According to tradition, the Gallic leader who captured Rome about 390 BC.

2. (p. 259) *as the Inquisition*. A reference to the general proscription practised by the English Bench which took place under the lead of the second Exclusionist Parliament following the alleged 'Popish Plot'. The Parliament was dissolved in January 1681, one month after the execution of Lord Stafford, who had been one of the most eminent figures wrongly impeached for complicity in the 'plot'.

3. (p. 262) *Mormon*. The prophet whose supposed revelations were recorded by Joseph Smith. Smith founded the Church of Jesus Christ of Latter-day Saints in 1830 at La Fayette, New York.

4. (p. 262) *Bentham*. Jeremy Bentham (1748–1832), the political speculator most associated with the principle of 'Utility'.

5. (p. 262) *Fifth-Monarchy men*. A sect of extreme puritans prominent during the years of the Commonwealth and the Protectorate, so called because of their belief that the time of the fifth monarchy was at hand – that is the monarchy that (according to a traditional interpretation of parts of the Bible) should succeed the Assyrian, Persian, Greek and Roman monarchies, and during which Christ should reign on earth for a thousand years.

Chapter 14

1. (p. 267) *notwithstanding Solomon*. Ecclesiastes 9:11.

Chapter 15

1. (p. 274) *Maimonides*. Moses Maimonides (1135–1204), Jewish philosopher, the most intellectual figure of medieval Judaism.

2. (p. 274) *Spinoza*. Benedict de Spinoza (1632–77), the independent Rationalist philosopher and religious thinker, came from refugee Portu-

guese Jewish stock. He studied non-Hebrew subjects privately and was excommunicated in 1656 by the local Jewish authorities for his non-traditional Biblical exegesis.

3. (p. 274) *a Pasta or a Grisi.* Giuditta Pasta (1798–1865) and Giulia Grisi (1811–69) were both sopranos.

BOOK V

Chapter 1

1. (p. 279) *Alcibiades.* (c.450–404 BC), brilliant but unscrupulous Greek politician and military leader.

2. (p. 280) *a Castle of Indolence.* 'The Castle of Indolence' is a poem, written in Spenserian stanzas, by James Thomson (1700–1748) and published in 1748. Once in the castle, visitors sink into idleness and delightful sights and sounds, but they soon become diseased and are thrown into a dungeon where they are left to languish.

Chapter 2

1. (p. 281) *necessarily.* The law as it then was required that Parliament be dissolved within six months of the sovereign's death.

2. (p. 282) *present of a commission.* Despite ecclesiastical abuses and the Oxford movement, the Church was not a particularly divisive subject in the mid-1830s as far as differences in Whig and Tory policy were concerned. Most of the legislation passed by the Whigs involved the attempted regulation of tithes and church rates. During his brief premiership of 1834–5 Peel had, in the main, followed the principles of the Whig policy, and in 1834 he had appointed a commission to inquire into the state of the Church in England and Wales. This commission issued four reports in 1835 and 1836, and its recommendations formed the basis of the Acts of 1836, revising diocesan boundaries; of 1838, dealing with pluralism; and of 1840, restricting the number of canons in every cathedral chapter.

3. (p. 283) *Periander or Thales.* Periander (c.625–585 BC) was ruler of Corinth and a patron of artists and poets. Thales of Miletus was a Greek philosopher of the late seventh century BC, and the first of the Ionian physical scientists.

4. (p. 283) *chaired.* It was the custom, after a parliamentary election, for the successful candidate to be placed in a chair and carried aloft in triumph by his supporters. As with most of the people involved with an election, these 'supporters' would be paid for their services.

5. (p. 284) *the cause for which … the scaffold.* i.e. the Whig cause. John Hampden (1594–1643) was killed whilst fighting for the parliamentary forces in the Civil War at Chalgrove Field on 18 June 1643. Algernon Sidney (1622–83) was executed for complicity in the so-called Rye

House Plot. Disraeli uses the phrase in a slightly different form in *Sybil*, Book I, Chapter 3.

6. (p. 284) *Harrington*. James Harrington (1611–77), political philosopher whose major work, *The Common-wealth of Oceana* (1656), was a restatement in seventeenth-century English terms of Aristotle's theory of constitutional stability and revolution.

7. (p. 284) *Sydney*. At Sidney's trial, passages from the manuscript of his *Discourses Concerning Government* (published in 1698) were introduced as evidence that he believed in the right of revolution.

8. (p. 284) *to change the ministry*. John Campbell, 2nd Duke of Argyll (1678–1743), was instrumental in getting the dying Queen Anne to accept Shrewsbury as Lord High Treasurer – a proposition which practically annihilated the Stuart cause. Charles Talbot, Duke of Shrewsbury (1660–1718), as Lord High Treasurer was largely responsible for the peaceful succession of the Hanoverian George I to the English throne in 1714.

Chapter 3

1. (p. 292) *high-lows*. Laced boots reaching up over the ankles.

Chapter 4

1. (p. 299) *his successor*. Lord Stanley.

2. (p. 300) *a Demosthenic impulse*. Demosthenes (384–322 BC), generally considered to be the greatest Greek orator, is said, in an apocryphal story, to have overcome a speech impediment by declaiming on the seashore against the noise of the waves with a mouth full of pebbles.

3. (p. 304) *The blunt's going like the ward-pump*. i.e. it was raining very heavily. 'Blunt' is an old regional word for a rain or snow storm.

Chapter 6

1. (p. 314) *by special license*. Such licences allowed marriages to take place without the formality of banns, etc. Thomas Poynter, a proctor of Doctors' Commons, recorded in 1822 that since 1759 special licences were the privilege of aristocrats.

Chapter 8

1. (p. 322) *the present King*. Louis Philippe, King of France from 1830 to 1848.

BOOK VI
Chapter 2

1. (p. 331) *Carlists*. Spanish political counter-revolutionaries and con-

servatives who supported the claims of the first Don Carlos to the throne on the death of his brother King Ferdinand VII in 1833.

2. (p. 332) *Soubise.* Charles de Rohan, Prince de Soubise (1715–87), commanded the French armies during the Seven Years' War.

3. (p. 332) *De Lauragais.* Louis-Léon-Félicité, Comte de Lauraguais (1733–1824).

4. (p. 333) *Œil de Bœuf. Œil-de-bœuf* windows are small circular or oval windows usually resembling wheels. This reference is to the small chamber in the Versailles palace called the *œil-de-bœuf* room, which is lighted by such a small, round window.

5. (p. 333) *Isthmus of Panama.* As early as the sixteenth century the Spanish conceived the idea of constructing a canal across the isthmus. In 1880 the French Panama Canal Company, under the leadership of Ferdinand de Lesseps, began the first attempt to construct a canal. After several delays and reorganizations, the canal was first opened to traffic on 15 August 1914.

6. (p. 336) *Monsieur Thiers.* (Louis-)Adolphe Thiers (1797–1877), statesman and historian, was a founder and first President of the Third Republic.

7. (p. 336) ἑταῖραι. Companions.

8. (p. 336) *Aspasia.* (5th century BC), mistress of the Athenian statesman Pericles and a prominent figure in Athenian society.

9. (p. 338) *Talmudical.* From the Talmud, the main authoritative compilation of ancient Jewish law and tradition.

10. (p. 338) *Athenæus.* (c. AD 200), Greek grammarian and author of *Deipnosophistai* ('The Gastronomers'). The value of this work lies partly in the large number of quotations it preserves from lost works of antiquity, and partly in the variety of unusual information it contains about the ancient world.

Chapter 3

1. (p. 340) *Finality men and progressive Reformers.* Progressive reformers saw the Reform Bill as one stage in a process. Those who wanted a 'final' measure were those keen to preserve the essentials of aristocratic power. In other words, the 'Finality men' wanted a Reform Bill which would settle the question of the electoral system at least for their time.

2. (p. 343) *Orangeman.* A member of the political society formed in 1795 to uphold the Protestant religion and Protestant supremacy in Ireland. Disraeli always associates what he calls 'political religionism' with Whiggism.

3. (p. 344) *the Corresponding Society.* These societies were informal political education groups in the seventeenth and eighteenth centuries.

BOOK VII

Chapter 1

1. (p. 364) *Icarian flight.* As in Icarus, the son of Daedalus, who

made him wings of feathers and wax so that both could escape from Crete. Icarus flew too near the sun, and when the wax melted he fell into the sea and was drowned.

Chapter 2

1. (p. 371) *Acts of 1827–8–32.* Most particularly the moves towards Catholic emancipation and constitutional reform in the years following the retirement of Lord Liverpool.

2. (p. 373) *locofoco.* An invented word in the 1830s for self-igniting matches in the United States, it was soon applied to the American 'Equal Rights' party after they had used such matches to light candles at a political meeting when the gas-lights had been extinguished in the tumult. The press then dubbed this radical section of the Democratic party the 'Loco-Foco party'.

3. (p. 377) *L'État c'est moi.* As said by Louis XIV.

4. (p. 377) *twenty Hoadleys.* Benjamin Hoadley (1676–1761), as the prominent and aggressive leader of the extreme latitudinarian party in Church and State, was an obvious figure for attack, especially from Tory and High-Church interests.

5. (p. 377) *James II ... to an Anglican see.* An oversimplification. James II promoted Roman Catholics to key positions throughout 1686, and an ecclesiastical commission, set up to silence Anglican critics, succeeded in depriving the Bishop of London of his functions. In the following year the King's Jesuit adviser, Father Petre, was introduced to the Privy Council, and a Roman Catholic head was forced upon an Oxford college.

6. (p. 377) *Nicholas Breakspear.* Breakspear (1100–1159), as Pope Adrian IV (1154–59), was the only Englishman to occupy the papal throne.

7. (p. 379) *Thou art the man.* 2 Samuel 12:7.

Chapter 4

1. (p. 385) *This was the period ... three days.* In May 1839, following Melbourne's resignation as premier, Peel was invited to form an administration. His proposals to Queen Victoria included changes in the Ladies of the Bedchamber. The Queen would hear of no such thing, and Peel would not consent to form a ministry without what he called 'such public proof of your Majesty's entire support and confidence, as would be afforded by the permission to make some changes in your Majesty's Household, which your Majesty resolved on maintaining entirely without change'. There was an interregnum of a few days, and then Melbourne, the Queen's favourite, claiming that he would not abandon his sovereign, returned to office. The fault for the 'crisis' lay with the attitudes of both parties concerned; the gaucherie of Peel, and the favouritism of the Queen.

2. (p. 387) *Geneva beat Venice.* A reference to Parliament's attempts to

achieve something akin to a constitutional monarchy via peaceful means prior to the ascendancy of the 'war party' and the ensuing Civil War, which brought the puritan interest to the fore.

Chapter 7

1. (p. 398) *Ausonian breezes.* From Ausonius (AD 310–c.395). a Gallo-Roman teacher of rhetoric and a prolific poet. HIs best poem, *Mosella*, is a poetic guidebook to the river Moselle.

Chapter 8

1. (p. 400) *Caryatides.* Draped female figures used instead of columns as architectural supports.

2. (p. 401) *blue-books.* Parliamentary reports, so called because of their blue covers.

BOOK VIII
Chapter 1

1. (p. 409) *Carlton House.* First erected by Lord Carlton in 1709, it was pulled down in 1828. Some of the Corinthian columns which formed the colonnade of the house were used in the portico of the National Gallery, others in the chapel at Buckingham Palace.

2. (p. 410) *qui vive.* On the alert; from the French sentry's challenge, literally '(long) live who?'.

3. (p. 411) *Goldsmith.* Oliver Goldsmith (1730–74). His works include a life of Bolingbroke (1770) and a history of England (1771).

4. (p. 414) *the ladies.* Of the Bedchamber.

Chapter 2

1. (p. 420) *never paired off.* If two Members of Parliament from opposite sides 'pair', they agree to abstain from voting on a particular issue, or for a specified duration of time. This arrangement is usually entered into if a Member knows in advance that he will be unable to attend the House because of some engagement, or through illness.

Chapter 3

1. (p. 427) *those Irish corporations.* The Union Act of 1800 swept away a large number of rotten corporations in Ireland, and the Reform Act of 1832, with its imposition of the £10 householder franchise in urban constituencies, broke the corporation monopolies and close nomination system in over half of the remaining Irish boroughs. The following year an inquiry began to look into municipal reform in Ireland, and, in pursuance of its report, a Bill was introduced early in 1836 for the better regulation of Irish corporations. Due, however, to Tory opposition, it was only in

1840, when Peel acknowledged that a settlement of the question was indispensable, that a Bill to this effect was finally passed.

2. (p. 427) *the real mischief.* Catholic emancipation.

3. (p. 429) *O'Connell.* Daniel O'Connell (1775–1847), first of the great nineteenth-century Irish leaders in the House of Commons.

4. (p. 429) *Irish Registration Bill.* 1840 saw Lord Stanley introduce for the Tories a Bill for the registration of Irish voters which, at the time, was vigorously opposed by many Whigs in the government.

5. (p. 430) *Grey would have gone to Ireland.* Late in 1829 Grey's attitude to Wellington's ministry was one of friendly neutrality. He was moved from this position by two things. In December 1829 he learned that Wellington did not mean to offer him office, although it had earlier been rumoured that Grey was to be offered the Lord-Lieutenant of Ireland. As it happens, Grey would probably have refused any such post, but it was a blow to his pride not to have it offered. The second thing was Grey's concern about the government's insensibility to the 'distress' in the country as a whole.

6. (p. 430) *Conservative Associations.* The expansion of the influence of local Conservative Associations was largely a feature of the election of 1834 and the ensuing months of office.

Chapter 4

1. (p. 434) *The die was cast.* When Julius Cæsar crossed the Rubicon (the river which marked the boundary between Italy and Gaul) in 49 BC, it was tantamount to a declaration of war on Pompey. Suetonius says that Cæsar saw a vision of a superhuman figure which beckoned him across, and gives him the words 'alea iacta est', meaning 'the die is cast'.

Chapter 5

1. (p. 436) *Sue.* Eugene Sue (1804–57), author of sensational novels about the seamy side of urban life.

Chapter 6

1. (p. 438) *Rowland Hill ... of the cheap postage.* Rowland Hill (1772–1842), a general in the Peninsular War, stormed Almarez on 19 May 1812. Rowland Hill (1795–1879), who was knighted in 1860, was the originator of the penny postage system.

2. (p. 439) *Nottingham Castle in flames.* Following the defeat of the Reform Bill in the House of Lords on 8 October 1831, there was much rioting throughout the country. At Nottingham the disturbances culminated in the destruction by fire of the ancient castle, once the property of the Duke of Newcastle, who had given offence by his rash declaration with regard to his voters at Newark that he had a right to do what he pleased with his own.

Chapter 7

1. (p. 452) *the Albany*. Albany Chambers, Piccadilly, take their name from Frederick, Duke of York and Albany, second son of George III. Lord Byron lived there from 1814 to 1815, and Gladstone was a resident from 1833 until his marriage in 1839.

2. (p. 453) *Boccaccio*. Giovanni Boccaccio (1313–75), Italian writer and humanist, author of *The Decameron*.

3. (p. 456) *a Joe Miller*. Meaning a stale joke. Joseph Miller (1684–1738) was a comedian. After his death his reputation was made by John Mottley who, in 1739, was commissioned to compile a collection of jokes, which he unwarrantably entitled *Joe Miller's Jests, or the Wit's Vademecum*.

BOOK IX

Chapter 1

1. (p. 459) *Lord of Misrule ... Abbot of Unreason*. The Lord of Misrule in England, or the Abbot of Unreason (as the post was known in Scotland), was the official in the late medieval and early Tudor period responsible for managing the Christmas festivities held at court, in the houses of noblemen or in colleges and Inns of Court. The Lord would preside over the affairs with a mock court, receiving 'homage' from the revellers. The English court ceased to appoint a Lord of Misrule after the death of Edward VI in 1553, and his function was probably taken over by a full-time official, the Master of the Revels. The office of Abbot of Unreason was suppressed in 1555.

2. (p. 459) *the Mummers, the Hobby-horse not forgotten*. Mummers were originally bands of masked persons who paraded the streets during winter festivities in Europe, entering houses to dance and play dice in silence. Here the association is with the English mummers who performed (and still do in some parts of the country) a traditional dramatic entertainment known as the mumming play, the origins of which are obscure. Although contemporary references to it do not begin to appear until the late eighteenth century, the narrative framework was first popularized at the end of the sixteenth century – the story of St George and the Seven Champions of Christendom. The hobby-horse referred to is a figure of a horse made of wickerwork which is fastened to the waist of a performer in some traditional plays and in some morris dances.

3. (p. 460) *'a knife and fork question'*. The *OED* ascribes this phrase only to William Gresley (1801–76), the Tractarian divine who apparently used it in his religious and social tale *Charles Lever, or the Man of the Nineteenth Century*.

4. (p. 460) *Hippocras*. A cordial drink made of wine flavoured with spices.

Chapter 3

1. (p. 472) *a red ribbon.* The Order of the Bath.
2. (p. 472) *the Great Seal.* The Lord Chancellorship.

Chapter 5

1. (p. 481) *Brown and Laudohn.* Maximilian Ulysses, Graf von Browne (1705–57), of Irish ancestry, and Gideon Ernst, Freiherr von Laudon (1717–90), of Scottish descent, were both Austrian field-marshals during the Seven Years' War (1756–63).

Chapter 6

1. (p. 483) *link-boys.* i.e. boys who carry 'links' (torches of tow and pitch) to light people along the streets.
2. (p. 483) *a much-wronged lady's name.* William IV's wife, Queen Adelaide (1792–1848), had become unpopular with the supporters of Reform because of her supposed interference during the passage of the Reform Bill through Parliament.
3. (p. 485) *Tidd and Chitty.* Probably the *Practice of the Court of King's Bench* (1790 and 1794) by William Tidd (1760–1847), to which Uriah Heep refers in Chapter 12 of *David Copperfield*: 'I am going through Tidd's Practice. Oh, what a writer Mr Tidd is, Master Copperfield!' Joseph Chitty the elder (1776–1841) was another leading legal writer.
4. (p. 491) *the Odd Fellows.* The Oddfellows' societies seem to have originated in the late eighteenth century in imitation of the Freemasons.
5. (p. 491) *Paulus Emilius returning from Macedon.* Lucius Aemilius Paullus Macedonicus (c.229–160 BC), the Roman general whose victory over the Macedonians at Pydna ended the Third Macedonian War (171–168 BC).

MORE ABOUT PENGUINS
AND PELICANS

For further information about books available from Penguins please write to Dept EP, Penguin Books Ltd, Harmondsworth, Middlesex UB7 ODA.

In the U.S.A.: For a complete list of books available from Penguins in the United States write to Dept DG, Penguin Books, 299 Murray Hill Parkway, East Rutherford, New Jersey 07073.

In Canada: For a complete list of books available from Penguins in Canada write to Penguin Books Canada Ltd, 2801 John Street, Markham, Ontario L3R 1B4.

In Australia: For a complete list of books available from Penguins in Australia write to the Marketing Department, Penguin Books Australia Ltd, P.O. Box 257, Ringwood, Victoria 3134.

In New Zealand: For a complete list of books available from Penguins in New Zealand write to the Marketing Department, Penguin Books (N.Z.) Ltd, P.O. Box 4019, Auckland 10.

THE PENGUIN ENGLISH LIBRARY

BENJAMIN DISRAELI
SYBIL
Introduced by R. A. Butler
and edited by Thom Braun

One of the most important of English political novels, *Sybil* caused a sensation when it was first published in 1845. So vivid was its exposure of the gross inequalities of Victorian society – from the desperate poverty of the industrial workers to the gross and irresponsible excesses of the wealthy – that its subtitle *The Two Nations* has passed into the language.

But Disraeli, the man who was to become one of Britain's most famous Prime Ministers, did not produce in *Sybil* merely a political tract on behalf of Tory democracy as the answer to the Hungry Forties. This is a dramatic novel of romance, full of wit and irony; a love story which ranges through adventure, mystery and political intrigue while questioning many of the basic assumptions of the Victorian social structure.

This edition includes an introduction by Lord Butler as well as notes, a note on the text, an appendix on Disraeli's view of history and a bibliography.

THOMAS CARLYLE
SELECTED WRITINGS
Edited by Alan Shelston

Now remembered mainly as the impressionistic historian of the French Revolution and as a forerunner of the authoritarian ideologies of the twentieth century, Carlyle enjoyed in his long lifetime an immense reputation as a prophet and preacher. For an anonymous correspondent he was 'an honoured and trusted teacher', for Charles Dickens the man who 'knows everything', for Matthew Arnold a 'moral desperado'. Certainly the voice of Thomas Carlyle is one of the most compelling of nineteenth-century England.

This selection is intended to be representative of all stages of his career, rather than a 'Best of Carlyle'. It includes the whole of *Chartism* and chapters from *Sartor Resartus*, *The French Revolution*, *Heroes and Hero-Worship*, *Past and Present* and the history of *Frederick the Great*.

J. S. MILL
ON LIBERTY
Edited by Gertrude Himmelfarb

'The only purpose for which power can be rightfully exercised over any member of a civilized community, against his will, is to prevent harm to others . . . Over himself, over his own body and mind, the individual is sovereign.'

To this 'one very simple principle' the whole of Mill's essay *On Liberty* is dedicated. If liberty has come to be the God to whom we all, from the anarchist to the communist, pay lip-service today, it is worth looking back at the text of the man who first supplied it with a Bible.

THE PENGUIN ENGLISH LIBRARY

THOMAS HOBBES
LEVIATHAN
Edited by C. B. Macpherson

From the turmoil of the the English Civil War, when life was truly 'nasty, brutish, and short', Hobbes's *Leviathan* (1651) speaks directly to the twentieth century. In its over-riding concern for peace, its systematic analysis of power and its elevation of politics to the status of a science, it mirrors much modern thinking. And despite its contemporary notoriety – Pepys called it 'a book the Bishops will not let be printed again' – it was also, as Professor Macpherson shows, a convincing apologia for the emergent seventeenth-century market society.

WILLIAM HAZLITT
SELECTED WRITINGS
Edited by Ronald Blythe

With his uncompromising contempt for lies, cant, and injustice, William Hazlitt (1778–1830) notably contributed to the literature of radical protest by flaying the standards of a depraved age. Never a good-natured man, he embarrassed his contemporaries by his fierce personal involvement in what he wrote and dismayed them by his unbudging championship of Bonaparte. Hazlitt's catholicity and that magnificent style which at once makes a friend or an enemy of the reader are well represented among these autobiographical pieces; essays and extracts on literature, art, religion, and philosophy; portraits (of Pitt, Wordsworth. Coleridge, Lamb, and others); and in his racy report of a fight between Bill Neate and the Gasman, or his obituary on a famous fives-player.

THE PENGUIN ENGLISH LIBRARY

ELIZABETH GASKELL
MARY BARTON
Edited by Stephen Gill

Mary Barton was only one of several books written in the 1840s about what came to be known as the 'condition of England' question. It is a tale of Dives and Lazarus, of the comfortable pinnacle and the miserable base of the Victorian social pyramid. It is told, however, without over-simplification, without bigotry, and, above all, without hatred. With an artist's sensitivity not just to economic and social facts but to individual human responses, Mrs Gaskell diagnoses men's tragic ignorance of each other as the root of the evil. *Mary Barton*, as Stephen Gill writes in his Introduction, is 'social history as it should be understood, on the pulses of the people who made it'.

WIVES AND DAUGHTERS
With an Introduction by Laurence Lerner

'The most underrated novel in English' is how Laurence Lerner describes *Wives and Daughters*, Mrs Gaskell's last work: and certainly the story of Mr Gibson's new marriage and its influence on the lives of those closest to him is a work of rare charm, combining pathos with wit, intelligence, and a perceptiveness about people and their relationships equalled only by Jane Austen and George Eliot. As in *Cranford* she surrounds her fiction with a fragrant evocation of English village life, but in *Wives and Daughters* this is underpinned by a sense of social change and of the more basic realities of birth and death.

Also published
THE LIFE OF CHARLOTTE BRONTË
CRANFORD AND COUSIN PHILLIS
NORTH AND SOUTH